The Critics Hail Marion Zimmer Bradley's Darkover Novels:

"A rich and highly colored tale of politics and magic, courage and pressure . . . Topflight adventure in every way!"
—Lester Del Rey in *Analog* (for *The Heritage of Hastur*)

"May well be [Bradley's] masterpiece."
—*New York Newsday* (for *The Heritage of Hastur*)

"Literate and exciting."
—*New York Times Book Review* (for *City of Sorcery*)

"Suspenseful, powerfully written, and deeply moving."
—*Library Journal* (for *Stormqueen!*)

"A warm, shrewd portrait of women from different backgrounds working together under adverse conditions."
—*Publishers Weekly* (for *City of Sorcery*)

"I don't think any series novels have succeeded for me the way Marion Zimmer Bradley's Darkover novels did."
—*Locus* (general)

"Delightful . . . a fascinating world and a great read."
—*Locus* (for *Exile's Song*)

"Darkover is the essence, the quintessence, my most personal and best-loved work."
—Marion Zimmer Bradley

THE FOUNDING:

A "lost ship" of Terran origin, in the pre-empire colonizing days, lands on a planet with a dim red star, later to be called Darkover.

DARKOVER LANDFALL

THE AGES OF CHAOS:

1,000 years after the original landfall settlement, society has returned to the feudal level. The Darkovans, their Terran technology renounced or forgotten, have turned instead to freewheeling, out-of-control matrix technology, psi powers, and terrible psi weapons. The populace lives under the domination of the Towers and a tyrannical breeding program to staff the Towers with unnaturally powerful, inbred gifts of *laran*

STORMQUEEN!

HAWKMISTRESS!

THE HUNDRED KINGDOMS:

An age of war and strife retaining many of the decimating and disastrous effects of the Ages of Chaos. The lands which are later to become the Seven Domains are divided by continuous border conflicts into a multitude of small, belligerent kingdoms, named for convenience "The Hundred Kingdoms." The close of this era is heralded by the adoption of the Compact, instituted by Varzil the Good. A landmark and turning point in the history of Darkover, the Compact bans all distance weapons, making it a matter of honor that one who seeks to kill must himself face equal risk of death.

TWO TO CONQUER

THE HEIRS OF THE HAMMERFELL

THE FALL OF NESKAYA

ZANDRU'S FORGE

THE RENUNCIATES:

During the Ages of Chaos and the time of the Hundred Kingdoms, there were two orders of women who set themselves apart from the patriarchal nature of Darkovan feudal society: the priestesses of Avarra, and the warriors of the Sisterhood of the Sword. Eventually these two independent groups merged to form the powerful and legally chartered Order of Renunciates or Free Amazons, a guild of women bound only by oath as a sisterhood of mutual responsibility. Their primary allegiance is to each other rather than to family, clan, caste or any man save a temporary employer. Alone among Darkovan women, they are exempt from the usual legal restrictions and protections. Their reason for existence is to provide the women of Darkover an alternative to their socially restrictive lives.

THE SHATTERED CHAIN
THENDARA HOUSE
CITY OF SORCERY

AGAINST THE TERRANS
—THE FIRST AGE (Recontact):

After the Hastur Wars, the Hundred Kingdoms are consolidated into the Seven Domains, and ruled by a hereditary aristocracy of seven families, called the Comyn, allegedly descended from the legendary Hastur, Lord of Light. It is during this era that the Terran Empire, really a form of confederacy, rediscovers Darkover, which they know as the fourth planet of the Cottman star system. The fact that Darkover is a lost colony of the Empire is not easily or readily acknowledged by Darkovans and their Comyn overloads.

REDISCOVERY (*with Mercedes Lackey*)
THE SPELL SWORD
THE FORBIDDEN TOWER
STAR OF DANGER
WINDS OF DARKOVER

AGAINST THE TERRANS
—THE SECOND AGE (After the Comyn):

With the initial shock of recontact beginning to wear off, and the Terran spaceport a permanent establishment on the outskirts of the city of Thendara, the younger and less traditional elements of Darkovan society begin the first real exchange of knowledge with the Terrans—learning Terran science and technology and teaching Darkovan matrix technology in turn. Eventually Regis Hastur, the young Comyn lord most active in these exchanges, becomes Regent in a provisional government allied to the Terrans. Darkover is once again reunited with its founding Empire.

THE DARKOVER ANTHOLOGIES:

These volumes of stories edited by Marion Zimmer Bradley, strive to "fill in the blanks" of Darkovan history, and elaborate on the eras, tales and characters which have captured readers' imaginations.

A WORLD DIVIDED

STAR OF DANGER

THE BLOODY SUN

THE WINDS OF DARKOVER

Marion Zimmer Bradley

DAW BOOKS, INC.

DONALD A. WOLLHEIM, FOUNDER

375 Hudson Street, New York, NY 10014

ELIZABETH R. WOLLHEIM
SHEILA E. GILBERT
PUBLISHERS

http://www.dawbooks.com

STAR OF DANGER
Original copyright © 1965 by Ace Books, Inc.
Copyright © renewed 1993 by Marion Zimmer Bradley

THE BLOODY SUN
Original copyright © 1965 by Ace Books, Inc.
Copyright © renewed 1992 by Marion Zimmer Bradley
"To Keep the Oath"
Copyright © 1979 by Marion Zimmer Bradley

THE WINDS OF DARKOVER
Copyright © 1970 by Marion Zimmer Bradley

A WORLD DIVIDED
Copyright © 2003 by The Marion Zimmer Bradley
Literary Works Trust

All Rights Reserved.

Cover art by Romas

DAW Book Collectors No. 1278.
DAW Books are distributed by the Penguin Group (USA).

All characters and events in this book are fictitious.
Any resemblance to persons living or dead is strictly coincidental.

First Paperback Printing, December 2003
1 2 3 4 5 6 7 8 9

DAW TRADEMARK REGISTERED
U.S. PAT. OFF. AND FOREIGN COUNTRIES
—MARCA REGISTRADA.
HECHO EN U.S.A.

PRINTED IN THE U.S.A.

CONTENTS

Star of Danger
To my son Patrick, but for whose help this book
would have been written much sooner

The Bloody Sun
For showing me universes without number;
in loving memory, Henry Kuttner

STAR OF DANGER

CHAPTER ONE

It didn't look at all like an alien planet.

Larry Montray, standing on the long ramp that led downward from the giant spaceship, felt the cold touch of sharp disillusion and disappointment. Darkover. Hundreds of light-years from Earth, a strange world under a strange sun—and it didn't look different at all.

It was night. Below him lay the spaceport lighted almost to a daytime dazzle by rows of bluewhite arclights; an enormous flat expanse of concrete ramps and runways, the blurred outlines of the giant starships dim through the lights; levels and stairways and ramps leading upward to the lines of high streets and the dark shapes of skyscrapers beyond the port. But Larry had seen spaceships and spaceports on Earth. With a father in the service of the Terran Empire, you got used to seeing things like that.

He didn't know what he'd expected of the new world—but he hadn't expected it to look just like any spaceport on Earth!

He'd expected so much. . . .

Of course, Larry had always known that he'd go out into space someday. The Terran Empire had spread itself over a thousand worlds surrounding a thousand suns, and no son of Terra ever considered staying there all his life.

But he'd been resigned to waiting at least a few more

years. In the old days, before star travel, a boy of sixteen could ship out as cabin boy on a windjammer, and see the world. And back in the early days of star travel, when the immense interstellar distances meant years and years in the gulfs between the stars, they'd shipped young kids to crew the starships—so they wouldn't be old men when the voyages ended.

But those days were gone. Now, a trip of a hundred light-years could be made in about that many days, and men, not boys, manned the ships and the Trade Cities of the Terran Empire. At sixteen Larry had been resigned to waiting. Not happy about it. Just resigned.

And then the news had come. Wade Montray, his father, had put in for transfer to the Civil Service on the planet Darkover, far out in the edge of the Milky Way. And Larry—whose mother had died before he was old enough to remember her, and who had no other living relatives—was going with him.

He'd ransacked his school library, and all the local reading rooms, to find out something about Darkover. He didn't learn much. It was the fourth planet of a medium-sized dark red star, invisible from Earth's sky, and so dim that it had a name only in star-catalogues. It was a world smaller than Earth, it had four moons, it was a world at an arrested cultural level without very much technology or science. The major products exported from Darkover were medicinal earths and biological drugs, jewel stones, fine metals for precision tools, and a few luxury goods—silks, furs, wines.

A brief footnote in the catalogue had excited Larry almost beyond endurance: *Although the natives of Darkover are human, there are several intelligent cultures of non-humans present on this planet.*

Nonhumans! You didn't see them often on Earth. Rarely, near one of the spaceports, you'd see a Jovian trundling by in his portable breathing-tank of methane gas; Earth's oxygen was just as poisonous to him as the gas to an Earthman.

And now and again, you might catch a curious, exciting glimpse of some tall, winged man-thing from one of the outer worlds. But you never saw them up close. You couldn't think of them as *people*, somehow.

He'd badgered his father with insistent questions until his father said, in exasperation, "How should I know? I'm not an information manual! I know that Darkover has a red sun, a cold climate, and a language supposed to be derived from the old Earth languages! I know it has four moons and that there are nonhumans there—and that's all I know! So why don't you wait and find out when you get there!"

When Dad got that look in his eye, it was better not to ask questions. So Larry kept the rest of them to himself. But one evening, as Larry was sorting things in his room, deciding to throw away stacks of outgrown books, toys, odds and ends he'd somehow accumulated in the last few years, his father knocked at his door.

"Busy, son?"

"Come in, Dad."

Wade Montray came, nodding at the clutter on the bed. "Good idea. You can't take more than a few pounds of luggage with you, even these days. I've got something for you—picked it up at the Transfer Center." He handed Larry a flat package; turning it over, Larry saw it was a set of tapes for his recording machine.

"Language tapes," his father said, "since you're so anxious to learn all about Darkover. You could get along all right in Standard, of course—everyone around the Spaceport and the Trade City speaks it. Most of the people going out to Darkover don't bother with the language, but I thought you might be interested."

"Thanks, Dad. I'll hook up the tapes tonight."

His father nodded. He was a stern-looking man, tall and quiet with dark eyes—Larry suspected that his own red hair and gray eyes came from his unremembered mother—and he hadn't smiled much lately; but now he smiled at Larry.

"It's a good idea. I've found out that it helps to be able to speak to people in their own language, instead of expecting them to speak yours."

He moved the tapes aside and sat down on Larry's bed. The smile slid away and he was grave again.

"Son, do you really mind leaving Earth? It's come to me, again and again, that it's not fair to take you away from your home, out to the edge of nowhere. I almost didn't put in for that transfer thinking of that. Even now—" he hesitated. "Larry, if you'd rather, you can stay here, and I can send for you in a few years, when you're through with school and college."

Larry felt his throat go suddenly tight.

"Leave me here? On Earth?"

"There are good schools and universities, son. Nobody knows what sort of education you'd be getting in quarters on Darkover."

Larry stared straight at his father, his mouth set hard to keep it from trembling. "Dad, don't you want me along? If you—if you want to get rid of me, I won't make a fuss. But—" he stopped, swallowing hard.

"Son! Larry!" His father reached for his hands and held them, hard, for a minute. "Don't say that again, huh? Only I promised your mother you'd get a good education. And here I am dragging you halfway across the universe, off on a crazy adventure, just because I've got the itch in my bones and don't want to stay here like a sensible man. It's selfish to want to go, and worse to want to take you with me!"

Larry said, slowly, "I guess I must take after you, then, Dad. Because I don't want to stay in one spot like what you call a sensible man, either. Dad, I *want* to go. Couldn't you figure that out? I've never wanted anything so much!"

Wade Montray drew a long sigh. "I hoped you'd say that—how I hoped you'd say that!" He tossed the tapes into a pile of Larry's clothes, and stood up.

"All right, son. Brush up on the language, then. There must be more than one sort of education."

Listening to the language tapes, moving his tongue around the strange fluid tones of the Darkovan speech, Larry had felt his excitement grow and grow. There were strange new concepts and thoughts in this language, and hints of things that excited him. One of the proverbs caught at his imagination with a strange, tense glow: *It is wrong to keep a dragon chained for roasting your meat.*

Were there dragons on Darkover? Or was it a proverbial phrase based on legend? What did the proverb mean? That if you had a fire-breathing dragon, it was dangerous to make him work for you? Or, did it mean that it was foolish to use something big and important for some small, silly job of work? It seemed to open up a crack into a strange world where he glimpsed unknown ideas, strange animals, new colors and thoughts through a glimmer of the unknown.

His excitement had grown with every day that passed, until they had taken the shuttle to the enormous spaceport and boarded the ship itself. The starship was huge and strange, like an alien city; but the trip itself had been a letdown. It wasn't much different than a cruise by ocean liner, except that you couldn't see any ocean. You had to stay in your cabin most of the time, or in one of the cramped recreation areas. There were shots and immunizations for everything under the sun—under *any* sun, Larry corrected himself—so that he went around with a sore arm for the first two weeks of the trip.

The only moment of excitement had come early in the voyage; just after breakaway from Earth's sun, when there had been a guided tour of the ship for everyone who wasn't still struggling with acceleration sickness. Larry had been fascinated by the crew's quarters, by the high navigation deck with its rooms full of silent, brooding computers, the robots which handled, behind leaded-glass shields, any needed repairs on the drive units. He'd even seen into the drive rooms themselves, by television. They were, of course, radioactive, and even crew members could enter them only in the gravest emergencies. Most exciting of all had been the single glimpse from the Captain's bridge—the tiny glass dome with its sudden panorama of a hundred million twinkling stars. Larry, pressing himself for his brief turn against the glass, felt suddenly very lost, very small and alone in this wilderness of giant, blazing suns and worlds spinning forever against the endless dark. When he moved away he was dazed and his eyes blurred.

But the rest of the trip had been a bore. More and more he had lost himself in daydreams about the new world at the end of the journey. The very name, *Darkover*, had its curious magic. He envisioned a giant red sun lowering in a lurid sky, four moons in strange colors; his mind invented fantastic and impossible shapes for the mysterious nonhumans who would crowd around the spaceship's landing. By the time they were sent to their staterooms to strap down for the long deceleration, he was simmering with wild excitement.

He had watched the landing on TV; their approach to the planet in its veil of swirling sunset-orange clouds that had thinned into the darkness of the night side as they came near; he'd felt the shudder and surge of new gravity, the tingle of strangeness when one of the small iridescent moons swam across the camera field. He wondered which of the moons it was. Probably Kyrrdis, he thought, with its blue-green shimmer, like a peacock's wing. The names of the moons were a siren song of enchantment; Kyrrdis, Idriel, Liriel, Mormallor, *We're here*, he thought, *we're really here*.

He waited, impatient but well-disciplined, for the loudspeaker announcement which permitted passengers to unfasten their straps, collect their belongings and gather in the discharge entrance. His father was silent at his side, and his face gave away nothing; Larry wondered how anyone could be so impassive, but not wanting to seem childishly eager, Larry kept silence too. He kept his eyes on the metal door which would open on the strange world. When the crewman in his black leather began undogging the seals, Larry was almost literally shaking with excitement. A strange pinkish glow filtered around the first crack of the door. *The red sun? The strange sky?*

But the door swung open on night, and the pink glow was only the fiery light of welding torches from a pit nearby, where workmen in hoods were working on the metal hull of another great ship. Larry, stepping out onto the ramp, felt the cold touch of disappointment. It was just another spaceport, just like Earth!

Behind him on the ramp, his father touched his shoulder and said, in a gently rallying tone, "Don't stand there staring, son; your new planet won't run away. I know how excited you must be, but let's move on down."

Heaving a deep sigh, Larry began to walk down the ramp. He should have know it would turn out to be a gyp. Things you built up in your mind usually were a let-down.

Later, he was to remember his sense of disillusion that morning, and laugh at himself; but at the moment, the flat disappointment was so keen he could almost taste it. The concrete felt hard and strange after weeks of uncertain gravity in the spaceship. He swayed a little to get his balance, watching the small, buzzing cargo dollies that were whirring around the field, the men in black or grayish leather uniforms with the insignia of the Terran Empire, on which the hard blue arclights reflected coldly. Beyond the lights was a dark line of tall buildings.

"The Terran Trade City," his father pointed them out. "We'll have rooms in the Quarters buildings. Come on, we'd better get checked through the lines, there's a lot of red tape."

Larry didn't feel sleepy—it had been daytime on the starship, by the arbitrary time cycle—but he was yawning by the time they got through standing in line, having their passports and credentials checked, picking up their luggage from customs. As they came away from one booth, he looked up, idly, and then his breath caught. The darkness had thinned; the sky overhead, black when he had stepped from the spaceship, was now a strange, luminous grayed-pearl. In the east, great rays of crimson light, like a vast, shimmering Aurora Borealis, began to fan out and dance through the grayness. The lights trembled as if seen through ice. Then a rim of red appeared on the horizon, gradually puffing up into an enormous, impossibly crimson sun. Blood red. Huge. Bloated. It did not look like a sun at all; it looked like a large neon sign. The sky gradually shifted from gray to pink through the spectrum to a curious lilac-blue. In the new light the spaceport looked strange and lurid.

As the light grew, behind the line of skyscrapers Larry gradually made out a skyline of mountains—high, rough-toothed mountains with cliffs and ice-falls shining red in the sun. A pale-blue crystal of moon still hung on the shoulder of one mountain. Larry blinked, stared, kept turning to look at that impossible sun. It was still very cold; you couldn't imagine that sun warming the sky as Earth's sun did. Yet it was a huge red coal, an immense glowing fire, the color of—

"Blood. Yes, it's a bloody sun," said someone in the line behind Larry, "That's what they call it. Looks it, too."

Larry's father turned and said quietly "Seems gloomy, I know. Well, never mind, in the Trade City there will be the sort of light you're used to, and sooner or later you'll get accustomed to it." Larry started to protest, but his father did not wait for him to speak. "I've got one more line to go through. You might as well wait over there. There's no sense in you standing in line too."

Obediently, Larry got out of line and moved away. They had climbed several levels now, in their progress from line to line, and stood far above the level where the starships lay in their pits. About a hundred feet away from Larry there was a huge open archway, and he went curiously toward it, eager to see beyond the spaceport.

The archway opened on a great square, empty in the red morning light. It was floored with ancient, uneven flagstones; in the center there was a fountain, playing and splashing faintly pink. At the far end of the square, Larry saw, with a little shock of his old excitement, a line of buildings, strangely shaped, with curved stone fronts and windows of a long lozenge shape. The light played oddly on what looked like prisms of colored glass, set into the windows.

A man crossed the square. He was the first Darkovan Larry had seen; a stooped, gray-haired man wearing loose baggy breeches and a belted overshirt that seemed to be lined with fur. He cast a desultory glance at the spaceport, not seeing Larry, and slouched on by.

Two or three more men went by. Probably, Larry thought, workmen on their way to early-morning jobs. A couple of women, wearing long fur-trimmed dresses, came out of one of the buildings; one began to sweep the cobblestone sidewalk with an odd-looking fuzzy broom, while the other started to carry small tables and benches out on the walk from inside. Men lounged by; one of them sat down at a little table, signaled to one of the women, and after a time she brought him two bowls from which white steam sizzled in the frosty air. A strong pleasant smell, rather like bitter chocolate, reminded Larry that he was both cold and hungry; the Darkovan food smelled good, and he found himself wishing that he had some Darkovan money in his pocket. He remembered, experimentally, phrases in the language he had learned. He supposed he'd be able to order something to eat. The man at the table was picking up things that looked like pieces of macaroni, dipping them into the other bowl, and eating them, very tidily, with his fingers and a long pick like one chopstick.

"What are you staring at?" someone asked, and Larry

started, looking up, seeing a boy a little younger than himself standing before him. "Where did you come from, *Tallo?*"

Not till the final word did Larry realize that the stranger had spoken to him in the Darkovan language, now so familiar through the tapes. *Then I can understand it! Tallo*—that was the word for copper; he supposed it meant *redhead*. The strange boy was red-headed too, flaming hair cut square around a thin, handsome, dark-skinned face. He was not quite as tall as Larry. He wore a rust-colored shirt and laced-up leather jerkin, and high leather boots knee-length over close-fitting trousers. But Larry was surprised more by the fact that, at the boy's waist, in a battered leather sheath, there hung a short steel dagger.

Larry said at last, hesitantly in Darkovan, "Are you speaking to me?"

"Who else?" The strange boy's hands, encased in thick dark gloves, strayed to the handle of his knife, as if absent-mindedly. "What are you staring at?"

"I was just looking at the spaceport."

"And where did you get those ridiculous clothes?"

"Now look here," Larry said, taken aback at the rude tone in which the boy spoke, "why are you asking me all these questions? I'm wearing clothes I have—and for that matter, I don't think much of yours," he added belligerently. "What is it to you, anyhow?"

The strange boy looked startled. He blinked. "But have I made a mistake? I never saw—who are you?"

"My name is Larry Montray."

The boy with the knife frowned. "I can't take it in. Do you—forgive me, but by some chance do you *belong* to the spaceport? No offense is intended, but—"

"I just came in on the ship *Pantomime*," Larry said.

The stranger frowned. He said, slowly, "That explains it, I suppose. But you speak the language so well, and you look like—you must excuse my mistake, it was natural." He stood staring at Larry for another minute. Then, suddenly, as if breaking the dam: "I've never spoken before to an off-worlder! What is it like to travel in space? Is it true that there are many suns like this one? What are the other worlds like?"

But before Larry could answer, he heard his father's voice, raised sharply. "Larry! Where have you gotten to?"

"I'm here," he called, turning around, realizing that where he stood, he was hidden in the shadow of the arch-way. "Just a minute—" he turned back to the strange boy, but to his surprise and exasperation, the Darkovan boy had turned his back and was walking rapidly away. He disap-peared into the dark mouth of a narrow street across the square. Larry stood frowning, looking after him.

His father came quickly toward him.

"What were you doing? Just watching the square? I sup-pose there's no harm, but—" He sounded agitated. "Who were you talking to ? One of the natives?"

"Just a kid about my age," Larry said. "Dad, he thought—"

"Never mind now." His father cut him off, rather sharply. "We have to find our quarters and get settled. You'll learn soon enough. Come along."

Larry followed, puzzled and exasperated at his father's curtness. This wasn't like Dad. But his first disappointment at the ordinariness of Darkover had suddenly disappeared.

That kid thought I was Darkovan. Even with the clothes I was wearing. From hearing me speak the language, he couldn't tell the difference.

He looked back, almost wistfully, at the vanishing panorama of Darkover beyond the forbidden gateway. They were passing now into a street of houses and buildings that were just like Earth ones, and Larry's father sighed—with relief?

"Just like home. At least you won't be too homesick

here," he said, checked the numbers on a card he held, and pushed open a door. "Our rooms are in this building."

Inside, the lights had been set so that the light was that of Earth at noon, and the apartment—five rooms on the fourth floor—might have been the one they had left on Earth. All the while they were unpacking, dialing food from the dispensers, exploring the rooms, Larry's thoughts ran a new and strange pattern.

What was the point of living on a strange world if you did your best to make your house, the furniture, the very *light*, look exactly like the old one? Why not *stay* on Earth if you felt like that?

Okay, if they wanted it this way. That was okay with him. But he was going to see more of Darkover than this.

He was going to see what lay beyond that gate. The new world was beautiful, and strange—and he could hardly wait to explore it.

Homesick? What did Dad think he *was?*

CHAPTER TWO

Larry pushed back the heavy steel door of Quarters B building, and emerged into the thin cold cutting wind of the
courtyard between buildings. He stood there shivering,
looking at the sky; the huge red sun hung low, slowly dropping toward the horizon, where thin ice-clouds massed in
mountains of crimson and scarlet and purple.

Behind him Rick Stewart shivered audibly, pulling his
coat tight. "Brrr, I wish they had a passageway between
buildings! And I can't see a thing in this light. Let's get inside, Larry." He waited a minute, impatiently. "What are you
staring at?"

"Nothing." Larry shrugged and followed the other lad
into Quarters A, where their rooms were located. How could
he say that this brief daily passage between Quarters B—
where the school for spaceport youngsters, from kindergarten to pre-university, was located—and Quarters A, was
his only chance to look at Darkover?

Inside, in the cool yellow Earthlike light, Rick relaxed.
"You're an odd one," he said, as they took the elevator to
their floor. "I'd think the light out there would hurt your
eyes."

"No, I like it. I wish we could get out and explore."

"Well, shall we go down to the spaceport?" Rick chuckled. "There's nothing to see there but starships, and they're

an old story to me, but I suppose to you they're still exciting."

Larry felt exasperated at the patronizing amusement in Rick's voice. Rick had been on Darkover three years—and frankly admitted that he had never been beyond the spaceport. "Not that," he said, "I'd like to get into the town—see what it's like." His pent-up annoyance suddenly escaped. "I've been on Darkover three weeks, and I might as well be back on Earth! Even here in the school, I'm studying the same things I was studying at home! History of Terra, early Space Exploration, Standard Literature, mathematics—"

"You bet," Rick said. "You don't think any Terran citizens would stay here, if their kids couldn't get a decent education, do you? Requirements for any Empire university."

"I know that. But after all, living on this planet, we should know a little something about it, shouldn't we?"

Rick shrugged again. "I can't imagine why." They came into the rooms Larry shared with his father, and dumped their school books and paraphernalia. Larry went to the food dispenser—from which food prepared in central kitchens was delivered by pueumatic tube and charged to their account—and dialed himself a drink and a snack, asking Rick what he wanted. The boys stretched out on the furniture, eating hungrily.

"You *are* an odd one," Rick repeated. "Why do you care about this planet? We're not going to stay here all our lives. What good would it do to learn everything about it? What we get in the Terran Empire schools will be valid on any Empire planet where they send us. As for me, I'm going into the Space Academy when I'm eighteen—and goodness knows, that's reason enough to hit the books on navigation and math!"

Larry munched a cracker. "It just seems funny," he repeated with stubborn emphasis, "to live on a world like this and not know more about it. Why not *stay* on Earth, if their culture is the only one you care about?"

Rick's chuckle was tolerant. "This is your first planet out from Earth? Oh, well, that explains it. After you've seen a couple, you'll realize that there's nothing out there but a lot of barbarians and outworlders. Unless you're going in for archaeology or history as a career, why clutter up your mind with the details?"

Larry couldn't answer. He didn't try. He finished his cracker and opened his book on navigation. "Was this the problem that was bothering you?"

But while they put their heads together, figuring out interstellar orbits and plotting collision curves, Larry was still thinking with frustrated eagerness of the world outside—the world, it seemed now, he'd never know.

Rick didn't seem to care. None of the youngsters he'd met here in the Trade City seemed to care. They were Earthmen, and anything outside the Terran Zone was alien—and they couldn't have cared less. They lived the same life they'd have lived on any Empire planet, and that was the way they wanted it.

They'd even been surprised—no, thunder struck—to hear that he'd learned the Darkovan speech. They couldn't imagine why. One of the teachers had been faintly sympathetic; he'd shown Larry how to make the complicated letters of the Darkovan alphabet, and even loaned him a few books written in Darkovan. But there wasn't much time for that. Mostly he got the same schooling he'd have had on Earth. Darkover, even the light of Darkover's red sun, was barriered out by walls and yellow earth-type lights; and the closed minds of the Terran Zone personnel were even more of a barrier.

When Rick had gone, Larry put his books away and sat scowling, thinking it over, until his father came in.

"How's it going, Dad?"

He was fascinated by his father's work, but Wade Montray wouldn't talk about it much. Larry knew that his father worked in the customs office, and that his work was, in a general way, to see that no contraband was smuggled from Darkover to the Terran Zone, or vice versa. It sounded interesting to Larry, though his father kept insisting it was not much different from the work he'd done on Earth.

But today he seemed somewhat more communicative.

"How about dialing us some supper? I was too busy, today, to stop and eat. We had some trouble at the Bureau. One of the City Elders came to us, as mad as a drenched cat. He insisted that one of our men had carried weapons into the City, and we had to check it up. What happened was that some young fool of a Darkovan had offered one of the Spaceports Guards a lot of money to sell him one of his pistols and report it lost. When we checked with the man, sure enough, he'd done just that. Of course, he lost his rank and he'll be on the next spaceship out of Darkover. The confounded fool!"

"Why, Dad?"

Wade Montray leaned his chin on his hands. "You don't know much Darkovan history, do you? They have a thing called the Compact, signed a thousand years ago, which makes it illegal for anyone to have or to use any weapon except the kind which brings the man who uses it into the same risk as the man he attacks with it."

"I don't think I quite understand that, Dad."

"Well, look. If you wear a sword, or a knife, in order to use it, you have to get close to your victim—and for all you know, *he* may have a knife and be better than you are at using it. But guns, shockers, blasters, atomic bombs—you can use those without taking any risk of getting hurt yourself. Anyway, Darkover signed the Compact, and before they agreed to let the Terran Empire build a spaceport here for trade, we had to give them iron-clad guarantees that we'd help them keep contraband out of Darkover."

"I don't blame them," Larry said. He had heard the tales of the early planetary wars on Earth.

"Anyway. The man who bought this gun from our spaceforce guard has a collection of rare old weapons, and he swears he only wanted it as part of his collection—but nobody can be sure of that. Contraband *does* get across the border sometimes, no matter how careful we are. So I had quite a day trying to trace it down. Then I had to arrange for a couple of students from the medical schools here to go out into the back country on Darkover, studying diseases. We've arranged to admit a few Darkovans to the medical schools here. Their medical science isn't up to much, and they think very highly of our doctors. But it isn't easy even then. The more superstitious natives are prejudiced against anything Terran. And the higher caste Darkovans won't have anything to do with us because it's beneath their dignity to associate with aliens. They think we're barbarians. I talked to one of their aristocrats today and he behaved as if I smelled bad." Wade Montray sighed.

"They think we're barbarians," Larry said slowly, "and here in the Terran Zone, we think *they* are."

"That's right. And there doesn't seem to be any answer."

Larry put down his fork. He burst out, suddenly, "Dad, when am I going to get a chance to see something of Darkover?" All his frustration exploded in him. "All this time, and I saw more through a gate on the spaceport than I've seen since!"

His father leaned back and looked at him, curiously. "Do you want to see it so much?"

Larry made it an understatement. "I do."

His father sighed. "It's not easy," he said. "The Darkovans don't especially like having Terrans here. We're more or less expected to keep to our own Trade Cities."

"But why?"

"It's hard to explain," said Wade Montray, shaking his head. "Mostly they're afraid of our influence on them. Of course they're not all like that, but enough of them are."

Larry's face fell, and his father added, slowly, "I can try to get permission, sometime, to take you on a trip to one of the other Trade Cities; you'd see the country in between. As for the Old Town near the spaceport—well, it's rather a rough section, because all the spacemen in from the ships spend their furloughs there. They're used to Earthmen, of course, but there isn't much to see." He sighed again. "I know how you feel, Larry. I suppose I can take you to see the market, if that will get rid of this itch you have to see something outside the Terran Zone."

"When? Now?"

His father laughed. "Get a warm coat, then. It gets cold here, nights."

The sun hung, a huge low red ball on the rim of the world, as they crossed the Terran Zone, threaded the maze of the official buildings and came out at the edge of the levels which led downward to the spaceports. They did not go down toward the ships, but instead walked along the highest level. They passed the gate where—once before—Larry had stood to look out at the city; only this time they went on past that gate and toward another one, at the far edge of the port.

This gate was larger, and guarded by black-clad men armed with holstered weapons. Both of the guards nodded in recognition at Larry's father as they went through into the open square.

"Don't forget the curfew, Mr. Montray. All Zone personnel not on duty are supposed to be inside the gates by midnight, our time."

Montray nodded. As they crossed the square side by side, he asked, "How are you getting along on the new sleep cycle, Larry?"

"It doesn't bother me." Darkover had a twenty-eight hour period of rotation, and Larry knew that some people found it difficult to adjust to longer days and nights, but he hadn't had any trouble.

The open square between the spaceport and the Darkovan city of Thendara was wide, open to the sky, and darkly spacious in the last red light of the sun. At one side it was lighted with the arclights from the spaceport; at the other side, it was already dimly lit with paler lights in a medium pinkish color. At the far end there was a row of shops, and Darkovans and Earthmen were moving about in front of them. The wares displayed were of a bewildering variety: furs, pottery dishes, ornate polished knives with bright sheaths, all kinds of fruits, and what looked like sweets and candies. But as Larry paused to inspect them, his father said in a low voice, "This is just the tourist section—the overflow from the spaceport. I thought you'd rather see the old market. You can come here any time."

They turned into a sidestreet floored with uneven cobblestones, too narrow for any sort of vehicle. His father walked swiftly, as if he knew where he was going, and Larry thought, not without resentment, *He's been here before. He knows just where to go. Yet he never realized that I'd want to see all this, too.*

The houses on either side were low, constructed of stone for the most part, and seemed very old. They all had a great many windows with thick, translucent, colored or frosted glass set in patterns into the panes, so that nothing could be seen from outside. Between the houses were low stalls made of reeds or wood, and a variety of outbuildings. Larry wondered what the houses were like inside. As he passed one of them, there was a strong smell of roasting meat, and behind one of the houses he heard the voices of children playing. A man rode slowly down the street, mounted on a small brownish horse; Larry realized that he controlled the horse without bit or bridle, with only a halter and the reins.

The narrow street widened and came out into a much larger open space, filled with the low reed stalls, canvas tents with many-colored awnings, or small stone kiosks. It was dimly lighted with the flaring enclosed lights. Around the perimeter of the market, horses and carts were tied, and Larry looked at them curiously.

"Horses?"

Montray nodded. "They don't manufacture any surface transport of any sort. We've tried to get them interested in a market for autocars or helicopters, but they say they don't like building roads and nobody is in a hurry anyway. It's a barbarian world, Larry. I told you that. Between ourselves," he lowered his voice, "I think many of the Darkovan people would like some of our kind of machinery and manufacturing. But the people who run things want to keep their world just the way it is. They like it better this way."

Larry was looking around in fascination. He said, "I'd hate to see this market turned into a big mechanized shopping center, though. The ones on Earth are ugly."

His father smiled. "You wouldn't like it if you had to live with it," he said. "You're like all youngsters, you romanticize old-fashioned things. Believe me, the Darkovan authorities aren't romantic. It's just easier for them to go on running things their own way, if they keep the people doing things the way they always have. But it won't last long." He sounded quietly certain. "Once the Terran Empire comes in to show people what a star-travel civilization *can* be like, people will want progress."

A tall, hard-faced man in a long, wrapped cloak gave them a sharp, angry glance from harsh blue eyes, then lowered thick eyelashes and walked past them. Larry looked up at his father.

"Dad, that man heard what you said, and he didn't like it."

"Nonsense," his father said. "I wasn't speaking that loud, and very few of them can speak Terran languages. It's all part of the same thing. They trade with us, yet they want nothing to do with our culture." He stopped beside a row of stalls. "Can you see anything you'd like here?"

There was a row of blue-and-white glazed bowls in small and larger sizes, a similar row of green-and-brown ones. At the next stall there were knives and daggers of various sorts, and Larry found himself thinking of the Darkovan boy who had worn a knife in his belt. He picked up one and fingered it idly; at his father's frown, he laughed a little and put it back. What would he do with it? Earthmen didn't wear swords!

An old woman behind a low counter was bending over a huge pottery bowl of steaming, bubbling fat, twisting strips of dough and dropping them into the oil. Below the bowl, the charcoal fire glowed like the red sun, throwing out a welcome heat to where the boy stood. The strips of dough twisted like small goldfish as they turned crisp and brown; as she fished them out, Larry felt suddenly hungry. He had not spoken Darkovan since that first day, but as he opened his mouth, he found that the learning-tapes had done their work well, for he knew just what he wanted to say, and how.

"What is the price of your cakes, please?"

"Two sekals for each, young sir," she said, and Larry, fishing in his pocket for his spending money, asked for half a dozen. His father put down a scroll at the next stall, and came toward him.

"Those are very good," he said, "I've tasted them. Something like doughnuts."

The old woman was laying out the cakes on a clean coarse cloth, letting the sweet-smelling oil drain from them, dusting them with some pale stuff. She wrapped them in a sheet of brownish fiber and handed the package to Larry.

"Your accent is strange, young sir. Are you from the Cahuenga ranges?" As she raised her lined old face, Larry saw with a shock that the woman's eyes were whitish and unfocused; she was blind. *But she had thought his speech genuinely Darkovan!* He made a noncommittal reply, paying her for the cakes and biting hungrily into one. They were hot, sweet and crisp, powdered lightly with what tasted like crushed rock candy.

They moved down the twilit lane of booths. Now and again they encountered uniformed men from the spaceport, or occasional civilians, but most of the men, women and children in the market were Darkovans, and they regarded the Terrans, father and son, with faintly hostile curiosity.

Larry thought, *Everyone stares at us. I wish I could dress like a Darkovan and mix in with them somehow so they wouldn't take any notice of me. Then I could know what they were really like.* Gloomily he munched the doughnut cake, stopping to look over a display of short knives.

The Darkovan behind the stall said to Larry's father, "Your son is not yet of an age to bear weapons. Or do you Terrans not allow your young men to be men?" His smile was sly, faintly patronizing, and Larry's father frowned and looked irritated.

"Are you ready to go, Larry?"

"Any time you say, Dad." Larry felt faintly deflated and let down. What, after all, had he been expecting? They turned back, making their way along the row of stalls.

"What did that fellow mean, Dad?"

"On Darkover you'd be legally of age—old enough to wear a sword. And expected to use them to defend yourself, if necessary," Wade Montray said briefly.

Abruptly and with a rush, the red sun sank and went out. Immediately, like sweeping wings, darkness closed over the sky and thin swirling coils of mist began to blow along the alleys of the market. Larry shivered in his warm coat, and his father pulled up his collar. The lights of the market danced and flickered, surrounded by foggy shapes of color.

"That's why they call the planet Darkover," Larry's father said. Already he was half invisible in the mist. "Stay close to me or you'll get lost in the fog. It will thin out and turn to rain in a few minutes, though."

Through the thick mist, in the flickering lights, a form took shape, coming slowly toward them. At first it looked like a tall man, cloaked and hooded against the cold; then, with a strange prickling along his spine, Larry realized that the hunched, high-shouldered form beneath the cloak was not human. A pair of green eyes, luminescent as the eyes of a cat by lamplight, knifed in their direction. The non-human came slowly on. Larry stood motionless, half-hypnotized, held by those piercing eyes, almost unable to move.

"Get back!" Roughly, his father jerked him against the wall; Larry stumbled, sprawled, fell, one hand flung out to get his balance. The hand brushed the edge of the alien's cloak—

A stinging, violent pain rocked him back, thrust him, with a harsh blow, against the stone wall. It was like the shock of a naked electric wire. Speechless with pain, Larry picked himself up. The nonhuman, unhurried, was gliding slowly away. Wade Montray's face was dead white in the flickering light.

"Larry! Son, are you hurt?"

Larry rubbed his hand; it was numb and it prickled. "I guess not. What was that thing, anyhow?"

"A *Kyrri*. They have protective electric fields, like some kinds of fish on earth." His father looked somber. "I haven't seen one in a human town for years."

Larry, still numbed, gazed after the dwindling form with respect and strange awe. "One thing's for sure, I won't get in their way again," he said fervently.

The mist was thinning and a fine spray of icy rain was beginning to fall. Not speaking, Wade Montray hurried toward the spaceport; walking fast to keep up—and not minding, because it was freezing cold and the rapid pace kept him warm—Larry wondered why his father was so silent. Had he simply been afraid? It seemed more than that.

Montray did not speak again until they were within their own rooms in Quarters A, the warmth and bright yellow light closing around them like a familiar garment. Larry, laying his coat aside, heard his father sigh.

"Well, does that satisfy your curiosity a little, Larry?"

"Thanks, Dad."

Montray dropped into a chair. "That means no. Well, I suppose you can visit the tourist section and the market by yourself, if you want to. Though you'd better not do too much wandering around alone."

His father dialed himself a hot drink from the dispenser, came back sipping it. Then he said, slowly, "I don't want to tie strings on you, Larry. I'll be honest with you; I wish you hadn't been cursed with that infernal curiosity of yours. I'd like it better if you were like the other kids here—content to stay an Earthman. It would take a load off my mind. But I'm not going to forbid you to explore if you want to. You're old enough, certainly, to know what you want. If you'd been brought up here, you'd be considered a grown man—old enough to wear a sword and fight your own duels."

"How did you know that, Dad?"

His father did not look at him. Facing the wall, he said, "I spent a few years here before you were born. I never should have come back. I knew that. Now I can see—"

He broke off sharply, and without another word, he went off into his own bedroom. Larry did not see him again that night.

CHAPTER THREE

If Larry's father had hoped that this glimpse of Darkover would dim Larry's hunger for the world outside the Terran Zone, he was mistaken. The faint, far-off glance at strangeness had whetted Larry's curiosity without satisfying it.

But after all, he didn't forbid me to leave the Terran Zone. Larry told himself that, defiantly, every time he crossed the gates of the spaceport and went out into the city. He knew his father disapproved, but they never spoke of it.

On foot, alone, he explored the strange city; at first staying close to the walls of the spaceport, within sight of the tall landmark-beacon of the Quarters Building. Terrans were a familiar sight, and the Darkovans of the sector paid little attention to the tall, red-haired young Terran. Some of the shopkeepers, when they found that he could speak their language, were inclined to be friendly.

Heartened by these expeditions into the city, Larry gradually grew bolder. Now and again he ventured out of the familiar spaceport district, exploring an unusually alluring side street, walking through an unfamiliar court or square.

One afternoon he stood for an hour near the door of a forge, watching a blacksmith shoeing one of the small, sturdy Darkovan horses with light strong metal shoes. You didn't see things like that on Earth, not in this day and age. Horses were rare animals, kept in zoos and museums.

He was aware, now and then, of curious or hostile
glances following him. Terrans were not overly popular in
the city. But he had been brought up on Earth, a quiet and
well-policed world, and hardly knew what fear was. Certainly, he thought, he was safe on the public streets during
the day light hours!

It was a few days after he had watched the blacksmith at
work. He had gone back to that quarter, fascinated by the
sight; and then, lured by a street lined with gardens of
strange, low-hanging trees and flowers, he had walked down
court after court. After a time, he began to realize that he had
taken little heed of his bearings; the street had turned and
twisted several times, and he was no longer very sure which
way he had come. He looked around, but the high houses
nearby concealed the beacons of the spaceport, and he was
not sure which way to go.

Larry did not panic. He felt sure that he need only retrace
his steps a little way to come back into familiar ground; or,
perhaps, to go on a little further, and he would come out into
a part of the city that he knew.

He went on a little way. The garden street suddenly ran
out, and he found himself in a part of the city where he had
never been before. It was so unlike anything he had seen so
far that he seriously began to wonder if he had strayed into
a nonhuman district. The sun was low in the sky, and Larry
began to worry a little about it. Could he, after all, find his
way?

He looked around, trying to orient himself in the dimming light. The streets were irregular here, and twisting; the
houses close together, made of thatch and chinked pebbles
daubed with what looked like coarse cement, windowless
and dark. The street seemed empty; and yet, as he stopped
and looked around, Larry had the disconcerting notion that
someone was watching him.

"Come on," he said aloud, "don't start imagining things."

He started seriously to take stock of his position. The spaceport lay to the east of the town, so that he should put his back to the sun, and keep on going that way.

Somebody's watching me. I can feel it.

He turned around slowly, getting his bearings. He ought to turn this way, into this street, and keep on eastward, then he couldn't possibly miss the spaceport. It might be a long walk, but before long he ought to get into some familiar district. *Before dark, I hope.* He looked back, nervously, as he turned into the narrow street. Was that a step behind him?

He ordered himself to stop imagining things. *People live here. They have a right to walk down the street, so what if there is somebody behind you? Anyway, there's nobody there.*

Abruptly the street turned a blind corner, ran into a small open square, and dead-ended in a low stone wall and the blank rear entrances of a couple of houses. Larry scowled, and felt like swearing. He'd have to try again, damn it! And if the sun went down and he had to start wandering around in the dark, he'd be in fine shape! He turned to retrace his steps, and stopped dead.

Across the square, several indistinct forms were coming toward him. In the lowering light, purple-edged, they seemed big and looming, and they seemed to advance on Larry with steady purpose. He started to walk on, then hesitated; they were moving—yes, they had cut off his return from the way he had come.

He could see them clearly now. They were boys and young men, six or eight of them, about his own age or a little younger, shabbily dressed in Darkovan clothes; their rough-cut hair was lying on their shoulders, and one and all, they had a look of jeering malice. They looked rough, rowdy, and not at all friendly, and Larry felt a touch of panic. But he told himself, sternly, *They're just a batch of kids. Most of them look younger than I am. Why should I assume they're after me—or that they have any interest in me at*

*all? For all I know, they might be the local chowder and
marching society out for an evening on the town!*

He nodded politely, and began to walk toward them, confident that they would part and let him through. Instead, the
ranks suddenly closed, and Larry had to stop to keep from
bumping headlong into the leader—a big, burly boy of sixteen or so.

Larry said politely, in Darkovan, "Will you let me pass,
please?"

"Why, he talks our lingo!" The burly boy's dialect was so
rough that Larry could hardly make out the words. "And
what's a *Terranan* from behind the walls doing out here in
the city?"

"What you want here anyway?" one of the young men
asked.

Larry braced himself hard, trying not to show fear, and
spoke with careful courtesy. "I was walking in the city, and lost
myself. If one of you would tell me which way I should take
to find the spaceport, I would be grateful."

The polite speech, however, was greeted with guffaws of
shrill laughter.

"Hey, he's lost!"

"Ain't that too bad!"

"Hey, *chiyu*, you expect the big boss of the spaceport to
come looking for you with a lamp?"

"Poor little fellow, out alone after dark!"

"And not even big enough to carry a knife! Does your
mammy know you're out walking, little boy?"

Larry made no answer. He was beginning to be dread-
fully afraid. They might simply take it out in rough language—but they might not. These Darkovan street urchins
might be just children—but they carried wicked long knives,
and they were evidently toughs. He began to measure the
leader with his eyes, wondering if he would stand up to them
if it came to a fight. He might—the big bully looked fat and

out of condition—but he certainly couldn't handle the whole gang of them at once.

Just the same, he knew that if he showed fear once, he was lost. If they were simply baiting him, a bold manner might bluff them away. He clenched his fists, trying with the gesture to hold his voice tight, and stepped up to the bully.

"Get out of my way."

"Suppose you *knock* me out of it, Terran!"

"Okay," said Larry between his teeth, "you asked for it, fat guy."

Quickly, with one hard punch, he drove his fist into the big boy's chin. The youngster let out a surprised "Ugh!" of pain, but his own fists came up, driving a low, foul blow into Larry's stomach. Larry, shocked as well as hurt, was taken aback. He staggered to recover his balance, gasping for breath.

The big boy kicked him. Then, in a rush, the whole gang was on him shoving and jostling him rudely, yelling words Larry did not understand. They shouldered him back, hustling him, forming a circle around him, pushing him off balance every time he recovered it, closing in to shove and jeer. Larry's breath came in sobs of rage.

"*One* of you fight me, you cowards, and you'll see—"

A kick landed in his shins; someone drove an elbow into his stomach. He slid to his knees. A fist jammed into his face, and he felt blood break from his lip. Cold terror suddenly gripped through him as he realized that no one in the Terran Zone so much as knew where he was; that he could be not only mauled but killed.

"Get away from him, you filthy gutter rabbits!"

It was a new voice, clear and contemptuous, striking through the rude jeers and yells. With little gulps and gasps of consternation, the street urchins jostled back, and Larry, coming up slowly to his knees, wiping at his bloody face in the respite, blinked in the sudden light of torches.

Two tall men, green-clad, stood there carrying lights; but

the lights, and all eyes, were focused on the young man who stood between the torches.

He was tall and red-haired, dressed in an embroidered leather jacket and a short fur cloak; his hand was on the hilt of a knife. His eyes, cold gray, were blazing as he whipped them with stinging words.

"Nine—ten against one, and he was still giving a good account of himself to you! So this proves that Terrans are cowards, eh?"

His eyes swung to Larry, and he gestured. "Get up."

The fat bully-boy was literally shaking. He bowed his head, whining, "Lord Alton—"

The newcomer silenced him with a gesture. The smaller roughnecks looked sullen or overawed. The youngster in the fur cloak took a step toward Larry, and a cold, bleak smile touched his lips.

"I might have known it would be you," he said. "Well, we're under bond to keep peace in the city, but it seems to me you were asking for trouble. What were you doing here?"

"Walking," Larry said. "I got lost." Suddenly he resented the cool, arrogant air of authority in the newcomer's voice. He flung his head back, set his chin and looked the strange boy straight in the eye. "Is that a crime?"

The fur-cloaked boy laughed briefly, and suddenly Larry recognized the laugh and the face. It was the same insolent redhead he had seen his first day on Darkover; the youngster who'd spoken to him at the spaceport gate.

The Darkovan boy looked around at the little knot of roughs, who had drawn back and were shouldering one another restlessly. "Not so brave now, eh? Don't worry, I didn't come to stop your fight," he said, and his voice was contemptuous and clear. "But you might as well make it mean something." He looked back at Larry, then back to the gang. "Pick out someone of your number—someone his own size—and *one* of you take him on." His eyes raked

Larry's and he added consideringly, "Unless you're afraid to fight, Terran? Then I can send you home with my body-guards."

Larry bristled at the suggestion. "I'll fight any five of them, if they fight fair," he said angrily, and the Darkovan threw back his head with a sharp laugh.

"One's plenty. All right, you bully boys," he snarled suddenly at the gang, "pick out your champion. Or isn't any one of you willing to stand up to a Terran without the whole rat-pack behind you?"

The street boys crowded together, looking warily at Larry, and the two looming guards, at the young Darkovan aristocrat. There was a long moment of silence. The Darkovan laughed, very softly.

Finally one of the gang, a long lean young man almost six feet tall, with a broken tooth and a rangy, yellowed, evil face, spat on the cobblestones.

"I'll fight the—" Larry did not understand the epithet. "I'm not afraid of any Terran from 'ere to the Hellers!"

Larry clenched his fists, sizing up his new opponent. He supposed the street boy was a year or so older than himself. Tall and stringy, with huge fists, he looked a nasty customer. This wasn't going to be easy either.

Suddenly the boy rushed him, landing a pounding succession of blows before Larry could counter a single punch. Larry was forced backward. One fist smashed into his eye; a second landed on his chin. He struggled to stay upright, hearing the street toughs yelling encouragement to their mate. The sound suddenly made Larry angry. He rushed forward, head down, and brought up his fist in a hard, rocking blow to the roughneck's chin; followed it up with a fast punch to the nose. The street boy's nose began to trickle blood. He struck out at Larry, furiously, but Larry, his rage finally roused, easily countered the wildly flailing blows. He realized that in spite of the street boy's longer reach, he didn't have the advantage of knowing what he was doing.

The ruffian got in one or two low body punches, but Larry, carefully mustering his knowledge of boxing, slowly forced him back and back, stepping on his toes, keeping him off balance, driving punch after punch at the boy's nose and chin. Head down, the roughneck tried to clinch; grabbed Larry around the waist and grappled with him, struggling to bring his knee up; but Larry knocked his elbow across the boy's face, managed to pry him loose, and drove up one single, hard punch in the eye.

The street boy reeled back, swayed, stumbled and crashed down full length on the cobblestones.

"Come on," said Larry, standing over him in a rage. "Get up and fight!"

The tough stirred. He struggled halfway to his knees, swayed again, and collapsed in a heap.

Larry drew a long breath. His mouth was split and tasted of blood, his eye hurt, and his ribs were bruised; and his fists, knuckles skinned raw, felt as if he'd been banging on a brick wall with them.

The Darkovan aristocrat motioned to one of his bodyguards, who bent to look at the unconscious street boy.

"Now, the rest of you rough fellows—make yourselves scarce!" His voice held stinging contempt. One by one, the gang melted away into the lowering mists of darkness.

Larry stood with his knuckles throbbing, until no one was left in the square but himself, the Darkovan boy, and the two silent guards.

"Thanks," he said, at last.

"No need to thank me," the Darkovan lad said brusquely. "You handled yourself well. I wanted to see how you'd come off." Suddenly, he smiled. "As far as I'm concerned, you've earned the freedom of the city. You've done something to deserve it. I've had an eye on you for several days, you know."

Larry stared. "What?"

"Do you think a redheaded Terran can walk in places

where no other Terran ever dared to go, without half the city knowing it? And things come to the ears of the *Comyn*."

Comyn . . . Larry didn't know the word.

The boy went on, "I was sure it was only a matter of time until you got into trouble, and I wanted to see whether you'd handle it like the typical Terran" —again there was a trace of contempt in his voice— "and try to scare off your attackers with cowards' weapons, like your guards with their guns, or shout for the police to come and help you out of your troubles. No Terran ever settles his own affairs." Then he grinned. "But you did."

"I couldn't have without your help, though."

The boy shook his head in disclaimer. "I didn't lift a hand. I only made sure that the settlement was an honorable one—and as far as I'm concerned, you can go where you like in the city, from now on. My name is Kennard Alton. What's yours?"

"Larry Montray."

Kennard spoke a formal Darkovan phrase, inclining his head. Then, suddenly, he grinned.

"My father's house is only a few steps away," he said, "and I'm off duty for the night. You can't possibly go back to the Terran Zone looking like that!" For the first time, he looked as young as he was, the formal soberness disappearing in boyish laughter. "You'd frighten your people out of their wits—and if your mother and father worry the way mine do, it's nothing to look forward to! Anyway, you'd better come home with me."

Without waiting for Larry's answer, he turned, motioning to his guards, and Larry, following without a word, felt a smothered excitement. What looked like a nasty situation was turning into an adventure. Actually invited into a Darkovan house!

Kennard led the way to one of the high houses. A wide, low-walled garden surrounded it; there were flights of stone

steps up which Kennard led Larry. He made some curious
gesture and the door swung wide; he turned.

"Enter and welcome; come in peace, Terran."

The moment seemed to demand a formal acknowledgment, but Larry could only say, "Thank you." He stepped
into the wide hall of a brightly-lit house, blinking in the
brilliant entryway, and looking around with curiosity and
wonder.

Someone, somewhere, was playing on a stringed instrument that sounded like a harp. The floors under his feet were
translucent stone; the walls were hung with bright thin panels of curtain. A tall, furry nonhuman with green intelligent
eyes came forward and took Kennard's cloak, and at a signal Larry's torn jacket also.

"It's my mother's reception night, so we won't bother
her," Kennard said, and, turning to the nonhuman, added,
"Tell my father I have a guest upstairs."

Larry followed Kennard up another long flight. Kennard
flung open a dark door, hummed a low note, and the room
was filled suddenly with bright light and warmth.

It was a pleasant room. There were low couches and
chairs, a rack of knives and swords against the wall, a
stuffed bird that looked like an eagle, a framed painting of a
horse, and, on a small high table, something that looked like
a chessboard or checkerboard with crystal pieces set up at
each end. The room was luxurious, but for all that it was not
tidy; various odds and ends of clothing were strewn here and
there, and there was a table piled high with odd items Larry
could not identify. Kennard threw open another door, and
said, "Here. Your face is all blood, and your clothes a mess.
You'd better clean up a little, and you might as well put on
some of my things for the time being." He rummaged behind a panel, flung some curiously shaped garments at
Larry. "Come back when you're presentable."

The room was a luxurious bathroom, done in tile of a
dozen colors, set in geometric patterns. The fixtures were

strange, but after a little experimenting, Larry found a hot-water faucet, and washed his face and hands. The warm water felt good on his bruised face, and he realized—looking into a long mirror—that between the gang-jostling and the fight, he had really been given quite a roughing up! He began to worry a little. What would his father say?

Well, he'd *wanted* to see Darkovan life close at hand, and he'd worry about getting home late, some other time! Dad would understand when he explained. He took off his torn and dirty clothes, and got into the soft wool trousers and the fur-lined jerkin which Kennard had lent him. He looked at himself in the mirror; why, except for his red hair, cut short, he might be any young Darkovan! Come to think of it, except for Kennard, he hadn't seen any red-haired Darkovans. But there must be some!

When he came out, Kennard was lounging in one of the chairs, a small table drawn up before him with several steaming bowls of food on it. He motioned to Larry to sit down.

"I'm always starved when I come off duty. Here, have something to eat." He hesitated, looking a little curiously at Larry as the other picked up the bowl and the long pick like a chopstick, then laughed. "Good, you can manage these. I wasn't sure."

The food was good, small meat rolls stuffed with something like rice or barley; Larry ate hungrily, dipping his rolls in the sharp fruity pickle-sauce as Kennard did. At last he put down the bowl and said, "You told me you've been watching me, while I've been exploring the city. Why?"

Kennard reached for the bowl containing some small crisp sticky things, took a handful and passed them to Larry before answering. He said, "I don't quite know how to say it without insulting you."

"Go ahead," Larry said. "Look, you probably saved me from getting badly hurt, if not killed. Say anything you want to. I'll try not to take offense."

"This is nothing against you. But nobody in Thendara wants trouble. Terrans have been mauled or murdered, here in the city. They usually bring it on themselves. I don't mean that you would have brought anything on yourself—those street boys are alley rats and they'll attack perfectly harmless people. But other Terrans *have* made trouble in the city, and our people have treated them as they deserve. So it should be settled—a troublemaker has been punished, and the affair is over. But you Terrans simply will not accept that. Any time one of your people is hurt, no matter what he has done to deserve it, your spaceforce men come around prying into the whole matter, raking up a scandal, insisting on long trials and questioning and punishment. On Darkover, any man who's man enough to wear breeches instead of skirts is supposed to be able to protect himself; and if he can't, it's an affair for his family to settle. Our people find it hard to understand your ways. But we have made a treaty with the Terrans, and responsible people here in the city don't want trouble. So we try to prevent incidents of that sort—when we can do it honorably."

Larry munched absentmindedly on one of the sweet things. They were filled with tart fruit, like little pies. He was beginning to see the contrast between his own world—orderly, with impersonal laws—and Darkover, with a fierce and individualistic code of every man for himself. When the two clashed—

"But it was more than that," Kennard said. "I was curious about you. I've been curious about you since the first day I saw you at the spaceport. Most of you Terrans like to stay behind your walls—they won't even take the trouble to learn our language! Why are you different?"

"I don't know. I don't know why they are the way they are, either. Just—well, call it curiosity." Something else occurred to Larry. "So you didn't just *happen* to come along then? You've been watching me?"

"Off and on. But it was just luck I came along then. I was

off duty and coming home, and heard the racket in the
square. And, on duty or off, that's part of my work."

"Your work?"

Kennard said, "I'm a cadet officer in the City Guard. All
the boys in my family start as cadets, when they're fourteen
winters old, working three days in the cycle as peace offi-
cers. Mostly, I just supervise guards and check over the duty
lists. What sort of work do you do?"

"I don't do any work yet. I just go to school." It made him
feel, suddenly, very young and ill at ease. This self-
possessed youngster, no older than Larry himself, was already doing a man's work—not frittering his time away,
being treated like a schoolboy!

"And then you have to start in doing your man's work
full time, without any training? How strange," Kennard said.

"Well, your system seems strange to me," Larry said,
with a flare of resentment against Kennard's assumption that
his way was the proper one, and Kennard grinned at him.

"Actually, I had another reason for wanting to get to
know you—and if this hadn't happened, sooner or later I
suppose I'd have managed it somehow. I'm wild to know all
about space travel and the stars! And I've never had a
chance to learn anything about it! Tell me—how do the Big
Ships find their way between stars? What moves the ships?
Do the Terrans really have colonies on hundreds of worlds?"

"One question at a time!" Larry laughed, "and remember
I'm only learning!" But he began to explain navigation to
Kennard, who listened, fascinated, asking question after
question about the spaceships and the stars.

He was describing his one view of the drive rooms on the
starship when the door swung open and a very tall man came
in. Like Kennard, he had red hair, graying a little at the temples; his eyes were deepset, hawk-keen and stern, and he
looked upright, handsome and immensely dignified in his
scarlet embroidered jacket. Kennard got quickly to his feet,
and Larry got up, too.

"So this is your friend, Kennard?" The man made a formal bow to Larry. "Welcome to our home, my boy. Kennard tells me you are a brave fellow, and have won the freedom of the city. Please consider yourself free of our house as well, at any time. I am Valdir Alton."

"Larry Montray, *z'par servu*," said Larry, bowing as he had seen Kennard do and using the most respectful Darkovan phrase, "At your service, sir."

"You lend us grace." The man smiled and took his hand. "I hope you will come to us often."

"I would like that very much, sir."

"You speak excellent Darkovan. It is rare to find one of your people who will do us even the small courtesy of learning our language so well," Valdir Alton said.

Larry felt inclined to protest. "My father speaks it even better than I do, sir."

"Then he is wise," Valdir replied.

"Father," Kennard cut in excitedly; he might be a poised young soldier in the streets, but here, Larry saw, he was just a kid like Larry himself. "Father, Larry has promised to lend me some books about space travel and about the Empire! And, to get permission, if he can, to show me over the spaceport!"

"For that last, of course, you must not be disappointed if permission is refused," Valdir warned the boys, smiling indulgently. "They might think that you were a spy. But the books will be welcome; I myself shall enjoy seeing them. I can read a little of the Terran Standard language."

"I thought about that," Larry said. "I wasn't sure if Kennard could. These are mostly pictures and photographs."

"Thanks," Kennard laughed, "I *can* read our scripts if I have to—well enough for duty lists and the like—but I'm too busy for a scholar's work! Oh, I can write my name well enough to serve, but why should I spoil my eyes for the hunt by learning what any public scribe can do for me? If it's a

question of pictures, though—that's something worth seeing!"

Larry, too startled to wonder whether it was polite,
blurted out, "You can't even read your own language? Why,
I can read Darkovan!"

"You *can*?" Kennard sounded honestly awed. "Why, I
thought you weren't even old enough to bear arms—and you
read two languages and can write too! Are you a scholar by
trade, then?"

Larry shook his head.

"But how old are you? If you can read already?"

"I was sixteen three months ago."

"I'll be sixteen in the Dark Month," Kennard said. "I
thought you were younger."

Valdir Alton, idly eating sweets from one of the bowls,
interrupted, saying, "I should be sorry to fail in hospitality,
Lerrys"—he spoke Larry's name with an odd, Darkovan accent—"but it is late and your spaceport curfew will be en-
forced. I think, Kennard, you must have your guest escorted
home—unless you would like to spend the night? We have
ample room for guests, and you would be welcome."

"Thank you, sir, but I'd better not. My father would
worry, I'm afraid. If someone can tell me the way—"

"My bodyguards will take you," Kennard said, "but
come again very soon. I'm on duty tomorrow and the next
day, but—the day after? Could you come and spend the afternoon?"

"I'd like to," Larry promised.

"You had better wear those clothes," Valdir said; "your
own, I fear, are fit only to clean floors. These are outworn
ones of Kennard's brother; you need not return them."

Kennard went to the door with him, repeating his cordial
urgings to come again, and Larry, escorted by the silent
guard, found his way quickly to the spaceport. His mind still
on his adventure, he was brought up with a shock when the
spaceport guard stopped him with a sharp challenge.

"What do you think you're doing here at this time of night? Nobody admitted now but spaceport personnel!"

With a shock, Larry remembered his Darkovan clothing. He produced his identity card, and the guard stared. "What the deuce you doing in *that* rig, kid? And you're late; half an hour more and I'd have had to put you on report for the Commandant. Don't you know it's not safe to go prowling around at night?" He caught sight of Larry's bruised and reddened knuckles, his slowly blackening left eye. "Holy Joe, you look like you found that out. I bet you catch it when your Dad sees you!"

Larry was beginning to be a little afraid of that, himself. Well, there was nothing to do but face it.

It had been worth it, whatever Dad said. Even worth a licking, if it turned out that way.

CHAPTER FOUR

It was worse than he had thought it would be.

As he came through the doors of the apartment in Quarters A, he saw his father, intercom in hand, and heard Wade Montray's sharp, preoccupied voice, with overtones of trouble.

"—went out after school, and hasn't come in; I checked with all his friends. The guard at the western gate saw him leave, but hasn't seen him come back. . . . I don't want to sound like an alarmist, sir, but if he'd wandered into the Old Town—you know as well as I do what could have happened. Yes, I know that, sir, and I'll take all the responsibility for letting it happen; it was foolish of me. Believe me, I realize that now—"

Larry said hesitantly "Dad—?"

Montray started, half dropping the cap of the intercom.

"Larry! Is that you?"

Montray said into the intercom, "Forget it. He just came in. Yes, I know, I'll attend to it. . . . All right, Larry, come in where I can get a good look at you."

Larry obeyed, bracing himself for a storm. As he came into the main room, and the light fell on his bruised face, Montray turned pale.

"Larry, your face! Son, what's happened? Are you all right?" He came forward, quickly, taking Larry by the shoulders and turning him toward the light; Larry tensed, trying to pull away.

"It's all right, Dad; I got into a fight. A bunch of toughs. It's all right." He added quickly, "It looks worse than it is."

Montray's face worked, and for a moment he turned away. When he looked at Larry again, his face was controlled and grim, his voice level. "You'd better tell me about it."

Larry began the story, trying to make light of the roughing up he had had, but his father interrupted, harshly, "You could have been killed! You know that, don't you?"

"I wasn't, though. And really, Dad, it's an incredible piece of luck, meeting Kennard and everything. It was worth a little trouble—Dad, what's wrong, what is it?"

Montray said, "I made a mistake ever letting you go into the town alone. I know that, now. That's all over. It could have been very serious. Larry, this is an order: You are not to leave the Terran Zone again—not at any time, not under any conditions."

Startled, outraged, hardly believing, Larry stared at his father. "You can't mean that, Dad!"

"But I do mean it."

"But you haven't even been listening to me, then! Nothing like that would happen again! Kennard said I had the freedom of the city, and his father invited me to come again—"

"I heard you perfectly well," his father cut in, "but you've had your orders, Larry, and I don't intend to discuss it any further. You are not to leave the Terran Zone again—at any time. No"—he raised his hand as Larry began to protest—"not another word, not one. Go and wash your face and put something on those cuts and get to bed. Get going!"

Larry opened his mouth and, slowly, shut it again. It wasn't the slightest use; his father wasn't listening to him. Fuming, outraged, he stalked toward his room.

It wasn't like Dad to treat him this way—like a little kid

to be ordered around! Usually, Dad was reasonable. While he washed his bruised face and painted his skinned knuckles with antiseptic, he stormed silently inside. Dad *couldn't* mean it—not now, not after the trouble he'd had getting accepted!

Finally he decided to let it ride until morning. Dad had been worried about him; maybe when he'd had a chance to think it over, he'd listen to reason. Larry went to bed, still thinking over, with excitement, the new friend he'd made and the opportunity this opened up—the chance to see the real Darkover, not the world of the spaceport and the tourists but the strange, highly colored world that lay alien and beautiful beyond them.

Dad would *have* to see it his way!

But he didn't. When Larry tackled him again, over the breakfast table, Montray's face was dark and forbidding, and would have intimidated anyone less determined than Larry.

"I said I didn't even want to discuss it. You've had your orders, and that's all there is to it."

Larry bit his lip, scowling furiously into his plate. Finally, flaming with indignation, he raised his head and stared defiantly at his father.

"I'm not taking that, sir."

Montray frowned again. "What did you say?"

Larry felt a queer, uneasy sensation under his belt. He had never openly defied his father since he was a toddler of four or five. But he persisted:

"Dad, I don't want to be disrespectful, but you can't treat me that way. I'm not a kid, and when you say something like that, I have a right, at least to an explanation."

"You'll do as you're told, or else you'll—" Montray checked himself. At last he laid down his fork and leaned forward, his chin on his hands, his eyes angry. But all he said was, "Fair enough, then. Here's the story. Suppose, last night, you'd been badly hurt, or killed?"

"But I—"

"Let me finish. One silly kid goes exploring, and it could create an interplanetary incident. If you'd gotten into real trouble, Larry, we would have had to use all the power and prestige of the Terran Empire just to get you out of it again. If we had to do that—especially if we had to use force and Terran weapons—we'd lose all the good will and tolerance that it's taken us years to build up. It would all have to be done over again. Sure, if it came to a fight, we'd win. But we want to *avoid* incidents, not win fights which cost us more than we gain by winning them. Do you honestly think it's worth it?"

Larry hesitated.

"Well, do you?"

"I suppose not, when you put it that way," Larry said slowly. Mentally he was comparing this with what Kennard had said: how the Darkovans resented the use of the whole power of Terra, just to "pry into" what should be a private quarrel between one troublemaker and the people he had offended. It would also mean that if Larry had been harmed, the Terrans would have held all of Darkover responsible, not just the few young toughs who had actually committed the incident.

He was trying to think how he could explain this to his father, but Montray left him no time. "That's the situation. No more exploring on your own. And no arguments, if you don't mind; I don't intend to discuss it any further with you. That's just the way it's got to be." He pushed away his plate and stood up. "I've got work to do."

Larry sat on at the empty breakfast table, a dull and simmering resentment burning through him. So Kennard had been right, after all. It seemed that all of Darkover and all of the Terran Empire had to be dragged into it.

His head throbbed and he could hardly see out of his black eye, and his knuckles were so swollen that he found it hard to handle a fork. He decided not to go to school, and spent most of the morning lying on his bed, bitterly resentful. This meant the end of his adventure. What else was there? The dull world of Quarters and spaceport, identical with the world he'd left on Earth. He might as well have stayed there!

He got out the books he had promised Kennard. So he couldn't even keep that promise! And Kennard would think his word wasn't worth anything. How could he get word to his Darkovan friend about the punishment imposed on him? Kennard, and Kennard's father, had shown him friendship and hospitality—and he couldn't even keep his word!

Well, they'd started out by not thinking much of the Terrans—and now their opinion would just be confirmed that Terrans weren't to be trusted.

The day dragged by. The next day he went back to school, turning aside queries about his black eye with some offhand story of falling over a chair in the darkness. But the day after, as the hour approached when he had promised the Altons to visit them, his conflict grew and grew.

Damn it, he'd *promised*.

His father, looking into his glowering face at breakfast, had said briefly, "I'm sorry, Larry. This isn't pleasant for me—to deny you something you want so much. Some day, when you're older, perhaps you'll understand why I have to do this. Until then, I'm afraid you'll just have to accept my judgment."

He thinks he'll cut off my interest in Darkover just by forbidding me to go outside the Terran Zone, Larry thought resentfully. *He doesn't know anything about it, really—or about me!*

The day wore away, slowly. He considered, and rejected, the idea of a final appeal to his father. Wade Montray seldom gave an order, but when he did, he never rescinded it, and Larry could tell his father's mind was made up on this subject.

But it wasn't fair—and it wasn't right, or just! Painfully,

Larry faced a decision that all youngsters face sooner or later: the knowledge that their parents are not always right—that sometimes they can be dead wrong!

Wrong, or not, he thinks I ought to have to obey him anyhow! And that's the bad thing. What else can I do?

I can refuse to obey him, the thought came suddenly, as if he had never had it before.

He had never deliberately defied his father. The thought made him uncomfortable.

But this time, I'm right and he's wrong, and if he can't see it, I can. I made a commitment, and if I break my word, that in itself is going to make a couple of Darkovans—and important people—think that Terrans aren't worth much.

This is one time where I'm going to *have* to disobey Dad. Afterward, I'll take any punishment he wants to hand out to me. But I'm not going to break my word to Kennard and his father. I'll explain to them why I may not be able to come again, but I won't insult their hospitality by just disappearing and not even letting them know why I never came back.

Kennard saved me from a mauling—maybe from being killed. I promised him something he wants—some books— and I owe him that much.

He was uneasy about disobeying. But he still felt, deep down, that he was right.

If I'd been born on Darkover, he told himself, I'd be considered a man; old enough to do a man's work, old enough to make my own decisions—and take the consequences. There comes a time in your life when you have to decide for yourself what is right and what is wrong, and stop accepting what older people say. Dad may be right as far as he knows, but he doesn't know the whole story, and I do. And I've got to do what I think is right.

He wondered why he felt so bad about it. It hurt, suddenly, to realize that he'd made a decision he could never go back on. He might be punished like a child, when he got back; but suddenly he understood that he'd never feel like one again. It wasn't just the act of disobeying his father—any kid could do that. It was that he had decided, once and for all, that he no longer was *willing* to let his father decide right and wrong for him. If he obeyed his father, after this, it would be because he had thought it over and decided, on a grown-up basis, that he wanted to obey him.

And it hurt. He felt a funny pain about it, but it never occurred to him to change his mind. He'd decided what he was going to do. Now he had to decide how he was going to do it.

His father had mentioned that if he, Larry, got into trouble, it might drag the whole Terran Zone into it. That was something to consider. That was fair enough. Larry wanted to be sure there was no danger of that.

Then he thought: *I could be taken for a Darkovan, except for my clothes. I have been mistaken for a Darkovan by my accent. If I'm not dressed as a Terran, then I won't be into any trouble.*

And, he added to himself rather grimly, *if anything does happen to me, the Terrans won't be dragged into it. It will be my own responsibility.*

Quickly, he got out of his own clothes and put on the Darkovan ones Kennard had lent him. He glanced briefly at himself in the mirror. Part of himself recognized, a little ironic awareness, that he was enjoying the masquerade. It was exciting, an adventure. The other half of his awareness was a little grim. By deliberately taking off everything that could identify himself as Terran, he was deliberately giving up his right to the protection of the Empire. Now he was on his own. He'd walk down into the city with no more protection than his two hands and his knowledge of the language could give him.

As if I were really Darkovan born, and entirely on my own!

He had halfway anticipated being stopped at the gate, but

he passed through the archway without challenge, and went out into the city.

It was the hour when workmen were returning home, and the streets were crowded. He walked through them without attracting a glance, a strange breathless excitement growing under his ribs, and bursting in him. With every step, he seemed somehow to leave the person he had been, further behind. It was as if his present dress was not a masquerade, but rather as if he had simply discovered a deeper layer of himself, and was living with it. The pale cold sun hung high in the sky, casting purple shadows across the narrow streets and alleys; he found his way through the outlying reaches of the city with the instinct of a cat. He was almost sorry when he finally reached the distant quarter where the house of the Altons lay.

The nonhuman he had seen before opened the door for him, but Kennard was standing in the hallway, and Larry wondered briefly if the Darkovan boy had been waiting for him.

"You did make it," Kennard said, with a grin of satisfaction. "Somehow I'd had the feeling you wouldn't be able to, but when I looked this afternoon, I realized you would."

The words were confusing; Larry tried to make sense of them, finally decided that they must be some Darkovan idiom he didn't understand too well. He said, "I thought, for a while, that I couldn't come," but he left it at that.

The nonhuman moved toward him, and Larry flinched and drew away involuntarily, remembering his encounter with one in the streets. Kennard said quickly, "Don't be afraid of the *kyrri*. It's true that if strangers brush against them they give off sparks, but he won't hurt you now he knows you. They're been servants to our families for generations."

Larry allowed the nonhuman to take his cloak, looking curiously at the creature. It was erect and vaguely manlike, but covered with a pelt of long grayish fur, and it had long prehensile fingers and a face like a masked monkey. He wondered where the *kyrri* came from and what sort of curious relationships could exist between human and nonhuman. Would he ever know?

"I brought you the books I promised," he told Kennard, and the other boy took them eagerly. "Oh, good! But I'll look at them later. We needn't stand here in the hall. Do you know how to play darts? Shall we have a game?"

Larry agreed with interest. Kennard showed him the game in a big downstairs room, wide and light, with translucent walls, evidently a game-room of some sort. The darts were light and perfectly balanced, feathered with crimson and green feathers from some exotic bird. Once Larry grew accustomed to their weight and balance, he found that they were well matched in the game. But they played it desultorily, Kennard breaking off now and again to leaf through the books, stare fascinated at the many photographs, and ask endless questions about star-travel.

They were in one such lull in the game when the curtained panels closing off the room swirled back and Valdir Alton came in, followed by another man—a tall Darkovan, with copper hair sweeping back from a high stern forehead marked with two wings of white hair. He wore an embroidered cloak of a curious cut. The boys broke off in their game, and Kennard, with a start of surprise, made the stranger a deep and formal bow. The newcomer glanced sharply at Larry, and, not wishing to seem rude, Larry repeated the gesture.

The man spoke some offhand phrase of polite acknowledgment, nodding pleasantly to both boys; but as his gray gaze crossed Larry's, he started, narrowed his brows, then, turning his head to Valdir, said, "Terran?"

Valdir did not speak, but they looked at one another for a moment. The stranger nodded, crossed the room and stood in front of Larry. Slowly, as if compelled, Larry looked up at him, unable to draw his eyes away from his intense and compelling stare. He felt as if he were being weighed in the balance, sorted out, drawn out; as if the old man's searching look went down beneath his borrowed clothes, down to the alien bones under his flesh, down to his deepest thoughts and memories. It was like being hypnotized. He found himself suddenly shivering, and then, suddenly, he could look away again, and the man was smiling down at him, and the strange gray eyes were kind.

He said to Valdir, speaking past the boys, "So this is why you brought me here, Valdir? Don't worry; I have sons of my own. Introduce me to your friend, Kennard."

Kennard said "The lord Lorill Hastur, one of the Elders of the Council."

Larry had heard the name from his father, spoken with exasperation but a certain degree of respect. He thought, *I hope my being here doesn't mean trouble, after all,* and for a brief instant almost regretted coming, then let it pass. The tension in the room slackened indefinably. Valdir picked up one of the books Larry had brought Kennard, turning the pages with interest; Lorill Hastur came and looked over his shoulder, then turned away and began examining the darts. He drew back his arm and tossed one accurately into the target. Valdir put the book down and looked up at Larry.

"I was sure that you would be able to come today."

"I wanted to. But I may not be able to come again," Larry said.

Valdir's eyes were narrowed, curious: "Too dangerous?"

"No," said Larry, "that doesn't bother me. It's that my father would rather I didn't." He stopped; he didn't want to discuss his father, or seem to complain about his father's unreasonableness. That was something between his father and himself, not to be shared with outsiders. The conflict touched him again with sadness. He liked Kennard so much better than any of the friends he had made in Quarters, and yet this friendship must be given up almost before it had a chance to be explored. He took up one of the darts and turned it, end for end, in his hand; then flung it at the target board, missing his aim. Lorill Hastur turned and faced him again.

"How is it that you were willing to risk trouble and even punishment to come today, Larry?"

It did not occur to Larry to wonder—not until much later—how the Elder had known his name, or the inner conflict that had forced a choice on him. Just then it seemed natural that this old man with the searching eyes knew everything about him. But he still wasn't ready to sound disloyal.

"I didn't have a chance to make him understand. He would have realized why I had to come."

"And breaking your word would have been an insult," Lorill Hastur said gravely. "It is part of the code of a man to make his own choices."

He smiled at the boys, and turned, without formal leave-taking. Valdir took a step to follow him, turned back to Larry.

"You are welcome here at any time."

"Thank you, sir. But I'm afraid I won't be able to come again. Not that I wouldn't like to."

Valdir smiled. "I respect your choice. But I have a feeling we'll meet again." He followed Lorill Hastur out of the room.

Alone with Kennard, Larry found room for wonder. "How did he know so much about me?"

"The Hastur-Lord? He's a telepath, of course. What else?" Kennard said, matter-of-factly, his face buried in a book of views taken in deep space. "What sort of camera do they use for this? I never have been able to understand how a camera works?"

And Larry, explaining the principle of sensitized film to Kennard, felt an amused, ironic surprise. *Telepath, of course!* And to Kennard this was the commonplace and something like a camera was exotic and strange. It was all in the point of view.

Far too soon, the declining sun told him it was time to go. He refused Kennard's urgings to stay longer. He did not want his father to be frightened at his absence. Also, at the back of his mind, was a memory like a threat—if he was missing, might his father set the machinery of the Terran Empire into motion to locate him, bring down trouble on his friends? Kennard went a little way with him, and at the corner of the street paused, looking at him rather sadly.

"I don't like to say goodbye, Larry," he said. "I like you. I wish—"

Larry nodded, a little embarrassed, but sharing the emotion. "Maybe we'll see each other again," he said, and held out his hand. Kennard hesitated, long enough for Larry to feel first offended, then worried for fear he had committed some breach of Darkovan manners; then, deliberately, the Darkovan boy reached both hands and took Larry's between them. Larry did not know for years how rare a gesture this was in the Darkovan caste to which the Altons belonged. Kennard said softly, "I won't say good-bye. Just—good luck."

He turned swiftly and walked away without looking back.

Larry turned his steps toward home, in the lowering mist. As he moved between the dark canyons of the streets, his feet steadying themselves automatically on the uneven stones, he felt a flat undefined sorrow, as if he were seeing all this with the poignancy of a farewell. It was as if life had opened a bright door, and then slammed it again, leaving the world duller by contrast.

Suddenly, his feeling of sadness thinned out and vanished. This was only a temporary thing. He wouldn't be a kid forever. The time would come when he'd be free and on his own, free to explore all the worlds of his own choosing—and Darkover was only one of many. He had tasted a man's freedom today—and some day it would be his for all time.

His head went up and he crossed the square toward the spaceport, steadily. He'd had his fun, and he could take whatever happened. It had been worth it.

He had the curious sense that he was re-living something that had happened before, as he entered their apartment in the Quarters building. His father was waiting for him, his face drawn, unreadable.

"Where have you been?"

"In the city. At the home of Kennard Alton."

Montray's face contracted with anger, but his voice was level and stern.

"You do remember that I forbade you to leave the Terran Zone? You're not going to tell me that you forgot?"

"I didn't forget."

"In other words, you deliberately disobeyed."

Larry said quietly, "Yes."

Montray was evidently holding his anger in check with some effort. "Precisely why, when I did forbid it?"

Larry paused a moment before answering. Was he simply making excuses about having done what he wanted to do? Then he was sure, again, of the rightness of his position.

"Because, Dad, I'd made a promise and I didn't feel it was right to break it, without a better reason than just that you'd forbidden it. This was something *I* had to do, and you were treating me like a kid. I tried to make sure that you wouldn't be involved, or the Terran Empire, if anything had happened to me."

His father said, at last, "And you felt you should make the decision for yourself. Very well, Larry, I admire your honesty. Just the same, I refuse to concede that you have a right to ignore my orders on principle. You know I don't like punishing you. However, for the present you will consider yourself under house arrest—not to leave our quarters except to go to school, under any pretext." He paused and a bleak smile touched his lips. "Will you obey me, or shall I inform the guards not to let you pass without reporting it?"

Larry flinched at the severity of the punishment, but it was just. From his father's point of view, it was the only thing he could do. He nodded, not looking up.

"Anything you say, Dad. You've got my word."

Montray said, without sarcasm, "You have shown me that it means something to you. I'll trust you. House arrest until I decide you can be trusted with your freedom again."

The next days dragged slowly by, no day distinguishing itself from the last. The bruises on his face and hands healed, and his Darkovan adventure began to seem dim and pallid, as if it had happened a long time ago. Nevertheless, even in the dullness of his punishment, which deprived him even of things he had previously not valued—freedom to go about the spaceport and the Terran city, to visit friends and shops—he never doubted that he had done the right thing. He chafed under the restriction, but did not really regret having earned it.

Ten days had gone by, and he was beginning to wonder a little when his father would see fit to lift the sentence, when the order came from the Commandant.

His father had just come in, one evening, when the intercom buzzed, and when Montray put the phone down, he looked angry and apprehensive.

"Your idiotic prank is probably coming home to roost," he said angrily. "That was the Legate's office in Administration. You and I have both been ordered to report there this evening—and it was a priority summons."

"Dad, if it means trouble for you, I'm sorry. You'll have to tell them you forbade me to go—and if you don't, I will. I'll take all the blame myself." For the first time, Larry felt that the consequences might really go beyond himself. *But that's not my fault—it's because the administration is unreasonable. Why should Dad be blamed for what I did?*

He had never been in the administration building before, and as he approached the great white skyscraper that loomed over the whole spaceport complex, he was intrigued to the point of forgetting that he was here for a reproof. The immense building, glimmering with white metal and glass, the wide halls, and the panoramic view from each corridor window of the Darkovan city below and the mountains beyond, almost took his breath away. The Legate's office was high up, bright and filled with lowering red sunshine; for a moment, as he stepped into the brilliant glassed-in room, a curious thought flashed through Larry's mind; *He sees more of this world than he wants anyone to know about.*

The Legate was a stocky man, dark and grizzled, with thoughtful eyes and a permanent frown. Nevertheless he had dignity, and something which made Larry think quickly of Lorill Hastur. *What is it? Is it that they're used to power, or to making decisions that other people have to live with?*

"Commander Reade—my son Larry."

"Sit down." It was a peremptory command, not an invitation. "So you've been roaming around in the city? Tell me about it—tell me everything you've done there."

His face was unreadable; without anger, but without friendliness. Reserving judgment. Neither kind nor unkind. But there was immense authority in it, as if he expected Larry to jump at once to obey him; and after ten days of sulking in Quarters, Larry wasn't feeling especially humble.

"I didn't know it was against any rules, sir. And I didn't hurt anyone, and nothing happened to me."

Reade made a noncommittal sound. "Suppose you let me decide about that. Just tell me about it."

Larry told the whole story: his wanderings in the city day after day, his meeting with the gang of toughs, and the intervention of Kennard Alton. Finally he told of his last visit to the Alton house, making it clear that he had gone without his father's knowledge and consent. "So don't blame Dad, sir. *He* didn't break any laws, at least."

Montray said quickly, "Just the same, Reade, I'll take the responsibility. He's my son, and I'll be responsible for his not doing it again."

Reade gestured him to silence. "That's not the problem. "We've heard from the Council—on behalf of the Altons. It seems that they are deeply and gravely offended."

"What? Why?"

"Because you have refused your son permission to pursue this friendship—they say you have insulted them, as if they were unfit to associate with your son."

Montray put his hands to his temples, wearily. He said, "Oh, my God."

"Exactly," Reade said in a soft voice. "The Altons are important people on Darkover—aristocrats, members of the Council. A snub or slight from a Terran can create trouble."

Suddenly his voice exploded in wrath. "Confound the boy anyhow! We aren't ready for this sort of episode. We should have thought of it ourselves and made preparations for it, and now when it hits us, we can hardly make good use of it! How old is the boy?"

Montray gestured at Larry to answer for himself, and Reade grunted. "Sixteen, huh? Here, they're men at that age—and we ought to realize it! What about it, young Larry? Are you intending—have you ever considered going into the Empire service?"

Puzzled by the question, Larry said, "I've always intended that, Commander."

"Well, here's your chance." He tossed a small squarish slip of paper across the table. It was thick and bordered, and had Darkovan writing on it, the straight squarish script of the city language. He said, "I understand you can read some of this stuff. God knows why you bothered, but it makes it handy for us. Figure it out later when you get the chance; as it happens, I can read it too, though most people in Administration *don't* bother. It's an invitation from the Altons— coming through Administration as a slap in the face: they don't like the way Terrans tend to go through channels on every little thing—for you, Larry, to spend the next season at their country estate, with Kennard."

Montray's face went dark as if a shutter had dropped over his eyes. "Impossible, Reade. I know what you have in mind, and I won't go along with it."

Reade's face did not change. "You see the position this puts us in. The boy's not prepared for the tremendous opportunity this opens up, but we've still got to grab this chance. We simply can't afford to let Larry refuse this invitation. For God's sake, do you realize that we've been trying to get permission for someone to visit the outlying estates, for fifteen years? It's the first time in years that any Terran has had this chance, and if we turn it down, it may be years before it comes again."

Montray's mouth twisted. "Oh, there have been a few."

"Yes, I know." Reade did not elaborate, but turned to Larry. "Do you understand why you're going to have to accept this invitation?"

Suddenly, with the visual force of a hallucination, Larry saw again the tall figure of Valdir Alton, and heard him say, as clearly as if he had been in that white Terran room with them, *I have a feeling we'll see you again before long.* It was so real that he shook his head to clear it of the abnormally intense impression.

Reade persisted. "You *are* going to accept?"

Larry felt a delayed surge of excitement. To see Darkover—not only the city, but far outside the Terran Zone entirely, the real world, untouched by Terra! The thought was a little frightening and yet wildly exciting. But a tinge of caution remained and he said warily, "Would you mind telling me why you are so eager to have me, sir? I understood that the Terrans were afraid of any—fraternization with Darkovans."

"Afraid of it causing trouble," Reade said. "We've been trying to arrange something like this, though, for years. I suppose they felt we were a little too eager, and were afraid we'd try something. Larry, I can explain it very easily. First of all, we don't want to offend Darkovan aristocrats. But more than that. This is the first time that Darkovans of power and position have actually made an advance of personal friendliness to any Terran. They trade with us, they accept us here, but they don't want to have anything to do with us personally. This is like a breach in that wall. You have a unique opportunity to be—a sort of ambassador for Terra. Perhaps, to show them that we aren't anything to fear. And then, too—" he hesitated. "Very few Terrans have ever seen anything of this planet except what the Darkovans wanted us to see. You should keep very careful records of everything you see, because something you don't even realize is important might mean everything to us."

Larry saw through that at once.

"Are you asking me to *spy* on my friends?" he asked, in outrage.

"No, no," Reade said quickly, even though Larry felt very clearly that Reade was thinking that he was a little too clever. "Just keep your eyes open and tell us what you see. Chances are they will be expecting you to do that anyhow."

Montray interrupted, pacing the floor restlessly. "I don't like having my son used as a pawn in power politics. Not by Darkovans trying to get next to us—and not by the Terran Empire trying to find out about Darkover, either!"

"You're exaggerating, Montray. Look, at least a few of the higher Darkovan caste may be telepaths; we couldn't plant the kid on them as a spy, even if we tried. It's just a chance to know a little more about them."

He appealed directly to Larry: "You say you liked this Darkovan youngster. Doesn't it make sense—to try and build friendly relations between the two of you?"

That thought had already crossed Larry's mind. He nodded. Montray said reluctantly, "I still don't like it. But there's nothing I can do."

Reade looked at him and Larry was shocked at the quick expression of triumph and power in the man's face. He thought, *He enjoys this.* He wondered, suddenly, why he could see into the man this way. He was sure he knew more about Commander Reade than Reade wanted him to know. Reade said softly over Larry's head to Wade Montray, "We've got to do it this way. You son is old enough, and he's not scared—are you, Larry? So all we have to do is tell the Altons that he'll be proud and honored to visit them—and say when."

Back again in their own apartment in Quarters A, Larry's father swore under his breath, ceaselessly, for almost a quarter of an hour. "And now you see what you've gotten yourself into," he finished at last, viciously. "Larry, I don't like it, I don't like it, I don't *like* it! And damn it, I suppose you're overjoyed—you've got what you want!"

Larry said, honestly, "It's interesting, Dad. But I am a little scared. Reade wants me to go for all the wrong reasons."

"I'm glad you can see *that*, at least," Montray snapped. "I ought to let you hang yourself. You got yourself into this. Just the same—" He grew silent; then he got up and came to his son, and took Larry by the shoulders again, looking very searchingly at him. His voice was gentler than Larry could remember hearing it in years.

"Listen, son. If you really don't want to get into this, I'll get you out of it, somehow. You're my son, not just a potential Empire employee. They can't force you to go. Don't worry about their putting pressure on me—I can always put in for a transfer somewhere else. I'll *leave* the damned planet before I let them force you to play their games!"

Larry, feeling his father's hands on his shoulders, suddenly realized that he was being given a chance—perhaps the last chance he would ever have—to return to the old, protected status of a child. He could be his father's son again, and Dad would get him out of this. So the step he had taken, in declaring himself a man, was not quite irrevocable

after all. He could return to the safe age, and the price was
very small. His father would take care of him.

He found himself wanting to, almost desperately. He'd
bitten off more than he could chew, and this was his chance
to get out of it. The alternative would put him on his own, in
a strange world, playing a strange part, representing his Terran world all alone.

*And the Altons would know that his man's decision had
been a lie, that he clung to the safety of being a Terran child
hiding behind his society—*

He drew a long breath, and put his hands up over his father's.

"Thanks, Dad," he said, warmly, meaning it. "I almost
wish I could take you up on that. Honestly. But I have to go.
As you say, I got myself into this, and I might as well get
some good out of it—for all of you. Don't worry, Dad—it's
going to be all right."

Montray's hands tightened on his shoulders. His eyes met
his son's, and he said, "I was afraid you'd feel that way,
Larry—and I wish you didn't. But I guess, being who you
are, you'd have to. I could still forbid you, I guess"—a wry
smile flitted across his face—"but I've found out you're too
old for that, and I won't even try." He dropped his hands, but
then a wide grin spread across his worried face.

"Damn it, son—I still don't like it—but I'm proud of
you."

CHAPTER FIVE

The morning mist had burned off the hills, but still lay thick in the valley. Above the bank of pinkish cloud, the red sun hung in a bath of thinning mist. Larry looked down at the treetops emerging from the top of the cloud, and drew a deep breath, savoring the strange scents of the alien forest.

He rode last in the little column of six men. Ahead of him, Kennard looked round briefly, lifted a hand in acknowledgment of his grin, and turned back.

Larry had been at Armida, the outlying country estate of the Altons, for twelve days now. The journey from the city had been tiring; he was not accustomed to riding, and though at first it had been pleasant novelty, he found himself thinking regretfully of the comfortable ground-cars and airships of Terran travel.

But the slow trip through forests and mountains had gradually won him to its charm: the high rocky trails reaching summits where crimson and purple landscapes lay rainbow-lovely below them, the deep shadowed roads through the forests, with here and there tall white towers rising high against the horizon, or glowing faintly luminescent in the night. At night they had either camped along the roadway, or now and again been guests in some outlying farmhouse where the Darkovans had treated Valdir and Kennard with extreme deference—and Larry had come in for his own

share of this respect. Valdir had told no one that his son's
guest and companion was one of the alien Terrans.

The home of the Altons was a great gray rambling structure, too low for a castle, too imposing to be a house. He
found himself fitting into the place easily, riding with Kennard, helping him train his hunting dogs, learning to shoot
with the curiously shaped crossbows they used for sport, savoring the strangeness of the life he lived. It was all very interesting, but certainly nothing that he could tell Reade
which might be of benefit to the Terrans—and he was glad
of it. He hadn't liked the idea of being what amounted to a
spy.

Mostly the days were too full for much introspection, but
sometimes when he was in bed at night, he found himself
wondering why the invitation had been issued in the first
place. He liked Kennard, they were friends, but would that
alone cause Valdir Alton to ignore the long tradition on
Darkover of ignoring the Terrans?

He found himself wondering if Valdir's reason for issu-
ing the invitation was not very much the same as Reade's
reason for wanting Larry to accept it—that Valdir just
wanted to know something about the Terrans, close up.

He was, by now, used to riding, and a three-day hunt had
been arranged partly for his benefit. He had managed to
shoot well enough to bring down a small rabbitlike beast on
the first day, which had been cooked over the campfire that
evening, and he was proud of that, even though it was the
only thing he had hit during the long hunt.

At the top of the hill he drew even with Kennard, and
they sat breathing their horses, side by side, looking across
the valley.

"It's nice up here," Kennard said at last. "I used to ride
this way fairly often, a couple of seasons ago. Father feels
that now it's too dangerous for me to come alone." He gestured at their escort, Darkovans Larry did not know: one a

well-dressed young redhead from a nearby estate, the others men from the Alton farms, workmen of various sorts. One was in the uniform of the Guards, but Kennard himself was wearing old riding-clothes, slightly too small for him.

"Dangerous? Why?"

"It's too near the edge of the forests," Kennard said, "and during the last few seasons, trailmen have spread down into these forests. Usually they stay in the hills. They're not really dangerous, but they don't like humans, and we stay out of their way, as a rule. Then, too, this is on the border of mountain country, and men from the Cahuengas—"

He broke off, stiffening in his saddle, looking intently across the valley.

"What is it, Kennard?" Larry asked.

The Darkovan boy pointed. Larry could see nothing, but Kennard called to his father, a shrill insistent shout, and Valdir turned his horse and came cantering back.

"What's wrong, Ken?"

"Smoke. The mist lifted just for a minute, over there—" Kennard pointed, "and I saw it. Right at the edge of the Ranger station."

Valdir frowned, narrowing his eyes, shading them with his thin brown hand. "How sure are you? It's a good hour's ride out of our way—damn this mist, I can't see anything." He flung back his head like a deer sniffing the wind, peering into the distance, and finally nodded.

"A trace of smoke. We'll ride and check." He glanced at Larry. "I hope you don't mind the extra riding."

"Not at all, but I hope nothing's wrong, Lord Alton."

"So do I," Valdir said, his brows drawn down with worry, and touched his horse's flank with a light heel. They were off down the trail, the sound of hoofs making a dull clamor on the leaves underfoot. As they neared the bottom of the valley, the mist lifted slightly and the men pointed and shouted. Larry's nostrils twitched at a faint, acrid whiff of strange smoke. The sun had swung southward, and they

were turning their horses up a widened trail that led to the
top of a little hill, when Valdir Alton let out a great curse, rising in his stirrups and pointing; then he clapped his heels to
his horse's side and vanished over the top of the rise. Kennard spurred after him, and Larry, urging his horse forward,
felt a surge of excitement and fear as he followed. He came
over the rise in the road and heard Kennard cry out in consternation; he pulled up his horse and looked down, in dismay, at a grove of trees from which black smoke was coiling
upward.

Kennard slid from his horse and began to run. The man
in the Guardsman's uniform called to him and drew his
crossbow up to rest, and Larry realized, with a shiver, that
they were all looking warily at the surrounding trees. What
might lie behind them?

Valdir leaped from his saddle; the other men followed suit,
and Larry slid down with the rest. The deathly silence seemed
more ominous because it was cut through with the soft chirp-
ing of birds from a distance, twittering in the grove.

Then Kennard called; he was kneeling in the road beside
what Larry thought to be a gray boulder, but he put out his
hand to turn it and Larry, his stomach cramping in horror,
saw that it was the hunched body of a man in a gray cloak.

Valdir bent over the man; straightened. Larry stood
frozen, looking down at death. He had never seen a dead
body before, let alone the body of a man dead by violence.
The dead man was young, little more than a boy, a shadow
of thin beard on his face. A great wound in his chest gaped
black and bloody. He had been dead some time.

Kennard was looking pale. Larry turned away, feeling
faint and sick, and struggling not to show it, as Valdir turned
away from the dead man.

"Cahuenga—his cloak is Cahuenga from the far hills," he
said, "but boots and belt are from Hyalis. A raider—but no
beacon flared when this station was attacked." He stepped
warily around the corpse. The Guardsman shouted, "don't

go up there alone, Lord Alton!" and, sliding from his saddle, crossbow lowered, ran to follow him. Kennard followed, and Larry, as if compelled, ran after them.

A blackened ruin, still smoking, showed the vague outline of a building. On a little stretch of green at one side lay the crumpled body of a man. When Kennard and Larry reached Valdir's side, Valdir was already kneeling beside the body. After one glance, Larry turned away from the glazed, pain-ridden eyes; the man was bleeding from a great gash across his side, and from his lips a little dark-flecked foam stirred with his rasping breath.

Over the inert body the other Darkovan aristocrat looked at Valdir; gripped the limp wrist. His forehead was ridged with dismay. Valdir, looking up, said, "He must speak before he dies, Rannirl. And he's dying anyway."

Rannirl's mouth was set. He nodded, fumbled at his belt, and from a leather wallet drew forth a small, blue-glazed vial stoppered with silver. Handling it carefully, and keeping his own face free of the small fumes that coiled up from the open mouth of the vial, he measured a few cautious drops in the cap: Valdir forced the man's mouth open and Rannirl let the fuming liquid fall on the man's tongue. After a moment a great shudder ran through the frame of the dying man, and the eyes fluttered.

His voice sounded harsh, far away. "*Vai dom*—we did what we could—the beacon—fire—"

Valdir gripped the limp hands, his face terrible and intent. There was something in his hands, something that glittered cold and blue; he pressed it to the dying man's forehead, and Larry saw that it was a clear jewel. Valdir said, "Do not spend your strength in speaking, Garin, or you will die before I learn what I must know. Form your thought clearly while you can, and I will understand. And forgive me, friend. You may save many lives with this torment." He bent close to the dying face, his own features a grim mask, lighted blue as the strange jewel suddenly flared and burned as if with inner flame. A spasm of terrible anguish passed over the dying Ranger's face; he shuddered twice and lay still, and Valdir, with a painful sigh, released his hands and straightened up. His own forehead was beaded with sweat; he swayed, and Kennard leaped to steady his father.

After a minute Valdir passed his hand over his wet brow, and spoke: "They didn't sell their lives cheaply," he said. "There were a dozen men; they came from the North, and hacked Balhar to pieces while he was trying to reach the beacon and set it aflame. He thought at first that they were Cahuenga, but two were tall pale men who were hooded almost like the *kyrri*, and one was masked. He saw them signal; they carried a mirror-flash device of some sort. After he fell, Garin saw them ride away northward toward the Kadarin."

Rannirl whistled softly. "If they could spare so many to prevent one beacon being lighted—this doesn't look like a few bandits out after a raid on the farms in the valley!"

Valdir swore. "There aren't enough of us to go after them," he said, "and we've only hunting weapons. And Zandru alone knows what other devil's work has been done along here. Kennard"—he turned to his son—"go and light the beacon, at least. Quickly! Garin tried to crawl there, when they had left him for dead, but his strength failed—" His voice went thin in his throat; he bent and covered the dead face with the Ranger's cloak.

"He didn't fight me," he said. "Even for a man weakened with many wounds and after a dose of that devil's drug of yours, Rannirl, that takes a rare kind of courage."

He sighed, then, recovering himself, told two of the workmen to bury the dead Rangers. The sound of mattock and pick rang dully in the grove; after a few minutes, Kennard came running back.

"No way to light the beacon, father. Those devils took the time to drench it with water, just in case!"

Valdir swore, again, moodily, biting his lip. "The people

along the valley should be warned, and someone should track them and find which way. We can't go to all four winds at once!" He stood for a moment, scowling, thoughtful. "If we had enough men we might take them at the fords, or if we could warn the countryside by beacon—"

Abruptly he seemed to come to a decision.

"There aren't enough of us to follow them, and they've too big a head start in any case. But this probably means a good-sized raid. We've got to warn the people in the valley—and we can find a tracker there who can get on their trail and follow it better than we could. Nothing's likely to happen before night." He glanced up at the sun, trembling crimson at the zenith. "The hunt's over; we'll eat a bit and then start back. Kennard, you and Larry—" he hesitated. "I'd like to send you both back to Armida, but you can't cross this country by yourselves. You'll have to ride with us." He looked at Larry. "It may mean some hard riding, I'm afraid."

The men had finished burying the Rangers; Valdir vetoed making a cookfire, directing the men to get cold food from their saddlebags. They sat eating, grimly discussing the burnt station and the dead Rangers in a dialect of which Larry could understand little. He could not eat; the food stuck in his throat. It was his first sight of violence and death and it had sickened him. He had known that violence was not unheard-of on Darkover, he had himself had a brief brush with it in his fight with the street boys, but now it assumed a dark and frightening aspect. With an almost painful nostalgia, he wished he were back in the safety of the Terran Zone.

Or was that safety, too, a mere illusion? Was there violence and cruelty and fear there, too, hidden behind the façades, and was he just now becoming aware of all these things? He choked over the piece of dry biscuit he was eating, and turned his eyes away form Kennard's too-searching gaze.

Valdir Alton's tall form shadowed him, and the Darkovan lord dropped on the grass at his side. He said, "Sorry that your hunt had to end this way, Lerrys. It wasn't what we planned."

"Do you really think I'd be worrying about a hunt when people are dead?" Larry asked.

Valdir's eyes were shrewd. "Nothing like this in your life before? Nothing like this in your world? Everything in the Terran Zone very neat and law-abiding?" Once again Larry had the feeling that—as with Lorill Hastur—his thoughts were being read. He remembered, with a small twinge of fear, how Valdir Alton had probed the mind of the dying Ranger.

He said, "I suppose there are law-breakers on Earth and in the Terran Zone, too. Only here it seems so—"

"So close up and personal?" Valdir asked. "Tell me something, Lerrys: Is a man more or less dead when he is killed neatly by a gun or a bomb, than when he is—" He moved his head toward where the dead Ranger had lain. His face was suddenly bitter as he added, "That seems to be the main difference between your people and ours. At least the men who killed poor Garin did not do their killing while they were a safe distance away!"

Larry said—glad to have something between himself and the memory of a dead man with a bleeding wound in his chest—"The main thing is that most of our people don't do any killing at all! We have laws and police to handle that sort of thing for us!"

"While here we feel that every man should handle his own affairs for himself, before they spread into wars," Valdir said steadily. "If any man offends me, damages my property or my family, steals my goods—it's my personal duty to revenge myself on that man—or forgive him, if I see fit, without dragging in others who really have no part in the quarrel."

Larry was trying to fit that together—the contrast between the fierce individualism of the Darkovan code, and the Terran's acceptance of an orderly society, based on rules and laws. "A government of laws and not of men," he said, and at Valdir's raised eyebrow, explained, "that's supposed to be the original theory behind the Terran governments."

"While ours is a government of men—becasue laws can't be anything but the expression of men who make them," Valdir said. His face was grave and serious and Larry knew that while he might have started this conversation for the purpose of taking his young guest's mind off the scene of unfamiliar violence, now he was deeply involved in what he was saying. "It's one reason we want little to do with the Terrans, as such," he said. "Without offense to you personally. It's true that we have wars on Darkover, but they are small local hand-to-hand skirmishes; they seldom get bigger than this—" Again he motioned toward the blackening ruin of the Ranger station. "The individual who makes trouble is promptly punished and the matter ends there, without involving a whole countryside."

"But—" Larry hesitated, remembering he was Valdir's guest. The older man said encouragingly, "Go ahead."

"Kennard has told me something of this, sir. You have long-lived feuds and when a trouble-maker is punished, his family takes revenge, and doesn't this lead to more and more trouble over the years? Your way doesn't really *settle* anything. Really lawless people—like these bandits—ought to be dealt with by the law, shouldn't they?"

"You're entirely too clever," Valdir said, with a bleak smile. "That's the one flaw in the system. We use their own methods to revenge ourselves on them; they raid us, we raid them back, and we're as bad as they are. Actually, Larry, it goes deeper than that. Darkover seems to be in one of those uncomfortable times to live in—a time of change. And having the Terrans here hasn't helped. Again—without offense to you personally—having a highly technical civilization among us makes our people dissatisfied. We live the way men were meant to live—in close contact with real things, not huddled in cities and factories." He looked around, past the burnt station, at the high mountains, and said, "Can't you see it, Larry?"

"I can see it," Larry admitted, but a brief stab of doubt struck at him. When he had said the same thing, his own father had accused him of being a romantic. The Darkovans seemed to want to go on living as if change did not exist, and whether they liked it or not, the space age was here— and they *had* chosen to let the Terran Empire come here for trade.

"Yes," Valdir said, reading his thoughts. "I can see that too—change is coming, whether we like it or not. And I want it to come in an orderly fashion, without upheaval. Which means I've made myself awfully damned unpopular with a lot of people in my own caste. For instance, I organized this defense system of border stations and Rangers, so that every farm and estate wouldn't have to stand alone against raids by bandits from across the Kadarin. And there are some people who find this a clear violation of our code of individual responsibility." He stopped. "What's the matter?"

Larry blurted out, "You're reading my mind!"

"Does that bother you? I don't pry, Larry. No telepath does. But when you're throwing your thoughts at me so clearly—" he shrugged. "I've never known a Terran to be so open to rapport."

"No," Larry said, "It doesn't bother me." To his own surprise, that was true. He found that the idea didn't bother him at all. "Maybe if more Terrans and Darkovans could read each other's minds they'd understand one another better, and not be afraid of each other, any more than you and I are afraid of each other."

Valdir smiled at him kindly and stood up. "Time to get on the road again," he said; then breaking off, added very softly, "But don't deceive yourself, Larry. We are afraid of you. You don't know, yourself, how dangerous you can be."

He walked away, quickly, while Larry stared after him, wondering if he had heard right.

The road into the valley was steep and winding, and for some time Larry had enough to do to keep his seat in the saddle. But soon, the road widened and became easier, and he realized that he had been smelling, again, the smoke from the burned station. Had the wind changed? He raised his head, slowing his horse to a walk. Almost at the same moment, Valdir, riding ahead, raised his arm in signal, and stopped, turning his head into the wind and sniffing, nostrils flared wide.

He said, tersely, "Fire."

"Another station?" one of the Darkovans asked.

Valdir, moving his head form side to side—almost, Larry thought, as if he expected to hear the sound of flames—suddenly froze, statue-still. At the same moment Larry heard the sound of a bell: a deep-toned, full-throated bell tone, ringing through the valley. It tolled over and over, ringing out in a curious pattern of sound. While the little party of riders remained motionless, still listening intently, another bell farther away, fainter, but repeating the same slow rhythm, took up the ringing, and a few minutes later, still farther away, a third bell added a deep note to the choir.

Valdir said, harshly, "It's the fire-bell! Kennard, your ears are better than mine—which ring is it?"

Kennard listened intently, stiffening in his saddle. He tapped out the rhythm with his fingers, briefly. "That's the ring from Aderis."

"Come on, then," Valdir rapped out. In another minute they were all racing down the slope; Larry, startled, jerked his reins and rode after them, as fast as he could. Keeping his seat with an effort, not wanting to be left behind, he wondered what it was all about.

As they came over the brow of a little hill, he cold hear the still-clamoring bell, louder and more insistent, and see, lying in the valley below them, a little cluster of roofs—the village of Aderis. The streets were filled with men, women and children; as they rode down from the slope into the streets of the village, they were surrounded by a crowd of men who fell silent as they saw Valdir Alton.

Valdir slid from his saddle, beckoned his party closer, Larry drawing close with them. He found himself beside Kennard. "What is it, what's going on?"

"Forest fire," Kennard said, motioning him to silence, listening to the man who was still pointing toward the hills across the valley. Larry, raising his head to look where the man pointed, could see only a thick darkening haze that might have been a cloud—or smoke.

The crowd in the village street was thickening, and through it all the bell tolled on.

Kennard, turning to Larry, explained quickly, "When fire breaks out in these hills, they ring the bells from the village that sees it first, and every village within hearing takes it up. Before tonight, every able-bodied man in the countryside will be here. That's the law. It's almost the only law we have that runs past the boundaries of a man's own estate."

Larry could see why; even in a countryside that scorned impersonal laws, men must band together to fight the one great impersonal enemy of fire. Valdir turned his head, saw the two boys standing by their horses, and came swiftly toward them. He looked harried and remote again, and Larry realized why some men were afraid of the Alton lord when he looked like this.

"Vardi will take the horses, Kennard. They're going to send us forward into the south slopes; they need fire-lines there. Larry—" he frowned slightly, shaking his head. Finally he said, "I am responsible for your safety. The fire may sweep down this slope, so the women and children are being sent to the next town. Go with them; I will give you a message to someone there who can have you as a guest until the emergency is over."

Kennard looked startled, and Larry could almost read his thoughts; the look in Kennard's eyes was too much for him. Should he, the stranger, be sent to safety with the women, the infirm, the little children?

"Lord Alton, I don't—"

"I haven't time to argue," The Darkovan snapped, and his eyes were formidable. "You'll be safe enough there."

Larry felt a sudden, sharp-flaring rage, like a physical thing. *Damn it, I won't be sent out of the way with the women! What do they think I am?* Valdir Alton had begun to turn away; he stopped short, so abruptly that Larry actually wondered for a moment if he had spoken his protest aloud.

Valdir's voice was harsh. "What is it, Larry? Be quick. I have a place to fill here."

"Can't I go with the men, sir? I—" Larry sought for words, trying to put into words some of the angry thoughts that struggled in his mind.

As if echoing his thoughts, Valdir said, "If you were one of us—but your people will hold me responsible if you are harmed. . . ."

Larry, catching swiftly at what Valdir had told him of Darkovan codes, retorted, "But you're dealing with me, not with all my people!"

Valdir smiled, bleakly. "If that's the way you want it. It's hard, rough work," he said, warningly, but Larry did not speak, and Valdir gestured. "Go with Kennard, then. He'll show you what to do."

Hurrying to join Kennard, Larry realized that he had crossed another bridge. He could be accepted by the Darkovans on their own terms, as a man—like Kennard—and not as a child to be guarded.

After a confused interval, he found himself part of a group of horsemen, Valdir in the lead, Kennard at his side, half a dozen strange Darkovans surrounding him, riding to-

ward the low-lying haze. As they rode, the smell of smoke
grew stronger, the air heavy and thick with curious smells;
flecks of dust hung in the air, while bits of black soot fell on
their faces and stung their eyes. His horse grew restive,
backing and whinnying, as the smoke thickened. Finally
they had to dismount and lead their horses forward.

As yet, the fire had been only a smolder of smoke lying
against the sky, an acrid and stinging stench; but as they
came between the two hills that cut off their view of the
forested slopes, Larry could see a crimson glow and hear a
strange dull sound in the distance. A small rabbitlike beast
suddenly scudded past, almost under their horses' hooves,
blindly fleeing.

Valdir pointed. He made a sharp turn past a high hedge,
and came out into a broad meadow whose grayish high grass
was trampled and beaten down. A large number of men and
boys were milling around at the center; there was a tent
pitched at the edge, and after a moment of confusion Larry
realized that the random groupings were orderly and busi-
nesslike. An elderly man, stooping and hobbling, came to
lead their horses away; Larry gave up his reins and hurried
after Kennard to the center of the field.

A boy about his own age, in a coarse sacking shirt and
leather breeches, motioned to them. He nodded to Kennard
in recognition, looked at Larry with a frown and asked,
"Can you use an axe?"

"I'm afraid not," Larry said.

The Darkovan boy listened briefly to his accent, but
shrugged it aside. "Take this then," he said, and from a pile
of tools handed Larry a thing like a long-toothed, sharp rake.
He waved him on. Raising his eyes to the far end of the
meadow, Larry could see the edge of the forest. It looked
green and peaceful, but over the tops of the trees, far away,
he saw the red glare of flame.

Kennard touched his arm lightly. "Come on," he said,

and gave Larry a brief wry grin. "No doubt about which way we're going, that's for sure."

Larry put the rake over his shoulder and joined the group of men and boys moving toward the distant glow.

Once or twice during that long, confused afternoon, he found himself wondering, remotely, why he had gotten himself into this, but the thought was brief. He was just one of a long line of men and boys spread out, with rakes and hoes and other tools, to cut a fire-line between the distant burning fire and the village. Crude and simple as it was, it was the oldest known technique for dealing with forest-fires—create a wide space where there was nothing for it to burn. With rakes, hoes, spades and shovels, they cleared away the dry brush and pine-needles, scraped the earth bare, chopped up the dry grass and made a wide swath of open ground where nothing could burn. Men with axes felled the trees in the chosen space; smaller boys dragged the dead trees and brush away, while behind them came the crew that scraped and shoveled the ground clear. Larry quickly had an ache in his muscles and his palms stung and smarted from the handle of the rake, but he worked on, one anonymous unit in the dozens of men that kept swarming in. When one spot was cleared they were moved on to another. Younger boys brought buckets of water around; Larry drank in his turn, dropping the rake and lowering his lips to the bucket's edge. When it was too dark to see, he and Kennard were called out of the line, their places taken by a fresh crew working by torchlight, and they stumbled wearily down the slope to the camp, lined up for bowls of stew ladled out by the old men keeping the camp, and, wrapping themselves in blankets, threw themselves down to sleep on the grass, surrounded by young men and old.

Larry woke before dawn, his throat and lungs filled with smoke. He sat up. The roar of the fire sounded ominous and harsh in his ears; men were still gathered at the center of the camp space. He recognized the tall form of Valdir Alton, heard the sound of excited voices. He wriggled out of his blanket and stood upright, then was aware of Kennard, rising to his feet beside him. Against the dimness, Kennard was only a blurred form. He said, "Something's happening over there, Let's go and see."

The two boys picked their way carefully through the rows of sleeping men. As they came closer to the lighted fire, the firelight shone on a tall man in a somber gray cloak, dull-red hair splotched with white, and Larry recognized the stern, ascetic face of Lorill Hastur; close at his side, in a close-wrapped cape, shivering, was a slight and fragile woman with masses of burning, fire-red hair.

Kennard whistled softly. "*A leronis*, a sorceress—and the Hastur-Lord! The fire must be worse than we thought!" He tugged at Larry's wrist. "Come on—this I want to hear!"

Quietly they crept to the outskirts of the little group. Valdir Alton had spread a blanket on the trampled grass for the woman; she sat down, staring at the glow of the distant fire as if hypnotized.

"The fire's leaped the lines on the North slope," Valdir said. "They were too close to the flames, and had to leave the area. We brought up donkey-teams to plow lines and clear away faster, but there weren't enough people working there. We had only one clairvoyant, and he couldn't see too clearly where the fire was moving."

Lorill Hastur said, in his deep voice, "We came as quickly as we could. But there's not much we can do until the sun rises." He turned to the woman. "Where are the clouds, Janine?"

Still staring fixedly at the sky, the woman said, "Too far, really. And not enough. Seven *vars* distant."

"We'll have to try it, though," Valdir said. "Otherwise it will cross the hill to the west, and burn down—Zandru's hells, it could burn all the way to the river! We can't afford to lose that much timberland."

Larry heard the words with a strange little prickle of

dread. He found himself thinking, painfully, of his own world.

With tractors and earth-movers they could cut firelines twenty feet wide in a few hours! With chemicals, they could douse the fire from the air, and have it out within an hour! Here, they didn't even have helicopters or planes to see from the air which way the fire was moving!

Kennard looked at him a little wryly, and Larry again wondered if he had spoken aloud, but the Darkovan boy said nothing. The darkness was thinning, and through the thick sooty air the sky was flushing purple with dawn.

"What are they going to do?" Larry asked.

Kennard did not answer.

The woman motioned to Lorill Hastur; he lowered himself and sat, cross-legged, on the blanket before her. Valdir Alton stood behind them, his face wiped clean of expression, intent and calm.

The woman was holding something in her hand. It was a blue jewel, glimmering, pale in the purplish dawn, and Larry thought suddenly of the blue jewel Valdir had held in his hand when he probed the mind of the dying Ranger. A curious little prickle of apprehension ran down his spine, and he shivered in the chilly, soot-laden wind.

The three forms were motionless, tense and still as carven images. Kennard gripped at Larry's arm and Larry felt the taut excitement in his friend; he wanted to ask a dozen questions, but the intentness of the three redheaded forms held him speechless. He waited.

Minutes dragged by, slowly, and the blue jewel gleamed in the woman's hand, and Larry could almost see the tension radiating between the three of them. The pale dawn brightened, and far away at the eastern horizon a dimmer crimson glow lightened the lurid red of the faraway fire. The light strengthened, grew brighter in the pale clear sky.

Then the woman sighed softly, and Larry felt it as a palpable darkening and chill. Kennard gripped his arm, pointed upward. Clouds were gathering—thickening, moving in the pale windless sky, centering, clustering from nowhere. Thick, heavy, high-piled cumulus, thin wispy fast-moving cirrus, raced from the horizon—from all the horizons! Not moving with normal wind, but coming, collecting from all corners of the compass, the clouds gathered and darkened, piling high and higher above them. The sun was blurred away, the meadow gradually darkened and Larry shivered in the sudden chill—but not with cold. He let out his breath in a long sigh.

Kennard loosed his clenched fists. He was staring at the sky. "Clouds enough," he muttered, "if only they would rain! But with no wind, if the clouds just *sit* there—"

Larry took the murmured words as license to break his silence. Questions tumbled one over another, condensed themselves to a blurted, "How did they do that? *Did* they bring those clouds?"

Kennard nodded, not taking it very seriously. "Of course. Nothing much to that—I can do it myself, a little. On a good day for it. And they're Comyn—the most powerful psi powers on Darkover."

Larry felt the chill run up and down his spine with cold feet. Telepathy—and now clouds moved by the power of trained minds!

His Terran training said, *Impossible, superstitious rubbish! They observed which way the clouds were moving and bolstered up their reputation by predicting that clouds would pile up for rain.* But even as he said it, he knew it was not true. He was not in the safe predictable world of Terran science now, but where these powers were more common than a camera.

"What now?" he asked, and as if in answer, Valdir said from the center of the circle, "Now, we pray for rain. Much good may it do us."

Then, raising his head, he saw the boys, and beckoned to them.

"Have some breakfast," he said. "As soon as it's a little lighter they'll send you out on the fire-lines again. Unless it rains."

"Evanda grant it," said the woman huskily.

Lorill Hastur raised his still face and gave Kennard a smile of greeting, which turned impassive as he saw Larry. Larry, under the man's gaze, was suddenly aware of his soot-stained face, his raw and blistered hands, the torn and sweaty state of his clothes. Then he realized that Valdir Alton was in little better state. He had vaguely noticed, yesterday, that the men on the fire-lines were of all sorts: some soft-handed, in the rich clothing of aristocrats, some in the rags of the poorest. Evidently rank made no difference; rich and poor alike worked against this common danger. Of all those in the field, only the two telepaths were unstained by hard work.

Then he saw the gray look of fatigue in the eyes of the woman, the deep lines in the face of the Hastur. *Maybe their work has been the hardest of all—*

Kennard nudged him, and he accepted, from one of the old men, a lump of bread and a battered cup of a bitter-chocolaty drink. They found an unmuddied stretch of grass and sat to eat, their ears tuned to the distant roaring of the fire.

Kennard said, grimly, "They can bring the clouds and pile them up, but they can't make them rain. Although sometimes just the sheer weight of the clouds will condense them into rain. Let's hope."

"If you had airplanes—" Larry said.

"What for?"

"On Terra, they can make rain," Larry said slowly, thinking back to half-learned lessons of his schooldays. "They seed the clouds with some chemical—crystals—silver iodide," he used the Terran word, not knowing the Darkovan one, "or even dry ice will do. I'm not sure how it works, but it condenses the clouds into rain—"

"How can ice be dry?" Kennard demanded, almost rudely. "It sounds like nonsense. Like saying dry water or a live dead man."

"It's not real ice," Larry corrected himself. "It's a gas—a frozen gas, that is. It's carbon dioxide—the gas you breathe out. It crystallizes into something like snow, only it's much, much colder than ice or snow—and it burns if you touch it."

"You're not joking?"

"I hope not," said Valdir abruptly from behind them. "Kennard, what was Larry saying to you just now? I picked it up, but I can't read him—"

With a curious prickly sensation again, Larry realized that Valdir had been well out of earshot. The Darkovan lord was looking down at him with an almost fierce intensity. He said, "Make rain? It sounds, then, as if the Terrans have a magic greater than ours. Tell me about this rain-making, Larry."

Larry repeated what he had said to Kennard, and the older man stood scowling, deep in thought. Without a word, Lorill Hastur and the frail, flame-haired woman had approached them, and stood listening.

Lorill Hastur said, "What about it, Valdir? You know something of atomic structures. Is it practical at all?"

The men who had slept in the meadow were collecting their tools now, forming in groups, getting their orders for the day's work. Larry looked at the forest edge. How green it looked. Yet above it rose the blanket of smoke and the omnipresent dull roar of the fire. Valdir turned, too, and looked at the cloud that hung over the burning woods.

He said, "Fire throws off the same gas as breath. There must be an enormous quantity of carbon dioxide going off into the air."

"We can move it into the cold of the outer sky," Lorill Hastur said. "That's easy enough. And from there, if it falls on the clouds—"

"There's no time to waste," the woman said. Her eyes

were closed, her voice remote, as she added, "A fire-storm has broken out on the far side of the forest, and the main blaze is racing toward the villages there. The fire-lines will never contain it. Rain is the only hope. There is enough moisture in those clouds to kill the fire—if we could only get it out of them."

"We can try," Valdir said. The three of them went into one of those intent silences again, the very air between their still forms seeming to tremble with invisible force.

Larry looked at Kennard. "Do you know what they're going to do? How can the—?"

"They can teleport the gas above the clouds," Kennard said. "If the cold can freeze it—"

Larry was becoming a little hardened to these curious powers now. If telepathy was possible, teleportation was only a minor step—

"If they can teleport, why don't they just teleport enough water from a river, or something, to put out the fire?"

"Too much weight involved," Kennard said gravely. "Even the clouds—they didn't move the clouds themselves, just enough air to create a wind to move them here." He fell silent, his eyes on his father, and when Larry started to speak, motioned him, impatiently, to silence.

The silence in the dawnlit meadow deepened; there was no sound at all, except for the distant, indistinct sound of the fire. The clouded sky seemed to darken, grow thick and dreary. Larry watched a group of men moving away toward the fire-lines; he and Kennard should have been with them. And they stood here, waiting, watching the three telepaths—

Abruptly there was a great WHOOSH from the distant fire; Larry, whirling round, saw a tremendous uprushing billow of smoke and flame, and seemed to feel, rather than hear, the wild roaring sound. Then silence again, hushed, tense and deep.

Above his head the clouds moved, writhed, seeming to form and reform into tossing shapes and worms of moisture;

théy curdled, coalesed, the sky darkened and darkened as the cloud-gray deepened.

Then the sky and cloud-layer suddenly *dissolved*—that was the only way Larry could describe it, afterward—and flowed into dark, thick lines of teeming, pouring rain. The burning forest sizzled, crackled in a sort of desperation. Great thick clouds of smoke and steam and soot billowed upward, and a rushing wind flung great sparks upward. Larry was soaked through in a moment, before the rain localized itself, pouring heavily down over the forest, but leaving the meadow untouched except by the brief spit of rain. The flames, visible over the treetops, sank and died beneath the upsurge of steam and smoke. The hissing sound grew louder, roared, then dimmed and was still.

The rain stopped.

Soaked, shivering, Larry stared in blank wonder at Valdir and the two gray-clad telepaths. They had cornered the clouds; they had harnessed the very force of the rain to combat the fire!

Valdir beckoned to the boys. They walked across the damp grass, Larry still a little dazed. He had boasted of Terran science; could it match *this?*

"That's over with, at least," Valdir said, in a tone of profound relief. "Larry, I wanted to thank you; without what you told us, none of us would have known how to do that. I hardly know how to thank you."

It was more confusing than ever. These men had forces and powers undreamed of by science—and yet they were ignorant of a simple notion like cloud-seeding! Because he could not have spoken without revealing that mixture of awe, mingled with surprise at the incompleteness of the knowledge, Larry was silent. Valdir turned to Lorill Hastur and said, "Now you can see my point, perhaps! Without their knowledge—"

But before he could finish the sentence, a wild clamor of bells broke out from the village below. Valdir stiffened; the two telepaths darted looks at one another. From further away another bell and another sounded the alarm; not now in the known pattern to signal a fire, but a wild, clamorous cry of warning. The men in the camp, the men trooping back from the dead fire, dropped their tools and axes and looked up, startled. There was a rising murmur of apprehension, of dread.

Valdir swore, furiously. "We might have known—"

Kennard looked at him in astonishment. "What is it, Father?"

Valdir's mouth twisted bitterly. "A trick—the fire was obviously set to draw us away from the villages, so that the bandits could attack in peace—and find no one to meet them but women and old men and little children!"

The fire camp, until now so orderly, was suddenly a scene of milling confusion as men formed into groups, stirred around restlessly, broke away for their horses, and within a few minutes the crowded field was almost empty, men vanishing silently in all directions. Valdir watched, tight-mouthed.

"The raiders may get a surprise," he said, at last. "They'll never guess we could have conquered such a fire so quickly. Just the same"—he looked grim and angry—"I had no chance—Tell me, Larry, how would your people handle such an attack?"

"I suppose we'd all get together and fight it," Larry said, and Valdir's mouth moved in a brief, mirthless laugh.

"Right. But they won't understand that it's as urgent as a fire—" he broke off, with a violent gesture. "Zandru seize them all! Kennard, where did they take our horses?"

Fifteen minutes later they were riding away from the village, Valdir still silent and grim. Kennard and Larry not daring to break in on his anger. Larry was still struggling with the sense of wonder. The powers these Darkovans had—and the slipshod, unsystematic way they used them!

He was beginning to formulate a theory as to why Valdir

had invited him to his estate. Valdir evidently had some inkling of the value of a quality which seemed alien to the Darkovan way of life, something the Terrans had. Larry hardly knew how to describe it. It was the thing Kennard had jeered at when he said, "You Terrans can't handle your personal problems by yourselves—you have to call in everyone else." Perhaps it could be called a community spirit, or the ability to work together in groups. They didn't know how to organize; even in firefighting there had been no single leader but each group had worked separately. Even now, there was no way they could get together against the common danger of the bandits. And Valdir, who could see the history of failure behind these scattered efforts, hoped to change this old pattern. But they hadn't given him a chance.

The other Darkovans who had originally been a part of the three-day hunt—how long ago that seemed!—rode several places behind, not wanting to break in on their master's preoccupation. To Larry, Valdir's feelings seemed as clear as if he, himself, had felt them. Kennard, too, riding silently at Larry's side, was mulling it over in his mind, the disparity behind the old codes and his father's attempt to change things. To Larry it seemed almost as if Kennard spoke his thoughts aloud—his father could do no wrong, and yet how had he come to these conclusions?

Once away from the site of the fire, there was no sign of clouds or of the brief rain; only the high-hanging cloud of smoke and soot over the forest told where the fire had been. Even that had vanished behind the hills by the time they paused, where the road forked at the foot of a thickly wooded slope, to breathe the horses and to eat cold food from their saddlebags.

Kennard said idly, "It's going to be good to be home."

Larry nodded. He still ached from the unaccustomed labor in the fire-lines, and his hands were raw and blistered.

"Mine too," Kennard said, displaying his hands ruefully. "Though you'd think they were hardened enough by now.

The arms-master in the city guard wouldn't have much sympathy for me. He'd say I'd shirked sword-practice too many times."

Larry reached in his saddle-bag for the small first-aid kit he had brought along. It had the emblem of the Medical HQ on it, and Kennard looked at it curiously as Larry opened it and glanced at the small bottles and tubes.

"Here. Try some of this on your blisters," he suggested diffidently, sprinkling the powder on his own. Kennard followed suit, smelling the antiseptic curiously.

"May I see it?" Kennard examined the small bottles and tubes with interested curiosity. "Your people make the damndest things!"

"Some of yours are just as strange," Larry retorted. "The idea of telepathy still seems weird to me. And teleportation!"

Kennard shrugged. "I suppose so, though of course to me it's very simple." He looked at his father; Valdir, looking somewhat less unapproachable now, turned, nodded to his son, fished in the pocket of his jerkin and tossed something to Kennard. Kennard caught the small object—it was shrouded in a small chamois bag and wrapped in silk—and from it, drew a glimmering blue jewel.

"Of course I'm not as good at it all as my father, but still—here, take a look in this."

Gingerly, Larry touched the blue jewel. It felt faintly warm. He hesitated, remembering how Valdir had probed the mind of the dying Ranger.

"It's all right," Kennard said gently, reassuringly. "You don't think I'd hurt you, do you?"

Abashed at his own fear, Larry looked into the blue jewel. Within the depths, faint colors seemed to move and writhe; suddenly, as he looked up at Kennard, some barrier seemed to drop. The Darkovan boy seemed nearer, and easier to understand. Larry caught, in one quick flash of understanding, a sudden blaze of Kennard's thoughts, as if the

essence of his friend's personality was made clear to him:
Kennard's intense pride of family, his tremendous sense of
responsibility for his work, the fears with which he sometimes struggled, the warmth Kennard felt for his father and
his young foster-sister, even—to Larry's shy embarrassment—the warm friendliness Kennard felt for Larry himself, and the emotion verging on awe with which he
regarded Larry's travels in space and his Terran origin. . . .

All this in a brief flash, as the blueness of the jewel
blazed; then it faded, the barrier dropped in place again, and
Kennard was smiling at him, somewhat tentatively. It occurred to Larry that Kennard now knew as much about him
as he knew about Kennard. He didn't mind—but it took
some getting used to!

At least, having had a sample of it, he couldn't doubt the
existence of telepathy!

Kennard shrouded the jewel again. Larry, realizing that
the medical kit was still in his other hand, thrust it quickly
into his pocket.

He had no way of knowing that the moment of rapport
between himself and Kennard was to save both their
lives. . . .

CHAPTER SIX

They had mounted again, and had ridden for an hour, when they came to a narrow canyon between two forested hills. Between the slopes and the dark trees the place lay in shadow, for the sun was declining; Valdir, riding ahead, slowed his horse to a walk and waited for the others to come up with him.

Kennard's eyes rested questioningly on his father, and Larry, riding beside him, could follow his thoughts in that way that was still so strange to him: *I don't like this place. Every clump of brushwood could have a dozen bandits behind it. It's a perfect set-up for an ambush. . . . It would be my first fight. The first time I've been this close to real danger, not just lolling around the city streets chasing home troublemakers. I wonder if Father knows that I'm afraid.*

Larry's skin prickled, in a strange mixture of excitement and fear. Within the last three days his peaceful life had suddenly plunged into a maelstrom of violence and danger. It was new to him, but, somehow, not unpleasant.

They were halfway down the little valley when Larry heard, through the hoofbeats, a curious sound from deep within the bushes. He stiffened in the saddle; Valdir, alert, saw the move and reined in, looking warily around. Then, from the shelter of the trees came a harsh and raucous cry— and then mounted men were all sweeping down on them.

Valdir cried out a warning. Larry, in that first instant of petrified shock, saw the riders, tall men in long furred cloaks, long-haired and bearded, mounted on huge rangy horses of a strange breed, racing down on them at incredible speed. There was no time to flee, no time to think. Suddenly he was in the middle of the attackers, saw the Darkovans had drawn their swords; Kennard, his face very white, had his dagger in his hand and was fighting to control his horse with the other.

He had a bare moment to see all this—and a strange, up-rushing sense of panic that he, of all his party, was unarmed and knew nothing of fighting—before it all melted into a mad confusion of horses pushing against horses, cries in a strange tongue, the dull clash of steel on steel.

Larry's horse reared upright and plunged forward. He gripped wildly at the reins, felt them slide through his fingers, burning his blistered hands with a brief stab of pain. Then he felt himself losing his balance and slid to the ground, legs crumpling beneath him. Half stunned, he had just sense enough to roll from beneath the pawing hooves of his frantic horse. Someone tripped over his prostrate body, stumbled, fell forward on the grass; roused up with a hoarse cry of rage, and a moment later came at Larry with a knife. Larry rolled over on his back, balling up, kicking with one booted foot at the descending knife. With a split-second sense of weird unreality—*This isn't real, it can't be!*—he saw the knife spin away in a high arc and fall ten feet away. The man, knocked off balance, reeled and staggered back; recovered himself and dived at Larry, getting hold of him with both hands. Larry drew his elbows up, pushed with all his might and freed himself momentarily. He struggled up to his knees, but his attacker was on him again and the man's face—rough, bearded, with evil yellow eyes—came close and menacing. His breath stank hot in Larry's face; his hands sought for Larry's throat. Larry, frightened and yet suddenly cool-headed, found himself thinking, *He hasn't got a knife, and he's fat and out of condition.*

He went limp, relaxing and falling backward, dragging the man with him, before his attacker could recover his balance, Larry drew up his feet to his chest in an almost convulsive movement: thrust out with all his strength. The kick landed in the man's stomach. The bandit gave a yell of agony and crumpled, howling, his hands gripping his belly in oblivious anguish.

Larry pulled himself up to his knees again, braced himself, and put the whole weight of his body into one punch, which struck the man fairly in the nose.

The man dropped, out cold, and lay still.

And as Larry straightened, recovering his balance, finding a moment to feel fright again, something struck him hard on the back of the head.

The clashing of swords and knives became a thunder, an explosion—then slid into a deathly, unreal silence. He felt himself falling. But he never felt himself strike the ground.

It was dark. He was sore and cramped; his whole body ached, and there was a throbbing jolting pain in his head. He tried to move, made a hoarse sound, and opened his eyes.

He could see nothing. He knew a split-second of panic; then he began to see, dimly, through the coarse weave of cloth over his face. He tried to move his hands and felt that they were bound with cords at his side. The jolting pain went on. It felt like hoofbeats. It was hoofbeats. He was lying on his stomach, bent in the middle, and against his hands was the hairy warmth of a horse's body.

He realized, fuzzily, that he was blindfolded and flung doubled over the saddle of a horse. With the realization, he panicked and struggled to move his arms, and then felt a sharp steel point, pricking through his clothes, against his ribs.

"Lie still," said a harsh voice, in so barbarous a dialect

that Larry could barely understand the words. "I know that orders are not to kill you, but you'd be none the worse for a little bloodletting—and much easier to carry! Lie still!"

Larry subsided, his head spinning. Where was he? What had happened? Where were Valdir, Kennard? Memory of the fight came rushing back. They had been outnumbered. Had the others, too, been taken prisoner? How long had he been unconscious? Where were they taking him? Cold fear gripped the boy; he was in the hands of Darkovan bandits, and he was alone and far from his own people, on a strange world whose people were hostile to Terra.

What would they do to him?

The jolting hoofbeats went on for what seemed hours before they slowed, stopped, and Larry was pulled roughly to the ground.

"A good prize," said a voice, speaking the same harsh and barbarous dialect, "and earnest for good behavior from those sons of Zandru. The heir of Alton, no less—see the colors he wears?"

"I thought Alton's son was older than this," said another voice.

"He's small for his years," said the first voice, contemptuously, "but he bears the mark of the Comyn—hair of flame, and no commoner ever wore such clothes, or rode one of the Alton-bred horses."

"Except when we come back from a raid," guffawed another voice.

Larry went cold with fright. Was Kennard a prisoner too?

Rough hands pulled Larry forward again; the folds of muffling cloth were jerked away from his face, and someone pushed him forward. It was twilight, and it was raining a little, thin fine cold drops that made him shiver. He blinked, wishing he could get his bound hands to his head, and looked around.

They stood in the shadow of an ancient, ruined building,

sharp-edged stones rising high around them. An icy wind
was blowing. Larry's captor shoved him forward.

There were a good dozen of the roughnecks in the lee of
the ruin, but he saw no sign of Kennard, Valdir, or of any of
his companions.

Before him stood a tall, strong man, cloaked in a soiled
crimson mantle, much cut and torn. Under it was a dark
leather vest and breeches which had once been finely cut
and embroidered. The hood of the mantle was pushed back
but the man's face was invisible; a soft leather mask, cut to
lie close to nose and cheeks, concealed all his features to the
thin, cruel lips. He had six fingers on each hand. His voice
was rough and husky, but he spoke the city dialect without
the barbarous accent of the others.

"You are Kennard Alton-Comyn, son of Valdir?"

Larry looked around, in dismay, but no one else was visible, and suddenly his mind flashed across the mistake they
had made.

They thought *he* was Kennard Alton—they had taken
him as a hostage—and he dared not even tell them they had
made a mistake! What would they do to one of the alien Terrans?

The man's words returned to him—*An earnest of good
behavior . . . the heir to Alton!* That sounded as if they
didn't want to kill him—not right away, at least. But how
could he keep them from discovering his Terran identity?
What would Kennard do?

The masked man repeated his question, harshly. Larry let
out his breath, slowly and tensely. What would Kennard
do—or say?

He thought of Kennard's arrogance, facing the street
roughnecks a few weeks ago. He drew himself to his full
height and said, clearly, slowly because he was searching for
the right words and colloquial phrases, but it gave an effect
of dignity, "Is it not courtesy in your land to declare the
host's name before asking the name of a—a guest?"

He knew he was playing for his life. He had watched the arrogance of the Darkovan aristocrats, and he sensed that their contempt for these bandits was as great as their hatred for them. He shrugged his cloak around his shoulders— thank God he had been wearing Darkovan clothes!—and stood unflinching before the man's masked stare.

"As you wish," the masked man said, his lips curling, "yet build no hope on courtesy, son of the *Hali-imyn*. I am called Cyrillon of the Forest Roads—and you are Kennard N'Caldir Alton-Comyn."

Larry said, "Would it profit anything to deny it?"

"Very little." Behind the mask, Larry felt Cyrillon's eyes sharp on him.

"What do you want with me?"

"Not your death, unless"—the cruel lips hardened—"you make it necessary. A pawn you are, son of Alton, and of value to us, but a time could come—never doubt it—where your death would be wiser than your life in our hands. So don't build too heavily on your safety, *chiyu*, or think that you can make whatever move you please and that we won't dare to kill you for it."

He regarded Larry for a moment, with eyes so grim that Larry flinched. He was cold with terror; he felt like breaking down, shrieking out the mistake they were making.

At last Cyrillon released his eyes. "We have a long way to ride, in rough country. You will come with us, or be carried like a bundle of blankets. But on the roads we will travel, men need their limbs, their wits, and the use of their eyes. The passes are not easy even for free men. If I leave you free, and give you the use of all three, will you pledge me your honor as *comyn* to make no attempt to escape?"

It occurred to Larry that a promise made under threats was no honorable promise, and involved nothing. He would, doubtless, save himself a lot of trouble by giving his parole. He wavered a moment; then, clearly as sight, he seemed to see the face of Kennard—stern, with boyish pride and the severe Darkovan concept of honor. Could a Terran do anything less? That pride stiffened his voice as he resolved to play his part.

"A pledge of honor to a thief and an outlaw? A man who"—again his thoughts raced, remembering stories Valdir had told about the codes of battle—"a man who carries away his enemy's son muffled in a cloak, rather than cutting him down openly in fair fight?"

He hesitated, then the words came to him, almost as if he heard Valdir's self speak them. "You who break laws of the road and the laws of war have no right to exchange words of honor with honorable men. I will speak to you as an equal only with the sword. Since you are without honor, I will not soil even my bare word. If you want me to go anywhere, you will have to take me by force, because I will not willingly go one step in the company of renegades and outlaws!"

Breathless, he fell silent. Cyrillon regarded him in deadly silence, his lips set and menacing, for so long that Larry quailed, and it was all he could do to keep his face impassive. Why had he burst out like that? What nonsensical impulse to play the part of an Alton had impelled those words? They had rushed out without his conscious control; without even a second thought! It might have been wiser not to enrage the outlaw.

And enrage him he had; Cyrillon's odd hands were clenched on his knife-hilt till the knuckles stood out, white and round; but he spoke quietly.

"Fine words, my boy. See, then, that you do not whimper at their results. Tie him, Kyro, and make a good job of it this time," he said to someone behind Larry.

The man cut the cords on Larry's wrists, then pulled his hands forward. He tied them together with a thick wool scarf which he took from his own throat; then the wool padding was crossed with tight leather thongs which, without the padding, would have bitten deep into his flesh. They left his feet free, but passed a rope about his waist, securing it by a long loop to the saddle of his captor. Then the man took water and wet the leather knots. Cyrillon watched these proceedings grimly and, at last, said, "I speak these orders in your presence, Alton, so that you will know what to expect. I do not want you killed; you are more useful to me alive. Just the same, Kyro, if he tries to run from the path, cut the sinew in one of his legs. If he tries to drag and hamper our climbing, once we get on the mountain, cut his throat right away. And if he makes any disturbance whatsoever as we go along the Devil's Shelf, cut the rope and let him drop into the abyss, and good riddance to him."

Larry felt his heart suck and turn over; but although his cheeks blanched, his eyes did not falter, and, at last, Cyrillon said, "Good. We understand one another." He turned to mount, and Larry, somehow, sensed that he was disappointed.

He wanted me to be frightened and plead with him. He would get some kind of satisfaction out of seeing an Alton pleading—with him! How did I know that?

The man who had him captive lifted Larry to the back of his horse.

"For the moment we can ride," he said, grimly. He looked ill-pleased. "Don't give me any trouble, lad; I have no stomach for torturing even a whelp of the *Hali-imyn*. Never doubt he means what he says, either."

The other bandits were mounting. Larry, stiff and cold and frightened, looked up at the high wall of mountains that rose ahead.

And yet, for all his fear, a curious and unquenchable pulse of excitement and curiosity beat within him. He had wanted to see the strange and exciting life of the alien world—and here at the foot of the strange mountains, under a strange sun, he was seeing it undiluted. Even with Kennard, there had been the sense that somehow everything was a little different, because he was Terran, because he was alien.

He realized that he had really no grounds for even the slight optimism he felt. For all he knew, Valdir and Kennard, and all their companions, might be lying dead in the valley where they had been ambushed. He was being taken— alone, unarmed, a prisoner, an alien—into some of the wildest and most dangerous and impassable country on Darkover.

Yet the indefinite lift of optimism remained. He was alive and unhurt—and almost anything could happen next.

CHAPTER SEVEN

Larry was dreaming.

In his dream he was back on Earth, and Darkover was still a faraway, romantic dream. He was on a camping trip, sleeping out in an old forest (or why would he be so cold, with the cold dampness of rain in all his bones?).

Then, through the dream, there was a faint blue glimmer, and an urgent voice speaking. *Where are you? Where are you? We've been close enough for a long enough time, that if I can pick you up I can follow you and find you. But don't let them know you're Terran. . . .*

Half impatiently he tried to shut the urgent voice away, to recapture the peaceful dream. He was back in the Terran Zone; in a little while his father would come in and waken him. . . . Someone had left the air-conditioning turned up to maximum; it was cold in here, colder than even the Darkovan night . . . and what was the matter with his arm? Why was his bed so cold, had he fallen asleep on the floor? With a little groan, he rolled over, his eyes blinked open and he was back in the terrible present. He squeezed his eyes shut again, with a spasm of despair. He was in the mountain fort of the bandits, and he was very helplessly a captive and alone, and although during the day he could keep up some hope, just now he was only a frightened boy, frightened in a strange world.

His left arm had been cruelly forced backward and strapped behind his back, the left hand at the shoulderblade, in a sort of leather harness. The fingers had long ago gone numb. The first night of his capture, the man who had carried him along the mountain trail had lifted him—numb and helpless—from the saddle, and brought him to their fire; he had, half pityingly, thrown a blanket across him, and cut the thongs on his wrist so that he could eat. Then the masked man had given orders, and two of the men had brought the leather harness. They had begun to tie his right hand behind his back when Cyrillon, whose cold eyes seemed to be everywhere at once, said harshly, "Are you blind? The little *bre'suin* is left-handed."

They had not been gentle, but he had not tried to fight or struggle; the fear was still on him, but he would not give them the satisfaction of pleading. Only once, in despair, had he thought of the last resort—telling them he was not their coveted hostage—

But then what? They probably wouldn't even bother with a prisoner of no importance; they might even kill him out of hand. And he did not want to die; although now, cold, wretched and in pain, he thought it might be rather nice to be dead.

He turned over, painfully, and looked about his prison.

A grim, pale light was sneaking its way through windows curtained roughly with threadbare tapestry, and shuttered with nailed boards. The room was spacious, with worm-eaten paneling, the hangings musty with age. The bed on which he lay was large and elaborate, but there were neither bedcoverings nor sheets; only an old horsehair mattress and a couple of fur rugs. The other furniture in the chamber was rickety and depressing, but he supposed he was lucky that he wasn't in a dirty dungeon somewhere; his brief glimpse of the outside of the fort looked as if there were dungeons aplenty beneath the grim stone walls.

He had not, so far, been harmed. He had, such as it was,

the freedom of this room. He could feed himself after a fashion with his right hand, but he had never realized how helpless anyone was with only one arm; he could not even balance properly when he walked. Morning and night they brought him food; a sort of coarse bread stuffed with nuts, a rough porridge of some unknown cereal, strips of rather good meat, some anonymous soapy-tasting stuff that he supposed was a form of cheese.

Now he sat up, hearing steps in the hall. It might have been someone with his breakfast, but he recognized the heavy, uneven tread of Cyrillon des Trailles. Cyrillon had visited him only once before, to inspect, briefly, the contents of his pockets.

"No weapons," the man Kyro had told him, holding up the things Larry had carried. Cyrillon turned them over. At the Terran medical kit he frowned curiously, then tossed it into a corner; Larry's mechanical pencil he tested with a fingertip, thrust into his own pocket. The other items he looked at briefly and dumped beside the Terran boy; a few small coins, a crumpled handkerchief, a small notebook. Larry's folded pocketknife he looked at curiously, asked, "What's this?"

Larry opened it, then mentally kicked himself; he might have been able to use the knife somehow, even though the main blade was broken off—he used it mostly for cutting string or building models. It had a corkscrew, a magnetized smaller blade and a hood for opening food cartons too.

Kyro said, "A knife? You won't want to leave him that!"

Cyrillon shrugged contemptuously. "With a blade not as long as my little finger? Much good may it do him!" He dropped it with the other oddments. "I only wanted to know if he had any of the Comyn weapons." He had laughed loudly, and walked out of the room, and Larry had not seen him again until this morning, he heard his heavy tread.

He felt a childish impulse to crawl under the bed and hide; but he mastered it, and got shakily to his feet. Three men entered, followed in a moment by Cyrillon, still masked.

Larry had realized, by now, that for all his contempt, Cyrillon treated him with a respect that verged on wariness. Larry couldn't quite figure out why. Cyrillon stood back from the bed now, as he ordered, "Get up and come with us, Alton."

Larry rose meekly and obeyed. He had sense enough to know that any gesture of defiance wouldn't help anything— except his pride—and might bring more abusive treatment. He might as well save his strength until he could do something really effective.

They conducted him to a room where there was a fire, and Larry's shivering became so intense that Cyrillon, with a gesture of contempt, motioned him to the fireplace. "These Comyn brats are all soft . . . warm yourself, then."

When he was warmed through, Cyrillon gestured him to sit on a bench. From a leather pouch Cyrillon drew something wrapped in a cloth. He glanced at Larry, curling his lip.

"I hardly dare to hope you will make this easy for me— or for yourself, young Alton."

He took from the cloth a jewel stone that flashed blue— a stone, Larry realized abruptly, of the same strange kind Kennard had shown him. This one was set into a ring of gold, with two handles on either side.

"I require you to look into this for me," Cyrillon said, "and if you find it easier to your pride, you may tell your people, afterward, that you did so under the threat of having your throat cut."

He laughed, that horrible raucous laughter that was like the screaming of some bird of prey.

Did Cyrillon expect him to demonstrate some psi power? Larry felt a pang of fright. His impersonation of a Darkovan must certainly fail, now. He felt his hand tremble as Cyrillon put the stone into it. He raised his eyes . . .

Blinding pain thrust through his head and eyes; he squeezed them shut spasmodically against the unbearable sense of *twisting* . . . of looking at something that should not exist in normal space at all. He felt sick. When he opened his eyes, Cyrillon was looking at him in grim satisfaction.

"So. You have the sight but are not used to stones of such power. Look again."

Larry, eyes averted, shook his head in refusal.

Cyrillon rose; every movement instinct with menace. Quite calmly, without raising his voice, he said, "Oh, yes you will." He gripped Larry's bound arm, somehow exerting a pressure that made red-hot wires run through the injured shoulder. "Won't you?"

Half senseless, Larry slumped forward on the bench. The stone rolled from his lax hand and he felt himself sinking beneath a warm, dark and somehow pleasant unconsciousness.

"Very well," said Cyrillon, very far away, "give him some *kirian*."

"Too dangerous," protested one of the men. "If he has the power of some of the Altons . . ."

Cyrillon said impatiently, "Didn't you see him turn sick at the sight of the stone? He hasn't any power yet! We'll chance it."

Larry felt one of the men seize his head, force it backward; the other was, with great care, uncapping a small vial from which rose strange colorless fumes. Larry, remembering Valdir's probing of the dying Ranger—what had he done?—jerked his head back, struggling madly; but the man who held him pressed his thumbs on Larry's jaw, forcing it open, and the other emptied the vial into his mouth.

He struggled, expecting heat, acid, fumes, but to his surprise the liquid, though bitterly cold, was almost tasteless. Almost before it touched his tongue, it seemed to evaporate. The sensation was intensely unpleasant, as if some strange gas were exploding in his head; his sight blurred, steadied. Cyrillon held the stone before his eyes; he realized, to his sick relief, that it was now only a blue glare, with none of the sickening twisting.

Cyrillon watched, intently.

Like shadows moving in the blue glare, forms became clear to Larry. A group of men rode past, Valdir's tall form clearly recognizable, a pair of curiously configured hills behind them. This faded, blurred into the face of Lorill Hastur, shrouded in a gray hood, and behind it Larry dreamily recognized the outline of the spaceport HQ building. He saw blurs again, then a small sturdy figure on a gray horse, bent low and racing against the wind, gradually cleared before his eyes. . . .

Larry suddenly became aware of what was happening. Somehow, through this magical stone, he was seeing pictures and they were being transmitted to Cyrillon des Trailles—why, why? Was he trying to spy through Larry on the people of the valleys? With a cry, Larry threw his arm over his eyes and saw the pictures thin out, blur and dissolve. A blind fury surged up in him at the cruel man who was using him this way—using, he thought, Kennard Alton against his own people—and such a flare of hatred as he had never felt for a living being. He would like to blast him down. . . .

And as the wrath surged up high and red, Cyrillon des Trailles drew a gasping breath of agony, dashed the crystal out of his hand and, with agonized force, struck Larry across the face. Larry fell, heavily, to the floor, and Cyrillon, doubled over in anguish, aimed a kick at him, missed and sank weakly to the bench.

One of the men said, "I warned you not to give him *kirian*. You gave him too much."

Cyrillon said, his voice still thick, "I guessed better than I knew . . . the accursed race have whelped a throwback! The youngster didn't even know what he was doing! If I had one or two of that kind in my hands, the whole cursed race of Cassild' would flee back to their lake-bottoms and the

Golden-Chained one would reign again! Zandru, what we could do with one of them on our side!"

The other man said, "We ought to kill him out of hand, before they find some way to use him against us!"

"Not yet," said Cyrillon. "I wonder how old he is? He looks a child, but all those lowland brats are soft."

One of the men guffawed. "He seemed not so soft a moment ago, when he had you yelping like a scalded cat!"

Cyrillon said, very softly, "If he were really as young as he looks, I'd guarantee to—re-educate him in my own way. I may try, at any rate. I can bear more than that," he added with gentle menace, "until he learns to—control his powers."

Larry, lying on the floor very still and hoping they had forgotten him, struggled with puzzlement greater than fear. Had *he* done that? If so, how? *He* had none of these Darkovan powers!

One of the men bent. Not gently, he lifted Larry to his feet. Cyrillon said, "Well, Kennard Alton, I warn you fairly not to try that trick again. Perhaps it was sheer reflex and you do not know your own powers. If that is true, I warn you, you had better learn control. The next time I will kick your ribs through your backbone. Now—*look into the stone!*"

The blue glare blinded his eyes. Then, crystal bright, intense, there were figures and forms he could not interpret, coming and going. . . . How was Cyrillon doing this? Or was he simply being hypnotized?

The blueness suddenly flared again. Inside his mind, in a sudden blaze, the voice of his dream spoke, *I've blanked it. He's no telepath and he doesn't dare force you. Don't be afraid; he can't read what you're getting now—but I can't hold this for long. . . . It's not hopeless yet. . . .*

Kennard?

Larry thought, *I'm going out of my mind. . . .*

The blue glare spread, became unbearable. He heard

Cyrillon snarl something—a threat?—but he saw nothing but that fearful blue.

With utter, absolute relief, for the first time in his life, Larry Montray fainted.

CHAPTER EIGHT

Day followed slow day, in the room where Larry was imprisoned; gradually, his original optimism dimmed out and faded. He was here, and there was no way to tell whether or not he would ever leave the place. He now knew he was being held as a hostage against Valdir Alton. From scraps of information he had wormed out of his jailer, he had put together the situation. Cyrillon and others of his kind had preyed on the lower lands since time out of mind. Valdir had been the first to organize the lowlanders in resistance, to build the Ranger stations which warned of impending raids, and this struck Cyrillon, unreasonably enough, as unfair. It ran clear against the time-honored Darkovan code, that each man shall defend his own belonging. By holding Valdir's son prisoner, he hoped to stalemate this move, and ward off retaliations.

But they did *not* have Valdir's son; and sooner or later, Larry supposed, Cyrillon would find out. He didn't like to think what would happen then.

As the fourth day was darkening into night, he heard sounds in the distance; feet hurrying in the corridors, horses' hooves trampling in the courtyard, men calling to one another in command. He looked up, in frustration, at the high window which prevented him from seeing out; then dragged a heavy bench toward the window and clambered up on it.

He could just see over the broad, high sill, and down into the courtyard below.

Nearly two dozen men were milling around below, leading out and saddling horses, choosing weapons from a great pile in the corner of the bricked-in courtyard. Larry saw Cyrillon's form, tall and lean, striding through the men; here pausing to speak to one, here inspecting a saddle-girth, here lashing out, swift as a striking snake, to knock a man head-over-heels with a swift fist. The great gate was swinging open, the mounted men forming to ride through.

Was the castle empty, then? Unguarded? Larry looked down to the courtyard, in frustration. He was at least thirty feet above the bricks; a thirty-foot fall might kill him if he landed on grass, but on stone. . . ? The castle wall was smooth below him for at least ten feet; with the use of both hands, he might well have managed a foothold on the ledge below. With one hand tied behind his back, he might as well have tried to walk a tightrope to the nearest mountain peak.

He let himself slide down to the floor again. Doubtless they had left someone here . . . possibly only the feeble old man who brought Larry's food.

If he had a weapon . . .

They had left him his pocketknife; but the main blade was broken, and the magnetized blade remaining was less than two inches long. The furniture in the room was all old and too heavy to be broken up for a club of any sort. If he could somehow manage to club the man over the head when next he came in. . . .

There seemed nothing from which he could improvise even a simple weapon. With both hands, he might have thrown his jacket at the old man and managed to smother him with it. They seemed to be guarding against the Comyn telepathic tricks, but they had not tried to guard against ordinary attack . . . and yet there was nothing in the room that could be used as a weapon.

He sat, scowling, considering, for a long time. If he could

have smashed the window, perhaps a long splinter of glass
might serve.

He heard shuffling footsteps down the hall, and a
thought—almost too late!—occurred to him. He dropped to
the floor and, with his one free hand, fumbled to unlace his
boot. It was heavy, a Darkovan riding-boot, and it struck the
man on the back of the head—

But it was slow work with one hand and before he had it
off, a key moved in the lock, the door came open in one
burst, as if the man had stood back and kicked it open without coming inside. Then the man appeared in the door. He
had a tray with food balanced in one hand; the other held a
long, wicked-looking riding whip. He held it poised to
strike, saying in his barbarous dialect, "None of your tricks,
boy!"

Larry jerked off the boot, clumsily with his right hand,
and hurled it at the man's head.

As soon as he had thrown it, he knew that the throw, with
the wrong hand, would go wild: he saw the old man start
slightly, the dishes on the tray clashing together. The whip,
as if with a life of its own, flicked out and wrapped round
Larry's free wrist, with a stinging slap; the man jerked the
whip free, laughing harshly.

"I thought you might have some such little trick," he
jeered, raised the whip again and brought it down, not very
hard, across Larry's shoulders. Tears started to Larry's eyes,
but really it was more of a warning than a blow—for Larry
knew that a blow with such a whip, given seriously, would
cut through his clothes and an inch into the flesh.

"Want some more?" the man asked, with a grin.

Furious with frustration, Larry bent his eyes on the
ground.

The man said good-naturedly, "Eat your dinner, lad. You
don't try any tricks and I won't hurt you—agreed? No reason we can't get along very nicely while the Master is
away—is there?"

When the man had gone, Larry turned dispiritedly to the tray. He didn't feel like eating; yet he had eaten so little in the last four days that he was tormented with hunger. The final ignominy was that he couldn't even get his boot on with one hand. He took the dishes off the tray, listlessly. Then he raised his eyebrows; instead of the usual dried meat strips and coarse bread, there was some sort of grilled fish, smoking hot, and a cup of the same chocolate-like drink he had had in the Trade City.

Awkwardly, with his free hand, but hungrily, he gobbled down the fish, even gnawing on the bones. It was an unfamiliar fish and had a strange tang, but he was too hungry to be particular. He leaned back, sipping the drink slowly. He wondered about the change. Perhaps Cyrillon—who obviously was somewhat afraid of him since the episode with the crystal—considered him valuable as a hostage and, seeing the coarser food left uneaten, had decided he had to feed him better, and keep him in good health and good spirits.

The light from the high window crept across the floor. The shadows were pale purple, the light pink and sparkling. Strange motes danced in the pink beam.

Larry, feeling full and comfortably sleepy, leaned back, watching the motes. He realized suddenly that on each of the motes a tiny man rode, pink and purple and carrying an infinitesimal spear that looked like a fiber of saffron. Fascinated and curious, he watched the tiny men slide down the sunbeam and mass on the floor. They formed into regiments, and still they kept sliding down the beam of pink light, until their small forms covered the floor. Larry blinked and they seemed to merge and melt away.

A huge black insect, almost the width of Larry's hand, stuck his quivering head from a hole in the floor. He waggled huge phosphorescent whiskers at Larry and spoke . . . and to Larry's listless interest, the bug was speaking perfect Terran.

"You're drugged, you know," the bug said in a high,

shaky voice. "It must have been in the food. Of course, that's why it was so much better than usual this time, so you'd be sure to eat it."

The pink and purple men reappeared on the floor and swarmed over the bug, shrilling in incomprehensible voices, nonsense syllables: "*An chrya morgobush! Travertina fo mibbsy!*"

As each little man touched the bug's phosphorescent tendrils, he burst into a puff of green smoke.

The door swung open, invitingly. Someone said in the distance, "No tricks this time, hah?"

The man was standing there, and the twilight in the room darkened, brightened again into dawn. The man with the whip jeered from a corner. The little pink and purple men were crawling all over him and Larry laughed aloud to see his jailer covered with the swarming creatures; one of them disappeared into his pocket, another did a hornpipe on the man's bald head. Dimly he felt someone bend over him, shove up his closed eyelid. How could he see with closed eyes? He laughed at the absurdity of it.

"No tricks," said the jailer again; and all the little pink and purple men shouted in chorus, " 'No tricks,' he said!"

Behind the man the door opened and Kennard Alton, in dark-green cloak and a drawn dagger in his hand, stood there. The little pink and purple men swarmed up his legs and nearly blotted out his figure. He raised the dagger and it turned into a bunch of pink tulips as he brought it down toward the old bandit's back. Larry heard himself laugh, but the laugh came out like a trumpetblast as the pink tulips plunged into the man's back and a great flight of blackbirds gushed out, screaming wildly. Kennard kicked the fallen man, who disappeared into a swarming regiment of little pink and purple men laughing in isolated notes like small bells. Then Kennard strode across the room. The purple men swarmed up him, sat astride his nose, soared down the sunbeams, as Kennard stood over Larry.

"Come on! Every minute we're here, there's danger! Somebody might come. I'm not sure that old fellow's the only guard in the castle!"

Larry looked up at him and laughed idly. The little pink and purple mannikin on Kennard's nose was climbing up, digging footholds in Kennard's chin with a tiny ax of green light. Larry laughed again.

"Brush the gremlins off your chin first."

"Zandru!" Kennard bent over, pink tulips cascading from the front of his shirt. His hands clasped on Larry's shoulders like nutcrackers. "I want some nuts," Larry said, and giggled.

"Damn you, get up and come with me."

Larry blinked. He said clearly, in Terran, "You're not really here, you know. Any more than the little pink and purple gremlins are here. You're a figment of my imagination. Go away, figment. A figment with purple pigment."

The figment bent over Larry. In his hands there seemed to be a bowl of chili with beans. He began throwing it at Larry, handful by handful. It was unpleasant; Larry's head hurt and the beans, dripping off his chin, hurt like hard slaps. He yelled in Darkovan, "Save the beans! They're too hard! We might better eat them!"

The vision-Kennard straightened as if he had been knifed. He muttered, "*Shallavan*! But why did they give it to Larry? *He's* no telepath! Did they believe—"

Larry protested as Kennard turned into a steamshovel and lifted him sidewise. The next thing he knew, water was streaming down his face and Kennard Alton, white as a sheet, was standing and staring at him.

It was Kennard. He was real.

Larry said shakily "I—I thought you were—a steamshovel. Is it—"

He looked down at the floor of the room. The old man lay there, blood caked on his leather jacket, and Larry hastily turned away. "Is he dead?"

"I don't know and I don't care," Kennard said grimly, "but we'll *both* be dead unless we get out of here before the bandits get back. Where's your other boot?"

"I threw it at him." Larry's head was splitting. "I missed."

"Oh, well—" Kennard said, deprecatingly, "you aren't used to this sort of thing. Get it on again—" he broke off. "What in the devil—" He surveyed the leather harness, anger in his eyes. "Zandru's hells, what a filthy contrivance!" He drew his dagger and cut through the leather. Larry's hand, numb and cramped, fell lifeless to his side. He could not move the fingers, and Kennard, swearing under his breath, knelt to help him with the boot.

Larry realized that he had no idea how long he had been drugged. He had a vague sort of memory of his jailer having come in once or twice before, but was not sure. He was still too dazed to do more than stand, swaying and weak, before Kennard.

"How did you come to be here? How did you find me?"

"You were taken for me," Kennard said briefly. "Could I leave you to face the fate they meant for me? It was my responsibility to find you."

"But how? And why did you come alone?"

"We were in rapport through the crystal," Kennard said, "so I could trail you. I came alone, because we knew that with any assault in strength, they'd probably kill you at once. That can wait till later! Right now, we still have to get out of this place before Cyrillon and his devils come back!"

"I saw them ride away," Larry said slowly. "I think they're all gone except that one old man."

"No wonder they doped you, then," Kennard said. "They'd be afraid you'd play some telepathic trick. Most people are afraid of the Altons, though they wouldn't know if you were old enough to have the *laran*—the power. I don't have much of it myself. But let's get out of here!"

Carefully he went to the door and opened it a fraction.

"The way he yelled, if there was anyone within shouting distance, they'd be all over us," Kennard said. "I think maybe you're right. They all must have gone."

Carefully, they came out into the corridor; walking on tiptoe, stole down the long stairs. Once Kennard muttered, "I hope we don't meet anyone! If I don't go out the way I came in, it would be damned easy to get lost in this place!"

Larry had not realized how immense this bandit stronghold was. He came out of the prison room wavering, unsteady on his feet so that Kennard had to take hold of his arm and brace him until he could stand without shaking. Still groggy from the drug, it seemed that they hurried through miles of corridors, starting at every distant sound, flattening themselves against the walls when once something like a step echoed at the bottom of a flight of stairs. But it had died in the distance and the old castle was silent again, brooding.

A great gate loomed before them and Kennard, shoving Larry back against the wall, peered out, sniffing the wind like a hunter. He said, tersely, "Seems quiet enough. We'll chance it. I don't know where the other gates are. I saw them ride away and took the chance.

The fresh air, bitterly cold, seemed to bite at Larry's bones, but it cleared the last traces of the drug from his head, and he stood staring around. Behind them, a high steep mountain face towered, rocky, speckled faintly with a scruff of underbrush and trees. Before them the narrow trail led away downward, through the valleys and hills, through the mountains where they had come.

Kennard said, swiftly, "Come on—we'll make a dash for it. If anyone's watching from those windows—" He made an edgy gesture upward toward the bleak castle face behind them. "If that old fellow *isn't* dead, and there *are* other guards, we've got maybe an hour before they start beating the woods for us."

He poised, said briefly, "Now—run," and raced across

the yard toward the gates, Larry following. His arm ached fiercely where it had been strapped, and he was shaky on his feet, but even so, he reached the edge of the forest only a few seconds after Kennard, and the Darkovan boy looked at him a little less impatiently. They stood there, breathing hard, looking at each other in wordless question. What next?

"There's only one road through these mountains," Kennard said, "and that's the one the bandits used. We could follow it—keeping in sight of it, and hiding if we heard anyone. There's an awful lot of forest between here and home—they couldn't search it all. But"—he gestured—"I think they have watch-towers too, all through this country along the road. We ought to stay under cover of the trees, night and day, if we take that route. This whole stretch of country—" he stopped, thinking hard, and Larry saw vividly, in his mind's eye, the terrible journey over chasms and crags which had brought him here. Kennard nodded.

"That's why they don't guard their stronghold, of course; they think themselves guarded well enough by the mountain trail. You need good, mountain-bred, trail-broken horses to make it at all. I left my own horse on the other side of the mountain ridge. Somebody's probably picked her up by now, I'd hoped—"

The deep throat of an alarm bell suddenly clanged, raising echoes in the forest; a bird cried out noisily and flew away, and Kennard started, swearing under his breath.

"They've roused the whole castle—there must have been some of them left there!" he said, tensely, gripping Larry's arm. "In ten minutes this whole part of the woods will be alive with them! Come on!"

He ran—feeling twigs catch and hold at his clothing, stumbling into burrows and ridges, his breath coming short in the bitter cold. Before him Kennard dodged and twisted, half doubling back once and again, plunging through the trackless trees, and Larry, stumbling and racing in desperate haste to keep up, his head pounding, fled after him.

It seemed hours before Kennard dropped into a little hollow made by the fallen branches of a tree. Larry dropped at his side, his head falling forward against the icy-wet grass. For a few moments all that he could do was to breathe. Slowly the pounding of his heart calmed to something like normal and the darkness cleared from before his eyes. He raised himself half on his elbow, but Kennard jerked him down again.

"Lie flat!"

Larry was only too glad to obey. The world was still spinning; after a moment it spun completely away.

When he came up to consciousness again, Kennard was kneeling at his side, head raised, his ear cocked for the wind.

"They may have trackers on our trail," he said, tersely. "I thought I heard—Listen!"

At first Larry's ears, not trained to woodcraft, heard nothing. Then, very far away, lifting and rising in a long eerie wail, a shrill banshee scream that grew in intensity until his ears vibrated with the sound and he clasped his hands to his head to shut out the sheer torture of the noise. It faded away; rose again in another siren wail. He looked at Kennard; the older boy was stark white.

"What is it?" Larry whispered.

"Banshees," Kennard said, and his voice was a gasp. "They can track anything that lives—and they'll scent our body warmth. If they get wind of us we're done for!" He swore, gasping, his voice dying away in a half-sob. "Damn Cyrillon—damn him and his whole evil crew—Zandru whip them with scorpions in his seventh hell—Naotalba twist their feet on their ankles—" His voice rose to a half-scream of hysteria. He looked white with exhaustion. Larry gripped his shoulders and shook him, hard.

"That won't help! What will?"

Kennard gasped and was silent. Slowly the color came

back into his face and he listened, motionless, to the siren wail that rose and fell.

"About a mile off," he said tersely, "but they run like the wind. If we could change our smell—"

"They're probably tracking by my clothing-smell," Larry said. "They took away my cloak. If I—"

Kennard had risen; he darted forward, suddenly, and fell into a bank of grayish shrubs. For a moment Larry, watching him roll and writhe in the leaves, thought that the hardships of the mountain journey had driven the Darkovan boy out of his wits. But when Kennard sat up his face, though ashen, was calm.

"Come here and roll in this," he ordered, "smear it all over your boots especially—"

Suddenly getting the idea, Larry grabbed handfuls of the leaves. They stung his hands with their furry needles, but he followed the older boy's example, daubing the leaves on face and hands, crushing their juice into clothing and boots. The leaves had a pungent, acrid smell that brought tears to his eyes like raw onions; but he crushed handfuls of the leaves over his boots and legs.

"This might or might not work," Kennard said, "but it gives us a bare chance—unless the smell of this stuff is like catnip to a kitten for those devilish things. If I knew more about them—"

"What are they?"

"Birds. Huge things—taller than a tall man, with long trailing thin wings—they can't fly. Their claws could rip your guts out at a stroke. They're blind, and normally they live in the mountain snows, and can scent anything warm that moves. And they scream like—well, like banshees."

All the time he spoke, he and Larry were crushing the leaves, rubbing them into their skin and hair, soaking their clothing with the juice. The odor was sickening, and Larry thought secretly that anything with any sense of smell at all could trace them for miles, but perhaps the banshees were like Terran bloodhounds, set on by a particular smell and trained not to follow any other.

"Zandru alone knows how Cyrillon and his hordes managed to train those devilish things," Kennard muttered. "Listen—they're coming nearer. Come on. We'll have to run for it again, but try to move quietly."

They moved off through the brushwood again, working their way slowly up the hill, Larry trying to move softly; but he heard dead twigs snap beneath his feet, dry leaves crackle, the creak of branches as he moved against them. In contrast, Kennard moved as lightly as a leaf. And ever behind them the shrill banshee howl rose, swelled, died away and rose again, throbbing until it seemed to fill all space, till Larry felt he must scream with the noise that vibrated his eardrums and went rolling around in his skull until there was no room for anything but pulsing agony.

The path they were following began to rise, steeply now, and he had to catch at twigs and brushwood, and brace his feet against rocks, to force his way up the rising slope. His clothes were tattered, his face torn, and the stink of the gray leaves was all around them. The slope was in deep shadow; it was growing bitterly cold, and above them the thick evening fog was deepening, till Larry could hardly see Kennard's back, a few feet before him. They struggled up the slope and plunged down into a little valley, where Kennard's pace slackened somewhat and he waited for Larry to catch up with him. Larry breathed hard, pressing his hands to his aching skull to shut out the banshee noise.

It lessened for a moment, died away in a sort of puzzled silence; began in a series of fresh yelps and wails, then faded out again. It was dimming with distance; Kennard, his face only a blur in the gathering fog, sighed and fell, exhausted, to the ground.

"We can rest a minute, but not too long," he warned.

Larry fell forward, dropping instantly into dead sleep. It seemed only a moment later—but it was black dark and a fine drizzling rain was falling and soaking them—that Kennard shook him awake again. The banshee howls were again filling the air—and *on this side of the slope*!

"They must have found the patch of *eris* leaves and figured out what we'd done," he said, his voice dragging between his teeth, "and, of course, that stuff leaves a scent that a broken-down mule could follow from here to Nevarsin!"

Larry strained his eyes to see through the thin darkness. Far down the slope there seemed a glint, just a pale glimmer in the moonlight. "Is there a stream at the bottom of the valley?"

"There might be. If there is—" Kennard was swaying with weariness. Larry, though aching in every muscle, found that the last traces of the drug were gone from his mind, and the brief sleep had refreshed him. He put his arm around Kennard's shoulders and guided the other boy's stumbling steps. "If we can get into the water—"

"They'll figure that trick out too," Kennard said hopelessly, and Larry felt him shudder, a deep thing that racked his bones. He pointed upward, and Larry followed his gaze. At the top of the slope, outlined against the sky, was a sight to freeze the marrow of his bones.

Bird? Surely no bird ever had that great gaunt outline, those drooping wings like a huge flapping cloak, the skull-like head that dripped a great phosphorescent red-glowing beak. The apparition craned a long dark neck and a dreadful throbbing cry vibrated to air-filling intensity.

Larry felt Kennard go rigid on his arm; the boy was staring upward, fixedly, like a bird hypnotized by a weaving snake.

But to Larry it was just another Darkovan horror; dreadful indeed—but he had seen so many horrors he was numb. He grabbed Kennard, and plunged with him down the slope, toward the distant glimmer. The banshee howl rose and fell, rose and fell on their heels, as they plunged through underbrush, careless now of noise or direction. The gleam of water loomed before them. They plunged in, fell full length with a splash, struggled up and ran, splashing, racing, stumbling on stones. Twice Larry measured his length in the shallow icy stream and his clothing stiffened and froze in the icy air, but he dared not slacken his speed. The banshee howl grew, louder and louder, then slackened again in a puzzled, yelping wail, an almost plaintive series of cheated whimpers. It seemed to run round in circles. It was joined by further howls, yelps and whimpers. They splashed along in the stream for what seemed hours, and Larry's feet were like lumps of ice. Kennard was stumbling; he fell again and again to his knees and the last time he fell with his head on the bank and lay still. None of Larry's urging could make him rise. The Darkovan lad had simply reached the end of his fantastic endurance.

Larry dragged him out, on the far side of the stream, hauled him into the shelter of the forest, and sat there listening to the gradually diminishing wails and yelps of the frustrated banshees. Far away on the slope he saw torches and lights. They were beating the bushes, but with their tracking birds cheated, there was no way to follow their escaped prey. But would they pick up the scent again downstream? Larry, conscious that he was famished, remembered that a day or two ago—before the drugging—he had thrust a piece of the coarse bread into his pocket. He hauled it out and began to gnaw on it; then, remembering, broke it in half and stowed the other half in his other pocket for Kennard. As he did so, his hands touched metal, and he felt the smooth outline of his Terran medical kit. Small as it was, it probably contained nothing for his scratches and bruises, but—

Of course! He pulled urgently at Kennard's hand; when the Darkovan boy stirred and moaned, he put the bread in his hand, then whispered, "Listen. I think we can outwit them even if they pick up our scent downstream. Here. Eat that, and then listen!" He was fumbling in the dark, by touch, in his medical kit. He found the half-empty tube of burn ointment he had used after the fire, unscrewed the cap and smelled the sharp, unfamiliar chemical smell.

"This should puzzle them for a while," he said, smearing a thin layer of the stuff, first on his boots and then on Kennard's. Kennard, munching the bread, nodded in approval. "They might pick up *eris* leaves. Not this stuff."

They rested a little, then began cautiously to crawl up the far slope. There was plenty of cover, though the plants and thorny bushes of the underbrush tore at their faces and hands. Kennard's leather riding-breeches did not suffer so badly as Larry's cloth ones, but their hands and faces were torn and bleeding, and the red sun was beginning to thin away the dawn clouds, before they reached the summit of the slope and lay on the rocks exhausted, too weary to move another step. Behind them, in the valley they had left, there seemed no sign of men or banshees.

"They may have called off the hunt," Kennard muttered, "Banshees are torpid in the sunlight—they're nightbirds. We just might have got clean away."

Huddling his cloak round him, he knelt and looked down into the far valley. It was a huge bowl of land, filled to the brim with layered forest. Near the top, where they were, there was underbrush and low scrubby conifers, and snow lay in thin patches in hollows of the ground where the sun had not warmed. Lower down were tall trees and thick brushwood, while the valley was thick with uncleared forest. Not a house, nor a farm, not a cleared space of land, not even a moving figure. Only the wheeling of a hawk above them, and the silent trees below them, moved in response to their dragging steps. They had escaped Cyrillon's castle. But in the growing red light, their eyes met, and the same thought was in them both.

They had escaped bandits and banshees. But they were hundreds of miles from safe, known country—alone, on foot, almost weaponless, in the great trackless unexplored forests of the wildest part of Darkover.

They were alive.

And that was just about all that they could say.

CHAPTER NINE

The sun climbed higher and higher. In the high hollow where they lay, a little cold sun penetrated their retreat, and finally Kennard stirred. He took off his cloak and spread it in the sun to dry, then stripped to the skin and gestured to Larry to do likewise. When Larry, shivering, hesitated, Kennard said harshly, "Wet clothes will freeze you faster than cold skin. And take off your boots and dry your stockings."

Larry obeyed, shivering, crouching in the lee of a sun-warmed rock. While their clothes dried in the bitter wind of the heights, they took stock.

In addition to his medical kit—which contained only a few of the most ordinary remedies, and measured only four or five inches square—Larry had his knife with the broken blade, corkscrew, and tiny magnetized blade. Kennard looked at it with raised eyebrows and a rueful grin, and shrugged. He also had another piece of the coarse bread, a notebook, handkerchief and a coin or two.

Kennard, who had come provided for a long journey, was better armed with his razor-sharp dagger, a tinderbox and flints, and in the leather pouch at his waist he had some bread and dried meat. "Not much," he said. "I had more cached near where I left my horse; I'd hoped we could dare take that road. And there is food in the forests, though I'm not so sure here as I am in the woodlands nearer home. No, we won't starve, but there's worse than that."

At Larry's questioning look, he said reluctantly, "We're lost, Larry. I lost my bearings when we were getting away from the banshees last night. All I know is that we're west of Cyrillon's hold—and no lowlander or Comyn has ever come so far into these mountains. Never. At least, if they have, they haven't lived to tell about it. We can't go back eastward toward home—we'd have to cross Cyrillon's country—or make a wide circle northward and get into the Dry Towns." His face, though he tried to keep it impassive, trembled. "That's all desert land—sand, no water, no food, and we might as well go back and ask Cyrillon for a night's lodging. Southward there's the range of the Hellers—and not even professional guides or mountaineers will go into them without climbing equipment, and mountain gear. I've done a little rockclimbing, but I'm about as fit to climb through the Hellers as you are to navigate a Terran space-ship."

That left only one possibility. "Westward?"

"Unless we want to try to get through Cyrillon's country again, banshees and all. As far as I know, it's simply forest. It's unexplored, but if we follow the setting sun, we should come out somewhere near to the lands where Lorill Hastur has his holdings. We'll be passing north of the Hellers—" He drew a crude sketch-map on the ground. "We're here. And we want to get to here. But the gods alone know what's in between, or how long it will take us." He looked at Larry, steadily. "I wouldn't enjoy a trip like that, even with my father and a dozen of his huskiest soldiers. But, *bredu*, if you'll back me up, we'll try it."

He met Larry's eyes, and for an instant Larry was reminded of that moment of deep rapport between them, across the blue crystal of psychic power. The word, *bredu*, had startled him. It meant, literally, *friend*—but the ordinary word for friend was simple *com'ii*. *Bredu* could mean one close, as in a family relationship—cousin, or brother—or it could mean *beloved brother*. It was a word which showed him the trust that this Darkovan boy, who had saved his life, placed in him. Kennard had undertaken, alone, a desperate journey on his behalf—and was about to undertake another, with Larry's help.

It was the most solemn moment of Larry's life. He was almost paralyzed with his fear, and he could feel Kennard's fear as if it were his own; deeper, because Kennard knew more of the dangers. And yet—

Larry said quietly, "I'm ready to try it if you are—*bredu*."

And in that moment he knew that he would, if necessary, give his life for Kennard—as Kennard had risked his for him.

The moment lasted only a fraction of a second. Then Kennard broke the remaining piece of Cyrillon's bread, and said, "Let's finish this. We need the strength. Then I have this—" Briefly, from his pocket, he showed the silk-wrapped thing that held the blue crystal. "It helped me find you, because when you looked into it, your mind was keyed to it. So that when I was lost, all I had to do was to look in it and think of you—and it showed me the right direction."

Larry averted his eyes from the stone. It made him think of that moment in Cyrillon's power. "Cyrillon made me look into one of these things."

The result on Kennard was electrifying. His whole face changed and turned white. "Cyrillon—has one of *these*?"

Briefly, Larry told him about it, and Kennard wet dry lips with his tongue. "Avarra guard and guide us! He may not know how to use it, but if he should ever learn, or if he should whelp a telepath by one of his women, the Gods themselves couldn't save Darkover from their evil powers! Not to mention," he added grimly, "that he might track us with it—as I tracked you."

"He's afraid of it," Larry said, and told Kennard how he knew, but Kennard shook his head. "He might still risk it;

he'd evidently risk a lot to have you. Oh, Zandru, what shall I do, what shall I do! He covered his face with his hands and sat motionless, the blue stone clutched in his hand. Finally he looked up and his face was gray and drawn with terror.

"We—must destroy Cyrillon's stone," he said at last. "I know what I must do, but I'm afraid, Larry, I'm afraid!" It was a cry of terror. "But I must!"

"Why?"

Kennard looked grim. He rolled back his sleeve and showed Larry a curious mark, like a tattoo. "Because I am sworn," he said, grimly, "that I will die rather than let any of our Comyn weapons fall into the hands of such people."

Larry felt a cold wrench of terror twisting his insides. To go back, deliberately, into Cyrillon's power and destroy the stone . . .

"What do we do?" he asked, deliberately light and sarcastic, "walk up to his front door and ask him politely to let us have it?"

Kennard shook his head. "Worse than that," he said his voice barely audible, "and I can't do it alone. I'll have to have your help. Aldones guard us! If I could only reach father with this—but I can't—"

"What is it? What do you have to do?"

"You wouldn't understand—" Kennard began hotly; then with an effort, said, "Sorry. You're in this, too, and you'll have to help me. I have to take *this*"—he motioned toward the blue crystal in his hand—"and destroy Cyrillon's—with it. And we have to do it *now*."

"But how can I?" Larry was frightened and bewildered. "I am not a telepath."

"You must be," said Kennard urgently. "You fought Cyrillon to a standstill with the thing! I don't understand either. I never heard of a Terran telepath. But evidently you and I are in rapport. Maybe you got it from me, I'm not sure. But we'll try."

He unwrapped the crystal and Larry averted his eyes. The

thought of looking into the thing again made him literally sick to his stomach. The memory of Cyrillon's forcing made his abused shoulder ache in sympathy.

But Kennard had to do it—Kennard, who had risked death to save him. Larry said steadily, "What do I have to do?"

Kennard sat cross-legged, gazing into the stone, and Larry was inescapably reminded of the three Adepts who had brought the rain to the forest fire. Uncommanded, he took his place across from Kennard. Kennard said, silently, "Just go into link with me—and hold hard. Don't let go, whatever happens."

The twisting blueness of the crystal engulfed all space. Larry felt Kennard like a spot of fire and tensed, throwing all his energies, all his will toward supporting him—

He felt a blue blaze, slumbering, blaze up and waken. It flared out, flaming electric blue, and Larry felt himself struggling, drowning. His body ached, his whole head tingled, earth spun away, he reeled alone in blue space as blue flame met blue flame and he felt Kennard tremble, spin out and vanish in unfathomable distance. The fire was drowning him. . . .

Then from somewhere a huge surge of strength seemed to roar through him, the same strength that had flung Cyrillon howling across the room. He poured it against the alien blue. The flames met, merged, sank—

The forest was green and bright around them and Larry gulped in air like a drowning man. Kennard lay white and drained on the leaves, his hand limply clutching the crystal. But there was no blue fire in its heart now. It was colorless stone, which as Larry looked glimmered once or twice and evaporated in a tiny puff of blue vapor. Kennard's hand was empty.

Kennard sat up, his chest heaving. He said, "It's gone. I destroyed it—even though I had to destroy this one too. And it might have guided us to Lorill Hastur's lands." His frown was bitter. "But better than having a starstone in Cyrillon's possession. Now all we have to face are ordinary dangers. Well—" He shrugged, and struggled to his feet. "We've got a lot of country to cover, and all we have to do is to follow the sun's path westward. Let's get started."

Forcing back his multitude of question and curiosity, Larry reached out for his now-drying clothes and began to draw them on. He knew Kennard well enough, by now, to know that he had had all the explanation the other lad would ever give him. Silently, he pocketed his little knife, his medical kit, thrust his feet into his boots. Still silently, he followed Kennard as the Darkovan started down the western slope of the mountain, down into the trackless wasteland that lay between Cyrillon's castle and the lands of Lorill Hastur.

All that day and all the next they spent forcing their way down through the pathless underbrush, following the westward sun-route, sleeping at night in hollows of dead leaves, eating sparingly of the bread and meat remaining of Kennard's provisions. On the night of the second day it came to an end, and they went supperless to bed, munching a few dried berries like rose-hips, which were sour and flavorless, but which eased hunger a little.

The next day was dreadful, forcing their way through the thinning underbrush, but they halted early, and Kennard, turning to Larry, said, "Give me your handkerchief."

Obediently, Larry handed it over. It was crumpled and filthy, and he couldn't imagine what Kennard wanted it for, but he sat and watched Kennard rip it into tiny strips and knot them until he had a fairly long strip of twisted cloth. He searched, on silent feet, till he found a hole in the ground; then, bending a branch low, rigged a noose and snare. He motioned to Larry to lie flat and still, following suit himself. It seemed hours that they lay there silent, Larry's body growing cramped and stiff, and Kennard turning angry eyes on him when he ventured to ease a sore muscle by moving it ever so slightly.

A long time later, some small animal poked an inquisitive snout from the hole; instantly, Kennard jerked the noose tight and the small creature kicked, writhing, in the air.

Larry winced, then reflected that, after all, he had been eating meat all his life and this was no time to get squeamish. He watched, feeling vaguely useless and superfluous, as Kennard wrung the creature's neck, skinned and gutted it, and gathered dead twigs for a fire.

"It would be safer not to," he said, with a wry smile, "but I haven't any taste for raw meat—and if they're still on our trail after this long, we're out of luck anyhow."

The small furred thing was not much bigger than a rabbit; they finished every scrap of the meat and gnawed the bones. Kennard insisted on himself covering the fire and scraping leaves over the place where it had been, so that no sign of their camp remained.

When they slept that night, Larry lay long awake, feeling somehow ill at ease; half envying Kennard's woodcraft—he was lost and helpless in these woods without the other boy's knowledge—yet possessed by a nagging disquiet that had nothing to do with that. The woods were filled with strange noises, the far-away cries of night birds and the padding of strange beasts, and Larry tried to tell himself that he was simply uneasy about the strangeness of it all. The next morning when they prepared to go on, he kept glancing around until Kennard noticed and asked him, rather irritably, what was the matter.

"I keep hearing—and not quite seeing—things," Larry said reluctantly.

"Imagination," Kennard said, shrugging it off, but Larry's disquiet persisted.

That day was much like the former. They struggled down exhausting slopes, forcing their way through brushwood;

they scrambled through country that looked like smooth forest but was matted with dead trees and deep ravines.

At night Kennard snared a bird and was about to light a fire to cook it when he noticed Larry's disquiet.

"Whatever is the matter with you?"

Larry could only shake his head, silently. He knew—without knowing *how* he knew—that Kennard *must not* light that fire, and it seemed so senseless that he was ready to cry with the tension of it. Kennard regarded him with a look halfway between impatience and pity.

"You're worn out, that's what's the matter," he said, "and for all I know you're still half-poisoned by the drug they gave you. Why don't you lie down and have a sleep? Rest and food will help you more than anything else." He took out his tinderbox and began to strike the fire—

Larry cried out, an inarticulate sound, and leaped to grab his wrist, spilling tinder. Kennard, in a rage, dropped the box and struck Larry, hard, across the face.

"Damn you, look what you've made me do.

"I—" Larry's voice failed. He could not even resent the blow. "I don't know why I did that."

Kennard stood over him, fury slowly giving way to puzzlement and pity. "You're out of your head. Pick up that tinder—" When Larry had obeyed he stood back, warily. "Am I going to have trouble with you, damn it, or do we have to eat raw meat?"

Larry dropped to the ground and buried his face in his hands. The reluctant spark caught the tinder; Kennard knelt, coaxing the tiny spark into flame, feeding it with twigs. Larry sat motionless, even the smell of the roasting meat unable to penetrate through the thick, growing fog of distress. He did not see Kennard looking at him with a frown of growing dismay. When Kennard took the roasted bird from the fire and broke it in half, Larry only shook his head. He was famished, the smell of the meat made his mouth water and his eyes sting, but the fear, like a thick miasma around him, fogged away everything else. He hardly heard Kennard speak. He took the meat the Darkovan boy put into his hands, and put it into his mouth, but he could neither chew now swallow. At last he heard Kennard say, gently, "All right. Later, maybe, you'll want it." But the words sounded very far away through the thing that was thickening, growing in him. He could feel Kennard's thoughts, like seeing the glow of sparks through half-dead ash; Kennard thought that he, Larry, was losing his grip on reality. Larry didn't blame him. He thought so too. But the knowledge could not break through the numbing fear that grew and grew—

It broke, suddenly, a great cresting wave. He heard himself cry out, in alarm, and spring upright, but it was too late.

Suddenly the clearing was alive with darkly clustering swarms of crouching figures; Kennard yelled and leaped to his feet, but they were already struggling in the meshes of a great net of twisted vines that had jerked them closely together.

The fogged thickness of apprehension was gone, and Larry was clear headed, alert, aware of this new captivity. The net had drawn them close, but not off their feet; they could see the forms around them clearly in the firelight and the color of phosphorescent torches of some sort. And the new attackers were not human.

They were formed like men, though smaller; furred, naked save for bands of leaves or some woven matting around their waists; with great pinkish eyes and long prehensile fingers and toes. They clustered around the net, twittering in high, birdlike speech. Larry glanced curiously at Kennard, and the other lad said tersely. "Trailmen. Nonhumans. They live in the trees. I didn't know they'd ever come this far to the south. The fire probably drew them. If I'd known—" He glanced ruefully at their dying fire. The trailmen were circling round it, shrilling, poking at it gingerly with long sticks, throwing dirt at it, and finally they managed to cover it entirely. Then they stamped on it with what looked like glee, dancing a sort of victory dance, and finally one of the creatures came to the net and delivered a long speech in their shrill language; neither of the boys, of course, could understand a word, but it sounded enraged and triumphant.

Kennard said, "They're terrified of fire, and they hate humans because we use it. They're afraid of forest fire, of course. To them, fire means death."

"What are they going to do to us?"

"I don't know." Kennard looked at Larry curiously, but all he said, at last, was, "Next time I'll trust your hunches. Evidently you have some precognition too, as well as telepathy."

To Larry, the trailmen looked like big monkeys—or like the *kyrri*, only smaller and without the immense dignity of those other creatures. He hoped they did not also have the *kyrri* trick of giving off electric sparks!

Evidently they did not. They drew the net tight around the boys' feet, forcing them to walk by tugging at the vine ropes, but offered no further violence. A few hundred feet of this, and they came upon a widened path; Kennard whistled, softly, at sight of it.

"We've been in trailmen country, evidently, most of the day. Probably they've been watching us all day, but they might not have bothered us if I hadn't lit that fire. I ought to have known."

It was easier to walk on the cleared path. Larry had lost track of time, but was stumbling with weariness when, much later, they came to a broad clearing, lighted by phosphorescence which, he now saw, came from fungus growing on broad trees. After a discussion in their twittering speech, the trailmen looped the net-ropes around the nearest tree and began to swarm up the trunk of the next.

"I wonder if they're just going to leave us here?" Kennard muttered.

A hard jerk on the rope disabused them. Slowly, the net

began to rise, jerking them off their feet, so that they hung up, swaying, in the great bag. Kennard shouted in protest, and Larry yelled, but evidently the trailmen were taking no chances. Once the slow motion rise stopped, and Larry wondered if they were going to be hung up here in a sack like a pair of big sausages; but after a heart-stopping interval, they began to rise again.

Kennard swore, in a smothered voice. "I should have cut our way out, the minute they left us!" He drew his dagger and began feverishly to saw at one of the great vines enclosing them. Larry caught his arm.

"No, Kennard. We'd only fall." He pointed downward into the dizzying distance. "And if they see that, they'll only take the knife from you. Hide it! Hide it!"

Kennard, realizing the truth of what Larry said, thrust the knife into his shirt. The lads clung together as the great vine net ascended higher and higher toward the treetops; far from wishing, now, to cut their way out, they feared it would break. The light brightened as they neared the lower branches of the immense trees, and at last, with a bump that flung them against one another, the net was hauled up over a branch and on to the floor of the trailmen's encampment in the trees.

Larry said urgently, "One of us should be a match for any two of those little creatures! Perhaps we can fight our way free."

But the swarms of trailmen surrounding them put a stop to Larry's optimism. There must have been forty or fifty, men, women and a few small pale-fuzzed babies. At least a dozen of the men rushed at the net, bearing Larry and Kennard along with them. When, however, they ceased struggling and made signs that they would walk peacefully, one of the trailmen—he had a lean, furred monkeyface and green, intelligent eyes—came forward and began to unfasten the complicated knots of the snare with his prehensile competent fingers. The trailmen, however, were taking no chances on a sudden rush; they surrounded the two boys closely, ringing them round and giving them no chance to escape. Seeing for the moment that escape was impossible, Larry looked round, studying the strange world of the trail-city around him.

Between the tops of a circle of great trees, a floor had been constructed of huge hewn logs, covered over with what looked like woven rush-matting. It swayed, slightly and disconcertingly, with every movement and step; but Larry, seeing that it supported this huge shifting crowd of trailmen, realized that it must have been constructed in such a way as to support immense weights. How could so simple a people have figured out such a feat of engineering? Well, he supposed that if beavers could make dams that challenged the ingenuity of human engineers, these nonhumans could do just about the equivalent in the treetops.

A pale greenish light filtered in from the leaves overhead; by this dim light he saw a circle of huts constructed at the edges of the flooring. A thatch of green growing leaves had been trained over their roofs, and vines covered their edges, hung with clusters of grapes so succulent and delicious that Larry realized that he was parched.

They were thrust into one of the huts; a tough grating slammed down behind them, and they were prisoners.

Prisoners of the trailmen!

Larry slumped on the floor, wearily. "Out of the frying pan into the fire," he remarked, and at Kennard's puzzled look repeated the remark in rough-hewn Darkovan. Kennard smiled wryly. "We have a similar saying: 'The game that walks from the trap to the cookpot.'"

Kennard hauled out his knife and began tentatively to saw at the material of the vines comprising their prison. No use—the vines were green and tough, thickly knotted and twined, and resisted the knife as if they had been iron bars. After a long grimace, he put the knife away and sat staring gloomily at the moss-implanted floor of the hut.

Hours dragged by. They heard the distant shrill and twittering voices of the trailmen, birdsongs in the treetops, the strident sound of cricketlike insects. In the moss that grew on the hut floor there were numerous small insects that chirped and thrust inquisitive heads up, without fear, like house pets, at the two boys.

Gradually the green-filtered light dimmed; it grew colder and darker, and finally wholly dark; the noises quieted, and around them the trail-city slept. They sat in darkness, Larry thinking with an almost anguished nostalgia of the clean quiet world of the Terran Trade City. Why had he ever wanted to leave it?

There, there would be lights and sounds, food and company, people speaking his own tongue . . .

In the darkness Kennard stirred, mumbled something unintelligible and slept again, exhausted. Larry felt suddenly ashamed of his thoughts. His quest for adventure had led him here, against all warnings—and Kennard seemed likely to share whatever obscure fate was in store for them at the hands of the trailmen. By Darkovan standards he, Larry, was a man. He could at least behave like one. He found the warmest corner of the hut, hauled off his boots and his jacket, and, on an impulse, spread his jacket over the sleeping Kennard; then he curled himself up on the moss and slept.

He slept heavily and long; when he woke, Kennard was tugging at his sleeve and the wicker-woven door was opening. It opened, however, only a little way; a wooden tray was shoved inside and the door closed again quickly. From outside they heard the bar drop into place.

It was light, and warmer. With one impulse, the two boys fell on the tray. It was piled high with food; the luscious grapes they had seen growing, nuts with soft shells which Larry managed to open with the broken blade of his small knife, some soft, spongy, earthy things which smelled like excellent honey. They made a substantial meal, then put the tray down and looked at one another, neither wanting to be the first to speak of the apparent hopelessness of their position.

Larry spoke first, examining the intricate carving of the tray: "They have tools?"

"Oh, yes, Very fine flint knives—I've seen them in a museum of non-human artifacts in Arilinn," Kennard returned, "and some of the mountain people trade with them—give them knives and tools in return for certain things they grow: dye-stuffs, mostly, certain herbs for medicines. Nuts and fruits. That sort of thing."

"They seem to have a fairly complex culture of their own, then."

"They do. But they fear and hate men, probably because we use fire."

Larry, thinking of the forest fire—only a few days ago—could not really blame the trailmen for their fears. He examined the cup which had contained the honey. It was made of unfired clay, sun-baked and rough. What else could a culture do without fire?

There were still some fruits and nuts remaining on the tray, so abundant had been the meal. He said, "I hope they're not fattening us up for their Sunday dinner."

Kennard laughed faintly. "No. They don't even eat animals. They're completely vegetarian as far as I ever heard."

Larry exploded, "Then what the mischief do they want with us?"

Kennard shrugged. "I don't know—and I'm damned if I know how to ask them!"

Larry was silent, thinking that over. Then: "Aren't you a telepath?"

"Not a good one. Anyway, telepathy transmits worded thoughts, as a rule—and emotions. Two telepaths who don't speak the same language have such different concepts that it's almost impossible to read one another's minds. And trying to read the mind of a non-human—well, a highly skilled

Hasturlord, or a *leronis* (a sorceress like the one you saw at the fire) might be able to manage it. I couldn't even try it."

So that, it seemed, was that.

The day dragged by. No one came near them. At evening, another tray piled high with fruit, nuts and mushrooms was slid into their prison, and the old one deftly extracted. Still a third day came and went, with neither of the boys able to imagine a way to get out of their predicament. Their jailer entered their hut, now to give them food and take away their empty dishes. He was a large and powerful creature—for a trailman—but walked with a limp. He seemed friendly but wary. Kennard and Larry discussed the possibility of over-powering the creature and making their escape, but that would only land them in the trailmen's city—with, perhaps, hundreds of miles of trailmen's forest country to be tra-versed. So they contented themselves with discussing plan after futile plan. None of them seemed even remotely feasi-ble.

It seemed, by the growing light, to be noon of the fourth day when the door of their prison opened and three trailmen entered, escorting a fourth who seemed, from their air of deference, to be a person of some importance among them. Like the others, he was naked save for the belt of leaves about his waist, but he wore a string of clay beads mingled with crimson berries, and had an air of indefinable dignity which made Larry, for some reason, think of Lorill Hastur.

He bowed slightly and remarked in perfectly understand-able, though somewhat shrill Darkovan dialect: "Good morning. I trust you are comfortable and that you have not been harmed?"

Both boys leaped to their feet as if electrified. He spoke an understandable tongue! The guards surrounding the trail-man personage put their hands to their flint knives, but see-ing that neither boy made a move toward the man, stood back.

Kennard shouted, "Comfortable be damned! What the mischief do you mean by keeping us here anyhow!"

The trailmen murmured, twittering, in shock and dismay, and the Personage spun on his heel in obvious offense: Kennard instantly changed his tactics. He bowed deeply.

"Forgive me. I"—he looked wildly at Larry—"I spoke in haste. We—"

Larry said, speaking the same dialect, "We have been well fed and kept out of the rain, if that is what you mean, sir." The word he used would also have been translated "Your honor." "But would your very high honor condescend to explain to us why we are being taken from our road and put in this exceptionally damp and confining place at all?"

The trailman's face was stern. He said, "Your people burn down the woods with the red-thing-that-eats-the-woods. Animals die. Trees perish. You were being watched and when you built the red-thing-that-eats-woods, we seized you."

"Then will you let us go again?" Kennard asked.

The trailman slowly made a negative gesture. "We have one protection, and only one, against the red-thing-that-eats-the-woods. Whenever your people come into the country of the People of the Sky, they never leave it again. So that your people will fear coming into our world, and there will be no fear of the red-thing-that-eats-the-woods destroying more of our cities."

Kennard, with a furious gesture, rolled back his sleeves. There were still crimson burn scars on them. "Listen you—" he began; and with an effort, amended, "Hear me, your—your High Muchness. Just a few days ago, I and my family and my friends spend many, many days putting out a fire. It is not *my* kind of people who burn down woods. We are—we are running away from the evil kind of people who set fires to burn down woods."

"Then why were you building a—you call it *fire*?"

"To cook our food."

The trailman's face was severe. "And your kind of—of *man*"—the word was one of inexpressible contempt on his lips—"eats of our brothers-that-have-life!"

"Ways differ and customs differ," said Kennard doggedly, "but we will not burn down your woods. We will even promise not to build a fire while we are in your woods, if you will let us go."

"You are of the fire-making kind. We will not let you go. I have spoken."

He turned on his heel and walked out. Behind him, his guards stalked out, and the bolt fell into place.

"And that," said Kennard, "is very much *that*."

He sat down, chin in hands, and stared grimly into space.

Larry was also feeling despair. Obviously the trailmen would not harm them. Equally obviously, however, they seemed likely to be sitting here in this prison—well fed, well housed, but caged like alien horrid animals—until hell froze over, as far as the Personage was concerned.

He found himself thinking in terms of the trailmen's way of life. If you depend on the woods for very life, fire was your worst fear—and evidently, to them, fire was a wild thing that could never be controlled. He remembered their triumphant dance of joy when they had managed to put out Kennard's little cookfire.

He said thoughtfully, "You still have your flint and tinder, don't you?"

Kennard caught him up instantly. "Right! We can burn our way out with torches, and no one will dare to come near us."

Suddenly his face fell. "No. There is a danger that their city might catch fire. We would be wiping out a whole village of perfectly harmless creatures."

And Larry followed his thought. Better to sit here in prison indefinitely—after all, they were being well fed and kindly treated—than risk exterminating a whole village of these absolutely harmless little people. People who would not even kill a rabbit for food. Sooner or later they would find a way out. Until then, they would not risk harming the trailmen, who had not harmed them.

They were interrupted by the entry of their guard, limping heavily, carrying a tray of their food—the nuts, the honey, and what looked like birds' eggs. Larry made a face—raw eggs? Well, he supposed they were a treat to the trailmen, and they were at least giving their prisoner-guests of their best. But a boiled egg would be a pleasant enough meal.

Kennard was asking the trailman, by signs, how he had hurt his leg. The trailman sprang into a crouch, his head laid into a feral gesture; he actually looked like the great carnivore he was imitating. He made a brutal clawing gesture; he fell to the mossy floor of the hut, doubled, up, imitating great pain; then displayed the cruelly festering wound. Larry turned sick at the sight of it; the thigh was swollen to nearly twice its size, and greenish pus was oozing from the wound. The trailman made a stoical shrug, pointed to his flint knife, gestured, struggled like a man being held down, hopped like a man with one leg, folded his hands, closed his eyes, held his breath like a man dead. He picked up the tray and hobbled out.

Kennard, his face twisting, shook his head. "I suppose you got all that? He means they'll have to cut his leg off soon or he will die."

"And it's so damned unnecessary!" Larry said violently. "All it needs is lancing and antibiotics, and a little sterile care—" Suddenly, he started.

"Kennard! That pot they brought the honey in, do you still have it?"

"Yes."

"I'm no good at making a fire with flint and tinder. But can you make one? A very small one in the pot? Enough, say, to sterilize a knife? To heat water very hot?"

"What do you—"

"I have an idea," Larry said between his teeth, "and it just might work." He pulled his medical kit from his pocket. "I have some antiseptic powder, and antibiotics. Not much. But probably enough, considering that the fellow must have the constitution of—of one of these trees, to live through a clawing like that and still be walking around at all."

"Larry, if we kindle a fire they will probably kill us."

"So we keep it in the pot, covered. The old fellow looks intelligent—the one who spoke Darkovan. If we show him that it can't possibly get out of a clay pot—"

Kennard caught his thought. "Zandru's hells, it just might work, Larry! But, Gods above, are you then apprenticed to be a curer-of-wounds among your people, like my cousin Dyan Ardais?"

"No. This knowledge is as common with the boys of my people as—" he sought wildly for a simile, and Kennard, following his thought as usual, supplied one: "As the knowledge of sword-play among mine?"

Larry nodded. He took over then, giving instructions: "If the chap yells, we'll be swamped, and never have a chance to finish. So you and I will jump him and keep him from getting one squeak out. Then you sit on him while I fix up his leg. We'll get just one chance to keep him from yelling—so don't muff it!"

By evening their preparations were made. The light was poor, and Larry fretted; though the light from the fire-pot helped a little. They waited, breathless. Had their jailer been changed, had he died of his terrible wound? No, after a time they heard his characteristic halting step. The door opened.

He saw the pot and fire. He opened his mouth to scream.

But the scream never got out. Kennard's arm was across his throat, and a crude, improvised gag of a strip torn from Larry's shirt-tail was stuffed into his mouth. Larry felt slightly sick. He knew what must be done, but had never done anything even remotely like it before. He held the knife in the fire until it glowed red-hot, then let it cool somewhat, and, setting his teeth, made a long gash in the swollen, festering leg.

There was an immediate gush of greenish, stinking matter from the wound. Larry sponged it away. It seemed there was no end to the stuff that oozed from the wound, and it was a sickening business, but finally the stuff was tinged with blood and he could see clean flesh below.

He sponged it repeatedly with the hot water heated in the second pot; when it was clean as he could make it, he sprinkled the antibiotic powder into the wound, covered it with the cleanest piece of cloth he had—a fragment of bandage remaining in the medical kit—and took the gag from the man's mouth.

The man had long since ceased to struggle. He lay blinking in stuporous surprise, looking down at his leg, which now had only a clean gash. Suddenly he rose, bowed half a dozen times profoundly to the boys, and backed out of the room.

Larry slumped on the floor, exhausted. He wondered suddenly if what he had done had really endangered their lives. The trailmen's customs were so different from theirs, there was really no way of telling; they might consider this just as evil as killing a rabbit.

After a while, at Kennard's urging, he sat up and ate some supper. He needed it—even if he had the feeling that he might be eating his last meal. They fed the small fire with the fragments of vine from the dead leaves, and toasted their mushrooms over it. For a while they felt almost festive. Much later, they heard steps, and looked at one another, with no need for words.

This is it. Life or death?

Kennard said nothing, but reached silently for Larry's hand; he clasped it and the clasp slid up Larry's elbow until their arms were enlaced as well as their hands. Unfamiliar as the gesture was, Larry knew it was a sign not alone of friendship but of affection and tenderness. He felt faintly

embarrassed, but he said, in a low voice, "If it's bad news—
I'm sorry as hell I got you into this—but it's been damn nice
knowing you."

An instant before the door opened, Larry saw it, a clear
flash of awareness; the sight of the trailman chief, and his
face was grave, but he was alone, and unweaponed. It was
not, at any rate, instant death.

The trailman said, "I have seen what you did for Rhhomi.
I cannot believe that you are evil men. Yet you are of the
kind who make fire." With a sort of grave dignity, he seated
himself. "None is so young he cannot teach, or so old he
cannot learn. Am I to learn from you, strange men?"

Kennard said swiftly, "We have told you already that we
have no will to harm even the least of your people or creatures, Honorable One."

"Yes." But it was at Larry that the trailman chief looked.
He said, irrelevantly, it seemed, "Among my folk, my title is
Old One, and what is age if not wisdom? Have you wisdom
for me, son of a strange land?"

Larry reached behind him for the honey pot, containing
still a few glowing embers of fire. The Old One shrank, but
controlled himself with an effort. Larry tried to speak his
simplest Darkovan; after all, the language was strange to
both himself and this alien creature.

"It is harmless here," he said, searching for words. "See,
the walls of your clay pot keep it harmless so that it cannot
burn. If you feed it with—with dead twigs and little bits of
dead, dry wood, it will serve you and not hurt you."

The Old One reached out, evidently conquering an ingrained shrinking, and touched the pot. He said, "Then it can
be servant and not master?

"And a knife made clean in this fire will heal?"

"Yes," said Larry, bypassing the whole of germ theory,
"or a wound washed with water made very hot, will heal
better than a dirty wound."

The Old One rose, bearing the firepot in his hands. He

said, gravely, "For this gift, then, of healing, my people thank you. And as a sign of this, be under our protection within our woods. Wear this"—and he extended two garlands of yellow flowers—"and none of our people will harm you. But build no red-flames-to-eat-our-woods within the limits of these branches."

Larry, sensing that the Old One spoke to him, said gravely, "You have my pledge."

The Old One threw open the door of the hut.

"Be free to go."

Awkwardly they settled the crowns of yellow flowers over their heads. The trailmen surged backward as the Old One came forth, bearing in his hands the pot of fire. He said ceremoniously, handing it to a woman, "I place this thing in your hands. You and your daughters and the daughters of your daughters are to feed it and bear responsibility that it does not escape."

The scene had a grave solemnity that made Larry, for some reason—perhaps only relief—want to giggle. But he kept his gravity while they were escorted to the edge of the trailmen's village, shown a long ladder down which they could climb, and finally, with infinite relief, set foot again on the green and solid ground.

CHAPTER TEN

All that day they walked, through the trails of the forest. Now and again, from the corner of their eyes, they caught a glimpse of movement, but they saw not a sign of a trailman. They slept that night hearing sounds overhead, but now without fear, knowing that the yellow garlands would protect them in trailman country.

So far neither of them had spoken of their escape. There was no need for words between them now. But when, on the second day—a day clouded and sunless, with a promise of rain—they sat to eat their meal of berries and the odd fungus the trailmen had shown them, which grew plentifully along these paths, Kennard finally spoke.

"You know, of course, that there will be fires. Houses will burn. Maybe even woods will burn. They're not human."

"I'm not so sure," Larry said thoughtfully. "Among the Terrans, they would be called at least humanoid. They have a culture."

"Yet was it safe to give them fire? I would never have dared," Kennard said, "not if we died there. For more centuries than I can count, man and nonhuman have lived together on Darkover in a certain balance. And now, with the trailmen using fire—" He shrugged, helplessly, and Larry suddenly began to see the implications of what he had done.

"Still," he said stubbornly, "they'll learn. They'll make mistakes, there will be mis-uses, but they will learn. Their pottery will improve as it is fired. They will, perhaps, learn to cook food. They will grow and develop. Nothing remains static," he said. He repeated the Terran creed, "A civilization changes—or dies."

Kennard's face flushed in sudden, sullen anger, and Larry, realizing that for the first time since his rescue they were conscious of being alien to one another, knew something else. Kennard was jealous. He had been the rescuer, the leader. Yet Larry had saved them, where Kennard would have given up because he feared change. Larry had taken command—and Kennard, second place.

"That is the Terran way," Kennard said sullenly. "Change. For better or worse, but change. No matter how good a thing is—change it, just for the sake of change."

Larry, with a growing wisdom, was silent. It was, he knew, a deeper conflict than they could ever resolve with words alone; a whole civilization based on expansion and growth, pitted against one based on tradition. He felt like saying, "Anyhow, we're alive," but forbore. Kennard had saved his life many times over. It hardly would become him to boast about beginning to even the score.

That evening they came to the edge of the trailmen's rain forest and into the open foothills again—bare, trackless hills, unexplored, rocky, covered with scrubby brush and low, bunchy grass. Beyond them lay the mountain ranges, and beyond that—

"There lies the pass," Kennard said, "and beyond it lies Hastur country, and the home of Castle Hastur. We're within sight of home." He sounded hopeful, even joyous, but Larry heard the trembling in his voice. Before them lay miles of canyons and gullies, without road or track or path, and beyond that lay the high mountain pass. The day was dim and sunless, the peaks in shadow, but even at this distance Larry could see that snow lay in their depths.

"How far?"

"Four days travel, perhaps, if it were open prairie or forest," Kennard said. "Or one day's ride on a swift horse, if any horse could travel these infernal arroyos."

He stood frowning, gazing down into the mazelike network of canyons. "The worst of it is, the sun is clouded, and I find it hard to calculate the path we must follow. From here to the pass we must travel due westward. But with the sun in shadow—" He knelt momentarily, and Larry, wondering if he were praying, saw that instead he was examining the very faint shadow cast by the clouded sun. Finally he said, "As long as we can see the mountain peak, we need only follow it. I suppose"—he rose, shrugging wearily—"we may as well begin."

He set off downward into one of the canyons. Larry, envying him his show of confidence, stumbled after him. He was weary and footsore, and hungry, but he would not show himself less manly than Kennard.

All that day and all the next they stumbled and scrambled among the thorny, rocky slopes of the barren foothills. They went in no danger of hunger, for the bushes, so thorny and barren in appearance, were lush with succulent berries and ripening nuts. That evening Kennard snared several small birds who were feeding fearlessly on their abundance. They were out of trailmen country now, so that they dared to make fire; and it seemed to Larry that no festive dinner had ever tasted so good as the flesh of these nutty birds, roasted over their small fire and eaten half-raw and without salt. Kennard said, as they sat companionably munching drumsticks, "This place is a hunter's paradise! The birds are without fear."

"And good eating," Larry commented, cracking a bone for the succulent marrow.

"It's even possible that we might meet a hunting party." Kennard said hopefully. "Perhaps some of the men from the

Hastur country beyond the mountains hunt here—where the game roams in such abundance."

But they were both silent at the corollary of that statement. If no one hunted here, where the hunting was so splendid, then the mountain pass that lay between them and safety must be fearsome indeed!

The third day was cloudier than the last, and Kennard stopped often to examine the fainter and fainter shadows and calculate the sun's position by them. The land was rising now; the gullies were steeper and more thorny, the slopes harder to scramble up. Toward that evening a thin, fine drizzle began to fall, and even Kennard, with all his skill, could not build a fire. They gnawed cold roast meat from the night before, and dampish fruits, and slept huddled together for warmth in a rock-lined crevasse.

All the next day the rain drizzled down, thin and pale, and the purplish light held no hint of sun or shadow. Larry, watching Kennard grow ever more silent and tense, could not at last contain his anxiety. He said, "Kennard, we're lost. I know we're going the wrong way. Look, the land slopes downhill, and we have to keep going upward toward the mountains."

"I know we're going downhill, muffin-head," snapped Kennard, "into this canyon. On the other side the land rises higher. Can't you see?"

"With this rain I can't see a thing," said Larry honestly, "and what's more, I don't think you can either."

Kennard rounded on him, suddenly furious: "I suppose you think you could do better?"

"I didn't say that," Larry protested, but Kennard was tensely trying to find a shadow. It seemed completely hopeless. They were not even sure of the time of day, so that even the position of the sun would have been no help, could they have seen a shadow; this damp, darkish drizzle made no distinction between early afternoon and deep twilight.

He heard Kennard murmur, almost in despair, "If I could only get a sight of the mountain peak!"

It was the first time the Darkovan boy had sounded despair, and Larry felt the need to comfort and reassure. He said, "Kennard, it's not as bad as all that. We won't starve here. Sooner or later the sun will shine, or the rain will stop, and the pass will be before us clearly. Then any one of these little hilltops will show us our right direction. Why don't we find a sheltered place and just wait out the rainstorm?"

He had not expected instant agreement, but he was not prepared for the violence, the fury with which the Darkovan boy rounded on him.

"You damned, infernal, bumbling idiot," he shouted, "what do you *think* I'd do if it was only me? Do you think I can't have sense enough to do what any ten-year-old with sense enough to tie his own bootlaces would do in such a storm? But with you—"

"I don't understand—"

"You wouldn't," shouted Kennard. "You never understand anything, you damned—*Terranan*!" For the first time in all their friendship, the word on his lips was an insult. Larry felt his blood rise high in return. Kennard had saved his life; but there was a point beyond which he could not rub it in any further.

"If I have so little sense—?"

"Listen," Kennard said, with suppressed violence, "my father gave his surety to the *Terranan* lords for your safety. Do you think you can never let any man live his own life or die his own death? No, damn it. If you visit my people—and you vanish and are killed—do you suppose the Terrans will ever believe it was accident and not a deep-laid plot? You head-blind Terrans without even telepathy enough to know when a man speaks truth, so that your fumbling insolent idiots of people dared—they *dared*!—to doubt that my father, a lord of the Comyn and of the Seven Domains, spoke truth?

"It's true, I rescued you for my own honor and because

we had sworn friendship. But also because, unless I brought you safely back to your people, your damned Terrans will be poking and prying, searching and avenging!" He stopped. He had to. He was completely out of breath after his outburst, his face red with fury, his eyes blazing, and Larry, in sudden terror, felt the other's rage as a murderous, almost a deadly thing. He realized suddenly that he stood very close to death at that moment. The fury of an unleashed telepath—and one too young to have control over his power—beat on Larry with a surge of power like a ship. It rolled over him like a crashing surf. It pounded him physically to his knees.

He bent before it. And then, as suddenly as it had come, he realized that he had strength to meet it. He raised his eyes gravely to Kennard and said aloud, "Look, my friend—" (he used the word *bredu*) "—I did not know this. I did not make my people's laws, no more than you caused the feud that set the bandits on our hunting party." And he was amazed at the steady force with which he countered the furious assault of rage.

Slowly, Kennard quieted. Larry felt the red surges of Kennard's fury receding, until at last the Darkovan boy stood before him silent, just a kid again and a scared one. He didn't apologize, but Larry didn't expect him to. He said, simply, "So it's a matter of time, you see, Lerrys." The Darkovan form of Larry's name was, Larry knew, tacit apology. "And as you care for your people, I care for my father. And this is the first day of the rainy season. I had hoped to be out of these hills, and through the passes, before this. We were delayed by the trailmen, or we should be safe now, and a message of your safety on its way to your father. If I had the starstone still—" he was silent, then shrugged. "Well, that is the Comyn law." He drew a deep breath. "Now, which way did you say you thought was west?"

"I didn't say," Larry said, honestly. He did not know until much later just how rare a thing he had done; he had faced the unleashed wrath of an Alton and a telepath—and been unharmed. Later, he remembered it and shook in his shoes; but now he just felt relieved that Kennard had calmed down.

"But," he said, "there's no point in going in circles. All these canyons look exactly alike to me. If we had a compass—" He broke off. He began to search frantically in his pockets. The bandits had not taken it from him because the main blade was broken. The trailmen had not even seen it. As a weapon it was worthless. He had not even been able to use it to help Kennard clean and gut the birds they had eaten.

But it had a magnetized blade!

And a magnetized blade, properly used could make an improvised compass. . . .

The first turn-out of his pockets failed to find it; then he remembered that during their time with the trailmen, fearing they might regard any tool, however small, as a weapon, he had thrust it into his medical kit. He took it out, and snapped the magnetized blade off against a stone, then tested it against the metal of the broken main blade. It retained its magnetism. Now if he could only remember how it was done. It had been a footnote in one of his mathematics texts in childhood, half forgotten. Kennard, meanwhile, watched as if Larry's brain had snapped, while Larry experimented with a bit of string and finally, looking at Kennard's long, square-cut hair, demanded "Give me one of your hairs."

"Are you out of your wits?"

"No," Larry said. "I think I may be *in* them, at last. I should have thought of this from the beginning. If I could have taken a bearing when the sun was still shining, and we had a clear view of the pass ahead of us, I'd know—"

Without raising his head, he accepted the hair which Kennard gave him gingerly, as if he were humoring a lunatic. He knotted the hair around the magnetized blade and waited. The blade was tiny and light, hardly bigger than the needles which had been the first improvised compasses. It swung wildly for a few moments; stopped.

"What superstitious rigamarole—" Kennard began,

stopped. "You must have something on your mind," he conceded, "but what?"

Larry began to explain the theory by which the magnetic compass worked. Kennard cut him short.

"Everyone knows that a certain kind of metal—you call it a magnet—will attract metal. But how can this help us?"

For a moment Larry despaired. He had forgotten the level of Darkovan technology—or lack of it—and how could he, in one easy lesson, explain the two magnetic poles of a planet, the theory of the magnetic compass which pointed to the true pole at all times, the manner of taking a compass direction and following? He started, but he was making very heavy weather of explaining the magnetic field around a planet. To begin with, he simply did not have the technological vocabulary in Darkovan—if there was one, which he doubted. He was reminded of the trailman chief calling fire "the red thing which eats the woods." He felt like that while he tried to explain about iron filings and magnetic currents. Finally he gave up, holding the improvised compass in one hand.

He said helplessly, "Kennard, I can't explain it to you any more than you can explain to me how you destroyed that blue jewel of yours—or how your psychics herded a batch of clouds across the sky to put out a fire. But I helped you do it, didn't I? And it worked? We can't possibly be any worse off than we are already, can we? And the Terran ships find their way between the stars by using this kind of—of science. So will you at least let me *try*?"

Kennard was silent for a moment. At last he said, "I suppose you are right. We could not be worse off."

Larry knelt and drew an improvised sketch map on the ground, what he remembered of the mountain range he had seen from the distance. "Now here's the mountains and here is the edge of the trailmen's forest. How far had we come before you lost sure sight of exactly where we were going?"

Hesitantly, with many frowns and rememberings, Kennard traced out a route.

"And that was—exactly how long ago? Try to be as accurate as you can, Kennard; how many miles ago did you begin not to be absolutely sure?"

Kennard put his finger on the improvised map.

"So we're within about five hours walk from that point." He drew a circle around the point Kennard had shown as their last positive location. "We could be anywhere in this circle, but if we keep west and keep going west we'll have to hit the mountains—we can't possibly miss them." He tried not to think of what would lie before them then. Kennard thought of it as just the final hurdle, but the journey with the bandits through their own dreadful chasms and crags—bound and handcuffed like sacked luggage—had given him an enduring horror of the Darkovan mountains that was to last his lifetime.

"If this works . . ." Kennard said, skeptically, but immediately looked an apology. "What do I have to do first? Is there any specific ritual for the use of this—this amulet?"

Larry, by main force, held back a shout of half-hysterical laughter. Instead, he said gravely, "Just cross your fingers that it will work," and started questioning Kennard about the minor discrepancies, of the seasons, and the sun's rising and setting. Darkover—he knew from its extremes of climate—must be a planet with an exaggeratedly tilted axis, and he would have to figure out just how far north or south of true west the sun set at this season of the year in this latitude. How he blessed the teacher at Quarters B who had loaned him the book on Darkovan geography—otherwise he might not even have been sure whether they were in the southern, rather than the northern hemisphere. He boggled at the thought of trying to explain an equator to Kennard.

A degree or two wouldn't matter—not with a range of mountains hundreds of miles long, that they couldn't miss if they tried—but the nearer they came out to the pass itself, the sooner they would be home. And the sooner Kennard's father would be out of trouble. He was amazed at how responsible he felt.

The compass would steady, he realized, if he let it swing freely without his hand moving. All they had to do was take a rough bearing, follow it, checking it again and again every few miles.

Once again, he realized, he had taken the lead in the expedition, and Kennard, reluctantly, was forced to follow. It bothered him, and he knew Kennard didn't like it. He hoped, at least, that it wouldn't bring on another outburst of rage.

He stood up, looking at the muddy mess of their improvised map. He was cold and drenched, but he assumed an air of confidence which, in reality, he was far from feeling.

"Well, if we're going to risk it," he said, "west is that way. So let's start walking. I'm ready if you are."

It was hard, slow going, scrambling into canyons and up slopes, stopping every hour to swing the compass free and wait for it to steady and point, re-drawing the improvised compass card in the mud. Larry finally shortened this step by drawing one on a page of his battered notebook. The rain went on, remorselessly, not hard, never soaking, but always *there*—a thin, fine, chilling drizzle that eventually seemed worse than the worst and hardest downpour. His arm, the one the bandits had harnessed behind his back, felt both numb and sore, but there wasn't a thing he could do but set his teeth and try to think about something else. That night they literally dug themselves into a bank of dead leaves, in a vain attempt to keep some of the worst of the rain off. Their clothes were wet. Their skin was wet. Their boots and socks were wet. The food they munched was wet—berries, nuts, fruits and a sort of root like a raw potato. Kennard could easily enough have snared small game, but they tacitly agreed that even cold raw sour berries and mushrooms were preferable to raw wet meat. And Kennard swore that in this drizzle, at this season, in this kind of country, not even a *kyrri* could strike enough spark to kindle a fire!

But toward nightfall of the next day—Larry had lost count of time, nothing existed now but the trudging through wet gulleys and slopes and thorny brushwood—Kennard stopped and turned to him.

"I owe you an apology. This toy of yours is working and I know it now."

"How?" Larry was almost too exhausted to care.

"The air is thinner and the rain is colder. Don't you find it harder to breathe? We must be rising very rapidly now toward the mountain ranges—must have come up several thousand feet in the last few hours alone. Didn't you notice that the western edge of every new gully was higher and harder to climb than the last?"

Larry had thought it was just his own tiredness that had made it seem so; but now that Kennard confirmed it, it seemed indeed that the land had somehow changed character. It was barer; the ridges were longer and steeper, and the abundant berries and nuts and mushrooms had dwindled to a few of the sparser, sourer kind.

"We're getting into the mountains, all right," Kennard said, "and that means we'd better stop early, tonight, and find all the food we can carry. There's nothing in the passes except snow and ice and a few wild birds that nest in the crags and live on the berries up there—berries which happen to be poisonous to humans."

Larry knew he might have found a way out of a couple of serious dilemmas with Terran science, but without Kennard's woodcraft they would both have died many times over.

Food was far from easy to find; they spent hours gathering enough for a sparse supper and a few more meager meals, and during the next day, vegetation diminished almost to nothing. However, Kennard was almost jubilant. If they were actually that near to the mountains, they must be nearing the pass. And that evening, for a little while, like an unexpected gift, the fog and drizzle cleared briefly, and they saw the high peak and the pass that lay below it, shining with the mauve and violet glare of the red sun on the snow, clear before their eyes and less than ten miles away. The brief flash of sun lasted only five minutes or so, but it was long enough for Larry to adjust and check his improvised compass card, take an exact bearing on the pass, and lay out a proper course. After that, whenever any steep slope or rock-ledge forced them to deviate from a chosen direction, he marked it and could correct for it; so that now, instead of going in roughly the right direction, he knew they were going direct for their destination.

But, vindicated though he was in Kennard's eyes, the going was rough now, and getting rougher. There were steep rock-slopes on which they had to scramble on all fours, clutching for handholds on slippery ledges; and once they had to traverse a two-inch-wide track above a cliff-face that left Larry pale and sweating with terror. Kennard took these rock-scrambles quite in stride, and was getting back some of his old arrogant assurance of leadership, and it bothered Larry. Damn it, it wasn't his fault that he hadn't been trained to climb rock-faces, nor did it make him a passive follower, just because heights of this sort made him sick and dizzy. He gritted his teeth, vowing to himself that anywhere Kennard led, he'd follow—even though it seemed that Kennard could often have chosen easier paths, and was trying to re-establish his own leadership of the expedition by showing off his own superior mountain-craft.

Their provisions ran out that night; they slept, hungry, cold and wet, on a frost-rimed slope a little more level than most—or rather, Kennard slept; Larry had trouble even in breathing. The morning dawned, and long before it was full light, Kennard stirred. He said, "I know you're not asleep. We may as well start. If we're lucky we'll reach the pass before noon." In the bleak morning dimness Larry could not see his friend's face, but he did not need to see. The emotions there were as clear to him as if he were inside Kennard's mind: *On the other side of the passes, there is food, and inhabited country, and warmth, and people to turn to for help. But the pass is going to be hard going. I wouldn't like doing it even with a couple of experienced guides to help. If it doesn't snow, we might get through—if the snow's not already too deep. Can the Terran boy hold out? He's already about exhausted. If he gives in now . . .*

And the despair in that thought suddenly overwhelmed Larry; Kennard was thinking, *If he gives out now, I'll be alone . . . and it will all be for nothing. . . .*

Larry wondered suddenly if he were imagining all this, if the height and the hardship were affecting his own mind. This sort of mental eavesdropping didn't make sense. Also, it embarrassed him. He tried, desperately, to close his mind against it, but Kennard's misgivings were leaking through all barriers:

Can Larry hold out? Can he make it? Have I got strength enough for both of us?

Silently, grimly, Larry resolved that if one of them gave out, it would not be himself. He was cold, hungry and wet, but by damn, he'd show this arrogant Darkovan aristocrat something.

Damn it! He was sick of being helped along and treated like the burden and the weaker one!

Terrans weak? Hadn't the Terrans been the first to cross space! Hadn't they taken the blind leap in the dark, before the stardrives, traveling years and years between the stars, ships disappearing and never being heard of again, and yet the race from Terra had spread through all inhabited worlds! Kennard could be proud of his Darkovan heritage and bravery. But there was something to be proud of in the Terrans, too! They had, in a way, their own arrogance, and it was just as reasonable as the Darkovan arrogance.

Here he had assumed, all along, that he was somehow inferior because, on a Darkovan world and in a Darkovan society, he was a burden to Kennard. Suppose it was reversed? Kennard did not understand the workings of a compass. He would be utterly baffled at the drives of a spaceship or a surface-car.

But even if he died here in the mountain passes, he was going to show Kennard that where a Darkovan could lead a Terran could follow! And then, damn it, when they got back to *his* world, he'd challenge Kennard to try following *him* a while in the world of the Terrans—and see if a Darkovan could follow where a Terran led!

He got up, grinned wryly, turned his pockets inside out in the hope of a stray crumb of food—there wasn't one—and said, "The sooner the better."

The grade was steeper now, and there began to be snow underfoot; they went very carefully, guarding against a sideslip that could have meant a ghastly fall. His injured arm felt numbed and twice it slipped on handholds, but he proudly refused Kennard's offers of help.

"I'll manage," he said, tight-mouthed.

They came to one dreadful stretch where frost-sheathed stones littered a high ledge without a sign of a track; Kennard, who was leading, set his foot tentatively on the ledge, and it crumbled beneath him, sending pebbles crashing down in a miniature rockslide whitened with powdery snow. He staggered and reeled at the edge of the abyss, but even before he swayed Larry had moved, catching the flash of fear at the touch, and grabbed and held him, hard—the older boy's weight jerking his hurt arm almost from the socket— until Kennard could recover his balance. They clung together, gasping, Kennard with fear and relief and Larry with mingled fright and pain; something had snapped in the injured shoulder and his arm hung stiff and immovable at his side, sending shudders of agony down his side when he as much as moved a finger.

Kennard finally wiped his brow. "Zandru's hells, I

thought I was gone," he muttered. "Thanks, Lerrys. I'm all right now. You—" He noted Larry's immobility. "What's the trouble?"

"My arm," Larry managed to get out, shakily.

Kennard touched it with careful fingers, drew a deep whistle. He moved his fingertips over it, his face intent and concentrated. Larry felt a most strange, burning itch deep in his bones under the touch; then Kennard, without a word of warning, suddenly seized the shoulder and gave it a violent, agonizing twist. Larry yelled in pain; he couldn't help it. But as the pain subsided, he realized what Kennard had done.

Kennard nodded. "I had to slip the damned thing back into the socket before it froze the muscles around it. Or it would have taken three men to hold you down while they worked it back into place," he said.

"How did you know—?"

"Deep-probed," Kennard said briefly. "I can't do it often, or very long. But I—" he hesitated, did not finish his sentence. Larry heard it anyhow: *I owed you that much. But damn it, now we're both exhausted!*

"And we've still got that devilish ledge to cross," he said aloud. He began unfastening his belt; tugged briefly at Larry's. Larry, curiously, watched him buckle them together and slip the ends around their waists.

"Shame you can't use your left hand," he said tersely. "Too bad they found out you were left-handed. Now we'll start across. Let me lead. This is a hell of a place for your first lesson in climbing this kind of a rock-ledge, but here it is. Always have at least three things all together hanging on. Never move one foot without the other foot and both hands anchored. And the same with either hand." His unfinished sentence again was perfectly clear to Larry: *Both our lives are in his hands, because he's the weakest.*

For the rest of his life, Larry remembered the agonizing hour and a half it took them to cross the twenty-foot stretch of rock-strewn ledge. There were places where the least

movement started showers of rocks and snow; yet they
could only cling together like limpets to their handholds and
to the face of the rock. Above and below was sheer cliff;
there was no help there, and if they retraced their steps, to
find an easier way, they would never get across. Half a
dozen times, Larry slipped and the belt jerking them back
together saved him from a very long drop into what looked
like nothingness and fog below. Halfway across a thin fine
powdery snow began to fall, and Kennard swore in words
Larry couldn't even begin to follow.

"That was all we needed!" Suddenly he seemed to
brighten up, and placed his next foot more cautiously. "Well,
Larry, this is it—this has got to be the worst. Nothing worse
than this could possibly happen. From now, things can only
get better. Come on—left foot this time. Try that greyish
hunk of rock. It looks solid enough."

But at last they were on firm ground again, dropping
down as they were in the snow, exhausted, to breathe deep
and slow and gasp like runners just finished with a ten-mile
race. Kennard, accustomed to the mountains, was as usual
the first to recover, and stood up, his voice jubilant.

"I told you it would get better! Look, Larry!"

He pointed. Above them the pallid and snowy light
showed them the pass, less than a hundred feet away, leading between rock-sheltered banks—a natural walkway,
deeply banked with the falling snow, but sloping only gradually so that they could walk erect.

"And on the other side of that pass, Larry, there are people—my people—friends, who will help us. Warmth and
food and fire and—" he broke off. "It seems too good to be
true."

"I'd settle for dry feet and something hot to eat," Larry
said, then froze, while Kennard still moved toward the pass.
The terrible creeping tension he had felt just before their
capture by the trailmen was with him again. It gripped him
by the throat; forced him to run after Kennard, grabbing at

him with his good arm, holding him back by main force. He couldn't speak; he could hardly breathe with the force of it. The wave surged and crested, the precognition, the fore-knowing of terrible danger. . . .

It broke. He could breathe again. He gasped and caught at Kennard and pointed and heard the older boy shriek aloud, but the shriek was lost in the siren screaming wail that rose and echoed in the rocky pass. Above them, a huge and ugly craning head, bare of feathers, eyeless and groping, snaked upward, followed by a huge, ungainly body, dimly shining with phosphorescent light. It bore down upon them, clumsily but with alarming speed, cutting off their approach to the pass. The siren-like wailing scream rose and rose until it seemed to fill the air and all the world.

It *had* been too good to be true.

The pass was a nest of one of the evil banshee-birds.

CHAPTER ELEVEN

For an instant, in blind panic, Larry whirled, turning to run. The speed with which the banshee caught the change in direction of movement paralyzed him again with terror; but during that split second of immobility, he felt a flash of hope. Kennard had begun to run, stumbling in helpless panic; Larry took one leap after him, wrenching him back, hard.

"*Freeze*," he whispered, urgently. "It senses movement and warmth! Keep perfectly still!"

As Kennard struggled to free himself, he muttered swiftly, "Sorry, pal," swung back his fist and socked Kennard, hard, on the point of the chin. The boy—exhausted, worn, defenseless—collapsed into the snowbank and lay there, motionless, too stunned to rise or to do more than stare, resentfully, at Larry. Larry flung himself down, too, and lay without moving so much as a muscle.

The bird stopped in mid-rush, turning its blind head confusedly from side to side. It blundered back and forth for a moment, its trundling walk and the trailing wings giving it the ungainly look of a huge fat cloaked man. It raised its head and gave forth that terrible, paralyzing wail again.

That's it, Larry thought, resisting the impulse to stuff his hands over his ears. Things hear that awful noise and they run—and the thing *feels them moving*! It's got something like the electrostatic fields of the *kyrri*—only what it senses is their movement, and their smell.

In this snowbank . . .

Very slowly, moving a fraction of an inch at a time, fearing that even the slightest rapid motion might alert the banshee again, he scrabbled slowly in his pocket for his medical kit. It was almost empty, but there might just be enough of the strongly chemical-smelling antiseptic so that they would not smell like anything alive—or, he thought grimly, good to eat.

"Kennard," he whispered, "can you hear me? Don't move a muscle now. But when I slop this stuff around, dive into that snowbank—and burrow as if your life depended on it." *It probably does,* he was thinking.

"*Now!*"

The smell of the chemical was pungent and sharp; the banshee, moving its phosphorescent head against the wind, made strange jolting motions of distaste. It turned and blundered away, and in that moment Larry and Kennard began to dig frantically into the snowbank, throwing up snow behind them, scrabbling it back over their bodies.

They were safe—for the moment. But how would they get across the pass?

Then he remembered Kennard's earlier words about the banshees. They're night-birds, torpid in the sunlight. The phosphorescence of their heads proved that they were no creatures of normal sunlight.

If they could live through the night . . .

If they didn't freeze to death . . .

If some other banshee couldn't feel their warmth through the snow around them . . .

If the sun shone tomorrow, brightly enough to quiet the great birds . . .

If all these things happened, then they just *might* live through their last hurdle.

If not . . .

Suddenly all these *ifs*, coming at him like blasts of fear from Kennard, stirred fury in him. Damn it, there *had* to be a way through! And Kennard seemed to have given up; he was just lying there in the snow, silent, apparently ready for death.

But they hadn't come so far together to die here, at the last. Damn it, he'd get them over that pass if he had to burrow through the damned snowbank with his bare hands. . . .

The banshee seemed to have gone; cautiously, he lifted his head, ever so slightly, from the snowbank. Then, thinking better of it, he plastered the freezing stuff over his head before lifting it up, quickly surveying the pass above them. Less than a hundred feet. If they could somehow crawl through the snow . . .

Urgently, he shook Kennard's shoulder. The Darkovan boy did not move. This last terror had evidently finished his endurance. He muttered, "Right back where we were—when we left Cyrillon's castle—"

Larry's fury exploded. "So after dragging me halfway across the country, within sight of safety you're going to lie here and die?"

"The banshees—"

"Oh, your own god Zandru take the banshees! We'll get through them or else we won't, but by damn we'll *try*! You Darkovans—so proud of your courage when it's a matter of individual bravery! As long as you could be a *hero*"—he flayed Kennard, deliberately, intently, with his words—"you were brave as could be! When you could make me look small! But now when you have to work *with* me, you konk out and lie down to die! And Valdir thinks he can do anything with your people? What the hell—his own son can't shut up and listen and co-operate! He's got to be a goddamn hero, or he won't play, and just lies down to die!"

Kennard swallowed. His eyes blazed fire, and Larry braced himself for another outburst of that flaying, dreadful Alton rage, but it was checked before it began. Kennard clenched his fists, but he spoke grimly, through his teeth.

"I'll kill you for that, some day—but right now, you'll see whether a Terran can lead an Alton on his own world. Try it."

"That's the way to talk," Larry said, deliberately jovial to infuriate Kennard's despairing dignity. "If we're going to die anyhow, we might as well do it while we're *doing* something about it! To hell with dying with dignity! Make the blasted beast fight for his dinner if he wants it—kicking and scratching!"

Kennard laid his hand on his knife. He said "He'll get a fight—"

Larry gripped his wrist, "*No*! Warmth and movement are what he senses! Damn you and your heroics! Common sense is what we need. Hell, I know you're *brave*, but try showing some brains too!"

Kennard froze. He said through barely moving lips, "All right. I said I'd follow your lead. What do I do now?"

Larry thought fast. He had pulled Kennard out of his fit of despair, but now he had to *offer* something. If he was going to take the lead, he had to lead—and do it damned fast!

The banshee sensed warmth and movement.

Therefore, it must be something like the *kyrri*; and the only way to outwit it was with cold, and stillness. But they could freeze to death and it could outwait them. Or else—

The idea struck him.

"Listen! You run one way and I'll run the other—"

Kennard said, "Drawing lots for death? I accept that. Whichever one of us he takes, the other goes free?"

"*No*, idiot!" Larry hadn't even thought of that. It was a noble Darkovan concept and honorable, but it seemed damned unnecessary. "We both get free—or neither. No, what I'm thinking about is to *confuse* the damned thing. I move. He's drawn off after me. Then I stop, burrow in a snowbank, stay still as a mouse—and while he's trying to scent me again, *you* start running around. Somewhere else. He'll start to move in *that* direction. Then you freeze and I start again. Maybe we can confuse him, keep him running back and forth long enough to get across the pass."

Kennard looked at him with growing excitement. "It just might *work*."

"All right, get ready—*freeze!*"

Larry jumped up and started running. He saw the huge lumbering bird twitch toward him as by a tropism, then come speeding. He yelled to Kennard, dived into a snowbank, scrabbled frantically in and lay still, not daring to move or hardly to breathe.

He felt, rather than seeing, the great bird stop short, clumsily twitch around, jerking in irritation. How had its prey gotten over *there*? Kennard dashed about twenty yards toward the pass, shouted and dived. Larry jumped up again. This time he tried to run too far; the evil creature's foul breath was actually hot on his neck and his flesh crawled with anticipation of the swift, disemboweling clawing stroke. He fell into the snow, burrowed in and lay still. The siren wail of the confused bird rose, filling the air with screaming terror, and Larry thought, *Oh, God, don't let Kennard panic again.* . . .

He raised his head cautiously, watched Kennard dive down, rose again and dashed. The bird twitched, began to lumber back, suddenly howled and began to dash madly in circles, its huge head flopping and flapping.

The banshee howl fell to terrified little yelps and the creature fell on its back, twitching.

Larry yelled to Kennard, "Come on! Run!" He was remembering psychology courses. Animals, especially very stupid animals, faced with a situation wholly frustrating and outside their experience, go completely to pieces and crack up. The banshee was lying in the snow squealing with a complete nervous breakdown.

They ran, gasping and trembling. The clouds seemed suddenly to thin and lift, and the pale Darkovan sun burst suddenly forth in morning brilliance.

Larry hauled himself up, exhausted, to the summit of the pass. He rested there, gasping, Kennard at his side.

Before them lay a trail downward, and far away, a countryside patched with quiet fields, smoke rising from small houses and hearthstones, the tree-laden slopes of low foothills and green leaves.

Exhausted, wearied, famished, they stood there feasting their eyes on the beauty and richness of the country that lay below. Kennard pointed. Far away, almost out of sight range, a gray spire just visible through the mist rose upward.

"Castle Hastur—and we've won!"

"Not yet," Larry said, warningly. "It's a long way off yet. And we'd better get right out of the high snows while this sun is bright enough to keep any of that big fellow's sisters and his cousins and his aunts from coming around!"

"You're right," Kennard said, sobering instantly, and they trudged off down the narrow trail, not really liking to think what had made it. But at least the sun was bright, and for the moment they were safe.

Larry had leisure to feel, now, how weary he was. His dislocated shoulder ached like the very devil. His feet were cold and hot by turns—he was sure he had frostbite—and his fingers were white and cold from scrabbling in the snow. He sucked them and slapped them together, trying hard to keep from moaning with the pain of returning circulation. But he kept pace with Kennard. He'd taken over the leadership—and he wasn't going to give out now!

The slopes on this side were heavily wooded, but the woods were mostly conifers and spruce, and there was still no sign of food. Lower down on the slope, they found a single tree laden with apples, damp and wrinkled after the recent storm, but still edible; they filled their pockets, and sat down to eat side by side. Larry thought of the peaceful time, so few days ago really, when they had sat side by side like this, before the alarm of forest-fire. What years he seemed to have lived, and what hills and valleys he had crossed—figuratively as well as literally—since then!

Kennard was frowning at him and Larry remembered, with an absolute wrench of effort, that they had exchanged harsh words in the pass.

Kennard said, "Now that we are out of danger—you spoke words to me beyond forgiveness. We are *bredin*, but I'm going to beat them down your throat!"

Oh no! Not that again!

"Forget it," he said. "I was trying to save both our lives; I didn't have time to be tactful."

Kennard is sulking because I saved our lives when he couldn't. He wants to settle it the Darkovan way—with a fight. Larry said, aloud, "I won't fight with you, Ken. You saved my life too many times. I would no more hit you than—than my own father."

Kennard looked at him, trembling with rage. "Coward!"

Larry took a deliberate bite out of his apple. It was sour. He said, "Calling me names won't hurt me. Go ahead, if it makes you feel better." Then he added, gently, "Anyhow, what would it prove, except that you are stronger than I? I've never doubted that, even for a moment. We'd *still* be in this thing together. And after coming through all this together—why should we end it with a fight, as if we were enemies instead of friends?" Deliberately, he used the word *bredin* again. He held out his hand. "If I said anything to hurt you, I'm sorry. You've hurt me a time or two, so even by your own codes we're even. Let's shake hands and forget it."

Kennard hesitated, and for a flooding, bitter moment Larry feared he would rebuff the gesture, and for that same moment Larry almost wished they had died together in the pass. They had grown as close as if their minds were one—and being closed away, now, hurt like a knife.

Then, like sunlight breaking through a cloud, Kennard smiled. He held out both hands and clasped Larry's in them.

"Have another apple," was all he said. But it was enough.

CHAPTER TWELVE

The trail downward was hard, rough going; but with the fear of the banshees behind them, and Larry's growing skill at rock-climbing, they managed the descent better than the ascent. Weary, half starved, Larry felt a relief all out of measure to their present situation—for in a trackless, almost foodless forest, they had still several days walking to cover before they came to inhabited country. They had seen it from the pass, but it was far away.

And yet the optimism seeded in him, growing higher and higher, like a cresting wave, like . . .

Like the growth of his fear when they had been in the acute danger of capture by the trailmen and he had not yet known it!

What kind of freak am I? How did I get it? I'm no telepath. And it can't be learned.

Yet he felt this cresting, flooding hope—almost like a great joy. The woods seemed somehow greener, the sky a more brilliant mauve, the red sun to shine with brilliance and glory overhead. Could it be only relief at escape? Or—

"Kennard, do you suppose we might meet a hunting party who are in these woods?"

Kennard, learned in woodcraft, chuckled wryly. "Who would hunt here—and what for? There seems to be not a sign of game in these woods, though later we may find fruit or berries. You looked damned optimistic," he added, rather sullenly still.

He's mad because I faced him down. But he'll get over it.

They scrambled their way to the lip of a rocky rise in the land, and stood looking down into a green valley, so beautiful that in the grip of this unexplained joy Larry stood almost ecstatically, entranced by the trees, by the little stream that ran silver at the bottom. Songbirds were singing. And through the birdsong, and the clear-running water, there was another sound—a clear voice, singing. The voice of a human creature.

In another moment, through the trees, a tall figure appeared. He was singing, in a musical, unknown tongue.

Kennard stood half-enraptured. He whispered, "A *chieri*!"

Human?

The creature was, indeed, human in form, though tall and of such a fragile slenderness that he seemed even more so. He? Was the creature a woman? The voice had been clear and high, like a woman's voice. It wore a long robe of some gleaming grayish silky substance. Long pale hair lay across the slim shoulders. The beckoning hand was white and almost translucent in the sunlight, and the bones of the face had an elfin, delicate, triangular beauty.

Flying around the head of the elfin creature were a multitude of singing birds, whose melodious voices mingled with that of the *chieri*. Suddenly the *chieri* looked sharply upward, and called in a clear voice, "You there, you evil tramplers! Go, before you frighten my birds, or I put an ill word on you!"

Kennard stepped forward, raising his hands in a gesture of surrender and respect. Larry remembered the respect the Darkovan boy had shown Lorill Hastur. This was more than respect, it was deference, it was almost abasement.

"Child of grace," he said, half-audibly, "we mean no harm to you or your birds. We are lost and desperate. My friend is hurt. If you can give us no help, give us at least none of your evil will."

The beautiful, epicene face, suddenly clear in the patch of sunlight, softened. Raising the thin hands, the *chieri* let the birds fly free, in a whirling cloud. Then the creature beckoned to them, but as they began to trudge wearily down the slope, it ran lightly upward to them.

"You are hurt! You have cuts and bruises; you are hungry, you have come through that dreadful pass haunted by evil things—?"

"We have," Kennard said faintly, "and we have crossed all the country from the castle of Cyrillon des Trailles."

"What are you?"

"I am Comyn," Kennard said, with his last scraps of dignity, "of the Seven Domains. This—this lad is my friend and *bredu*. Give us shelter, or at least no harm!"

The *chieri*'s fair and mobile face was gentle. "Forgive me. Evil things come sometimes from the high passes, and foul my clear pools and frighten my birds. They fear me, fortunately—but I do not always see them. But you—" The *chieri* looked at them, a clear piercing gray gaze, and said, "You mean no harm to us."

The glance held Larry's eyes spellbound. Kennard whispered, "Are you a mighty *leronis*?"

"I am of the *chieri*. Are you wiser, son of Alton?"

"You know my name?"

"I know your name, Kennard son of Valdir, and your friend's. Yet I have none of your Comyn powers. But you are weary, and your friend, in pain; so no more talk now. Can you walk a steep path?" The *chieri* seemed almost apologetic. "I must guard myself, in this land."

Larry, drawing himself upright, said, "I can go where I must."

Kennard said, "You lend us grace, child of light. And blessed was the lord of Carthon when he met with Kierestelli beside the wells of Reuel."

"Is that tale still known?" The alien, elfin face was merry. "But time enough later for tales and old legends, son of the Seven Domansa. No more talk now. Come."

The *chieri* turned, taking an upward path. It was a long climb and Larry was sweating in exhaustion, his injured arm feeling ready to drop off, before they reached the top. At the end, Kennard was half carrying him. But even Kennard was too weary to do more, and the *chieri* came, put an arm around each, and supported them. Frail, almost boneless as the creature looked, it was incredibly strong.

They came out upon a flat space, screened with living boughs, and entered a door of woven wicker into the strangest room he had ever seen.

The floor was of earth, not mud or of sun-dried brick, but carpeted thickly with grass and living moss in which a cricket chirped; it felt warm and fragrant under their feet.

The *chieri* bent and removed his sandals, and at his signal, the boys removed their wet and soaking boots and worn socks. The grass felt comfortable to their weary feet.

The walls were of woven wicker, screened lightly with thin hangings of cloth, heavy but not coarse, which admitted light but could not be seen through. In the roof of thatch, vines with great trumpet-shaped blossoms were growing, which pervaded the whole place with a fragrance of green and growing things. It smelled fresh, and sweet. An opened door at the back led to an enclosed garden where a fountain splashed into a stone bowl, running out and away in a little rivulet. A fire burned there in a small brazier of hardened clay, and over it was a metal crane on which a steaming kettle swung, giving forth a good smell of hot food. The lads felt their eyes watering at this steam. Furniture there was little, save for a bench or chest or two, and at the edge of the room an upright loom with a strung web on it.

As they entered, the *chieri* raised its hands, saying in its clear voice, "Enter in a good hour, and let no fear or danger trouble you within these walls." That done, it turned to

Larry, saying "You are hurt and in pain, and you flee from evil things. I sensed your minds within the pass. I will ask no more till you have had rest and food."

It went to the brazier, and Kennard, sinking down on the grass wearily, said, "Who are you, child of grace?"

"You may call me Narad-zinie," said the *chieri*, "which is my name among your people. My own would be strange to your ears and overlong." From a chest it took silver cups, plainly but beautifully worked, and poured drink into them. It offered a cup to each. Larry tasted; it was delicious, but very strong wine. He hesitated a moment, then his weariness and thirst overcame him; he drank it up anyhow. Almost at once the sense of complete exhaustion left him and he watched alertly as the *chieri* moved the kettle aside from the brazier.

"Porridge is slim food alone for footsore travelers," it said. "I will make you some cakes as well. No more wine until you have eaten, though! Meanwhile—" It gestured at the fountain, and Larry, suddenly abashed at his dirty and torn clothes, went to wash and douse his head under the fountain. Kennard followed suit.

When Larry came back, something like pancakes were baking on a flat griddle over the brazier. They smelled so good that his mouth watered. The *chieri* brought them food on flat, beautifully carved wooden trays, and there were also bowls of porridge, the flat pancakes which had a yeasty, puffy texture, bowls of hot milk, honey and what tasted like cheese. The flavors were oddly pungent, but the boys were far too hungry to care; they demolished everything in sight, and the *chieri* brought them second helpings of pancakes and honey. Replete at last, they leaned back and surveyed the room, and Larry's first words were oddly irrelevant.

"The trailmen might evolve something like this instead of what you fear, Kennard."

The *chieri* answered for Kennard. "The trailfolk, in the far-back times, were our kinfolk, but then we left the trees and built fire, they feared it and our ways moved apart. They are our younger brother, to grow more slowly in wisdom. But perhaps it is time, indeed, for what this child of two worlds has done."

Larry stared up at the alien's strange beautiful face. "You—know all this?"

"The Comyn powers are *chieri* powers, little brother," the *chieri* said. It stretched out its long body on the green turf. "I suppose you have no patience with long tales, so I will say only this, Kennard—the *chieri* lived on Darkover long before you Terrans came, to drive us into the deep and deeper woods."

Kennard said, "But I am not Terran," and Larry felt his amazed anger. "Larry is the Terran!"

The *chieri* smiled. "I forgot," he said gently, "that to your people, the passing of a lifetime is as a sleep and a sleep to our folk. Children of Terra are you both. I was here, a youngling of my people, when the first ship from Terra arrived, a lost ship and broken, and your people were forced to remain here. The time came when they forgot their origins; but the name they gave to this world—Darkover—indeed reflects their speech and their customs."

It was a strange tale he told, and Kennard and Larry, lying at ease and almost in disbelief, listened while the *chieri* told his tale.

The Terran ship had been one of the first early starships to cross space. Their crew, some hundred men and women, had been forced to remain, and after dozens of generations—which had seemed like only a little while to the *chieri*-folk—they had spread over most of the planet.

"There is a tale you spoke of," the *chieri* said, "of the lord of Carthon—one of your people, Kennard—who met with a woman of my folk Kierestelli; and she loved him, and bore him a son, and therewith she died, but the blood had mixed. And this son, Hastur, loved a maiden of your people, Cas-

silda, and from this admixture in their seven sons came the
Seven Domains in which you take such pride."

Interbreeding to produce these new telepathic powers in
greater intensity had led to seven pure strains of telepathy,
each with its own Domain, or family; and each with its own
kind of *laran*, or psi power.

"The Hasturs. The Aillard. The Ridenow. The Elhalyn.
The Altons—your clan, young Kennard. And the Aldaran."

"The Aldaran," said Kennard with a trace of bitterness,
"were exiled from the Comyn—and they sold our world to
the Terrans!"

The *chieri's* beautiful face was strange. "You mean,
when the Terrans came again, for the second time, the Aldaran first welcomed their long-forgotten brothers to their
own people who had forgotten their ancestry," he said. "Perhaps among the Aldarans, their Terran heritage was never
forgotten. But as for you, little son of Darkover and of
Terra"—and he looked at Larry with great gentleness—"you
are weary; you should sleep. Yet I know very well why you
are in haste. Even now—" his face became distant "—Valdir
Alton answers for your fate to these new Terrans who have
also forgotten that these men of Darkover are their brothers.
As, indeed, all folk are brothers, though there are many,
many times when they forget it. And because you are both
of my people, I will help you—though I would love to speak
more to you. For I am old, and of a dying race. Our women
bear no more children, and one day the *chieri* will be only a
memory, living on only in the blood of those, their conquer-
ers." He sighed. "Beautiful were our forests in those days.
Yet time and change come to all men and all worlds, and you
are right to speak with reverence of Kierestelli and to call
Cassilda blessed, who first mingled blood with blood and
thus assured that the *chieri* would survive in blood if never
in memory. But I am old—I talk too much. I should act instead."

He got to his feet. With those strange gray eyes—eyes

like the eyes of Lorill Hastur, Larry realized—he enspelled them both, until nothing but those gray eyes remained; space whirled away and reeled—

Bright hot light struck their eyes. Yellow light. They were standing on a brilliantly tiled floor in a brightly glassed-in room overlooking the spaceport of Darkover, and before them, in attitudes of defiance, stood Valdir Alton, Commander Reade—and Larry's father.

CHAPTER THIRTEEN

They had slept. They were rested and fed and re-clothed, Kennard this time in some spare garments of Larry's, and once again they sat before Valdir Alton and Wade Montray and Commander Reade, finishing the tale of their adventures.

Valdir said at last, his face very grave, "I have heard of the *chieri*-folk; but I did not know that any of them still lived, even in the deep woods. And what you tell me of our mixed heritage is strange—and troubling," he added honestly, his eyes meeting those of Wade Montray with a confused newness in them. "Yet the old *chieri* spoke only a truth I already knew. Time and change come to all worlds, even to ours. And if our sons could cross the mountains together in harmony—and neither alone could have lived, but both needed the other's ways—then perhaps our worlds are the same."

"Father," said Kennard gravely, "I decided something on the way back. Don't be angry; it's something I must do. I will do it with your consent now, or without your consent when I come of age. But I am going to take ship for Terra, and learn all that they can teach me there, in their schools. And after me, there will be others."

Valdir Alton looked troubled; but finally he nodded.

"You are a man, free to choose," he said, "and perhaps

the choice is wise. Time only will tell. And you, Lerrys," he added, for Larry had raised his head to speak.

"I want to learn your languages and your history, sir. It's foolish to live here without learning them—not only for me, but for all Terrans who come here."

Valdir nodded again, gravely. "Then you shall do it as a son in my house," he said. "You and my son are *bredin*; our house is yours."

"Ah, some day," Reade said, "a school will be established for sons of both worlds to learn about the other." He looked wryly at the boys and said, "I appoint you both Special Consultants on the Bureau of Terran-Darkovan Liaison. Hurry up and finish that interplanetary education of yours, boys."

"One more thing," Valdir said. "I think we need to learn from Terra about such things as forest fires, and what to do about bandits and banshees. And then, to use the knowledge in our own way." He looked straight at Wade Montray and said, "Forgive me for intruding, but I am Alton. I think you should tell you son, now, why the *chieri* could call them both his kindred."

Wade Montray stood before his son. "You've grown," he said. "You're a man." Then he wet his lips.

"Larry, you were born on Darkover," he said, "of a woman of the high Darkovan caste of the Aldaran, who forsook her people for me, and returned with me to Terra. For years I would not bring you back. I didn't want you torn apart between two worlds, as I had been. I tried to keep you away from Darkover, but the call was too strong for you. As the call had been too strong for me." His face worked. "So you'll be torn between two alien worlds—as I was—"

"But," Larry said quietly, and he stretched a hand to his father, "Darkovans are not alien. Once they were Earthmen. And Earthmen are akin to Darkovans, even those who have not the *chieri* blood in their veins. The call is not of alien worlds—but of blood brothers, who want to understand one another again. It won't be easy. But"—his eyes sought out Kennard's—"it's a beginning."

Wade Montray nodded, slowly and painfully, and Valdir Alton suddenly did a thing unprecedented for a Darkovan aristocrat. Awkwardly, the gesture unpracticed, he held out his hand to Wade Montray, and the two men shook hands, while Commander Reade beamed.

They had, indeed, made a beginning. Trouble would come—as all change brings trouble in its wake. But it was a beginning, and, as with the bringing of fire to the trailmen, the benefits would outweigh the risks.

The first step had been taken.

Larry and Kennard would take the next.

After them, thousands.

The brother worlds were once again reconciled.

THE BLOODY SUN

The stranger who comes home
dos not make himself at home
but makes home strange.

Prologue: Darkover

The Leronis

Leonie Hastur was dead.

The ancient *leronis*, sorceress of the Comyn, Keeper of Arilinn, telepath, trained with all the powers of the matrix sciences of Darkover, died as she had lived, alone, sequestered high in the Tower of Arilinn.

Not even her priestess-novice-apprentice, Janine Leynier of Storn, knew the hour when death came quietly into the Tower and took her away into one of the other worlds she had learned to walk as skillfully as within her own enclosed garden.

She died alone; and she died unmourned. For, although Leonie was feared, revered, worshipped almost as a Goddess throughout all the Domains of Darkover, she was not loved.

Once she had been greatly loved. There had been a time when Leonie Hastur had been a young woman, beautiful and chaste as a distant moon, and poets had written of her glory, comparing her to the exquisitely shining face of Liriel, the great violet moon of Darkover; or to a Goddess come down to live among men. She had been adored by those who lived under her rule at Arilinn Tower. Once, despite the austerity of the vows under which she lived (which would have made it blasphemy unspeakable for any man to touch her fingertips) Leonie had been loved. But that had been long ago.

And now, as the years had passed over her head, leaving her more and more alone, further from humanity, she was loved less; and feared and hated more. The old Regent Lorill Hastur, her twin brother (for Leonie had been born into the royal house of the Hasturs of Hastur, and if she had not chosen the Tower, she would have stood higher than any Queen in the land), was long dead. A nephew she had seen but a few times stood behind the throne of Stefan Hastur-Elhalyn and was the real power in the Domains. But to him Leonie was a whisper, an old tale and a shadow.

And now she was dead and lay, as the custom was, in an unmarked grave within the walls of Arilinn, where no human being save those of Comyn blood might ever come; in death no more secluded than in life. And there were few left alive to weep.

One of the few who wept was Damon Ridenow, who had married years ago into the Domain of Alton, and briefly been Warden of that Domain for the young Heir of Alton, Valdir of Armida.* When Valdir had come of age and taken a wife, Damon and all his household, which was large, had removed to the estate of Mariposa Lake, which lay in the pleasant upland country in the foothills of the Kilghard Hills. When Leonie was young, and Damon was young, and he a mechanic in the Tower of Arilinn, he had loved Leonie; loved her chastely, with never a touch or a kiss or any thought of breaking the vows that bound her. But he had loved her, nonetheless, with a passion that had given form and color to all his life afterward; and when he heard of her death, he went apart to his own study and there he shed the tears he would not shed before his wife or his wife's sister, who had once been Leonie's novice-Keeper at Arilinn, or

*This story is told in *The Forbidden Tower*.

before any of his household. But if they knew of his grief—
and in a household of Comyn telepaths such things could
not well be hidden—no one would speak of it; not even his
grown sons and daughters asked why their father grieved in
secret. Leonie, to them, of course, was only a legend with a
name.

And so, when the news spread through the domains, there
was much excited speculation, even in this most distant of
remote corners in the Domains, about the question that now
quickened and burned all over the Domains, from the
Hellers to the Plains of Arilinn: *Who now will be Keeper of
Arilinn?*

And to Damon, one day soon after that, in the privacy of
his own study, came his youngest daughter Cleindori.

She had been given the old fashioned name, legendary
and traditional, of Dorilys: *Golden-flower*. But as a child her
hair had been pale sunny gold, and her eyes so big and blue
that her nurses dressed her always in blue frocks and blue
ribbons; her foster-mother, Damon's wife Ellemir, said that
she looked like a blue bell of the *kireseth* flower, covered
with its golden pollen. so they had nicknamed her, when she
was only a toddler, Cleindori, *Golden Bell*, which was the
common name for the *kireseth* flower: And as the years
passed, most people had all but forgotten that Dorilys Aillard (for her mother had been a *nedestro* daughter of that
powerful Domain) had ever borne any other name but
Cleindori.

She had grown into a tall, shy, serious young woman,
thirteen years old now, her hair sunny, copper-golden. There
was Drytown blood in the Ridenow clan, and her mother's
father, too, had been, it was whispered, a Drytown bandit
from Shainsa; but that old scandal had been long forgotten.
Damon, looking up at the womanly body and serious eyes of
his last-born daughter, felt for the first time in his life that he
was approaching old age.

"Have you ridden all the way from Armida today, my child? What had your foster-father to say to that?"

Cleindori smiled and went to kiss her father on the cheek. "He said nothing, for I did not tell him," she said gaily, "but I was not alone, for my foster-brother Kennard rode here with me."

Cleindori had been sent to fosterage at nine years old, as the custom was in the Domains, to grow to womanhood under a hand less tender than that of a mother. She had been fostered by Valdir, Lord Alton, whose lady, Lori, had only sons and longed for a daughter to rear. There was a distant understanding that when Cleindori was old enough to marry, she might be wedded to Lord Alton's elder son, Lewis-Arnad; but as yet, Damon supposed, there was not thought in Cleindori of marriage; she and Lewis and Valdir's youngest son Kennard were sister and brothers. Damon greeted Kennard, who was a sturdy, broad-shouldered, grey-eyed boy a year younger than Cleindori, with a kinsman's embrace, and said, "So I see my daughter was well-guarded on her way here. What brings you here, children? Were you hawking and late returning, and chose to ride this way, thinking there would be cakes and sweets for runaways here when there would be only the bread and water of punishment at home?" But he was laughing.

"No," Kennard said seriously. "Cleindori said she must see you; and my mother gave us leave to ride, but I do not think she knew fully what we asked or what she answered, for there was such hullabaloo at Armida on this day, ever since the news has come."

"What news?" Damon asked, leaning forward, but already he knew, and felt his heart sink. Cleindori curled herself up on a cushion at his feet, looking up at him. She said, "Dear father, three days ago the Lady Janine of Arilinn came riding to Armida on her search for one to bear the name and dignity of the Lady of Arilinn who is dead; the *leronis* Leonie."

"It took her long enough to come to Armida," Damon commented with a curl of his lip. "No doubt she had tested in all the Domains before this."

Cleindori nodded. "I think so," she said, "for after she knew who I was, she looked at me as if she smelled something bad, and said, 'Since you are from the Forbidden Tower, have you been taught in any of their heresies?' For when Lady Lori told her my name, she was angry, and I had to tell her that my mother had given me the name of Dorilys. But Janine said, 'Well, by law I am required to test you for *laran*. I cannot deny you that.'"

She screwed up her face in imitation of the *leronis*, and Damon put his hand across the lower part of his face, as if in thought, but actually to conceal a grin; for Cleindori had a knack for mimicry and she had caught the sour tone and disapproving stare of the *leronis* Janine. Damon said, "Aye. Janine was among those who would have had me burned alive or blinded when I fought with Leonie for the right to use the *laran* gods had given me as I myself chose, and not only as Arilinn demanded. It would not make her love you, child, that you are my daughter."

Cleindori smiled again, gaily. "I can live well enough without her love; I can well believe that she has never loved even a pet kitten! But I was trying to tell you, Father, what she said to me and what I said to her . . . she seemed pleased when I told her that you had taught me nothing as yet, and that I had been fostered since I was nine at Armida; and so she gave me a matrix and tested me for *laran*. And when she had done, she said that she wanted me for Arilinn; and then she frowned and told me that she would not have chosen me for this, but that there were few others who could bear the training; and that she wished to train me as Keeper."

Damon's breath caught in his throat; but the cry of protest died unspoken, for Cleindori was looking up at him with her eyes shining. "Father, I told her, as I knew I must, that I could not enter a Tower without my father's consent; and then I rode away here to ask for that consent."

"Which you shall not have," said Damon harshly, "not while I am above ground and unburied. Or after, if I can prevent it."

"But Father—to be Keeper of Arilinn! Not even the Queen—"

Damon's throat tightened. So after all these years the hand of Arilinn was reaching out again toward one that he loved. "Cleindori, no," he said and reached out, touching her fair curls, which shone with the light of alloyed copper and gold. "You see only the power. You do not know the cruelty of that training. To be Keeper—"

"Janine told me. She said that the training is very long and very cruel and very difficult to bear. She told me something of what I must vow and what I must give up. But she said also that she thought I was capable of it."

"Child—" Damon swallowed hard. He said, "Human flesh and blood cannot endure it!"

"Now that is foolish," Cleindori said, "for you endured it, Father. And so did Callista, who was once Leonie's novice-Keeper at Arilinn."

"Have you any idea what it cost Callista, child?"

"You made sure I should know, before I was out of childhood," Cleindori said. "And so, too, did Callista, telling me before I had come to womanhood what a cruel and unnatural life it was. I cut my teeth on that old tale of how you and Callista fought Leonie and all of Arilinn in a duel that lasted nightlong. . . ."

"Has the tale grown so much?" Damon interrupted with a laugh. "It was less than a quarter of an hour; though indeed the storm seemed to rage through many days. But we fought Arilinn; and won the right to use *laran* as we would and not as Arilinn should decree."

"But I can see, too," Cleindori argued, "that you, who were trained in Arilinn, and Callista, too, trained in the Way of Arilinn, are superbly skilled; while those who have been taught *laran* here have fewer skills and are clumsy in the use of their gifts. And I know, too, that all the other Towers in this land still hold to the Way of Arilinn."

"These powers and skills—" Damon paused and collected himself, trying to speak calmly, for he was shouting. Then he said, "Cleindori, since I was a young man I have believed that the Way of Arilinn—and of all the other Towers on whom the people of Arilinn force their will—is cruel and inhuman. I believe this; and I fought, laying my life as forfeit, so that men and women in the Towers need not give up all their lives to a living death, sealed within Tower walls. Such skills as we have can be learned by any man or woman, Comyn or Commoner, if they possess the inborn talent. It is like playing the lute; one is born with an ear for music and can learn the way of plucking the strings, but even for that difficult vocation no one should be asked to give up home and family, life or love. We have taught much to others; and we have won the right to teach them without penalty. A day will come, Cleindori, when the ancient matrix sciences of our world will be free to any who can use them, and the Towers will be no more needed."

"But we are still outcaste," argued Cleindori. "Father, if you had seen Janine's face when she spoke of you, calling it the Forbidden Tower. . . ."

Damon's face tightened. "I do not love Janine so much that her evil opinion of me will lose me any sleep of nights."

"But Cleindori is right," Kennard said. "We are renegades. Here in the countryside people hold to your ways; but all over the Domains they turn only to the Towers to know of *laran*. I too am to go to a Tower, Neskaya perhaps, or perhaps to Arilinn itself, when I have done my three years' service in the Guards; if Cleindori goes to Arilinn, they said I could not go until she had completed her years of seclusion, for a Keeper in training cannot have a foster-brother near, or anyone to whom she is bound by affection—"

"Cleindori is not going to Arilinn," Damon said, "and there's an end of it." And he repeated, even more vehemently, "Human flesh and blood cannot endure the Way of Arilinn!"

"And again I say that is foolish," Cleindori said, "for Callista endured it; and the lady Hilary of Syrtis; and Margwenn of Thendara; and Leominda of Neskaya; and Janine of Arilinn; and Leonie's self; and nine-hundred-and-twenty-odd Keepers before her, so they say. And what they endured, I can endure if I must."

She leaned her chin on her folded hands, looking up at him seriously. "You have told me often enough, since I was only a child, that a Keeper is responsible only to her own conscience. And that everywhere, among the best of women and men, conscience is the only guide for that they do. Father, I feel it is laid upon me to be a Keeper."

"You can be Keeper among us, when you are grown," said Damon, "without such torment as you must endure at Arilinn."

"Oh!" She rose angrily to her feet and began to pace in the chamber. "You are my father, you would keep me always a little girl! Father, do you think I do not know that without the Towers of the Domains, our world is dark with barbarism? I have not been very far abroad, but I have been to Thendara, and I have seen the spaceships of the Terrans there, and I know that we have resisted their Empire only because the Towers give our world what we need, with our ancient matrix sciences. If the Towers go dark, Darkover falls into the hands of the Empire, like a ripe plum, for the people will cry out for the technology and the trade of the Empire!"

Damon said quietly, "I do not think that this is inevitable. I have no hatred for the Terrans; my closest friend was Terran-born, your uncle Ann'dra. But it is for this I am working, that when every Tower is dark, there will be enough *laran* among the populace of the Domains that

Darkover may be independent, and not go begging to the Terrans. That day will come, Cleindori. I tell you, a day will come when every Tower in the Domains stands bare and empty, the haunt of evil birds of prey—"

"Kinsman!" Kennard protested swiftly, and made a quick sign against evil. "Do not say such things!"

"It is not pleasant hearing," Damon said, "but it is true. Every year there are fewer and fewer of our sons and daughters with the power or the will to endure the old training and give themselves over to the Towers. Leonie once complained to me that she had trained six young girls and of them all, only one could complete the training to be Keeper; this was the *leronis* Hilary, and she sickened and would have died if they had not sent her from Arilinn. Three of the Towers—Janine would not tell you this, Cleindori, but I who am Arilinn-trained know it well—three of the Towers are working with a mechanic's circle because they have no Keeper, and their foolish laws will not allow them to take a Keeper to their circles unless she is willing to be a cloistered symbol of virginity. They say her strength and her *laran* powers are less important than that she should be a virgin goddess, sequestered and held in superstitious awe. There are, at a guess, a hundred women or more in the Domains who could do the work of a Keeper, but they see no reason to undergo a training that will make them, not women, but machines for the transmission of power! And I do not blame them! The Towers will go. They must go. And when they are gone, standing bare as ruined monuments to the pride and the madness of the Comyn, the *laran* power, and the matrix stones that help us to use it, can be used as they were meant to be used; science, not sorcery! Sanity, not madness! I have worked for this all my life, Cleindori."

"Not to overthrow the Towers, Uncle!" Kennard sounded shocked.

"No. Never that. But to be there when they have been

abandoned or forsaken, so that our *laran* sciences need not perish for lack of Towers to work them."

Cleindori stood beside him, her hand lightly on his shoulder. She said, "Father, I honor you for this. But your work is too slow, for they still call you outcaste and renegade and worse things. And that is why it is so much more important that young people like I, and like my half-sister Cassilde, and Kennard—"

Damon said, shocked, "Is Cassilde, too, going into Arilinn? It will kill Callista!" For Cassilde was Callista's own daughter, four or five years older than Cleindori.

"She is too old to need consent," Cleindori said. "Father, it is necessary that the Towers shall not die until the time has come, even if the day must come when they are no longer needed. And I feel it laid upon my conscience to be Keeper of Arilinn." She held out her hand to him. "No, Father, listen to me. I know *you* are not ambitious; you flung away the chance to command the City Guard; you could have been the most powerful man in Thendara; but you threw it away. I am not like that. If my *laran* is as powerful as the Lady of Arilinn told me, I want to be Keeper in a way that will let me *do* something useful with it; more than ministering to the peasants and teaching the village children! Father, I want to be Keeper of Arilinn!"

"You would put yourself into that prison from which we freed Callista at such great price!" Damon said, and his voice was unspeakably bitter.

"That was *her* life," Cleindori flared, "this is *mine*! But listen to me, Father," she said, kneeling beside him again. The anger was gone from her voice and a great seriousness had taken its place. "You have told me, and I have seen, that Arilinn declares the laws by which *laran* is used in this land, save for you few here who defy Arilinn."

"They may be doing things otherwise in the Hellers or at Aldaran and beyond," Damon qualified. "I know little of that."

"Then—" Cleindori looked up at him, her round face very serious. "If I go to Arilinn and learn to be Keeper, by their own rules the most orthodox of the ways by which *laran* can be used—if I am Keeper by the Way of Arilinn, then I can change those laws, can I not? If the Keeper of Arilinn makes the rules for all the Towers, then, Father, I can change them, I can declare the truth; that the Way of Arilinn is cruel and inhuman—and because I have succeeded at it, they cannot say I am simply a failure or an outcaste attacking what I myself cannot do. I can change these terrible laws and cast down the Way of Arilinn. And when the Towers no longer give men and women over to a living death, then the young men and women of our world will flock to them, and the old matrix sciences of Darkover will be reborn. But these laws will never be changed—not until a Keeper of Arilinn can change them!"

Damon looked at his daughter, shaken. It was indeed the only way in which Arilinn's cruel laws could be changed; that a Keeper of Arilinn should herself declare a new decree that should be binding on all the Towers. He had tried his best, but he was renegade, outcaste; he could do nothing from outside the walls of Arilinn. He had accomplished little—no one knew better than he how little he had accomplished.

"Father, it is fated," Cleindori said, and her young voice trembled. "After all Callista suffered, after all you suffered, perhaps it was all for this, that I should go back and free those others. Now that you have proven that they can be freed."

"You are right," Damon admitted, slowly. "The Way of Arilinn will never be thrown down until the Keeper of Arilinn herself shall throw it down. But—oh, Cleindori, not you!" Agonized, despairing, he clasped his daughter to him. "Not you, darling!"

Gently she freed herself from his embrace, and for a moment it seemed to Damon that she was already tall, impres-

sive, aloof, touched with the alien strength of the Keeper,
clothed in the crimson majesty of Arilinn. She said, "Father,
dear Father, you cannot forbid me to do this; I am responsible only to my own conscience. How often have you said to
all of us, beginning with my foster-father Valdir, who never
tires of repeating it to me, that conscience is the only responsibility? Let me do this; let me finish the work you have
begun in the Forbidden Tower. Otherwise, when you die, it
will all die with you, a little band of renegades and their
heresies perishing unseen and good riddance. But I can
bring it to Arilinn, and then all over the Domains; for the
Keeper of Arilinn makes the laws for all the Towers and all
the Domains. Father, I tell you, it is fated. I *must* go to Arilinn."

Damon bowed his head, still reluctant, but unable to
speak against her young and innocent sureness. It seemed to
him that already the walls of Arilinn were closing around
her. And so they parted, not to meet again until the hour of
her death.

CHAPTER ONE

The Terran

Forty Years Later

This is the way it was.

You were an orphan of space. For all you knew, you might have been born on one of the Big Ships; the ships of Terra; the starships that made the long runs between stars doing the business of the Empire. You never knew where you had been born, or who your parents had been; the first home you knew was the Spacemen's Orphanage, almost within sight of the Port of Thendara, where you learned loneliness. Before that somewhere there had been strange colors and lights and confused images of people and places that sank into oblivion when you tried to focus on them, nightmares that sometimes made you sit up and shriek out in terror before you got yourself all the way awake and saw the clean quiet dormitory around you.

The other children were the abandoned flotsam of the arrogant and mobile race of Earth, and you were one of them, with one of their names. But outside lay the darkly beautiful world you had seen, that you still saw, sometimes, in your dreams. You knew, somehow, that you were different; you belonged to that world outside, that sky, that sun; not the clean, white, sterile world of the Terran Trade City.

You would have known it even if they hadn't told you;

but they told you often enough. Oh, not in words; in a hundred small subtle ways. And anyway you were different, a difference you could feel all the way down to your bones. And then there were the dreams.

But the dreams faded; first to memories of dreams, and then to memories of memories. You only knew that *once* you had remembered something other than this.

You learned not to ask about your parents, but you guessed. Oh, yes, you guessed. And as soon as you were old enough to endure the thrust of a spaceship kicking away from a planet under interstellar drives, they stuck your arm full of needles and they carried you, like a piece of sacked luggage, aboard one of the Big Ships.

Going home, the other boys said, half envious and half afraid. Only you had known better; you were going into exile. And when you woke up, with a fuzzy sick headache, and the feeling that somebody had sliced a big hunk out of your life, the ship was making planetfall for a world called Terra, and there was an elderly couple waiting for the grandson they had never seen.

They said you were twelve or so. They called you Jefferson Andrew Kerwin, Junior. That was what they'd called you in the Spacemen's Orphanage, so you didn't argue. Their skin was darker than yours and their eyes dark, the eyes you'd learned to call animal eyes from your Darkovan nurses; but they'd grown up under a different sun and you already knew about the quality of light; you'd seen the bright lights inside the Terran Zone and remembered how they hurt your eyes. So you were willing to believe it, that these strange dark old people could have been your father's parents. They showed you a picture of a Jefferson Andrew Kerwin when he was about your age, thirteen, a few years before he'd run away as cargo boy on one of the Big Ships, years and years ago. They gave you his room to sleep in, and sent you to his school. They were kind to you, and not more than twice a week did they remind you, by word or look, that you were not the son they had lost, the son who had abandoned them for the stars.

And they never answered questions about your mother, either. They couldn't; they didn't know and they didn't want to know, and what was more, they didn't care. You were Jefferson Andrew Kerwin, of Earth, and that was all they wanted of you.

If it had come when you were younger, it might have been enough. You were hungry to belong somewhere, and the yearning love of these old people, who needed you to be their lost son, might have claimed you for Earth.

But the sky of Earth was a cold burning blue, and the hills a cold unfriendly green, the pale blazing sun hurt your eyes, even behind dark glasses, and the glasses made people think you were trying to hide from them. You spoke the language perfectly—they'd seen to *that* in the orphanage, of course. You could pass. You missed the cold, and the winds that swept down from the pass behind the city, and the distant outline of the high, splintered teeth of the mountains; you missed the dusty dimness of the sky, and the lowered, crimson, blazing eye of the sun. Your grandparents didn't want you to think about Darkover or talk about Darkover and once when you saved up your pocket money and bought a set of views taken out in the Rim planets, one of them with a sun like your home sun of Darkover, they took the pictures away from you. You belonged right here on Earth, or so they told you.

But you knew better than that. And as soon as you were old enough, you left. You knew that you were breaking their hearts all over again, and in a way it wasn't fair because they had been kind to you, as kind as they knew how to be. But you left; you had to. Because you knew, if they didn't, that Jeff Kerwin, Junior, wasn't the boy they loved. Probably, if it came to that, the *first* Jeff Kerwin, your father, hadn't been that boy either, and that was why *he* had left. They loved something they had made up for themselves and called their son, and perhaps, you thought, they'd even be happier with memories and no real boy around to destroy that image of their perfect son.

First there was a civilian's job in the Space Service on Earth, and you worked hard and kept your tongue between your teeth when the arrogant *Terranan* stared at your height or made subtle jokes about the accent you'd never—quite—lost. And then there was the day when you boarded one of the Big Ships, awake this time, and willingly, and warranted in the Civil Service of the Empire, skylifting for stars that were names in the roll call of your dreams. And you watched the hated sun of Earth dwindle to a dim star, and lose itself in the immensity of the big dark, and you were outward bound on the first installment of your dream.

Not Darkover. Not yet. But a world with a red sun that didn't hurt your eyes, for a subordinate's job on a world of stinks and electric storms, where albino women were cloistered behind high walls and you never saw a child. And after a year there, there was a good job on a world where men carried knives and the women wore bells in their ears, chiming a wicked allure as they walked. You had liked it there. You had had plenty of fights, and plenty of women. Behind the quiet civil clerk there was a roughneck buried; and on that world he got loose now and then. You'd had good times. It was on that world that you started carrying a knife. Somehow it seemed right to you; you felt a sense of completion when you strapped it on, as if somehow, until now, you had been going around half dressed. You talked this over with the company Psych, and listened to his conjectures about hidden fears of sexual adequacy and compensation with phallic symbols and power compulsions; listened quietly and without comment, and dismissed them, because you knew better than that. He did ask one telling question.

"You were brought up on Cottman Four, weren't you, Kerwin?"

"In the Spacemen's Orphanage there."

"Isn't that one of the worlds where grown men wear swords at all times? Granted, I'm no comparative anthropologist, but if you saw men going around wearing them, all the time. . . ."

You agreed that probably that was it, and didn't say any more, but you kept on wearing the knife, at least when you were off duty, and once or twice you'd had a chance to use it, and proved quietly and to your own satisfaction that you could handle yourself in a fight if you had to.

You had good times there. You could have stayed there and been happy. But there was still a compulsion driving you, a restlessness, and when the Legate died and the new one wanted to bring in his own men, you were ready to leave.

And by now the apprentice years were over. Until now you'd gone where they told you. Now they asked you, within reason, where you wanted to go. And you never hesitated.

"Darkover." And then you amended: "Cottman Four."

The man in Personnel had stared awhile. "God in heaven, why would anyone want to go *there*?"

"No vacancies?" By now you were half resigned to letting the dream die.

"Oh, hell, yes. We can never get volunteers to go there. Do you know what the place is *like*? Cold as sin, among other things, and barbaric—big sections of it barred off to Earthmen, and you won't be safe a step outside the Trade City. I've never been there myself, but the place, from what I hear, is always in an uproar. Added to which there's practically no trade with the Darkovans."

"No? Thendara Spaceport is one of the biggest in the Service, I heard."

"True." The man explained gloomily, "It's located between the upper and lower spiral arms of the Galaxy, so we have to recruit enough personnel to staff a major re-routing station. Thendara's one of the main stops and transfer points for passengers and cargo. But it's a hell of a place; if you go there, you might be stuck for years before they could locate a replacement for you, once you get tired of it. Look," he added persuasively, "you're getting on too well to throw yourself away out there. Rigel 9 is crying out for good men, and you could really get ahead there—maybe work up to Consul or even Legate, if you wanted to get into the Diplomatic branch. Why waste yourself on a half-frozen lump of rock way out at the edge of nowhere?"

You should have known better; but you thought, for once, maybe he really wanted to know; so you told him.

"I was born on Darkover."

"Oh. One of *those*. I see." You saw his face change, and you wanted to smash that smirk off his pink face. But you didn't do it; you only stood there and watched him stamp your transfer application, and you knew that if you had ever had any intention of transfer to the Diplomatic Branch, or any hopes of working up to Legate, whatever he had stamped on your card had just killed them off; but you didn't care. And then there was another of the Big Ships, and a growing excitement that gnawed at you so that you haunted the observation dome, searching for a red coal in the sky that grew at last to a blaze haunting your dreams. And then, after a time that seemed endless, the ship dropped lazily toward a great crimson planet that wore a necklace of four tiny moons, jewels set in the pendant of a carmine sky.

And you were home again.

CHAPTER TWO

The Matrix

The *Southern Crown* made planet-fall at high noon on dayside. Jeff Kerwin, swinging efficiently down the narrow steel rungs of the ladder from the airlock, dropped to the ground and took a deep breath. It had seemed that the very air should hold something rich and different and familiar and strange.

But it was just air. It smelled good, but after weeks of the canned air inside the spaceship, any air would smell good. He inhaled it again, searching for some hint of his elusive memory in the fragrance. It was cold and bracing, with a hint of pollen and dust; but mostly it held the impersonal chemical stinks of any spaceport. Hot tar. concrete dust. The stinging ozone of liquid oxygen vaporizing from bleeder valves.

Might as well be back Earthside! Just another spaceport!

Well, what the hell! He told himself roughly to come off it. *The way you built it up in your mind, getting back to Darkover, you made it such a big deal that if the whole city came out to meet you with parades and fanfares, it would still fall flat!*

He stepped back, out of the way of a group of Spaceforce men—tall in black leather, booted, blasters concealing their menace behind snug holsters—with stars blazing on their sleeves. The sun was just a fraction off the meridian—huge,

red-orange, with little ragged fiery clouds hanging high in
the thin sky. The saw-toothed mountains behind the spaceport cast their shadows over the Trade City, but the peaks lay
bathed in the sullen light. Memory searched for landmarks
along the peaks. Kerwin's eyes fixed on the horizon, he
stumbled over a cargo bale, and a good-natured voice said,
"Star-gazing, Redhead?"

Kerwin brought himself back to the spaceport, with a
wrench almost physical. "I've seen enough stars to last me
awhile," he said. "I was thinking that the air smells good."

The man at his side grinned. "That's one comfort. I spent
one tour of duty on a world where the air was high-sulfur
content. Perfectly healthy, or so the Medics said, but I went
around feeling as if someone had thrown a whole case of
rotten eggs at me."

He joined Kerwin on the concrete platform. "What's it
like—being home again?"

"I don't know yet," said Kerwin, but he looked at the
newcomer with something like affection. Johnny Ellers was
small and stocky and going bald on top, a tough little man in
the black leather of a professional spaceman. Two dozen
stars blazed in a riot of color on his sleeve; a star for every
world where he had seen service. Kerwin, only a two-star
man so far, had found Ellers a fund of information about almost every planet and every subject under the sun—any sun.

"We'd better move along," Ellers said. The process crew
was already swarming over the ship, readying it for skylift
again within a few hours. Favorable orbits waited for no
man. The spaceport was already jammed with cargo trucks,
workhands, buzzing machinery, fuel trucks, and instructions
were being yelled in fifty languages and dialects. Kerwin
looked around, getting his bearings. Beyond the spaceport
gates lay the Trade City, the Terran Headquarters Building—and Darkover. He wanted to run toward it, but he
checked himself, moving with Ellers into the line that was
forming, to verify their identities and assignments. He gave

up a fingerprint and signed a card verifying that he was who he said he was, received an identity certificate, and moved on.

"Where to?" asked Ellers, joining him again.

"I don't know," Kerwin said slowly. "I suppose I'd better report to the HQ for assignment." He had no formal plans beyond this moment, and he wasn't sure he wanted Ellers butting in and taking over. Much as he liked Ellers, he would have preferred to get reacquainted with Darkover on his own.

Ellers chuckled. "Report? Hell, you know better than that. You're no greenie, still bug-eyed about his first off-planet assignment! Tomorrow morning is time enough for the red tape. For tonight—" He waved an expansive hand toward the spaceport gates. "Wine, women and song—not necessarily in that order."

Kerwin hesitated, and Ellers urged, "Come on! I know the Trade City like the back of my hand. You've got to fit yourself out—and I know all the markets. If you do your shopping at the tourist traps, you can spend six months' pay without half trying!"

That was true. The Big Ships were still too weight-conscious to permit transshipping of clothing and personal gear. It was cheaper to dispose of everything when you transferred, and buy a new outfit when you landed, than to take it along and pay the weight allowances. Every spaceport in the Terran Empire was surrounded with a ring of shops, good, and indifferent, all the way from luxury fashion centers to second-hand rag markets.

"And I know all the high spots, too. You haven't lived till you've tried Darkovan *fifi*. You know, back in the mountains they tell some funny stories about that stuff, especially its effect on women. One time, I remember—"

Kerwin let Ellers lead, listening with half an ear to the little man's story, which was already taking a familiar turn. To hear Ellers talk, he had had so many women, on so many worlds, that Kerwin sometimes wondered vaguely how he'd had time in between to get into space. The heroines of the stories ranged all the way from a Sirian bird-woman, with great blue wings and a cloak of down, to a princess of Arcturus IV surrounded by the handmaidens who are bound to her with links of living pseudoflesh till the day she dies.

The spaceport gates opened into a great square, surrounding a monument raised on high steps, and a little park with trees. Kerwin looked at the trees, their violet leaves trembling in the wind, and swallowed.

Once he had known the Trade City fairly well. It had grown some since then—and it had shrunk. The looming skyscraper of Terran HQ, once awesome, was now just a big building. The ring of shops around the square was deeper. He did not remember having seen, as a child, the loom of the massive, neon-fronted Sky Harbor Hotel. He sighed, trying to sort out the memories.

They crossed the square and turned into a street paved with hewn blocks of stone, so immense in size that it paralyzed his imagination to guess who or what had laid down those vast slabs. The street lay quiet and empty; Kerwin supposed that most of the Terran population had gone to see the starship touch down, and at this hour few Darkovans would be on the street. The real city still lay out of sight, out of hearing—out of reach. He sighed again, and followed Ellers toward the string of spaceport shops.

"We can get a decent outfit in here."

It was a Darkovan shop, which meant that it spilled out halfway along the street and there was no clear distinction between outside and in, between the merchandise for sale and the owner's belongings. But this much concession had been made to custom of the alien Terrans, that some of the goods for sale were on racks and tables. As Kerwin passed beneath the outer arch, his nostrils dilated in recognition of a breath of the familiar; a whiff of scented smoke, the incense that perfumes every Darkovan home from gutter to palace. They hadn't used it, not officially, in the Spacemen's Orphanage in the Trade City; but most of the nurses and matrons were Darkovan, and the resinous fumes had clung to their hair and clothing. Ellers wrinkled his nose and made an "Ugh!" sound, but Kerwin found himself smiling. It was the first touch of genuine recognition in a world gone strange.

The shopkeeper, a little withered man in a yellow shirt and breeches, turned and murmured an idle formula: "*S'dia Shaya.*" It meant *you lend me grace*, and without thinking about it, Kerwin muttered an equally meaningless polite formula; and Ellers stared.

"I didn't know you spoke the lingo! You told me you left here when you were just a kid!"

"I only speak the City dialect." The little man was turning to a colorful rack of cloaks, jerkins, silken vests and tunics, and Kerwin, exasperated with himself, said curtly in Terran Standard, "Nothing like that. Clothing for *Terranan*, fellow."

He concentrated on picking out a few changes of clothing—underwear, nightgear, just what he could get along with for a few days until he found out what the job and climate would demand. There were heavy mountain-weight parkas, intended for the mountains in the climbing preserves of Rigel and Capella Nine, lined with synthetic fibers, guaranteed to safeguard body heat down to minus thirty Centigrade or well below, and he shrugged it aside, though Ellers, shivering, had already bought one and put it on; it wasn't *that* cold even in the Hellers, and here in Thendara it felt like shirtsleeve weather to him. He warned Ellers in an undertone against buying shaving gear.

"Hell, Kerwin, going native? Going to grow a beard?"

"No, but you'll get better ones in the Service canteens inside the HQ: Darkover is metal-poor, and what metals they have aren't as good as ours, and cost a hell of a lot more."

While the shopkeeper was making up the parcels, Ellers drifted to a table near the entry-way.

"What sort of outfit is this, Kerwin? I've never seen anyone on Darkover wearing anything quite like *this*. Is it native Darkovan costume?"

Kerwin flinched; *native Darkovan costume* was a concept, like *the Darkovan language*, which consisted only in the simplifications of Empire outsiders. There were nine Darkovan languages he knew about—although he could speak only one well, with a smattering of words from two others—and costume on Darkover varied enormously, from the silks and fine-spun colors of the lowlands to the coarse leathers and undyed furs of the far mountains. He joined his friend at the table, where a tangle of odd garments, all more or less worn, most of them the utilitarian coarse breeches and shirts of the city, were flung at random there; but Kerwin saw at once what had attracted Eller's eye. It was a thing of beauty, green and dull yellows blended, richly embroidered in patterns that seemed familiar to him; he suspected he was more fatigued than he realized. He held it up and saw that it was a long, hooded cloak.

"It's a riding-cape," he said. "They wear them in the Kilghard Hills; and from the embroidery it probably belonged to a nobleman; could be his house colors, though I don't know what it signifies, or how it came here. They're warm and they're comfortable, especially for riding, but even when I was a kid, this kind of cloak was going out of fashion down here in the city; stuff like that—" he pointed to the offworld synthetic parka Ellers was wearing—"was cheaper and just as warm. These cloaks are handmade, hand dyed, hand embroidered." He took the cloak from Ellers. It was not a woven fabric, but a soft, supple leather, fine as woven wool, flexible as silk, and richly embroidered in metallic threads: The rich dyes were a riot of color spilling over his arm.

"It looks as if it had been made for a prince," commented Ellers in an undertone. "Look at the fur! What kind of beast is *that* from?"

The shopkeeper burst out into a voluble sales pitch about the costliness of the fur, scenting customers; but Kerwin laughed and cut him off with a gesture.

"Rabbithorn," he said. "They raise them like sheep. If it was wild *marl*-fur, this *would* be a cloak for a prince. As it is, I suppose it belonged to some poor gentleman attached to a nobleman's household—one with a talented and industrious wife or daughter who could spend a year embroidering it for him."

"But the embroideries, nobles, the patterns, fit for *Comyn*, the richness of the dyed leather . . ."

"What it looks, is *warm*," Kerwin said, settling the cloak over his shoulders. It felt very soft and rich. Ellers stepped back, regarding him with consternation.

"Good lord, are you going native already? You aren't going to wear *that* thing around the Terran Zone, are you?"

Kerwin laughed heartily. "I should say not. I was thinking it might be something to wear around my room in the evenings. If bachelor quarters in HQ are anything like they were at my last assignment, they're damn stingy with the heat, unless you want to pay a double assessment for energy use. And it gets fairly cold in the winter, too. Of course it's nice and warm here now—"

Ellers shivered and said gloomily, "If this is *warm*, I hope I'm at the other end of the Galaxy when it gets *cold*! Man, your bones must be made of some kind of stuff I don't understand. This is *freezing*! Oh, well, one man's planet is another man's hell," he said, quoting a proverb of the Service. "But man, you aren't going to spend a month's pay on that damn thing are you?"

"Not if I can help it," Kerwin replied out of the corner of his mouth, "but if you don't shut up and let me bargain with him, I just might!"

In the end he paid more than he had expected, and told himself he was a fool as he counted it over. But he wanted the thing, for no reason he could explain; it was the first

thing that had taken his fancy after his return to Darkover.
He wanted it, and in the end he got it for a price he could afford, though not easily. He sensed, toward the end of the
bargaining, that the shopkeeper was uneasy, for some reason, about haggling with him, and gave in much easier than
Kerwin had expected. He knew, if Ellers didn't, that he had
really gotten the thing for somewhat less than its value. Considerably less, if the truth be told.

"That kind of money would have kept you happily drunk
for half a year," Ellers mourned as they came out on the
street again.

Kerwin chuckled. "Cheer up. Fur isn't a luxury on a
planet like this, it's a good investment. And I've still got
enough in my pocket for the first round of drinks. Where can
we get them?"

They got them in a wineshop on the outer edge of the sector; it was clear of tourists, although a few of the workhands
from the spaceport were mingled with the Darkovans
crowded around the bar or sprawled on the long couches
along the walls. They were all giving their attention to the
serious business of drinking, talking, or gambling with what
looked like dominoes or small cut-crystal prisms.

A few of the Darkovans glanced up as the two Earthmen
threaded their way through the crowd and sat down at a
table. Ellers had cheered up by the time a plump, dark-
haired girl came to take their order. He gave the girl a pinch
on her round thigh, ordered winc in the spaceport jargon,
and, hauling the Darkovan cloak across the table to feel the
fur, launched into a long tale about how he had found a particular fur blanket particularly worthwhile on a cold planet
of Lyra.

"The nights up there are about seven days long, and the
people there just shut down all their work until the sun
comes up again and melts off the ice. I tell you, that babe
and I just crawled inside that fur blanket and never put our
noses outside . . ."

Kerwin applied himself to his drink, losing the thread of the story—not that it mattered, for Ellers's stories were all alike anyhow. A man sitting at one of the tables alone, over a half-emptied goblet, looked up, met Kerwin's eyes, and suddenly got up—so quickly that he upset his chair. He started to come toward the table where they were sitting; then he saw Ellers, whose back had been turned to him, stopped short and took a step backward, seeming both confused and surprised. But at that moment Ellers, reaching a lull in his story, looked round and grinned.

"Ragan, you old so-and-so! Might have known I'd find you in here! How long has it been, anyhow? Come and have a drink!"

Ragan hesitated, and it seemed to Kerwin that he flicked an uneasy glance in his direction.

"Ah, come on," Ellers urged. "Want you to meet a pal of mine. Jeff Kerwin."

Ragan came and sat down. Kerwin couldn't make out what the man was. He was small and slight, with a lithe sunburnt look, the look of an outdoor man, and callused hands; he might have been an undersized mountain Darkovan, or an Earthman wearing Darkovan clothes, though he wore the ubiquitous climbing jacket and calf-high boots. But he spoke Terran Standard as well as either of the Earthmen, asking Ellers about the trip out, and when the second round of drinks came, he insisted on paying for them. But he kept looking at Kerwin sidewise, when he thought he wouldn't be noticed.

Kerwin demanded at last: "All right, what is it? You acted as if it was me you recognized, before Ellers called you over—"

"Right. I didn't know Ellers was in yet," Ragan said, "but then I saw him with you, and saw you wearing—" He gestured at Kerwin's Terran outfit. "So I knew you couldn't be who I thought you were. I *don't* know you, do I?" he added, with a puzzled frown.

"I don't think so," Kerwin said, sizing the man up, and wondering if he could have been one of the kids from the Spaceman's Orphanage. It was impossible to tell, after—how long? Ten or twelve years, Terran reckoning; he'd forgotten the conversion factors for the Darkovan year. Even if they'd been childhood friends, that amount of time would have wiped it out. And he didn't remember anyone named Ragan, although that didn't mean anything.

"But you're not Terran, are you," Ragan inquired.

The memory of a clerk's sneer—*one of those*—rushed through Kerwin's mind; but he shoved it aside. "My father was. I was born here, brought up in the Spaceman's Orphanage. I left pretty young, though."

"That must be it," Ragan said. "I spent a few years there. I do liaison work for the Trade City when they have to hire Darkovans: guides, mountaineers, that kind of thing. Organize caravans into the mountains, into the other Trade cities, whatever."

Kerwin was still trying to decide whether the man had a recognizably Darkovan accent. He finally asked him. "Are you Darkovan?"

Ragan shrugged. The bitterness in his voice was really appalling. "Who knows? For that matter, who cares?"

He lifted his glass and drank. Kerwin followed suit, sensing that he would be drunk fairly soon; he never was much of a drinker and the Darkovan liquor, which of course as a child he had never tasted, was strong stuff. It didn't seem to matter. Ragan was staring again and that didn't seem to matter either.

Kerwin thought, *Maybe we're a lot the same. My mother was probably Darkovan; if she'd been Terran, there'd have been records. She could have been anything. My father was in the Space Service; that's the one thing I know for sure. But apart from that, who and what am I? And how did he come to have a halfbreed son?*

"At least he cared enough to get Empire citizenship for

you," Ragan said bitterly, and Jeff stared, not realizing that he had actually been saying all this aloud. "Mine didn't even care that much!"

"But you've got red hair," Jeff said and wondered why he had said it, but Ragan seemed not to hear, staring into his glass, and Ellers interrupted, with an air of injury:

"Listen, you two, this is supposed to be a celebration! Drink up!"

Ragan leaned his chin in his hands, staring across the table at Kerwin. "So you came here, at least partly, to try and locate your parents—your people?"

"To find out something about them," Kerwin amended.

"Had it ever occurred to you that you might be better off not knowing?"

It had. He'd been all the way through that and out the other side. "I don't care if my mother was one of those girls," he said, nodding toward the women who were coming and going, fetching drinks, stopping to chaff with the men, exchanging jokes and innuendos. "I want to *know* about it."

To be sure which world can claim me, Darkover or Terra. To be certain . . .

"But aren't there records at the orphanage?"

"I haven't had a chance to look," Kerwin said. "That's the first place to go, anyhow. I don't know how much they can tell me. But it's a good place to start."

Kerwin fumbled, with fingers made clumsy by drink, at the copper chain that had been around his neck as long as he could remember. He said, "Only this. They told me, in the orphanage, that it was around my neck when I came there."

They didn't like it. The matron told me I was too big to wear lucky charms, and tried to get it away from me. I screamed . . . why had I forgotten that? . . . and fought so hard that they finally let me keep it. Why in the hell would I do that? My grandparents didn't like it, either, and I learned to keep it out of sight.

"Oh, nuts," interrupted Ellers rudely. "The long-lost talisman! So you'll show it to them and they'll recognize that you're the long-lost son and heir to the Lord High Muckety-Muck in his castle, and you'll live happily ever after!" He made an indescribable sound of derision. Kerwin felt angry color flooding his face. If Ellers really believed that rubbish. . . .

"Can I have a look at it?" Ragan asked, holding out his hand.

Kerwin slipped the chain off his neck; but when Ragan would have taken it, he cradled it in his palm; it had always made him nervous for anyone else to touch it. He had never wanted to ask them, in Psych, just why. They probably would have had a pat and ready answer, something slimy about his subconscious mind.

The chain was of copper, a valuable metal on Darkover. But the blue stone itself had always seemed unremarkable to him; a cheap trinket, something a poor girl might treasure; not even carved, just a pretty blue crystal, a bit of glass.

But Ragan's eyes narrowed as he looked at it, and he gave a low whistle. "By the wolf of Alar! You know what this is, Kerwin?"

Kerwin shrugged. "Some semiprecious stone from the Hellers, I suppose. I'm no geologist."

"It's a matrix jewel," Ragan said, and at Kerwin's blank stare, elaborated, "a psychokinetic crystal."

"I'm lost," Ellers said, and stretched out his hand to take the small gem. Quickly, protectively, Kerwin closed his hand over it, and Ragan raised his eyebrows.

"Keyed?"

"I don't know what you're talking about," Kerwin said, "only I somehow don't like people touching it. Silly, I suppose."

"Not at all," Ragan said, and suddenly seemed to make up his mind.

"I have one," he said. "Nothing like that size; a little one, the kind they sell in the markets for suitcase locks and children's toys. One like yours—well, they don't just lie around in the street, you know; it's probably worth a small fortune, and if it was ever monitored on any of the main banks, it won't be hard to tell who it belonged to. But even the little ones like mine—" He took a small wrapped roll of leather out of an inside pocket and carefully unrolled the leather. A tiny blue crystal rolled out.

"They're like that," he said. "Maybe they have a low-level form of life, no one has ever figured out. Anyway, they're definitely one-man jewels; seal a lock with one of them, and nothing will ever open it except your own *intention* to open it."

"Are you saying they're magic?" Ellers demanded angrily.

"Hell, no. They register your brainwaves and their distinct EEG patterns, or something like that; like a fingerprint. So somehow you are the only person who can open that lock; a great way to protect your private papers. That's what I use this one for. Oh, I can do a few tricks with it."

Kerwin stared at the small blue jewel in Ragan's palm. It was smaller than his own, but the same distinctive color. He repeated it slowly: "Matrix jewel."

Ellers, sobering briefly, stared at Kerwin and said, "Yeah. The big secret of Darkover. The Terrans have been trying to beg, borrow, or steal some of the secrets of matrix technology for generations. There was a big war fought here about that, twelve, twenty years ago—I don't remember, long before my time. Oh, the Darkovans bring little ones into the Trade City, like Ragan's there, and sell them; trade them off for drugs, or metals, usually daggers, or small tools, or camera lenses. Somehow, they transform energy without fission by-products. But they're so small; we keep hearing rumors of big ones. Bigger ones even than yours, Jeff. But no Darkovan will talk about them. Hey," he said, grinning, "maybe you *are* the lost heir to the Lord High Muckety-Muck in his castle after all! It's for sure no bar girl would be wearing a thing like that!"

Kerwin cradled the thing in his hand, but he did not look at it. It made his eyes blur with a strange dizzy sickness. He tucked it inside his shirt again. He did not like the way Ragan was staring at him. Somehow it *reminded* him of something.

Ragan shoved his own small crystal—it was no longer than the bead a woman might braid at the end of a long tress—toward Kerwin. He said, "Can you look into it?"

Someone had said that to him before. At some time someone had said, Look into the matrix. *A woman's voice, low. Or had she said,* Do not look into the matrix. . . . His head hurt. Pettishly he pushed the stone away. Ragan's eyebrows went up again in appraisal. "That much, huh? Can you use yours?"

"Use it? How? I don't know *one damn thing* about it," he said rudely. Ragan shrugged; he said, "I can only do tricks with mine. Watch."

He up-ended the rough green-glass goblet to drink the last few drops from it, then turned it bottom-up and laid the tiny blue crystal on the foot of the goblet. His face took on an intent, concentrated stare; abruptly there was a small eye-hurting flash, a sizzling sound, and the rigid stem of goblet melted, sagged sidewise, slid into a puddle of green glass. Ellers gasped and swore. Kerwin passed his hand over his eyes; the goblet sat there, bowed down with the wilted stem. There was a Terran artist, he remembered from a course in art history, who had painted things like fur teacups and limp watches. History had judged him a lunatic, rather than a genius. The goblet, stem lolling to one side, looked just as surrealistic as his work.

"Could I do that? Could anybody?"

"With one the size of yours, you could do a hell of a lot more," Ragan said, "if you knew how to use it. I don't know how they work; but if you concentrate on them, they can move small objects, produce intense heat, or—well, other things. It doesn't take much training to play around with the ones this size."

Kerwin touched the lump at his chest. He said, "Then it isn't just a trinket."

"Hell, no. It's worth a small fortune—maybe a big one; I'm no judge. I'm surprised they didn't take it away from you before you left Darkover, considering how hard the Terrans have been trying to get hold of some of the larger ones, to experiment with them and test their limits."

Another of those dim memories surfaced. Drugged, on the Big Ship that had taken him to Terra, a stewardess or attendant of some sort fumbling with the jewel; waking, screaming, nightmares. He had thought it a side-effect of the drugs. He said somberly, "I think maybe they tried."

"I'm sure the authorities at the HQ would give a lot to have one that size to play around with," Ragan said. "You might consider turning it over to them; they'd probably give you anything you wanted for it, within reason. You might be able to get a really good assignment out of them."

Kerwin grinned. He said, "since I feel like hell whenever I take it off, that would present—some difficulties."

"You mean you never take it off?" Ellers demanded drunkenly. "That must present some troubles. You don't take it off even in the bath?"

Kerwin said, with a chuckle, "Oh, I *can*. I don't like to; I feel—oh, I don't know, *weird*—when I take it off. Or leave it off for any amount of time." He had always berated himself for being superstitious, irrational, compulsive, treating the thing as a fetish.

Ragan shook his head. "Like I say, they're a strange kind of thing. They—hell, this makes no sense, but it *happens*: I don't know how it works, I just know it does; maybe they *are* a low form of life. See, they *attach* themselves to you; you can't just walk away and leave them behind, and nobody I heard of ever lost one. I know a man who kept losing his keys until he got one of these to tag on his keyring, and whenever he left it behind, believe me, he *knew* where it was."

That, Kerwin thought, explained a lot. Including a child, screaming as if he were half his age, when a Terran no-nonsense matron deprived him of his "lucky charm." They had had to give it back to him in the end. He wondered, with a shiver, what would have happened if they had *not*. He didn't think he wanted to know. He touched the hidden jewel again, shaking his head, remembering his childish sureness that this held the key to his hidden past, to his identity and the identity of his mother, to his obscured memories and half-forgotten dreams.

"Of course," he said with heavy irony, "I was hoping it was that amulet that really *would* prove I was the long-lost son and heir of your Lord-High-Something-or-Other. Now all my illusions have been shattered." He raised the goblet to his lips, calling the Darkovan girl to bring them more of the same.

And as he did so, his eyes fell on the goblet whose stem Ragan had melted. Hell, was he drunker than he'd ever believed?

The goblet stood upright on a solid green stem, unbroken, unsagging. There was nothing whatever wrong with it.

CHAPTER THREE

The Strangers

Three drinks later Ragan excused himself, saying he had a commission at the HQ and had to report on it before he could get paid. When he had gone, Kerwin scowled impatiently at Ellers, who had matched Ragan drink for drink. This wasn't the way he had wanted to spend his first night back on the world whose image he'd carried in his mind since childhood. He didn't know quite what he *did* want—but it wasn't to sit in a spaceport bar all night and get drunk!

"Look, Ellers—"

Only a gentle snore answered him; Ellers had slid down in his seat, out cold.

The plump Darkovan bar girl came with refills—Kerwin had lost track of how many—and looked at Ellers with a professional mixture of disappointment and resignation. Then, with a quick glance at Kerwin, he could see her shift her focus of interest; bending to pour, she brushed artfully against Kerwin. Her loose robe was unpinned at the throat so that he could see the valley between her breasts, and the familiar sweet smell of incense clung to her robe and her hair. A thread of awareness plucked a string deep in his gut, as he breathed in the scent of Darkover, of woman; but he looked again and saw that her eyes were hard and shallow, and the music of her voice frayed at the edges when she crooned, "You like what you see, big man?"

She spoke broken Terran Standard, not the musical idiom of the City dialect; that, Kerwin knew afterward, was what had bothered him most. "You like Lomie, big man? You come 'long with me, I nice and warm, you see . . ."

There was a flat taste in Kerwin's mouth that wasn't just the aftertaste of the wine. Whatever the sky and sun, whatever they called the world, the girls around the Terran Trade City bars were all the same.

"You come? You come—?"

Without knowing quite what he was going to do, Kerwin grabbed the edge of the table and heaved himself up, the bench going over with a crash behind him. He loomed over the girl, glaring through the dim and smoky light, and words in a language long forgotten rushed from his lips:

"Be gone with you, daughter of a mountain goat, and cover your shame elsewhere, not by lying with men from worlds that despise your own! Where is the pride of the Cahuenga, shameful one?"

The girl gasped, cowered backward, a convulsive hand clutching her robe about her bared breasts, and bent almost to the ground. She swallowed, but for a moment her mouth only moved, without sound; then she whispered, *"S'dia shaya . . . d'sperdo, vai dom alzuo. . . . "* and fled, sobbing; the sound of the sob and the scent of her musky hair lingered in the room behind her.

Kerwin clung, swaying, to the edge of the table. *God, how drunk can you get! What was all that stuff I was spouting, anyway?* He was bewildered at himself; where did he get off anyway, scaring the poor girl out of her wits? He was no more virtuous than the next man. What Puritan remnant had prompted him to rise up in wrath and demolish her that way? He'd had his share of the spaceport wenches on more worlds than one.

And what language had he been speaking, anyway? He *knew* it hadn't been the city dialect, but what *was* it? He could not remember; try as he might, not a syllable remained

of the words that had come into his mind; only the form of
the emotion remained.

Ellers, fortunately, had snored through the whole thing;
he could imagine the ribbing the older man would have
given him, if he hadn't. He thought, *We'd better get out of
here while I can still navigate—and before I do something
else that's crazy!*

He bent and shook Ellers, but Ellers didn't even mumble.
Kerwin remembered that Ellers had drunk as much as Kerwin and Ragan put together. He did this in every spaceport.
Kerwin shrugged, set the bench he'd knocked over back on
its legs, lifted Eller's feet to them, and turned unsteadily toward the door.

Air. Fresh air. That was all he needed. Then he'd better
get back inside the Terran Zone; at least, inside the spaceport
gates, he knew how to behave. But, he thought confused, I
thought I knew how to behave here on Darkover. What got
into me?

The sun, bleared and angry-looking, lay low over the
street. Shadows of deep mauve and indigo folded the huddled houses in a friendly gloom. There were people on the
streets now, Darkovans in colorful shirts and breeches,
wearing heavy woven capes or the commonplace imported
climbing jackets; women muffled to the eyebrows in fur;
and once, gliding along, a tall form invisible beneath a hood
and mantle of strange cut and color; but the gliding form
was not human.

And even as he paused, looking up at the flaming sky, the
sun sank with a rush and the swift dark came swooping
across the sky, a darkness like great soft wings, folding to
blot out the brilliance; the fast-dropping night that gave this
world its name. Leaping out in a sudden glare came the
crown of vast white stars; and three of the small jeweled
moons were in the sky, jade-green, peacock-blue, rose-pearl.

Kerwin stood staring upward, his eyes wet, unashamed
of the sudden tears that had started to them. It was not illu-

sion, then, despite the commonplace spaceport bars and the disillusion of the streets. It was real; he was home again; he had seen the falling dark over the sky, the blaze of the crown of stars they called Hastur's Crown after the legend . . . He stood there until, with the sudden cooling of the air, the thick nightly mist gathered and the blaze dimmed, then vanished.

Slowly, he walked on. The first thin misty traces of rain were stirring; the tall beacon of the HQ in the sky gave him his bearings, and he moved, reluctantly, in that direction.

He was thinking of the Darkovan girl in the bar, the one he had rebuffed so unexpectedly—and so strangely. She had been warm and lissome, and she was clean, and what more could a man want for a welcome home? Why had he sent her away—and sent her away like *that*?

He felt strangely restless, at loose ends. Home? A home meant more than a familiar sky and stars overhead. A home meant people. He had had a home on Earth if that was what he wanted. No, he thought soberly; his grandparents had never wanted him, only a second chance to remake his father in their own image. In space? Ellers, perhaps, was the closest friend he had, and what was Johnny Ellers? A bum of the spaceports, a planet-hopper. Kerwin felt the sudden hunger for roots, a home, for a people and a world he had never known. Never been allowed to know. The words he had said, self-deriding, to Ellers, came back to his mind: *I had hoped it was the amulet that would prove I was the long-lost son and heir. . . .*

Yes; he knew it now, that was the dream that had lured him back to Darkover, the fantasy that he would find a place where he belonged. Otherwise, why should he have left the last world? He'd liked it there; there had been plenty of fights, plenty of women, plenty of easygoing companionship, plenty of rough and ready adventure. But all the time, driving him, there had been that relentless compulsion to get back to Darkover; it had caused him to turn down what he knew, now, had been a sure route to advancement; and further, to kill off any hope of serious promotion.

And now that he was back, now that he had seen the four moons and the swift dark of his dreams, would all the rest be anticlimax? Would he find that his mother was just such another spaceport wench as the one who had rubbed up against him tonight, eager to take home some of the plentiful spaceport pay? If so, he didn't admire his father's taste. His father? He had heard a lot about his father, in those seven years he'd stuck it out with his grandparents, and the picture he'd gotten from them wasn't quite like that. His father, he assumed, had been a fastidious man. But that was only, perhaps, how he had seemed to his grandmother. . . . Well, at least he had cared enough to get Empire citizenship for his son.

Well, he'd do what he'd come here to do. He would try to trace his mother, and decide why his father had abandoned him in the spaceport orphanage and how and where he had died. And then? *What then?* The question nagged him—what would he do then?

I will fly that hawk when his pinions are grown, Kerwin said to himself, realizing afterward that he had spoken the Darkovan proverb without thinking about it.

The nocturnal mist had condensed now, and a thin cold rain was beginning to fall. It had been so warm during the day that Kerwin had almost forgotten how swiftly daytime warmth, at this season, was blotted out in sleety rain and snow. Already there were little needles of ice in the rain. He shivered and walked faster.

Somehow he had taken a wrong turning; he had expected to come out into the square fronting on the spaceport. He was on an open square, but it was not the right one. Along one edge there was a line of little cafés and cookshops, taverns and restaurants. There were Terrans there, so it was certainly not off limits to spaceport personnel—he knew that some of them were, he had been carefully briefed about

that—but horses were tethered outside, so there was a Darkovan clientele also. He walked outside them, picked one that
smelled richly of Darkovan food, and walked inside at random. The smell made his mouth water. Food; that was what
he needed, good solid food, not the tasteless synthetics of
the starship. In the dim lights faces were all a blur, and he
didn't look for any of the men from the *Southern Crown*.

He sat down at the corner table and ordered, and when
the food came, he sank his teeth into it with pleasure. Not far
away a couple of Darkovans, rather better dressed than
most, were idling over their food. They wore gaily colored
cloaks and high boots, jeweled belts with knives stuck into
them. One had a blazing red head of hair, which made Kerwin raise his eyebrows; the city Darkovans were a swarthy
lot, and his own red hair had made him an object of curiosity and stares when, as a child, he'd gone out into the city.
His father and grandparents, too, had dark hair and eyes, and
he had blazed like a beacon among them. In the orphanage
they'd called him *Tallo*—copper; half in derision, half, he
recognized it now, in a kind of superstitious awe. And the
Darkovan nurses and matrons had been at such pains to sup-
press the nickname that even then it had surprised him. He
had collected the notion somehow, though the Darkovan
nurses were forbidden to talk local superstitions to the children, that red hair was unlucky, or taboo.

If it was unlucky the redhead certainly didn't seem to
know about it or care.

On Earth, perhaps because red hair was really not all that
uncommon, the memory of that superstition had dimmed.
But maybe that explained Ragan's early stare. If red hair
was all that uncommon, obviously you would assume, if you
saw a red-haired man at a distance, that he was the man you
knew, and be surprised when it turned out to be a stranger.

Though, come to think of it, Ragan's own hair had a rusty
dull-red look to it; he might have been redheaded as a child.
Kerwin thought again that the little man had looked famil-

iar, and tried again to remember if there had been any red-heads, other than himself, in the orphanage. Surely he had known a couple of them when he was very small. . . .

Maybe before I went to the orphanage. Maybe my mother was redheaded, or had some relatives who were. . . . But try as he might, he could not uncover the blankness of the early years. Only a memory of disturbing dreams . . .

A loudspeaker on the wall hiccupped loudly, and a metal-lic voice remarked, "Your attention please. All spaceport personnel, your attention please."

Kerwin lifted his eyebrows, staring at the loudspeaker with definite resentment. He'd come in here to get away from things like that. Evidently some of the other patrons of the restaurant felt the same way; there were a couple of de-risive noises.

The metallic voice remarked, in Terran Standard, "Your attention please. All HQ personnel with planes on the field report immediately to Division B. All surface transit will be cancelled, repeat, will be cancelled. The *Southern Crown* will skylift on schedule, repeat, on schedule. All surface air-craft on the field must be moved without delay. Repeat, all HQ personnel with private surface aircraft on the field . . ."

The redheaded Darkovan Kerwin had noticed before said in an audible and malicious voice—and in the City dialect everyone understood—"How poor these Terrans must be, that they must disturb us all with that squawking box up there instead of paying a few pennies to a flunkey to bring their messages." The word he used for "flunkey" was a par-ticularly offensive one.

A uniformed spaceport official near the front of the restaurant stared angrily at the speaker, then thought better of it, settled his gold-lace cap on his head and tramped out into the rain. A blast of bitter cold blew into the room—for he had started a small exodus—and the Darkovan nearest Kerwin said to his companion, "*Esa so vhalle Terranan ac-qualle . . .* " and chuckled.

The other replied something even more insulting, his eyes lingering on Kerwin, and Kerwin realized that he was the only Terran left in the room. He felt himself trembling. He had always been childishly sensitive to insults. On Earth he had been an alien, a freak, a Darkovan; here on Darkover, suddenly, he felt himself a Terran; and the events of the day hadn't been calculated to sweeten his disposition. But he only glared and remarked—to the empty table at his left, "The rain can only drown the mud-rabbit if he hasn't the wit to keep his mouth shut."

One of the Darkovans—not the redhead—pushed his bench back and swung around, upsetting his drink in the process. The thin crash of the metal goblet, and the bleat of the waiter, drew all eyes to them, and Kerwin edged out of his seat. Inside he was watching himself with dismay. Was he going to make *two* scenes, in *two* bars, and would this rip-rousing welcome to Darkover end up by getting him hauled off to the local brig for being drunk and disorderly?

Then the man's companion grabbed his elbow and said something urgent that Kerwin didn't hear. The first man's eyes traveled slowly upward, rested on Kerwin's head, now clearly illumined by a lamp in a bracket over him, and he said with a little gulp, "No! I want no trouble with Comyn. . . ."

Kerwin wondered what in the hell he was talking about. The would-be fighter looked at his companion, found no encouragement there; then he flung up his arm before his face, mumbled something that sounded like "*Su serva, vai dom . . .* ", barged across the room, avoiding tables like a sleepwalker, and plunged out into the rain.

Kerwin realized that everybody left in the little restaurant was staring at him; but he managed to meet the eyes of the waiter long enough to drive him away. He sat down and picked up his cup, which contained the local equivalent of coffee—a caffeine-rich beverage tasting remotely like bitter chocolate—and sipped. It was cold.

The remaining well-dressed Darkovan, the redheaded one, got up, came over, and slid into the empty seat across from Kerwin.

"Who the hell are you?"

He spoke Terran Standard, to Jeff's surprise; but he spoke it badly, forming each word with care.

Kerwin set his cup down wearily.

"Nobody you know, friend. Go away, will you?"

"No, I am serious," the red-haired man said. "What is your name?"

And suddenly Kerwin was exasperated. What right did this chap have to come over and demand that he give an account of himself?

"Evil-eye Fleegle, a very ancient god," he said. "And I feel every millennium of it. Go away or I'll put the whammy on you like I did on your friend."

The red-haired man grinned—a mocking, unfriendly grin. "He's no friend of mine," he said, "and it's obvious you're not what you seem; you were more surprised than anyone when he ran out of here. Obviously, he thought you were one of us." He broke off and amended: "One of my relatives."

Kerwin said politely, "What is this, Old Home Week? No, thank you. I come from a long line of Arcturian lizard-men." He picked up the coffeelike stuff and buried his head in his mug again, felt the redhead's puzzled gaze on the top of his head. Then the man turned away, muttering, "*Terranan*" in that tone that made the single word into a deadly insult.

Now that it was too late, Kerwin wished he had answered more politely. That was the second time tonight that someone had thought they recognized him. If he closely resembled someone in Thendara, wasn't this what he had come here to find out? He had a tardy impulse to go after the man and demand an explanation. But the sure knowledge that this would only mean a new rebuff prevented him. Feeling frustrated, he put some coins down on the bar, picked up the bundle from the spaceport shop—and went out again.

By now the rain had become icy sleet; the stars were gone. It was dark and cold, with a howling wind, and he fought his way along, shivering in the thin uniform jacket. Why hadn't he brought along something warm to wear after dark? He knew what the weather was like here at night! Hell—he *had* something warm with him. A little peculiar-looking, perhaps, but he could put it on till he got out of this wind. With stiff fingers he fumbled with the bundle and got out the fur-lined, embroidered cloak. He settled it over his shoulders with a shrug, feeling the supple warmth of the fur closing around him like a caress.

He turned into a side street and there was the open square fronting on the spaceport, the neon lights of the Sky Harbor Hotel facing it across from the gates. He should go into the HQ, get assigned to quarters; he hadn't reported, he didn't even know where he was going to sleep. He walked toward the gates; then, on impulse, turned back toward the hotel for a final drink and some time to think before going back into the world of white walls and yellow lights. Maybe he would take a room for the night.

The clerk, busily sorting records, hardly glanced up at him.

"You go through there," he said curtly, and returned to his book.

Kerwin, startled—had the Civil Service reserved accommodations here?—started to protest, then shrugged and went through the indicated door.

And stopped, for he had stepped into a room prepared for a private party; a long table was laid in the center with some kind of buffet supper and there were flowers in tall crystal vases; at the far end of the room a tall red-headed man in a long embroidered cape stood hesitantly looking at him— then Kerwin realized that the black wall was a pane of glass opening on night, and darkness behind it made it a mirror;

the cloaked Darkovan was himself. He looked as if he had never seen himself before; a big man, with red hair flattened from the rain, and a lonely and introspective face, the face of an adventurer who has for some reason been cheated of adventure. The sight of his own face rising above the Darkovan cloak arrested him with a strange surge of—of memory? When had he seen himself dressed like this before? Or—or *someone else*?

Kerwin scowled, impatient. Of course he looked familiar to himself. What was the *matter* with him? And this was the answer, too; the clerk had simply taken him for a Darkovan, perhaps someone he knew by sight, and directed him into the reserved room. In fact, that would explain Ragan, too, and the redhead in the restaurant; he had a double, or near-double on Darkover, some big redhead of about his size and coloring, and that deceived people, with a quick look.

"You're here early, *com'ii*," said a voice behind him, and Kerwin turned and saw her.

He thought at first that she was a Terran girl, because of the red-gold hair clustered in curls atop her small head. She was slight and slim, wearing a simple gown that clung to dainty curves. Kerwin quickly averted his eyes—staring at a Darkovan woman in public is insolence punishable by a beating or worse, if any of the woman's relatives are around and care to take offense—but she returned his gaze frankly, smiling with welcome, and so, even on second thoughts, he believed for a moment she was a Terran, despite her Darkovan speech.

"How did you get here? I thought we had decided to come with our respective Towers," she said, and Kerwin stared. He felt his face heating, and not from the fire. "My apologies, *domma*," he said in the language of his childhood. "I didn't realize that this was a private room; I was directed here by mistake. Forgive the intrusion; I will go at once."

She stared at him, her smile fading. "But what are you

thinking of?" she demanded. "We have many things to discuss—" She stopped. Then she said, uncertainly, "Have I made a mistake?"

Kerwin said, "Somebody's made one, that's for sure." His voice trailed away on the last words, realizing that she was *not* speaking the language of Thendara, but some language he had never heard before. And yet he had understood her, so well that for a moment he had not realized that she had spoken an unfamiliar language.

Her mouth dropped open, and she said, "In the name of the Son of Aldones and his divine Mother, who are you?"

Kerwin started to say his name; then realized it could not possibly mean anything to her, and that red imp of anger, held in abeyance for a few moments because he was talking to a beautiful woman, deviled him again. This was the second time tonight—no, the third. Damn it, that double of his must be quite a fellow, if he was recognized simultaneously in a spaceport dive, and in the private reserved suite of Darkovan aristocracy—for the girl could not possibly be anything else.

He said with the heaviest irony he could manage, "don't you recognize me, lady? I'm your big brother Bill, the black sheep of the family, who ran away to space when he was six years old and I've been held captive by space pirates in the Rim Worlds ever since. Find out in the next installment."

She shook her head, uncomprehending, and he realized that language, and satire, and the allusions he had made, would mean less than nothing to her. Then she said in that language he understood, if he didn't think too hard about it, "But surely you are one of us? From the Hidden City, perhaps? Who are you?"

Kerwin scowled impatiently, too annoyed to carry the game any further. He almost wished that the man she had mistaken him for would walk in right now so he could punch him in the face.

"Look, you're mistaking me for someone else, girl. I

don't know anything about your Hidden City—it's hidden too well or something. What planet is it on? You're not Darkovan, are you?" For her manners were certainly not those of a Darkovan woman.

If she had seemed startled before, now she appeared thunderstruck. "And yet you understood the language of Valeron? Listen to me," she began again, and this time she was speaking the City dialect of Thendara. "I think we must have this clearly understood. There is something very strange here. Where can we talk together?"

"We're dong fine, right here and now," Kerwin said. "I may be new to Darkover, but not *that* new; I'm not crazy about having your relatives file an intent-to-murder on me before I've been here twenty-four hours, in case you have some touchy male relatives. If you *are* Darkovan."

The small pixielike face screwed up in a puzzled little smile. "I can't believe this," she said. "You don't know who I am, and what's worse, you don't know *what* I am. I was sure that you must be from one of the remoter Towers, someone I have never seen before face to face, but only in the relays. Perhaps someone from Hali, or Neskaya, or Dalereuth. . . ."

Kerwin shook his head.

"I'm no one you know, believe me," he said. "I wish you'll tell me who you mistook me for; I'd like to meet him, whoever he is, if I have a double in this city. It might answer a few questions for me."

"I can't do that," she said, hesitant, and he sensed that now, under his opened Darkovan cloak, she had seen the Terran uniform. "No, please don't go. If Kennard were here—"

"Tani, what is this?" A low, harsh voice broke in, and in the mirrored wall Kerwin saw a man walking toward them. He turned to face the newcomer, wondering—so mad had the world become—if he would see a mirror image of himself. But he didn't.

The newcomer was slight, tall, fair-skinned, with thick red-gold hair. Kerwin detested him on sight, even before he recognized the red-haired man with whom he'd had that brief and unsatisfactory confrontation in the bar. The Darkovan took in the scene at a glance, and his face took on the look of scandalized conventionality.

"A stranger here, and you alone with him, Taniquel?"

"Auster, I only wanted—" the girl protested.

"A *Terranan!*"

"I thought, at first, he was one of us, perhaps from Dalereuth."

The Darkovan favored Kerwin with a contemptuous glance. "He's an Arcturian lizard-man—or so he told me," he said with a sneer. Then he spoke to the girl, a rush of words in, Kerwin thought, the same language she had spoken, but so rapidly that he could not understand a single word of what the man said. He didn't need to; the tone and gestures told Kerwin all he needed to know. The redhead was mad as hell.

A deeper, mellower voice interrupted. "Come, Auster, it can't be as bad as all that. Come, Taniquel, tell me what this is all about, and don't tease, child." A second man had come into the room. And he too was one of the redheads. Where were they all coming from, tonight? This one was heavy-set, a burly man, tall and strongly built; but his red hair was dashed with long streaks of grey, and a close-cut, greying beard surrounded his face. His eyes were almost hidden behind ridged brows so thick as to approximate deformity. He walked stiff-legged, leaning on a thick, copper-headed walking stick. He looked straight at Kerwin and said, "*S'dia shaya*; I'm Kennard, third in Arilinn. Who is your Keeper?"

Kerwin was sure he said *Keeper*. It was a word that could also be translated as *Warden* or *Guardian*.

"They usually let me out without one," he said dryly. "At least they have so far."

Auster said, quickly and mockingly, "You're wrong too,

Kennard. Our friend is an—an Arcturian crocodile-man, or so he claims. But, like all Terrans, he lied."

"Terran!" Kennard exclaimed, "but that's impossible!" And he seemed as shocked as the girl.

Kerwin had had enough of this. He said sharply, "Far from being impossible, it is perfectly true; I am a citizen of Terra. But I spent my early years on Darkover, and I learned to speak the language well. Now, if I have intruded or offended, please accept my apologies; and I wish you a good night." He turned on his heel and started to leave the room.

Auster mutter something that sounded like "crawling rabbithorn!"

Kennard said, "Wait." Kerwin, already halfway out the door, paused at the man's courteous, persuasive voice. "If you have a few minutes, I'd really like to talk with you, sir. It could be important."

Kerwin glanced at the girl Taniquel, and almost yielded. But one look at Auster decided him. He didn't want any trouble with that one. Not on his first night on Darkover. "Thank you," he said pleasantly. "Another time, perhaps. Please accept my apologies for intruding on your party."

Auster spat out a mouthful of words, and Kennard gave in gracefully, bowed, and spoke a polite formula of farewell. The girl Taniquel stared after him, sobered and stricken, and he hesitated again, on an impulse, realizing that he should stop, change his mind, demand the explanation that he suspected Kennard could give. But he had gone too far to back down and keep any dignity at all. He said, "Again, good night," and felt the door swing shut between himself and the redheads. He felt a curious sense of defeat and apprehension as he crossed the lobby. A group of Darkovans, most of them in long ceremonial capes like his own—crossed the lobby in the other direction and went through the door he had just vacated. Kerwin noticed that there were some redheads among them, too, and there was murmuring among the crowd in the lobby; again he caught the murmured word *Comyn*.

Ragan had spoken the word, about the jewel he had around his neck; *fine enough for Comyn.* Kerwin searched his memory; the word meant, only, *equals*—those who stood in rank equal to one's own. That wasn't how they had used the word, though.

Outside, the rain had dissolved into stinging mist. A tall man in a green and black cape, red head held high, brushed past Kerwin and said, "Inside, quick, you'll be late," and went on into the Sky Harbor Hotel. It seemed like a curious place for a group of Darkovan aristocrats to hold a family reunion, but what did he know about it? A wild thought darted into his mind that perhaps he ought to crash the party and demand to know if anyone had lost a young relative about thirty years ago. But it was only a wild notion, dismissed as soon as it had arisen.

In the dark street, glazed underfoot now with the icy rain, which froze as it fell, the thick sleet cut off moon or stars. The lights of the HQ gates burned with a yellow glare. Kerwin knew that there he would find warmth and familiar things, shelter, assigned place and even friends. Ellers had probably wakened, found him gone, and returned to the HQ.

But what would he find there if he did return? A set of assigned rooms exactly like those on his last planet, cold and bare with the antiseptic institutional smell; a library of films carefully censored so as not to raise too many unmanageable emotions; meals exactly the same as he would have had on any other Terran Empire planet, so that the workers likely to be transferred at any moment would not have to suffer any digestive discomforts or period of adjustment; and the society of other men like himself, who lived on fantastically alien worlds by turning their backs on them to live in the same dull familiar world of the Terrans.

They lived on alien worlds under alien suns just as they lived on Terra—unless, that was, they wanted to go out and raise hell; when they sought the worst, not the best of that alien beauty. Potent drink, women who were willing, if not too appealing, and a place to spend their spare pay. The real worlds lay, would always lie, a million miles out of their reach. As far out of their reach as the red-haired, smiling girl who had smiled and greeted him as *com'ii*, friend.

He turned, again, away from the gates of the HQ. Outside the circle of spaceport bars, tourist traps, whorehouses, and exhibitions, there must be a real Darkover out there somewhere, the world he had known when he was a boy in the city; the world that had haunted his dreams and jerked him out from his new roots on Terra. But why had he ever had those dreams? Where had they come from? Certainly not from the clean, sterile world of the Spacemen's Orphanage!

Slowly, as if wading through mud, he walked toward the old town, his fingers knotting the fastenings of the Darkovan cloak about his throat. His Terran-made boots rang hard on the stone. Whatever people took him for, it wouldn't hurt to go looking around a little. This was his own world. He had been born here. He was no naive Terran spaceman, unsafe outside the spaceport quarter. He knew the city, or had known it once, and knew the language. All right, so Terrans weren't specially welcome in the Old Town. He wouldn't go as a Terran! Wasn't it a Terran who had once said, *Give me a child till he is seven years old, and anyone who wants him can have him after that.* That grim old saint had the right idea; by that reckoning, Kerwin was Darkovan and always would be, and now he was home again and he wasn't going to be kept away!

There were not many people in the streets now. A few, in cloaks and furs, moving head-down against the bitter biting wind. A shivering girl, hugging an inadequate fur smock about her, gave Kerwin a hopeful glance and murmured to him in the old tongue of the city, which Kerwin had spoken before he could lisp three words of nursery Terran (how did he knew that?). And he hesitated, for she was shy and soft-voiced and wholly different from the hard-eyed girl in the spaceport bar, but then her eyes raised to his red hair and she murmured unintelligibly and fled.

A little dwarfed creature pattered by, giving Kerwin a swift upward glance from green eyes that glowed, catlike, in the dark, but had unmistakable human intelligence behind them; Kerwin moved quickly aside, for the *kyrri* were strange creatures who fed on electrical energy and could give unwary strangers painful, though not fatal, shocks if they were jostled or crowded.

Kerwin walked on through the market of the Old Town, savoring the unfamiliar sounds and smells. An old woman was selling fried fish in a little stall; she dropped the bundles of fish into a thick batter, then into the bowl of clear green oil. She looked up and with voluble words in a dialect too thick for understanding, handed him the fresh fish. He started to shake his head, but it smelt good and he shrugged and fumbled for coins in his purse, but she looked at him, startled, and the coins dropped on the ground as she backed away. In her babble he caught again the word *Comyn*, and frowned. The devil! He seemed to have the knack, tonight, of innocently scaring people half to death. Well, with the city full of redheaded men and women on some kind of family reunion, Kerwin decided red hair was even unluckier than they'd told him in the orphanage!

Maybe it was this fantastic nobleman's cloak he was wearing. He'd take it off, but it was too cold for his thin Terran uniform; besides, he surmised that in his Terran clothes he couldn't be really safe in this part of the city.

He admitted it to himself, now; he had had just this kind of imposture in mind when he bought the cloak. But too many people were staring. He turned, deciding he had better take the faster route back to the HQ.

He walked swiftly now through dark, deserted streets. He heard a step behind him—a slow, purposeful step; but told himself not to be suspicious; he wasn't the only man who might have a good reason to be out in the rain tonight! The step kept pace with him, then quickened to overtake him, and Kerwin stepped aside to let the follower pass in the narrow street.

That was a mistake. Kerwin felt a searing pain; then the top of his head exploded and from somewhere he heard a voice crying out strange words:

Say to the son of the barbarian that he shall come no more to the plains of Arilinn! The Forbidden Tower is broken and the Golden Bell is avenged!

That didn't make sense, Kerwin thought in the split second before his head struck the pavement and he knew no more.

CHAPTER FOUR

The Search

It was dawn, and it was raining hard, and somebody somewhere was talking right in his ear.

"Lie still, *vai dom*, no one will hurt you! Vandals! What has come to the city, when Comyn can be attacked . . ."

And another voice, rougher: "Don't be a donkey; can't you see the uniform? The man's *Terran* and somebody's head will roll for this. Go and call the watch, quickly!"

Someone tried to lift his head, and Kerwin decided it was his head that was going to roll, because it exploded and he slid back into unconsciousness again.

Then, after confused noises and pain, a bright white light seemed to shine into the innermost recesses of his brain. He felt someone mauling his head, which hurt like hell, and grunted in pain, and someone took the light out of his eyes.

He was lying in an antiseptic white bed in an antiseptic white room, and a man in a white smock, wearing the caduceus emblem of Medic and Psych, was bending over him.

"All right now?"

Kerwin started to nod, but his head exploded again and he thought better of it. The doctor handed him a small paper cup of red liquid; it burned his mouth and stung all the way down, but his head stopped hurting.

"What happened?" Kerwin asked.

Johnny Ellers put his head around the door; his eyes

looked bloodshot. "You ask that? *I* pass out—but you're the one gets slugged and rolled! The greenest kid, on his first planetside assignment, ought to know better than that! And why the hell were you wondering around the native section? Didn't you study the off-limits map?"

There was a warning in his words. Kerwin said, slowly, "Yeah. I must've got lost."

How much of what he remembered was true? Had he dreamed all the rest—his bizarre wanderings in the Darkovan cloak, all the people who had mistaken him for *someone else*. . . . Had it all been wishful thinking, based on his desire to belong?

"What day is this?"

"Morning after the night before," Ellers said.

"Where did it happen? Where did I get knocked out?"

"God knows," the doctor said. "Evidently someone found you and got scared; dragged you to the edge of the spaceport square and dumped you there about dawn." The doctor moved out of eye range and Kerwin found that it hurt his head to try and follow him, so he went back to sleep. Ragan, the girl in the wineshop, the redheaded aristocrats and the strange encounter in the Sky Harbor Hotel drifted in his mind as he slipped away. If he'd started by thinking that this return to Darkover was an anticlimax to his dreams, at least he'd had enough adventure now to last him fifty years.

No satirical demon whispered in his ear that he hadn't started yet.

His head was still bandaged when he reported to the Legate for assignment the next morning, and the Legate regarded him without enthusiasm.

"I need Medics and technicians, mapmakers and linguists, and what do they send me? Communications men! Hell, I know it's not your fault, they send me what they can get. I hear you actually requested transfer out here, so maybe I can keep you a while; usually what I get are greenies who transfer out as soon as they have enough seniority credits. I hear you got yourself smashed up a little, wandering around alone in the native quarter. Didn't they tell you that's not smart, here?"

Kerwin just said, "I got lost, sir."

"But why the hell were you wandering around outside the spaceport area anyhow? There's nothing interesting back there." He scowled. "Why would you want to go exploring on your own?"

Kerwin said doggedly, "I was born here, sir." If they were going to discriminate against him because of that, he wanted to know it right away. But the Legate only looked thoughtful.

"You may be fortunate," he said. "Darkover is not a popular assignment; but if it's home to you, you won't hate it quite as much. Maybe. I didn't volunteer, you know; I got in with the wrong political crowd, and I'm serving—you might say—a sentence here. If you actually like the place, you might have quite a career ahead of you; because, as I told you, under normal conditions nobody stays much longer than they have to. So you think you'll like it here?"

"I don't know. But I did want to come back." He added, feeling somehow that he could trust this man, "It was almost a compulsion. What I remembered as a child."

The Legate nodded. He was not a young man, and his eyes were sad. "God, don't I know!" he said, "The longing for the smell of your own air, the color of your own sun. I know, lad. I've been out for forty years, and I've seen Alpha twice in that time, and I hope I die there. What's the old saying . . . *Though stars like weeds be thickly sown, no world of stars can match your own . . .*" He broke off. "Born here, huh? Who was your mother?"

Kerwin thought of the women in the spaceport café and then tried not to think about them. At least his father had cared enough about his son to get citizenship for him, to leave him in the Spacemen's Orphanage.

"I don't know, sir. That's one of the things I hoped would be recorded here."

"Kerwin," the Legate mused. "I seem to have heard the name. I've only been here four or five years, local time. But if your father had married here, it would be in Records, downstairs. Or the Orphanage would have records. They're fairly careful who they take in there; ordinary foundlings get turned over to the Hierarchs of the City. And then, you were sent back to Earth; that's *very* rare. Normally you would have been kept here and given work or training by the Department, mapping worker, interpreter, something where it would be an advantage to you to know the language like a native."

"I've thought I was probably Darkovan . . ."

"I doubt that; your hair. We Terrans have a lot of redheads—hyperadrenal types, we go in for adventurous life. With certain exceptions, there aren't many redheaded Darkovans . . ."

Kerwin started to mention that he'd run into at least four, last night, and then could not speak the words. Literally he *could not*; it was like a fist rammed at his throat. Instead he listened to the Legate talking about Darkover.

"It's a funny place," he said. "We hold scraps of it for trade, Trade Cities here and in Caer Donn up in the Hellers, the spaceport here and the big airfield out at Port Chicago, just as we do elsewhere. You know the routine. We leave governments alone, usually. After the people of the various planets have seen what we have to offer in the way of advanced technology and trade, membership in a galactic civilization, they start to get tired of living under primitive or barbarian conditions and hierarchies and monarchies and autarchies; and they petition to come into the Empire. And we're here to enforce plebiscites and protect them against entrenched tyrannies. It's almost a mathematical formula; you can predict the thing. A class-D world like this will hold out maybe a hundred, hundred and ten years. But Darkover isn't following the pattern, and we don't quite know why."

He struck his clenched fist on his acres of desk. "They say we just don't have a damned thing they want. Oh, they trade with us, sometimes; give us silver, or platinum, or jewels, or small matrix crystals—you know what they are?—for things like cameras and medical supplies and cheap down or synthetic mountain gear, ice axes, that sort of thing. Metal tools, especially; they're metal-starved. But they don't have the faintest interest in setting up industrial or technological exchange with us, they haven't asked for technological experts or advice, they don't have anything resembling a commercial system. . . ."

Kerwin remembered some of this from his briefing on the ship. "Are you talking about the government or the common people?"

"Both," the Legate snorted. "The government's a little hard to locate. At first we thought there wasn't any. Hell, there might as well *not* be!"

The Darkovans, according to the Legate, were ruled by a caste who lived in virtual seclusion; they were incorruptible and, especially, unapproachable. A mystery, a riddle.

"One of the few things they do trade for, is *horses*," the Legate told him. "Horses. Can you figure that? We offer them planes, surface transit, roadbuilding machinery—and what do they buy? Horses. I gather there are big herds of them, out on the outer steppes, the plains of Valeron and Arilinn, and in the uplands of the Kilghard Hills. They say they don't want to build roads, and from what I know of the terrain, it wouldn't be easy, but we've offered them all kinds of technical help and they don't want it. They buy a few planes, now and then. God knows what they do with them. They don't have airstrips and they don't buy enough fuel, but they do buy them." He leaned his chin on his hands.

"It's a crazy place. I never have figured it out. To tell the truth, I don't really give a damn. Who knows? Maybe you'll figure it out some day."

When he next had free time, late the next day, Kerwin went out through the more respectable section of the Trade City, toward the Spacemen's Orphanage. He remembered every step of the way. It rose before him, a white cool building, strange and alien as it had always been among the trees, set back at the end of a long walk from the street; the Terran star-and-rocket emblem blazed over the door. The outer hall was empty, but through an open door he saw a small group of boys working industriously around a globe. From behind the building he could hear the high cheery sound of children playing.

In the big office that had been the terror of his childhood, Kerwin waited until a lady dressed respectably in muted Darkovan clothing—loose skirt, furred jacket over all—came out and inquired in a friendly manner what she could do for him.

When he told her of his errand, she held out her hand cordially. "So you were one of our boys? I think you must have been before my time. Your name—?"

"Jefferson Andrew Kerwin, Junior."

Her forehead ridged in a polite effort at concentration. "I may possibly have seen the name in Records, I don't remember offhand. I think you must have been before my time. When did you leave? At thirteen? Oh, that is unusual. Mostly our boys stay until they are nineteen or twenty; then, after testing, we find them work here."

"I was sent to my father's family on Earth."

"Then we will surely have records on you, Jeff. If your parents are known—" She hesitated. "Of course, we try to keep complete records, but it's possible we may only have one parent's name; there have been—" She hesitated, trying to find a courteous way to phrase it. "—unfortunate liaisons—"

"You mean, if my mother was one of the women of the spaceport bars, my father may not have bothered tell you who she was?"

She nodded, looked ruffled at this plain speaking. "It does happen. Or one of your young women may choose to have a child without informing us of the father, though in your case that wouldn't seem to apply. If you'll wait a minute." She went into a little side office. Through the open door he caught a glimpse of office machines and a trim Darkovan girl wearing Terran uniform. After a few minutes the lady came back looking puzzled and a little annoyed, and her voice was curt.

"Well, Mr. Kerwin, it seems there is no record of you in our orphanage. It must have been some other planet."

Kerwin stared, in amazement. "But that's impossible," he said reasonably. "I lived here until I was thirteen years old. I slept in Dormitory Four, the matron's name was Rosaura. I used to play ball on that field back there." He pointed.

She shook her head. "Well, we certainly have no records of you, Mr. Kerwin. Is it possible you were registered here under another name?"

He shook his head. "No, I was always called Jeff Kerwin."

"Furthermore we have no record of any of our boys being sent to Terra in his thirteenth year. That would be very unusual, not our regular procedure at all, and it would certainly have been carefully recorded. Everyone here would certainly remember it."

Kerwin took a step forward. He leaned over the woman, a big man, menacing, furious. "What are you trying to say? What do you *mean*, you have no records on me? In God's name, what possible reason would I have for lying about it? I tell you, I lived here thirteen years, do you think I don't *know*? Damn it, I can prove it!"

She shrank away from him. "Please—"

"Look," Kerwin said, trying to be reasonable. "There has

got to be some kind of mistake. Could the name be misfiled, could your computer have malfunctioned? I need to know what kind of records were kept on me. Will you check the spelling again, please?" He spelled it again for her, and she said coldly, "I checked that name, and two or three possible spelling variations. Of course, if you had been registered here under another name—"

"No, damn it," Kerwin shouted. "It's *Kerwin*! I learned to *write* my name—in that schoolroom right at the end of that corridor, the one with a big picture of John Reade on the north wall!"

"I am sorry," she said. "We have no record of anyone called Kerwin."

"What kind of half-headed, fumbled-fingered idiot have you got tending your computer, then? Are they filed under names, fingerprints, retinal prints?" He had forgotten that. Names could be altered, changed, misfiled, but fingerprints did not change.

She said coldly, "If it will convince you, and you know anything about computers . . ."

"I've been working in Comm Terra with a Barry-Reade KSO4 for seven years."

Her voice was icy. "Then, sir, I suggest you come in here and check the banks yourself. If you feel the name may have been misrecorded, misspelled, or misfiled, every child who has passed through the Orphanage is coded for fingerprint access." She bent silently and handed him a card form, pressed his fingers, one by one, against the special molecular-sensitive paper that recorded, invisibly, the grooves and whorls of the raised lines, pore-patterns, skin type and texture. She faced the card into a slot. He watched the great silent face of the machine, the glassy front, like blind eyes staring.

With uncanny speed a card was released, slid down into a tray; Kerwin snatched it up before the woman could give it to him, disregarding the cold outrage on her face. But as he turned it over his triumph and assurance that she had, for some reason, been lying to him, drained away. A cold terror gripped at his stomach. In the characterless capitals of mechanical printing it read:

NO RECORD OF SUBJECT

She took the card from Kerwin's suddenly lax fingertips.

"You cannot accuse a machine of lying," she said coldly. "Now, if you please, I'll have to ask you to leave." Her tone said clearer than words that unless he did she would have someone come and put him out.

Kerwin clawed desperately at the counter edge. He felt as if he had stepped into some cold and reeling expanse of space. Shocked and desperate, he said, "How could I be mistaken? Is there another Spacemen's Orphanage on Darkover? I—I *lived* here, I tell you—"

She stared at him until a sort of pity took the place of her anger. "No, Mr. Kerwin," she said gently. "Why don't you go back to the HQ and check with Section Eight there? If there is a—a mistake—maybe they could help you."

Section Eight. Medic and Psych. Kerwin swallowed hard and went, without any further protest. That meant she thought he was deranged, that he needed psychiatric help. He didn't blame her. After what he had just heard, he kind of thought so himself. He stumbled out into the cold air, his feet numb, his head whirling.

They were lying, lying. Somebody's lying. She was lying and he knew it; he could feel her lying. . . .

No; that was what every paranoid psychotic thought; somebody was lying, *they were all lying, there was a plot against him. . . .* Some mysterious and elusive *they* was conspiring against him.

But how could he have been mistaken? Damn it, he thought as he walked down the steps, I used to play ball over there; kickball and catch-the-monkey when I was little, more structured games when I was older. He looked up at the windows of his old dormitory. He had climbed into them often enough after some escapade, aided by convenient low branches of that very tree. He felt like climbing up into the dormitory to see if the initials he had carved into the window-frame were still there. But he abandoned the notion; the way his luck was running, they'd just catch him and think he was a potential child molester. He turned and stared again at the white walls of the building where he had spent his childhood . . . *or had he?*

He clasped his hands at his temples, searching out elusive memories. He could remember so much. All his conscious memories were of the orphanage, of the grounds where he stood now, running around these grounds; when he was very small he had fallen on these steps and skinned his knee . . . how old had he been then? Seven, perhaps, or eight. They had taken him up to the infirmary and said they were going to sew up his knee, and he had wondered how in the world they would get his knee into a sewing machine; and when they showed him the needle, he had been so intrigued at how it was done that he had forgotten to cry; it was his first really clear memory.

Did he have any memories *before* the orphanage? Try as he might, he could remember only a glimpse of violet sky, four moons hanging like jewels and a soft woman's voice that said, "Look, little son, you will not see this again for years. . . ." He knew, from his geography lessons, that a conjunction of the four moons together in the sky did not come very often; but he could not remember where he had been when he saw it, or when he had seen it again. A man in a green and golden cloak strode down a long corridor of stone that shone like marble, a hood flung loose over blazing red hair; and somewhere there had been a room with blue light . . . and then he was in the Spacemen's Orphanage, studying, sleeping, playing ball with a dozen other boys his age, in a cluster of kids in blue pants and white shirts. When he was ten he had had a crush on a Darkovan nurse called—what had been her name? Maruca. She moved softly in heel-less slippers, her white robes moving around her with fluid grace, and her voice was very gentle and low. *She tousled my hair and called me Tallo, though it was against the rules, and once when I had some kind of fever, she sat by me all night in the infirmary, and put cold cloths on my head, and sang to me. Her voice was deep contralto, very sweet.* And when he was eleven he'd bloodied the nose of a boy named Hjalmar for calling him *bastard*, yelling that at least he *knew* his father's name, and they'd been pulled apart, kicking and spitting gutter insults at each other, by the grey-haired mathematics teacher. And just a few weeks before they bundled him, scared and shaking and listless from the drugs, aboard the starship that would take him to Terra, there'd been a girl named Ivy, in a class higher than his. He had hoarded his allotment of sweets for her, and they had held hands shyly, walking under those trees at the far edge of the playground; and once, awkwardly, he had kissed her, but she had turned away her face so that he had kissed only a mouthful of fine, pale-brown, sweet-scented hair.

No, they couldn't tell him he was crazy. He remembered too much. He'd go to the HQ as the woman said, only not to Medic and Psych, but Records. They had a record there of everyone who had ever worked in the Empire service. Everyone. They'd know.

The man in Records sounded a little startled when Kerwin asked for a check, and Kerwin couldn't exactly blame him. After all, you don't usually walk up and ask for your own record, unless you're applying for a job transfer. Kerwin fumbled for an excuse.

"I was born here. I never knew who my mother was, and there might be records of my birth and parentage. . . ."

The man took his fingerprint and punched buttons disinterestedly. After a time a printer began clattering, and finally a hard copy slid out into the tray. Kerwin took it up and read it, at first with satisfaction because it was obviously a full record, but with growing disbelief.

KERWIN, JEFFERSON ANDREW. WHITE. MALE. CITIZEN TERRA. HOME MOUNT DENVER. SECTOR Two. STATUS single. HAIR red. EYES grey. COLORING fair. EMPLOYMENT HISTORY age twenty apprentice CommTerra. PERFORMANCE satisfactory. PERSONALITY withdrawn. POTENTIAL high.

TRANSFER age 22. Sent as warranted Comm Terra certificate junior status, Consulate Megaera. PERFORMANCE excellent. PERSONALITY acceptable, introverted. POTENTIAL very high. DEMERITS none. No entanglements known. PRIVATE LIFE normal as far as known. PROMOTIONS regular and rapid.

TRANSFER age 26. Phi Coronis IV. CommTerra ratings expert. Legation. PERFORMANCE excellent; commendations for extraordinary work. PERSONALITY introverted but twice reprimanded for fights in native quarter. POTENTIAL very high, but in view of repeated requests for transfer possibly unstable. No marriages. No liaisons of record. No communicable diseases.

TRANSFER age 29, Cottman IV, Darkover. (requested for personal reasons, unstated.) Request approved, granted, suggest Kerwin not be transferred again except at loss of accumulated seniority. PERFORMANCE no records as yet, one reprimand for intrusion into quarter off limits. PERSONALITY APPRAISAL excellent and valuable employee but

significant personality and stability defects. POTEN-
TIAL excellent.

There was no more. Kerwin frowned. "Look that's my
employment record; what I wanted was birth records, that
kind of thing. I was born here on Cottman IV."

"That's your official transcript, Kerwin. It's all the computer has on you."

"No birth records at all?"

The man shook his head. "If you were born outside the
Terran Zone—and your mother was a native—well, it
wouldn't be recorded. I don't know what kind of birth
records they keep out there—" He waved an inclusive hand
at the view of distant mountains—"but it's for sure they're
not in *our* computer. I'll try you in Birth Records; and I can
try pass rights for orphans. If you were sent back to Terra at
thirteen, that would be under Section Eighteen, the Repatri-
ation of Spacemen's Orphans and Widows Act." He
punched buttons for several minutes, then shook his head.

"See for yourself," he said. It kept coming up: NO
RECORD OF SUBJECT.

"Here are all the birth records we have for Kerwin; we
have an Evelina Kerwin, born to one of our nurses here, died
at six months. And there's an employment record on a Hen-
derson Kerwin black, male, age 45, who was an engineer in
Thendara spaceport and died of radiation burns after an accident to the reactor. And under pass rights for orphans I
found a Teddy Kerlayne, who was sent to Delta Ophiuchi
four years ago. Not relevant, huh?"

Kerwin mechanically shredded the paper into bits, his
fingers knotting with the frustration he felt. "Try one more
thing," he said. "Try my father. Jefferson Andrew Kerwin,
senior." He crushed his own printout in his hands, remembering it had said, no marriages, no recorded liaisons. His
father's marriage, or liaison, with his unknown mother,
would have *had* to be recorded, in order for the older Jeff

Kerwin to get Empire citizenship for his son. The procedure had been carefully explained to him when he joined the Civil Service; how to record native marriages—few Empire planets were as tough on fraternization and mixing with natives as Darkover—and how to legitimize a child, with or without Terran marriage. He knew how it would have to be done. "See when and where my father filed a 784-D application, will you?"

The man shrugged. "Buddy, you sure are hard to convince. If you had ever been listed on a 784, it would have showed up on that employment record."

But he started to punch buttons again, staring at the glassed-in surface where the information appeared before the hard copy was printed. Abruptly, he started; his lips pursed. Then he turned and said civilly, "Sorry, Kerwin; no records. Somebody's steered you wrong; we don't have any record of a Jeff Kerwin in Civil Service. Nobody but you."

Kerwin snapped, "You've got to be lying! Or what are you gawping at on that screen? Damn it, move your hand and let me see it myself!"

The clerk shrugged. "Suit yourself." But he had punched another button and the screen was blank.

Fury and frustration surged up in Kerwin like a cresting wave. "Damn it, are you trying to tell me I don't exist?"

"Look," the clerk said wearily, "you can erase an entry in a ledger. But show me anybody who can tamper with the memory banks of CommTerra records, and I'll show you a cross between a man and a crystoped. According to official records, you came to Darkover for the first time two days ago. Now go down and see Medic and Psych, and quit bothering me!"

How naive do they think I am? CommTerra can be fudged so no outsider can get at the records, if you have the right codes for access. Someone, for some obscure reason, had fixed it so that he couldn't get access to the data.

But why would they bother?

The alternative was what the woman had said. She had thought he was crazy, confabulating, that he had never been on Darkover before, that for some reason he was inventing an elaborate Darkovan past for himself. . . .

Kerwin reached into his pocket, extended a folded bill.

"Try my father again. Okay?"

The clerk looked up, and now Kerwin knew that his guess had been right. It was worth the money, though he couldn't afford it, to know that he wasn't crazy. Greed and fear wavered in the man's face, and finally he said, whisking the bill quickly into his pocket, "Okay. But if the banks are being monitored, it could be my job. And whatever we get, that's *it*; no more questions, okay?"

Kerwin watched the programming this time. The machine burped slowly to itself. Then the panel flashed a red light, blink-blink-blink, an urgent panic signal. The clerk said softly, "Shunting circuit."

Red letters flashed on the panel.

REQUESTED INFORMATION AVAILABLE ON PRIORITY CODE ONLY: CLOSED ACCESS. GIVE VALID ACCESS CODE AND AUTHORITY FOR FURTHER ACCESS.

The letter flashed on and off with hypnotic intensity. Kerwin finally shook his head and motioned and the clerk shut off the lights. The screen stared back at them, blank and enigmatic.

"Well?" the clerk asked. Kerwin knew he wanted another bribe to try and break the access code, but Kerwin had as good a chance of breaking it as the clerk did. Anyhow, that proved there was *something* there.

He didn't know what. But it explained the way the woman at the Orphanage had acted, too.

He turned and went out, resolve slowly hardening in him.

He had been drawn back to Darkover—only to find greater mysteries awaiting him. Somewhere, somehow, he would find out what they were.

Only he didn't know where to start.

CHAPTER FIVE

The Technician

He let it alone for the next few days. He had to; breaking in on a new job, however simple the job was, and however similar to the one on his last planet, demanded all his attention. It was a highly specialized branch of Communications—the testing, calibrating, and occasional repair of the intercom equipment both in the HQ building itself and from point to point in the Terran Zone. It was time consuming and tedious rather than difficult, and he often found himself wondering why they bothered to bring Terran personnel in from outside, rather than training local technicians. But when he put the question to one of his associates, his friend only shrugged:

"Darkovans won't take the training. They don't have a technical turn of mind—no good with this sort of thing." He indicated the immense bank of machinery they were inspecting. "Just naturally that way, I guess."

Kerwin snorted brief, unamused laughter. "You mean something inborn—some difference in the quality of their minds?"

The other man glanced at him warily, realizing that he had trodden on a sore place. "You're Darkovan? But you were brought up by Terrans—you take machinery and technology for granted. As far as I know, they don't have anything resembling it—never have had." He scowled. "And they don't want it, either."

Kerwin thought about that, sometimes, lying in his bunk in the bachelor quarters of the HQ building, or sitting over a solitary drink in one of the spaceport bars. The Legate had mentioned that point—that the Darkovans were immune to the lure of Terran technology, and had kept out of the mainstream of Empire culture and trade. Barbarians, beneath the veneer of civilization? Or—something less obvious, more mysterious?

During his off-duty hours, sometimes, he strolled down into the Old Town; but he did not wear the Darkovan cloak again, and he made sure that his headgear covered the red head. He was giving himself time to work it through, to be sure what his next move would be. If there was a next move.

Item: the orphanage had no record of a boy named Jefferson Andrew Kerwin, Junior, sent to Terran grandparents at the age of thirteen.

Item: the main computer banks at the HQ refused to disclose any information about Jefferson Andrew Kerwin, Senior.

Kerwin was debating what these two facts might have in common—added to the fact that the Terran HQ computer was evidently set in such a way as to give the casual inquirer no information whatever—not even that such a person as his father had ever existed.

If he could find someone he had known at the orphanage, presumably that would be proof, of a sort. Proof at least that his memories of a life there were real—

They were real. He *had* to start from there because there was no other place to start. If he began doubting his own memories, he might as well open the door right now to chaos. So he would go on the assumption that his memory was real, and that for some reason or other, the records had been altered.

During the third week he became aware that he had seen

the man Ragan just a little too frequently for coincidence. At first he thought nothing of it. In the spaceport café, when he saw Ragan at a far table each time he entered, he nodded a casual greeting and that was that. After all, the place was public, and there were doubtless many steady customers and habitués. He was well on the way to being one himself, by now.

But when an emergency failure in the spaceport dispatch office kept him on duty overtime one evening, and he saw Ragan in his usual place at well past the usual hour, he began to notice it. So far, it was just a hunch; but he began to shift his mealtimes and eat at odd hours—and four times out of five he saw the swart Darkovan there. Then he did his drinking in another bar for a day or two; and by now he was sure that he was being shadowed by the man. No, shadowed was the wrong word; it was too open for that. Ragan was making no effort to keep out of Kerwin's sight. He was too clever to try to force himself on Kerwin as an acquaintance—but he was putting himself in Kerwin's path and Kerwin had the curious hunch that he wanted to be charged with it, questioned about it.

But why? He thought it through, long and slowly. If Ragan was playing a waiting game, perhaps it was tied in somehow with the other oddities. If he held aloof, and seemed not to notice, maybe they—whoever "they" were— would be forced to show a little more of their hand.

But nothing happened, except that he settled down to the routine of his new job and his new life. In the Terran Zone, life was very much like life in the Terran Zone of any other Empire planet. But he was very conscious of the world beyond that world. It called to him with a strange hunger. He found himself straining his ears in the mixed society of the spaceport bars for scraps of Darkovan conversation; absentmindedly heard himself answer one too many casual questions in Darkovan. And sometimes at night he would take the enigmatic blue crystal from its place around his neck and stare into its strange cold depths, as if by wanting it fiercely he could bring back the confused memories to which it now seemed a key. But it lay in his palm, a cold stone, lifeless, giving back no answer to the pounding questions in him. And then he would thrust it back into his pocket and walk restlessly down to one of the spaceport bars for a drink, again, straining ears and nose for a whiff of something beyond. . . .

It was three full weeks before the waiting suddenly snapped in him. He spun around from the bar on impulse, not giving himself time to consider what he would do or say, and strode toward the corner table where the little Darkovan, Ragan, sat over a cup of some dark liquid. He jerked out a chair with his foot and lowered himself into it, glowering across the ill-lighted table at Ragan.

"Don't look surprised," he said roughly. "You've been on my tail long enough." He fingered in his pocket the edges of the crystal, drew it out, slapped it on the table between them. "You told me about this, the other night—or was I drunker than I think? I've got the notion you have something to say. Say it."

Ragan's lean, ferret face looked wary and guarded. "I didn't tell you anything that any Darkovan couldn't have told you. Almost anyone would have recognized it."

"Just the same, I want to know more about it."

Ragan touched it with the tip of a finger. He said, "What do you want to know? How to use it?"

Briefly, Kerwin considered that. No; at present, at least, he had no use for such tricks as Ragan had done with the crystal, to melt glasses or—whatever else it might do. "Mostly I'm curious to know where it came from—and why I happened to have one."

"Some assignment," Ragan said dryly. "There are only a few thousand of them, I should imagine." But his eyes were narrowed, not casual at all, although his voice was elaborately casual. "Some of the people at the Terran HQ have been experimenting with the small ones. You could probably get a sizable bonus, or something, by turning this one over to them for experimental purposes."

"No!" Kerwin heard himself speak the negative before he even knew he had rejected the idea.

"But why come to me?" Ragan asked.

"Because lately I've stumbled over you every damn time I turn around, and somehow I don't think it's just because you've got a yen for my company. You know something about this business, or you want me to think so. First of all, you might tell me who you mistook me for, that first night. Not just you. Everybody who saw me thought I was somebody else. That same night I got slugged and rolled in an alley. . . ."

Ragan's mouth dropped open; Kerwin could not doubt that he was genuinely shocked.

". . . and pretty obviously, it was because I looked like that same *somebody*—"

"No, Kerwin," Ragan said. "There you're wrong. That would have protected you, if anything. It's a messy business. Look," he said, "I've got no grudge against *you*. I'll tell you this much; it's because of your red hair—"

"Hell, there are redheaded Darkovans. I've met them—"

"You have?" Ragan's eyebrows lifted. "*You?*" He snorted brief, unamused laughter. "Look, if you're lucky, you got yours from the Terran side. But I'll tell you this much; if I were you, I'd be on the first ship offplanet, and I wouldn't stop till I was halfway across the Empire. That's my advice, dead sober."

Kerwin said with a bleak smile, "I like it better when you're drunk," and signaled the waiter for refills. "Listen, Ragan," he said when the waiter had gone, "if I have to, I'll put on Darkovan clothes and go down in the Old Town—"

"And get your throat cut?"

"You just said red hair would protect me. No. I'll go

down in the Old Town and stop everybody I meet on the street and ask them who they think I am, or who I look like. And sooner or later I'll find *somebody* to tell me."

"You don't know what you're monkeying with."

"And I won't, unless you tell me."

"Stubborn damned fool," Ragan said. "Well, it's your neck. What do you expect *me* to do? And what's in it for me?"

Now Kerwin felt on safer ground. He would have distrusted it if the shrewd Darkovan had offered to help him.

"Damned if I know, but there must be something you want from me, or you wouldn't have spent so much time hanging around waiting for me to ask you questions. Money? You know how much a Communications man makes with the Empire. Enough to live on, but no big rake-offs. I expect—" his mouth twisted—"that you'll be expecting some pickings whatever happens. And that you have a good reason to expect them. Start with this." He picked up the matrix crystal on its chain. "How do I find out about it?"

Ragan shook his head. "I gave you the best advice I could; I'm not going to get mixed up in that part of it. If you have to know more, there are licensed matrix mechanics, even in the Terran Zone. They can't do much. But they can give you answers. I still say keep out of it. Get as far away as you can. You haven't the slightest idea what you're monkeying with."

Of all of this Kerwin had fastened only on the strange knowledge that there were licensed matrix mechanics. "I thought it was this big secret the Terrans didn't know anything about!"

"I told you; they trade for the little ones. Like mine. And the small ones, almost anybody can learn to handle. The way I do. A few tricks."

"What does a matrix mechanic do?"

Ragan shrugged. "Say you have legal papers you want to lock up, and you don't even feel safe about trusting them to a banker; you buy one of the smaller matrixes—if you can afford it, they're not cheap, even the tiny ones—and get the mechanic to key it to your personal pattern; your own brain-waves, like a fingerprint. Then you decide shut that box, and the matrix will seal those edges so that nothing in the world, not a sledgehammer or a nuclear explosion, will ever open them again; nothing except your own personal decision, your own mental 'Open Sesame.' You think *Open* at it, and it opens. No combination to remember, no secret bank-account number, nothing."

Kerwin whistled. "What a gadget! Come to think of it, I can imagine some pretty dangerous uses for that kind of thing."

"Right," Ragan said drily. "I don't know a lot of Darko-van history, but the Darkovans aren't letting any of the big-ger matrixes out of their hands. Even with the little ones you can do some fairly nasty tricks, even though they can't han-dle more than the smallest measure of energy. Suppose, for instance, you have a business rival who owns some sensi-tive machinery. You concentrate on your crystal—even a little one like mine—and raise the heat in a thermostat, say, three degrees Centigrade, and melt the most important cir-cuits. You want to put your competitor out of business? You hire an unscrupulous matrix mechanic to sabotage him, mess up his electrical equipment, short out his circuits, and you can still prove you never went near the place. I think they're scared green, up at HQ, that the Darkovans will play some trick with matrixes—wipe the memory banks of their computers, mess up the navigational control center of their starships. The Darkovans have no reason to do such a thing. But the very fact that that kind of technology exists, indi-cates to the Terrans that they ought to know how it works and how to guard against it." Again he grinned, wryly. "That's why I say they'd probably give you a small fortune, or let you write your own ticket, if you turned that one of yours over to them. It's the biggest one I ever saw."

Kerwin recalled fragmentary memories; a Terran starship's stewardess, fumbling at the shirt of a drugged and screaming child. "So tell me, how the hell did *I* get one that size?"

Ragan shrugged. "Kerwin, my friend, if I knew the answer to that, I'd go to the Terran Zone and let them beg me to write *my* own ticket. I'm no fortuneteller"

Kerwin thought about that for a minute. He said, "Maybe a fortuneteller or something like it is what I need. Well, I've heard there are telepaths and psychics all over Darkover."

"You don't know what you're playing around with," Ragan said, "but if you're bound and determined to risk it, I know a woman, down in the Old Town. She used to be— well, no matter. If anybody can tell you, she can. Give her this." He fumbled in his pocket for a bit of paper, scribbled briefly on it. "I've got contacts in the Darkovan Zone; it's how I make my living. I warn you; it'll cost you plenty. She'll be risking something and she'll make you pay for it."

"And you?"

Ragan's brief, dry chuckle sounded loud. "For a name and an address? Hell, you bought me a drink, and maybe I've got a score to settle with another redhead or two. Good luck, *Tallo*." He raised his hand and Jeff watched him go, wondering. What was he being steered into? He studied the address, realizing that it was in the most unsavory part of Thendara, in the Old Town, the haunt of thieves and pimps and worse. He wasn't anxious to go there in Terran uniform. He wasn't anxious to go there at all. Even as a kid, he'd known better.

In the end he made cautious inquiries about matrix mechanics in the better part of town and found out that they operated quite openly; he found the names of three licensed and bonded ones in the most respectable part of the city, and chose one at random.

It lay in a district of wide, high houses, with walls of translucent building stone; here and there he saw a park, a public building of some sort, a walled compound bearing a small placard saying it was the Guild House of the Order of Renunciates—he wondered if that was something like a convent or monastery—and the streets were wide and well-kept without paving stones. In an empty square men were working on an unfinished building whose walls rose gaunt, half completed; men laying stones with mortar, sawing, hammering. In the next street was a market where shawled women bargained for food, small children clinging to their skirts, or sat in little clusters at a stall selling fried fish and deep-fried sweet cakes and mushrooms. The very common-place minutiae of everyday life were reassuring; women gossiping, children playing catch-the-monkey in and out of the stalls and teasing their mothers for sweets or fried mush-rooms. They called this culture *barbarian*, Jeff thought re-sentfully, because they had no complicated transit or technology and felt no need for it. They had no rocket-cars, no great roadways and skyscrapers, no spaceports; but they had no steel factories, or stinking chemical refineries, none of what some Terran writer had called "dark Satanic mills," no dark mines filled with slave labor or robot machinery. Kerwin chuckled dryly to himself; he was romanticizing. Looking at a livery stable where horses were being packed and saddled, he reflected that shoveling horse manure on a morning when the snow lay three feet deep wasn't all that much better than working in a mill or a mine, either.

He located the address he was looking for and was ad-mitted by a quietly dressed woman, who showed him into an enclosed room, a kind of study hung with pale draperies. *In-sulating draperies,* Jeff found himself thinking, and raised a mental eyebrow at himself. What the hell! A woman and a man came toward him; they were tall and stately, fair-skinned with grey eyes and an air of quiet authority and poise. But they both seemed startled, almost awed.

"*Vai dom*," said the man, "you lend us grace. How may we serve you?"

But before Kerwin could answer the woman curled her lip in swift disdain. "*Terranan,*" she said with flat hostility. "What do you want?"

The man's face mirrored the change in hers. They were enough alike to be brother and sister and Kerwin noted in the fluid light that although both were dark of hair and grey-eyed, there were pale reddish glints, hardly noticeable, in the hair of both. But they had nothing like the red hair and aristocratic bearing of the three redheads in the Sky Harbor Hotel that night.

He said, "I want information about this," and extended the matrix to them. The woman frowned, motioned it away, went to a bench and picked up a length of something sparkling, like a silk shot with metallic or crystalline glitter. She shrouded her hand carefully with the stuff, and as she returned and carefully picked up the matrix out of his hand so that her bare hands did not touch it, Kerwin was struck with a brief, painful *déjà vu*.

I saw someone do that, before, that gesture . . . but where? When?

She scanned it briefly, the man looking over her shoulder. Then the man said, with sharp hostility, "Where did you get this? Did you steal it?"

Kerwin knew perfectly well that the accusation did not have quite the force it would have had in the Terran Zone; just the same it made him angry. He said, "No, damn it. I have had it ever since I can remember, and I don't know how I came by it. Can you tell me what it is or where it came from?"

He saw them exchange a glance. Then the woman shrugged and sat down at a small desk, the matrix in her hand. She examined it carefully with a hand lens, her face thoughtful and withdrawn. Before the desk was a heavy glass plate, opaque, dark, with small lights glittering deep inside the glass; the woman made another of those familiar-strange gestures and lights began to wink on and off inside the glass with a hypnotic effect. Kerwin watched, still in the grip of the *déjà vu* thinking, *I have seen this before.*

No. It's an illusion, something to do with one side of your brain seeing it a split second before the other side, and the other side, catching up, remembers seeing it. . . .

The woman said, her back to Kerwin, "It is not on the main monitor screen."

The man bent over her, wrapped his hand in a fold of the insulating stuff, and touched the crystal. Then he looked at the woman, startled, and said, "Do you suppose he knows what he has here?"

"Not a chance," the woman said. "He is from off-planet; how would he know?"

"Is he a spy sent to draw us out?"

"No; he is ignorant, I sense it. But we cannot afford to risk it; too many have died who were touched even by the shadow of the Forbidden Tower. Get rid of him."

Kerwin wondered with a little annoyance if they were going to keep talking right past him Then, in shock, he realized that they were not speaking the dialect of Thendara, nor even the pure *casta* of the mountains. They were speaking that language whose form he somehow knew without being able to understand consciously a single syllable.

The woman raised her head and said to the man, "Give him a chance. Perhaps he is really altogether ignorant and he could be in danger." Then she said to Kerwin in the language of the spaceport, "Can you tell me anything about how you came by this crystal?"

Kerwin said slowly, "I think it was my mother's. I don't know who she was." Then, hesitantly, aware that it was relevant, he repeated the words he had heard the night he was struck down in the Old Town.

"Say to the son of the barbarian that he shall come no more to the plains of Arilinn, that the Golden Bell is avenged. . . ."

The woman suddenly shuddered; he saw her perfect

poise split and crack. Hastily she stood up and the man extended the crystal to Kerwin as if their movements were somehow synchronized.

"It is not for us to meddle in the affairs of the *vai leroni*," she said flatly. "We can tell you nothing."

Kerwin said, shocked, "But—you know something— you can't—"

The man shook his head, his face blank and unreadable. *Why do I feel as if I ought to be able to know what he was thinking?* Kerwin wondered.

"Go, *Terranan*. We know nothing."

"What are the *vai leroni*? What—"

But the two faces, so alike, distant and arrogant, were closed and impassive; and behind the impassivity, frightened; Kerwin knew it.

"It is not for us."

Kerwin felt as if he would explode with frustration. He put out his hand in a futile, pleading gesture, and the man stepped back, avoiding the touch, the woman withdrawing fastidiously.

"But, my God, you can't leave it like that, if you know something—you have to tell me—"

The woman's face softened slightly. "This much, I will say; I thought *that*—" she indicated the crystal, "had been destroyed when—when the Golden Bell was broken. Since they saw fit to leave it with you, they may some day see fit to give you an explanation. But if I were you, I would not wait for it. You—"

"*Latti*!" The man touched her arm. "Leave it! Go," he added to Kerwin, "you are not welcome here. Not in our house, not in our city, not on our world. We have no quarrel with you; but you bring danger on us even with your shadow. Go." And from that, there was no appeal. Kerwin went.

Somehow he had halfway expected this. Another door slammed in his face; like the computer, coded so he could not read the records of his own birth. But he could not drop it here, even though he wanted to, even though he was beginning to be frightened.

He took the precaution of covering his hair; and although he didn't wear the Darkovan cloak, he carefully took off all the insignia of the Service, so that when he went into the Old Town there was nothing that could identify him with the spaceport people.

The address was in a crumbling slum; there was no bell, and after he knocked he stood waiting a long time. He had half resolved to turn away again when the door opened and a woman stood there, holding to the doorframe with an unsteady hand.

She was small and middle-aged, clad in nondescript shawls and bundled skirts, not quite rags and not really dirty, but she gave a general impression of unkempt slovenliness. She looked at Kerwin with dreary indifference; it seemed to him that she focused her eyes with difficulty.

"Do you want something?" she asked, not caring.

"A man named Ragan sent me," he said, and handed her the scribbled slip. "He said you were a matrix technician."

"I was once," she said, still with that deadly indifference. "They cut me off from the main relays years ago. Oh, I can still do some work, but it'll cost you. If it was legal, you wouldn't be here."

"What I want's not illegal, as far as I know. But maybe it's impossible."

A faint spark of interest flickered behind the dull eyes. "Come in." She motioned him into the room. Inside it was clean enough; it had a pungent-familiar smell, herbs burning in a brazier; the woman stirred the fire, sending up fresh clouds of the pungent smoke, and when she turned, her eyes were more alert.

But Kerwin thought he had never seen so colorless a person. Her hair, coiled loose on her neck, was the same faded grey as her bundled shawl; she walked wearily, stooping a

little as if in some chronic pain. She lowered herself carefully into a chair and gestured him, with a tired, abrupt motion of her head, to sit.

"What do you want, *Terranan*?" At his look of surprise,
her faded lips stretched faintly, not quite a smile. "Your
speech is perfect," she said, "but remember what I am.
There is another world in your walk and the set of your
head, in what you do with your hands. Don't waste our time
in lies."

At least she hadn't mistaken him for his mysterious double somewhere, Kerwin thought thankfully, and pushed
back his headgear. He thought, *Maybe if I level with her,
she'll level with me.* He fumbled at his neck and laid down
the crystal in front of her.

"I was born on Darkover," he said, "but they sent me
away. My father was Terran. I thought it would be very simple to find out more about myself."

"It should be, with this," she said. "Fit for a Keeper, it is."
She leaned forward; unlike the other mechanics, she did not
shroud her hand when she touched it. Kerwin flinched; he
hated to have it touched, for some reason. She saw the gesture and said, "So you know *that* much. Is it keyed?"

"I don't know what you mean."

She raised her eyebrows. Then she said, "Don't worry; I
can guard against it, even if it is. I'm not superstitious, and
I learned a long time ago, from the old man himself, that any
halfway-competent technician can do a Keeper's work. I've
done it enough. Let me take it." She picked it up; he felt only
a faint shock. The hands were beautiful, younger than the
rest of her, smooth and supple and the nails well-kept; he
had expected them, somehow, to be gnawed and dirty. Again
the gesture seemed familiar.

"Tell me about it," she said, and Kerwin told her everything, feeling suddenly secure; the way in which he had
been mistaken for some mysterious *other*, the attack in the
street, the failure to find records in the orphanage, the re-

fusal of the two matrix mechanics to tell him anything. At
that she frowned scornfully.

"And they say they are free of superstition! Fools," she
said.

"What can you tell me?"

She touched the crystal with one beautifully manicured
fingertip. She said, "This much: It's not on the main banks.
It may have come from one of the Forbidden Tower people.
I don't recognize it offhand," she said. "But it's hard to believe you have any Terran blood at all. Though there have
been a few, and once I saw old *Dom Ann'dra*. . . . But that's
neither here nor there." She went to a cupboard and rummaged in it, taking out something wrapped in a length of the
insulating silk. Before her on the table she placed a small
wicker-wood frame, then carefully untwisting the silks, she
laid something in the frame. It was a small matrix; smaller
than his own, but considerably larger than the one Ragan
had showed him. Small lights played in it; Kerwin, looking
at them, felt sick and nauseated. The woman looked into her
own matrix, then into Kerwin's, rose, stirred the brazier
again so that clouds of the choking smoke rose, and Kerwin's head began to swim. The smoke seemed to contain
some potent drug, for the woman, inhaling it deeply, stared
at him with a sudden live glitter in her eyes.

"You," she said, "you are not what you seem." Her words
slurred strangely. "You will find what you seek, but you will
destroy it too. You were a trap that missed its firing, they
sent you away to safety, from the blizzard to feed the banshee. . . . You will find the thing you desire, you will destroy
it but you will save it, too. . . ."

Kerwin said rudely, "I didn't come here to have my fortune told."

She seemed not to hear, muttering almost incoherently. It
was dark in the room, except for the dim glow of the brazier,
and very cold. Impatient, Kerwin stirred; she made an imperative gesture and he sank back, surprised at the authority

of the movement. *Muttering, drugged old witch! What the hell was she doing now?*

The crystal on the table, his own crystal, glowed and shimmered; the crystal in the wicker frame, between the woman's slender hands, began slowly to glow with blue fire.

"The Golden Bell," the woman muttered thickly, slurring the words and making them one, *Cleindori*. "Oh yes, Cleindori was beautiful, long, long they sought her in the hills across the river, but she had gone where they could not pursue, the proud superstitious fools preaching the Way of Arilinn. . . ."

All the light in the room, now, was focused on the woman's face, the light that seemed to pour from the blue center of the crystal. Kerwin sat there a long, long time, while the woman stared into the crystal and muttered something to herself. Finally he wondered if she had gone into a trance, if she were a clairvoyant who could answer his questions.

"Who am I?"

"You are the one they managed to send away, the brand snatched from the burning," she said thickly. "There were others, but you were the most likely. They didn't know, the proud Comyn, that you had been snatched away from them. That they had hidden the prey inside the hunter's door, hidden the leaf inside the forest. All of them, Cleindori, Cassilde, the *Terran*, the Ridenow boy. . . ."

The lights in the crystal seemed to coagulate into a brilliant flash of flame. Kerwin flinched as it knifed through his eyes, but he could not move.

And then a scene rose before his eyes, clear and distinct, as if imprinted on the inside of his eyelids:

Two men and two women, all of them in Darkovan clothing, all seated around a table on which lay a matrix crystal in a cradle; and one of the women, very frail, very fair, was bending over it, gripping the cradle so tightly that he could see the knuckles of her hands whitened by that desperate grip. Her face, framed in paling reddish hair, seemed eerily familiar. . . . The men watched, intent, unmoving. One of them had dark hair and dark eyes, animal eyes, and Kerwin heard himself thinking, The Terran, *and knew at the back of his mind that he looked on the face of the man whose name he would bear, and they all watched spellbound while the cold lights played on the woman's face like some strange aurora; and then the tall redheaded man suddenly wrenched the woman's hands from the cradle; the blue fires died and the woman sank back senseless in the dark man's arms. . . .*

The scene swept away; Kerwin saw moving clouds, cold drenching rain falling in a courtyard, a man in a jeweled cloak fastened high at the neck; a tall arrogant man, and Kerwin gasped, recognizing the dream-face of his earliest memories. The scene narrowed again to a high-walled chamber. The women were there, and one of the men. Kerwin seemed to see the scene from a strange perspective, as if he were either up very high or down very low, and he realized that he was *there*, horror and sudden dread making him tremble. He seemed to look away from the four grouped around the matrix, at a closed door, a turning door-handle that moved slowly, very slowly, then was suddenly flung back, blotted out by dark forms that filled the doorway and blotted out the light, rushing forward . . .

Kerwin screamed. It was not his own voice, but the voice of a child, thin and terrible and terrifying, a shriek of utter despair and panic. He slumped forward across the table, the scene darkening before his eyes, remembered screams ringing and ringing on and on in his ears long after his cry had jolted him up to consciousness again.

Dazed, he straightened and passed his hand slowly across his eyes. His hand came away wet with clammy sweat—or tears? Confused, he shook his head. He was *not* in that high-walled room filled with vague shapes of terror. He stood in the stone-walled cottage of the old matrix technician; the fire in the brazier had burned out, and the room was dark and cold. He could just see the woman; she had collapsed forward, her body lying across the table and atop the wicker frame, which had turned sidewise and spilled the crystal out on to the table. But there was no blue light in her crystal now. It lay blank, grey, a featureless piece of glass.

Kerwin looked down at the woman, angry and puzzled. She had shown him *something*—but what did it mean? Why had he screamed? He felt cautiously at his throat. His voice felt frayed.

"What the hell was that all about? I suppose the dark man was my father. But who were the others?"

The woman neither stirred nor spoke, and Kerwin scowled. Drunk, drugged? Not gently, he reached to shake her shoulder. "What was that? What did it mean? Who were they?"

With nightmarish, slow grace, the woman slid down and toppled sideways to the floor. Swearing, Kerwin vaulted the table and knelt at her side, but he already knew what he would discover.

The woman was dead.

CHAPTER SIX

Re-Exile

Kerwin's throat still hurt, and he felt a ragged hysteria gripping at him.

All the doors keep closing in my face!

Then he looked down at the dead woman with pity and a painful guilt. He had dragged her into this, and now she was dead. This unknown unlovely woman, whose name he didn't even know, and he had involved her in the mysterious fate that was tracking him.

He looked at her matrix, lying grey and featureless on the table. Had it died when the woman died, then? Gingerly, he picked up his own and put it into his pocket, looked down at the dead woman again with regret and futile apology, and then, turning away, he went and called the police.

They came, green-clad, cross-belted Darkovans of the City Guard—equivalent of metropolitan police, what there was of it on Darkover—not at all happy to see a Terran there, and they showed it. Reluctantly, with rigid politeness, they allowed him the legal privilege of summoning a Terran consul before questioning, a privilege Kerwin would just as soon have waived. He wasn't at all eager for the HQ to know he had been making inquiries down here.

They asked him questions, and then they didn't like the answers. Kerwin held back nothing, except the fact of his own matrix, or why he had been there to consult the woman in the first place. But in the end, because there wasn't a mark on her, and because the woman had obviously not been sexually molested, and because a Terran medic and a Darkovan both gave their independent opinion that she had died of a heart attack, they let him go, and escorted him formally to the edge of the spaceport. They said goodbye to him there with a certain grim formality that warned him, without words, that if he was found in that part of the city again, they wouldn't be responsible for what happened.

He thought, then, that he had seen the worst of it, when the blind alley led to a dead end and a dead woman. Alone in his quarters, pacing the floor like a caged animal, he reviewed it again and again, trying to make sense of it.

Damn it, there was *purpose* behind it! Some one, or something, was *determined* he should not trace down his own past. The man and woman, refusing to help him, had said, "It is not for us to meddle in the affairs of the *vai leroni*."

That word was unfamiliar to him; he tried to puzzle out the component parts. *Vai*, of course, was simply an additional honorific, meaning something like *worthy* or *excellent*; as in *vai dom*, which meant, roughly, *worthy lord, good sir, your Excellency*, depending on context. *Leroni* he found under *leronis* (singular; mountain dialect) and defined as "probably derived from *laran*, meaning power or inheritance right, especially inherited psychic power; *leronis* can usually be translated *sorceress*."

But, Kerwin wondered, frowning, who then were the *vai leroni*, the worthy sorceresses, and why in the world—*any* world—should anyone believe he was entangled in their affairs?

An intercom buzzer struck through his preoccupation; he growled response into it, then braced himself, for the face of the Legate, in the screen, looked very grim indeed.

"Kerwin? Get yourself up to Administration—on the double!"

Kerwin did as ordered, riding the long elevators to the high, glass-walled penthouse that was the Legate's staff quarters. As he waited outside Administration, he stiffened, seeing through the open door two of the green cross-belted uniforms of City Guardsmen; they came out, walking stiffly on either side of a tall, straight, silver-haired man whose rich dress and short, jeweled, blue-and-silver cloak betokened high Darkovan aristocracy. All three of them looked straight through Kerwin, and Kerwin felt a nagging sensation that the worst had yet to come.

The receptionist motioned him in. The Legate scowled at him and this time did not ask him to sit down.

"So, it's the Darkovan," he said, not kindly. "I might have known. What the hell have you been getting yourself into now?"

He didn't wait for Kerwin's answer.

"You were warned," he said. "You got yourself into trouble before you'd been here a full twenty-eight hours. That wasn't enough; you had to go looking for trouble."

Kerwin opened his mouth to answer, but the Legate gave him no time. "I called your attention to the situation on Darkover; we live here under an uneasy truce at best; and, such as it is, we have agreements with the Darkovans. Which includes keeping nosey tourists out of the Old Town."

The injustice of that made Kerwin's blood boil.

"Look here, sir, I'm not a tourist! I was born and brought up here—"

"Save it," the Legate said. "You got me just curious enough to investigate that cock-and-bull story you told me about having been born here. Evidently you made the whole thing up, for some obscure reason of your own; there's no record of any Jeff Kerwin anywhere in the Service. Except," he added grimly, "the damned troublemaker I'm looking at right now."

"That's a lie!" Kerwin burst out in anger. Then he

stopped himself. He had seen it himself, the red priority circuit for coded access warning. But he had bribed the man; and the man said, *it's my job on the line.*

"This is no world for snoops and troublemakers," the Legate said. "I warned you once, remember; but I understand you had to do some pretty extensive nosing around. . . ."

Kerwin drew breath, trying to present his case calmly and reasonably. "Sir, if I made this whole thing up out of whole cloth, why would anyone be bothered by what you call my 'nosing around'? Can't you see that if anything this proves my story—that there's something funny going on?"

"All it proves to me," said the Legate, "is that you're a nut with a persecution complex; some notion that we're all in a plot to keep you from finding out something or other."

"It sounds so damned logical when you put it that way, doesn't it?" Kerwin said, and his voice was bitter.

"Okay," the Legate said, "just give me one good reason why anyone should bother plotting against one small-time civil servant, son of—as you claim—a spaceman in the Empire, somebody nobody ever heard of? Why would you be that important?"

Kerwin made a helpless gesture. What could he say to that? He knew his grandparents had existed, and he had been sent back to them, but if there was no record on Darkover of any Jeff Kerwin except himself, what could he say? Why would the woman at the orphanage lie? She had said herself that they were eager to retain contact with their boys. What proof did he have? Had he built the whole thing up from wishful thinking? His sanity reeled.

With a long sigh he let the memories go, and the dream.

"All right, sir, I'm sorry. I'll stay out of it; I won't try to find out anything more—"

"You won't have the chance," the Legate said coldly, "you won't be here."

"I won't—" Something struck, grim and knife-cold, in Kerwin's heart. The Legate nodded, his face rigid.

"The City Elders put your name on a list of *persona non grata*," he said. "And even if they hadn't, official policy is to take a dim view of anybody who gets too mixed up in native affairs."

Kerwin felt as if he had been pole-axed; he stood motionless, feeling the blood drain from his face, leaving him cold and lifeless. "What do you mean?"

"I mean I put you down for transfer out," the Legate said. "You can call it that if you want to. In plain words, you've stuck your big nose into too many corners, and we're making damned sure you don't do it again. You're going to be on the next ship out of here.

Kerwin opened his mouth and then shut it again. He steadied himself against the Legate's desk, feeling as if he might fall over if he didn't. "You mean I'm being deported?"

"That's about it," the Legate confirmed. "In practice, it's not that bad, of course. I signed it as if it were a routine transfer application; God knows, we get enough of them from out here. You have a clean record, and I'll give you a clean-sheet recommendation. Within limits, you can have any assignment you've got the seniority for; see the Dispatch board about it."

Kerwin said, through a queer thickening lump in his throat, "But sir, Darkover—" and stopped. It was his home. It was the only place he wanted to be.

The Legate shook his head, as if he could read Kerwin's thoughts. He looked tired, worn, an old man, a weary man, struggling with a world too complex for him. "I'm sorry, son," he said, kindly. "I guess I know how you feel. But I've got a job to do and not an awful lot of leeway in how I do it. That's the way it is; you're going to be on the next ship out of here. And don't put in an application to come back, because you won't get it." He stood up. "I'm sorry, kid," he said, and offered his hand.

Kerwin did not touch it. The Legate's face hardened.

"You're relived from duty as of now; inside twenty-eight hours, I want a formal transfer request filled out, with your preferred routing for assignment; if I have to do it for you, I'll put you through for the penal colony on Lucifer Delta. You're confined to quarters till you leave." He bent over his desk, shuffling the papers there. Without looking up, he said, "You can go."

Kerwin went. So he had lost, then—lost entirely. It had been too big for him, the mystery he faced; he had run up against something entirely beyond him.

The Legate had been lying. He had known that, when the man offered him his hand at the last. The Legate had been forced to send him into exile, and he didn't particularly want to. . . .

Going back into his bleak rooms, Kerwin told himself not to be a fool. Why would the Legate lie? Was he a dreamer, a fool with delusions of persecution, compensating for his orphan childhood with dreams of grandeur?

He paced the floor, went restlessly to the window, staring at the red sun dipping toward the hills. *The bloody sun.* Some romantic poet had given Cottman's Star that name a long time ago. As the swift dark came rushing from the mountains, he clenched his fists, staring into the sky.

Darkover. It's the end of Darkover for me. The world I fought for, and it's kicking me out again. I worked and schemed to get back here, and it's all going for nothing. All I get is frustration, closed doors, death. . . .

The matrix is real. I didn't dream that, or invent it. And that belongs to Darkover. . . .

He put his hand into his pocket and drew out the blue jewel. Somehow this was the key to the mystery, the key to all the closed doors slammed in his face. Maybe he should have shown it to the Legate . . . no. The Legate knew perfectly well that Kerwin was telling the truth; only, for some reason, he had chosen not to admit it. Faced with the matrix, he would simply have invented some other lie.

Kerwin wondered how he knew the man had been lying. But he *knew*. Beyond a doubt, without hesitation, he knew the man had been lying, for some obscure reason of his own. But *why*?

He drew the curtains against the blackness outside, the lights of the spaceport below, and set the crystal on the table. He paused, hesitant, seeing in his mind's eye the picture of a woman sprawled in unlovely death, the terror that had risen in him. . . .

I saw something when she was looking into the matrix, but I can't remember what it was. I only remember that it scared the hell out of me. . . . A woman's face flickered in his mind, dark forms against an opening door. . . . He set his teeth against the surging panic, battering against the closed door of his memory, but he could not remember; only the fear, the scream in a child's voice and darkness.

He told himself sternly not to be a fool. The man Ragan had used this crystal and it hadn't hurt him. Feeling self-conscious, he laid the crystal on the table and shaded his eyes as the woman had done, staring into it.

Nothing happened.

Damn it, maybe there was a special knack to it, maybe he should have hunted up Ragan and persuaded him, or bribed him, to teach him how to use it. Well, too late for that now. He stared fiercely into the crystal, and for a moment it seemed that a pale light flickered inside it, crawling blue lights that made him feel vaguely sick. But it vanished. Kerwin shook his head. He had a crick in his neck and his eyes were playing tricks on him, that was all. The old "crystal-gazing" trick was just a form of self-hypnosis, he'd have to guard against that.

The light remained. It crept, a small faint pinpoint of color moving inside the jewel. It *flared*, and Kerwin jumped;

it was like a red-hot wire touching something inside his brain. And then he heard something, a voice very far away, calling his name . . . no. There were no words. But it was speaking to *him*, to no one else who had ever existed, a vastly *personal* message. It was something like, *You. Yes, you. I see you.*

Or, even more, I *recognize you.*

Dizzily he shook his head, gripping at the edge of the table with his fists. His head hurt, but he could not stop now. It seemed that he could hear speech, just random syllables . . . a low murmuring voice, or voices, that went on and on just below the threshold of awareness, like a running, whispering stream murmuring over sharp stones.

Yes, he is the one.

You cannot fight it now.

Cleindori worked too hard for this to waste it.

Does he know what he has or what is happening?

Be careful! Don't hurt him! He's not accustomed . . .

A barbarian, Terranan . . .

If he is to be any good to us, he must find his way alone and unaided, that much of a test I must insist upon.

We need him too much for that. Let me help . . .

Need that? A Terranan—

That voice sounded like the redhead in the Sky Harbor Hotel, but when Kerwin whirled, half expecting to find that the man had somehow made his way into the very room, there was no one there and the bodiless voices were gone.

He leaned forward, staring into the crystal. And then, as it seemed to expand, to fill the room, he saw the face of a woman.

For a moment, because of the glint of red hair, he thought it was the small, pixielike girl they had called Taniquel. Then he realized that he had never seen her before.

Her hair was red, but a pale red, almost more golden than red; she was small and slender, and her face was round, childish, unmarred. She could not, Kerwin thought, be very far out of her teens. She looked straight at him, with wide, dreamy grey eyes that seemed to look, unfocused, *through* him.

I have faith in you, she said somehow, wordlessly, or at least the words seemed to reverberate inside his head, *and we have such need of you that I have convinced the others. Come.*

Kerwin's hands clenched on the table.

"Where? *Where?*" he shouted.

But the crystal was blank and blue again, and the strange girl was gone; he heard his own cry echo foolishly on empty walls.

Had she ever been there? Kerwin wiped his forehead, damp with cold sweat. Had his own wishful thinking tried to give him an answer? He swept the crystal into his pocket. He couldn't waste time on this. He had to pack for space, dispose of his gear, and leave Darkover, never to return. Leave his dreams behind, and the last of his youth. Leave behind all those vague memories and teasing dreams, those will-o'-the-wisps that had led him halfway to destruction. Make a new life for himself somewhere, a smaller life, bounded by the KEEP OUT sign of the old dead hopes and longing, make a life somehow out of the fragments of his old aspirations, with bitterness and resignation. . . .

And then something rose up inside Jeff Kerwin, something that was not the meek CommTerra employee, something that stood up on its hind legs and pawed the ground and said, cold and clean and unmistakable: *No.*

That wasn't the way it was going to be. The *Terranan* could never force him to go.

Who the hell do they think they are, anyway, those damned intruders on our world?

The voice from the crystal? No, Kerwin thought, the inner voice of his own mind, flatly rejecting the commands of the Legate. This was *his* world, and he'd be damned if they were going to force him off it.

He realized that he was moving automatically, without thought, like a long-buried other self. Kerwin watched himself moving around the room, discarding most of his gear; he thrust half a dozen minor keepsakes into a pocket, left the rest where they were. He put the matrix on its chain around his neck and tucked it carefully out of sight. He started to unbutton his uniform, then shrugged, left it the way it was, but went to a wardrobe and got out the embroidered Darkovan cloak he had bought his first night in Thendara, drew it around his shoulders and did up the fastenings. He glanced briefly in the mirror. Then, without a backward glance, he walked out of his quarters, the thought dimly skittering across the surface of his mind that he would never see them again.

He walked through the central living rooms of bachelor quarters, took a short cut through the deserted dining commons. At the outer door of the section he paused; a clear and unmistakable inner voice said, *no, not now, wait.*

Not understanding, but riding the hunch—what else was there to do?—he sat down and waited. He felt, oddly, not impatient at all. The waiting had the same wary certainty of a cat at a mousehole; a secureness, a—a *rightness*. He sat quietly, hands clasped, whistling a monotonous little tune to himself. He did not feel restless. Half an hour, an hour, an hour and a half went by; his muscles began to feel cramped and he shifted automatically to relieve the tension, but he went on waiting, without knowing what he was waiting for.

Now.

He stood up and stepped out into the deserted corridor. As he walked swiftly down the hall, he found himself wondering if there would be a pickup order out for him if he should be missed from his quarters. He supposed so. He had no plans, except the very basic one of refusing to obey the deportation order. This meant he must somehow get out, not only of the HQ, but of the Spaceport Zone and the entire Terran Zone unobserved. What would come after he did not know and, strangely, did not care.

Still riding the strange hunch, he turned out of the main corridor where he might meet off-duty acquaintances heading for the quarters, and went toward a little-used freight elevator. He told himself that he ought, at least, to take off the Darkovan cloak; if anyone met him wearing it, inside the HQ it would lead to question and discovery. He put up his hand to unfasten the clasps and sling it over his arm; back in uniform, he'd just be another invisible employee walking in the halls.

No.

Clear, unmistakable, the negative warning in his mind. Puzzled, he dropped his hand and let the cloak be. He emerged from the elevator into a narrow walkway and paused to orient himself; this part of the building was not familiar to him. There was a door at the end of the walkway; he pushed it open and emerged into a crowded lobby. What looked like a whole shift of maintenance workers in uniform was milling around, getting ready to go off duty. And a large group of Darkovans in their colorful dress and long cloaks were making their way through the crowd toward the outer door and the gates. Kerwin, at first taken aback by the crowd, realized quickly that no one was paying the slightest attention to him. Slowly, unobtrusively, he made his way through the crowd, and managed to join the group of Darkovans. None of them took the slightest notice of him. He supposed they were some formal delegation from the city, one of the committees that helped administer the Trade City. They formed a random stream in the crowd, going in their own special direction, and Kerwin, at the edge of the group, streamed along with them, into the street, outside the HQ, through the gateway that led out of the enclosure. The

Spaceforce guards there gave them, and Kerwin, only the most cursory of glances.

Outside the gate the group of Darkovans began to break up into twos and threes, talking, lingering. One of the men gave Kerwin a polite look of non-recognition and inquiry. Kerwin murmured a formal phrase, turned quickly and walked at random into a side street.

The Old Town was already shadowed with dimness. The wind blew chill, and Kerwin shivered a little in the warm cloak. Where was he going, anyhow?

He hesitated at the corner of the street where, once in a restaurant, he had faced Ragan down. Should he seek out the place and try and see if the little man could be useful to him?

Again the clear, unmistakable *no* from that inner mentor. Kerwin wondered if he was imagining things, rationalizing. Well, it didn't matter much, one way or the other, and it had gotten him out of the HQ; so whatever the hunch he was riding, he'd stay with it a while. He looked back at the HQ building, already half wiped out in the thickening mist, then tuned his back on it and it was like the slamming of a mental door. That was the end of that. He had cut himself adrift and he would not look back again.

A curious peace seemed to descend over him with this decision. He turned his back on the known streets and began to walk quickly away from the Trade City area.

He had never come quite so far into the Old Town, even on that day he sought out the old matrix mechanic, the day that had ended with her death. Down here the buildings were old, built of that heavy translucent stone, chill against the blowing wind. At this hour there were few people in the streets; now and then a solitary walker, a workman in one of the cheap imported climbing jackets, walked head down against the wind; once a woman carried in a curtained sedan chair on the shoulders of four men; once, moving noiselessly in the lee of the building, a silver-mantled, gliding nonhuman regarded him with uninvolved malice.

A group of street gamins in ragged smocks, barefoot, moved toward him as if to pester him for alms; suddenly they drew back, whispered to each other, and ran off. Was it the ceremonial cloak, the red hair they could see beneath the hood?

The swift mist was thickening; now snow began to fall, soft thick heavy flakes; and Kerwin became quickly aware that he was hopelessly lost in the unfamiliar streets. He had been walking almost at random, turning corners on impulse, with that strange, almost dreamish sensation that it didn't matter which way he went. Now, in a great and open square, so unfamiliar that he had not the slightest idea how far he had come, he stopped, shaking his head, coming up to normal consciousness.

Good God, where am I? And where am I going? I can't wander around all night in a snowstorm, even wearing a Darkovan cloak over my uniform! I should have started out by looking for a place to hide out for a while; or I should have tried to get right out of the city before I was missed!

Dazed, he looked around. Maybe he should try and get back to the HQ, take whatever punishment was coming. No. That way lay exile. He had already settled that. But the curious hunch that had been guiding him all this way seemed to be running out, and now it deserted him entirely. He stood staring this way and that, wiping snowflakes from his eyes and trying to decide which way he should go. Down one side of the square there was a row of little shops, all fast-shuttered against the night. Kerwin mopped his wet face with a wet sleeve, staring through the thick snow at a solitary house; a mansion, really, the town house of some nobleman. Inside there were lights, and he could see, through the translucent wall, dark blurred forms. Drawn almost magnetically to the lights, Kerwin crossed the square and stood just outside the half-open gate. Inside was a flight of shallow steps, which led to the invisible pull of that door.

What am I doing? I can't just walk in there, into a strange house! Have I gone completely crazy?

No. This is the place. They're waiting for me.

He told himself that was madness; but his steps carried him on, automatically, toward the gate. He put a hand on it, and when nothing happened, he opened it and went through and stood on the lower step. And there he stopped, sanity and madness fighting in him, and the worst part of it was, Kerwin wasn't quite sure which was which.

You've come this far. You can't stop now.

You're being an awful God-damned fool, Jefferson Andrew Kerwin. Get out—just turn right around and get the hell out of here before you get yourself into something you really can't handle. Not just something predictable like being slugged and rolled in an alley.

Step by slow step, he went up the sleet-slipperied steps toward the lighted doorway. *Two late to turn back now.* He grasped the handle, noticing peripherally the design, in the shape of a phoenix. He twisted it slowly, and the door opened and Kerwin stepped inside.

Miles away, in the Terran Zone, a man had gone to a communicator and requested a specially coded priority circuit to speak with the Legate.

"Your bird's flown," he said.

The Legate's face on the screen was composed and smug.

"I thought so. Push hard enough and they'd have to make a move. I knew they wouldn't let us deport him."

"You sound awfully sure, sir. He sounds like an independent cuss. Maybe he just walked off on his own; went over the wall. He wouldn't be the first. Not even the first one named Kerwin."

The Legate shrugged. "We'll soon find out."

"You want him tailed any further, then?"

The answer was immediate. "No! Hell, no! These people are nobody's fools! In the state he was in he might not have spotted a tail; it's for damn sure *they* would. Let him go; no strings. It's their move. Now—we wait."

"We've been doing that for more than twenty years," the man grumbled.

"We'll wait twenty more if we have to. But the catalyst's working now; somehow I don't think it will be that long. Wait and see."

The screen went blank. After a while the Legate pushed another button and hit a special access code marked KER-WIN.

He looked satisfied.

CHAPTER SEVEN

Homecoming

Kerwin stood blinking against the warmth and light of the spacious hallway. He mopped snow from his face again, and for a moment all he could hear was the wind and snow outside, slapping against the closed door. Then a bright tinkle of laughter broke the silence.

"Elorie has won," said a light, girlish voice, somehow familiar to him. "I told you so."

A thick velvet curtain parted, just before him, and a girl stood there, a slender young woman with red hair in a green dress with a high collar, and a pixie-pretty face. She was laughing at him. Behind her two man came through the curtains, and Kerwin wondered if he had somehow wandered into a daydream—or nightmare. For they were the three redheads from the Sky Harbor Hotel; the pretty woman was Taniquel, and behind her, the feline and arrogant Auster, the thickset, urbane man who had introduced himself as Kennard. It was Kennard who spoke now.

"Did you doubt it, Tani?"

"The *Terranan*!" Auster stood glowering; Kennard gently moved Taniquel out of his way, and came toward Kerwin, who stood bewildered, wondering if he ought to apologize for this intrusion. Kennard stopped a step or two from Kerwin and said, "Welcome home, my boy."

Auster said something sarcastic, curling his lip in an ironic smile.

Kerwin said, shaking his head, "I don't understand any of this."

"Tell me," Kennard countered, "how did you find this place?"

Kerwin said, too baffled for anything but the truth, "I don't know. I just came. Hunch, I guess."

"No," Kennard said gravely, "it was a test; and you passed it."

"A *test*?" Suddenly Kerwin was both angry and apprehensive. Ever since he landed on Darkover, somebody had been pushing him around; and now, when he made what he thought was an independent move to break away, he found himself led here.

"I suppose I ought to be grateful. Right now all I want is an explanation! Test? What for? Who *are* you people? What do you want with me? Are you still mistaking me for someone else? Who do you think I am?"

"Not who," said Taniquel, "what." And at the same time Kennard said, "No, we knew *who* you were all along. What we had to find out—" And the two of them stopped, looked at each other and laughed. Then the girl said, "You tell him, Ken. He's *your* kinsman."

Kerwin jerked up his head and stared at them, and Kennard said, "We are all your kinsmen, if it comes to that; but I knew who you were, or at least I guessed, from the beginning. And if I had not known, your matrix would have told me, because I have seen it before and worked with it before. But we had to test you, to see if you had inherited *laran*, if you were genuinely one of us."

Kerwin frowned and said, "What do you mean? I am a Terran."

Kennard shook his head and said, "That's as may be. Among us the child takes the rank and privilege of the parent of higher caste. And your mother was a woman of the Comyn; my foster-sister, Cleindori Aillard."

There was a sudden silence, while Kerwin heard the word *Comyn* echo and re-echo in the room.

"Remember," Kennard said at last, "that we mistook you for one of ourselves, that night in the Sky Harbor Hotel. We were not so wrong as we thought—not so wrong as you told us we were."

Auster interrupted again with something unintelligible. It was strange how clearly he could understand Kennard and Taniquel, and hardly a word of Auster's speech.

"Your foster-sister?" Kerwin asked. "Who are you?"

"Kennard-Gwynn Lanart-Alton, Heir to Armida," the older man said. "Your mother and I were fostered together; we are blood kin as well, though the relationship is—complicated. When Cleindori—died—you were taken away; by night and by stealth. We tried to trace her child; but there was, at that time, a—" Again he hesitated. "I'm not trying to be secretive, I give you my word; it's only that I can't imagine how to make it clear to you without giving you a long history of the political complications of forty-odd years ago in the Domains. There were—problems, and when we knew where you were, we decided to leave you there for a time; at least you were safe there. By the time we could try and reclaim you, they had already sent you to Terra, and all we could do was wait. I was reasonably sure of who you were, that night in the hotel. And then your matrix turned up on one of the monitor screens . . ."

"What?"

"I can't explain just now. Any more than I can explain Auster's stupidity when he met you in the bar, except that he'd been drinking. Of course, you weren't exactly cooperative, either."

Again Auster exploded into unintelligible speech, and Kennard motioned him to silence. "Save your breath, Auster, he's not getting a word of it. Anyway, you passed the first test; you have rudimentary *laran*. And because of who you are, and—and certain other things—we're going to find out if you have enough of it to be useful to us. I gather you want to stay on Darkover; we offer you a chance at that."

Dazed, still off balance, and feeling somewhere inside himself that Kennard's explanations were only confusing the issue further, Kerwin could do nothing but stare.

Well, he had followed his hunch; and if it had led him from the trap to the cookpot, he had only himself to thank.

Well, here I am, he thought. *The only trouble is, I haven't the foggiest notion of where "here" is!*

"What is this place?" he asked. "Is it—" He repeated the word he had heard Kennard say: "Armida?"

Kennard shook his head, laughing. "Armida is the Great House of the Alton domain," he said. "It's in the Kilghard Hills, more than a day's ride from here. This is the town house belonging to my family. The rational thing would have been to bring you to Comyn Castle; but there were some of the Comyn who didn't want anything to do with this—" he hesitated "—this experiment until they knew what was going to happen, one way or another. And it was better that we shouldn't let too many people in on what was happening."

Kerwin looked around at the rich draperies, the walls hung with panels of curtain. The place seemed familiar, somehow, familiar and strange, out of those long-ago, half-forgotten dreams. Kennard answered his unspoken thought:

"You may possibly have been here once or twice. As a very young child. I doubt if you would remember, though. Anyhow—" He glanced at Taniquel and Auster. "We should go, as soon as we can. I want to leave the city as quickly as possible. And Elorie is waiting." His face was suddenly somber. "I don't have to tell you that there are—some people—who will take a very dim view of all this, and we want to present them with something already accomplished." His eyes seemed to go right through Kerwin as he said, "You've already been attacked once, haven't you?"

Kerwin didn't waste time wondering how Kennard knew that. He said, "Yes," and Kennard looked grim. He said, "I thought, at first, that Auster was behind it. But he swore to me that he wasn't. I had hoped—those old hates, superstitions, fears—I had hoped a generation would quiet them down." He sighed, turned to Taniquel.

"Let me just say goodnight to the children. Then I'll be ready to go with you."

A little airship, buffeted by the treacherous winds and currents of flowing atmosphere above the crags and ridges of the mountains, flew through the reddening dawn. They had left the storm behind; but the rough terrain, a dizzy distance below, was softened by layers of mist.

Kerwin sat with legs folded up uncomfortably beneath him, watching Auster manipulate the unseen controls. He would not have chosen to share the small forward pilot-cabin with Auster, but there was barely room for Kennard and Taniquel in the small rear cabin, and he had not been consulted about his preference. He was still baffled by the speed with which events had moved; almost at once they had hurried him to a small private landing field at the far edge of the city, and put him aboard this plane. At least, he thought wryly, he now knew more than the Terran Legate, who couldn't imagine what use the Darkovans had for aircraft.

Kerwin still didn't know what they wanted with him; but he wasn't frightened. They weren't exactly friendly; but they somehow—well, they *accepted* him, much as his grandparents had done; it had nothing to do with his character and personality, or whether they liked him—and Auster, at least, definitely *didn't*—they accepted him, like family. Yes, that was it; like family. Even when Kennard had brusquely cut off his flood of questions with "Later, later!" there had been no offense.

The ship had no visible instruments except for some small calibrator dials. One of those Auster had adjusted when they boarded, apologizing curtly for the discomfort— an unpleasant vibration that made Kerwin's ears and teeth ache. It was necessary, Auster told him in a few grudging words, to compensate for the presence of an undeveloped telepath inside the aircraft.

Since then Auster had barely leaned forward, now and then, from his folded-up kneeling posture, stirring a hand languidly as if signaling some unseen watcher. Or, thought Kerwin, as if he were shooing away flies. He had asked, once, what powered the ship.

"Matrix crystal," Auster said briefly.

This made Kerwin purse his lips in a soundless whistle. He had not even remotely guessed that the power of these thought-sensitive crystals could be so enormous. It wasn't psi power alone. He was sure of that. Kerwin had guessed, from what Ragan had told him and what little he had seen, that matrix technology was one of those sciences that Terrans lumped together under the general name of *noncausative sciences*; cyrillics, electromentry, psychokinetics; and Kerwin knew very little of these. They were usually found on nonhuman worlds.

Kerwin was, despite all his fascination, plainly and unequivocally scared. And yet—he had never thought of himself as Terran except by accident of birth. Darkover was the only home he had ever known, and now he knew that he really belonged here, that he was somehow related to their highest nobility, to the Comyn.

The Comyn. He knew very little about them; just what every Terran assigned to Cottman Four knew, which wasn't much. They were a hereditary caste who chose to have as little as possible to do with the Terrans, though they had ceded the spaceport lease and allowed the building of the Trade

Cities. They were not kings, autocrats, priesthood, or government; he knew more about what they were *not* than what they were. But he had had a taste of the fanatical reverence with which they were treated, these red-haired noblemen.

He tried cautiously to unkink his legs without kicking out a bulkhead. "How much further is this city of yours?" he asked Auster.

Auster did not deign to look at him. He was very thin, with a suggestion of the feline in his shoulders and the curl of his arrogant mouth; but he looked familiar somehow, too, in a way Kerwin couldn't quite identify. Well, they were all related somehow; Kennard had said they were all his kinsmen. Maybe Auster looked like Kennard.

"We do not speak the Cahuenga here," Auster said tersely, "and I cannot understand you, or you me, with the telepathic damper adjusted." He made a small gesture toward the calibrator.

"What's wrong with Cahuenga? You can speak it all right—I heard you."

"We are capable of learning any known human tongue," said Auster, with that unconscious arrogance that irritated Kerwin so much, "but the concepts of our world are expressible only in the nexus of our own semantic symbology, and I have no desire to converse in crocodile with a half-breed on trivial matters."

Kerwin fought an impulse to hit him. He was thoroughly tired of his offhand statement about lizard-men, and tireder of having Auster throw it back at him every time he opened his mouth. He'd never known a man quite so easy to dislike as Auster, and if the man was his kinsman, he decided blood relationships didn't mean as much as they were supposed to mean. He found himself wondering just how closely they were related. Not too closely, he hoped.

The sun was just touching the rim of the mountains when Auster stirred slightly, his satirical face relaxing a little, and pointed between twin mountain peaks.

"It lies there," he said, "the plains of Arilinn, and the City, and the Arilinn Tower."

Kerwin moved his cramped shoulders, looking downward at the city of his forefathers. From this altitude it looked like any other city, a pattern of lights, buildings, cleared spaces. The little craft slanted downward in response to one of those shoofly motions of Auster's hands; Kerwin lost his balance, made a wild grab to recover it, and involuntarily fell against Auster's side.

He was wholly unprepared for Auster's reaction. The man forgot the operation of the ship and with a great sweep of his arm, jerked backward, his elbow thrusting out to knock Kerwin away from him, hard. His forearm struck Kerwin a hard blow across the mouth; the aircraft lurched, swerved, and behind them, in the cabin, Taniquel screamed. Auster, recovering himself, made swift controlling movements.

Kerwin's first impulse—to swat Auster in the teeth and be damned to the consequences—died unacted. He held himself in his seat by an act of will, clenching his fists to keep control. He said in Cahuenga, "Fly the damn ship, you. If you're spoiling for a fight, wait till we get landed, and it will be my pleasure to oblige you."

Kennard's head appeared in the narrow doorway between control and rear cabin; he said something questioning, concerned, in a language Kerwin didn't know, and Auster snarled, "Then let him keep his crocodile's paws to himself, damn him!"

Kerwin opened his mouth—it was Auster's sharp movement that had flung him against the other man—and then shut it again. He hadn't done anything to apologize for! Kennard said in a conciliating tone, "Kerwin, perhaps you did not know that any random movement can throw the aircraft off course, when it is being operated by matrix control." He looked at Kerwin thoughtfully, then shrugged. "We'll be landing in a minute, anyway."

The little ship came down smoothly on a small landing field where a few lights were blinking. Auster unfastened a door and a swart Darkovan in a leather jerkin and breeches threw up a short ladder.

"Welcome, *vai dom'yn*," he said, throwing up one hand in a courtly gesture vaguely like a salute. Auster stepped down the ladder, gesturing Kerwin to follow, and they repeated the salute for him. Kennard came down the ladder, fumbling with his feet for the rungs. Kerwin had not realized how excruciatingly lame the older man was; one of the men came, deferentially, to assist Kennard, who accepted the man's arm with good grace. Only a little tightening of his jaw showed Jeff Kerwin what Kennard really thought of accepting the man's help. Taniquel scrambled down the ladder, looking sleepy and cross; she said something to Auster with a scowl and they stood talking together in an undertone. Kerwin wondered if they were married, or lovers; they had a sort of easy intimacy that he associated only with long-term couples. Then she looked up at Kerwin, shaking her head.

"There's blood on your mouth. Have you and Auster been fighting already?"

There was a teasing malice in her voice; she tilted her head to one side, looking first at one of them and then the other. Auster glowered.

"An accident and a misunderstanding," Kennard said quietly.

"*Terranan*," Auster muttered.

"How can you expect him to be anything else? And whose fault is it that he knows nothing of our laws?" Kennard asked. Then he pointed, drawing Kerwin's gaze with the gesture.

"There it lies; the Tower of Arilinn."

It rose upright, squat, and yet, on closer look, incredibly high, fashioned of some brown and glareless stone. The sight seemed to stir in Kerwin some buried *déjà vu* again, as he looked at the Tower rising against the sky, and he said, his voice shaky, "Have I—have I been here before, sir?"

Kennard shook his head. "No, I don't think so," he said. "Perhaps the matrix—I just don't know. Does it seem so familiar to you?" He laid his hand briefly on Kerwin's shoulder—a gesture that surprised the younger man, in view of the taboo that seemed to surround a random touch among these people. Kennard withdrew his hand quickly, and said, "It is not the oldest, or even the most powerful of the Comyn Towers. But for a hundred generations and more our Keepers have worked the Arilinn Tower in an unbroken succession of Comyn blood alone."

"And," said Auster behind them, "with the hundred and first we bring the son of a Terran and of a renegade *leronis* here!"

Taniquel turned on him fiercely. She said, "Are you going to question the word of Elorie of Arilinn?"

Kerwin swung angrily on Auster. He had taken enough from him already; now the man had started on his parents! *The son of a Terran and a renegade* leronis . . .

Kennard's deep voice was harsh:

"Auster, that's enough; I said it before we came here, and I will say it for the last time. The man is not responsible for his parents or their fancied sins. And Cleindori, I remind you, was *my* foster-sister, and *my* Keeper, and if you speak of her again in that tone, you will answer, not to her son, but to *me*!"

Auster hung his head and muttered something; it sounded like an apology. Taniquel came to Kerwin's side and said, "Let's get inside, not stand around on the airfield all day!"

Kerwin felt curious eyes on him as he crossed the field. The air was damp and cold, and it crossed his mind that it would be pleasant to get under a roof, and get warm, and relax, and that he would very much like a bath, and a drink, and some supper—hell—breakfast! Anyhow, he'd been up all night.

"All in good time," Kennard said, and Kerwin jumped, realizing he would have to get used to that trick Kennard had of reading his thoughts. "First, I'm afraid, you'll have to meet the others here; naturally we're anxious to know all about you, especially those of us who haven't had a chance to meet you face to face yet."

Kerwin wiped off the blood still oozing from his lip. He wished they'd let him clean up before thrusting him into the presence of strangers. He had not yet learned that telepaths seldom paid any attention to what a man looked like on the outside. He walked across the bricked-in quadrangle of a building that looked like a barracks, and through a long passageway barred with a wooden gate. A familiar smell told him that horses were stabled nearby. Only as they neared the Tower did he become aware of the way in which the clean sweep of its architecture was marred by the cluster of low buildings around its foot. They went across two more outer courtyards, and finally reached a carven archway across which shimmered a thin, rainbow mist.

Here Kennard paused momentarily, saying to Kerwin, "No living human, except those of pure and unbroken Comyn blood, has ever crossed this Veil."

Kerwin shrugged. He felt he should be impressed or something, but he was running low on surprise. He was both tired and hungry, he hadn't slept in forty-eight hours, and it made him nervous to realize that they were all, even Auster, watching to see what he would say or do when faced with this. He said irritably, "What is this, a test? My hat's fresh out of rabbits, and anyway, you're writing the script. Do we go this way?"

They kept on waiting, so he braced himself and stepped through the trembling rainbow.

It felt faintly electric, like a thousand pins and needles, as if his whole body were a foot that had gone to sleep, and when he looked back he could not see the others except as the vaguest of shadows. Suddenly he began to shake; had this all been an elaborate build-up to some kind of trap? He stood alone in a tiny windowless cubicle, a cul-de-sac, only the rainbow behind him showing the faintest of lights.

Then Taniquel stepped through the rainbow shimmer, Auster and Kennard following. Kerwin let out a sigh of foolish relief . . . if they'd meant him any harm, they wouldn't have had to bring him this far!

Taniquel made signals with her fingers, not unlike those Auster had used controlling the aircraft, and the cubicle shot upward, with such suddenness that Kerwin swayed and almost fell again. It shivered and stopped and they stepped out through another open archway into a lighted room that opened, in turn, on a broad terrace.

The room was huge, rising to echoing space, yet paradoxically gave an impression of warmth and intimacy. The floor was laid with old tiles worn uneven, as if they had seen many feet walking on them. At the far end of the room was a fire that smelled of fragrant smoke and incense, and something furry and dark and not human crouched there, doing something to the fire with a long, oddly-shaped bellows. As Kerwin came in, it turned large pupilless green eyes on him, fixing him with an intelligent stare of question.

To the right of the fire was a heavy carven table of some glossy wood, a few scattered armchairs, and a big dais or divan covered with heaps of cushions. Tapestries hung on the walls. A middle-aged woman rose out of one of the chairs and came toward them. She stopped a step away from Kerwin, regarding him with cool, intelligent grey eyes.

"The barbarian," she said. "Well, he looks it, with blood on his face. Any more fighting, Auster, and you can go back to the Nevarsin House of Penitence for a full season." She added, considering, "In winter."

Her voice was husky and harsh; there was grey liberally salted in hair that had once been gingery red. Her body was thick and compact beneath the heavy layers of skirts and shawls she wore, but was too sturdy to look fat. Her face was humorous and intelligent, wrinkled around the eyes.

"Well, what name did the *Terranan* give you?"

Kerwin told the woman his name, and she repeated it, her lip curling slightly.

"Jeff Kerwin. I suppose that was to be expected. My name is Mesyr Aillard, and I am your very remote cousin. Don't think I'm proud of the relationship. I'm not."

Among telepaths, polite social lies would be meaningless. Don't judge their manners by Terran standards. Kerwin thought that in spite of her rudeness, there was something about this hearty old lady that he rather liked. He only said courteously, "Perhaps, one day, I can change your mind, Mother." He used the Darkovan word that meant, not precisely *mother*, nor yet *foster-mother*, but a general term for any female relative of a mother's generation.

"Oh, you can call me Mesyr," she snapped. "I'm not *that* old! And close your face, Auster, the hole in it would swallow a banshee! He hasn't the faintest notion that he's being offensive, he doesn't know our customs, how would he?"

"If I have given offense when I intended courtesy—" Kerwin began.

"At that you call me *Mother* if you want to," Mesyr said. "I never go near the screens any more, not since my cub Corus was old enough to work in them; *that* much of a taboo I still observe. My son, Corus; what do we call you, *Jefferson*—" She stumbled a little over the name. "*Jeff*?"

A long-limbed youngster in his teens came and gave Kerwin his hand, as if it were a formal act of defiance. He grinned quirkily in a way that reminded Kerwin of Taniquel and said, "Corus Ridenow. Have you been off-world, in space?"

"Four times. Three other planets, including Terra itself."

"Sounds interesting," Corus said, almost wistfully. "I've never been further than Nevarsin, myself."

Mesyr scowled at Corus and said, "This is Rannirl. Our technician.

Rannirl was about Kerwin's own age, a thin, tall competent-looking fellow with a shadow of red beard, and heavy cal-lused muscular hands. He did not offer to shake hands with Jeff, but bowed formally and said, "So they found you. I didn't expect it, and I didn't expect you could make it through the Veil. Kennard, I owe you four bottles of Ravnet wine."

Kennard said with a cordial grin, "We'll drink it together next holiday—all of us. I believe you made a wager with Elorie, too? Your passion for a bet will ruin you some day, my friend. And where is Elorie? She should be on hand to claim the hawk she wagered, if nothing more."

"She will be down in a few minutes," said a tall woman, whom Kerwin decided to be about Mesyr's age. "I am Neyrissa." She was redheaded, too, red glints on rusty-brown hair, tall and angular and plain, but she met Jeff's eyes with a quick, direct stare. She didn't look friendly, but she wasn't hostile, either. "Are you going to be working as monitor here? I don't like to work outside the circle, it's a waste of my time."

"We haven't tested him yet, Rissa," Kennard said, but the older woman shrugged.

"He has red hair, and he made it through the Veil without being hurt, and that's enough test for me; he's Comyn," she said. "But I suppose you have to find out which *donas* he has. Cassilda grant he's Alton or Ardais, we need the power of that. We're over-balanced on Ridenow gifts—"

"I resent that," said Taniquel gaily. "Are you going to stand there and let her say that, Corus?"

The teenager laughed and said, "In these days we can't afford to be choosy; that's what this is all about, isn't it, that we can't find enough people to work at Arilinn? If he has Cleindori's talents, that's splendid, but don't forget he has Ridenow blood, too."

"We won't know for a while whether he will make monitor or mechanic, or even a technician," Kennard said. "That will be for Elorie to say. Here's Elorie now."

They turned to the door; and then Kerwin realized that the silence in the room was his own imagination, for Mesyr and Rannirl and Neyrissa were still talking, and only in his own mind did a silence move around the girl who stood framed in the doorway. In that instant, as her grey eyes lifted to his, he recognized the face he had seen in the matrix crystal.

She was small and delicately made, and Kerwin realized that she was very young; perhaps even younger than Taniquel. Copper hair, sunrise gold, lay in straight pale strands around her sun-browned cheeks. Her dress was a formal robe of heavy crimson, pinned at the shoulders with clasps of heavy metal; dress and clasps seemed too weighty for her slenderness, as if the slim shoulders drooped under their burden; a child burdened with the robes of a princess or a priestess. She had the long-legged walk of a child, too, and a child's full sulky underlip, and her eyes, framed in long lashes, were grey and dreamy.

She said, "This is my barbarian, I suppose?"

"Yours?" Taniquel lifted her eyebrows at the girl in the crimson robe and giggled, and the grey-eyed girl said in her soft light voice, "Mine."

"Don't fight over me," Kerwin said. He couldn't help feeling a little amused.

"Don't flatter yourself," Auster snarled. Elorie raised her head and gave Auster one sharp, direct look, and to Kerwin's astonishment Auster lowered his head like a whipped dog.

Taniquel looked at Kerwin with that special smile—it was, Kerwin thought, as if they shared some secret—and said, "And this is our Keeper, Elorie of Arilinn. And now that's really all of us, so you can sit down and have something to eat and drink and recover your wits a little. I know this has been a long night, and hard for you."

Kerwin accepted the drink she put into his hand. Kennard lifted his glass to Kerwin and said, with a smile, "Welcome home, my lad." The others joined in, gathering around him, Taniquel with her kittenish grin, Corus with that odd mixture of curiosity and diffidence, Rannirl with a reserved, yet friendly smile, Neyrissa openly studying and appraising him. Only Elorie neither spoke nor smiled, giving Kerwin a grave direct glance over the rim of her goblet, then lowering her eyes. But he felt as if she, too, had said, "Welcome home."

Mesyr set her glass down firmly.

"That's that. And now, since we all stayed up all night to see whether they'd be able to get you back safely, I suggest we all get to bed and have some sleep."

Elorie rubbed her eyes with childish doubled fists and yawned. Auster moved to Elorie's side and said angrily, "You've exhausted yourself again! For *him*," he added, with a furious glance at Kerwin. He went on speaking, but he had switched to a language Kerwin couldn't understand.

"Come along," Mesyr said, jerking her head at Kerwin. "I'll take you upstairs and find you a room. Explanations can come later, when we've all had some sleep."

One of the nonhumans went before them, bearing a light, as Mesyr led the way through a wide echoing hallway, up a long flight of mosaic stairs.

"One thing we're not short of is houseroom," she said. "So if you don't like this one, look around and find one that's empty and move into it. This place was built to hold twenty or thirty, they used to have three complete circles here, each with its own Keeper, and there are eight of us— nine, with you. Which, of course, is why you're here. One of the *kyrri* will bring you anything you want to eat, and if you need someone to help you dress, or anything like that, ask it for help. I'm sorry we have no human servants, but they can't come through the Veil."

Before he could ask any more questions, Mesyr said, "I'll

see you at sunset. I'll send someone to show you the way,"
and went away. Kerwin stood and looked around the room.

It was huge and luxurious, not just a room but a suite of
rooms. The furnishing were old, and the hangings on the
walls were faded. In an inner room was a great bed on a
dais; the prints of generations of feet had worn depressions
in the tiles, but the bedding was fresh and white and smelled
faintly of incense. There were some old books and scrolls on
shelves, and a couple of musical instruments on a shelf. Kerwin wondered who had last lived in this room, and how long
ago. The little furry nonhuman was opening curtains to let in
the light in the outer room, closing them to shade the inner
room, turning down the bed. Exploring the suite, Kerwin
found a bath of almost sybaritic luxury, with a sunken tub
deep enough to swim in; and other fixtures to match, alien-
looking, but, he discovered, provided with everything a
human could want and a few things he wouldn't have
thought of for himself. There were a few small, carved
ivory-and-silver jars on a shelf; curiously he opened one. It
was empty, except for a little dried, resinous paste at the bottom. Cosmetic or perfume, a ghost of some long-dead
Comyn *leronis* who had once inhabited these rooms. Was
the room filled with ghosts? The perfume stabbed another of
those half-memories buried in his mind; he supposed he
must have smelled it when he was very young, and he stood
very still, fumbling for the memory; but it eluded him . . . he
shook his head resolutely, closed the jar. The memory receded, a dream within a dream.

He went back into the sitting-room of the suite. A painting hung there—a slender copper-haired woman struggling
in the grip of a demon. Kerwin's childhood memories of
Darkovan legend identified the mythical figures, the ravish-
ment of Camilla by the demon Zandru. There were other
paintings from Darkovan legend; he recognized some from
the *Ballad of Hastur and Cassilda*, the legendary Cassilda at
her golden loom, bending over the unconscious form of the

Son of Light on the shores of Hali, Camilla bringing cherries and fruits to him, Cassilda with a starflower in her hand, Alar at his forge, Alar chained in hell with the she-wolf gnawing at his heart, Sharra rising in flames . . . Camilla pierced with the shadow-sword. Vaguely he remembered that the Comyn claimed to be descended from the mythical Hastur, Son of Light. He wondered what the God of the legends had to do with the present-day Hasturs of the Comyn. But he was too tired to wonder for long, or ask any more questions. He went and threw off his clothes and crawled into the big bed, and after a time he fell asleep.

When he woke the sun was declining, and one of the soft-footed nonhumans was moving around in the bathroom, drawing water from which came a faint perfume. Remembering what Mesyr had said about a meeting at sunset, Kerwin bathed, shaved, ate some of the food the nonhuman brought him. But when the furry creature gestured toward the bed, where he had laid out some Darkovan clothing, Kerwin shook his head and dressed in the dark uniform of Terran Civil Service. He was sourly amused at himself. Among Terrans he felt a need to emphasize his Darkovan blood, but here he felt a sudden compulsion not to deny his Terran heritage. He wasn't ashamed of being the son of a Terran, whatever Auster said, and if they wanted to call him barbarian, well, let them!

Without a knock, or the slightest word of warning the girl Elorie came into his room. Kerwin started, taken aback by the intrusion; if she'd come in two minutes earlier, she'd have caught him in his bare skin! Even though he was dressed, except for his boots, it disconcerted him!

"Barbarian," she said with a low laugh. "Of course I knew! I'm a telepath, remember?"

Flushing to the roots of his hair, Kerwin put his foot into his other shoe. Obviously the conventions of life in a group of telepaths wouldn't be what he was accustomed to.

"Kennard was afraid you'd get lost, trying to come down

to the big hall; and I told him I'd come and show you the way."

Elorie was no longer wearing the heavy formal robe, but a filmy gown, embroidered with sprays of starflowers and bunches of cherries. She was standing just beneath one of the legendary paintings, and the resemblance was immediately apparent. He looked from the painting to the girl and asked, "Did you sit for your portrait?"

She glanced up indifferently. "No; that was my great-great-grandmother," she said. "The women of the Comyn, a few generations ago, had a passion for being painted as mythological characters. I copied the dress from the painting, though. Come along."

She wasn't being very friendly, or even very polite; but she did seem to take him for granted, as they all had done.

At the end of the hallway, about to lead the way down a flight of long stairs, Elorie paused and went to a window where a deep embrasure in the wall looked over a sunset landscape.

"Look," she said, and pointed. "From here you can see just the tip of the mountain peak at Thendara—if your eyes are trained to look. There is another Comyn Tower there. Though most of them are empty now."

Kerwin strained his eyes but could see only plains and the far away foothills dying into bluish haze. He said, "I'm still confused. I don't really know what the Comyn is, or what the Towers are, or what a Keeper is—aside," he added, smiling, "from being a very beautiful woman."

Elorie simply looked at him, and before the direct, leveled stare, Kerwin lowered his own eyes; she made him feel that the compliment had been both rude and intrusive.

Then she said, "It would be easier to explain what we do than what we *are*. What we *are* . . . There are so many legends, old superstitions, and somehow we have to live up to them all . . ." She looked into the distance for a moment, then she said, "A Keeper, basically, works in the central po-

sition, centerpolar if you wish, of a circle of matrix technicians. The Keeper—" A faint frown appeared between Elorie's pale eyebrows, as she obviously considered how to put
it into words he could understand "A Keeper is, technically,
no more than a specially trained matrix worker who can
gather up all of her circle of telepaths into a single unit, act
as a kind of central coordinator to make the mental linkages.
The Keeper is always a woman. We spend our entire childhood training for it, and sometimes—" She turned to the
window, looking over the mountains—"We lose our powers
after only a few years. Or give them up of our own accord."

"Lose them? Give them up? I don't understand," Kerwin
said, but Elorie only shrugged slightly and did not answer.
Kerwin was not to know until a long time later just how
much Elorie overestimated his telepathic abilities. She had
never in her life known any man, or for that matter anyone
at all, who could not read at such close quarters any thought
she chose. Kerwin knew nothing, as yet, of the fantastic
seclusion in which the young Keepers lived.

At last she went on. "The Keeper is always a woman—
not since the Ages of Chaos have men lawfully worked as
Keeper. The others—monitors, mechanics, technicians—
can be men or women. Although in these days it is easier to
find men for the work. But not very easy, even then. I hope
that you will accept me as Keeper and that you will be able
to work very closely with me."

"That sounds like nice work," Kerwin said, looking ap-
preciatively at the lovely girl before him. Elorie whirled and
stared at him, her mouth wide open in disbelief. Then, her
eyes blazing, her cheeks aflame, she said, "Stop it! *Stop it!*
There was a day on Darkover, you barbarian, when I could
have had you killed for looking at me like that!"

Kerwin, dismayed and amazed, backed away a step. He
said, feeling numb, "Take it easy, miss—Miss Elorie! I
didn't mean to say anything to offend you. I'm sorry—" he

shook his head, not comprehending—"but remember, if I offended you, I haven't the slightest idea how, or why!"

Her hands gripped on the rail, so hard that he could see the white knobs of her knuckles. They looked so frail, those white hands, narrow, with delicate tapered fingers. After a moment of silence, a long moment that stretched, she let go of the rail, tossing her head with a little impatient movement.

She said, "I had forgotten. I heard you insulted Mesyr, too, without the slightest idea that you had done so. If Kennard is to stand as your foster-father here, he had better teach you something of elementary courtesy! Enough of that, then. You said you didn't even know what the Comyn were—"

"A governing body, I thought—"

She shook her head. "Only recently, and not very much; originally, the Comyn were the seven telepath families of Darkover, the Seven Domains, each holding one of the major Gifts of *laran*."

Kerwin blurted, "I thought the whole place was crawling with telepaths!"

She shrugged that off. "Everyone alive has some small degree of *laran*. I'm speaking of special psychokinetic and psi gifts, the Comyn Gifts, bred into our families in the centuries past—in the old days it was believed that perhaps they were inherited, that the Comyn were descended from the seven children—some people say the seven sons, but personally I find that hard to believe—of Hastur and Cassilda; maybe it's because in the old days the Comyn were known as the Hastur-kin, or the Children of Hastur. Specifically, the Gifts of *laran* center upon the ability to use a matrix. You know what a matrix is, I take it."

"Vaguely."

Her pale eyebrows lifted again. "I was told you had the matrix belonging to Cleindori, whose name is written here as Dorilys of Arilinn."

"I do," Jeff said, "but I haven't the faintest idea what it *is*, essentially, and even less notion of what it's good for." He had decided, a long time ago, that the sort of thing Ragan did with his small matrix was essentially irrelevant; and these people were very serious about it.

She shook her head, almost in wonder. "And yet we found you, guided you with it!" she said. "That proved to us that you had inherited some of the—" She paused and said angrily, "I'm *not* evasive! I'm trying to put it into words you can understand, that's all! We traced Cleindori's matrix through the monitor banks and relays, which proved to us that you had inherited the mark of our caste. A matrix, essentially, is a crystal that receives, amplifies, and transmits thought. I could talk about space lattices, and neuro-electronic webs, and nerve channels, and kinetic energons, but I'll let Rannirl explain all that; he's our technician. Matrixes can be as simple as this—" she touched a tiny crystal, that, in total defiance of gravity, suspended her filmy gown from her throat—"or they can be enormous, synthetically-made screens—the technical term is *lattices*—with immensely complex man-made interior crystalline structures, each crystal of which responds to amplification from a Keeper. A matrix—or rather, the power of thought, of *laran* controlled by a skilled matrix technician or Keeper's circle— can release pure energy from the magnetic field of a planet, and channel it, either as force or matter. Heat, light, kinetic or potential energy, the synthesis of raw materials into usable form—all those things were once done by matrix. You do know that thought rhythms, brain waves, are electrical in nature?"

Kerwin nodded. "I've seen them measured. We call the instrument an electro-encephalograph—" He spoke the words in Terran Standard, not knowing if the Darkovans had a word for it, and began to explain how it measured and made visible the electrical energies of the brain, but she shrugged impatiently.

"A simple and clumsy instrument. Well, in general, thought waves, even those of a telepath, can't have much effect in the material universe. Most of them can't move a single hair. There are exceptions, special forces—well, you'll learn about that. But in general, the brain waves themselves can't move a single hair. But the matrix crystals somehow act to transform force into form. That's all."

"And the Keepers—"

"Some matrixes are so complex that one person can't handle them; it takes the energy of several minds, linked together and feeding through the crystal, to form a nexus of energy. A Keeper handles and coordinates the forces. That's all I can tell you," she said abruptly, and turned, pointing down the stairs. "Straight down that way." She turned and walked away in a flutter of filmy draperies, and Kerwin watched her go, startled. Had he done something, again, to offend her? Or was this some childish whim? She *looked* childish enough, certainly!

He went down the stairs, finding himself again in the great firelit hall where, this morning at sunrise, they had welcomed him—welcomed him *home*? His home? The room was completely empty, and Kerwin dropped into one of the cushioned chairs, burying his head in his hands. If someone didn't explain things fairly soon, he was going to go crazy with frustration!

Kennard found him there, that way; Kerwin looked up at the older man and said helplessly, "It's too much. I can't take it all in. It's too much, coming all at once. I don't understand it, I don't understand any of it!

Kennard looked down at him with a curious mixture of compassion and amusement. "I can see how it would be," he said. "I lived a few years on Terra; I know all about culture shock. Let me get off my feet." He lowered himself, carefully, to the mass of cushions, and leaned back, hands clasped behind his head. "Maybe I can clear it up for you. I owe you that."

Kerwin had heard that the Darkovans, the nobility anyhow, had little to do with the Empire; the news that Kennard
had actually lived on Terra amazed him, but no more than
anything else that had happened in the last day or so, no
more than his own presence here. He was all but immune to
further shock. He said, "Start with this. Who am I? Why the
devil am I here?"

Kennard ignored the question, staring into space over
Kerwin's head. After a while he said, "That night in the Sky
Harbor Hotel; do you know what I saw?"

"Sorry. Not in the mood for guessing games." Kerwin
wanted to ask straight questions and get straight answers; he
definitely didn't want to answer more questions himself.

"Remember, I hadn't the least notion who you were. You
looked like one of us, and I knew you weren't. I saw a Terran, but I'm an Alton, I have one of those screwy, out-of-
phase time perceptors. So I looked at the Terran and I saw a
child, a confused child, one who had never known who or
what he was. I wish you had stayed and talked to us, then."

"I do, too," Kerwin said slowly. *A child who had never
known who or what he was.* Kennard had put it very precisely. "I grew up, all right. But I left myself somewhere."

"Maybe you'll find yourself here." Kennard got slowly to
his feet, and Kerwin rose too; he held out a hand to assist the
older man, but Kennard drew away; after a moment, Kennard smiled self-consciously and said, "You're wondering
why—"

"No," said Kerwin, suddenly understanding that all of
them had deftly avoided touching him. "I hate people
jostling me; I've never gotten along with most people at
close quarters. And I feel like hell in a crowd. Always have."

Kennard nodded. "*Laran*," he said. "You have just
enough to find physical contact distasteful—"

Kerwin chuckled. "I wouldn't go so far as to say *that*—"

Kennard said, with a sardonic shrug, "Distasteful except
in circumstances of deliberate intimacy. Right?"

Kerwin nodded, thinking over the rare personal encounters of his life. He knew he had gravely distressed his Terran grandmother by his violent distaste for demonstrations of affection. And yet he had grown fond of the old lady, had loved her in his own way. His work associates—well, it occurred to him that he had treated them as Auster had treated him on the plane: violently rebuffing the slightest personal contact, shrinking physically from a random touch. It hadn't made him particularly popular.

"You're how old? Twenty-six, twenty-seven? Of course I know how old you are, Darkovan—I was one of the first ones Cleindori told—but I never can convert that to Terran reckoning. It was too long ago I lived on Terra. Hell of a long time to live outside your proper element!"

"Proper element hell," Kerwin retorted." Show me where I fit into this mess, will you?"

"I'll try." Kennard went to a table in the corner and poured himself a drink from an assortment of bottles there; lifted his eyebrows in question at Kerwin.

"We'll have drinks when the others come down; but I'm thirsty. You?"

"I'll wait," Kerwin said. He'd never been that much of a drinker. Kennard's bad leg must be giving him considerable pain if he'd break custom this way, the thought flickered through his mind and he wondered impatiently where it had come from, as the older man came cautiously back to his seat.

Kennard drank, set the glass down, locked his fingers meditatively. "Elorie told you; there are seven families of telepaths on Darkover, a ruling family for each of the Seven Domains. The Hasturs, the Ridenow, Ardais, the Elhalyn, the Altons—my family—and the Aillard. Yours."

Kerwin had been counting. "That's six."

"We don't talk about the Aldarans. Although some of us have Aldaran blood, of course, and Aldaran gifts. And there's been some intermarriage—well, we won't talk about that, that's a long story and a shameful one; but the Aldarans were exiled from the Domains a long time ago; I couldn't tell you all about that now, even if I knew it all, and even if we had the time—which I don't and we don't. But, with only six main telepath families—have you any idea how inbred we are?"

"You mean that normally you marry only within your caste? Telepaths?"

"Not entirely. Not—deliberately," Kennard said, "but, being a telepath, and being isolated in the Towers, only with others of our own kind—it's like a drug." His voice was not quite steady. "It completely unfits you for—for contact with outsiders. You, well, you get lost in it, and when you come up for air, as it were, you find you can't breathe ordinary air any more. You find you can't stand having outsiders around, people who aren't tuned to your thoughts, people who—who jostle against your mind. You can't come close to them; they aren't quite real to you. Oh, it wears off, after a while, or you couldn't live outside the Tower at all, but—but it's a temptation. Non-telepaths feel to you like barbarians, or like strange animals, alien, wrong . . ." He was staring into space, over Kerwin's head. "It spoils you for any kind of contact with ordinary people. With women. Even at your level, I should imagine, you've had trouble with women who can't—can't share your feelings and thoughts. After ten years at Arilinn, anything else is like—like bedding with a brute beast . . ."

The silence stretched while Kerwin thought about that, about the curious alienation, the sense of difference, which had come between him and every woman he had ever known. As if there had to be something more, deeper than the most intimate contact. . . .

Abruptly with a little shiver, Kennard recalled himself, and his voice sounded harsh.

"Anyway. We're inbred mentally, even more than physically; just because of that inability to tolerate outsiders. And

the physical inbreeding is bad enough; some very strange re-
cessives have come up. A few of the old Gifts are bred out
altogether; I haven't seen more than one or two catalyst
telepaths in my lifetime That's the old Ardais gift, but Dom
Kyril didn't have it, or if he did he never learned to use it,
and he's mad as a banshee in a Ghost Wind. In the Aillards,
the Gift has become sex-linked; shows up only in the
women, and the men don't carry it. And so forth, and so
on. . . . If you learn anything about genetics, you'll find out
what I mean. A solid outbreeding program might still save
us, if we could do it; but most of us can't. So—" he
shrugged. "Every generation fewer and fewer of us are born
with the old *laran* Gifts. Mesyr told you; once there were
three circles here at Arilinn, each with its own Keeper. Once
there were over a dozen Towers; and Arilinn was not the
largest. Now—well, there are three other Towers working a
mechanic's circle; we are the only Tower with a fully qualified Keeper, which means Elorie is virtually the only Keeper
on Darkover. And, within the Comyn, and the minor nobility connected to us by blood, there are hardly enough of us,
in each generation to keep them alive. So there are two lines
of thought within the Comyn." He spoke briskly now, without a trace of the earlier remoteness. "One faction felt we
should cling to our old ways while we could, resist every
change, until we died out, as we inevitably would in a generation or two, and it didn't matter any more; but at least we
would remain what we were. Others felt that, with change
inevitable, or at least the only alternative to death, we should
make what changes we could tolerate, before intolerable
ones were forced upon us. These people felt that matrix science could be taught to anyone with the rudiments of skill at
laran, developed and trained to work in the same ways that
a Comyn telepath could do. There were a few of this faction
in power in the Comyn a generation ago, and during those
few years, matrix mechanics came into being as a profession. During that time we discovered that most people have

some psi power—enough to operate a matrix, anyway—and could be trained in the use of matrix sciences."

"I've met a couple," Kerwin said.

"You've got to remember," Kennard told him, "that this was complicated by a lot of intense, very emotional attitudes. It was virtually a religion, and the Comyn were almost a priesthood at one time. The Keepers, especially, were objects of religious fanaticism that amounted to worship. And now we come to where you fit into the story."

He shifted his weight, uncomfortably, sighed and stared at Jeff Kerwin. Finally he said, "Cleindori Aillard was my foster-sister. She was a *nedestro* of her clan; that means she was not born in a legitimate marriage, but was the daughter of an Aillard woman and one of the Ridenow, a younger son of that clan. She carried Aillard name because among us a child takes the name of the parent of higher rank, not necessarily the father's name as you do on Terra. She and I were brought up together from the time she was a small girl, and she was handfasted—which is a sort of pledge of marriage, more between the families than the persons concerned—to my older brother Lewis. Then she was chosen to be trained as Keeper at Arilinn."

Kennard was still, his face bitter and remote again. Then he said, "I don't know all the story; and I swore an oath—they forced me to swear, when I came back to Arilinn—there are things I can't tell you. Anyway, during part of it I was away, fostered on Terra; that's a long story, too. My father chose a Terran foster-son, and I went to Terra as what you'd call, I suppose, an exchange student, while Lerrys was fostered here. And so I did not see Cleindori for six or seven years, and when I came back she was Dorilys of Arilinn. Keeper. Cleindori was—in some ways—the most powerful person in the Comyn, the most powerful woman on Darkover. Lady of Arilinn. She was a *leronis* of surpassing skill; and, like all Keepers, she was pledged virgin, living in seclusion and a rigid isolation . . . she was the last. Even

Elorie was not trained as Cleindori had been trained, in the old ways; Cleindori accomplished that much, at least." He slid away for a moment into the bitter remoteness again. Then, sitting upright on his cushions, his voice dry and emotionless, he said: "Cleindori was a fighter; a rebel. She was a reformer at heart; and, as Lady of Arilinn, and one of the last surviving Aillard women in the direct line, she had considerable power and Council status in her own right. So she tried to change the laws of Arilinn. She fought bitterly against the new Council, and the conviction they held, that Comyn Towers should maintain their secrecy and their old, protected, semi-religious status. She tried to bring in outsiders to the Towers—she succeeded in that, a little. Neskaya Tower, for example, will take anyone with telepathic power—Comyn, commoner, or beggar born in a ditch. But then, they have not had a real Keeper for half a hundred years. But then she began to attack the taboos around her own special status. And that was too much, that kind of heresy raised up rebellion . . . Cleindori broke the taboos again and again, insisting that she could break them with impunity because, as Keeper, she was responsible only to her own conscience. And at last she ran away from Arilinn."

Kerwin had begun to suspect that it would end there, but even so it was a shock. He said very low, "With an Earthman. With my father."

"I am not sure whether she left the Tower with him, or whether he came later," Kennard evaded. "But yes, this is why Auster hates you, why there are many, many people who think your very existence is a sacrilege. It was not unheard of that a Keeper should lay down her powers and marry. Many have done so. But that a Keeper should leave the Towers and give up her ritual virginity and remain a Keeper . . . no, that they would not tolerate." The bitterness in his voice deepened. "After all, a Keeper is not so unusual; it was discovered, or rediscovered, in my father's time, that any halfway competent technician can do a Keeper's work. Including some men. I can, if I must, do it myself, though I am not especially skillful at it. But the Keeper of Arilinn—well, she is a symbol. Cleindori said once to me that what the Comyn really needed was a child's waxen doll on a stick, to wear the crimson robe and speak the right words at the proper time, and there would be no need for Keepers at Arilinn; and since the doll could remain virgin forever without fuss or pain or sacrifice, all the troubles of Arilinn would be forever solved. I don't suppose you can imagine just how shocking that was to the more conservative men and women of the Council. They were very bitter against Cleindori's—sacrilege."

He scowled at the floor. "Auster too has a special reason to hate you. He too was born among the Terranan, although he does not remember; for a time he too was in the Spacemen's Orphanage, although we got him back from them before he had even learned their language. I have not heard him speak a word of Terran, or *cahuenga*, since he was thirteen years old; but that's neither here or there. That's a strange story." Kennard raised his head and looked at Kerwin, saying, "It's fortunate for you that the Terrans sent you to the Kerwins on Terra. There were plenty of fanatics who would have considered that they had done a virtuous deed—to avenge the dishonor of a *vai leronis* by killing the child she had borne to her lover."

Kerwin found that he was shivering, although the room was warm. "If that's the case," he said, "what in the hell am I doing here at Arilinn?"

"Times have changed," Kennard said. "As I told you, we're dying out. There just aren't enough of us any more. Here at Arilinn, we have a Keeper, but there are not more than two or three Keepers in all of the Domains, and a couple of little girls growing up who might grow *into* Keepers. The fanatics have died off or mellowed into old age; and even if there are still a few around, the ones who are left

have learned to listen to the voice of expediency. I ought to
say, of stark necessity; we cannot afford to waste anyone
who might be carrying Aillard or Ardais gifts, or . . . others.
You have Ridenow blood, and Hastur blood not too many
generations back, and Alton. For a variety of reasons—" He
checked himself. He said, "Different people are ruling the
Council. When you came back to Thendara . . . well, it
didn't take me long to guess who you must be. Elorie saw
you in the monitor screens—saw Cleindori's matrix,
rather—and confirmed it. That night in the Sky Harbor
Hotel, half a dozen of us from the few remaining Towers
gathered there—outside Comyn Castle, so that we could talk
freely about it—and the reason we met was to try and reach
some agreement about standards for admissions to the Towers, so that we could keep more than one or two of them
working. When you walked in—well, you remember what
happened; we thought you were one of us, and it wasn't just
that you had red hair. We could sense what you were. So we
called you. And you came. And here you are."

"Here I am. An outsider—"

"Not really, or you could never have passed the Veil. You
have guessed that we don't like having non-telepaths
around; that's why we have no human servants, and why
Mesyr stays and keeps house for us even though she's past
working in the screens. You passed the Veil, which means
you have Comyn blood. And I feel at ease with you. That's
a good sign."

Kerwin felt his eyebrows lift. Kennard might feel at ease
with him, but it sure as hell wasn't mutual, not yet. He was
inclined to like the older man, but that was a good long way
from feeling at home with him.

"He's wishing he felt the same way about you," Taniquel,
popping her head into the room. "You will, Jeff. You've just
lived among barbarians too long."

"Don't tease, *chiya*," Kennard said, in indulgent reproof.
"He's not used to you either, which doesn't necessarily

mean he's a barbarian. Get us a drink and stop making mischief, why don't you? We're going to have trouble enough."

"No drinks yet," said Rannirl, pausing beneath the arch into the room. "Elorie will be down in a minute. We'll wait."

"That means she's going to test him," Taniquel said. She came over to the cushions and dropped gracefully, catlike, her head leaning against Kennard's knee. She flung out her arms, one of them striking Kerwin; she yawned, crooked her arm carelessly round his foot, giving it a little, absent-minded pat with her hand. She let her hand rest on his ankle, her eyes glinting up at him in a mischievous smile. He was uncomfortably conscious of the touch. He had always disliked being touched, and he felt Taniquel knew it.

Neyrissa and Corus drifted into the room, found places on the cushions; they shifted, making room for Kennard's lame leg, and Taniquel moved restlessly until she was between Kerwin and Kennard, snuggled into the cushions like a kitten, an arm across the lap of each. Kennard patted her curly head affectionately, but Kerwin drew uneasily away. Damn it, was the girl just an outrageous tease? Or was she simply naive, relaxing, childlike, among men she found as neutral as if they were brothers or close relatives? Certainly she treated Kennard—and he, her—as if he were a favorite uncle, and there was nothing provocative in the way she touched him, but somehow it was subtly different with Kerwin, and he was conscious of the difference, and wondered if *she* was. Was he just imagining things? Once again, as when Elorie had walked unannounced into his room before he had finished dressing, Kerwin felt troubled. Damn it, the etiquette of a telepath group was still a mystery to him.

Elorie, Mesyr and Auster came together into the room. Auster's glare instantly sought out Kerwin, and Taniquel straightened herself and drew just a little away from Kerwin. Corus went to a cabinet, evidently from long habit. "What will you drink? Your usual, Kennard, Mesyr? Neyrissa, what will you have? Elorie, I know you never drink anything stronger than *shallan* . . ."

"She will tonight," Kennard said. "We'll have *kirian*."

Corus turned, startled, for confirmation. Elorie nodded. Taniquel rose and went to help Corus, filling low goblets from a curiously shaped flask. She brought a glass to Kerwin, not asking if he wanted it.

The liquid in the glass was pale and aromatic; Kerwin glanced at it and felt that they were all watching him. Damn it, he was getting tired of that performance! He set the goblet, untasted, on the floor.

Kennard laughed. Auster said something Kerwin didn't catch, and Rannirl frowned, murmuring a reproving reply. Elorie watched them, smiling faintly, raising her own goblet to her lips and barely tasting the liquid within. Taniquel giggled, and Kennard exploded:

"Zandru's hells! This is too serious for a joke! I know you like your fun, Tani, but just the same—" He accepted the glass Corus brought him, staring into it with a frown. "I seem to be cast in the role of schoolmaster too much of the time!" He sighed, lifted the goblet and said to Kerwin, "This stuff—it isn't pure *kirian*, in case you know what that is, but *kirian* liqueur—it's not exactly a drug or a stimulant, but it does lower the threshold of resistance against telepathic reception. You don't have to drink it unless you want it, but it helps. Which is why we're all sharing it." He sipped his own briefly and went on: "Now that you're here, and you've had a chance to rest a bit, it's fairly important that we test you for *laran*, find out how much of a telepath you are, what *donas* you may be carrying, how much training you'll need before you can work with the rest of us—or the other way round. We're gong to test you half a dozen ways; it's more efficient in a group. Hence—" he drank another sip— "*kirian*."

Kerwin shrugged and picked up the glass. The liquid had a sting and a curious volatile smell; it seemed to evaporate on his tongue even before he could taste it. It wasn't his idea of a good way to get drunk. It was more like inhaling perfume than drinking anything. The flavor was vaguely lemony. Four or five sips finished the glass, but you had to take it slowly; the fumes were simply too strong to drink it like an ordinary drink. He noticed that Corus made a face over his, as if he violently disliked the taste. The others were apparently accustomed to it; Neyrissa swirled it in her glass and inhaled the fumes as if it were a fragrant brandy. Kerwin decided the stuff was very much of an acquired taste.

He finished the goblet and set it down.

"Now what happens?" To his surprise, the words, on his tongue, sounded curiously thick; he had some trouble framing them, and when he had finished speaking, he was not sure what language he had been speaking. Rannirl turned toward him and with a grin that Kerwin knew was meant to reassure him said, "Nothing to worry about."

"I don't know why this is necessary," Taniquel said. "He's already been tested for *laran*. They saved us that much trouble with the monitor screens." As she spoke, a picture flickered, unbidden, in Kerwin's mind, the brother and sister who had studied his matrix, arrogantly told him he was not welcome in their house or on their world.

"They had the damned insolence!" Corus said angrily. "I didn't know that!"

Taniquel said, "As for the rest—"

Kerwin looked down at the girl curled up close to his knee, her face upturned to him, her eyes, meeting his, bright and sympathetic. She was very close to him. Kerwin could have bent down and kissed her.

He did.

Taniquel leaned against him, smiling, her cheek resting against his. She said, "Mark him positive for empathy, Kennard."

Kerwin started, startled, at his own arms around Taniquel; then laughed and relaxed, suddenly not worrying about it. If the girl intended to object, she would have done it already; but he sensed that she was pleased, nestling within his arm as if she was quite content to be there. Auster exploded into a mouthful of unintelligible syllables, and Neyrissa shook her head reprovingly at Taniquel.

"*Chiya*, this is a serious matter!"

"And I was perfectly serious," said Taniquel, smiling, "even if my methods strike you as unorthodox." She laid her cheek against Kerwin's; suddenly, surprisingly, Kerwin felt a lump in his throat, and for the first time in years he felt tears gathering and blurring his eyes. Taniquel was not smiling now; she moved away from Kerwin a little, but left her hand cradling his cheek, like a promise.

She said softly, "Can you think of a better test for an empath? If he didn't belong, no harm would be done, for he wouldn't receive from me; and if he did—then he deserves it." Kerwin felt her soft lips touch his hand, and felt an almost overwhelming emotion. The gentleness and intimacy of that small gesture was somehow more meaningful to him than anything any woman had ever done in his whole life. He felt that it had been an absolute acceptance of him, as a man and as a human being, that somehow, here before them all, Taniquel and he had suddenly become more intimate than lovers.

The others had suddenly ceased to exist. His arm was round her; he drew her head to his shoulder, and she leaned against him, tenderly, comfortingly, a gesture of reassurance and warmth unlike anything he had ever felt. He raised blurred eyes, and blinked, embarrassed at this display of emotion; but he saw only understanding and kindliness.

Kennard's grim face looked a little less craggy than usual. "Taniquel's the expert on empathy. We could have expected that—he has Ridenow blood. Though it's damned unusual for a man to have it to this degree."

Taniquel said, still clinging to Kerwin, "How lonely you must have been." The words were barely audible.

All my life. Not belonging, never belonging anywhere.
But you belong here now.

All the looks were not benevolent. Auster met Kerwin's eyes, and Kerwin had the definite feeling that if looks could burn, he would be lying in a sizzled cinder on the floor. Auster said, "Much as I dislike to interrupt this touching display . . ."

Taniquel, with a resigned shrug, dropped Kerwin's hand. Auster was still speaking, but he had dropped back into that language Kerwin did not understand. Kerwin said, "I'm sorry, I don't understand you," and Auster repeated it, but in the same language Kerwin didn't know. Auster turned to Kennard and said something, raising his eyebrows with a sardonic grin.

Kennard said, "Aren't you getting it at all, Jeff?"

"No, and it's damned funny, because I understand you and Taniquel just fine."

Rannirl said, "Jeff, you've understood most of what I said, haven't you?"

Kerwin nodded. "All but a few words now and then."

"And Mesyr?"

"Yes, perfectly."

"You *should* understand Auster," Rannirl said. "He has Ridenow blood and is the closest kinsman you have here, except perhaps—" He frowned. "Jeff, answer me quickly. What language am I speaking?"

Kerwin started to say, the language I learned as a child, the Thendara dialect, then stopped, confused. He didn't know. Kennard nodded, slowly. "That's right," he said. "That's what I noticed about you first of all. I've spoken to you in three different languages tonight and you never hesitated about answering me in any of them. Taniquel spoke a fourth. Yet Auster tried you in two languages that you had understood when Rannirl and I spoke, and you didn't understand a word. But even when Auster is speaking Cahuenga, you only understand him part of the time. You're

a telepath, all right. Haven't you always been an exceptionally good linguist?" He nodded, not waiting for Kerwin's
answer. "I thought so. You catch the thought without waiting for the words. But you and Auster simply don't resonate
enough to one another for you to pick up what he says."

"It may come in time," Elorie said diffidently, "as they
know one another better. Don't jump to conclusions too
quickly, Uncle." She used the word that was slightly more
intimate than, simply, *kinsman*; it was a catch-all term for
any close relative of a father's generation. "So we have ver-
ified that he has basic *laran*, telepathy, and a high degree of
empathy; Ridenow gift, full measure. He's probably carrying an assortment of minor talents—we'll have to sort them
out one by one, perhaps in rapport. Jeff—" She seemed
somehow to turn to him, even though she was looking off
into the distance and, though he tried to catch her eye, she
did not glance in his direction. "You have a matrix. Do you
know how to use it?"

"I haven't the faintest idea."

She said, "Rannirl. You're the technician."

Rannirl said, "Jeff, can you let me see your matrix?"

Kerwin said, "Of course," and pulled it out, slipped the
chain over his head and handed it to Rannirl. Shielding his
hand with a silk kerchief, the tall man took it from him; but
to his surprise, as the man took it between his fingers, Kerwin felt a vague, crawling discomfort. Automatically, without conscious thought, he reached out and snatched it back
into his own hands. The discomfort faded. He stared,
amazed, at his own hands.

"I thought so." Rannirl nodded. "He's managed to key
himself to it, roughly."

Kerwin said, "that never happened before!" He was still
staring at the matrix within his hands, shocked at the way he
had acted without thought to protect himself against the
touch.

"Probably it happened while we were guiding you to us,"

Elorie said. "You were in rapport with the crystal for a long time; it's how we reached you." She extended her slender fingers and said, "Give it to me, if you can."

Bracing himself, Kerwin let Elorie take the crystal. He felt the touch as if her delicate hands were actually touching his nerves; it was not acutely painful, but he was excruciatingly aware of it, as if the indefinable touch might become agony at a moment's notice . . . or unendurable pleasure.

"I'm a Keeper," she said. "One of the skills I must have is to handle matrixes that are not keyed to me. Taniquel?"

Kerwin felt the hypersensitive awareness ebb away as Taniquel took the matrix from Elorie; she smiled and said, "That's no fair test; Jeff and I are close in rapport just now. It feels as if you were handling it yourself, doesn't it?"

He nodded.

"Corus?" Taniquel handed it on.

Kerwin flinched uncontrollably at the rough prickling sensation all over his body as Corus touched the matrix; Corus shuddered as if the touch hurt him, and quickly handed the crystal to Kennard.

Kennard's touch was not acutely painful, although Kerwin was extremely conscious of it, unpleasantly so. The discomfort lessened somewhat, as Kennard held the crystal in his hand, to a sense of not-unpleasant warmth; but it was still intrusive, an unwelcome intimacy, and Kerwin was relieved when Kennard passed it on to Neyrissa.

Again, the excruciatingly close, almost painful sensitivity that lessened, somewhat, as Neyrissa held it; he could feel her warm breath on the crystal, which made no sense because she was halfway across the room from him. She said quietly, "I'm accustomed to monitor work; I can do what Tani does, resonate to your body's magnetic field, although not so well because we're not so closely in rapport. So far, so good. That leaves only Auster."

Auster gasped and dropped the matrix as if it were a live coal. Kerwin felt the pain like a shock all along his nerves, felt Taniquel shiver under his hand as if she, too, felt the pain. Neyrissa glanced at the dropped crystal without venturing to touch it and said, "Tani? Will you—"

The pain stopped as Taniquel cradled the matrix in her hand; Kerwin drew a deep, shaking breath. Auster, too, was white and shaking.

"Zandrus's hells!" His look at Kerwin was not so much malevolence, now, as fear. He spoke Cahuenga—Kerwin got the feeling that he wanted to be clearly understood, this time. "I'm sorry, Kerwin, I swear I didn't do that deliberately."

"He knows that, he knows that," Taniquel soothed; she dropped Jeff's hand and went to Auster, laying an arm around his waist, gently caressing his hand. Kerwin watched, in surprise and sudden, jealous amazement. How could she pull out of such close, emotional contact with him, and go straight to that—that so-and-so, Auster—and start making a fuss over him? Jealously intent, he watched Taniquel draw Auster down, watched the lines in Auster's lean face smoothing out and calming.

Elorie met Kerwin's eyes as he tucked away the matrix. She said, "It's evidently been keyed to you. First lesson in proper handling of a matrix—even under *kirian*, like this, never again let anyone handle it except in your own circle, and only when you are very sure they are in rapport with you. We were all trying for maximum attunement, even Auster; and it seems, except for him, to have worked well enough. But from an outsider, you could have had a *really* painful shock."

Kerwin wondered what a really painful shock would be like, if Elorie didn't think that one from Auster was very important. He glowered at Taniquel and Auster, feeling wrathful and deserted.

Rannirl grinned his lean sardonic grin and said, "All that, just to find out what we could have guessed this morning when we saw Kerwin with blood on his face; they aren't sympathetic and they can't attune."

"They'll have to," Elorie said tensely. "We need them both, and we can't have that kind of friction here!"

Auster said, his eyes closed, "I said I would abide by the majority decision. You know my feelings in the matter, but I promised, and I said I would do my best. I meant it."

"That's all anyone could expect of you," Taniquel soothed, and Kennard said, "Fair enough. What next?"

Rannirl said, "He can key into the circle when we help him; but can he *use* his matrix? Try a pattern test."

Kerwin grew suddenly apprehensive again; for Kennard looked tense and drawn, and Taniquel came and held his hand again. She said, "If he managed to key his own matrix, maybe he can get the pattern spontaneously."

"Maybe pigs can fly," Kennard said shortly. "We'll test for the possibility, but I think it would be forcing our luck to take it for granted. Let me have your goblet, Tani." He up-ended the glass on a low table. "Jeff, take the crystal—no, don't give it to me," he said, as Kerwin would have handed it over. "Just a test." He pointed at the goblet. "Crystallize it."

Kerwin looked at him, uncomprehending.

"Make a clear picture in your mind of that glass going to pieces. Careful, don't let it shatter or explode; nobody wants to be hit by flying glass. Use the matrix to see into its crystalline structure."

Suddenly Kerwin remembered the man Ragan doing something like that, in the spaceport cafe. It couldn't be so difficult, if Ragan could do it. He stared intently at the glass, then at the crystal, as if intense concentration could force the process into his mind, and felt a curious stirring. . . .

"No," Kennard said harshly, "don't help him, Tani. I know how you feel, but we have to be sure."

Kerwin stared into the crystal; his eyes began to ache and blur. "Sorry," he muttered. "I can't figure out how."

"Try," Taniquel insisted. "Jeff, it's so simple. Terrans, children, anyone can be taught to do it, it's nothing more than a trick!"

"We're wasting time," Neyrissa said. "You'll have to give him the pattern, Ken. He can't do it spontaneously."

Kerwin stared at them suspiciously, for Kennard was looking grim. "What now?"

"I'll have to show you how it's done, and the technique's nonverbal; I'll have to go straight in. I'm an Alton; that's our special technique, forced rapport." He hesitated; and it seemed to Kerwin that they were all watching him apprehensively. He wondered what was going to happen now.

Kennard said, "Watch my finger." He put it close to Kerwin's nose; Kerwin watched, startled, wondering if it would disappear or something, and what kind of demonstration of psi power *this* could possibly be, watched as Kennard very slowly drew it back. Then he felt the older man's hands, touching his temples, then . . .

He remembered no more.

He moved his head, groggily. He was lying back on the cushions, his head pillowed on Taniquel's lap. Kennard was looking down at him with friendly concern. Elorie's face, over Kennard's shoulder, was aloof, curious. Kerwin's head felt strange, as if he had a hangover.

"What the hell did you do to me?" he demanded.

Kennard shrugged. "Nothing, really. Next time you won't consciously remember this, but it will be easier." He handed Kerwin the goblet. "Here. Crystallize it."

"I just *tried* . . ."

Under Kennard's eyes he stared rebelliously at the matrix. Suddenly the goblet before him blurred, took on a strangeness. It was no longer a flat piece of glass; he seemed to be seeing it differently. It wasn't glass at all, glass was amorphous; the goblet was crystal, and within it he could see curious tensions and movements. He was conscious of a strange throb from the matrix crystal in his hand, an emotional tension, an equilibrium. . . . *The crystals lie in a plane,* he thought, suddenly perceiving the plane, and even as it became clear in his mind, he heard a faint *crack*; the new kind of sight blurred and vanished, and he stared down, unbelieving, at the goblet lying on the cushions before him in two halves, split evenly down the center as if by a sharp knife. *Surrealistic*, he thought. A few drops of the pale kirian lay soaking into the cushions. He shut his eyes. When he opened them, it was still there.

Kennard nodded in satisfaction. "Not bad, for a first attempt. Not quite even, but pretty good. Your molecular perception will sharpen with practice. Zandru's hells—you've got strong barriers, though! Head ache?"

Kerwin started to shake his head no, realized it should be yes instead. He touched his temples gingerly. Elorie's grey eyes met his for a moment, cool and aloof.

"Mental defense," she said, "against intolerable stress. Typical psychosomatic reaction; you say to yourself, *if I'm in pain they'll stop hurting me and let me alone.* And Kennard's squeamish about hurting people; he stopped, to avoid hurting you more. Pain is the best defense against mental invasion. For instance, if anybody tries to pick your mind, and there's no damper, the best defense is simply to bit your lip until it bleeds. Damned few telepaths can get through that. I could give you a technical explanation about sympathetic vibrations and nerve cells, but why bother? I'll leave that to the technicians." She went to the cabinet where the drinks were kept, shook three flat green tablets from a small vial and put them into his hand, deftly, without touching him.

"Take these. In an hour or two it will be better. When you've had more practice, you won't need them because you can work on the channels directly, but for the meantime—"

Kerwin obediently swallowed the pills, looking again, without belief, at the goblet lying in neat halves, sundered along a clean line of cleavage. "Did I really do that?"

"Well, none of us did," Rannirl said dryly. "And I imagine you can estimate the probabilities of all the molecules losing their tension along a line like that by chance. Putting them at one in a hundred trillion would be *very* good odds."

Kerwin picked up the two halves, feeling the sharp fracture edge with his fingertips. He was trying to formulate some explanation that would satisfy the Terran half of his mind, playing with phrases like *subliminal perception of atomic structure*—Hell, for a minute he'd *seen* the way the crystals were held together by a pattern of living tensions and forces! During his schooling, he remembered, he had learned that atoms were just whirling aggregates of electrons, that every solid object really consisted of empty space occupied by infinitesimal forces in stasis. It made him feel dizzy.

"You'll learn," counseled Rannirl, "or you can always do like Tani does—think of it as magic. Concentrate, wave your hand, and there you are—*Poof!* All done by magic!"

"It's easier that way," Taniquel protested. "It *works*, even if I haven't figured out the exact forces involved in the molecular stresses. . . ."

"And that's just playing into the hands of the people who enjoy being superstitious about us!" Elorie said angrily. "I think you like it when they call you *sorceress* and *witch*—"

"They're going to do it anyway, no matter what I call myself," Taniquel said with equanimity "They said it of Mesyr, and she was one of the top technicians in her day. What does it matter what they think, Lori? We know what we are. Or what's that proverb Kennard's so fond of, about going to learn logic from the barkings of your dog?"

Elorie didn't answer. Kerwin took up the broken glass and fitted the edges together, staring at it fiercely. Once again the new kind of perception came, the insight as if seeing beneath the surface, all the forces and tensions in the *structure* of the crystal . . .

The glass lay whole in his hand, joined neatly, but a little out of true, a notch in the rim showing where the split had been.

Kennard smiled, as if relieved. He said, "That leaves only one test."

Kerwin was still staring at the slightly off-center goblet. He asked, "Can I keep this?"

Kennard nodded. "Bring it along."

Again Kerwin felt Taniquel's small fingers folding through his own, and he could sense that she was frightened, feel her fear like a pain somewhere inside him. "Is that really necessary, Kennard?" she appealed. "Can't you put him in the outer circle and see if he can be shocked open that way?"

Elorie gave her a pitying glance. "That almost never works, Tani. Not even in a mechanic's circle."

Kerwin began to be afraid again. He had come so well through the other tests, had begun to be proud of what he was accomplishing. "What is it? What now, Taniquel?"

But it was Elorie who answered, gently. "What Kennard means is only this; now we have to try you in a circle and see how you can fit into the relays—the nexus of power. We know you're a high-level empath, and you've passed the basic tests—you have enough PK for a good mechanic, when you learn how. But this is the real test—to see how you'll mesh with the rest of us." She turned to Kennard. "You tested him in rapport, you know how he works on pattern. How are his barriers?"

"Hellish," Kennard said. "How would you expect them to be, coming of age among the head-blind?" He explained to Kerwin, "She means that I forced rapport on you, to give you the pattern there—" He pointed to the broken-and-joined goblet, slightly out of line. "And so I had a chance to test how strong your defenses are. Everyone has some natural defense against telepathic invasion—the technical term we use is *barrier*; protective shielding among telepaths, to keep you from broadcasting your private thoughts all over the locality, and to protect you from picking up a lot of random telepathic static—after all, you don't need to hear the groom deciding which horse he'll curry first, or the cook wondering what to have for dinner. Everybody has it; it's a conditioned reflex, and the stronger the telepath, in general, the stronger the barrier. Well, when we work in a circle, we have to learn to lower that barrier, work without the protective reflex. Most of us started work when we were in our teens, and we learn how to keep the barriers up, or lower them, consciously. Growing up on a world of non-telepaths, you probably learned to keep them locked in place all the time. Sometimes the barrier won't drop at all, and has to be forced, or shocked, open. We have to know how hard it's going to be to work with you, and how much resistance you have."

"But why tonight?" Mesyr asked, speaking for the first time—Kerwin had a vague notion that she considered herself apart from the others, no longer a part of their inner circle. "He's doing so well; why hurry things? Can't you give him time?"

"Time is the one thing we don't have to give him," Rannirl said. "Remember, we're working against a deadline."

"Rannirl's right," Kennard said, looking at Kerwin almost in apology. "We brought Kerwin here because we were desperately short-handed here at Arilinn, and if we can't use him, you know as well as I do what's going to happen to us all." He looked around bleakly. "We need to get him in shape to work with us, damned fast, or else!"

We're wasting time," said Elorie, and rose, her pale draperies floating like some intangible drift of air around her. "But we'd better do it up in the matrix chamber."

One by one they rose; at Taniquel's tug on his hand, Kerwin stood up, too. Kennard looked pityingly at Taniquel and said, "I'm sorry, Tani; you know as well as I do why you can't be part of it. The link's already too strong. Neyrissa will monitor." To Kerwin he explained, "Taniquel is our empath, and in rapport with you. If she was part of this, she'd help you too much; she couldn't stand it otherwise. Later, the rapport between you will make the link stronger and help the circle, but not while we're testing you. Tani, you have to stay here."

Reluctantly, she let go of his hand. Kerwin felt cold and alone; evidently the sense of warmth, of confidence, had been part of what Taniquel was radiating and pouring into him. He felt, quite suddenly, scared.

Rannirl said, "Cheer up," and put his own arm lightly through Jeff's. The gesture was reassuring, but the tone wasn't; it sounded too much like an apology.

Kennard motioned and they went in a close group through the long hall, up a flight of stairs and through a corridor; and finally up another flight of stairs to a closed-in room Kerwin had not seen before. It was small, eight-sided. Along the walls were glass and mirrory surfaces that reflected random images, distorting their shapes out of recognition, and Kerwin saw himself, a lean streak of black uniform topped with a brief crimson flame of hair. At the center of the room was a sunken circle lined with padded seats, and Kerwin saw them moving into the circle in an order that seemed familiar, predetermined. At the central part of the circle there was a small flat table or stand, with a woven cradle like the one he had seen in the house of the *leronis*, giving Kerwin a brief painful flash of *déjà vu* again. In it lay a crystal, larger than any he had seen before. Rannirl murmured in his ear, "It's the relay lattice," which seemed to make no sense at all to Kerwin. Trying to explain himself, Rannirl added, "It's a synthetic lattice, not a natural matrix," but that explained nothing at all to Kerwin.

"Take us out of the relays, Neyrissa, just for tonight," Elorie murmured. "There's no reason those people at Neskaya should know what we're doing here, and I don't think Hali wants to know!"

Neyrissa went to the central seat, insulating her hands

with a length of the silk as the *leronis* in Thendara had done. She leaned over the crystal, and Kerwin covered his eyes with his hands, the *déjà vu* was so strong, as he watched her graceful gestures. What was wrong with him? He'd never been in a matrix chamber before, never seen a circle form . . . an illusion, a false perception of the two halves of the brain, he told himself fiercely, nothing more than that . . .

He heard the drift of thought, the random flickers around him, then clearly, though Neyrissa did not speak. *We are testing at Arilinn, we will be out of the relays for twenty-eight hours . . .*

Carefully, shielding her hand, Neyrissa removed the enormous crystal from the cradle. "We're shielded," she said, "and out of the screens." She put the crystal away in the cabinet, wrapping it carefully in its heavy silks, but she did not return to the central seat. She said to Elorie, with a curious formality, "The circle is in your hands, *tenerésteis*." Kerwin recognized the archaic term for Keeper, without quite knowing how.

Elorie laid her own crystal in the cradle, taking it from around her neck. She looked questioningly at the circle, at the others. Kennard nodded; Neyrissa and Rannirl followed suit. Auster looked briefly doubtful, but finally said, "I defer to your judgment, Elorie. I said all along I'll go with the majority decision."

Young Corus pursed his lips, looked skeptically at Kerwin. He said, "I think Mesyr was right, we ought to have waited. But I can manage, if you think he can."

Elorie was looking at Auster; he said something unintelligible to Kerwin, and Elorie nodded in agreement. Kennard leaned toward Kerwin and said, "As long as you and Auster can't resonate, we'll have to keep you on separate levels."

Elorie said, "I'll take Auster first, and bring Kerwin in last." She glanced from Rannirl to Kennard, finally said, "Kennard, you bring him in." She glanced quickly round the circle, shifted slightly in her seat, and Kerwin saw a slight, almost imperceptible communication run round the circle, nods, glances, a kind of mutual settling-down, small agreements needing no words. Elorie lowered her head, glanced for a moment into the matrix, then pointed a slender finger at Auster.

Kerwin, watching, apprehensive, sensitized to these currents, felt something like a palpable line of force connecting the delicate girl with Auster; felt a small electrical shock in the air as they dropped into rapport.

An overtone of emotion in the room like a sullen flame, a covered flame burning against the ice . . .

Rannirl . . .

Forces in tension, aligning, a strong bridge across an empty abyss . . .

"Corus," Elorie whispered aloud, and Kerwin knew, without knowing how, picking it up like flickers of thought, that Corus was young enough, and inexperienced enough, that he could not pick up the circle without the verbal cue. Grinning nervously, the youngster covered his face with his hands, his forehead screwed up into intense concentration. He looked very young. Kerwin, still tentatively feeling out the atmosphere in the room, sensed his curious visualization of hands and wrists interlocking, like the meshing grip of acrobats in midair, a tightening grip . . .

Neyrissa, came the silent command, and suddenly the room was filled with small electrical sparkles, a web of little shimmers interconnecting. For a moment Kerwin felt them all melt together, a blend of eyes, circling faces, and as he felt Kennard slip away from him and into the rapport, he sensed the flight of birds, wheeling as one, swooping, faces, waiting eyes . . .

"Easy," Kennard whispered to him. "I'll bring you in." Then Kennard's voice thinned, dimmed, seemed to hum in Kerwin's ears from an enormous distance. He could see them all now, not with his eyes, but like a circle of faces, waiting eyes . . . He knew he was hovering on the edge of the telepathic rapport; it looked to him like a web, delicately waving its strands . . .

Elorie whispered, "Jeff," but the soft word was like a shriek.

Just let go and slide into contact, it's easy. It was like the instructions he had been given about finding his way to them, random walking through the streets of Thendara. He could tell where they were, he could *feel* the circle waiting for him, somehow visualized them as a ring holding hands, a space left empty for him . . . but how to move toward it? He stood helpless, as if hanging back from their stretched hands, and suddenly felt as if he were swinging in midair over an immense gulf, awaiting a signal to jump for some moving target . . . He knew he was picking up a mental image from Corus, and didn't know why, but he felt the same nerve-twitching fear of the great height, paralyzing terror of the great gulf, the fall, the plunge down and down . . . what was he supposed to do? They seemed to think he knew.

You can do it, Jeff. You have the Gift. It was Kennard's voice, pleading.

No use, Ken. He can't quite make it.

The barrier's a conditioned reflex. After twenty years with the Terrans, he'd have gone mad without it. Kennard's face wavered in the curious light in the room, reflecting from Elorie's crystal, flashing prismatic flares of color all around them. He could see Kennard's lips move but he could not hear him speak. It's going to be rough. *Twenty years. It was hard enough for Auster after five, and he was pure Comyn.*

He moved blurrily through the light in the room; he seemed to be swimming underwater.

Try not to fight it, Jeff.

Abruptly, like a knife-stab, he felt the touch—indescribable, unbelievable, so alien and indefinable that it could be interpreted only as pain . . . in a fractional second, he knew that this was what Kennard had done before, that this was what could not be borne or remembered, this intolerable touch, intrusion, violation . . . It was like having his skull bored open with a dentist's drill. He stood it for about five seconds, then felt himself twitch convulsively all over, and heard someone scream from a million miles away as he slid into the darkness.

When he came out of it this time he was lying on the floor of the octagonal matrix chamber, and Kennard and Neyrissa and Auster were standing and looking down at him. Somewhere he heard muffled sobbing and saw, with the fringes of his mind, young Corus hunched over, his face buried in his hands. Rannirl was standing with his arm around Corus, holding the boy against him. Kerwin's head was a giant balloon filled with red-hot seething pain. It was so awful he couldn't breathe for a second; then he felt his lungs expand and a hoarse sound coming from him, without volition.

Kennard knelt beside him and said, "Can you sit up?"

Somehow he managed it. Auster put out a hand to help him, looking sick. He said, with an unusual friendliness in his voice, "Jeff, we've all been through it, one way or the other. Here, lean on me." Detached, surprised at himself, Kerwin accepted the other man's hand. Kennard asked, "Corus, are you all right?"

Corus raised a blotched, tear-stained face. He looked sick, but he said, "I'll live."

Neyrissa said with gentle detachment, "You're doing it to yourself, you know. You have a choice."

Elorie said, in a taut voice, "Let's get through it quickly. None of us can take much more." She was shaking, but she stretched a hand to Corus, and Kerwin felt, like a faint snap and jolt of electricity, felt it somewhere inside his mind, the re-building of the mesh. Auster, then Rannirl, Neyrissa, dropped into place; Kennard, still holding Kerwin, dropped away and was gone. Elorie did not speak, but suddenly her grey eyes filled up all the space in the room and Jeff heard her commanding whisper.

"Come."

With a jolt, the breath crashing from his body, he felt the impact of their meshed minds as if he had dropped into one facet of the carven crystal. A pattern flamed like a giant star of fire in his mind, and he felt himself run all around the circle, flowing like water, swirling in and out of contact; Elorie, cool, aloof, *holding him at the end of a lifeline* . . . Kennard's gentle sureness; a feather-touch of rapport, shaky, frightened, from Corus; a sullen flare from Auster, sparks meshing, jolting apart . . . Neyrissa, a soft searching touch . . .

"Enough," said Kennard sharply and suddenly Kerwin was himself again, and the others were not intangible energy-swirls in the room around him, but separate people again, standing grouped around him.

Rannirl whistled. "Zandru's hells, what a barrier! If we ever get it all the way down, Jeff, you'll be one hell of a technician, but we've got to get rid of that barrier first!"

Corus said, "It wasn't quite as bad the second time. He did make it, part way."

Kerwin's head was still one seething mass of fire. He said, "I thought, whatever it was you did to me—"

"We got rid of part of it," Kennard said, and he went on speaking, but suddenly the words had no meaning. Elorie glanced sharply at Kerwin; she said something, but the words were just noise, static in Kerwin's brain. He shook his head, not understanding.

Kennard said in Cahuenga, "Headache any better?"

"Yeah, sure," Kerwin muttered; it wasn't, if anything it was worse, but he didn't have the energy to say so. Kennard didn't argue. He took Kerwin firmly by the shoulders, led him into the next room and put him into a cushiony chair. Neyrissa said, "Here, this is my business," came and put her light hands on Kerwin's head.

Kerwin didn't say anything. He was past that now. He was rocking in a giant swing, faster and faster, on a pendulum of dizzy pain. Elorie said something. Neyrissa spoke to him in a tone of urgent question, but none of it made any sense to Kerwin. Even Kennard's voice was only a blur of meaningless syllables, verbal hash, word salad. He heard Neyrissa say, "I'm not getting through to him. Get Taniquel up here, fast. Maybe she can . . ."

Words rose and fell around him like a song sung in a strange language. The world blurred into grey fog and he was swinging on a giant pendulum further and further out, into darkness and pale lights, nothingness . . .

Then Taniquel was there, blurring before his eyes; she fell to her knees beside him with a cry of distress.

"Jeff! Oh, Jeff, can you hear me?"

How could he help it, Kerwin thought with the unreason of pain, when she was shouting right in his ear?

"Jeff, please look at me, let me help—"

"No more," he muttered. "No more of this. I've had enough for one night, haven't I?"

"Please, Jeff, I can't help you unless you let me—" Taniquel begged, and he felt her hand, hot and painful on his throbbing head. He twitched restlessly, trying to throw it off. It felt like hot iron. He wished they would all go away and let him alone.

Then slowly, slowly, as if some tense, full vein had been tapped, he felt the pain drain away. Moment by moment it receded until at last he could see the girl clearly again. He sat up, the pain just a dim throb at the base of his brain.

"Good enough," Kennard said briskly. "I think you'll work out, eventually."

Auster muttered, "It's not worth the trouble!"

Kerwin said, "I heard that," and Kennard gave a slow, grimly triumphant nod.

"You see," he said. "I told you so. I told you it was worth the risk." He drew a long, weary sigh.

Kerwin lurched to his feet and stood there, gripping the chair back. He felt as if he had been dragged through a wringer, but he was painfully at peace. Taniquel was slumped beside his chair, grey and exhausted, Neyrissa beside her, holding her head. She said, weakly, raising her eyes, "Don't worry about it, Jeff. I was just—just glad I could do something for you."

Kennard looked tired, too, but triumphant. Corus looked up and smiled at him, shakily, and it struck Kerwin, with a curious wrench, that the boy had been crying over his pain. Even Auster, biting his lip, said, "I've got to give you this. You're one of us. You can't blame me for doubting, but— well, don't hold it against me."

Elorie came and stood on tiptoe; close enough to embrace him, though she didn't. She raised one hand and touched his cheek, just a feather-touch with the tips of her fingers. She said, "Welcome, Jeff-the-barbarian," and smiled into his eyes.

Rannirl linked arms with him as they went down the stairs to the hall where they had met earlier that night. "At least, this time, we can decide for ourselves what we want to drink," he said, laughing, and Kerwin realized that he had come through the final ordeal. Taniquel had accepted him from the beginning, but now they all accepted him with the same completeness. He, who had never belonged anywhere, was now overwhelmed with the knowledge of how deeply he belonged. Taniquel came and sat on the arm of his chair. Mesyr came and asked if he wanted something to eat or drink. Rannirl poured him a glass of cool, fragrant wine that tasted faintly of apples, and said, "I think you'll like this; it comes from our estates." It was incongruously like a birthday party.

Sometime later that evening he found himself next to Kennard. Sensitized to the man's mood, he heard himself say, "You look happy about this. Auster isn't pleased, but you are. Why?"

"Why isn't Auster, or why am I?" Kennard asked with a twist of droll laughter.

"Both."

"Because you're part Terran," Kennard replied somberly. "If you *do* become a working part of a matrix circle—actually inside a Tower—and the Council accepts it, then there's a chance the Council will accept *my* sons."

He frowned, looking over Kerwin's head into a sad distance.

"You see," he said at last, "I did what Cleindori did. I married outside Comyn—married a woman who was part Terran. And I have two sons. And it sets a precedent. I would like to think that one day, my sons could come here . . ." He fell silent. Kerwin could have asked a dozen more questions, but he sensed that this wasn't the time. It didn't seem to matter. He belonged.

CHAPTER EIGHT

The World Outside

The days slipped by in Arilinn and Kerwin soon began to feel as if he had been there all his life. And yet, in a curious way, he was like a man lost in an enchanted dream, as if all his old dreams and desires had come to life and he had stepped into them and closed a wall behind him. It was as if the Terran Zone and the Trade City had never existed. Never, in any world, had he felt so much at home. Never had he belonged anywhere as he belonged here. It made him almost uneasy to be so happy; he wasn't used to it.

Under Rannirl's guidance, he studied matrix mechanics. He didn't get too far with the theory; he felt that maybe Tani had the right idea when she called it magic. Spacemen didn't understand the mathematics of an interstellar drive, either, but it worked. He was quicker in learning the simper psychokinetic feats with the small matrix crystals; and Neyrissa, the monitor, taught him to go into his own body, searching out the patterns of his blood flowing in his veins, to regulate, quicken or slow his heartbeats, raise or lower his blood pressure, watch over the flows of what she called the channels, and what Kerwin suspected would have been called, by Terran medics, the autonomic nervous system. It was considerably more sophisticated than any biofeedback technique he had ever known in the Terran Zone.

He made less progress in the rapport circle. He had

learned to take his turn—with Corus or Neyrissa at his
side—in the relays, the communication network of telepaths
between the Towers, which sent messages and news of what
was happening, between Neskaya and Arilinn and Hali and
faraway Dalereuth; messages that still meant little to Jeff,
about a forest fire in the Kilghard Hills, an outbreak of bandit raids far away on the fringes of the Hellers, an outbreak
of a contagious fever in Dalereuth, the birth of triplets near
the Lake Country; citizens, too, came to the Stranger's
Room of the Tower and asked that messages be sent through
the relays, matters of business or news of births and deaths
and the arrangement of marriages.

But in the working of the circle he was less successful.
He knew they were all anxiously watching his progress, now
that they had accepted him; it seemed sometimes that they
watched over him like hawks. Taniquel insisted they were
pushing him too fast, while Auster glowered and accused
Kennard and Elorie of coddling him. But as yet he could endure only a few minutes at a time in the matrix circle. It
wasn't, evidently, a process that could be hurried; but he
gained a few seconds a day, holding out longer each time
under the stresses of contact before he collapsed.

The headaches continued, and if anything they got worse,
but for some reason it didn't discourage any of them.
Neyrissa taught him to control them, a little, by regulating
the inner pressure of the blood vessels around the eye sock-
ets and inside the skull. But there were still plenty of times
when he found himself unable to endure anything but a
darkened room and silence, with his head splitting. Corus
made up rude jokes about him, and Rannirl predicted pes-
simistically that he'd get worse before he got better, but they
were all patient with him; once, even, when he was shut up
with one of the blinding headaches, he heard Mesyr—whom
he had thought disliked him—remonstrating with Elorie,
whom she obviously adored, for making noise in a hallway
outside the corridor of his room.

Once or twice, when it got too bad, Taniquel came unasked to his room and did the trick she had done the first night, touching his temples with light fingers and draining the pain away as if she had tapped a valve. She didn't like doing it, Kerwin knew; it exhausted her, and it scared Kerwin—and made him ashamed, too—seeing her so grey and haggard afterward. And it infuriated Neyrissa.

"He has got to learn to do it for himself, Tani. It is not good for you, or for him either, if you do for him what he can and must learn to do for himself! And now look at you," she scolded, "you have incapacitated yourself too!"

Taniquel said faintly, "I can't endure his pain. And since I have to feel it anyway, I may as well help him."

Then learn to barrier yourself," Neyrissa admonished. "A monitor must never become so deeply involved, you know that! If you go on like this, Tani, you know very well what will happen!"

Taniquel looked at her with a mischievous smile. "Are you jealous, Neyrissa?" But the older woman only frowned at Kerwin angrily, and went out of the room.

"What was all that about, Tani?" Kerwin asked, but Taniquel did not answer. Kerwin wondered if he would ever understand the small interactions among the people here, the courtesies and the things left unsaid in a telepathic society.

And yet he had begun to relax. Strange as the Arilinn Tower was, it wasn't a magical fairy-tale castle, just a big stone building where people lived. The gliding, silent, non-human servants still made him a little uneasy, but he didn't have to see much of them, and he was getting used to their silent ways and learning to ignore them as the others did, unless he wanted something. The place wasn't all wizard and hobgoblin. The enchanted tower wasn't enchanted at all. For some curious reason he felt pleased when he discovered a leak in the roof, right over his room, and since no workman or outsider could come inside the Veil, he and Rannirl had to climb up on the dizzily sloping roof and fix it themselves.

Somehow that prosaic incident made the place more real to him, less dreamlike.

He began to learn the language they spoke among themselves—they called it *casta*—for, while he could understand and telepathically, he knew that sooner or later he would have to deal with local non-telepaths. He read some history of Darkover from the Darkovan, not the Terran point of view; there weren't many books, but Kennard was something of a scholar, and had an extensive history of the days of the Hundred Kingdoms—which seemed, to Jeff, somewhat more complicated than that of medieval Europe—and another of the Hastur Wars which, at the end of the Ages of Chaos, had united most of the countryside under the Seven Domains and the Comyn Council. Kennard warned him that accurate history was all but unknown; these had been compiled from tradition, legend, old ballads, and stories, since for almost a thousand years writing had been left to the brothers of Saint Valentine at Nevarsin Monastery, and literacy had been all but lost. But from all this Jeff gathered that at one time, Darkover had had a highly developed technology of the matrix stones, and that its misuse had reduced the Seven Domains to a chaotic anarchy, after which the Hasturs had formed the system of Towers under the Keepers, pledged to chastity to avoid dynastic squabbles, and bound by vows and severe ethical principles.

He had begun to lose track of time, but he thought he had been at Arilinn for three or four tendays when Neyrissa, at the end of a training session, said unexpectedly, "I think you could function as monitor in a circle now, without too much difficulty. I'll certify you as monitor, and give you the oath, if you want me to."

Jeff regarded her in astonishment and dismay. She mistook his surprise and said, "If you would rather take the oath at Elorie's hands, it is your lawful right, but I assure you, in practice we don't trouble the Keeper with such things; I am fully qualified to receive your first oath."

Kerwin shook his head. He said, "I'm not sure I want to take any kind of oath! I wasn't told—I don't understand!"

"But you cannot work in the circle without the monitor's oath," Neyrissa said with a faint frown. "No one trained at Arilinn would ever consider it. Nor would anyone from another Tower be willing to work with you, unsworn—why don't you want to take the oath?" She regarded him with dismay and the suspicion that had vanished from all their eyes except Auster's. "Are you proposing to betray us?" It was a minute or two before Kerwin realized she had not spoken that last sentence aloud.

She was, he realized, old enough to be his mother; he wondered, suddenly, if she had known Cleindori, but would not ask. *Cleindori had betrayed Arilinn.* And Kerwin knew her son would never be free of that stigma, unless he earned the freedom.

He said slowly, "I wasn't told I would have to take oaths. It's not, in general, a Terran custom. I don't know what I would have to swear to." He added, on an impulse, "Would you take an oath you didn't know, without knowing to what it bound you?"

Slowly the suspicion and anger left her face. She said, "I hadn't thought of that, Kerwin. The monitor's oath is taken even of children when they are tested here. Other oaths may be asked of you later, but this one binds you only to basic principles; you swear never to use your starstone to force the will or conscience of any living thing, never to invade the mind of any other unwilling, and to use your powers only for helping or healing, and never to make war. The oath is very old; it goes back to the days before the Ages of Chaos, and there are those who say it was devised by the first Hastur when he gave a matrix to his first paxman; but that's a legend, of course. We *do* know it has been formally given in Arilinn since the days of Varzil the Good, and perhaps before." She added, with a scornful twist of her thin mouth, "Certainly there is nothing in a monitor's oath that could offend the conscience of Hastur himself, let alone a *Ter-ranan!*"

Kerwin thought about that a moment. It had been a long time since anyone had called him that; not since his first night here. Finally he shrugged. What had he to lose? Sooner or later he would have to put aside his Terran standards, choose Darkovan principles and ethics, and why not now? He shrugged. "I'll take your oath," he said.

As he repeated the archaic words—*to force no living thing against will or conscience, to meddle unasked with no mind nor body save to help or heal, never to use the power of the starstone to force the mind or conscience*—he thought almost for the first time of the truly frightening powers of the matrix in the hands of a skilled operator. The power to interfere with people's thoughts, to slow or speed their heartbeats, check the flow of blood, withdraw oxygen from the brain . . . a truly terrifying responsibility, and he suspected that the monitor's oath had much the same force as the Hippocratic oath in Terran medicine.

Neyrissa had insisted that the oath be taken in rapport—it was customary, she said, and he suspected that the reason was to monitor any mental reservations, a rudimentary form of lie-detector, which was so normal between telepaths that he realized it did not imply lack of trust. As he spoke the words—understanding, now, why they were being exacted, and realizing that he genuinely meant them—he was aware of Neyrissa's closeness; somehow it felt as if they were physically very close together, although actually the woman was sitting at the far end of the room, her head lowered and her eyes bent on her matrix, not even looking at him. As soon as Kerwin had finished, Neyrissa rose quickly and said, "I'm tired of being shut up indoors; let's go out into the air. Would you care for a ride? It's still early, and there's nothing much to do today, neither of us is listed for the relays. What would you say to hawking? I'd like some birds for supper, wouldn't you?"

He tucked away his matrix and followed her. He had learned to enjoy riding—on Terra it was an exotic luxury for rich eccentrics, but here on the Plains of Arilinn it was a commonplace means of getting around, since the air-cars, matrix-powered, were very rare and used only by the Comyn; and those only under very special circumstances.

He followed her to the stables without demur; but halfway down the stairs she said, "Perhaps we should ask one or two of the others to come?"

"Just as you like," he replied, slightly surprised. She hadn't been particularly friendly before and he hadn't expected that she had much interest in his company. But Mesyr was busy about some domestic affairs somewhere in the Tower, Rannirl had some unspecified business in the matrix laboratory—he tried to explain it, but Kerwin couldn't understand more than one word in five, he didn't have the technical background—Corus was in the relays, Kennard's bad leg was bothering him, and Taniquel was resting for her shift in the relays later that night. So in the end they went out alone, Auster having curtly refused an offer to join them.

Kennard had placed a horse at Kerwin's disposal, a tall rangy black mare from his own estates; Kerwin understood that the Armida horses were famous throughout the Domains. Neyrissa had a silvery-grey pony with gold-colored mane and tail, which she said came from the Hellers. She took her hawk on the saddle-block before her; she wore a grey-and-crimson cape and a long full skirt that Kerwin finally realized was a divided skirt cut like very full trousers. As she took the bird from the hawkmaster, she glanced at him and said, "There is a well-trained sentry-hawk that Kennard has given you leave to use; I heard him."

"I don't know anything of hawking," Kerwin said, shaking his head. He had learned to ride acceptably, but he didn't know how to handle hunting-birds and wasn't going to pretend he did.

There were a few curious stares and murmurs, which

Neyrissa ignored, as they rode through the fringes of the
town. He realized he had seen almost nothing of the city of
Arilinn—which, he had heard, was the third or fourth largest
city in the Seven Domains—and decided he would go exploring some day. Neyrissa's cape was flung back, revealing
her greying copper hair coiled in braids around her head.
Because it was cold, Kerwin had put his leather ceremonial
cape over his Terran clothing, and, hearing the murmurs,
seeing the awed faces, he realized that they took him for any
other member of the Tower circle. Was this what the people
in Thendara had thought, his first night on Darkover?

Outside the gates of Arilinn the plains stretched wide,
with clumps of bushes here and there, a few tracks and an
old cart road, now deserted. They rode for an hour or so beneath the lowering sky, in the pale-purple light of the high
sun. At last Neyrissa drew her horse to a walk, saying,
"There is good hunting here. We should get some birds, or a
rabbithorn or two . . . Elorie hasn't been eating much lately.
I'd like to tempt her with something good."

Kerwin had been thinking of hawking, actually, as an exotic sport, an alien thing done for excitement; for the first
time he realized that in a culture like this one, it was a very
utilitarian way to keep meat on the table. Perhaps, he
thought, he ought to learn it. It seemed to be one of the practical skills of a gentleman—or for that matter, he thought,
watching Neyrissa's small sturdy hands as she unhooded her
hawk, of a lady. One didn't think of noblewomen hunting
for the pot. But of course that was how hawking had begun,
as a way of pot-hunting for the kitchen! And while a lady
might not be able to do much with large meat animals, there
was no reason a woman shouldn't equal or surpass a man at
this skill. Kerwin suddenly felt very useless.

"Never mind," said Neyrissa, glancing up at him, and he
realized they were still touched by the fringes of rapport.
"You'll learn. Next time I'll find you a *verrin* hawk. You're
tall enough and strong enough to carry one."

She tossed the hawk high into the air; it took off, winging higher and higher, and Neyrissa watched the flight, her hands shading her eyes. "There," she said in a whisper, "he has sighted his prey . . ."

Kerwin looked, but could see no trace of the bird. "Surely you can't see that far, Neyrissa?"

She looked up impatiently. *Of course not, rapport with hawk and sentry-bird is one of our family gifts.* The thought was careless, with the very surface of her mind, and Kerwin realized that there was a strong rapport still between them, as with a part of his mind he *felt* flight, long pinions beating, the all-encompassing excitement of the chase, seeing the world wheeling below, stooping, striking a rush of ecstasy through his whole body . . . Shaking his head in wonder, Kerwin brought himself back to earth, following Neyrissa as she rode swiftly toward the spot where the hawk had brought his kill to the ground. She gestured to the falconer, following them at a distance, to take up the small dead bird and carry it on his saddle; the hawk stood on her glove, and Neyrissa took the head of the dead bird and fed it, still warm, to the hawk. Her eyes were closed, her face flushed; Kerwin wondered if she, too, had shared the excitement of that kill; he watched the hawk tearing at the blood and sinews with a sense of excitement combined with revulsion.

Neyrissa looked up at him and said, "She feeds only from my glove; no well-trained bird will taste her own kill until it is given her. Enough—" She wrenched the bloody tidbit away from the cruel beak, explaining, "I want another bird or so." Again she flung the hawk into the air and again Kerwin, sensing the thread of rapport between woman and hawk, followed it in his mind, knowing he was not prying, that she had somehow opened to him to share the ecstasy of flight, the long strong soaring, the strike, the gushing blood. . . .

As the falconer brought the head of the second bird to Neyrissa, through the excitement and revulsion, he became abruptly aware of how deeply he was sharing this with Neyrissa, of arousal, almost sexual, deep in his body. Angrily, Kerwin turned away from the thought, troubled and shamed lest Neyrissa should be aware of it. H wasn't trying to seduce her . . . he didn't even *like* her! And the last thing he wanted, here, was to complicate his life with any women!

Yet as the sun lowered, and the hawk climbed the sky again and again, striking and killing, Kerwin was drawn once more into the ecstatic rapport of woman and falcon, blood and terror and excitement. At last Neyrissa turned to the falconer, said, "No more, take the birds back," and drew her horse up, breathing in long, slow breaths as she watched him ride away. Kerwin was sure she had forgotten him. Without a word she turned her horse back toward the distant gates of Arilinn.

Kerwin rode after her, curiously subdued. A wind was rising, and he drew his cloak carefully around his head. Riding after Neyrissa's shrouded figure, with the dim red sun low in the sky and a crescent of violet moon low over a distant hill, pale and shadowy, he had the curious sense that he was alone on the face of this world with the woman, her head turned away, riding after her as the falcon had pursued the fleeing bird . . . He dug his heels into the flanks of his horse and rode after her, racing as if on the wings of the flying wind, lost in the excitement of the chase . . . clinging to his horse with his knees, by instinct, his whole mind caught up in the excitement of the chase, awareness surging in him. As he rode, he was faintly aware of the still-lingering rapport with the woman, the excitement in her own body, her awareness of the pursuing hoofs, the long chase, a strange hunger not unmixed with fear. . . . Images flooded his mind, overtaking her, snatching her from her horse, flinging her to the ground . . . it was a flooding, cresting sexual excitement, sharing it with her, so that unconsciously he speeded his mount, till he was at her very heels at the gate of the city. . . .

Realization flooded over him. What was he doing? He

was an invited guest here, a co-worker, now sworn to them; a civilized man, not a bandit or a hawk! The blood pounded in his temples, and he avoided Neyrissa's eyes as grooms came to take their horses. They dismounted; yet he sensed that she too was weak with excitement, that she could hardly stand. He felt ashamed and troubled by the prevalence of the sexual fantasy, aghast at the thought that she had shared it. In the small dimensions of the stable she moved past him, their bodies not quite touching, yet he was very aware of the woman under the folded cloak, and he ducked his head to conceal the color that flooded through his face.

Just beyond the Veil, on the inner staircase, she suddenly stopped and raised her eyes to him. She said quietly, "I am sorry. I had forgotten—please believe me, I did not do that willingly. I had forgotten that you would not—not yet be able to barricade, if it was unwelcome to you."

He looked at her, a little shamefaced, hardly taking it in that she had formed and shared that curious fantasy. Trying to be polite, he said, "It doesn't matter."

"But it does," she said angrily. "You don't understand. I had forgotten what it would mean to you, and it is not what it would mean to one of us." Abruptly her mind was open to him and he was shockingly aware of the taut excitement in her, nakedly sexual, now unmasked by the symbolism of the falcon-hunt. He felt troubled, embarrassed. She said, in a low, vicious voice, "I told you; you do not understand; I should not have done that to you unless your barriers were adequate to block it, and they were not. In a man—in one of our own—the fact that you accepted it and—and shared it— would mean something more than it does to you. It is my fault; it happens sometimes, after rapport. It is my failure. Not yours, Kerwin; you are not bound by anything. Don't trouble yourself; I know you don't want—" She drew a long breath, looking straight at him, and he could feel her anger and frustration.

Kerwin said, troubled, still only half understanding,

"Neyrissa, I'm sorry, I didn't mean to—to do anything to offend or hurt you—"

"I know that, damn you," she said in a rage. "I tell you: it happens sometimes. I have been a monitor for enough years that I know I am responsible for it. I misjudged the level of your barriers, that is all! Stop making a thing of it, and get control of yourself before we spread this all through Arilinn! I can handle it; you can't, and Elorie is young. I won't have *her* disturbed with this nonsense!"

It was like a sudden flooding with ice water, drowning it all, drenching his awareness of the woman, in shock and awareness, that the other telepaths here might pick up his fantasies, his needs . . . He felt naked and exposed, and Neyrissa's rage was like crimson lightning through the flooding shock. He felt stripped, shamed to the ultimate. Stammering a sickened apology, he fled up the stairs and took refuge in his own room. He was still not entirely aware what had happened, but it troubled him.

Long introspection told him that concealment of emotions was impossible in a telepath group; and when they met again, though he was worried for fear his shameful inability to block his own thoughts should have spoilt the ease with which he was accepted, no one spoke of it or even seemed to think about it. He was beginning to understand a little what it meant to be open, even to your innermost thoughts, to a group of outsiders. He felt flayed, embarrassed, as if he had been stripped nude and displayed; but he supposed none of them had gone through life without an embarrassing thought, and he'd simply have to get used to it.

And at least he knew, now, that there was no use trying to pretend with Neyrissa. She knew him, she had gone, as a monitor, deep into his body, and now into his mind too, even those bare spots he would rather she hadn't seen. And she still accepted him. It was a good feeling. Paradoxically he didn't like her any better than he had before, but now he knew that didn't matter; they had shared something, and accepted it.

He had been at Arilinn about forty days when it occurred again to him that he had seen nothing of the city, and one morning he asked Kennard—he was not sure of his status here—if he could go and explore. Kennard stared briefly, and said, "Why not?" Then, breaking out of reverie, said, "Zandru's hells, youngster, you don't have to ask permission to do anything you please. Go alone, or one of us will come and show you about, or take one of the *kyrri* to keep you from getting lost. Suit yourself!"

Auster turned from the fireplace—they were all in the big hall—and said sourly, "Don't disgrace us by going in those clothes, will you?"

Anything Auster said always roused Kerwin's determination to do exactly that. Rannirl said, "You'll be stared at in those things, Jeff."

"He'll be stared at anyway," Mesyr said.

"Nevertheless. Come along, I'll find you some of my things—we're just about the same height, I think—for the time being. And we ought to do something about getting you a proper outfit, too."

Kerwin felt ridiculous when he got into the short laced jerkin, the long blouse with loose sleeves, the full breeches coming down only to the top of his boots. Rannirl's notions of color were not his, either; if he had to wear Darkovan clothing—and he supposed he *did* look pretty silly in Terran uniform—he needn't go about in a magenta doublet with orange insets! At least, he hoped not!

He was surprised, though, to discover, glancing into a mirror, how the flamboyant outfit suited him. It showed to advantage the unusual height and coloring that had always made him feel awkward in Terran clothing. Mesyr cautioned him against wearing any headgear; Arilinn Tower telepaths showed their red heads proudly, and this protected them against accidental injury or insult. On a world of daily vio-

lence like Darkover, where street riots were a favorite form
of showing high spirits, Jeff Kerwin conceded that this probably made good sense.

As he walked in the streets of the city—he had chosen to
go alone—he was conscious of stares and whispers, and nobody jostled him. It was a strange city to him; he had grown
up in Thendara, and the dialect here was different, and the
cut of the clothing the women wore, longer skirts, fewer of
the imported Terran climbing jackets and more of the long
hooded capes, on men and women both. The footgear of a
Terran did not suit the Darkovan clothing he was wearing—
Rannirl, taller than Kerwin, had surprisingly small feet for a
man, and his boots had not fitted—so on an impulse, passing a street-shop where boots and sandals were displayed,
Kerwin went inside and asked to see a pair of boots.

The proprietor seemed so awed and respectful that Kerwin began to wonder if he had committed some social
error—evidently the Comyn rarely went into ordinary
shops—until the bargaining began. Then the man kept trying so hard to shift Kerwin from the modestly-priced boots
he had chosen to the most expensive and well-crafted pairs
in the shop, that Kerwin grew angry and began to bargain
hotly. The shopkeeper kept insisting with a beautifully-
genuine distress that these poor things were not worthy of
the *via dom*. Finally Kerwin settled on two pairs, one of riding boots, and one set of the soft low-cut suede boots that all
the men of Arilinn seemed to wear all the time indoors. Taking out his wallet, he asked "What do I owe you?"

The man looked shocked and offended. "What have I
done to merit this insult, *via dom*? You have lent grace to me
and to my shop; I cannot accept payment!"

"Oh, look here," Kerwin protested. "You mustn't do
that—"

"I have told you these poor things are not worthy of your
attention, *vai dom*, but if the High-lord would venture to accept from me a pair truly worthy of his notice—"

"Hells's bells," muttered Kerwin, wondering what was going on and what Darkovan taboo he'd blundered into, unknowing, this time.

The man gave Kerwin a sharp look, then said, "Forgive my presumption, *vai dom*, but you are the high-lord Comyn Kerwin-Aillard, are you not?"

Recalling the custom that gave a Darkovan child the name and rank of the highest-ranking parent, Kerwin admitted it, and the man said, firmly and respectfully, but rather as if he were instructing a retarded child in suitable manners, "It is not the custom to accept payment for anything that a Comyn high-lord condescends to accept, sir."

Kerwin gave in gracefully, not wanting to make a scene, but he felt embarrassed. How the devil could he get the other things he wanted? Just go and ask for them? The Comyn seemed to have a nice little racket going, but he wasn't larcenous enough to enjoy it. He was used to working for what he wanted, and paying for it.

He tucked the package under his arm, and walked along the street. It felt curiously different and pleasant, to walk through a Darkovan city as a citizen, not an outsider, not an interloper. He thought briefly of Johnny Ellers, but that was another life, and the years he had spent with the Terran Empire were like a dream.

"Kerwin?"

He looked up to see Auster, clad in green and scarlet, standing before him. Auster said, pleasantly for him, "It occurred to me that you might get lost. I had business in the city and I thought perhaps I might find you in the marketplace."

"Thanks," Kerwin said. "I wasn't lost yet, but the streets are a little confusing. Good of you to come after me." He was startled at the friendly gesture; Auster alone, of all the circle, had been persistently unfriendly.

Auster shrugged, and suddenly, as clearly as if Auster had spoken, Kerwin sensed it, clear patterned:

He's lying. He said that so I wouldn't ask his business down here. He didn't come to meet me and he's sore about it. But he shrugged the thought aside. What the hell, he wasn't Auster's keeper. Maybe the man had a girl down here, or a friend, or something. His affairs were none of Kerwin's business.

But why did he think he had to explain to me why he was in the city?

They had fallen into step together, turning their steps back in the direction of the Tower, which lay like a long arm of shadow over the marketplace. Auster paused.

"Care to stop somewhere and have a drink before we get back?"

Although he appreciated the friendly offer, Kerwin shook his head. "Thanks. I've been stared at enough for one day. I'm not much of a drinker, anyhow. Thanks all the same. Another time, maybe."

Auster gave him a quick look, not friendly, but understanding. He said, "You'll get used to being stared at—on one level. On another, it keeps getting worse. The more you're isolated with—with your own kind—the less you're able to tolerate outsiders."

They walked for a moment, shoulder to shoulder. Behind him, then, Kerwin heard a sudden yell. Auster whirled, giving Kerwin a hard, violent shove; Kerwin lost his footing, taken off balance, slipped and fell sprawling as something hurtled past and struck the wall behind him. A flake of stone ricocheted off, striking Kerwin's cheek, and laid it open to the bone.

Auster had slid off balance and fallen to his knees; he hauled himself to his feet, looking warily around, picked up the heavy paving-stone someone had hurled with what could have been a deadly accuracy.

Kerwin said, "What the hell!" He picked himself up, staring at Auster.

Auster said stiffly, "I apologize—"

Kerwin cut him short. "Forget it. You saved me a nasty bruise. If that thing had hit me amidships, I could have been killed." He touched his cheek with careful fingers. "Who threw that damn thing?"

"Some malcontent," Auster said, and looked round, unquiet. "Strange things are abroad in Arilinn these days. Kerwin, do me a favor?"

"I guess I owe you one at that."

"Don't mention this to the women—or to Kennard. We have enough to worry about now."

Kerwin frowned; but finally nodded. Silently, side by side, they walked up toward the Tower. It was surprising how much at ease he felt with Auster, in spite of the fact that Auster obviously disliked him. It was as if they'd known each other all their lives. *Being isolated with your own kind*, Auster had said. Was Auster his own kind?

He had two facts to chew on. One, Auster, who didn't like him, had moved—automatically, by instinct—to shield him from a thrown rock; by standing still, he could have let Kerwin be hurt and saved himself some aggravation and trouble. But even more than Auster's strange behavior, was the surprising event of the rock. Despite all the deference shown the Comyn by the people of Arilinn, there was *somebody* in Arilinn who would like to see one of them dead.

Or was it the half-Terran interloper who was supposed to be killed? Kerwin suddenly wished he had not given Auster his promise. He'd have liked to talk it over with Kennard.

When they joined the others in the hall that night, Kennard looked strangely at his bandaged cheek, and if Kennard had then asked a point-blank question, Kerwin might have answered—he had not promised Auster to lie about it—but Kennard said nothing, and so Kerwin only told him about the shopkeeper and the boots, mentioning his own disquiet at the custom. The older man threw back his head and guffawed.

"My dear boy, you've given the man prestige—I suppose

a *Terran* would say, free publicity—that will last for years! The fact that a Comyn of Arilinn, even one who's not very important, came into his shop and actually bargained with him—"

"Nice racket," said Kerwin sourly. He wasn't amused.

"Actually, Jeff, it makes excellent good sense. We give a good slice of our lives to the people, we can do things nobody else can do. They wouldn't think of letting us have a good excuse to do anything else. I spent some time as an officer in the Guards; my father is the hereditary Commander, it's an Alton post; and when he dies, I shall have to command it. I should be at his side, learning; but Arilinn was short-handed, so I came back. If my brother Lewis had lived—but he died, leaving me Heir to Alton, and with that, the command of the Guards." Kennard sighed. His eyes strayed into the distance. Then he said, abruptly recalling what he had been saying to Kerwin:

"In a sense, it's a way of keeping us prisoner here; a bribe. Anything we happen to want—any of us—we're given, so we have no shadow of excuse to leave the Tower on the grounds that there could be more for us elsewhere." He looked at the boots and frowned: "—and poor enough merchandise he gave you! The man should be ashamed; it speaks ill of him and his shop!"

Kerwin laughed. No wonder the man had tried so hard to steer him to a better pair! He said so, and Kennard nodded.

"Seriously, it would please the man if you went back when you next visit the town, and accepted the best pair in his shop. Or better yet, commission him to make a pair for you specially, from some design you happen to fancy! And while you're at it, let some clothingmaker fit you out with proper clothing for this climate, why don't you? The Terrans believe in heating their houses, not their bodies; I nearly suffocated when I was there. . . ."

Kerwin accepted the change of subject, but he still did not wholly understand what the Towers *did* that was so important. Messages, yes. He supposed the relays were simpler and less troublesome than a system of telephones or wireless radio communication. But if that was all they wanted, a radio system would be simpler. As for the other things, he hadn't yet connected the simpler tricks with crystal to the overwhelming importance that the Comyn telepaths seemed to have on Darkover.

And now there was another piece of the puzzle that did not fit; a rock, thrown in broad daylight, at two of the revered Tower telepaths. Not accident. Not mistaken aim on the fringes of a riot somewhere. A rock thrown deliberately, to disable or kill—and it had come near enough to doing it. It didn't fit, and he cursed having given his promise Auster.

He got the answer to one of his questions a couple of ten-days later. In one of the insulated rooms, supervised by Rannirl, Kerwin was working on elementary mechanics, practicing simple force-emission techniques, not unlike the glass-melting tricks Ragan had shown him. They had been at it for over an hour, and Jeff's head was beginning to throb, when Rannirl said abruptly, "Enough for now; something's going on."

They came out on the landing just as Taniquel darted up the stairs; she almost ran into them, and Rannirl reached out and steadied her.

"Careful, *chiya!* What's happening?"

"I'm not sure," she said. "But Neyrissa has had a message from Thendara; the Lord Hastur is coming to Arilinn."

"So soon," Rannirl murmured. "I'd hoped we'd have more time!" He looked at Kerwin and frowned. "You're not ready."

Kennard limped up the steps toward them, holding heavily to the rail. Kerwin asked, "Has this something to do with me?"

"We're not sure yet," Kennard said. "It might be. It was Hastur who gave his consent to bringing you here, you know—though we accepted responsibility."

Kerwin felt sudden fear constricting his throat. Had he been traced here? Were the Terrans going to enforce their deportation order? He did not want to leave Darkover, felt he could not bear, not now, to leave Arilinn. He belonged here; these were his people. . . .

Kennard followed his thoughts and smiled kindly to him.

"They have no authority to deport you, Jeff. By Darkovan law, citizenship follows the parent of higher rank; which means you are Darkovan by blood-right, and Comyn *Aillard*. No doubt, when Council season comes again, Lord Hastur will confirm you as Heir to Aillard, since there is no female heir to that line; Cleindori had no daughters, and she was herself *nedestro*." But he still looked troubled, and as he went up toward his room he looked over his shoulder, edgily, saying, "But, damn it, wear Darkovan clothes!"

Kerwin had had himself outfitted in the city; as he got into the somber blue-and-grey outfit he had chosen from the best tailor he could find, he thought, looking at himself in the mirror, that at least he *looked* Darkovan. He felt like one—most of the time, anyway. But he still had the sense of being on trial. Did Arilinn, or for that matter Comyn Council, really have the power to defy the Terran Empire?

That, Jeff decided, was a damn god question. The only problem was that he didn't know the answer, and couldn't even guess.

They gathered, not in the big hall they used evenings, but in a smaller, more formally arranged chamber high in the Tower, which Kerwin had heard called the Keeper's audience-chamber. The room was brightly lit with prisms suspended from silver chains; the seats were old, carved from some dark wood, and in their midst was a low table inlaid with patterns in pearl and nacre, a many-pointed star at the center. Neither Kennard nor Elorie was in the room; Kennard, he knew, had gone to the airfield to welcome the distinguished guest. Kerwin, taking one of the low seats around the table, noticed that one chair was higher and more imposing than the rest; he supposed that this was reserved for the Lord Hastur.

A curtain was drawn back by one of the nonhumans; Kennard hobbled in and took his seat. Behind him came a tall, dark, commanding man, slightly built, but with a soldierly air of presence. He said ceremoniously, "Danvan Hastur of Hastur, Warden of Hastur, Regent of the Seven Domains, Lord of Thendara and Carcosa—"

"And so forth and so forth," said a gentle, resonant voice. "You lend me grace, Valdir, but I beg of you, spare me all these ceremonies." And the Lord Hastur came into the room.

Danvan Hastur of Hastur was not a tall man. Simply clad in grey, with a blue cloak lined in silvery fur, he seemed at first just a scholarly, quiet man, edging past middle age; his hair was fair, silvering at the temples, and his manner was courteous and unassuming. But something—the stately straightness of his slim body, the firm line of his mouth, the swift, incisive look with which he summed up the room of people—made Kerwin aware that this was no elderly nonentity; this was a man of tremendous presence, a man accustomed to command and to be obeyed; a man absolutely secure in his own position and power, so secure that he did not even need arrogance.

Somehow, he seemed to take up more space in the room than he physically occupied. His voice filled it to the corners, without being loud.

"You lend me grace, children. I am glad to return to Arilinn."

The clear blue eyes fixed on Kerwin, and the man moved toward him. So compelling was that presence that Kerwin rose to his feet in automatic deference.

"*Vai dom*," he said. "I am here at your service."

"You are Cleindori's child, then, the one they sent to Terra," Danvan Hastur said. He spoke the Thendara dialect of Kerwin's own childhood. Somehow, not knowing precisely how he sensed it, Kerwin knew Hastur was not a telepath. "What name did they give you then, son of Aillard?"

Kerwin told the man his name; Hastur nodded thoughtfully.

"Well enough; although *Jeff* has an unnecessarily barbarian sound. You might well consider adopting one of the names of your clan; your mother would certainly have given you one of her family names, Arnad or Damon or Valentine. Had you thought about it? When you are presented before Council, surely, you should wear a name befitting an Aillard noble."

Kerwin said tightly, resisting the man's charm, "I'm not ashamed of wearing my father's name, sir."

"Well, please yourself," Hastur said. "I assure you I meant no offense, kinsman; and I had no intention of suggesting that you deny your Terran heritage. But you look Comyn. I wanted to see you myself and be sure of you."

Kennard said dryly, "You did not trust my word, Lord Danvan? Or—" He glanced at the dark sallow man he had called Valdir. "Or was it you who could not accept my word, my father?" A look half hostile, half affectionate passed between them, before he said formally to Kerwin, "My father, Valdir-Lewis Lanart of Alton, Lord of Armida."

Kerwin bowed, startled; Kennard's father?

Valdir said, "It did not occur to us that you would attempt to deceive us, Kennard, even if you could. But Lord Hastur wished to be certain that the Terrans had not duped you all into accepting an imposter." His sharp eyes studied Kerwin briefly, then he sighed and said, "But I can see that it is true." He added directly to Kerwin, "You have your mother's eyes, my boy; you are very like her. I was her foster-father; will you embrace me as a kinsman, nephew?" He stepped forward, embracing Jeff formally, pressing his cheeks to each of Kerwin's in turn. Kerwin, sensing—correctly—that this was a very meaningful act of personal recognition, bowed his head.

Hastur said, frowning a little, "These are strange days. I never thought I would welcome the son of a Terran to the Council. Yet if we must, we must." He sighed and said to Kerwin, "Be it so then; I recognize you." His smile was wry. "And since we have accepted the son of a Terran father, we must, I suppose, accept the son of a Terran mother. Bring Lewis-Kennard to Council, then, if you must, Kennard. How old is he now—eleven?"

"Ten, sir," Kennard said and Hastur nodded. "I cannot speak for what the Council will do. If the boy has *laran*— but then, he is too young to tell, and the Council may refuse to recognize him; but I, at least, will not fight you any further, Ken."

"*Vai dom*, you are too kind," said Kennard, in a voice heavily overlaid with sarcasm. Valdir said sharply, "Enough. We will fly that falcon when her pinions are grown. For the moment—well, Hastur, young Kerwin here would not be the first of Terran blood to stand before Comyn Council by marriage-right. Nor even the first to build a bridge between our two worlds, to the betterment of both."

Hastur sighed. "I know your views on that, Valdir; my father shared them, and it was by his will that Kennard was sent to Terra when he was no more than a boy. I do not know if he was right or wrong; only time will tell. For the moment, we are confronted with the consequences of that choice, and we must deal with them, will we nil we."

"Strange words for the Regent of Comyn," Auster said from his place, and Hastur gave him a fierce hawk-blue stare, saying, "I deal in realities, Auster. You live here isolated with your brothers and sisters of Comyn blood; I, at the very edge of the Terran Zone. I cannot pretend that the ancient days of Arilinn are still with us, or that the Forbidden Tower has never cast a shadow over every Tower in the Domains. If King Stephen—but he is dead, sound may he sleep, and I rule as Regent for a child of nine, and not a very clever or sound one; one day, if we are all fortunate, Prince

Derek will rule, but until that day comes, I do what I must in his place." He turned with a gesture of finality that silenced Auster, and took his seat—not, Kerwin noticed with astonishment, the high seat, but one of the ordinary seats around the table. Valdir did not seat himself but remained standing by the door. Although he wore no weapon, Kerwin somehow thought of a man with a hand on the hilt of his sword.

"Now, tell me, my children, how does it go with you in Arilinn?"

Kerwin, watching Lord Hastur, thought: *I wish I could tell that old fellow about the heaved rock! There's no nonsense to Lord Hastur; he'd know what to make of it, and no mistake!*

The curtains at the entrance moved. Valdir said ceremoniously, "The Lady Elorie, Keeper of Arilinn."

Once again her small stately body seemed weighted with the cruelly heavy ceremonial robes. The golden chains at her waist and fastening her cloak seemed almost fetterlike with their weight; they clasped at her shoulders, heavy, a burden. In silence, not looking at any of them, she moved to the thronelike chair at the head of the table. Valdir's deep bow startled Kerwin no less than the Lord Hastur, who rose in his place and bowed the knee deeply to Elorie.

Kerwin watched, paralyzed; this was the same girl who played with her pet birds in the great hall, and quarreled with Taniquel and made silly bets with Rannirl and rode like a hoyden with her hawks; he had not seen her before in the full regalia of the Keeper, and it was a shock and a revelation. He felt as if he too should bow, but Taniquel touched his wrist and he heard the unspoken thought:

The Tower Circle at Arilinn, alone in the Domains, need not rise for their Keeper. The Keeper of Arilinn is sacrosanct; but we are her own, her chosen. There was pride in Taniquel's thought, and Kerwin felt a flicker of it, too; even Hastur could not refuse deference to the Keeper of Arilinn.

So in a sense we are more powerful than the Regent of the Seven Domains. . . .

"Welcome, in the name of Evanda and Avarra," Elorie said in her soft throaty voice. "How may Arilinn serve the son of the Hasturs, *vai dom*?"

"Your words brighten the sky, *vai leronis*," Hastur replied, and Elorie motioned him to resume his seat.

Kennard said, "It's a long time since you honored us with a visit to Arilinn, Lord Hastur. And we are honored indeed, but if you'll forgive me, we know you didn't come to do us honor, or to have a look at Jeff Kerwin, or to bring me messages about the Council, or even to let me visit my father and ask about the health of my sons. Nor, I venture to say, even for the pleasure of our company. What do you want with us, Lord Hastur?"

The Regent's face crinkled up in a pleasant grin.

"I should have known you'd see through me, Ken," he said. "When Arilinn can spare you, we need someone like you in Council; Valdir is too diplomatic. You're right, of course; I came from Thendara because we have a delegation waiting—with the big question."

All of them, except Kerwin, seemed to know what he meant. Rannirl muttered, "So soon?"

"You haven't given us much time, Lord Hastur," Elorie said. "Jeff's making good progress, but it's slow."

Kerwin leaned forward, gripping at the chair arm.

"What's this all about, why are you looking at me?"

Hastur said, solemnly, "Because, Jeff Kerwin-Aillard, you have given us, for the first time in many years, a Tower Circle with a full complement of power, under a Keeper. If you do not fail us, we may be in a position to save the power and prestige of the Comyn—if you do not fail us. Otherwise—" He spread his hands. "The Terrans will have their entering wedge. The rest will follow and there won't be any way to stop it. I want you—all of you—to come and talk to the delegation. What about it, Elorie? Do you trust your Terran barbarian as much as that?"

In the silence that followed, Kerwin felt Elorie's glance, calm, childlike, resting on him.

Barbarian. Elorie's barbarian. I'm still that, to all of them.

Elorie turned to Kennard and said quietly, "What about it, Ken? You know him best."

By now Kerwin was used to being discussed before his face. In a telepath society there was no way to avoid it anyway. Even if they had tactfully sent him out of the room, he would have been aware of what was being said. He tried to keep his face impassive.

Kennard sighed and said, "As far as trusting goes, we can trust him, Elorie," he said. "But the risk is yours and so the decision has to be yours. Whatever you decide, we'll stand by you."

"I speak against it," Auster said passionately. "You know how I feel—you too, Lord Hastur!"

Hastur turned to the younger man and said, "Is it blind prejudice against Terrans, Auster?" His calm manner contrasted curiously with Auster's tense, knotted face and angry voice. "Or have you some reason?"

"Prejudice," Taniquel said angrily, "and jealousy!"

"Prejudice, yes," Auster admitted, "but not, I think, blind. It was entirely too easy to get him from the Terrans. How do we know that the whole thing wasn't concocted for our benefit?"

Valdir said, in his deep voice, "With Cleindori's face written on his own? He has Comyn blood."

"I think, by your leave," Auster said, "that you, too, are prejudiced, Lord Valdir. You, with your Terran foster-son and half-caste grandson—"

Kennard leaped to his feet. "Now, damn it, Auster—"

"And you speak of Cleindori!" As he spoke it, the word

was an epithet, a foulness. "She who was Dorilys of Arilinn—renegade, heretic—"

Elorie rose, angry and white. "Cleindori is dead. Let her lie in peace! And Zandru send scorpion whips to those who murdered her!"

"And to her seducer—*and all his blood!*" Auster flung back. "We all know Cleindori was not alone when she fled from Arilinn—"

New, unaccustomed emotions were battling in Jeff Kerwin. This was his father, his unknown mother, that they were cursing! For the first time in his life he felt a surge of sympathy for his Terran grandparents. Unloving and cold they had seemed; and yet they had taken him in as a son and never once had they reproached him with his unknown, alien mother or his mixed blood. He longed to rise, fling challenge at Auster; he half rose to his feet, but Kennard's angry look fixed him in his seat; and Hastur's ringing voice commanded, "Enough!"

"Lord Hastur—"

"Not a word!" Hastur's angry, emphatic voice silenced even Auster. "We are not here to rake up the deeds and misdeeds of men and women a generation dead!"

"Then, under favor, Lord Hastur, why are we here?" asked Neyrissa. "I have given Kerwin the monitor's oath; he will do for a mechanic's circle."

"But a Keeper's circle?" Hastur asked. "Are you all ready to risk him for that? To do again what Arilinn could do in Leonie's time and has not done since? Are you ready for that?"

There was silence, a deep silence, and Kerwin sensed that there was fear in it. Even Kennard was silent. At last Hastur added, urgently, "Only the Keeper of Arilinn can make that decision, Elorie. And the delegation awaits the word of Arilinn's Keeper."

"I don't think we ought to risk it," Auster said. "What is

the delegation to us? The Keeper should choose in her own good time!"

"The risk is *mine*—to accept or refuse!" Two spots of angry color burned in Elorie's cheek. "I have never before used my authority; I am not a witch, not a sorceress, I will not let men place on me the supernatural power. . . ." She spread her hands in a little, helpless gesture. "Yet, for good or ill, I am Arilinn; authority rests by law in me, Elorie of Arilinn. We will hear the delegation. There is no more to be said; Elorie has spoken."

There were bent heads, murmurs of assent, and Kerwin, watching, was shocked. Among themselves, they quarreled with Elorie and argued points with her without hesitation; this public assent had the feel of ritual.

Elorie turned to the door, stately and unbending. Kerwin watched her, and suddenly felt at one with her disquiet. He *knew*, not quite knowing how the knowledge had come to him, how Elorie hated to invoke her supreme and ritual authority; how much she disliked the superstitious awe surrounding her high office. Suddenly this pale, childish girl seemed *real* to him, her calmness merely a mask for passionate convictions, for emotions so severely controlled that they were like the eye of the hurricane.

And I thought her calm, emotionless? A mask she wears, no more, only a mask no one can remove, not even she herself. . . .

He felt Elorie's emotions as if they were his own.

So I've done what I swore I would never do. I've used their conditioned reverence for a Keeper, just to force them to do what I want! But I had to, oh, I had to, or we'd have another hundred years of this superstitious rubbish. . . . And then a thought that, Kerwin knew, shocked Elorie as much as it shocked him, a flaring, frightening question: *Was Cleindori right?* And he felt Elorie's thoughts flare into silence, knowing she had frightened herself with that last question.

CHAPTER NINE

Challenge to Arilinn

Riding down in the shaft, between Taniquel and Elorie, Kerwin was still shaken by the backlash of that contact with Elorie. What had Kennard called his gift? *Empath*—gifted with the power of sensing the emotions of others. He had accepted, intellectually, that this was true; had tested it a little under laboratory conditions and among the circle. Now, for the first time, it had hit him deep, on the level of his guts, and he *felt* it and knew it.

He didn't know where they were going. He followed the others. But they went down through the Veil and outside, and into a building near the Tower that Jeff had never seen before. It was a long, narrow, silk-hung hall, and somewhere a ceremonial gong rang out as they filed into the room. There were a few spectators in the seats, and before them, at a long table, were half a dozen men.

They were prosperous looking men, most of them middle aged and more, wearing Darkovan dress in the fashion of the cities. They waited silently while Elorie was announced and took the central chair. The Tower circle seated themselves quietly around Elorie, not speaking.

It was Danvan of Hastur who spoke, at last.

"You are the men who call yourselves the Pan-Darkovan Syndicate?"

One of the men, a heavy-set and swarthy man with fierce eyes, bowed.

"Valdri of Carthon, *z'par servu*, my lords and ladies," he confirmed. "By your leave I will speak for all."

"Let me review the situation," said Hastur. "You have formed a league—"

"To encourage the growth of manufacturing and trade on Darkover, in the Domains and beyond," Valdrin said. "I hardly need to tell you the political situation—the Terrans and their foothold on our world. The Comyn and the Council, saving your presence, Lord Hastur, have tried to ignore the Terran presence here and its implications for trade—"

Hastur said quietly, "That is not precisely the situation."

"I won't bandy words with you, *vai dom*," said Valdrin, respectfully but impatiently too. "The facts are these: In view of our agreements with the Terrans, we have an opportunity we've never had before, to bring the Domains out of our Dark Ages. Times change. Like it or not, the Terrans are here to stay. Darkover is being swept into the Empire. We can pretend they're not there, refuse to trade with them, ignore their offers of trade, and keep them locked up inside their Trade Cities, but the barriers we put up will come tumbling down in another generation, maybe two at most. I've seen it happening on other worlds."

Kerwin remembered what the Legate had said, that they left governments alone, but that the people saw what the Terran Empire had to give, and started demanding to come into it. *It's almost a mathematical formula—you can predict the thing.*

Valdrin of Carthon was saying the same thing, quite passionately.

"In short, Lord Hastur, we protest the decision of Comyn Council; we want some of the advantages that come with being a part of the Empire!"

Hastur said quietly, "Do you understand the decision of the Council, to retain the integrity of the Darkovan way of life, rather than becoming just another Empire satellite state?"

"With all respect, Lord Hastur, when you talk about the Darkovan way of life, you're talking about letting us stay a barbarian culture forever. Some of us want civilization and technology—"

Hastur said quietly, "I have seen the Terran civilization more closely than you. I tell you, Darkover wants none of it."

"Speak for yourselves, *vai dom*, not for us! Perhaps in the old days there was some justification for the rule of the Seven Domains; in those days, Comyn gave us something to compensate for what we gave them in the way of allegiance and support!"

Valdir Alton said, "Man, am I listening to treason against the Council and Hastur?"

Valdir of Carthon said heavily, "Treason? Not that, sir. God forbid. And we don't want to be part of the Empire any more than you do. We're talking about trade, technological advance. There was a day when Darkover had its own science and technology. But those days are gone, and we've got to have something to replace them, or else sink into a second Ages of Chaos. It's time to admit that they're gone, and find something to replace them. And if the Terrans want to be here, they can offer us something—trade, metals, tools, technological consultants. Because it's for certain that the old sciences of the Towers are gone forever."

Kerwin was beginning to see it clearly. By virtue of their inborn psi powers, once, the Comyn had been rulers—and, in a certain sense, slaves—of Darkover and the Domains. Through the tremendous energy of the matrixes, not the small individual ones, but the great ones demanding linked circles of Tower-trained telepaths linked under a Keeper, they had given Darkover her own science and her own technology. This explained the vast ruins of a forgotten technology, the traditions of ancient sciences. . . .

But what had the cost been, in human terms? The men and women possessed of these powers had lived, perforce, lives constrained and circumscribed, guarding their precious powers carefully, spoilt for ordinary human contacts.

Kerwin wondered if the natural drift of evolution, in nature, toward the norm and away from extremes, had been responsible for the waning of these powers. For they had waned. Arilinn, Mesyr had told him, had once held three circles, each with its own Keeper; and Arilinn had been only one of many Towers. Fewer and fewer were born in these days with a full measure of the precious *laran*. The science of Darkover had become a forgotten myth and a few psi tricks. . . . And this was not enough to keep Darkover independent of the lure of Terran trade and Terran technology.

"We have dealt with the Terrans," Valdrin of Carthon said, "and I think, also, that we have won most of the people to our side."

Valdir said, "In Thendara, the people are loyal to Comyn Council!"

"But, under favor, *vai dom*, Thendara is only a very small part of the Domains," Valdrin said, "and the Domains are not all of Darkover. The Terrans have pledged that they will lend us technicians, engineers, industrial developers and experts—everything necessary to begin extensive mining and manufacturing operations here. Metals and ores are the key, my lord. Before we have technology we must have machinery, and before we have machinery we must have—"

Hastur raised a hand. He said, "I know it all like an old song. Before you have mines you must have machinery, and someone must make the machinery, and someone must mine the materials to make the machinery. We are not a mechanized civilization, Valdrin—"

"True, more's the pity!"

"Is it such a pity? The people of Darkover are content on their farms and lands and cities. We have what industries we need; dairy farming, cheesemaking, the milling of grains, and weaving of cloth. There are papermills and felting-mills, the processing of nuts and cereals—"

"Transported at horseback pace!"

"And," Hastur said, "No men to slave at the building of roads to keep them in condition for monstrous robot vehicles to whiz over at breakneck speed and make our clean air rotten with their chemical fuels!"

"We have a right to industries and wealth—"

"And to factories? To wealth gained by forcing men to labor in inhuman conditions, to build things that men do not really need or want? To work done by automatic machinery, leaving men with nothing to do but drug their senses with cheap amusements, and work at repairing the machinery? To mines, and people herded together in cities to build and repair these machines, so they have no time to grow and prepare the food they need? So that the raising of food becomes another monster factory enterprise, and a man's children become a liability instead of an asset?"

Valdrin's voice was calm, tinged with contempt. "You are a romantic, my lord, but your biased picture will not convince those men who want something better than starving on their land from year to year and dying in a bad year. You cannot hold us back forever to a primitive culture, my lord."

"Do you really want to become a replica of the Terran Empire, then?"

"Not that," Valdrin said, "not what you think. We can take what we need from the Terran system without being corrupted by it."

Hastur smiled faintly and said, "That is a delusion that has seduced many people and worlds, my good man. Do you think we can fight the Terrans on their own ground? No, my friend; the world that accepts the good things that come from the Terran Empire—and I am not deceived, there are many—must also accept the evil that comes with it. And yet perhaps you are right; we cannot bar the way forever, and keep our people poor and simple, an agricultural society in

an interstellar age. It may be that your accusation is just.
Once we were more powerful than now; it is true that we are
just emerging from a Dark Age. But it is not true that we
must go Terra's way. What if the old powers were to return?
What if the Comyn could do again all the things that legend
said they could do? What if energy sources were available
again, without the endless search for fuels, without the evils
that blasted our land in the years before the Compact?"

"What if Durraman's donkey could fly?" asked Valdrin.
"It's a good dream, but there hasn't been a competent
Keeper, let alone a fully qualified circle, for years."

"There is now." Hastur turned with a gesture. "A Comyn
circle complete and ready to demonstrate their powers. I ask
only this; that you keep free of the Terrans, and their ru-
inous, dehumanizing methods. Don't accept their technicians and their engineers, to destroy our lands! And if you
must trade with Terra, do it as equals, not as poor protégés,
being helped up from barbarian status! Our world is old,
older than Terra dreams, and prouder. Don't shame us this
way!"

He had caught them on their pride and their patriotism,
and Kerwin saw it catch fire in the eyes of each of the delegation, although Valdrin still seemed skeptical.

"Can the Tower circle do this?"

"We can," Rannirl said. "I'm the technician; we have the
skill and we know how to use it. What do you need?"

"We've been dealing with a group of Terran engineers,
to make a survey of the natural resources in the Domains
for us," Valdrin said. "Our major needs are for metals: tin,
copper, silver, iron, tungsten. Then for fuels, for sulfur, hy-
drocarbons, chemicals—they promised us a complete in-
ventory, to locate with their surveying equipment all the
major accessible deposits of natural resources for mining—"

Rannirl held up a hand. "At the same time finding out
where they are," he drawled, "and spreading all over Dark-

over with their infernal machines instead of staying decently shut up in their Trade Cities!"

Valdrin said hotly, "I deplore that as much as you do! I have no love for the Empire, but if the alternative is to slip backward into primitivism . . ."

"There is an alternative," Rannirl said, "We can make your survey for you—and do the mining, too, if you like. And we can do it quicker than the Terrans."

Kerwin drew a deep breath. He should have guessed. If a matrix crystal could power an aircraft, what were the limits of that power?

God, what a concept! And to keep the Terran engineers out of the Domains . . .

Kerwin had not realized until this moment how deeply he felt on this subject; his years on Terra came back to his mind, dirty industrialized cities, men living for machinery, his dismay when he came back to Thendara and found the Trade City only a little corner of the Empire. With the passionate love of an exile for his home, he understood Hastur's dream; to keep Darkover what it was, keep it out of the Empire.

Valdrin said, "It sounds good, my lords, but the Comyn haven't been that strong, not for centuries—maybe never. My great-granfer used to tell stories of buildings raised by matrix power, and roads built, and such-like things, but in my time it's been all a man can do to get enough iron to shoe his horses!"

"It sounds good, yes," said another of the men, "but I think it more likely the Comyn are just trying to delay us until the Terrans lose interest and go elsewhere. I think we ought to deal with the Terrans."

Valdrin said, "Lord Hastur, we need more than vague talk about the old Comyn powers and the Tower circles. How long would it take you to make this survey for us?"

Rannirl glanced at Hastur, as if asking permission to

speak. He asked, "How long would the Terrans need to do it?"

"Theyve promised it to us in half a year."

Rannirl glanced at Elorie, at Kennard, and Kerwin felt that they shared an exchange from which he was excluded. Then he said, "Half a year, eh? What would you say to forty days?"

"On one condition," Auster broke in passionately. "That if we do it for you, you'll abandon all ideas of dealing with the Terran engineers!"

"That seems only fair," said Elorie, speaking for the first time, and Kerwin noticed how a silence dropped in the room as the Keeper spoke. "If we prove to you that we can do more for you than your Terran engineers, will you be content to be guided by the Council? Our only desire is that Darkover shall continue to be Darkover, not a replica of the Terran Empire . . . or a third-rate imitation! If we succeed, you will allow yourselves to be guided by Comyn Council and Arilinn in all things."

"That seems fair enough, my lady," Valdrin said. "But it's only fair it should go both ways. If you can't deliver what you say, will Comyn Council pledge itself to withdraw all objections, and let us deal with the Terrans without interference?"

Elorie said, "I can only speak for Arilinn, not for Comyn Council," but Hastur rose. In the quiet, resonant voice that filled the Council chamber without being loud, he said, "On the word of a Hastur, it shall be so."

Kerwin met Taniquel's eyes, seeing the shock in them. The word of Hastur was proverbial. And now it was all in their hands—if they could indeed do what Rannirl had said they could do, what Hastur had pledged they could do. The whole future direction of Darkover hung on their success or failure. And that success or failure hung on him, on Jeff Kerwin, on "Elorie's barbarian"—the newest member of the circle, the weak link in the chain! It was a paralyzing responsibility, and Kerwin was terrified by the implications.

The formalities of leavetaking were endless, and halfway through them Kerwin slipped away unseen, back through the courtyards and through the shimmering haze of the Veil.

It was too heavy a weight to be borne, that their success or failure should hang on him alone . . . and he had thought he would have more time to learn! He remembered the agony of the first rapports, and was horribly afraid. He turned into his room and flung himself down on his bed in silent despair. It wasn't fair to demand so much of him, so soon! It was too much, to insist that the whole fate of Darkover, the Darkover he knew and loved, should depend on his untried powers!

The ghostly scent in the room felt strong to him; in a flash of remote recognition, it penetrated a closed place in his memory.

Cleindori. My mother, who broke her vows to the Comyn, for an Earthman . . . must I pay for her betrayal?

A flash of something, recognition, memory, hovered at the edge of his senses, a voice that said *it was not betrayal.* . . . He could not identify the dark, closing door of memory, standing half-ajar, a voice . . .

Blinding pain struck through his head; it was gone. He stood in his room, crying out in despair. "It's too much! It's not fair, that it should all depend on me . . ." And heard the words echoing in his mind, as if from the walls, as if someone else had stood here, crying these words in the same despair.

A soft step in the room, a voice that whispered his name, and Taniquel was at his side, the web of rapport meshing between them. The girl's face, now solemn and free of mischief, was drawn and grieved with his trouble.

"But it's not like that, Jeff," she whispered at last. "We trust you, we all trust you. If we fail, it's not your doing alone. Don't you know that?" Her voice broke and she clung to him, holding him in her arms. Kerwin, shaken with a new, violent emotion, crushed the girl to him. Their lips met; and Kerwin knew that he had been wanting this since he first saw her, through the smoke of a Terran room. The woman of his own people, the first to accept him as one of themselves.

"Jeff, we love you; if we fail, it's not your failure, it's ours. You won't be the one to blame. But you won't fail, Jeff. I know you won't. . . ."

Her arms sheltered him, their thoughts blended, and the upsurge of love and desire in him was something he had never known, never guessed.

Here was no easy conquest, no cheap girl from the space-men's bars, to give his body a moment's ease but leave his heart untouched. Here was no encounter to leave the after-taste of lust in his memory, and the sickening of loneliness when he sensed, as he had sensed so often, the woman's emptiness as deep as his own disillusion.

Taniquel. Taniquel, who had been closer than any previous lover from that first instant of rapport between them, from her first accepting kiss. How was it that he had never known? He shut his eyes, the better to taste this closeness, the closeness that was more intense than the touch of lips or arms.

Taniquel whispered, "I've sensed . . . your loneliness and your need, Jeff. But I was afraid to let myself share them until now. Jeff, Jeff—I've taken your pain to myself, let me share this too."

"But," Kerwin said hoarsely, "I'm not afraid now. I was afraid only because I felt alone."

"And now," she spoke his thoughts, sinking into his arms with a surrender so absolute that he seemed never to have known a woman before, "you'll never be alone again."

CHAPTER TEN

The Way of Arilinn

If Kerwin had visualized the planetary survey as something to be done by magic, concentration into the matrixes, a quick mental process, he was quickly shown how wrong he was. The actual rapport work, Kennard told him, would come later; meanwhile there were preparations to be made, and only the Tower telepaths themselves could make them.

It was almost impossible to focus telepathic rapport, so they explained to him, unless the object or substance had first been brought into a rapport with the telepath who would be using it. Kerwin had imagined that the gathering of the materials would be done by outsiders or menials; instead, he himself, as the least skilled in actual telepathic matrix work, was put to several small technical jobs in the preliminary stages. He had learned something of metallurgy on Terra; assisted by Corus, they located samples of various metals, and, working in a laboratory that reminded Jeff of an Earth-history conception of an alchemist's study, smelted them down and with primitive but surprisingly effective techniques, reduced them to pure form. He wondered what on earth they were going to do with those miniature samples of iron, tin, copper, lead, zinc, and silver. He was even more confused when Corus started making molecular models of these metals, kindergarten affairs with little clay balls on sticks, pausing at times to concentrate on the metals and "sound" the atomic structure with his matrix. Kerwin quickly picked up the trick of this—it was not unlike his early experiments with glass and crystal structure.

Meanwhile Taniquel was out daily in the air-launch with Auster and Kennard, examining great maps, carefully coordinating them with photographs (made on excellent Terran cameras) of the terrain. Sometimes they were away for two or three days at a time.

Taniquel had explained to Kerwin why they needed the maps and pictures of the countryside. "You see," she explained, "the picture—and the map—becomes a symbol of that piece of ground, and we can establish rapport with it through the picture. There was a time when a good psychic could find water, or minerals in the ground, but he had to be walking over it at the time."

Kerwin nodded; even on Earth, where psi powers were still not much regarded, there were water-finders and dowsers. But on a *map*?

"We don't find them on the map, silly," Taniquel said. "The map is a device to establish contact with that piece of land, the territory *represented* by the map. We could find it by pure psychism, but it's easier if we have something that directly represents it; like a photograph. We use the map to establish the contact, and to mark what we find there."

Kerwin supposed the principle was the same as the folktale of the man who killed his enemy by sticking pins in his image; but as the memory came into his mind, Taniquel blanched and said, "No one trained at Arilinn would ever, *ever* do such a wicked thing!"

"But the principle is the same," Kerwin said, "using an object as a focus for the powers of the mind." But Taniquel still would not admit it. "It isn't the same at all! That's meddling with the mind, and it's unlawful and—*dirty*," she said vehemently, then looked at him with suspicion. "You took the monitor's oath, didn't you?" she demanded, as if wondering how anyone sworn that way could even have such thoughts. And Kerwin sighed, knowing he would never understand Taniquel. They shared so much, they had been so often in rapport, he felt that she was utterly known to him: And yet there were times when, as now, she became alien, wholly a stranger.

While they were making the maps and checking their accuracy with the Terran photographs (Kerwin, who knew something of cameras from his years on Terra, was pressed into service developing, printing, and enlarging the enormous aerial views), Corus finished the work of making the metal samples; then Elorie brought them in on the work of constructing the matrix lattices, or "screens."

This was hard, demanding work, both mentally and physically; they worked with molten glass, whose amorphous structure was nevertheless solid enough to hold the matrix crystals in the desired structure, a solid network encased in glass. Corus, whose PK potential was enormously high, had the task of holding the glassy stuff in a state of liquid pliancy without heat. Kerwin attempted this several times, but it frightened him to see Elorie plunge her frail white hands into the apparently boiling mass. Rannirl said dryly that if Kerwin lost his nerve and his control they could all be badly hurt, and refused to let him have control of the glass while they were working inside it. Layer after layer of the glass was poured, Elorie activating, with her own matrix, the tiny sensitized crystals suspended inside each layer; Rannirl standing by to take control when hers faltered; and meanwhile following the whole process on a monitor screen not unlike the one Kerwin had seen in the house of the two matrix mechanics in Thendara, monitoring the complex interior crystalline structures being built up in the layers of glass, by a process analogous to the monitoring process that Taniquel, or Neyrissa, could do with the body of one of them.

Rannirl said once, at the end of a long stint working with the lattices, "I shouldn't say this; but Elorie is wasted as a Keeper. She has the talent to be a technician; and she never

will be, because we need Keepers too badly. If there were
more women willing to work as Keepers—a Keeper doesn't
need that kind of talent, a Keeper doesn't even have to learn
to monitor; she simply has to hold the energon flows. Zandru's hells, we could use a damned *machine* for that. I could
build an amplifier that would do it, one that any good mechanic could handle! But it's traditional, using a Keeper's
polarities and energy flows. And I can't even teach Elorie as
much as she wants to know about mechanics; she needs all
her energy for the work she does in the circle! Damn it—"
He lowered his voice and said, as if he expected to be overheard and blasted, "Keepers are an anachronism in this day
and age. Cleindori was right, if they could only see it!" But
when Kerwin stared and asked him what he had meant, Rannirl shook his head, tightened his mouth and said, "Forget I
said it. It's a dangerous point of view." He would say no
more, but Kerwin caught a fragment of thought about fanatics who thought that a Keeper's ritual virginity was more
important than her efficiency at the matrixes, and that this
point of view was going to destroy the Towers sooner or
later, if it hadn't already.

Working with them, he felt his own sensitivity growing,
day by day. He had no trouble now in visualizing almost any
atomic structure; the work he had done with Neyrissa, in
learning to monitor his own internal organs and processes,
was beginning to carry over to seeing energy fields and
atomic processes, and he had no trouble in maintaining the
stasis in any crystalline structure. He was beginning to
sense the internal structure of other substances now; once
he found himself aware of oxidation of the iron in a slowly-
rusting doorhinge; in his first unsupervised effort, he pulled
out his matrix and with a fierce mental effort reversed the
process.

He still got the splitting headaches when he was actually
working with the screens—though now he could handle a
shift in the relay nets unassisted—and the effort was tremen-

dous, racking, each expenditure of psychic energy leaving him spent and drained, his body demanding enormous quantities of food and sleep.

He understood, now, the gargantuan appetites they all had—Elorie, for instance; he had been amused at her child-like greediness for sweets, and had been astonished at seeing so frail and dainty a little girl put away quantities of food that would have satiated a horse-drover. But now he realized that he was hungry all the time; his body, drained of energy, demanded replacements with ravenous hunger. And when the day's work was completed—or called to a halt because Elorie could not endure any more of the strain—and Kerwin could rest, or when Taniquel had a little leisure to spend with him, he found that he could only fling himself down beside her and sleep.

"I'm afraid I'm not a very ardent lover," he apologized once, half sick with chagrin; Taniquel close to him, loving and willing, but the only desire in his body was an exhausted hunger for sleep. Taniquel laughed softly, bending to kiss him.

"I know; I've been around matrix workers all my life, remember? It's always that way when there's work in hand—you have only so much energy, and it all goes into the work, and there's nothing left. Don't worry about it." She laughed, a small mischievous chuckle. "When I was training at Neskaya, we used to test ourselves, sometimes, one of the men and I; we'd lie down together—and if either of us could even *think* of anything but sleep, we'd know we'd been cheating, not giving all we had to the matrix work!"

He felt a sudden inner storm of jealousy for the men she had known that way; but he was really too tired to care.

She stroked his hair. "Sleep, *bredu*—we'll have time together when this is over, if you still want me."

"*If* I still want you?" Kerwin sat upright, staring at the girl. She lay back on the pillow, her eyes closed, the freckles pale on her pixie face, her hair loosened, sunbright on the sheets. "What do you mean, Tani?"

"Oh, people change," she said vaguely. "Never mind that now. Here—" She pulled him gently down, her light hands caressing his forehead. "Sleep, love; you're worn out."

Weary as he was, the words had driven sleep from his mind. How could Taniquel doubt—or was the girl in the grip of some premonition? Since they had been lovers, he had been happy; now, for the first time, disquiet moved in him, and he had a sudden mental flash of Taniquel, hand in hand with Auster, walking along the battlements at the tower. What had been between Taniquel and Auster?

He *knew* Taniquel cared for him in a way he had never guessed possible with any woman. They were in total harmony. He knew, now, why his casual affairs with women had never gone beneath the surface; the unrecognized telepathic sensitivity in him had picked up the fundamental shallowness of the kind of women he had known; he had chided himself for being an idealist, wanting more than any woman could give. Now he knew it was possible; his relationship with Taniquel had brought a whole dimension into focus; his first taste of shared passion and emotion, real intimacy. He *knew* Taniquel cared for him; could she possibly care for him so deeply, if she cared for someone else that way?

Many disquiets began to come into focus as he lay awake, his head throbbing, of course. Now it was clear to him; everyone in the Arilinn Tower knew they were lovers. Small things he had not noticed at the time, a smile from Kennard, a meaningful glance from Mesyr, even the small interchange with Neyrissa—*Are you jealous?*—now took on significance.

And I never realized; in a telepath culture they would take it for granted, there would be no such thing as privacy and I never understood . . . Suddenly the thought was violent, embarrassing: Telepaths all, were they reading his thoughts, his emotions, spying on what he had shared with Taniquel? Scalding embarrassment flooded him, as if he had had some shameful dream of walking naked in the public square and waked to find that it was true. . . .

Taniquel drowsily holding his hand, curled against him, jerked awake as if touched by a live wire. Indignation flamed in her face.

"You—you *are* a barbarian," she raged. "You—you *Terranan!*" She scrambled out of bed and caught up her dressing-gown; quickly she was gone, her light footsteps dying away with an angry pattering on the uneven floor. Kerwin, baffled at her sudden rage, lay with his head throbbing. He told himself that this would not do, he had work to do the next day, and lay down, trying hard to apply the techniques Neyrissa had taught him, relaxing his body, slowing his breathing to normal, trying to calm the tensions in his body by controlling his breath, to ease the blood pounding in his temples. But he was too confused and dismayed for much success.

But when they met again, she was gentle and affectionate as ever, greeting him with her spontaneous embrace. "Forgive me, Jeff, I shouldn't have been angry. It was unfair of me. It's not for me to blame you, that you've lived among the *Terranan* and picked up some their—their strange ways. You'll come to understand us better, in time."

And with the reassurance of her arms around him, her emotions meshing with his, he could not doubt the sincerity of her feelings.

Thirteen days after Hastur's visit to Arilinn, the matrixes were prepared; and later that same day, in the great hall, Elorie told them, "We can begin the first surveying operation tonight."

Kerwin felt last-minute panic. This would be his first experience in the prolonged rapport of a matrix circle.

"Why at night?" he asked.

It was Kennard who answered. "Most people sleep during the dark hours; we get less telepathic interference—in radio you'd call it static. There's telepathic static, too."

"I want all of you to get some sleep during the day," Neyrissa said. "I want you all fresh and rested for tonight."

Corus winked at Kerwin and said, "Better give Jeff a sedative; otherwise he'll lie awake fretting." But there was no malice in his words. Mesyr looked at him, questioningly.

"If you want something—"

He shook his head, feeling foolish. They talked a few minutes longer, then Elorie, yawning, said she was going to take her own advice, and went upstairs. One by one, they began to drift away from the fireside. Kerwin, not sleepy in spite of his weariness, waited, hoping Taniquel would join him. Perhaps, if she were with him, he might be able to forget the impending ordeal and relax.

"Neyrissa meant it, youngster," said Kennard, pausing beside him. "The monitor's word is law, in cases like this. Better get some rest, or tonight will be too much for you."

A moment of silence; then Kennard's heavy brows went into his hairline. "Oh," he said, "it's like that, is it?"

Kerwin exploded. "Damn it, is there no privacy at all here?"

Kennard looked at him with a wry, apologetic smile. "I'm sorry," he said. "I'm an Alton; we're the strongest telepaths in the Comyn. And—well, I've lived on Terra; I married a Terran woman. So perhaps I understand more than some of the younger ones would. Don't be offended, but—may I say something, as I would to—to a younger brother or a nephew?"

Touched against his will, Kerwin said, "Yes, of course."

Kennard thought for a minute, then said, "Don't blame Taniquel for leaving you alone just now, just when you feel that you need her most. I know how you feel—Zandru's hells, how well I know!" He chuckled as if at some private joke. "But Tani knows, too. And when a matrix operation is in train, a big one like this especially, celibacy is the rule, and necessary. She knows better than to play around with that. For that matter, one of us should have talked to you about it before."

"I don't think I understand," Kerwin said slowly, rebelling. "Why should it make any difference?"

Kennard answered with another question. "Why do you think the Keepers are required to be virgins?"

Kerwin hadn't the faintest idea, but it suddenly struck him that it explained Elorie. On the surface, she was a lovely young woman, certainly as beautiful as Taniquel, but as sexless as a child of seven or eight. Rannirl had said something about ritual virginity—and Elorie was certainly as unconscious of her own beauty and desirability as the youngest, most unaware of children. Or more so; most little girls, by eight or nine, were quite aware of their own femininity and one could see in them the seeds of desirability. Elorie, somehow, seemed entirely unaware of her own womanhood.

"In the ancient days it was regarded as a ritual thing," Kennard said. "I think that's drivel. The fact remains that it's terribly dangerous for a woman to work in the center-polar position in a matrix circle, holding the energon flows, unless she's a virgin; it has something to do with nerve currents. Even on the edges of the circle, the women observe strict chastity for a considerable time beforehand. As for you—well, you are going to need every scrap of your nervous energy and strength tonight, and Taniquel knows that. Hence, you get some sleep. Alone. And I might as well warn you, if you haven't already found it out, that you won't be much good to a woman for some days afterward. Don't let it worry you; it's just a side effect of the energy drains." He laid a kindly, almost fatherly hand on Kerwin's wrist. "The trouble is, Jeff, you've become so much a part of us that we forget you haven't always been here; we take it for granted that you'll know all these things without being told."

Jeff said in a low voice, touched by Kennard's warmth, "Thank you—kinsman." He used the word without selfconsciousness, for the first time. If he had been foster-brother to Cleindori, Jeff's mother—Kerwin already knew that fosterage, on Darkover, created family ties that were, in many cases, stronger than those of blood.

He asked on an impulse, "Did you know my father, Kennard?"

Kennard hesitated. Then he said, slowly, "Yes. I suppose you could say I knew him quite well. Not—not as well as I could have wished, or things might have been different. It didn't help me to change anything."

"What was my father like?" Kerwin asked.

Kennard sighed. He said, "Jeff Kerwin? Not much like you; you look like my sister. Kerwin was big and dark and practical; a no-nonsense kind of man. But he had imagination, too. Lewis—my brother—knew him better than I did. He introduced him to Cleindori." Kennard frowned suddenly and said, "Look this is no time for this. Go and rest." He sensed that Kennard was troubled. Abruptly, whether because he sensed something, picked up an image form Kennard's mind, Kerwin asked:

"Kennard, how did my mother die?"

Kennard's jaw set in a tight line. He said, "Don't ask me, Jeff. Before they consented to let you come here—" He stopped, obviously considering what to say, and Kerwin sensed that the older man was holding himself tightly blocked against Kerwin picking up even a fragment of thought. He said, "I was at Arilinn, too, then. And they asked me to come back because they were so short-handed, after—after what happened. But before they consented to let you come here, they made me—made me swear I wouldn't answer certain questions, and that's one of them. Jeff, the past is *past*. Think of today. Everybody at Arilinn, everybody in the Domains, has to put the past behind us and think of what we're doing for Darkover and for our people." There was a hint of old pain in his face, but he was still tightly barriered.

"Jeff, when you came here, we were all very doubtful about you. But now, win or lose, you're one of us. True Darkovan—and true Comyn. That thought may not be as reassuring as it would be to have Tani with you," he added, with an attempt at flippancy, "but it should help, just a little. Now go and sleep—kinsman."

They sent for him at moonrise. The Arilinn Tower felt strange and still in the deep night, and the matrix chamber was filled with the strange resonating quiet. They gathered, speaking in hushed voices, feeling the stillness as a living thing around them, a very real presence they hated to disturb. Kerwin felt slack, empty, exhausted. He noticed that Kennard was limping more than usual; Elorie looked sleepy and cross, and Neyrissa spoke sharply when Rannirl made some jocular remark.

Taniquel touched Kerwin's forehead, and he felt the faint feather-touch of her thoughts, the swift sure rapport. He did not flinch away from it now. "He's all right, Elorie."

Elorie glanced from Taniquel to Neyrissa. "You monitor, Tani. We need Neyrissa in the circle," she explained, at Neyrissa's injured glance. "She's stronger; and she's been working longer." To Kerwin, she explained, "when we're working in a circle like this, we need a monitor outside the circle, and Taniquel's the best empath we have; she'll stay in rapport with all of us, so if one of us forgets to breathe, or gets a muscle cramp, she'll know it before we do, and keep us from being too depleted or damaged. Auster, you hold the barriers," she directed, adding, for the benefit of the newcomer, "we all drop our individual barriers, and he puts up a group barrier which keeps out telepathic eavesdropping; and he'll sense it if anyone tries to interfere with us. In the old days there were alien forces on Darkover; perhaps, for all we know, there still are. The barrier around the gestalt formed by our minds will protect us."

Kennard was holding a smaller matrix lattice—one of the glass-surfaced screens like the one they had constructed. He was turning it this way and that, toward each of them, frowning and making some small adjustments on a cali-brated dial. Lights glowed here and there in its depth. He said, absentmindedly, "Auster's barrier should hold, but just for safety's sake I'll put a damper on, and focus it around the Tower. Second level, Rannirl?"

"Third, I think," Elorie said.

Kennard raised his eyebrows. "Everyone in the Domains will know that something's going on in Arilinn tonight!"

"Let them," Elorie said indifferently. "I already asked them to take Arilinn out of the relay net tonight. It's our af-fair."

Kennard finished what he was doing with the damper, and began to lay the maps out on the table in front of them; and with them a large number of colored crayons. He asked, "Do you want me to mark the maps? Or shall we have Ker-win do it?"

"You mark them," Elorie said. "I want Corus and Jeff in the outer circle. Corus has enough PK that sooner or later we'll be able to do mining with him, and Jeff has a fabulous sense of structural perception. Jeff—" She placed him just beyond Rannirl. "And Corus here."

The great matrix lattice lay in its cradle before her.

Auster said, "Ready here."

To Kerwin the moonlit silence in the room seemed to deepen; in the quiet air, it seemed that they were somehow insulated, their very breathing deepening, echoing around them. A faint picture floated through his mind, and he knew that Corus had touched him with a fragment of rapport, *a strong glass wall surrounding us, clearly seen through, but impenetrable . . .* He could sense the very walls of the Ar-ilinn Tower, not the real Tower somehow but a mental picture of it, like but unlike, an archetypal Tower, and he heard someone in the circle thinking, *It has stood here like this for hundred and hundreds of years* . . .

Elorie's hands were folded before her; he had been cautioned again and again, *never touch a Keeper, even accidentally, within the circle,* and indeed none of them ever touched Elorie, though sometimes Rannirl, who was the technician, would support her briefly with a light hand on her shoulder; and Elorie never touched anyone. Kerwin had noticed that; she could come very close to them, could hand him pills, stand close to him, but she never actually *touched* anyone; it was simply part of the taboo that surrounded a Keeper, banning even the most fragmentary physical touch. And yet, even though he could see her slender hands folded on the table, he *felt* her reach out her hands to them, and all round the circle it seemed that they linked hands, meshing into a tight grip all round; and yet to Kerwin it seemed, and he knew that each of them shared the sensation, that Elorie held one hand, and Taniquel, the monitor, the other. Kerwin swallowed, his mouth suddenly dry, as Elorie's grey eyes met his; they glimmered, like the molten shimmer of the matrix, and he felt her pick them up like a meshed web drawn between her strong hands, a net of sparkling threads in which they were embedded like jewels, each its own flashing color; the warm rose-grey of Taniquel's watchfulness, the diamond-hard brilliance of Auster, Corus with a bright colorless luster, each of them with his or her own individual sound and color in the moon glow net that was Elorie. . . .

Through Kennard's eyes they saw the map spread on the table. Kerwin floated toward it, and somehow felt himself soaring out, as if he flew, bodiless, wingless, over a great expanse of countryside, with the magnet strength of the pure metallic sample that lay in the cradle beside the matrix lattice. He seemed to stretch out, infinitely extended, unaware of the limits of his body; then Rannirl projected a swift, whirling pattern, and Kerwin, without surprise, found himself tracing, with all of his mind and consciousness, a molecular model as once his fingers had traced the clay balls and sticks of the kindergarten model. Through Corus's sensitive fingertips he felt the whirling electrons, the strange amalgam of nucleus, protons, the atomic structure of the metal they sought.

Copper. Its structure seemed to glow and swirl from the map, attuned as it was to the terrain which the map had suddenly become, he could *feel* the metal there. It was not, quite, like sinking into the crystal structure of the glass. It was curiously different, as if, through map and photographs that had, somehow, the texture of soil and rock and grass and trees, he traced the palpable magnetic currents and brushed aside all irrelevant atomic patterns. He was hundreds of times as sensitive to the terrain under his—hands? Surely not! Under his mind, his thoughts, but still, somehow, he was sifting the very soil in search of the glowing and complex structure of copper atoms, to where they clustered . . . rich deposits of ore . . .

Dull, throbbing pain knifed him; he twisted *through* the copper atoms, he had *become* copper, hiding within the ground, entangled with other unfamiliar electrons, other structures, so thickly entangled that it was impossible to breathe, atoms whirling and meshing and colliding. He was *in* the energy currents; he wandered in them and flowed in them. For a moment, disembodied sentience, he looked out through Rannirl's eyes at the complex patterns, looked down on a strange flat-squeezed countryside, which he knew intellectually was the map, but which was still somehow the great aerial perspective of the Kilghard Hills spread out below him, hilltop eyries and crags and chasms, rocks and trees—and through it all he traced the sequences of copper atoms. . . . He saw and felt through Kennard's eyes, moved on the tip of an orange crayon down to the surface of the map, a mark that meant nothing, absorbed as he was in the whirl of structures and patterns, pure copper atoms entangled painfully into the complex molecules of rich ores . . . Kennard, he knew, followed him, measuring distances and transmuted them into measurements and marks on the maps . . . he moved on, interwoven with the meshing, sparkling layers of the matrix lattice, had, somehow, become the map and the very surface of the planet. . . .

He never knew, for time ceased entirely to have meaning, how long he whirled and probed and flashed, soil, rock, lava, riding magnetic currents, how many times Rannirl's perceptions picked him up and he rode down on the tip of Kennard's crayon, for his whole substance to be transmuted into markings on the map. . . . But at last the whirling slowed and stilled. He felt Corus (a liquid crystallizing, cooling into crystal) drop out of the mesh with a sensation like a shattering crash; heard Rannirl slide out of some invisible gap; felt Elorie gently open her hand and drop Kennard (invisible fingers set a doll on a table) out of the web; then pain, like the agony of breathing water, racked Kerwin as he felt himself drop in free-fall into nowhere; Auster (a glass shattering, freeing a prisoner) made a thick sound of exhaustion, sliding forward with his head on the table. An invisible rope broke and Neyrissa fell, crumpled, as if from a great height. The first thing Kerwin saw was Taniquel, sighing wearily, straightening her cramped body. Kennard's knotted fingers, swollen and tight with pain, released a stump of crayon, and he grimaced, holding one hand with the other. Kerwin could see the swelling in the fingers, the tension in them, and for the first time was aware of the joint-disease that had crippled Kennard and would some day paralyze him if he lived so long. The map was covered with cryptic symbols. Elorie put her hands over her face with a sound like a sob of exhaustion, and Taniquel rose and went to her, bending over her with a look of concern and dismay, running her hands over her in the monitor's touch, an inch away from her forehead.

Taniquel said, "No more. Corus's heart nearly stopped; and Kennard is in pain."

Elorie came on unsteady tiptoe to stand behind Rannirl and Kennard, looking at the maps. She touched Kennard's swollen hand with the lightest of fingertip-touches, more a symbolic gesture than a real one. She said, with a swift side-long glance at Kerwin, "Jeff did all the structural work; did you notice?"

Kennard raised his head to grin unsteadily at Kerwin. He was still absentmindedly rubbing his hands, as if they hurt him, and Taniquel came and took them gently into her own, holding them cradled softly between her soft fingers. Kerwin saw the taut lines of pain leaving the older man's face. Kennard said, "He was there all the time, holding all the structures; it was easy with him in the net. He's going to be as good a technician as you are, Rannirl."

"That wouldn't take much doing," Rannirl said. "I'm a mechanic, not a technician; I can do a technician's work, but I look pretty bad when there's a real technician around. Kerwin can have my place any time he wants it; *you* could, Ken, if you were strong enough."

"Thanks. I'll leave it to Jeff, *bredu*," Kennard said, with an affectionate smile at Rannirl. He leaned forward, resting his head for minute on Taniquel's shoulder, and Kerwin caught a fragment of her thought, *he's too old for this work,* and a furious surge of resentment, *we're so damned short-handed. . . .*

"But we did it," said Corus, looking at the map, and Elorie touched the surface of the map with a light finger. "Look, Kennard has measured every copper deposit in the Kilghard, and all the places where the ores are richest, as well as those places where they are so mixed with other ores as to be prac-tically useless. Even the depth is marked, and the richness, and the chemical composition of the ores so they will know

what equipment they will need for assaying and refining."
Suddenly, through her heavy-eyed weariness, her eyes were
exultant. "Show me the Terrans who could do so much, for
all their technology!"

She stretched, catlike. "Do you realize what we've
done?" she demanded. "It worked, all of you—it worked!
Now are you glad you listened to me? Who's a barbarian
now?" She went to Jeff, stretched her hands to him, and her
delicate fingertips just touched his; a gesture, he sensed, as
meaningful to Elorie, behind the structure of taboo and un-
touchability, as another girl's spontaneous hug would have
been. "Oh, Jeff, I knew we could do it with you, you're so
strong, so powerful, you helped us so much!"

Impulsively, his hands tightened on hers; but she drew
away, her face suddenly white, and her eyes met his; he
could see the flash of panic in them. She clasped her hands
together in a terrified gesture, and there was sudden appeal
in her eyes; but it was only a moment. Then she slumped,
and Neyrissa caught the girl in her arms.

"Lean on me, Elorie," she said gently. "You're exhausted, and no wonder, after all that."

Elorie swayed tiredly and covered her eyes, childishly,
with her clenched fists. Neyrissa lifted her into strong arms,
and said, "I'll take her to her room and see that she eats
something."

Kerwin was aware again of his own agonizingly cramped
muscles; he stretched and turned to the window, where the
sun was flooding in, already high in the sky. He had not been
aware of its rising. They had been within the matrix, and in
rapport, for more than an entire night!

Rannirl folded the map carefully. "We'll try again in a
few days with iron samples," he said. "Then tin, lead, alu-
minum—it will be easier next time, now that we know what
Jeff can do in the network." He grinned at Jeff and said, "Do
you know this is the first time there's been a full circle at Arilinn in twelve years or more?" He looked past Auster,

frowning. "Auster, what's the matter with you, kinsman? This is a time for rejoicing!"

Auster's eyes were fixed on Kerwin with steady, unblinking malevolence. And Kerwin knew: *He's not happy that I did it.*

He wanted me—us—to fail. But why?

CHAPTER ELEVEN

Shadows on the Sun

The depression lingered even after Kerwin had slept away
the fatigue. As he dressed himself to join the others, near
sunset, he told himself that he should not let Auster's malice
soil this for him. He had come through the acid test of full
rapport within the Tower Circle, and it was his triumph.
Auster had never liked him; it might even be that he was
jealous of the fuss they were making over Kerwin. Probably
there was no more to it than that.

And now, he knew, there would be a free interval, and he
looked forward to spending some of it with Taniquel. Despite Kennard's warning, he felt fresh and rested, eager to
join her. He wondered if she would consent, as she had done
often, to spend the night with him, and there was a pleasant
anticipation in his thoughts as he went downstairs. But there
was no hurry; if not tonight, then later.

The others had all wakened before him and were gathered in the hall. The very casualness of their greetings
warmed him; he belonged, he was family. He accepted a
glass of wine and sank down in his accustomed seat.
Neyrissa came over to him, trailing an armful of some kind
of needlework, and settled down near him. He felt a little
impatient, but there was time. He looked around for
Taniquel, but she was near the fireplace, talking to Auster,
her back to him, and he could not catch her eye.

"What are you making Neyrissa?"

"A coverlet for my bed," she said. "You do not know how cold it is here in the winter; and besides, it keeps my hands busy." She turned it to show him. It was a white quilt, with cherries in three shades of red stitched on in clusters, with green leaves, and bands of the same three shades of red at the edges; and the whole now being quilted with delicate stitches in a pattern of loops and curls. He was astonished at the amount of work and thought that must have gone into the design; it had never occurred to him that Neyrissa, monitor of Arilinn and a Comyn lady, would occupy herself with a such tedious stitchery.

She shrugged—"As I say, it keeps my hands busy when there is nothing else to do," she said. "And I am proud of my handiwork."

"It is certainly very beautiful," he said. "A piece of handiwork like this would be priceless on most of the planets I have visited, for most people now have their bedding made easily and quickly by machine."

She chuckled. "I do not think I would care to sleep under anything that had been made by machinery," she said. "It would be like lying down with a mechanical man. I understand they have such things on other worlds, too, but I do not suppose women are very pleased with them. I prefer genuine handiwork on my bed as well as in it."

It took Jeff a moment to understand the double entendre—which was somewhat more suggestive in *casta* than in the language he spoke—but no one with a scrap of telepathic force could misunderstand her meaning, and he chuckled, a little embarrassed. But she met his eyes so forthrightly that he could not retain his embarrassment and laughed heartily. "I suppose you're right, some things are better when they're the work of nature," he agreed with her.

"Tell me something about your work for the Empire, Jeff. If I had been a man, I sometimes think, I would like to have gone offworld. There is not a great deal of adventure in the

Kilghard Hills, and certainly not for a woman. Have you lived on many worlds?"

"Two or three," he conceded, "but in the Civil Service you don't see much of them; it's mostly working with communications equipment."

"And you do the same thing with your communications machinery that we can do with the relay-nets?" she said, curiously. "Tell me a little of how they work, if you can. I have been working in the relays since I was fourteen years old; it would seem strange to do this with machinery. Are there truly no telepaths in the Terran Empire?"

"If there are," Kerwin said, "They're not telling anyone."

He told Neyrissa about the CommTerra communications network that linked planet with planet by interstellar relay systems, explaining the difference between radio, wireless, and interstellar hypercomm. He found that she had a quick mechanical intelligence and swiftly picked up the theory involved, although she found the thought of communicating by machinery somewhat distasteful.

"I would like to experiment with some of them," she said. "But only as a toy. I think the Tower relays are more reliable and swifter, and they do not get out of order so easily, I suppose."

"And you have been doing this all your life?" Kerwin asked, wondering again how old she was. "What made you want to go into a Tower, Neyrissa? Have you never married?"

She shook her head. "I never had any wish to marry," she said, "and for a woman in the Domains, it is marriage or the Tower—unless," she laughed—"I wished to crop my hair and take up the sword and the oath of a Renunciate! And I had seen my sisters marry, and spend their lives catering to the whims of some man and bearing babe after babe till at twenty-nine they were thick and ugly, their bodies worn with childbearing, and their minds worn as narrowly into the track of nursery and laundry and hen-yard! Such a life, I thought, would not suit me; so when I was tested for *laran*, I came here as a monitor; and the work suits me, and the life."

It occurred to Kerwin that when she was a young woman she must have been a beauty; the materials of beauty were there still, the aristocratic bones of her face, the rich color of her hair, only a little tinged with grey, and her body was slim and erect as Elorie's own. He said, gallantly, "I am sure there were many to protest that decision."

Her eyes met his, just a flicker. She said, "You are not naive enough to think I took Keeper's vows as well? I bore Rannirl a child ten years ago, hoping it would inherit my *laran*; my sister has fostered her, but I had no wish to drag a babe round at my heels. I would have given Kennard one as well, for he had no heirs and the Council was wroth with him, but he chose instead to marry. They did not like the woman he married, but she bore him two sons, and they have accepted the oldest son as his Heir—though it was hard enough to get them to do it. And I am well-enough pleased, for I am very much needed here, though not quite so much, now that Taniquel has been discovered to have enough *laran* for a monitor. Still, Tani is young. It is likely that she may decide to leave the Tower and marry; many of the younger women do so. I was surprised when Elorie came here; but she is the daughter of old Kyril Ardais, and he has spread the tale of his lecheries from Dalereuth to the Hellers; after seeing what her own mother suffered, I am sure Elorie had no wish to marry, and began with a fear and dread of all men. She is my half-sister, you know; I am one of old Dom Kyril's bastards." She spoke with dispassionate calm. "I was responsible for bringing her here, you know. The old man would have had her to sing and entertain his drinking companions, and once, when she was still very small, one of them laid rough hands on her—our brother came near to killing him. And after that, he complained to the Council, and Elorie was brought to Arilinn, and Dyan petitioned them to set Father aside and name him Regent of the Domain, so when Father's wits are not with him, the Domain will not be brought into disrepute because of his indecencies and debaucheries. It cost Dyan something to do this; he is a gifted musician, and a healer; he wished to study all the healing arts at Nevarsin, and now he has the weight of the Domain on his shoulders. But I am gossiping," she added with a faint smile. "At my age, I think I can be excused for it. I brought Lori here, as I say, and I had hoped she would make a monitor, perhaps even a technician; she has a good mind. Instead, they chose to try and teach her the Keeper's way, and so we are the only Tower on Darkover with a Keeper qualified in the old way. I suppose we should be proud of it; but I am sorry for Elorie. It is a hard life; and since she is the only Keeper we have—although there is a little girl at Neskaya who is being taught—she will not feel free to leave the Tower, as most Keepers in past ages have felt free to do when the weight of their work grows too heavy. It is a dreadful burden," she added, meeting his eyes, "and despite the fact the Lady of Arilinn stands higher than the queen, I would not want it for myself; nor for any child of mine."

Her glass was empty; she leaned forward and asked him to refill it. Rising, Kerwin went to the table where the drinks were kept. Corus and Elorie were playing some sort of game with cut-crystal dice. Rannirl had a scrap of leather in his hands and was stitching it into a falcon's hood.

Taniquel was near the fireplace, deep in conversation with Auster; Kerwin tried to catch her eye, to make an unobtrusive signal that she should join him; a signal she knew well. He fully expected her to make some light-hearted excuse to Auster and join him.

But she only gave him a little eye-blink of a smile, and lightly shook her head. Startled, rebuffed, he looked at her hand lying in Auster's, their heads close together. They seemed quite absorbed. Kerwin filled Neyrissa's glass and took it to her, his puzzlement growing. The girl had never seemed half so desirable as now, when her laughter, her impish smile were all for Auster. He went back and sat down by Neyrissa, giving her the glass, but from irritation he proceeded to bewilderment, and then to resentment. How could she do this to him? Was she nothing, then, but a heartless tease?

As the evening passed, he sank deeper and deeper into depression. He listened to Neyrissa's gossip with half an ear, the attempts of Kennard and Rannirl to engage him in conversation fell flat; after a time they assumed he was still weary and left him to himself. Corus and Elorie finished their game and started another; Neyrissa went to show Mesyr her needlework and ask for advice, the two women sorting a lapful of threads and comparing the colors of dyes. It was a perfectly comfortable domestic scene except for Kerwin's knifelike awareness of Taniquel, her head resting on Auster's shoulder. A dozen times Kerwin told himself that he was a fool to sit and watch it, but bewilderment and resentful anger strove in him. Why was she doing this, why?

Later Auster rose to refill their glasses, and Kerwin rose abruptly; Kennard looked up, troubled, as Kerwin crossed the room and bent to touch Taniquel on the arm.

"Come with me," he said. "I want to talk to you."

She looked up, startled and not pleased, but with a quick glance around—he could almost feel her exasperation, mingled with her resolve not to make a scene—she said, "Let's go out on the terrace."

The last remnants of the sunset had long vanished; the mist was condensing into heavy splatters of rain that would, before long, be a downpour. Taniquel shivered, dragging her yellow knitted shawl close around her shoulders. She said, "It's too cold to stand out here very long. What's the matter, Jeff? Why have you been staring at me like that, all evening?"

"You don't know?" he flung at her. "Haven't you any heart? We've had to wait—"

"Are you *jealous?*" she asked, good-naturedly. Jeff drew her into his arms and kissed her violently, crushing her mouth under his; she sighed, smiled and returned the kiss, but with tolerance rather than passion. He seized her by the elbows, saying hoarsely, "I should have known you were just deviling me, but I couldn't stand it—watching you with Auster, right under my very eyes—"

She held herself away from him, puzzled and, he sensed, angry.

"Jeff, don't be so dense! Can't you see that Auster needs me now? Can't you understand that? Have you *no* feelings, no kindness at all? This is your triumph—and his defeat, can't you see?"

"Are you trying to say you've turned against me?"

"Jeff, I simply don't understand you," she said, frowning in the half-light from the window behind them. "Why should I have turned against you? All I'm saying is that Auster needs me—now, tonight—more than you do." She raised herself on tiptoe, kissing him coaxingly, but he held her roughly at arm's length, some hint of her meaning beginning to reach him.

"Are you saying what I think you're saying?"

"What is the *matter* with you, Jeff? I can't seem to get through to you at all tonight!"

He said, his throat tight, "I love you. I—I want you; is that so hard to understand?"

"I love you, Jeff," she said, with a faint undertone of impatience in her words. "But what has that to do with it? I think you're overtired, or you wouldn't talk this way. What is it to do with you, if for this one night Auster needs me more than you do, and I choose to comfort him in the way he needs me most?"

He asked flatly, "Are you trying to tell me you're going to sleep with him tonight?"

"Why, yes, certainly!"

His mouth felt dry. "You little bitch!"

Taniquel stepped back as if he had struck her. Her face, in the dim light, was dead white, the freckles standing out like dark blotches.

"And you are a selfish brute," she retorted. "Barbarian as Elorie called you, and worse! You—you Terrans think women are *property!* I love you, yes; but not when you act like this!"

He felt his mouth twitch, painfully. "*That* kind of love I can buy in the spaceport bars!"

Taniquel's hand went up, hard and stinging, flat across his cheekbones. "You—" she stammered, speechless. "I belong to *myself*, do you hear? You take what I give and think it right; but if I give it to another, you are ready to name me whore? Damn you, you filthy-minded *Terranan!* Auster was right about you all along!"

She moved swiftly past him, and he heard her steps receding, swift and final; somewhere a door slammed inside the Tower.

His face burning, Kerwin did not follow. The rain was heavy now, blowing around the cornice of the Tower, and there were traces of ice in the heavy drops; he brushed it from his smarting cheek. What had he done? On a numb, shamed impulse to hide himself—they must all have seen Taniquel's rejection of him, the way she had turned to Auster, they must all have known what it meant—he went swiftly along the passageway and up the stairs to his own room; but before he reached it, he heard an uneven footfall and Kennard stood behind him in the doorway.

"Jeff, what's the matter?"

He did not want to face the older man's craggy, knowing face just now. He went on into his room, muttering, "Still tired—guess I'll go to bed, get some more sleep."

Kennard came behind him, put his hands on the younger man's shoulders and, with surprising strength, physically turned him around to face him. He said, "Look, Jeff, you can't keep it from us like that. If you'll talk about it—"

"Damn it," Jeff said, his voice cracking, "is there no privacy in this place at all?"

Kennard slumped and sighed. He said, "My leg's giving me hell; can I sit down?"

Kerwin could not refuse; Kennard dropped into an armchair. He said, "Look son, among us, things have to be—well, they have to be faced; they can't be hidden away to fester. For better or for worse, you're a member of our circle—"

Jeff tightened his mouth again. He said, "Keep out of this. It's between me and Taniquel, and none of your business."

"But it's not between you and Taniquel at all," Kennard said. "It's between you and Auster. Look, everything that happens in Arilinn affects us all. Tani is an empath; can't you understand how she feels when she senses—when she has to *share*—that kind of need, and hunger, and loneliness? You were broadcasting it everywhere; we all picked it up. But Tani is an empath, and vulnerable. And she answered that need, because she's a woman, and kind, and an empath, and she couldn't endure your unhappiness. She gave you what you needed most, and what it was natural for her to give."

Kerwin muttered, "She said she loved me. And I believed her."

Kennard put out his hand, and Kerwin sensed the sympathy in him. He said, "Zandru's hells, Jeff—words, words, words! And the way people use them, and what they mean by them!" It was almost like an imprecation. He touched Jeff lightly on the wrist, the accepting, telepath's touch, which somehow meant more than a handclasp or an embrace. He said gently, "She loves you, Jeff. We all do, every one of us. You are one of us. But Tani—is what she is. Can't you understand what that means? And Auster—try and imagine what it means to be a woman, and an empath, and feel the kind of despair and need that was in Auster tonight?

How can she feel that, and not—not respond to it? Damn it," he said, despairingly, "if you and Auster understood each other, if you had empathy with him, you'd feel his pain too, and you'd understand what Taniquel was feeling!"

Against his will, Jeff began to grasp the concept; in a close-knit circle of telepaths, emotions, needs, hungers, did not affect only the one who felt them, but everyone who was near him. He had been disrupting them all with his loneliness and his hunger for acceptance, and Taniquel had responded to it, as naturally as a mother quiets a crying child. But now, when Jeff was happy and triumphant, and Auster apparently defeated, it was Auster's pain she desired to sooth. . . .

Human flesh and blood couldn't endure it, he thought savagely. Taniquel, whom he loved, Taniquel, the first woman who had ever meant anything to him, Taniquel in the arms of a man he hated. . . . He closed his eyes, trying to barricade away the thought, the pain of it.

Kennard looked at him, and Kerwin, uncomfortably, recognized his expression of pity.

"It must be very difficult for you. You spent so much time among the Terrans, you've taken their neurotic codes to yourself. The laws of the Tower are not the same as the laws of the Domains; among telepaths they can't be. Marriage is a fairly recent development on Darkover; what you call monogamy is more recent yet. And it's never been really accepted. I'm not blaming you, Jeff. You are what you are, just as Tani is what she is. I only wish you weren't so unhappy about it." He hauled himself wearily out of his chair and went away, and Kerwin caught the trail and overflow of his thought. Kennard, too, had married a Terran, known the pain of a man caught between two worlds and belonging to neither, seen his two sons rejected because he could not father a son on the suitable wife the Council had given him, but whom, too sensitive to unspoken emotions, he could not love. . . .

Lying awake, aflame with jealous rage, Kerwin fought a solitary battle, and toward morning came to grim equilibrium. The woman wasn't worth it. He wasn't going to let Auster wreck things for him. They had to work together, somehow or other. It was galling to lose out to Auster, but after all, it was only his pride that was involved. If Taniquel wanted Auster, she was welcome to him. She'd made her choice, and she could just stick to it.

It wasn't ideal, but it worked, after a fashion. Taniquel was polite and icily remote, and he took his tone from her. Once again they began the work of building matrix screens, keying them into maps and aerial photographs; again they gathered for the circle, searching out iron deposits, and a few days later, silver and zinc. The day before they were to go into a fourth rapport search, Jeff came in from a solitary ride in the foothills to find Corus waiting for him, pale and excited.

"Jeff! Elorie wants us all in the matrix chamber, quickly!"

He followed the kid, wondering what had happened. The others were already gathered there, Rannirl with the maps in hand.

"Trouble," he said. "I had word from our clients, just after I passed this map to them. In three separate places, here, here, and here——" he indicated on the marked maps, "the people from across the Hellers, and damned Aldarans and their men, have moved in and filed claims on the lands we marked as being the richest deposits of copper; you know as well as I do that the Aldarans are pawns of the Terrans, with their Trade City at Caer Donn; they're fronting for the Empire, claiming the land to set up a Terran industrial colony there. It's empty land in the Hellers, not good for agriculture, and I don't think anyone's ever guessed it was good for mining; it's too inaccessible. How did they know?"

"Coincidence," Neyrissa said. "You know the people from Aldaran are close to the forge-folk. They're always prospecting for metals, and they use fire-talismans in the hills the way we use matrix circles."

Auster said angrily, "I can't believe it's coincidence! That this should happen the very first time Jeff is part of the circle! The front men for Terra move in on the richest claims, leaving us nothing to offer our clients but some weak ores, almost impossible to smelt! Not one, not two, but *three* of the claims!" He swung around angrily to face Kerwin. "How much did the Terrans pay you to betray us?"

"If you believe that, damn you, you're more of a fool than I ever thought!"

Taniquel said angrily, "I know you don't like Jeff, Auster, but this is outrageous! If you believe that, you'd believe anything!"

"It's bad luck," Kennard said, "but that's all it is; sheer bad luck."

Auster raged, "Once, I would believe coincidence; twice, coincidence and bad luck. But three times? *Three?* It's coincidence like work for the midwife after a Ghost Wind is coincidence!"

Elorie frowned. She said, "Hush, hush! I won't have this brawling! there is one way to settle it, Kennard. You're an Alton. He can't lie to you, Uncle."

Kerwin knew immediately what she meant, even before she turned to him and said, "Will you consent to telepathic examination, Jeff?"

Rage surged through him. "Consent to it? I *demand* it," he said, "And then, damn it, I'll make you eat those words, Auster. I'll cram them down your throat with my fist!" He faced Kennard, rage making him oblivious to the fear of facing that nightmarish probe. "Go ahead! Find out for yourself!"

Kennard hesitated. "I don't really think—"

"It's the only way," said Neyrissa briskly. "And Jeff is willing."

Kerwin closed his eyes, bracing himself for the painful

shock of forced rapport. No matter how often it was done, it never became easier. He endured it for a moment, incredible intrusion, nightmarish violation, before the grey and merciful haze blotted out the pain. When he came to he was standing before them, gripping the edges of the table to keep from falling over. He heard his own breathing loud in the silent room.

Kennard was looking back and forth from him to Auster.

"Well?" Jeff demanded, his voice angry and defensive.

"I have always said that we could trust you, Jeff," Kennard said quietly, "but there is something here. Something I do not understand. There is some blocking of your memory, Jeff."

Auster said, "Could the Terrans have given him some kind of post-hypnotic conditioning? Planted him on us—a time bomb?"

"I assure you," Kennard said, "you overestimate their knowledge of the mind. And I can assure you, Auster, that Jeff is not feeding them information. There's no guilt in him."

But a cold bleak horror had suddenly gripped Jeff by the throat.

Ever since arriving on Darkover he had been pushed around by some mysterious force. It had certainly not been the Comyn who destroyed his birth records, and the records of Jeff Kerwin who had claimed him, and gotten Empire citizenship for him, in the Terran computers. It had not been the Comyn who kept pushing him around until he had no place to go, and he had escaped; escaped to the Comyn.

Had he been planted on them, an unconscious spy within the Arilinn Tower?

"I never heard anything so damnably foolish," Kennard said angrily. "I'd as soon believe it of you, Auster; or of Elorie herself! But if there's this kind of suspicion among us, no one will benefit but the Terrans!" He took up the map.

"More likey it's one of the Aldarans; they have some telepaths there, and they work with unmonitored matrixes, outside the Tower relays. Your barrier may have slipped, Auster; that's all. Call it bad luck and we'll try again."

CHAPTER TWELVE

The Trap

He tried to dismiss the idea from his mind. After all, Kennard had warranted him guiltless after telepathic examination. That was, he knew, legal defense anywhere. But once roused, the idea persisted like pain in a nagging tooth.

Would I even have to know it, if the Terrans had planted me here?

I was so damned glad to be free of the Terran Zone that I didn't even ask questions. Like, why did the computer at the Spaceman's Orphanage have no records of me? They said that Auster, too, was born among the Terrans. I wonder if there's a record of him *there? Is there any reason why a telepath with a matrix, as Ragan suggested, couldn't wipe the memory bank of a computer—clear it of one specific record?* Everything he knew of computers, and everything he knew of matrixes, suggested that that wouldn't be a difficult trick at all.

He went through the days silent and morose, lying on his bed for hours and trying to think of nothing, riding alone in the hills. He was conscious of Taniquel's eyes watching him whenever he was with the others, feeling her sympathy (*damned bitch, I don't want her pity!*) and the pain of her awareness. He avoided her when he could, but the memory of their little time as lovers cut like a knife. Because it had gone so much deeper with him than any casual relationship, it could not be casually dismissed; it stayed with him, painful.

He was vaguely aware that she was trying to encounter him, alone; he took perverse pleasure in evading her. One morning, however, he met her face to face on the stairs.

"Jeff," she said, reaching out her hand to him. "Don't run away—please, don't keep running away. I want to talk to you."

He shrugged, looking over her head. "What's there to say?"

Her eyes filled with tears, and spilled over. "I can't stand this," she said, brokenly. "The two of us like enemies, and the Tower filled with—with spear-points of hate and suspicion! And jealousy—"

He said, the ice of his resentment giving way before the genuineness of her pain, "I don't like it either, Tani. But it wasn't my doing, remember."

"Why must you—" She controlled her temper, biting her lip. She said, "I'm sorry you're so unhappy, Jeff. Kennard explained to me, a little, how you felt about it, and I'm sorry, I didn't understand—"

He said, knifing the words with heavy sarcasm, "If I'm unhappy enough, would you come back to me?" He took her, not gently, by the shoulder. "I suppose Auster's got you to thinking the worst of me, that I'm a spy for the Terrans, or something like that?"

She was quiet between his hands, making no effort to break away. She said, "Auster isn't lying, Jeff. He's only saying what he believes. And if you think he is happy about it, then you are very much mistaken."

"I suppose his heart would be broken if he managed to drive me away?"

"I don't know, but he doesn't hate you the way you feel that he does. Look at me, Jeff, can't you tell I'm telling you the truth?"

"I suppose you ought to know just what Auster's feeling," he said, but Taniquel's shoulders were trembling, and somehow the sight of Taniquel, the mischievous, the carefree, in tears, hurt worse than the suspicions of all the others. That was the hell of it, he thought wearily. If Auster had been lying out of malice, if Taniquel had left him for Auster in order to hurt him, to make him jealous, he could at least have *understood* that kind of motivation. As it was, it was a complete mystery to him. Taniquel neither attacked nor defended, even in thought; she simply shared his pain. She fell against him, sobbing, clinging helplessly.

"Oh, Jeff, we were so happy when you came, and it meant so much to us to have you here, and now it's all spoilt! Oh, if we could only know, if we could only be sure!"

He faced them down that night in the hall, waiting until they had gathered for their evening drinks before rising aggressively, hands clenched behind his back. Defiantly he had put on Terran clothes; defiantly, he spoke Cahuenga.

"Auster, you made an accusation; I submitted to telepathic examination, which should have settled it, but you didn't accept my word or Kennard's. What proof would you demand? What would you accept?"

Auster rose to his feet, slender, graceful, cat-lean; he said, "What do you want from me, Kerwin? I cannot call challenge on your Comyn immunity—"

"Comyn immunity be—" Kerwin used a word straight from the spaceport gutters. "I spent ten years on Terra, and they have an expression there which can be roughly translated as put up or shut up. Tell me, right here and now, what proof you *will* accept, and give me a chance here and now to prove it to your satisfaction. Or shut your mouth on the subject once and forever, and believe me, brother, if I hear one damned syllable, or pick up one single telepathic insinuation, I'll beat the stuffing out of you!" He stood, fists clenched, and when Auster stepped to one side Jeff moved too, keeping straight in front of him. "I'm saying it again. Put up, or shut up and stay shut forever."

There was a shocked silence in the room, and Jeff heard it with satisfaction. Mesyr made a small, remonstrating noise, almost an admonitory cluck; *Now, children. . . .*

"Jeff's right," Rannirl said. "You can't keep this up, Auster. Prove what you're insinuating, or apologize to Jeff and keep your mouth buttoned about it afterward. Not just for Jeff's sake; you owe it to all of us. We can't live this way; we're a circle. I don't insist that you swear the oath of *bredin*, but you must somehow manage to live together in harmony. We can't live like this, divided into two factions, with each group snarling at the other half. Elorie has enough to cope with, as it is."

Auster looked at Kerwin. If looks could kill, Kerwin thought, Auster wouldn't have any problem. But when he spoke, his voice was calm, considerate. "You're right. We owe it to all of you to find out the truth once and for all. And Jeff himself has pledged to abide by the result. Elorie, can you build a trap matrix?"

"I can," she flared. "But I won't! Do your own dirty work!"

"Kennard can," Neyrissa said, and Auster frowned. "Yes. But he's prejudiced—in Jeff's favor. He's standing foster-father to him here!"

Kennard's voice was quiet and dangerous. "If you dare assume that I, who have been mechanic at Arilinn since before the Changes, would falsify my oath—"

Rannirl raised his hand to stop them both. "I'll build it," he said. "Not because I'm on your side, Auster, but because we have to settle this one way or the other. Jeff—" He turned to Kerwin. "Do you trust me?"

Kerwin nodded. He wasn't sure what a trap matrix was; but with Rannirl in charge of it, he was sure the trap wouldn't be set for *him*.

"All right, then," Rannirl said. "That's settled. So until we can set the trap matrix for the next circle, can't you two declare a truce?"

Jeff felt like saying, *the hell I can*, and he knew, looking at Auster's sullen face, that the other man was equally unwilling. How could telepaths pretend? But Taniquel was on the edge of tears; and Jeff suddenly shrugged. What the hell, it wouldn't hurt him to be civil; Auster only wanted to know the truth, and that was one thing they were agreed on anyhow. He said with a shrug, "I'll let him alone if he lets me alone. Agreed?"

Auster's taut face relaxed. He said, "Agreed."

With the decision made, the tension relaxed and the next phase of the work began with an atmosphere that was, by contrast, almost friendly. This time they had to build a matrix lattice for the work known as "clearing"—which had not been done on this scale since the great days of the Comyn, when Towers dotted the land, giving power and technology to all the Domains.

They had located mineral and ore deposits and marked them for richness and accessibility. In the next step they would separate the deposits from the other minerals that contaminated them, so that the copper and other metals could be mined in a pure form without need for refining. Drop by drop, atom by atom, deep within the earth, by tiny shiftings of energy and force, the pure metals would be separated from the ores and the rock. Corus spent more time with his molecular models, fussing over precise weights and proportions. And this time, Elorie, with Rannirl, specially asked for Kerwin's help in placing the crystals within their lattices. He was required to hold complex molecular patterns clearly visualized on a monitor screen, so that Elorie and Rannirl could place the blank crystals precisely inside the amorphous layers of glass. He learned things about atomic structure that even the Terran scientists did not know—his education in physics, for instance, had told him nothing about the nature of *energons*. It was wearying work, monotonous and nerve-racking rather than physically taxing, and always at the back of his mind was the knowledge of the test that would come with the trap matrix, whatever that was.

I want to know the truth, whatever it is.

Whatever it is?

Yes. Whatever it is.

One day they were working in one of the matrix laboratories, Jeff holding the complex internal crystal structure visualized for the monitor screen, when suddenly he saw the lattice structure blur together; melt into a blue flare and streak. Pain knifed through him; hardly knowing what he did, Jeff acted on pure instinct. He swiftly cut the rapport between Rannirl and Elorie, blanked the screens, and caught Elorie's fainting body as she fell. For a panicked moment he thought she was not breathing; then her eyelashes moved and she sighed.

"Working too hard, as usual," said Rannirl, staring down at the lattice. "She *will* keep on, even when I beg her to rest. Good thing you caught her, Jeff, just when you did; otherwise we'd have the whole lattice to rebuild, and that would cost us a tenday. Well, Elorie?"

Elorie was crying weakly in exhaustion, lying limp in Jeff's arms. Her face was deathly white, and her sobs shallow as if she no longer had the strength to breathe. Rannirl took her from Jeff's arms, lifting her like a small child, and carried her out of the lab. He flung back over his shoulder, "Get Tani up here, and hurry!"

"Taniquel went with Kennard in the airlaunch," Kerwin said.

"Then I'd better go up and try to get them in the relays," Rannirl said, kicked the nearest door open with his foot. It was one of the unused rooms; it looked as if no one had set foot in it for decades. He laid the girl down on a couch covered with dusty tapestry, while Kerwin stood helplessly in the door. "Anything I can do?" he asked.

"You're an empath," Rannirl said, "and qualified as a monitor; I haven't done it in years. I'll go up and try to get

Neyrissa, but you'd better monitor her and see if her heart's all right."

And suddenly Kerwin remembered what Taniquel had done for him on that first night of testing, taking his pain into herself, when he collapsed with the breaking of his barriers.

"I'll do what I can," he said, and came closer to her. Elorie moved her head from side to side, like a fractious child. "No," she said irritably. "No, let me be, I'm all right." But she had to breathe twice while she said it and her face was like scraped bone.

"She's always like this," Rannirl said. "Do what you can, Jeff, I'll go and find Neyrissa."

Jeff came and bent over Elorie.

"I don't suppose I'm as good at it as Tani or Neyrissa," he said, "but I'll do what I can." Quickly, heightening his sensitivity, he ran his fingertips along her body, an inch or two away, feeling deep into the cells. Her heart was beating, but thin, irregular, threadlike; the pulse was faint, almost unreadable. Her breathing was so faint he could hardly feel it. Cautiously, he reached for rapport, seeking, with that heightened awareness, the limits of her weakness, trying to take her exhaustion upon himself as Taniquel had taken his pain. She stirred and made a faint movement, reaching with her hands for his, and he remembered how Taniquel had taken his hands in her own. The searching movement of her hands went on, and after a moment Jeff put his own between them, feeling the faint effort she made to close hers over them. She was almost unconscious. But gradually, as he knelt there with her hands in his, he could feel her breathing steady, sensed that her heart had begun to beat smoothly again, and saw the deathly white of her face beginning to transmute into a healthy color again. He did not realize how frightened he had been until he heard her breathing, calm and steady; she opened her eyes and looked at him. She was still a little pale, her soft lips still colorless.

"Thank you, Jeff," she whispered weakly, and her hands tightened on his; then, to his astonishment, she put out her arms, reaching up to him in appeal. Quickly responding, he gathered her close to him, sensing that she wanted the reassurance of contact; he held her for a moment, feeling her close to him, soft and limp, still weak. And then, without surprise, Kerwin felt the soft and exquisite blending of perceptions as their lips met.

He felt it with an intensely heightened dual consciousness, Elorie's limp slight body in his arms, sensing the fragility mingled with steely strength, the childlike quality blended with the calm, ageless wisdom of her caste and her training. *(And dimly through all these things he felt what Elorie felt, her weakness and lassitude, the terror she had known when her heart faltered and she felt herself near to death, the need for the reassurance of contact, the strength of his own arms around her; he felt the lassitude and the eagerness with which she accepted his kiss, a strange and half-understood wakening in her senses; he shared with the woman her own wonder and surprise at this touch, the first touch she had ever known that was not fatherly and impersonal; shared her shy and shameless surprise at the strength of his man's body, at the sudden rising heat in him; felt her reach out to him, unmistakably, for a deeper contact, and answered it. . . .)*

"Elorie," he whispered, but it was like a triumphant shout. "Oh, Elorie—" And only to himself he whispered, *my love*, and for a moment he felt everything in the woman move toward him, felt her sudden warmth and flooding longing for his kiss. . . .

Then there was a spasmodic moment of shattering, convulsive fear, clawing with anguish at every nerve in him; the rapport between them smashed like a breaking crystal, and Elorie, white and terrified, was straining away from him, fighting like a cat in his arms.

"No, no," she gasped. "Jeff, let me go, let me go—don't—"

Dazed, numb with shock, Kerwin released her; she scrambled quickly up and away from him, her hands crossed in terror over her breasts, which rose and fell with soundless, anguished sobs. Her eyes were wide with horror, but she was barriered tightly against him again. Her childish mouth moved silently, her face screwed up in a little girl's grimace against tears.

"No," she whispered, again, at last. "Have you forgotten—forgotten what I am? Oh, Avarra pity me," she said in a broken gasp, covered her face with her hands and fled blindly from the room, half tripping over a stool, evading Jeff's automatic reach to steady her, slipping through the door and running, running away down the hall. Far away, far up in the Tower, he heard the closing of a door.

He did not see Elorie again for three days.

For the first time, that night, she did not join them for the evening ritual of drinks in the great hall. Jeff, from the moment Elorie fled from him, felt cut off and alone, a stranger among them in a world suddenly cold and strange.

The others seemed to take Elorie's seclusion for granted; Kennard said with a shrug that all Keepers did that now and then, it was part of being what they were. Jeff, holding his barriers firm against involuntary betrayal (of himself? Of Elorie?) said nothing. But Elorie's eyes, luminous and haunted with dismay and that shocking, sudden fear, as well as the memory of her warmth in his arms, seemed to swim before his eyes in the darkness every night before he slept; he felt, with an almost tactile memory, her kiss on his mouth, her frail and frightened body in his arms, and the shock after she had broken away and run from him. At first he had been half angry: *She* had initiated the contact. Why now should she break away as if he had attempted rape?

Then, slowly and painfully, understanding came.

He had broken the strictest law of the Comyn. A Keeper was a pledged virgin, trained lengthily for her work, body and brain given lengthy conditioning for the most difficult task on Darkover. To every man in the Domains, Elorie was inviolate. A Keeper, *tenerésteis*, never to be touched by lust or even by the purest love.

He had heard what they said—and worse, felt what they felt—about Cleindori, who had broken this vow. (And she, too, with one of the despised Terrans.)

In his old life Kerwin might have defended himself, saying that Elorie had invited his advances. She had first touched him, first raised her lips to his. But after a time of training in the unsparing self-honesty of Arilinn, there were no such easy evasions. He had been aware of the taboo, and of Elorie's ignorance; he was aware of the forthright way with which she showed affection to the others of her circle, completely confident in the taboo that protected her; to all of them, she was sexless and sacrosanct. She had accepted Jeff in the same way—and he had betrayed her trust!

He loved her. He knew now that he had loved her from the first time he laid eyes her; or perhaps before, when their minds touched through the matrix and he had heard her soft *I recognize you*. And now he saw nothing ahead of him but pain and renunciation.

Taniquel—his infatuation with Taniquel now seemed like a dream. He knew now that it had been gratitude for her acceptance, for her kindness and warmth; he was still fond of her, but what had been between them, for a time, could not survive any interruption of the sexual tie between them. It had never been anything like this overwhelming thing that swallowed up his whole consciousness; he knew that he would love Elorie for the rest of his life, even if he could never again touch her and she never showed the slightest sign of returning his love.

(But she had, she had. . . .)

But worse than this was a terrible fear, knifing at his con-

sciousness. Kennard had warned him of the dangers of
nervous exhaustion, counseling him to remain apart from
Taniquel during the days immediately before a heavy load of
matrix work, to avoid depleting his energies. The Keepers,
he knew, keyed themselves completely, body and mind, into
the matrixes they operated; this was why they must never be
touched by a hint of emotion, and far less by sexuality. His
memory went back to his first night in Arilinn; Elorie's dismay at the mildest flirtatious or gallant remark, her comment that Keepers trained lifelong for their work and
sometimes lost the ability for it after a very short time.
Neyrissa had underlined that there were no other Keepers,
so that Elorie, unlike Keepers in the past, was not free to set
aside her high office for marriage—or for love.

And now, when perhaps the very fate of Darkover rested
upon the strength of the Arilinn Tower—and perhaps upon
Elorie alone, when the strength of Arilinn rested upon the
fortitude of their cherished Keeper—he, Jeff Kerwin, the
stranger in their midst, the outsider they had taken to their
hearts, had betrayed them and struck through the defenses of
their Keeper.

And at this point in his thoughts Kerwin sat up and buried
his head in his hands. He tried to blank out his thoughts
completely. This was worse than Auster's accusation that he
was a spy, feeding information to the Empire.

Alone in the night he fought his way to the end of a hard-
won battle. He loved Elorie; but his love for her could destroy her as Keeper. And without a Keeper, they would fail
in the work they were doing for the Pan-Darkovan Syndicate, and the Syndicate would take that as permission to
bring in the Terrans, experts in the remodeling of Darkover
into the image of the Empire.

A traitor part of himself asked: *Would that be so bad?*
Sooner or later, Darkover would fall into line. Every planet
did.

And even for Elorie, he told himself, it would be better.

No young woman should have to live like this, in seclusion, avoiding everything that made life worthwhile. No woman should have to know that her body is no more than a machine to transform the energies of matrix work! Even Rannirl had rebelled, and Rannirl was the chief technician of Arilinn. Rannirl had said that Keepers like Elorie were an anachronism in this day and age. If the Arilinn Tower and matrix technology could not survive except by the sacrifice of the lives of young women like Elorie, perhaps it did not deserve to survive at all. If their work for the Pan-Darkovan Syndicate failed, then Elorie need not be Keeper, and she was free.

Traitor! he accused himself bitterly. The people of Arilinn had taken him in, a stranger, homeless, exile of two worlds, and accepted him as one of themselves, given him kindness and love and acceptance. And he was ready to strike at their weakest point; he was willing to destroy them!

Lying there in the night, he willed himself to give up Elorie. She was the one that mattered; and her choice was to be Keeper, and remain Keeper. At whatever cost to himself in renunciation and agony, her peace of mind must never be endangered.

On the morning of the fourth day he heard her voice on the stairs. He had fought himself to acceptance, but at the sound of her soft voice it all surged up; he went back and flung himself down blindly, willing himself to calm through the blind ache and rebellion in him. *Oh, Elorie, Elorie . . .* He could not face her yet.

Later he heard Rannirl's voice at his door.

"Jeff? Will you come down?"

"Give me just a minute," Jeff said, and Rannirl went away. Left alone, Kerwin fought to apply all the techniques of control that he had been taught, steadying his breathing, forcing himself to relax; and when he knew that he could face them all without revealing his pain or his guilt, he went downstairs.

The circle of Arilinn was gathered before the fire, but Kerwin had eyes only for Eloric. She had put on again the filmy gown embroidered with cherries, anchored at her throat with a single crystal; her copper hair was twisted up in an elaborate coiffure of looped braids, caught with a blue flower dusted with gold; the *kireseth* flower, colloqually called the golden bell—*cleindori*. Was she testing his control? Or, he wondered suddenly, her own?

She raised her eyes, and he remembered how to breathe. For her smile was gentle, aloof, indifferent.

Had she felt nothing, then. Had he imagined it all? Had her reaction to him been no more than fear, then, as if he had reawakened the old fear—he remembered Neyrissa's story; one of her mad father's drinking-companions had laid rude hands on the girl, and her brother had brought her here for safety and refuge.

Kennard laid his hand gently on Jeff's shoulder; somehow, through the touch, an unspoken awareness passed through them both. *The Keepers are trained, in ways you could hardly guess at, to keep themselves free of all emotion.* Somehow, in those three days of seclusion, Elorie had managed to bring herself back to remote calm, untouched peace. Her smile was almost exactly as it had always been. *Almost.* Kerwin sensed that it was brittle, wary, a thin skin of control over panic; and with a surge of compassion and pain, he thought, *I must do nothing, nothing to trouble her. She wants it this way. I must not infringe on her control even with a thought.*

She said quietly, "We have arranged the separating operation for tonight; and Rannirl tells me that the trap matrix is ready for you, Auster."

"I'm ready," Auster said. "Unless Jeff wants to back out."

"I said I'd abide any test you gave me. But what the hell is a trap matrix?"

Elorie made one of her childish faces. "It's a filthy perversion of an honest science," she said.

"Not necessarily," Kennard protested. "There are valid ones. The Veil outside Arilinn is one kind of trap matrix; it keeps out everyone not accepted as Comyn and blood-related. And there are others in the *rhu fead*, the holy place of Comyn. What kind is yours, Auster?"

"Trap set on the barrier," Auster said. "When we put up the group barrier around our circle, I'll set the trap matrix in synch with it. Then, if anyone is picking a mind within the circle, it will hold him and immobilize him, and we can get a look at him afterward in the monitor."

"Believe me," said Kerwin, "if anyone's spying through *my* mind, I'm as anxious to find it out as you are!"

"We'll start then." She hesitated, bit her lip and moved to the cupboard where the drinks were kept. "I want some *kirian*." At Kennard's disapproving look she brushed past him, poured it for herself. "Anyone else who doesn't trust himself tonight? Auster? Jeff? Stop looking at me like that, Neyrissa, I know what I'm doing, and you're not my mother!"

Rannirl said roughly, "Lori, if you're not feeling ready for the clearing operation, we could delay it a few days—"

"We've already delayed three days, and I am as ready as I shall ever be," she said, and lifted the *kirian* to her lips. But she glanced at Jeff when she thought he did not see her, and her eyes struck Kerwin to the heart.

So it was that way for her, too. He had thought himself hurt that she could set it all aside, that she had been able to forget or ignore what had been between them. Now, seeing the hurt in her eyes, Kerwin wished with all his heart that Elorie had been truly untouched by what had happened. He could endure the suffering, if he must. But he did not know if he could endure what it had done to Elorie.

He could, because he must. He watched her finish the *kirian* liqueur, and went, with the others, upstairs to the matrix chamber.

They were placed as before, Taniquel monitoring,

Neyrissa within the circle, Auster holding the group barrier, Elorie at the center, holding in her slender hands the forces that could tap the magnetic field of a planet, gathering up all their joined minds and directing their mingled forces into the matrix lattice designed for this operation.

Kerwin felt the waiting like a pain, bracing himself for control against the moment when Elorie's grey eyes, turned on him, would pull him into the rapport of the circle. He felt it taking shape around him; Auster, strong and protective; the intangible strength that was Kennard, so at odds with the man's crippled body; Neyrissa, kindly and detached; Corus a flood of tumbling images.

Elorie.

He felt her firm, directing presence guiding him into the layers of the crystal lattice that somehow, was also the map lying before Kennard and the countryside of the Domains, extending his awareness beyond time and space, sending him out to travel, deep in the core of the world. . . .

He came out of it hours later, coming slowly up to consciousness to see dawn light in the room and the faces of the Tower circle around him. And Auster; drawn, hostile—triumphant. Wordless, he gestured them around him.

Kerwin had never seen a trap matrix before. It looked like a bit of strangely shiny metal, studded with crystals here and there, the glassy surface enlaced with little ribbons of gleaming light deep inside. Auster said, "Tired, Elorie? Take the monitor screen for a minute, Corus, let's see what we have in here." He pointed a finger at the beautiful, deadly thing in his lap. "I set it for anyone who tried to work through the group barrier; and I felt the trap sprung. Whoever it was, he's immobilized here, and we can get a good look at him."

Fastidiously, as if he touched something dirty, Corus picked up the trap matrix. He moved a calibration on the big monitor screen, and lights began to blink inside it. Then, in the glassy surface, a picture slowly formed. It hovered over the city of Arilinn; passed landmark after landmark. Then, gradually, it centered upon a small, mean room, almost bare, and the figure of a man, bent in soundless concentration, motionless as death.

"Whoever he is, we've got him in stasis," Auster said. "Can you get his face, Corus?"

The picture focused; and Jeff cried out as he recognized the face.

Ragan!"

Of course. The little bitter man from the spaceport gutters, who had all but admitted being a Terran spy, who had dogged Jeff's footsteps and taught him to use a matrix and pushed him at every step.

Who else could it have been?

Suddenly he was swept by a great, calm, icy rage. Some atavistic thing in him, all Darkovan, shook loose everything but his wrath and injured pride at having been manipulated like this, is his mind picked. Ancient words sprang without thought to his mind.

"Com'ii, *this man's life is mine!* When, how, and as I can, I claim his life, one to one, and who takes it before I do, answers to me!"

Auster—braced, Kerwin knew, to fling new challenges and charges, stopped cold, his eyes wide and shocked.

Kennard met his eyes. He said "*Comyn* Kerwin-Aillard, as your nearest kinsman and Warden here, I hear your claim and allot this life to you; to claim or spare as you will. Seek it, take it, or give your own."

Jeff heard the ritual words almost without understanding. His hands literally ached to tear Ragan limb from limb. He said tersely, gesturing the picture off the screen, "Can that thing hold him long enough for me to get to him, Auster?"

Auster nodded, the trap matrix still held between his hands. Taniquel broke into the silence, her voice shrill.

"You can't let him do this! It's murder; Jeff has no idea

how to use a sword, and do you think that—that *sharug*, that cat-spawn, will even fight fair?"

"I may not be able to handle a sword," Jeff said tautly, "but I'm damn good with a knife. Kinsman, give me a dagger, and I can take him," he added, turning to Kennard, who had acknowledged him.

But it was Rannirl who unbuckled the knife he wore at his waist. He said slowly, "Brother, I'm with you. Your foes are mine; let there never be a knife drawn between us." He held the knife out, hilt first, to Kerwin. Kerwin took it in a daze. From somewhere he remembered that on Darkover this had a very serious meaning. He didn't know the ritual words, but he remembered that this exchange had the ritual force of an oath of brotherhood, and even through his all-encompassing rage he was warmed by it. He caught Rannirl into a quick embrace. All he could think of to say was, "Thank you—brother. Against my foes—and yours." It must have been the right thing to say, or something near to it, for Rannirl turned his head and, somewhat to Jeff's embarrassment, kissed him on the cheek.

"Come on," he said, "I'll see fair play done in your name, Kennard. If you doubt it, Auster, come along."

Kerwin took the knife, balancing it in his hands. He had no doubt in his ability to handle himself. There had been a couple of fights on other worlds; he had found that inside himself there was a roughneck buried, and he was glad, now, to know it. The code of his childhood, the code of blood-feud, seemed to fill him to the roots of his whole being.

Ragan was going to get a damned big surprise.

And then he was going to get very, very dead.

CHAPTER THIRTEEN

Exile

They came out of the Tower, through the Veil, into dim red sunlight, the Bloody Sun rising over the foothills far away to the east. Jeff walked with his hand on his knife, feeling strange and cold. At this hour the streets of Arilinn were deserted; only a few startled onlookers in the street saw the three redheads, moving shoulder to shoulder, armed and ready for a fight; and those who did, suddenly discovered that they had urgent business in a couple of other directions.

They went through the outlying district, through the market where in a happier day Jeff had chosen a pair of boots, and into a crowded and dirty suburb. Auster, his hands still on the trap matrix, said in a low voice, "This won't hold him much longer."

Kerwin's grin stretched his mouth, mirthless. "Hold him long enough for me to *find* him, and then let him go any damn time you please."

They went through a narrow alley, a filthy courtyard cluttered with rubbish, a stable with a couple of ill-kept animals. A half-witted stableman in rags, his mouth hanging open, watched them briefly, then turned and fled. Auster pointed up a steep, crazy flight of stairs to an outside gallery with a couple of rooms opening off it. As they climbed the stairs, a girl in a torn skirt and scarf came out on the gallery, her mouth a wide O of astonishment. Rannirl made an angry, abrupt gesture, and she bolted back into one of the rooms and slammed the door.

Auster stopped outside the other door. He said, "Now," and his bony hands did something to the trap matrix that Jeff didn't see. From inside the room came a long cry of rage and despair as Kerwin, leaping forward, kicked the door open and burst in.

Ragan, still in the held-fast posture of the trap matrix, suddenly broke free and whirled on them like a trapped cat, knife flashing from his boot. He backed off and faced them, naked steel between them, baring his teeth with a snarl. "Three against one, *vai dom'yn?*"

"Just one!" Kerwin rasped, and with his free arm, motioned Rannirl and Auster to stand back. In the next moment he reeled under the impact of Ragan's body crashing into his. He felt the slash of the point along his arm as he whipped his knife up, but it had only torn his sleeve. He countered with a fast thrust, shoving Ragan off balance; then they were locked into a deadly clinch, and he was struggling to keep Ragan's knife from his ribs. He felt his own knife rip leather; it came away red. Ragan grunted, struggled, made a sudden swift feint—

Auster, watching like a cat at a mousehole, suddenly flung himself against them. He knocked Jeff off balance, and Kerwin, hardly believing that this was really happening—*he should have known he couldn't trust Auster!*—felt Ragan's knife rip along his arm and go in a few inches below the armpit. Numbness, then burning pain, spread in him; the knife dropped from his left hand and he snatched it up with the other, fighting Auster's death grip, dragging his arm down. Kerwin swore, brutally, kicking out with booted feet.

"Get away, damn you—is this your notion of a fair fight?" And Rannirl ran to fling his arms around Auster from behind, grab him and drag him away, taking a slash from

Ragan's knife that tore along his forearm and down the back of his hand. He was swearing.

"Man, are you crazy?" he panted.

Ragan wrenched loose. There was a crash, the sound of running feet on the staircase, the clatter of rubbish kicked loose on the staircase. Auster and Rannirl fell, still struggling, to the ground. Auster, somehow, had Ragan's knife. Rannirl panted, "Jeff! Get the knife!"

Kerwin dropped his own knife, flung himself on the struggling bodies, and forced Auster's hand back. Auster struggled briefly, then his hand relaxed and he dropped it, sanity coming slowly back to his eyes. There was a long slash on his cheek—Kerwin didn't know from which knife—and his eye was darkening, blood streaming from his nose, where Jeff's elbow had smashed at him.

Rannirl picked himself up, wiping the blood from his forearm. The knife had not gone into him at all; it was a cut less than skin deep. He stared down at Auster in shock and horror. Auster started to get up and Kerwin made a menacing gesture. For two cents he'd have kicked Auster's ribs right in. "Stay right where you are, damn you."

Auster wiped blood from his nose and mouth, and stayed where he was. Kerwin went to the window and looked into the dirty courtyard. Ragan, of course, was gone. There wasn't a chance they'd find him again.

He walked back to Auster and said, "Give me one good reason I shouldn't kick your brains out!"

Auster sat up, bloody, but not beaten. "Go ahead, *Terranan*," he said. "Pretend we owe you the protection of our codes of honor!"

Rannirl stood over him, menacing. "Do you dare call *me* traitor?" he said. "Kennard accepted the challenge; you did not speak to it then. And I have given this man my knife; he is my brother. By rights, Auster, I could kill you!" He looked ready to do it, too.

"Kennard gave him the right—"

"To murder his accomplice, so that we'd never know the truth! Didn't you see he was set to kill the man before we could question him? Didn't you see that he recognized him? Oh, yes, he put on a good show for us," Auster said. "Damned clever; kill him before any of us could get at the truth. I wanted to take him alive, and if you'd have the sense of a rabbithorn, we'd have him, now, for questioning and telepathic interrogation!"

He's lying, lying, Kerwin thought hopelessly, but doubt had begun to cloud even Rannirl's face. As usual, Auster had managed to confuse the issue, to put him on the defensive.

"Come on," he said wearily, "we might as well get back." He felt weary and anticlimactic; his arm was beginning to ache where Ragan had stabbed him. "Help me get this shirt off and stop the bleeding, will you, Rannirl? I'm bleeding like a summer slaughterhouse!"

There were more people in the streets now, and more to stare at the three Comyn, one with his face smeared from a bloody nose, and one with his arm pinned up in an improvised sling from Rannirl's undertunic. Kerwin felt all the weariness of a night spent at matrix work descending on him; he felt as if every step was his last effort. Auster, too, was staggering with weariness. They passed a cookshop where workmen were clustered, eating and drinking, and the smell of food reminded Kerwin that after a night in the matrix screens they had eaten nothing and that he was starving. He glanced at Rannirl and with one unspoken movement they went into the shop. The proprietor was awed and voluble, pouring out promises to set his finest before them, but Rannirl shook his head, caught up a couple of long loaves of fresh hot bread and a pan of cooked sausages, flung some coins at the cook and jerked his head at his companions. Outside he broke the bread, handed a portion to Kerwin and, glaring, one to Auster; they strode on through the streets of Arilinn, munching at the coarse food with wolfish hunger. It felt like the tiniest of between-meal snacks, a dainty morsel for a small and finicky child, but it did restore his strength somewhat. When they reached the Tower, and passed through the Veil, the faint stinging seemed to drain the last of Kerwin's strength.

"Jeff," said Rannirl, "I'll come and bandage that for you."

Kerwin shook his head. Rannirl looked exhausted, too, and it hadn't even been his fight. "Go and rest—" awkwardly, he added—"brother. I'll manage."

Rannirl hesitated, but he went, and Kerwin, relieved to be alone, went into his own room and flung the door shut. In the luxurious bath he ripped off sling and shirt, awkwardly raising his arm with a grimace of pain. Rannirl had crudely stanched the bleeding with a heavy pad from his torn shirt; he worked it loose and examined the wound. A flap of skin had been sliced away, skin and flesh hanging down like a bloody rag, but as far as he could tell the wound was simply a flesh one. He stuck his head into the fountain; raised it, dripping but clear-headed.

The furry nonhuman who served him glided into the room and stood dismayed, green pupilless eyes wide in consternation; he went quickly and came back with bandages, some thick yellow stuff he smeared on the wound; and deftly, with his odd thumbless paws, bound it up. That done, he looked at Kerwin in question.

"Get me something to eat," Kerwin said, "I'm starving." The bread and sausages they had shared on the way back had only begun to fill the vast crater of emptiness inside him.

He had eaten enough for three hungry horse-breakers after a fall round-up when the door opened, and Auster came, unannounced, into the room. He had bathed and changed his clothes, but, Kerwin was gratified to see, he had a splendidly black eye that would take a good while to heal. Kerwin wiped his mouth, shoved his plate away, and gestured at Rannirl's knife on the table.

"If you've had another brainstorm, there's a knife," he said. "If not, get the hell out of my room."

Auster looked pale. He touched his eye as if it hurt. Jeff hoped it did. "I don't blame you for hating me, Jeff," he said, "but I have something to say to you."

Kerwin started to shrug, found that it hurt, and didn't. Auster watched him and flinched as if the pain had been his own. "Are you badly hurt? Did the *kyrri* make sure there was no poison on the knife?"

"A hell of a lot you care," Kerwin said, "but that's a Darkovan trick; Terrans don't fight that way. And what the hell are you worrying about, when you did your level damnedest to make sure I got knifed in the first place?"

Auster said, "I deserve that, maybe. Believe anything you want to. I only care about one thing—two things, and you're destroying them both. Maybe you don't realize—but, damn it, it's worse than if you did!"

"Get to the point, Auster, or get out."

"Kennard said there was a block in your memory. Look, I'm not accusing you of betraying us on purpose—"

"That's damn good of you," Kerwin said with heavy sarcasm.

"You don't want to betray us," Auster said, his face suddenly cracking and going to pieces, "and you still don't realize what this *means*! It means that *the Terrans planted you on us!* They put that block in your memory, probably before you ever left the Spacemen's Orphanage, before you ever went to Terra. And when you came back here, they set it up, hoping that just this would happen—that we'd come to accept you, think of you as one of us, depend on you—*need* you! Because it was so obvious that you were one of us—" His voice broke; in shock, Kerwin realized that Auster was fighting back tears, shaking from head to foot. "So we fell for it, Kerwin, and for you—and how can we even hate you for it—brother?"

Kerwin shut his eyes. This was the very thought he had been pushing away.

He had been maneuvered every step of the way, from the first moment when Ragan had met them in the shops. Perhaps Johnny Ellers had been set up to introduce him to Ragan; he would never know. Who but the Terrans could have done it? Maneuvered into his experiments with the matrix. Maneuvered into confrontation with the Comyn. And at last threatened with deportation, to force the Comyn to move and reclaim him.

He was an elaborate booby trap! Arilinn had taken him in—and at any moment, he might explode in their faces!

Auster took Jeff gently by the arm, careful not to injure his wounded shoulder. "I wish we'd liked each other better. Now you must think I'm saying this because we haven't been friends."

Kerwin shook his head. Auster's pain and sincerity were obvious to anyone with a scrap of *laran*. "I don't think that. Not now. But what could they hope to achieve?"

"I'm not sure. Perhaps they thought the Tower Circle would disintegrate with you in it; perhaps they wanted information, leaked to them through the break in the barrier. I know they're curious about how matrix science operates, and they haven't been able to find out very much. Not even from Cleindori, when she ran away with your damned father. I don't know. How the hell would *I* know what the Terrans want? You should; you're one of them. You've lived with them. You tell me what they want!"

Kerwin shook his head. "Not now. I left them, didn't I? I never was one of them, except on the surface," he said slowly. "But now that we have the spy, now that we know what they're doing—can't we guard against it?"

"If it were only that, Jeff," Auster said earnestly. "But there's something else; the thing I've been trying not to see." His face was set and white. "What have you done to Elorie, my brother?"

Elorie. What have you done to Elorie.

And if Auster knew, they all knew.

He could not speak. His guilt, Auster's fear, was like a miasma in the room. Auster let him go and said earnestly, "Go away, Jeff. For the love of any Gods you know about on Terra, go away before it's too late. I know it's not your fault. You didn't grow up with the taboo. It isn't deep in your blood and bone. But if you care about Elorie, if you care about any of us, go away before you destroy us all."

He turned and went out, and Kerwin went and threw himself face down on his bed, seeing it clearly for the first time.

Auster was right. He heard, like a grim echo, the words of the matrix mechanic who had paid with her own life for showing him a scrap of his own past. *You are the one who was sent, a trap that missed its firing.* But she had said something else too. *You will find the thing you love, and you will destroy it; but you will save it, too.*

True, her prophecy, that old and unlovely and doomed woman whose name or history he was never to know. He had found what he loved, and already he had come close to destroying it. Could he save it, if he went away now, or was it already too late?

Oh, Elorie, Elorie! But he must not even whisper her name. Even a thought could disturb her hard-won peace. Kerwin rose, grim-faced, knowing what he must do.

Slowly he stripped off the suede-leather breeches and laced boots, the bright jerkin; he dressed himself again in the Terran uniform he had laid aside—forever, he thought—when he came here.

He hesitated over the matrix stone, cursing, torn, wanting to fling it from the highest window of the Tower and shatter it on the stones; but at last he put it into his pocket. He was under enough stress now, and he had always felt uneasy when it was, physically, out of his reach.

It was my mother's. It went with her into exile. It can go with me, too.

He hesitated, too, over the embroidered ceremonial cloak lined with fur that had begun this chain of events; but at last he put it round his shoulders. It was his, honestly bought with money earned on another world; and, sentiment aside, it was a bulwark against the bitter cold of the Darkovan night. He was still wearing the slash of Ragan's knife (was this all the Comyn could give him, knife wounds in his body, keener wounds in his soul?) and he couldn't afford to get chilled. And—another immensely practical consideration—on the streets of Arilinn, a man in Terran uniform would show up like a starflower on the bare glaciers of the Hellers. The cloak would keep him decently anonymous until he was a good long way away from here.

He went to the door of his room. There was a good smell of hot food somewhere; knife fights, blood feuds, endless telepathic operations within the matrix chamber could come and go, but practical Mesyr would plan their dinners, persuade the *kyrri* to cook them as she wished, chide Rannirl for spoiling his appetite with wine before dinner, search out new ribbons for Elorie's filmy dresses, scold the men for flinging muddy boots in the great hall after riding or hunting. He heard her cheery calm voice with a wrench of nostalgia. This was the only home he had ever known.

I always wanted my grandmother Kerwin to be just like her.

He passed an open door. The drift of Taniquel's delicate, flowery perfume wafted out, and he heard her singing somewhere in the suite. A brief vision caught at him, of her slim, pretty body half-submerged in greenish water, her curls piled atop her head as she scrubbed. Tenderness overwhelmed him; she had slept away the weariness of the night's work, and did not yet know of the aftermath of the knife fight . . . nor did Kennard.

The thought froze him. Soon now, if not already, the

touch of rapport would begin to drift among them as they gathered for the evening, and then they would all know what he planned. He must go quickly, or he would not be able to go at all.

He flung the hood over his head, slipped down the stairs unseen, and out through the Veil. Now he was safe; the Veil insulated thought, too. Moving resolutely, holding his weariness at bay, he went through the cluster of buildings near the Tower, across the airstrip, and toward the city of Arilinn.

His plans were vague. Where could he go? The Terrans had not wanted him. Now there was no place for him on Darkover either, no safety; wherever he hid, from Dalereuth to Aldaran, there was no refuge so remote that the Comyn could not find him; certainly not while he bore the matrix of the renegade Cleindori.

Back to the Terrans, then. Let them deport him, stop fighting his fate. They might simply deport him. But if they had actually planted him on the Comyn, a giant booby trap, what would they do when they discovered that he had sabotaged their plan, a carefully-laid plan that had taken two generations to bring to fruition?

Did it matter? They could do their worst.

Did anything matter now?

He raised his eyes, looked directly into the great red bloodshot eye of what some romantic Terran, a few generations ago, had dubbed the Bloody Sun. It was sinking behind the Arilinn Tower; he watched it vanish, and with it came the swiftly lowering darkness, the chill and silence. The last gleam of the bloody sun went out; the Tower lingered a minute, a pale afterimage on Jeff's eyelids, then dissolved in stinging rain. A single blue light shone from near the tip of the Tower, battling valiantly to pierce the mist and rain; then vanished as if it had never been. Kerwin wiped the rain from his eyes (was the rain salt and warm, stinging his face?)

turned his back resolutely on the Tower and walked into the city.

He found a place where they did not recognize him either as Terran or Comyn, but looked only at the color of his money, and gave him a bed, and privacy, and enough to drink—he hoped—to blot out thought and memory, blur the vain, unavoidable reliving of those brief weeks in Arilinn.

It was a monumental drunk. He never knew how many days it lasted, or how many times he staggered into the streets of Arilinn for more to drink and back to his hole like a wounded animal. When he slept, the darkness was blurred with faces and voices and memories he could not endure; he came at last up to consciousness from a long forgetfulness, more sleep than stupor, and found them all around his bed.

For a moment he thought it was the aftermath of bad whiskey, or that his overloaded mind had cracked. Then Taniquel made an uncontrollable sound of dismay and pity and flung herself down on her knees beside the filthy pallet where he was lying. And then he knew they were really there.

He rubbed a hand over his unshaven chin, wet his cracked lips with his tongue. His voice wouldn't obey him.

Rannirl said, "Did you really think we would let you go like this, *bredu*?" He used the inflection that made the word mean *beloved brother*.

Kerwin said thickly, "Auster—"

"Doesn't know everything," Kennard said. "Jeff, can you listen to us sensibly now, or are you still too drunk?"

He sat up. The squalor of the hideout room, the empty bottle at the foot of the tangled blanket, the ache, still sharp, in the neglected knife wound, seemed all part of the same thing, his own misery and defeat. Taniquel was holding his hand, but it was the monitor's touch of Neyrissa that he felt on his mind.

"He's sober enough," she said.

He looked around at them. Taniquel, her firm little fingers

pressing his; Corus, looking troubled, almost tearful; Rannirl, troubled and friendly; Kennard, sad and concerned; Auster, bitterly aloof.

Elorie, her face a white mask, the eyes red and swollen; Elorie, in tears!

Kerwin sat up, gently letting Taniquel's hand go. He said, "Oh, God, why must we go through all this again? Didn't Auster tell you?"

"He told us a lot of things," Kennard said, "all rooted in his own fears and prejudices."

"I don't even deny that," Auster said. "I ask if the fears and prejudices weren't justified. That spy—what did Jeff say his name was? Ragan. He's another of them. It's fairly obvious—damnt it, I *recognize* the man. I'd swear he's a *nedestro* of Comyn, maybe Ardais or even Aldaran! With Terran blood. Just right to spy on us. And Jeff—He could even come through the Veil! And fool Kennard on telepathic interrogation!"

Rannirl said angrily, "I think you see Terran spies under every pillow, Auster!"

Taniquel reached for Kerwin's hand again. She said, "We can't let you go, Jeff. You're one of us, you're a part of ourselves. Where will you go? What will you do?"

Kennard said, "Wait, Tani. Jeff, bringing you to Arilinn was a calculated risk; we knew that before we called you through the matrix, and we all agreed on the risk. And it was more than that. We wanted to strike a blow against dark magic and taboo, take a first step toward making matrix mechanics a science, not a— thing of sorcery. To prove it could be learned by anyone, not by a sacrosanct—priesthood."

"I don't know that I agree with Kennard on that," Neyrissa said. "I want no shadow of the Forbidden Tower, with their dirty ways and their forsworn Keepers, to touch Arilinn. But we've reclaimed Arilinn; and Jeff, Tani is right, you're one of us. We all agreed on the risk."

"But can't you understand?" Kerwin's voice broke. "I'm

not willing to take the risk. Not when I'm not sure that I'm—I'm a free agent, not a planted spy; when I don't know what they might make me do. When they might make me destroy you."

"Maybe *this* was how you were meant to destroy us," Corus said, and his voice was bitter. "To make us trust you—and then, when we can't work without you, to walk out on us."

"That's a damnably unfair way of putting it, Corus," Jeff said hoarsely. "I'm trying to save you; I can't be the one to destroy you!"

Taniquel bent her head and put her cheek against his hand. She was crying without a sound. Auster's face was hard. "Kerwin is right, Kennard, and you know it. He's got guts enough to want to do the right thing, anyway. And you're only hurting us all by prolonging this."

Kennard stood leaning heavily on his stick, looking down at them all with contempt, with lip-biting repressed anger.

"Cowards, all of you! Now that we have a chance to *fight* this damned nonsense! Rannirl, you know what's right! You've said it yourself—"

Rannirl clenched his teeth. He said, "My private beliefs are one thing; the will of the Council is another. I refuse to make a political statement about my career in Arilinn. I'm a technician, not a diplomat. Jeff is my friend. I gave him my knife. I call him brother, and I will defend him against his enemies. He doesn't have to go back to the Terrans. Jeff—" He turned to the man on the bed and said, "When you leave here, you don't need to go back to the Terrans; go to my family home in the Kilghard Hills. Ask anyone where to find Lake Mirion. Tell anyone there that you are my sworn brother; show them the knife I gave you. When this is settled, perhaps you can come back to Arilinn."

"I didn't think you were such a coward, Rannirl," Kennard said. "Defend him here, why don't you? If he needs a home, Armida is his; or, as Cleindori's child, Mariposa

Lake. But isn't there anyone with the guts to stand up for him at Arilinn? He's not the first Terran—"

"You're too damn transparent, Kennard," Auster said. "All you care about is getting that half-caste boy of yours into Arilinn some day, and you'll even put up with a Terran spy to create a precedent! Can't your damned son make it into Arilinn on his own merits, if he has any? I don't wish Jeff any harm now; Zandru seize this hand—" he laid it briefly on the hilt of his dagger—"if I wish him any harm. But he must not return to Arilinn; we cannot risk a Terran spy actually within a matrix circle. If he returns to Arilinn, I will go."

"And I," said Neyrissa. Rannirl, looking bitterly ashamed, said, "I am sorry. So will I."

"Cowards," Corus flung at them fiercely. "The Terrans have broken our circle after all, haven't they? They didn't need to make Jeff their spy. They just had to make us suspect him!"

Kennard shook his head in disbelieving disgust. He said, "Are you really going to do this, all of you?"

Kerwin wanted to cry out: *I love you all, stop torturing me this way!* He said thickly, "Now that you know it can be done, you'll find someone to take my place."

"Who?" Elorie asked bitterly. "Kennard's half-caste son? He's not ten years old yet! Old Leominda from Neskaya? The Heir to Hastur, who's only four years old, or the Heir to Elhalyn, who's nine years old and not much better than a half-wit? My madman of a father, perhaps? Little Callina Lindir from Neskaya?"

Kennard said, "We went all over this when we decided to bring Jeff here. In all the Seven Domains we could find no other candidates. And now, when we have a fully qualified and functioning Keeper's Circle at Arilinn, you are going to throw that away and let Jeff go? After all we went through to get him here?"

"No!" Elorie startled them all with her cry. She flung herself forward; afraid she would fall, Kerwin put out a hand to catch her. He would have let her go at once, respectfully, but she clung to him, her arms tightening around him. Her face was whiter than when she had collapsed in the matrix chamber.

"No," she whispered. "No, Jeff, no, don't go! Stay with us, Jeff, whatever happens—I beg you, I can't bear to see you go—"

For an instant Kerwin held her tight, his own face like death. He whispered, under his breath, "Oh, Elorie, Elorie . . ." But then, steeling himself, he put her gently away.

"Now do you see why I must go?" he said, almost in a whisper, speaking to her alone. "I *must* go, Elorie, and you know it was well as I. Don't make it harder for me."

He saw shock, anger, compassion, accusation dawning in the faces all around him. Neyrissa came to take Elorie away, murmuring to her, but Elorie flung off her hand. Her voice was high and shrill.

"No. If this is what Jeff has decided, or what you force on him, then I have decided too, and it is over. I—I can't give up my life for it this way anymore!" She faced them all, her eyes enormous, looking like bruises in her pale face.

"But Elorie, Lori," Neyrissa pleaded. "You know why you cannot withdraw, you know how much you are needed—"

"And what am I, then? A doll, a machine to serve the Comyn and the Tower?" she cried, her voice high and hysterical. "No. No. It's too much! I cannot stand it, I renounce it—"

"Elorie—*breda*," Taniquel pleaded. "Don't say that—not like this, not now, not here! I know how you feel, but—"

"You say you know how I feel! You dare to say that to me, you who have lain in his arms and known his love! Oh, no, you have not denied yourself, but you are all too ready to tell me what I must do—"

"Elorie," Kennard's voice was tender. "You don't know what you are saying. I beg of you, remember who you are—"

"I know who I am supposed to be!" she cried, sounding frantic, beside herself. "A Keeper, a *leronis*, a sacred virgin without mind or heart or soul or life of my own, a machine for the relays—"

Kennard closed his eyes in agony, and Kerwin, looking at the old man's face, seemed to hear words spoken like this, years before, and saw, mirrored in Kennard's mind and memory, the face of his mother. *Cleindori. Oh, my poor sister!* But aloud Kennard only said, very gently, "Lori, my darling. Everything you suffer, others have suffered before you. When you came to Arilinn, you knew it would not be easy. We cannot allow you to renounce us, not now. Another Keeper is being trained, and when that day comes you can be freed. But not now, *chiya*, or you throw away all we have done."

"I cannot! I cannot live like this!" Elorie cried. "Not now, when at last I know what it is I swore to renounce!"

"Lori, my child—" Neyrissa said softly, but Elorie turned on her like a fury. "You have lived as you saw fit, you found freedom, not slavery in the Tower! For you it was a refuge; for me it has never been anything but a prison! You and Tani both, you are quick to urge me to give up forever what you have known, love and shared joy and children—" her voice broke. "I didn't know, I didn't know, and now—" She flung herself into Jeff's arms again; he could not put her away.

Auster said in a low voice, staring at Elorie in horror, "This is worse treachery than the Terrans could ever compass. And to think, Jeff, that I believed you had done this innocently!"

Rannirl shook his head, staring at them in dismay. He said in a low, vicious voice, "I gave you my knife. I called you brother. And you have done this to us, done this to *her*!" He spat. "There was a day when the man who seduced a Keeper would be torn on hooks, and the Keeper who violated her oath—" He could not continue. He was too angry.

"And so history repeats itself—Cleindori and this filth of a Terran!"

"You said it yourself," Elorie cried out in torment. "You said that any mechanic could to a Keeper's work, that a Keeper was an anachronism, that Cleindori was right!"

"What I believe, and what we can do at Arilinn, are two different things," he spat at her, contemptuously. "I had not believed you were such a fool! Nor did I think you weak enough to go whoring after this handsome Terran who has seduced us all with his charming ways! Yes, I too was charmed by him—and he used this, damn him, he used it to break the Tower!" Rannirl swore, turned his back on them.

"Dirty bitch," Neyrissa said, and raised her hand to slap Elorie. "No better than that dirty old man, our father, whose filthy lecheries—"

Kennard moved swiftly to grab Neyrissa's hand in midair. "What? Lay a hand on your Keeper?"

"She has forfeited that," said Neyrissa, curling up her lip in contempt.

Auster said, staring somberly at them, "In days past, it would have been death for you, Elorie—and death by torture for *him*.

In shock and dismay Kerwin realized the mistake they were making; for Elorie was clinging to him, white and terrified, her face hidden against his breast. He stepped forward quickly, to deny the accusation, to reaffirm Elorie's innocence. The words were already on his lips: *I swear that she has been sacred to me, that her chastity is untouched—*

But Elorie flung back her head, white and defiant. "Call me what you will, Neyrissa," she said. "All of you; it's no use. I have renounced Arilinn; I proclaim myself unfit to be Keeper by Arilinn's laws—"

She turned then to Kerwin, sobbing bitterly, and flung her arms around him again, hiding her face on his breast. The words still unspoken—*This is only an innocent girl's fantasy. I have not betrayed her, or you—*died forever on his lips. He could not rebuff or repudiate her now; not as he saw the shock and disbelief on their faces changing to revulsion and disgust. She was clinging helplessly, holding herself to him with desperate force, her whole body shaken with her weeping.

Deliberately, accepting, he bowed his head and faced them, his arms sheltering Elorie.

"They should die for this!" Auster cried.

Rannirl shrugged. "What's the use? They've sabotaged everything we tried to do, everything we've accomplished. Nothing we could do now would make any difference. Wish them joy of it!" He turned his back on them and walked out.

Auster and Corus followed; Kennard lingered a moment, his face lined and miserable with despair. "Oh, Elorie, Elorie," he said in a whisper, "if you had only come to me, warned me in time—" and Kerwin knew that he was not speaking to Elorie, but to a memory. But she did not raise her head from Jeff's breast and after a time Kennard sighed, shaking his head and went away.

Stunned, still shaken by the force of her lie, Kerwin heard the door closing behind them. Elorie had quieted a little; now she began to weep again, brokenly, like a child; Kerwin held her in his arms, not understanding.

"Elorie, Elorie," he entreated. "Why did you do it? Why did you lie to them?"

Sobbing and laughing at once, hysterical, Elorie leaned back to look at him. "But it wasn't a lie," she sobbed. "I couldn't have lied to them again! It was my being Keeper that had become a lie, ever since I touched you—oh, I know you would never have touched me, because of the law, because of the taboo, and yet when I spoke to them they knew I was telling the truth! Because I had come to want you so, to love you so, I couldn't have endured it, to turn myself into a robot again, a machine, a dead-alive automation as I did before—" Her sobbing almost drowned out the words. "I knew I could never endure it again, to go on being Keeper—

and when you went away, I thought at first without you there I could perhaps go back to being what I was, but there was nothing, nothing anymore in my world, and I knew that if I never saw you again, I would be more dead than alive—"

"Oh, Elorie! Oh, God, Elorie!" he whispered, overwhelmed.

"So now you have lost everything—and you're not even free," she said wildly. "But I have nothing, no one else, if you do not want me, I have nothing, nothing—"

Kerwin picked her up in his arms like a child, cradling her close to him. He was awed at the immensity of her trust; shaken and dismayed at what she had given up for him. He kissed her wet face; laid her down on the tumbled bed and knelt at her side.

"Elorie," he said, and the words were a prayer and a pledge, "I don't care if I have lost everything else, now that I have you. My only regret in leaving Arilinn was because I thought I was leaving you."

The words were not true and he knew as he spoke them that they were not true, and he knew that Elorie knew. Yet the only thing that mattered now was to reassure Elorie with a deeper truth. "I love you, Elorie," he whispered, and that at least was true. "I will never let you go." He leaned forward, kissing her on the lips, and gathered her childish body again into his arms.

CHAPTER FOURTEEN

Doorway to the Past

Thendara, in the dying light, was a mass of black towers and shapes; the Terran HQ below them was a single brightly lighted spike against the sky. Jeff pointed it out to Elorie through the window of the Terran airliner.

"It may not be very beautiful to you now, my darling. But somewhere I'll find a world to give you."

She leaned against his shoulder. "I have all the world I want."

The seat-belt sign flashed, and he helped her to buckle her straps; she put her hands over her ears, hating the noise, and he put his arm around her, holding her tight.

The last three days had been day of joy and discovery for both of them, even through their shared sense of being outcaste, driven from the only home either of them had ever wanted. Neither spoke of this; they had too much else to share with one another.

He had never known a womanlike Elorie. Once he had thought her aloof, passionless; then he had come to see that calm as a deep-seated control, not as absence of passion.

She had come to him frightened, desolate, innocent almost to ignorance, and terrified. And she had given him her fear as she had given the rest of herself, without pretense and without shame. That utter trust frightened Kerwin, too—how could he ever be worthy of it? But it was typical of Elorie that she could do nothing by halves or meanly; as Keeper she had kept herself clear even from the fringes of passion; even in imagination, she had never thought of love. And having discarded that place, she had given herself over to Jeff with all of her long-controlled passion and dedication.

Once he had said something of this to her; his surprise, his fear that she would be frightened or frigid, his overwhelming surprise and delight at her response to his passion. Somehow he had believed that a woman who could live the life of a Keeper would be cold at the core, without passion or desire.

She had laughed aloud, shaking her head. "No," she said. "Kennard explained this once to me; outsiders would think that a passionless woman, who would not suffer in living alone and loveless, would be right for a Keeper. But anyone who knew anything of *laran* would know better. *Laran* and sexuality arise from the same place within, and are closely akin, and a woman who could be keeper without suffering would not have enough *laran* to be a Keeper, or anything else!"

Now, as they landed, she drew her cloak over her bright hair; he held her arm on the hard and unfamiliar metal steps. He must seem resolute for her sake, even if he was not. "I know it is strange to you, darling. But it won't be strange for long."

"No place will be strange to me where you are," she said valiantly. "But—but will they allow this? They won't—won't separate us?"

On that he could reassure her. "I may be Darkovan under your laws," he said, "but I have Terran citizenship and they cannot deny me that. And any woman who legally marries a citizen of the Empire is automatically given citizenship." He remembered the bored, incurious clerk in the Trade City at Port Chicago who had married them three days ago. Port Chicago was beyond the Domains; the clerk had glanced briefly at Jeff's identity disk, heard Elorie give her name as "Elorie Ardais" without a ripple of interest; probably he had never heard of the Comyn, or of the Arilinn Tower. He brought in a woman in his office to witness the marriage; she had been chirpy and friendly, saying to Elorie that with their two red heads they should have a quite a crop of red-headed children. Elorie had blushed, and Kerwin had felt a great and unexpected tenderness. The thought a child of Elorie's touched him in a way he had not thought he could be moved.

"You are my wife in Empire law, wherever we go," he repeated. He added, gently, "We may have to leave Darkover, though."

She nodded, biting her lip. The Comyn might be as anxious, now, to have Jeff deported as, before, they had been anxious to prevent it.

Kerwin secretly felt it would be better that way. Darkover could never be, for either of them, more than a reminder of what they had lost. And there were worlds enough, out there.

Nervously, he approached the barrier. He might, just possibly, be taken into custody as a man under sentence of deportation. There were certain legal formalities he could invoke, appeal, delays to which he was legitimately entitled. It hadn't seemed worth it, for himself. For Elorie, he would do all he could to evade the summary judgment, turn it in his favor.

The tall Spaceforce man in black leather stared at Kerwin's shabby Terran clothing, at the shrinking, veiled girl on his arm. He glanced at Jeff's identity certification.

"And the woman?"

"My wife. We were married in Port Chicago three days ago."

"I see," said the Spaceforce man, slowly. "In that case there are certain formalities."

"Just as you like."

"If you'll come inside the HQ please."

He led them inside, Jeff squeezing Elorie's arm reassuringly. He tried to hide the apprehension he felt. The marriage would have to be recorded through Records, and once Jeff surrendered his identification, the computer would immediately come up with the information that he was under sentence of deportation and suspension.

He had considered returning to the Terran Zone anonymously, at least for a day or two. But the peculiarity of Empire law concerning native women and marriage made that unthinkable. She had insisted, when he explained, that she did not care. But Jeff said firmly, asserting himself over her protest for the first time, "*I* care," and had left her no room for argument.

The Empire Civil Service consists largely of single men; few Terran women care to accompany their men halfway across the Galaxy. This means that on every planet liaisons with native women, both formal and informal, are taken for granted. To avoid endless complications with various planetary governments, the Empire makes a very clear distinction.

An Empire citizen may marry any woman, on any planet, by the laws of her own world and her own customs; it is a matter between the individual Terran, the woman, her family, and the laws under which she lives. The Empire has no part in it. Whether the marriage is formal or informal, temporary or permanent, or no marriage at all, is a matter for the private ethical and moral standards of the parties involved. And that man is carried as single on the Records of the Empire, making such provision for his wife as he privately chooses; although he may, if he wishes, file for citizenship for any child of the marriage, and obtain certain privileges for him. As the elder Jeff Kerwin had done for his son.

But if he chooses to register the marriage through Terran records, or signs any Empire document speaking of any native woman on any world, legally, as his wife, she is so in fact. From the moment their marriage contract was signed, and went through the Records, Elorie was entitled legally to all the privileges of a citizen; and if Jeff had died in the next breath after signing, she would still have been entitled to all the privileges of a citizen's widow. Kerwin was uncertain as to what the future would hold; but he had wanted to protect Elorie and provide for her in this way. Words spoken in bitterness still rang in his ears and turned up in his nightmares.

In the old days it would have been death for you, Elorie—and death by torture for him! And an old terror was upon him. There were those who might feel compelled to avenge the honor of a Keeper.

Kennard had said—what had Kennard said? Nothing. But still, Jeff was afraid without knowing why. So he watched with relief as a registry clerk took his thumbprint, and Elorie's, and tapped out information for Records. Now there was no way for the long arm of the Comyn to reach out and snatch Elorie from him.

He hoped.

Watching the details disappear into the computer, he was sure he had set trouble in motion for himself. Within a few hours he would have questions to answer, he might have to face deportation. He had a blot on his record, but he was a civilian, after all, and leaving his job without formal permission was only a minor offense against his seniority, not a crime. Somehow, he had to arrange to make a living. He had to decide whether to go to Terra or take a chance on another world—he was fairly sure his Terran grandparents wouldn't really welcome Elorie—but all those details could wait.

Most of his knowledge of Thendara was of bars and similar places, where he couldn't take Elorie. He could have claimed quarters in the HQ, putting in a requisition for married personnel, but he wouldn't do that until he had to. Equally unwise would be to find quarters in the Old Town— he had had a taste in Arilinn of how the Comyn were treated when recognized. A hotel in the Trade City was the obvious temporary solution.

He pointed out to her, as they passed, the Spaceman's Orphanage. "That's where I lived until I was twelve years old," he said, and let the silent puzzlement strike him again: *Or did I? Why, then, did the place have no records of me?*

"Elorie," he asked, when they were alone in their hotel, "did the Comyn have anything to do with destroying my records in the Orphanage?" A matrix, he supposed, could easily wipe out the data on a computer. At least, with what he knew of computers and matrixes, he could easily have devised a way to do it.

"I don't know," she said. "I do know we got Auster back from them when he was a small child, and *his* records were destroyed."

Kennard had referred to that as a curious story, and had implied that he would tell Jeff about it sometime. But he hadn't.

Long after Elorie slept, he lay awake at her side, thinking about the false leads and blind alleys that had obscured his search for his own background. When the Comyn found him, he had abandoned the search—after all, he had found out the main thing he wanted to know; where he belonged. But there were still mysteries to be solved, and before he left Darkover forever—and he supposed, now, that was only a matter of time—he was going to have a last try at solving them.

He told Elorie a little, the next day.

"There was no record of me there; I saw what the machine gave out. But if I could get into the place and check—there might even be someone there, one of the matrons or teachers, who remembered me."

"Would it be dangerous—to try and get in?"

"Not dangerous to life or limb, no. But I could be arrested for trespassing, or for breaking and entering. I wish to hell I knew a way a matrix could make me invisible."

Her smile was faint. "I could barricade you—throw what they call a *glamour* over you, so you could pass in among them unseen." She sighed. "It is unlawful for a Keeper who has given back her oath to use her powers. But I have broken so many laws already. And certain powers—I have lost."

She looked pale and wretched, and Kerwin felt his heart turn over at the thought of what she had given up for him. But why should it make so much difference? He would not ask, but she picked the question up directly from his mind, and said, "I do not know. I—I have always been told that a Keeper must be—must be virgin, and resigns her powers if she gives back her oath and takes a lover, or a husband."

Kerwin was startled by her acceptance of this; she had defied so many superstitions, had refused to accept her ritual authority, had hated the word *sorceress* when applied to her. But this one, perhaps, was so deeply ingrained in her that she could not resist it.

Kennard had called it superstitious rubbish. But whether she had really lost her powers, or only believed she had, the effect would be much the same. And perhaps there was some truth to it, too. He knew the terrible exhaustion and nervous drain of matrix work, even on his newcomer level. Kennard had counseled him to avoid sex for some time before serious work in the screens. It made sense that the Keepers must remain always at the peak of strength, guarding their powers in seclusion, sparing no energies for any other ties or concerns.

He remembered the day she had collapsed in the matrix screens; how he had thought her heart had stopped. Kerwin took her in his arms, holding her tight, thinking: *At least she is safe from that, now!*

But he had touched her, that day; had lent her strength. Had that contact destroyed her as Keeper?

"No," she said quietly, knowing his thoughts as she so often did. "From the first moment I touched you through the matrix, I knew that you would be—someone special, someone who would trouble my peace; but I was proud. I thought

I could keep my control. And there was Taniquel; I envied her, but I knew you would not be too much alone." Her eyes suddenly brimmed over.

"I shall miss Tani," she said softly, "I wish it could have been different, that we could have—could have left in a way that would not leave them hating us. Tani is so dear to me."

"You aren't jealous? Because she and I—"

She laughed a little. "Oh, you Terrans! No, darling. If things were different, if we could have lived among our own people, I would willingly have called her *bredhis*, it would have been Tani that I chose for your bed if I were ill or pregnant—does that seem so shocking to you?"

He kissed her, without speaking. Darkovan customs were idealistic, but they took some getting used to. And he was just as glad to have Elorie to himself.

But that made him think of something else.

"Taniquel was no virgin, certainly. And yet she worked in the matrix circle—"

"Taniquel was not a Keeper," Elorie said soberly, "and she was never required to do a Keeper's work, never required to gather the energons of the circle and direct them. Such vows, and such—such abstinence—were not required of her, nor of Neyrissa, no more than of any of the men. And a few generations ago—in the time of the Forbidden Tower—there was a Keeper who left Arilinn to marry, and continued to use her powers; it was a great scandal; I do not know all the story, it was such a tale as they did not tell to children. And I do not know how she did it." Quickly, as if she feared he would question further, she said, "Some things, I am sure, I can still do with my own matrix. Let me try."

But when she had taken it from the tiny leather case in which she kept it, wrapped in its insulating silks, she hesitated.

"I feel so strange. Not like myself. I don't seem to—to belong to myself any more."

"You belong to me," Kerwin said firmly, and she smiled.

"Are your Terran wives property? No, I think not, love; I belong to myself; but I will willingly share every moment of my life with you," she said.

"Is there a difference?" Kerwin asked.

Her soft laugh always delighted him. "To you, perhaps not. To me, it is very important. If I had wished to be some man's property, I could have wedded someone before I was out of childhood, and would never have gone to the Tower." She took the matrix in her hand; but Kerwin saw the tentative way in which she touched it, contrasting her hesitation with the sureness she had shown in the matrix chamber. She was frightened! He wanted to tell her he didn't give a damn, put it away, he didn't want her to touch the accursed thing—she was too precious to risk—and then he saw her eyes.

Elorie loved him. She had given up her whole world for him, all she was and all she could have been. Even now, Kerwin knew, he had only the dimmest, outsider's perception of what it meant to be a Keeper. If she needed this, he had to let her try. Even if it killed her, he had to let her try.

"But promise me, Elorie," he said, taking her shoulders in his hands and tipping her head back to look into her eyes, "no risks. If it doesn't feel right, don't try it."

He felt that she hardly heard him. Her slight fingers curved around the matrix; her face was distant and abstracted. She said, not to him, "The shape of the air here is different, we are among the mountains; I must be careful not to interfere with his breathing." She moved her head, an imperious small signal, and he felt her drop into rapport, intangibly, like a caress.

I don't know how long I can hold it, when there are Terrans around, but I will try. There. Jeff, look in the mirror.

He rose and looked into the mirror. He could see Elorie perfectly well, in her thin grey dress, her bright hair bent over the matrix in her hand; but he could not see himself. He looked down; he could see himself perfectly well, but he did not reflect in the mirror.

"But, but, I can see myself—"

"Oh, yes, and if anyone bumps into you, they will know perfectly well that you are there," she said with a sting of a smile. "You have not become a ghost, my love of a barbarian, I have only changed the look of the air around you, for a little while. But I think it will hold long enough for you to get into the orphanage unseen."

Her face held the triumph of a gleeful child. Jeff bent down to kiss her and saw the strangeness in the mirror, Elorie evidently lifted up and resting on nothing. He smiled. It was not a difficult matrix operation; he could probably have done it himself. But it had proved to her . . .

"That I'm not blind and deaf to it," she said, picking up his thought, and her voice sounded tight, though she was still smiling the childish smile. "Go, darling, I'm not sure how long I can hold it, and you shouldn't waste any time."

He left her there in the Terran hotel room, passing silently and unseen down the corridors. In the lobby people passed him, unseeing. He had a curious, lunatic sense of power. No wonder the Comyn were all but invincible—

But at what cost? Girls like Elorie, giving up their lives . . .

The Spacemen's Orphanage looked just as it had looked a few scant months ago. A few of the boys were doing something to the grounds, kneeling around a patch of flowers, supervised by an older boy with a badge on his arm. Silent as a ghost, Kerwin hesitated before walking up the white steps. What should he do first? Go unseen into the office, check files and records? Quickly he dismissed that notion; he might be invisible, but if he started handling books or punching buttons, the people in the office would see *something* even if it was only books and papers moving of their own accord; and sooner or later they'd start investigating.

And sooner or later someone would bump into him.

He stopped and considered. In the third-floor dormitory where he had slept with five other boys, he had carved his initials, at the age of nine, into a window-frame. The frame might have been repaired or replaced; but if it hadn't, and he could find the carving, it would prove something, to his own satisfaction; at least he wouldn't have to carry around the sneaking suspicion that he never *had* been there, that he had imagined the whole thing, that all his memories were hallucinations.

And after all, the dormitory was an old one and many of the boys had done the same thing. The Darkovan nurses and the children's counselors had left them a good deal of freedom in some areas. In his day the dormitory had been battered, orderly and clean enough, but bearing the imprint of many childish pranks and experiments with tools.

He went up through the halls, passing an open classroom door, trying to tread lightly, but two or three heads turned as he passed. *So they heard someone walking in the halls, so what?* Nevertheless, he rose on tiptoe and tried to make as little noise as possible.

A Darkovan woman, hair coiled low on her neck and fastened with a leather butterfly-clasp, her long tartan skirt and shawl faintly scented with incense, went along the hall, singing softly to herself. She went into one of the rooms and came out with a sleepy toddler cradled in her arms. Kerwin froze automatically, even though he knew himself invisible, and the woman seemed unconscious of him, still humming her mountain song.

"Laszlo, Laszlo, dors di ma main . . ."

Kerwin had heard the song of his own childhood, a silly rhyme about a little boy whose foster-mother stuffed him with cakes and sweets until he cried for bread and milk; he remembered, once, being told that the song went back to the historical period called the time of the Hundred Kingdoms, and the Hastur Wars that had ended them, and that the verses were a political satire about over-benevolent governments.

Kerwin drew aside as the woman passed him, feeling the rustle of her garments; but as they passed each other, she frowned curiously, and broke off her song; had she heard his breathing, smelled some unfamiliar scent from his clothing?

"*Laszlo, Laszlo . . .*" she began to croon her little song again, but the child in her arms twisted, turning his face over the woman's shoulder, looking straight at Kerwin. He said something in baby-talk, thrusting one chubby fist at Kerwin, and the nurse frowned, turning.

"What man? There's nobody there, *chiy'llu*," she scolded softly, and Kerwin turned and tiptoed down the hallway, his heart suddenly pounding. Could a child's eyes penetrate Elorie's illusion?

He paused at the top of the stairs, trying to get his bearings. Finally he turned toward what he thought was the right room.

It was quiet and sunlit, eight small, neatly-made cots in little cubicles around the edges of the room, and in the open play space between, a group of toy figures, men and buildings and spaceships, was arranged on a small table. Carefully stepping around the toys, he saw that a tall white skyscraper had been built at the center of the toy group, and sighed; the children had built the Terran HQ that loomed so large in their thoughts.

He was wasting time. He moved to the windows and moved his fingers along the molding at eye-level. No, there were no carvings . . . suddenly he realized what he was doing. Yes, he had carved his initials at eye-level, but the eye-level of a nine-year-old boy, not his present two meters and more!

He stooped and felt again at mid-level. Yes, there were carvings in the soft wood; rough crosses, hearts, tick-tack-toe crosses. And then, at the left, in the squarish letters of the

Terran Standard alphabet, he saw the childish work of his first pocketknife.

J. A. K. JR

Not until he saw the initials did he realize that he was shaking. His fists were clenched so hard that his nails hurt his palms. He did not realize, until now, that he had ever doubted finding them; but now, as he touched the childish, rude gouges in the wood, he knew that he had doubted his own sanity and that the doubt had gone deep.

"They lied, they lied," he said aloud.

"Who lied?" asked a quiet voice. "And why?"

Kerwin turned quickly toward the door. A short, sturdy, grey-haired man was standing there, looking straight at him. So Elorie's illusion had worn off; he had been seen, and heard—and found.

Now what?

CHAPTER FIFTEEN

Through the Barrier

The man's eyes, intelligent and kindly, rested on Kerwin without anger. "We never allow visitors in the dormitories," he said. "If you wanted to see a particular child, you should have asked to see him in the playroom." His eyes narrowed suddenly. "But I know your face," he said. "Your name is Jeff, isn't it? Kerradine, Kermit—"

"Kerwin," he said, and the man nodded.

"Yes, of course; we called you *Tallo*. What are you doing here, young Kerwin?"

Abruptly, Kerwin decided to tell the truth. "Looking for my initials, carved here," he said.

"Now why would you want to do that? Sentiment? Old times sake?"

"Not a bit of it. A few months ago I came here," Kerwin said, "and they told me in the office that there were no records of my ever having been here, no records of my parentage—that I was lying when I claimed to remember being brought up here. I don't blame the matron—she evidently was since my time—but when the computer showed no records of my fingerprints—well, I started doubting my own sanity." He pointed to the carved initials. "I'm sane, anyhow. I cut those initials here when I was a kid."

"Now why would that happen?" the man demanded. "Oh, I forgot—I don't suppose you remember my name; I'm

Jon Harley. I used to teach mathematics to the older boys. Still do, as far as that goes."

Jeff clasped the hand the man held out to him. "I remember you, sir. You stopped a fight I got into once, and bandaged up my chin afterward, didn't you?"

Harley chuckled. "I remember that, all right. You were a young rowdy, right enough. I remember when your father brought you to us. You were about five, I think."

Had his father lived so long? I ought to remember him, then, thought Kerwin, but try as he might there was only the elusive blank space in his memory, fragmentary memories of dreams.

"Did you know my father, sir?"

The man said, regretfully, "I saw him only that once, you know, when he brought you here. But, for goodness sake, young Kerwin, come downstairs and have a drink or something. Computers do get out of order, sometimes, I suppose; perhaps we should check the written files and school records."

Kerwin realized that he should have waited, demanded, tried to see someone who would actually *remember* him. Like Mr. Harley. "Is there anyone else still here who could remember me?"

Harley thought it over. "I don't think so," he said. "It's been a long time, and there's a considerable turnover. Some of the maids, perhaps, but I think I'm the only teacher who would remember you. Most of the nurses and teachers are young; we try to keep them young, children need young people about them. I go on and on, old fellow that I am, because it's hard to get good teachers to come out from Terra, and they want someone who speaks the language without accent." He said, with a deprecating shrug, "Come down to my office, young Jeff. Tell me what you're doing these days. I remember you were sent to Terra. Tell me how you happened to come back to Darkover."

In the old man's austere office, filled with the open-window noises of children playing outside, Jeff accepted a drink he didn't want, fighting unspoken questions to which, he supposed, old Harley wouldn't have the answer.

"You say you remember my father bringing me here. My mother—was she with him?"

Harley shook his head. "He said nothing about having a wife," he said, almost prissily.

But, Kerwin thought, he had acknowledged his son, and that wasn't easy under Terran Empire laws. "What was my father like?"

"As I say, I saw him only once, and it wasn't easy to tell what he looked like. His nose had been broken, and he'd been in some kind of fight; there was a lot of rioting in Thendara about then; some political upheaval. I never knew the details. He was wearing Darkovan clothing; but he had his Terran identifications. We asked you questions about your mother, but you couldn't talk."

"At *five years old?*"

"You didn't talk for another year or so," Harley said, frankly. "To be truthful, we thought you were mentally deficient. That's one reason I remember you so well; because we all spent a lot of time trying to teach you to talk; we had a speech therapist come from Thendara HQ to work with you. You didn't speak a word, either in Terran *or* Darkovan."

Kerwin listened in amazement as the old man talked on.

"Kerwin—yout father—finished up all the formalities for having you admitted here that night," he said. "Then he went away and we never saw him again. We were fairly curious, because you didn't look at all like him, and of course you had red hair; and that same week we had taken in another little red-headed fellow, a year or so younger than you."

Kerwin said with sudden curiosity, "Was his name— Auster?"

Harley frowned. "I don't know; he was in the younger division and I never saw much of him, though I know he had a Darkovan name. He was only here for a year or so, and that's very odd too. He was kidnapped and all his records stolen at the same time . . . well, I'm talking too much. I'm an old man and it's nothing to do with you. Why do you ask?"

"Because," Kerwin said slowly, "I think perhaps I know him."

"His records aren't here; as I said, they were stolen, but here's the record of the kidnapping," Harley said. "Shall I look it up?"

"No, don't bother." Auster was nothing to do with him now; whatever the curious story, and both Kennard and Harley had called it odd, he would never know. It was unlikely that he would have been listed here as *Auster Ridenow*, in any case. Perhaps Auster too was born of two of the Comyn traitors, who had fled with the renegade Cleindori and her Terran lover. Did it matter? He had been brought up among the Comyn and he had inherited all their powers and he had gone to Arilinn at the appointed time. And he, Kerwin, brought up on Terra, had gone to Arilinn and he had betrayed them. . . .

But he wouldn't think of that now. He thanked Harley, refused another drink, submitted to being shown around the new playground and dormitory buildings, and finally took his leave, filled with new questions to replace the old ones.

Where and how had Cleindori died?

How and why had the elder Jeff Kerwin, his nose broken, bruised and battered after a terrible fight, brought their son to the Spaceman's Orphanage?

And where had he gone after that, and where and how had he died? For surely he had died; if he had lived, surely, surely, he would have reclaimed his son.

And why had Jeff Kerwin's son, at five years old, been unable to speak a word in either of his parents' languages, for more than a year?

And why had Jeff Kerwin, grown, no memory of mother

or father, no memory at all except the curious half-memories of dreams—walls, arches, doors, a man who strode proudly, cloaked, through a castle corridor, a woman bending over a matrix, taking it up with a gesture that remained when all the rest of his memory had blurred . . . a child's scream . . .

Shuddering, he cut off the half-formed memory. He had found out a part of what he wanted to know, and Elorie would be waiting to know what had happened.

When he got back, she was asleep, flung across the bed in exhaustion, grey smudges under her long-lashed eyes; but she sat up as he came in, and put up her face to be kissed.

"Jeff, I'm sorry, I held it as long as I could . . ."

"It's all right."

"What did you find out?"

He hesitated, not sure he should tell her, Would the questions surging in him raise disquiet in her? What did she know of Cleindori, except that she had been taught to despise the "renegade"?

Her hand closed over his. "What would really hurt me," she said, "would be if you refused to share these things with me. As for Cleindori . . . how can I look down on her? She did only what I have done; and now I know why." Her smile made Kerwin feel that his heart would break. "Don't you know that *Elorie of Arilinn* will be written beside Ysabet of Dalereuth and Dorilys of Arilinn as renegade Keepers, who fled without giving back their oath or asking leave?" He had forgotten that Cleindori had been only his mother's nickname, not her real name; at Arilinn she was written as *Dorilys*.

He sat down close beside her, then, and told her everything; all that had happened since his first moment on Darkover, when he had encountered Ragan and learned what his matrix was, the frustration of his first visit to the orphanage, the matrix mechanics who had refused to help him and the old woman who had died trying to help; and then all the rest, including what Harley had told him.

"And time's running out," he concluded. "I ought to face facts; it's not likely that I'll ever find out any more. As soon as the report I put in at the spaceport HQ goes through, I'll probably have to face charges and perhaps a civil inquiry. But there it is; the story of my life, for what it's worth, Elorie. You've married a man without a country, darling."

As if in answer, the communicator in the corner of the room sounded and when he picked it up, a metallic mechanical voice said, "Jefferson Andrew Kerwin?"

"Speaking."

"Coordination and Personnel," said the mechanical recorded voice. "We are informed that you are within the Terran Zone, where a civil charge has been placed against you of unlawful flight to avoid deportation. You are hereby notified that the City Council of Thendara, acting in the name and with the authority of Comyn Council on a warrant signed by Danvan, Lord Hastur, Regent for Derek of Elhalyn, has declared you persona non grata. You are officially forbidden to leave the Terran Zone; and since proceedings have been instituted to declare your wife, Elorie Ardais Kerwin, a citizen of the Empire, this prohibition applies also to Mrs. Kerwin. This is an official order; you are forbidden to travel more than two Universal Kilometers from your present accommodations, or to leave them for more than two hours; and within fifty-two hours you are ordered to surrender yourself to the appropriate authorities, which may be accomplished by presenting yourself, with identification, to any member of Spaceforce in uniform, or to any employee of Coordination and Personnel. Do you understand the communication? Please acknowledge."

Jeff muttered, "Damn!"

The mechanical voice repeated patiently, "Please acknowledge," and waited.

Elorie whispered, "Do your Terran officials all talk like that?"

"Please acknowledge," the mechanical voice repeated a

third time, and Jeff muttered, "Acknowledged." Turning
from the communicator, he murmured, "Do we want to fight
this, darling?"

"Jeff, how would I know? I'll abide by your decision. Do
what you think best, love."

The mechanical voice was proceeding steadily. "Kindly
indicate whether you will accept the summons and surrender
within the time indicated, or whether you elect to file a legal
request for an appeal."

Jeff's mind was racing. It went against the grain to accept
the deportation order calmly. An appeal would give him a
tenday's automatic delay, and perhaps in that time he might
discover something further. He was resigned to leaving
Darkover; but if he acted as if he might make trouble, they
might offer him a better post when he was finally forced to
transfer.

"I request an appeal," he said at last, and the silence from
the communicator made him think of computers racing, se-
lecting the appropriate loop for communicating further.

"Kindly indicate the nature of your appeal and the legal
grounds on which you attempt to file the appeal," the voice
said, and Kerwin thought quickly. He was not a legal expert.
"I claim Darkovan citizenship," he said at last, "and I appeal
their right to declare me *persona non grata*."

It probably wouldn't do any good, he thought while the
communicator's patient taped voice repeated his words. But
he wasn't sure whether this was the old declaration of *persona non grata* after which he had fled from the HQ, or a
new one, filed against him since he had left Arilinn. He
didn't think the Arilinn Tower could have reached Hastur
yet and persuaded him to issue a new order so quickly. Anyhow, this would gain time. But if they had, not a soul on
Darkover would stand between him and legal deportation.

Kennard might help . . . if he could reach Kennard. But
Kennard was in Arilinn, a long way from here. And however

he might sympathize with them, he was bound by his oath to Arilinn.

And none of the questions would ever be answered. He would never know who Cleindori had been, or why she had died, or why she had left Arilinn. H would never know the secrets of his own childhood.

Elorie rose and came to him. She said, "I could—perhaps—get through the barrier in your memory with this, Jeff. Kennard said you had a fantastic degree of barrier; that was why he didn't spot the block in your mind at first. Only—Jeff, why do you want to know? We're done with the Comyn, and probably leaving Darkover forever. What does it matter, then? The past is past."

For a moment he was not sure how to answer. Then he said, "Elorie, all my life I've had this—this fantastic compulsion to get back to Darkover. It was an obsession, a hunger; I could have made a life for myself on other worlds, but Darkover was always at the back of my mind. Calling me. Now I begin to wonder if it was really me—or if the pushing-around really started way back during the time I can't remember anything."

He did not go on, but he knew Elorie followed his thoughts. If his hunger for Darkover was not real, but a compulsion implanted from outside, then what was he? A hollow man, a tool, a mindless booby trap, a programmed thing no more real than the mechanical taped voice of the communicator. What was reality? Who and what was he?

She nodded gravely, understanding. "I'll try, then," she promised. "Later. Not now. I'm still tired from the illusion. And—" she smiled faintly—"hungry. Can we get anything to eat in this hotel or near it, Jeff?"

Remembering the dreadful drain of matrix work, he took her to one of the spaceport cafés, where she ate one of her enormous meals. They walked about the Terran Zone for a little, and Jeff made a gesture at showing her some of the sights of the Zone, but he knew that she cared no more than he did.

Neither of them spoke of Arilinn, but Jeff knew that her thoughts, like his, kept returning there. What would this failure mean to Darkover, to the Comyn?

They had located and clarified the mineral deposits in the contract; but the actual work of mining was still to be done, the major operation of lifting them to the surface of the planet.

Elorie said once, as if at random, "They can work it with a mechanic's circle. Rannirl can do most of the work with the energons. Any halfway good technician can do most of a Keeper's work. They don't need me." And at another time, apropos of nothing at all, she said, "They still have all the molecular models we made, and the lattice is still workable. They ought to be able to handle it."

Jeff pulled her to him. "Regretting?"

"Never." Her eyes met his honestly. "But—oh, wishing it could have happened another way."

He had destroyed them. He had come back to the world he loved, and he had destroyed its last chance to remain as it was.

Later, when she took the matrix between her hands, he was filled with sudden misgiving. He recalled the matrix mechanic who had died in trying to read his memory. "Elorie, I'd rather never know, than risk harming you!"

She shook her head. "I was trained at Arilinn; I risk nothing," she said with unconscious arrogance. She cupped the matrix between her two hands, brightening the moving points of light. Her ruddy hair fell like a soft curtain along either cheek.

Kerwin was feeling frightened. The breaking of a telepathic barrier—he remembered Kennard's attempt—was not an easy process, and the first attempt had been painful.

The light in the crystal brightened, seemed to pour in a

thick flood over Elorie's face. Kerwin shaded his eyes from the light, but he was caught in the brilliant, reflecting patterns. And suddenly, as if printed plain before his eyes, the light thickened and darkened into moving shadows that suddenly cleared into color and form. . . .

Two men and two woman, all of them in Darkovan clothing, seated around a table. One of the women, very frail, very fair, bending over a matrix . . . *he had seen this before!* He froze, terror clawing at him, as the door opened, slowly slowly . . . on horror . . .

He heard his own cry, shrill and terrified, the shriek of a frightened child from the full throat of a man, just in the moment before the world blurred and went dark.

. . . He was standing, swaying, both hands gripping at his temples. Elorie, very white, was staring up at him, the crystal fallen into the lap of her skirt.

"Jeff, what did you see?" she whispered. "Avarra and Evanda guard you, I never dreamed of such a shock!" She breathed deeply. "I know now why the woman died! She . . ." Elorie swayed suddenly, fell back against the wall. Jeff moved to steady her, but she went on, not noticing. "Whatever she saw—and I'm not an empath, but whatever it was that struck you dumb as a child, that poor woman evidently caught the full backlash of it. If she had a weak heart, it probably stopped, literally frightened to death by something you saw more than a quarter of a century ago!"

Jeff took her hands. He said, "Let's forget it. It's too dangerous, Elorie, it's killed one woman already. I can live without knowing whatever it is."

"No," she said. "I think we have to know. There have been too many mysteries. No one knows how Cleindori died, and Kennard knows but has been sworn not to tell. I don't think he killed her," she went on, and Kerwin stared at her in shock; *that* had never occurred to him.

"No. I'd stake my life on Kennard's honesty." And, Kerwin thought, his very genuine affection for them both.

"I'm a trained Keeper, Jeff, there's no danger for me. And I'm as eager to know as you are. But wait, give me *your* matrix," she added. "It was Cleindori's. And let's start with something else. You said that you had only a very few memories before the orphanage; let's try and go back to them."

She looked into Kerwin's matrix; as always when it was in a Keeper's hands, Jeff felt only the faint threading of Elorie's consciousness through his own. He shut his eyes, remembering.

The light in the matrix brightened. There were colors, swirls like mist; there was a blue beacon shining somewhere, a low building gleaming white on the shores of a strange lake that was not water, a ghost of perfume; a low and musical voice singing an old song, and Kerwin knew, with a thrill of excitement, that the voice was the voice of his mother, Cleindori, Dorilys of Arilinn, renegade Keeper, singing a lullaby to the child who should never have been born.

Wrapped in a cloak of fur, he was carried through long corridors in the arms of a man with blazing red hair. It was not the face of Jefferson Kerwin, familiar to him from pictures on Terra; but Kerwin knew, in the strange alienated corner of his mind that was his adult self, that he looked on the face of his father. *But whose son am I, then?* He saw, briefly and in a glimpse, the face of Kennard, younger, unlined, a gay and light-hearted face. Other pictures came and went; he saw himself playing games in a tiled courtyard among flowering plants and bushes, with two smaller children, as alike as twins, except that one had the red hair of their caste, like his own, and the other was small and dark and swarthy. And there was a big burly man in strange dark clothing, who spoke to them in a strangely accented voice, and treated them all with rough kindness, and the twins called him father, and Jeff called him by a word very like it, which meant, in the mountain tongue, foster-father or Uncle; as he called Kennard; and the grown-up Jeff Kerwin felt the hair rising on his head as he knew that he looked on the face of the man whose name he bore; he was not like his pictures in the household of his grandparents, but this was the elder Jeff Kerwin. More hazy were the memories of the fair-haired woman, more blonde than copper-haired, and of another woman whose hair was dark with red glints in the sunlight, and of the hills behind the castle, sharp-toothed mountains, and an old high tower . . .

But that is Castle Ardais, that is my home . . . How did you come to be there, Jeff? Kennard and my half-brother Dyan were bredin, *they were much together in childhood. . . . And you were brought up in the Hellers, then? And that is the wall of Castle Storn. . . .*

How did you come to be reared in the Hellers, beyond the Seven Domains, then? Did Cleindori take refuge there, then, when she fled the Tower? What does my brother Dyan know of this, I wonder? Or was it only that my father was mad, and could not betray them all?

The memories moved on. Kerwin realized that his breath choked in his throat, that he was approaching the point of peril; he felt his own blood pounding in his ears. Suddenly there was a blaze of blue light, and a woman stood before him; a tall woman, slender and youthful, but no longer young; and he knew he looked on his mother. Why had he never been able to remember her face before this moment? She was wearing a curiously-cut crimson robe, the robe Elorie had cast aside forever, the ceremonial robe of a Keeper of Arilinn; but even as he looked on her it shredded and disappeared, to leave her standing before him in the old, workaday tartan skirt and white embroidered tunic embroidered in a pattern of butterflies that she wore every day; he could remember the very texture of the cloth.

Why did not Elorie see her? "Mother," he said in a whisper, "I thought you were dead." And he knew his voice as a child's voice. And then he knew she was not there, that it was her image he saw; the image of a woman many, many years dead; and he felt the tears coming into his throat and choking him, tears he knew he had never been able to shed before.

My mother. And she died, horribly, murdered by fanatics. . . .

But he heard her voice, distracted, desperate, sorrowing.

How can I do this to my child? My son, my little one, he is too young to bear such a weight, too young for the matrix, and yet . . . twice now I have so narrowly escaped death, and soon or late, they will have me and kill me, those fanatics who believe a Keeper's virginity is more important than her powers! Even when I have shown them what I can do. . . .

And another voice, a man's voice deep and gentle, sounded in his mind: *Did you expect anything else of Arilinn, my Cleindori?* And somehow through his mother's memory and perceptions, Kerwin saw, as a child and as a man, with a strange double vision, the face of the speaker—an old man, stooped with age, with a remote, scholarly face, his hair silver-grey, his eyes remarkably kind—but bitter. *They cast Callista forth, though I showed them what you tried to show them.*

Father, are all the folk of Arilinn such fools? It was a cry of despair. *Look, here is my son, your namesake, Damon Aillard; and they will not stop at killing me, and Lewis, and Cassilde; they will kill Jeff and Andres and Kennard and all the rest of us, down to Cassilde's little boys and the daughter she will bear to Jeff this summer! Father, father, what can I do? Have I brought death upon them all? I never meant any harm, I would have given them new laws, I would have cast down the cruel old laws of Arilinn, so that the women there might live in happiness, that the men and women of Arilinn might not give themselves up to a living death; and they would not listen, even though the Keeper of*

*Arilinn spoke! The Law of Arilinn is that the Keeper's word
is law; and yet when I would have given them this new dis-
pensation, they would not hear me, and persecuted me, and
Lewis, until we fled. . . . Father, father, how could I have
been so wrong? And now they have killed my son's father
and I know they will not stop until they have killed every last
child of the Forbidden Tower! Is there no way I can save
them?*

Kerwin shared, for a searing moment, the thoughts of
Damon Ridenow; all of them, everyone who had worked
within the walls of what they still called, defiantly, the Forbidden Tower, had drawn a death sentence, which sooner or
later would fall upon them all.

He felt the despair with which Damon spoke.

*There is no way to use reason with fanatics, Cleindori.
Reason and justice tell you that a Keeper is responsible to
her own conscience; but they are immune to reason and justice. You are not the matrix worker; it is not as a matrix
worker that they want you in Arilinn for Keeper, but what
they want in Arilinn is a sacred virgin, a sacrifice to their
own guilts and fears. I do not think the forces of reason have
any weight against fanatics and blind superstition, Cleindori.*

Father, you reared me to believe in reason!

I was wrong. Oh, my darling, I was wrong.

And then he heard the resolution.

*I could hide here forever, and be safe, or hide among
the Terrans. But if I must die, and I know now that soon or
late I must die, I will go to Thendara, and I will teach others the work I have learned can be done. You have taught
many matrix workers. I will teach others. They can kill me,
then, but they cannot forever hide what I have learned, and
what I have taught. There will be matrix workers outside the
Tower; and when the Arilinn Tower comes crashing down in
the ruins of its hatred and the living death of the souls of the
men and women who live there, blind to justice and right*

and truth, then there will be others, so that the old matrix sciences of Darkover will never die. Bid me farewell, Father, and bless my son. For I know now that we will never meet again.

They will kill you, Cleindori. Oh, my daughter, my golden bell, must I lose you too?

Soon or late, all men and women born of this earth must die. Bless me, father, and bless my son.

Kerwin, through his strange divided double consciousness, felt Damon's hand on his head. *Take my blessing, darling. And you, too, little one in whom my own name and my own childhood are reborn.* And then consciousness was swamped in the awareness of anguish, as father and daughter parted for the last time.

Kerwin, caught up in the memory, knew that tears were flooding down his face; but he was caught up in the matrix, caught up in the memory Cleindori had imprinted into her child; unwilling, for he was too young, but still knowing that some record must be kept, lest the knowledge of her death be forever hidden. . . .

Time had come and gone; he did not know how many days and nights she had lived in the hidden room, how many people had come and gone secretly to the house in Thendara where the work of teaching went on, led by Cleindori and the gentle woman he called foster-mother, whose name was Cassilde, the mother of Auster and Ragan, who were his playmates. She was, he knew vaguely as a child knows, soon to give them all a little sister. Already they called the unborn child Dorilys, which he knew was his own mother's name, for Cassilde said that was a fine name for a rebel. "And may she raise a storm over the Hellers as her namesake did in years gone by! For she will one day be our Keeper," Cassilde had promised. They had to play quietly, for no one must know that folk lived there, his mother said; and Jeff and Andres, coming and going from the spaceport, brought them food and clothing and whatever else they needed. Once he had asked why his foster-father Kennard was not with them.

"Because there are too many who could find him, Damon; he is trying to gain amnesty for us in Council, but it is long work, and he has not the ear of Hastur," his mother had replied, and he did not know what an amnesty was, but he knew it was very important, for his foster-father Arnad talked of nothing else. He never asked about his father; he knew vaguely that his father had gone away to fight, and that he would not come back. Valdir, Lord Alton, and Damon Ridenow, the old Regent of Alton, were fighting with the Council, and Jeff's child-mind wondered if they were fighting duels with swords and knives in the Council room and how many people they would have to fight before he and his mother and all of them could all go home again.

And then . . .

Jeff felt his heart pounding, the breath coming hard in his veins, and knew that the hour he could never remember, the terror that had blotted out mind and memory, was upon him, and suddenly, fighting the memory in terror, feeling Elorie's relentless will driving through the matrix, he *was* his own childish self, he was five years old, playing on the rug in the small, dark, cramped room, a little toy spaceship in his hands. . . .

. . . The tall man in Terran clothing stood up, letting the toy ship fall from his hands. The three of them began to squabble over it, but Jeff Kerwin silenced them with a gesture.

"Boys, boys—hush, hush, you must not make so much noise . . . You know better than that," he admonished in a whisper.

"It is hard to keep them so quiet," Cassilde said in a low voice. She was heavy, now, and clumsy, and Jeff Kerwin went and put her into a chair before he said, "I know. They ought not to be here; we should send them to safety."

"There is no safety for them!" Cassilde said, and sighed.

The twins were playing, now, with the toy ship, but the child Damon, who was one day to be called Jeff Kerwin, knelt a little apart from them, his eyes fixed on his mother, standing behind the matrix in its cradle.

"Cleindori, I have told you what you should do," Kerwin said, and there was tenderness in his eyes. "I have offered to find safety for all of you with the Empire. You need not tell them more than you think they should know; but even for that much they will be more than grateful; they will send you and the children to safety on any world you choose."

"Am I to go into exile because fools and fanatics yell and shout slogans in the streets of Thendara?"

Cassilde said, cradling her hands over her pregnant body as if to protect the child that sheltered there, "Fools and fanatics can be more dangerous than the wise men. I am not afraid of Hastur, nor of the Council. And the people of Arilinn itself—they may despise us, but they will not harm us; no more than Leonie harmed Damon, after the duel that won him the right to keep the Forbidden Tower. But I am afraid of the fanatics, the conservatives who want everything, including Arilinn and Hali, to go as they were in the times of our grandsires. I cannot go to Terra, not until after my child is born; and the children are too young for star-travel. But I think you should go, Cleindori. Leave your child in the care of the Terrans, and go. I will ask shelter of the Council; and I am sure they will have me at Neskaya."

"Oh, Evanda and Avarra guard you," Cleindori said despairingly, looking at her half-sister. "I endanger you simply by remaining, do I not? You are not a Keeper, Cassie, and you can go where you will and live as you will, but it is I, I that am the renegade and under sentence of death, from the moment I stood before them and proclaimed that I had made fools of them all, that Lewis and I had been lovers for more than a year and yet I continued to work as Keeper in their precious Arilinn! Lewis—" her voice broke.

"I loved him . . . and he died for my love! Kennard should hate me for it. And yet he continues to fight for me in the Council—"

Jeff said cynically, "The death of Lewis Lanart-Alton has made Kennard Heir to Alton, Cleindori."

"And yet you want me to beg for the protection of the Council, from Lord Hastur who has called me abominable things? Yet I will do it if you all ask me. Jeff? Cassie? Arnad?"

The tall man in the green-and-golden cloak came up behind Cleindori and put his arms around her, laughing. He said, "If any of us had any such thoughts we would be ashamed to show it before you, Golden Bell! But I think we must be realistic."

"Believe me," the Terran said, "I would rather defy them all, at least until the Council has made its decision. But I think Cassilde should go to Neskaya, or at least to Comyn Castle, until her child is born; no assassin can touch her there. The Council may disapprove of her, but they will protect her physically; she is under no sentence of death."

"Except," Cassilde said, "that I have borne children to the despised Terrans." Her mouth was wry.

Arnad said, "You are not the first; nor will you be the last. There have been intermarriages enough. No one, I think, cares, except the fanatics. And you, Cleindori, must go; leave your child with the Terrans, who will protect him— even in Comyn Castle, the child of a forsworn Keeper will not be safe from an assassin's knife, but the Terrans will protect him."

Cleindori's mouth quirked up in a smile. "And what would induce the Terrans to give refuge to the child of a renegade Keeper and the late Heir to Alton? What is he to them?"

"How are they to know he is not *my* son?" Kerwin asked. "The Terrans have none of your elaborate monitoring methods; the child calls me *foster-father*, and there are not enough language experts on Darkover to know the difference between the words. I am legally entitled to have my son reared in the Spacemen's Orphanage; even if I thought my child's mother unfit to rear him as befits the son of a Terran, they would accept him there." He came and touched Cleindori's shoulder, a gesture of great tenderness. "I beg you, *breda*; let me do this, and send you to Terra for a year or two on another world, until this fanaticism dies down, and then you can come back and teach, openly, what you teach secretly now. Already, Valdir and Damon managed to persuade the City Elders to license matrix mechanics as a profession; and they are working in Thendara and Neskaya, and one day they will work in Arilinn too. The Council does not like it, but how runs the proverb . . . *the will of Hastur is the will of Hastur, but it is not the law of the land.* Let me do this for you, *breda*. Let me send you to Terra."

Cleindori lowered her head. "As you will, if you all think it best. You will go to Neskaya, then, Cassie? What of you, Arnad?"

"I'm tempted to go with you to Terra," the red-haired man in green and gold said defiantly, "but if you're going under Jeff's protection, it wouldn't be wise; I suppose he'll have to call you his wife?"

Cleindori shrugged. "What do I care what it says on the Terran records? They live in computers and believe that because their record says a thing it is true; what do I care?"

"I'll go now, to make the arrangements," Jeff said, "but are you all safe here? I'm not sure . . ."

Arnad said, with an arrogant gesture, dropping his hand to his sword, "I have this; I'll protect them!"

Time seemed to spin out and drag endlessly when he had gone. Cassilde put the twins to bed behind a curtained alcove; Arnad paced the floor restlessly, his hand straying now and then to his sword hilt. The child Damon knelt forgotten on the rug, motionless, waiting, filled with the apprehension of the adults around him. At last Cleindori said, "Jeff should be back by now—"

"Hush," Cassilde said urgently. "Did you hear—quiet; there is someone in the street?"

"I heard nothing," Cleindori said impatiently. "But I am afraid of what has happened to Jeff! Help me, Arnad."

She drew the matrix from her breast and laid it on the table. The child tiptoed closer, staring in fascination. His mother had made him look into it so often, lately; she didn't know why, and Arnad said he was too young, that it could hurt him, but he knew that for some reason his mother wanted him able to handle and touch the matrix that no one else, not even his father, could ever touch, or any of his foster-fathers.

He moved closer, now, to the center of the glowing circle, reflected on the faces bending over the matrix; some slight sound distracted him; he turned to look, in growing terror, at the turning handle of the door. . . .

He shrieked and Arnad turned a moment too late; the door burst open and the room was full of hooded and masked forms; a deadly, thrown knife took him in the back and he fell with a gurgling cry. He heard Cassilde scream aloud and saw her fall. Cleindori bent and snatched up Arnad's knife, fighting and struggling with one of the masked men. The child ran, shrieking, struggling, pounding at the dark forms with small fists; biting, kicking, clawing like a small, enraged wild animal. Scratching and kicking, he ran right up the back of one of the men, sobbing wild threats.

"You let my mother alone—! Let her go, fight like a man, you coward—"

Cleindori shrieked and burst away from the man who held her. She caught up Damon to her breast, holding him tight, and he felt her terror like a physical agony reflected in a great blue glow like the glow of the matrix. . . . *There was one instant of blinding, blazing rapport, and the child knew,*

*in agony, exactly what they had done, knew every instant of
Cleindori's life, as her whole life flashed before her eyes. . . .*

The rough hands seized him; he was flung through the air
and struck his head, hard, on the stone flooring. Pain exploded in him and he lay still, hearing a voice crying out as
he went down into darkness:

*"Say to the barbarian that he shall come no more to the
plains of Arilinn! The Forbidden Tower is broken, and the
last of its children lie dead, even to the unborn, and so shall
we deal with all renegades until the last days!"*

Unbelievable, unbearable agony thrust a knife into his
heart; then, mercifully, the rapport burned out, and the room
went dark, and the world vanished into darkness. . . .

There was a pounding at the door. The child who lay unconscious on the floor stirred and moaned, probing, wondering if it was his foster-father, but felt only strangeness,
seeing only darkness and strange men bursting again into
the room. *They came back to kill me!* Memory flooded over
him like a trapped rabbit and he clutched his small fingers
over his mouth, squirming painfully under the table and
cowering there. The pounding on the door increased; it
broke open, and the terrified child, cowering under the table,
heard heavy boots on the floor and felt shock in the minds
of the men who stood holding a lamp high and looking at the
carnage in the room.

"Avarra be merciful," a man's voice muttered, "we were
too late, after all. Those murdering fanatics!"

"I told you we should have appealed directly to Lord
Hastur before this, Cadet Ardais," said another voice,
vaguely familiar to the child under the table, but he was
afraid to move or cry out. "I was afraid it would come to
this! Naotalba twist my feet, but I never guessed it would be
murder!" A fist struck the table in impotent wrath.

"I should have known," the first voice said, a harsh,
somehow musical voice, "when we heard that old Lord

Damon was dead, and Dom Ann'dra, and the rest. A fire, they said . . . I wonder whose hand set that fire?" Before the despairing wrath in that voice the concealed child cowered, clasped his fingers harder over his mouth to stifle his cries.

"Lord Arnad," the voice said, "and the lady Cassilde, and she so heavy with child that you would think even one of those murdering fanatics would have had pity on her! And—" his voice fell—"my kinswoman Cleindori. Well, I knew she was under sentence of death, even from Arilinn; but I had hoped the Hasturs would protect her." A long, deep sigh. The child heard him moving around, heard the curtain drawn from the alcove. "In Zandru's name—children!"

"But where's the Terran?" one of the men asked. "Dragged away alive for torture, most likely. Those must be Cassilde's children by Arnad; look, one of them has red hair. At least those fanatic bastards had decency enough not to harm the poor brats."

"Most likely, they didn't see them," retorted the first man. "And if they find out they left them alive—well, you know what will happen as well as I do, Lord Dyan."

"You're right—the more shame to us all," said the man he had called Lord Dyan, frowning. "Gods! If we could only reach Kennard! But he isn't even in the city, is he?"

"No, he went to appeal to Hali," the first man said, and there was a long silence. Finally Lord Dyan said, "Kennard has a town house here in Thendara. If the Lady Caitlin is there—would she shelter them until Kennard returns and can appeal to Hastur on their behalf? You're Kennard's sworn man; you know the Lady Caitlin better than I do, Andres."

"I wouldn't ask any favors of the Lady Caitlin, Lord Dyan," Andres said slowly. "She grows more bitter as the years go by and she is more certain of her barrenness; she knows well that Kennard must one day put her aside and father sons somewhere, and any child we asked her to shelter for Kennard's sake—well, she would certainly think them bastards of Kennard's fathering, and lift no one of her fingers to protect them. Besides, if assassins broke into Kennard's town house, they might well slaughter the Lady Caitlin too—"

"Which would be no grief to Kennard, I think," said Lord Dyan, but Andres drew a breath of horror.

"Still, as Kennard's sworn man, Lord Dyan, I am pledged to safeguard her too; he may not love his wife, but he honors her as he must by law; and I dare not endanger her by the presence of these children. No, by your leave, Lord Dyan, I will take them to the Terrans and find shelter for them there. Then, when the memory of these riots has died down, Kennard can appeal to Hastur for amnesty for them. . . ."

"Quick," said Lord Dyan. "Someone's coming. Bring the children and keep them quiet. Here, wrap the little one in this blanket—there, now, little copper-hair, keep still." Damon crept to the edge of the table, hiding in shadow, and saw the two men, one in Terran clothing, the other in the green-and-black uniform of the City Guard, wrapping his playmates in blankets and carrying them away. The room went dark around him. . . .

Then there was a terrible cry of anguish and Jeff Kerwin stood in the room. He was swaying on his feet; his clothes were torn and cut, his face covered in blood. The child hiding under the table felt something break inside him, some terrible pain, he wanted to scream and scream, but he could only gasp, he thrust aside the tablecloth, staggered out into the room, and heard Kerwin's cry of dismay as he was caught up into his foster-father's strong arms.

He was wrapped warmly in a blanket; snow was falling on his face. He was wet through and in pain, and he could feel the pain of his foster-father's broken nose. He tried to speak and he could not make his voice obey him. After a long time of cold and jolting pain he was in a warm room

and gentle hands were spooning warm milk into his mouth.
He opened his eyes and whimpered, looking into his foster-
father's face.

"There, there, little one," said the woman who was
feeding him. "Another spoonful, now, just a little one,
there's my brave fellow—I don't think it's a skull fracture,
Jeff; there's no bleeding within the skull; I monitored him.
He's just bruised and battered, those lunatics must have
thought him dead! Murdering devils, to try and kill a child
of five!"

"They killed my little ones, and dragged their bodies
away somewhere, probably flung them in the river," said his
foster-father, and his eyes were terrible. "They'd have killed
this one too, Magda, only they must have thought he was
dead already. They killed Cassilde, and her unborn babe
with her . . . fiends, fiends!"

The woman asked gently, "Did you see your mother die,
Damon?" But although he knew she was speaking to him, he
could not speak; he struggled to speak, in terror, but not a
single word would come through the fear and dread. It felt
as if a tight fist was holding his throat.

"Frightened out of his wits, I shouldn't wonder, if he saw
them all die," Kerwin said bitterly. "God knows if he'll ever
have all his wits again! He hasn't spoken a word, and he wet
and soiled himself, big boy that he is, when I found him. My
children dead, and Cleindori's son an idiot, and this is the
harvest we reap for seven years' work!"

"It may not be as bad as that," the woman Magda said
gently. "What will you do now, Jeff?"

"God knows. I wanted to keep away from the Terran authorities until we could make our own terms—Kennard and
Andres and young Montray and I. You know what we were
working for—to carry on what Damon and the rest had
started."

"I know." The woman cradled him in her lap. "Little
Damon here is all that's left of it; Cleindori's mother and I

were *bredini*, sworn sister, when we were girls . . . and now they are all gone. Why should I stay here?" Her eyes were bitter. "I know you tried, Jeff. I tried, too, to help Cleindori, but she wouldn't come to me. But she had agreed to go off-world—"

"And it was just a day too late," Kerwin said bitterly. "If only I had persuaded her a single day sooner!"

"There is no use in regretting," Magda said. "I would keep the child myself; but I could be transferred away from Darkover at any moment, and he is too young to travel on the Big Ships, even if drugged—"

"I'll take him to the Spacemen's Orphanage," Kerwin said. "I owe that to Cleindori, at least. And when I can manage to find Kennard—I think Andres is in the city, somewhere, I'll look for him and find out from him where Kennard has gone—then, perhaps, something can be done for him. But he will be safe with the Terrans."

The woman nodded, gently smoothed down Damon's aching head, drawing him against her for a final caress. Her hand tangled in the chain about his neck and she gave a cry of consternation.

"The matrix! Cleindori's matrix! Why didn't it die when she died, Jeff?"

"I don't know," Kerwin said. "But it was still alive. And though the boy didn't speak, he knew enough to grab for it. My guess is that she had let him play with it, touch it; it had keyed roughly into his consciousness and if he felt her die, through the matrix—well, it would account for the kid's state," he said bitterly. "It's safe enough where it is, round the neck of an idiot child. They won't be able to get it away without killing him. But they'll be kind to him. Maybe they can teach him something, sooner or later."

And then he was cold again, and he was held in his foster-father's arms, each step jolting his broken ribs, as he was carried through heavy rain and blowing sleet through the streets of Thendara. . . .

And then he was gone, he was nowhere, nothing. . . .

He was standing, white and shaken, tears on his face, in his room in the hotel in Thendara, still shaking with a child's terror. Elorie was staring up at him. She was crying, too. Jeff struggled to speak, but his voice would not obey him. Of course not, he could not speak a word . . . *he would never speak again.* . . .

"Jeff," Elorie said quickly. "You are here. Jeff—Jeff, come up to present time! *Come up to present time!* That was twenty-five years ago!"

Jeff put a hand to his throat. His voice was thick, but he could speak. "So that was it," he whispered. "I saw them all killed. Murdered. And—and I am not Jeff Kerwin. My name is Damon, and Kerwin was not my father; he was my father's friend. He befriended their child . . . but I am not Jeff Kerwin. *I'm not a Terran at all!*"

"No," Elorie said in a whisper. "Your father was Kennard's elder brother! By right you, not Kennard, are Heir to Alton—*and Kennard knows it!* You could displace Kennard's half-caste sons. Was that why he didn't speak up for you, at the last? He loves you. But he loves the sons of his second wife, his Terran wife, more than anything in the world. More than Arilinn. More, I think, than his own honor. . . ."

Jeff gave a short, hard laugh. "I'm a bastard," he said, "and the son of a renegade Keeper. I doubt if they'd want me as Heir to Alton, or anything else. Kennard can stop worrying. If he ever did."

"And then the final complication in this farrago of mistaken identity," Elorie said. "Cassilde's children were taken to the Spacemen's Orphanage—I know Kennard's man, Andres. But Lord Dyan—he is my half-brother, Jeff. I didn't know he knew Auster at all. But he must have known, and that is why he insisted on getting Auster from the orphanage; he must have thought he was Cassilde's child by Arnad Ridenow, because of his red hair."

"God, help us all," Jeff said. "No wonder Auster thought he recognized Ragan! They're twin brothers! They don't look all that much alike, but they are twins—"

"And the Terrans used Ragan to spy upon the Comyn," Elorie said. "For the telepath bond between the twin-born is the strongest known! It was Auster, not you, who was the time-bomb planted by the Terrans! They knew about the telepath link between twins. So they let them have Auster back—and kept Ragan, linked to him in mind, to spy on Auster. Even after he went to Arilinn!"

"And Jeff Kerwin took me to the Spacemen's Orphanage, and registered me there as his son," Jeff said. "And then— God knows; he must have been killed, too."

"Strange," Elorie said, "and sad, that when children were in danger, both factions should have realized that they'd be safer with the Terrans. Our laws of blood-feud are relentless; and the fanatics felt they must exterminate the Forbidden Tower even to the unborn children and the babies."

"I lived on Terra," Jeff said. "Most of them are good people. And it's true that they're a little less likely to drag children into adult affairs, or blame the sins of the fathers on the heads of the children."

He fell silent. Always, the knowledge that he was a Terran, an exile, had become part of his existence. And now, legally, he *was Terran;* and under sentence of deportation by the Terran Empire!"

"But I'm not Terran," he said. "I'm no relation to Jeff Kerwin, I haven't any Terran blood at all. My name isn't even Kerwin; it's—what would it be?"

"Damon," she said. "Damon Aillard, since the child takes the name of the parent of higher rank, and the Aillard rank higher in the Comyn than the Altons' just as our children, if we ever had any, would be Ardais instead of Aillard. . . .

Only if you married a Ridenow, or a commoner, would your children be Altons. But by Terran custom, you'd call yourself Damon Lanart-Alton, wouldn't you? They take the father's name, and you were brought up to that."

Her face suddenly whitened. "Jeff! We have to warn them at Arilinn!"

"I don't understand, Elorie."

"They may try the mining operation—though I think they'd be mad to try it without a Keeper—and Auster is still in mental link with Ragan, the spy—and doesn't know it!"

Cold struck at Jeff's heart. But he said, "My love, how can we warn them? Even if we owed them anything—and they cast us out, calling you filthy names—that's there, and we're *here*. Even if we could get out of the Terran Zone— and I'm under house arrest, remember—I doubt if we could *reach* Arilinn. Except, perhaps, telepathically; you can try that, if you want to."

She shook her head. "Reach Arilinn from Thendara, unaided? Not without one of the special relay screens," she said. "Not with my matrix alone. Not—" she hesitated, colored, and said—"not now. At one time—as Keeper of Arilinn—I might have done so. But not now."

"Then don't worry about them! Let them take their own risks!"

Elorie shook her head.

"Arilinn trained me; Arilinn made me what I am; I cannot stop caring what will happen to my circle," she said. "And there is a relay screen in Comyn Castle in Thendara. I could reach them through *that*."

"Fine," said Kerwin, with a sardonic smile. "I can just see it. You, the Keeper who was cast out of Arilinn, and I, the Terran under sentence of deportation, walking up to the Comyn Castle and asking politely for the use of the relay screen there."

Elorie bent her head. "Don't be cruel, Jeff," she said. "I know, well enough, that we are under the ban. But Council will not meet till summer. No one will be resident in Comyn Castle at this season except the Regent, Lord Hastur. Lady Cassilda was my mother's friend. And my half-brother, Lord Dyan, is an officer in the City Guard. I think—I think he will help me to gain audience with Lord Hastur."

"If he's that good a friend to Kennard," Jeff said, "he'd probably be glad to see me dead."

"He loves Kennard, yes. But he does not approve of his second marriage, nor of his Terran wife nor his half-Terran sons; and you are pure Darkovan," Elorie said. "Dyan wanted to serve at Arilinn; the Comyn means much to him. He would have gone there with Kennard when they were lads, I heard, but he was tested, and found—unsuitable. I think—I hope I can prevail upon him for audience with Hastur." She added, her mouth tight, "If all else fails I will appeal to Lord Alton; Valdir Alton loved his older son, too, and you are, after all, his elder son's only son."

Jeff still could not take it in. Lord Alton, the old man who had embraced him as a kinsman, was actually his grandfather.

But it went against the grain for Elorie to go begging on his account. "Arilinn has turned against us. Forget them, Elorie!"

"Oh, Jeff, no," she begged. "Do you want the Pan-Darkovan Syndicate to turn to Terra, and Darkover to become no more than a second-rate Terran colony?"

And that touched him. Darkover had been his home, even when he thought himself a son of Terra and a citizen of the Empire. Now he knew himself *really* Darkovan; he had not a scrap of legal right to call himself Terran. He was Comyn through and through, a true son of the Domains.

"Can't you see? Oh, I know failure is almost certain, especially if they try it with a mechanic's circle with Rannirl in charge, or if they're mad enough to try it with a half-trained Keeper," she said. "And I'm afraid that's what they'll do. They'll bring little Callina from Neskaya, and make *her* try to hold the matrix ring; and she's only twelve years old or so. I've spoken to her in the relays. She's gifted, but she's not Arilinn-trained, and Neskaya doesn't have the tradition of great Keepers anyway; the best ones were always from Arilinn. But," she added, "now that they know you're not Terran, *you* could go back, and the circle would be that much stronger!" Her face was pale and eager. "Oh, Jeff, it means so much to our world!"

"Darling," he said, wrung, "I'd try anything. I'd even go back into the matrix circle, if they'd have me; but that notice I got says we're prisoners! If we try to go more than a kilometer from the hotel, they'll arrest us. Just because we're not behind bars doesn't mean I'm not under arrest. I can appeal against the deportation, and if I can prove I'm not Kerwin's son by blood I may be able to stay here, but for the moment we're as much prisoners as if we were in the brig!"

"What right have they—" The arrogance of the princess, the sheltered, pampered, worshipped Lady of Arilinn, was in her voice now. She caught up her hooded cape—Jeff had bought it for her in Port Chicago to conceal her red hair, which marked her out as Comyn—and flung it over her shoulders. "If you will not come with me, Jeff, I will go alone!"

"Elorie—you're serious about this?" Her eyes answered for her, and he made up his mind. "Then I'll come with you."

In the streets of Thendara she moved so swiftly he could hardly keep up with her. It was late afternoon; the light lay blood-red along the streets and shadows crept, long and purple, between the houses. As they neared the edge of the Terran Zone, Kerwin wondered if this was insanity; they'd certainly be stopped at the gates. But Elorie moved so quickly that all he could do was to follow at her heels.

The great square was empty, and the gates of the Terran Zone were guarded desultorily by a single uniformed Space-force man. Across the square he could see little clusters of

Darkovan restaurants and shops, including the one where he had bought his cloak. As they approached the gate, the Spaceforce man barred their way briefly.

"Sorry. I have to see your identification."

Kerwin started to speak, but Elorie prevented him; swiftly she flung back the grey hood over her red hair, and the light of the Bloody Sun, setting, turned it to fire, as Elorie sent a high, clear cry ringing across the square.

And all through the square Darkovans turned round, startled and shocked at what Kerwin knew, somehow, was an ancient rallying-cry; someone shouted "Hai! A Comyn *vai leronis*, and in the hands of the Terrans!"

Elorie seized Jeff's arm; the guard stepped forward, threatening, but a crowd was already materialized, as if by magic, all through the square; the sheer weight of it rolled over the Terran guard—Jeff knew they had orders not to fire on unarmed people—and Elorie and Jeff were borne along on it, a way opening for them through the crowd, with deferential cries and murmurs following them. Breathless, startled, Jeff found himself in the mouth of a street opening on the square; Elorie caught his hand and dragged him away down the street, the sounds of riot dying away behind them.

"Quick, Jeff! This way or they'll be all around us wanting to know what it's all about!"

He was startled, and a little shocked. There could be repercussions; the Terrans would not be happy about a riot right on their doorstep. But, after all, no one had been hurt. He would trust Elorie, as she had trusted him with her life.

"Where are we going?"

She pointed. High above the city, Comyn Castle rose, vast, alien and indifferent. Except for a few of the highest dignitaries, no Terran had ever set foot there; and then only by invitation.

Only he wasn't a Terran, and he would have to remember it.

Funny. Ten days ago that would have made me very happy. Now I'm not so sure.

He followed her through the darkening streets, the steep climb to Comyn Castle, wondering what would happen when they got there, and if Elorie had any specific plan. The Castle looked both big and well-guarded, and he didn't suppose that two strangers could walk in and ask to speak to Lord Hastur without any formalities or so much as an appointment!

But he had reckoned without the enormous personal prestige of the Comyn themselves. There were guards, in the green and black of the Altons who had, so Kerwin had heard from Kennard, founded the Guard and commanded it from time out of mind. But at the sight of Elorie, even afoot and humbly clad, the Guard fell back in reverence.

"*Comynara*—" The guard looked at Jeff's red head, then at his Terran clothes, but decided to play it safe and amended, "*Vai Comynari*, you lend us grace. How may we best serve the *vai domna*?"

"Is Commander Alton within the castle?"

"I regret, *vai domna*, the Lord Valdir is away at Armida these ten days."

Elorie frowned, but hesitated only a moment. "Then say to Captain Ardais that his sister, Elorie of Arilinn, would speak with him at once."

"At once, *vai domna*." The guard still looked askance at Jeff's Terran clothes; but he did not question. He went.

CHAPTER SIXTEEN

The Broken Tower

It was not more than a few minutes before the guard came back; and with him was a tall, spare man in dark clothing—Kerwin supposed he was somewhere in his forties, though he looked younger—with a keen, hawklike face.

"Elorie, *chiya*," he said, lifting his eyebrows, and Kerwin flinched. He had heard before that harsh, musical, and melancholy voice; heard it as a frightened child, battered and left to die, crouching unseen under a table. But after all, Dyan Ardais had meant him no harm; would have certainly, if he had been appealed to, taken him under his protection as he had taken those other children, overlooked by the assassins. He knew Elorie's brother for a harsh man, but kindly, even soft-hearted toward young children, cruel as he could be to his peers.

"I heard you had fled from Arilinn," he said, looking at her humble garments and coarse cloak with distaste, "and with a Terran. Sorrow upon Arilinn, that twice within forty years this must happen to them. Is this the Terran?"

"He is no Terran, my brother," she said, "but the true son of Lewis-Arnad Lanart-Alton, elder son of Valdir, Lord Alton, by Cleindori; who laid down her office, though unpermitted, by the laws of Arilinn, to take a consort of her own rank and station; and this is her son. A Keeper, Dyan, is responsible only to her own conscience. Cleindori did only what the law would have permitted; she is not responsible for those who denied the right of the Lady of Arilinn to declare just laws for her circle."

He looked at her, frowning. His eyes, Kerwin thought, were colorless as cold metal, grey steel. He said, "Some of this I had from Kennard, who tried to tell me of Cleindori's innocence; though I called it folly. Lewis, too, was a foolish idealist. But he was Kennard's brother; and I owe to his son a kinsman's dues." His thin lips moved into a sarcastic grin. "So we have here a rabbithorn in the fur of a catman; Comyn in Terran garb, which is a change after the ranks of spies and imposters we have had to face from time to time. Well, what did they name you, then, Cleindori's son? Lewis, for your father, and with a better right to that name than Kennard's bastard?"

Kerwin had the uncomfortable feeling that Dyan was amused—no, that he took a positive pleasure—in his discomfiture. In years to come, knowing Dyan better, he knew that Dyan seldom missed an opportunity to twist a knife of malice. He said sharply, "I am not ashamed of bearing the name of my Terran foster-father; it would hardly be honorable to disown him at this stage of my life; but my mother called me Damon."

Dyan threw back his head and laughed, a long shrill laugh like the screaming of a falcon. "The name of one renegade for another! I had never suspected that Cleindori had such a sense of the right thing," he said, when he had done laughing. "Well, what do you want from me, Elorie? I don't suppose you want to take your husband—" actually the word he used was *freemate*; if he had shaded the word to make it mean *paramour*, Jeff would have struck him—"to our mad father at Ardais?"

"I need to see Lord Hastur, Dyan. You can arrange it, as *seconde* for Valdir!"

"In the name of all nine of Zandru's hells, Lori! Doesn't the Lord Danvan have enough troubles? Will you bring down the shadow of the Forbidden Tower on him again, after a quarter of a century?"

"I must see him," Elorie insisted, and her face crumpled. "Dyan, I beg you. You were always kind to me when I was a child; and my mother loved you. You saved me from Father's drunken friends. I swear to you—"

Dyan's mouth twisted and he said cruelly, "The standard oath is, Elorie, *I swear it by the virginity of the Keeper of Arilinn.* I doubt even you would have the insolence to take that oath now."

Elorie flared at him: "That is the kind of stupid madness and fanaticism that has kept the Keepers of Arilinn as ritual dolls, priestess, sorceresses. I thought better of you than to think you would throw it at me! Do you want the Tower of Arilinn to be the laughingstock of all our people, because they are more concerned with a Keeper's virginity than her powers as Keeper? You have a good mind, Dyan, and you are not a fool or a fanatic! Dyan, I beg of you," she said, her anger suddenly vanishing into seriousness. "I swear to you, by the memory of my mother, who loved you when you were a motherless boy, that I will not abuse the Lord Hastur's kindness, and that it is not a trivial or a frivolous request. Won't you take me to him?"

His face softened. "As you will, *breda,*" he said with unusual gentleness. "A Keeper of Arilinn is responsible only to her own conscience. I will show respect to yours until I learn otherwise, little sister. Come with me. Hastur is in his presence-chamber, and he should be finished now with the last delegation for today."

He led them into the Castle, through broad corridors and into a long pillared passageway; Jeff stiffened, shaking, again a child, carried through this long corridor. *One of the strange and colorful dreams that had haunted him in the Spacemen's Orphanage. . . .*

Dyan ushered them into a small anteroom; gestured to them to wait. After a little while he came back, saying,

"He'll see you. But Avarra protect you if you waste his time or try his patience, Lori, for I won't." He motioned them into a small presence-chamber, where Danvan Hastur sat on his high seat; bowed and went away.

Lord Hastur bowed to Elorie; his brows ridged briefly in displeasure as he saw Kerwin, but immediately the frown vanished; he was reserving judgment. He gave Kerwin the briefest possible polite nod of acknowledgment, and said, "Well, Elorie?"

"It is kind of you to see me, kinsman," Elorie said. Then, and Jeff could hear her voice shake, she said, "Or—don't you know—"

Danvan Hastur's voice was courteous and grave.

"Many, many years ago," he said, "I refused to listen when a kinsman begged for my understanding. And as result, Damon Ridenow and all his household were burned by a fire whose origin I refused to question, telling myself that it was the hand of the Gods that burned their household to cinders. And I stood by and raised no hand to help, and I have never felt guiltless of Cleindori's death. At the time I thought it the just vengeance of the Gods even though I did not sanction, and I knew nothing of the fanatical assassins who had actually compassed her death. I thought, may all the Gods forgive me, that the breaking of the Forbidden Tower, cruel as the deaths were, would restore our land and our Towers to the old, righteous ways. Oh, I had no hand in any of the deaths, and if the murderers had come into my hands I would have delivered them into the hands of vengeance; but I did not stretch out my hand to prevent the murders, either, or to discredit the fanatics who were responsible for the death of so many of the Comyn whom we could spare so ill. I told myself, when she appealed to me, that Cleindori had forfeited all right to my protection. I don't intend to make that mistake twice; if I can prevent it, there will be no more deaths in Comyn. Nor will I visit the sins of men long dead on the heads of their descendants. What do you want from me, Elorie Ardais?"

"Now just a minute here," said Kerwin, before Elorie could open her mouth, "let's get one thing straight. I didn't come here to ask for anybody's protection. The Arilinn Tower threw me out, and when Elorie stuck by me, they threw her out too. But coming here wasn't my idea, and we don't need any favors."

Hastur blinked; then, over his stern and austere face, an unmistakable smile spread. "I stand reproved, son. Tell it your way."

"To start with," Elorie said, "he isn't a Terran. He isn't Jeff Kerwin's son." She explained what she had found out.

Hastur looked startled. He said softly, "Yes. Yes, I should have known. You have a look of the Altons; but Cleindori's father had Alton blood, and so I never thought anything of it." Gravely, he bowed to Elorie. "I have done you a grave injustice," he said. "Any Keeper may, at the promptings of her own conscience, lay down her holy office and take a consort of her own rank and station. We wronged Cleindori; and now we have wronged you. The status of your *Comyn* husband shall be regularized, kinswoman; may all your sons and daughters be gifted with *laran*. . . ."

"Oh, the hell with that," Jeff said, in a sudden rage. "I haven't changed one damn bit from what I was four days ago, when they thought I wasn't good enough for Elorie to spit on! So if I marry her while they think I'm Jeff Kerwin, Junior, she's a bitch and a whore, but if I marry her after I find my father was one of your high-and-mighty Comyn, who couldn't even be bothered to notify his family that I existed, all of a sudden it's all right again—"

"Jeff, Jeff, *please*—" Elorie begged, and he heard her frightened thoughts, *nobody dares speak like this to the Lord Hastur*—"

"I dare," he said curtly. "Tell him what you came to tell him, Elorie, and then let's get the hell out of this place! You married me thinking I was a Terran, remember? I'm not ashamed of my name or the man who gave it to me when my own father wasn't around to protect me!"

He broke off, suddenly abashed before the old man's steady blue eyes. Hastur smiled at him.

"There speaks the Alton pride—and the pride of the Terrans, which is different, but very real," he said. "Take pride in your Terran fostering as well as your heritage of blood, my son; my words were to ease Elorie's heart, not to cast disparagement on your Terran foster-father. By all accounts he was a good and brave man, and I would have saved his life if I could. But now tell me, both of you, why you came here."

His face grew graver as he listened.

"I knew Auster had been in the hands of the Terrans," he said, "but it never occurred to me that they could use him in any way; he was so very young. Nor did I know that Cassilde had borne twins. We did the other child a grave injustice; and you say, Kerwin—" he stumbled a little over the name, making it nearer to the Darkovan name *Kieran*, "that he is embittered, and a Terran spy. Something must be done for him. Why, I wonder, did not Dyan tell me?"

Elorie said, shaking her head, "Dyan knew from Kennard something of the ways of the Forbidden Tower. The children were unlike; perhaps he thought one of them, being dark-haired and dark-eyed, was the son of the Terran; and he helped you only to reclaim the one he believed to be Arnad Ridenow's son."

"It is true that we acknowledged Auster as son to Arnad Ridenow," Hastur said. "He had the Ridenow gift; but he could have had it through Cassilde, who was Callista Lanart-Carr's daughter by Damon Ridenow." He shook his head with a sigh.

"The thing is, Lord Hastur," Jeff said, "that I thought *I* was the time-bomb the Terrans had planted; and it's Auster. *And he is still in the matrix circle at Arilinn!*"

"But he has *laran!* He grew up among us! He is Comyn!"
Hastur said in dismay, and Kerwin shook his head.

"No. He is Jeff Kerwin's son," Kerwin said, "and I'm
not." Auster, then, had been his foster-brother; they had
played together as children. He did not like Auster; but he
owed him loyalty. Yes, and love—for Auster was the son of
the man who had given him name and place in the Terran
Empire. Auster was his brother, and more, his friend within
the matrix circle. He did not want Auster used to break the
Arilinn Tower.

"But—a Terran? In Arilinn?"

"He thought he was Comyn," Kerwin said, a curious
yeasting excitement boiling within him as he began to understand. "He *believed* he was Comyn, he *expected* to have
laran—and so he had it, he never developed any mental
block against believing in his own psi powers!"

"But don't you see," Elorie interrupted. "We have to
warn them at Arilinn! They may try the mining operation—
and Auster is still linked to Ragan—and it will fail!"

Hastur looked pale. "Yes," he said. "They sent the little
Keeper from Neskaya there—and they were going to try it
tonight."

"Tonight," Elorie gasped. "We've got to warn them! It's
their only chance!"

Kerwin's thoughts were bitter as they flew through the
night. Rain beat and battered at the little airship; a strange
young Comyn knelt in the front of the machine, controlling
it, but Kerwin had neither eyes nor thought for him.

They had tried to warn Arilinn through the relay screen
high in Comyn Castle; but Arilinn had already been taken
out of the relay net. Neskaya Tower had told them that they
had closed the relays to Arilinn three days ago, when they
had sent for Callina Lindir.

So he was going back to Arilinn. Going, after all, to warn
them, perhaps to save them—for there was no question that

this, the greatest of the Tower operations, was the primary target of the Terrans who wanted Arilinn to fail; fail, so that the Domains would fall into the hands of the Terran advisers, engineers, industrialists.

The young Comyn flying the ship had looked with reverence at Elorie when the name of Arilinn was spoken. It seemed that they all knew about the tremendous experiment at Arilinn, which might keep Darkover and the Domains out of the hands of the Terran Empire.

But it would fail. They were racing through the night to stop it before it started; but if they didn't do it at all, it would be default, and default would have the same weight as failure, which was why they were trying this desperate experiment with a half-trained Keeper. Either way, it meant the end of the Darkover they knew.

If only I had never come back to Darkover!

"Don't, Jeff," she said softly. "It's not fair to blame yourself."

But he did. If he had not come back, they might have found someone else to take the vacant place at Arilinn. And Auster, without Jeff to antagonize him, would perhaps have discovered the truth about the Terran spy. But now they were all bound to abide by the success or failure of this experiment; and if it failed—and it would fail—then they were all pledged, on the word of Hastur, to offer no more resistance to Terran industrialization, Terran trade, the Terran culture, the Terran way.

Without Kerwin to lend them this false confidence, the Terran's spying would have yielded only minor information.

Elorie's hand felt cold as ice in his. Without asking, Kerwin wrapped his fur-lined cloak around her, remembering against his will one of Johnny Eller's stories. He could shelter Elorie against physical cold in his Darkovan cloak; but now that he knew he had no more right to his Terran citizenship than to Arilinn, where could he take her?

She pointed through the window of the plane. "Arilinn,"

she said, "and there is the Tower." Then she drew a deep breath of consternation and despair; for, faintly around the Tower, he could see a bluish, flickering, iridescence.

"We're too late," she whispered. "They've already started!"

CHAPTER SEVENTEEN

The Conscience of a Keeper

Kerwin felt as if he were sleepwalking as they hurried across the airfield, Elorie moving dreamlike at his side. They had failed, then, and it was too late. He caught at her saying, "It's too late! Accept it!" But she kept moving, and he would not let her go alone. They passed through the sparkling Veil, and Kerwin caught his breath at the impact of the tremendous, charged force that seemed to suffuse the entire Tower, radiating from that high room where the circle had formed. Incomplete, yes, but still holding incredible power. It beat in Kerwin like an extra heartbeat, and he felt Elorie, at his side, trembling.

Was this dangerous for her, now?

Swept on, dominated by her will and that mysterious force, Kerwin climbed the Tower. He stood outside the matrix chamber, sensing what lay within.

Auster's barrier was no more than a wall of mist to him. His body remained outside the room, but he was inside, too, and with senses beyond his physical eyes he touched them all: Taniquel, in the monitor's seat, Rannirl firmly holding the technician's visualization; Kennard bent over the maps; Corus in his own, Kerwin's place; and holding them together, on frail spiderweb strands, an unfamiliar touch, like pain. . . .

She was slight and frail, not yet out of childhood, yet she

wore the robe of a Keeper, crimson, not the ceremonial robe but the loose hooded robe they all wore within the matrix chamber, her robe crimson, so that no one would touch her even by accident when she was carrying the load of the energons. She had dark hair like spun black glass, still braided like a child's along her face, and a small, triangular, plain face, pale and thin and trembling with effort.

She sensed his touch and looked puzzled, yet somehow she knew it was not intrusion, that he *belonged* here. Quickly Kerwin made the rounds of the circle again, Rannirl, Corus, Taniquel, Neyrissa, Kennard—Auster . . .

Auster. He sensed something, from outside the circle as he was, like a sticky, palpable black cord, extending outside the barrier; the line that chained them, kept the matrix circle from closing their ring of power. *The bond, the psychic bond between the twin-born, that bound Auster's twin without his knowledge to the fringes of the circle . . .*

Spy! Terran, spy! Auster had sensed his presence, turned viciously in his direction . . . though his body, immobile in the rapport, did not move . . . but the tension rippled the calm of the circle, came near to breaking.

"Spy and Terran. But not I, my brother!" Kerwin moved into the circle, fell into full rapport and projected into Auster's mind the full memory of that room where Cleindori, Arnad, Cassilde had been murdered, Cassilde struck down still bearing Auster's sister, who was never born . . .

Auster screamed noiselessly in anguish. But as the barrier around the circle dropped, Kerwin caught it up in his own telepathic touch; flashed round the circle in a swift round, locking himself into it; and with one swift, deliberate thrust, cut through the black cord . . . (*sizzling, scorching, a bond severed*) and broke the bond forever.

(Miles away, a swart little man who called himself Ragan collapsed with a scream of agony, to lie senseless for hours, and wake with no knowledge of what had happened. Days later, they found him and took him to Neskaya, where, in the

Tower, the psychic wound was healed and Auster was ready, again, to greet his unknown twin; but that came later.)

Auster's mind was reeling; Kerwin supported him with a strong telepathic touch, dropping into deep rapport.

Bring me into the circle!

There was a brief moment of dizzy timelessness as he fell into the old rapport. A facet of the crystal, a bodiless speck floating in a ring of light . . . then he was one of them.

Far down beneath the surface of the world lie those strange substance, those atoms, molecules, ions known as minerals. His touch had searched them out, through the crystal structure in the matrix screen; now, atom by atom and molecule by molecule, he had sifted them from impurities so that they lay pure and molten in their rocky beds, and now the welded ring of power was to lift them, through psychokinesis, molding the circle into a great Hand that would bring them in streams to the place prepared for them.

They were poised, waiting, as the frail spiderweb touch of the child-Keeper faltered, trying to grasp them. Kerwin deeply in rapport with Taniquel, felt the monitor's despair as she felt the girl's wavering touch.

No! It will kill her!

And then, as the welded circle faltered, ready to dissolve, Kerwin felt again a familiar, secure, beloved touch.

Elorie! No! You cannot!

I am a Keeper, and responsible only to my own conscience. What matter? My ritual status, an old taboo that lost its meaning generations ago? Or my power to wield the energons, my skill as Keeper? Two women died so that I could be free to do this work I was born and trained to do. Cleindori proved it, even before she left Arilinn, she would have freed the Keepers from laws she had found to be pious frauds, meaningless and superstitious lies! They would not hear her; they drove her out to die! Now, with the Terrans waiting for us to fail, will you sacrifice the success of Arilinn for an old taboo? If you will, let Arilinn be broken, and let

Darkover fall to the Terrans; but the blame is upon you, not me, my brothers and my sisters!

Then, with infinite gentleness (a steadying arm slipped around the childish shoulders, a faltering and spilling cup held firmly in place), Elorie slid into the rapport, gently displacing the spiderweb-threads of the child-Keeper's touch with her own strong linkage, so gently that there was neither shock nor hurt.

Little sister, this weight is too strong for you. . . .

And the rapport locked suddenly into a closed ring within the crystal screen; the power flared, flowed . . . Kerwin was no longer a single person, he was not human at all, he was one with the circle, part of a tremendous, glowing, burning river of molten metal that surged upward, impelled by great throbbing power; it burst, spilled, flamed, engulfed them. . . .

Slowly, slowly, it cooled and hardened and lay inert again, awaiting the touch of those who had need of it, awaiting the tools and hands that would shape it into tools, energy, power, the life of a world.

One by one, the circle loosened and dissolved. Kerwin felt himself drop from the circle. Taniquel raised eyes, blazing with love and triumph, to welcome him back. Kennard, Rannirl, Corus, Neyrissa, they were all round him; Auster, deep shock in his cat's eyes, but burnt clean of hatred, came to welcome him with a quick, hard embrace, a brother's touch.

The little girl, the Keeper from Neskaya, lay fallen in a heap; she had physically fallen from the Keeper's seat to the floor, and Taniquel was bending over her, hands to her temples. The child looked boneless, exhausted, fainting. Taniquel said, troubled, "Rannirl, come and carry her. . . ."

Elorie! Kerwin's heart sucked and turned over. He leaped over the chairs to throw open the door of the room. He had no memory of how he had gotten into the room, but Elorie had not managed, however it was, to follow him. Her mind had come into the matrix ring . . . but her body lay outside the shielded room unguarded.

She was lying on the floor in the hall, sprawled there white and lifeless at his feet. Kerwin dropped to his knees, at her side, all his triumph, all his exaltation, melting into hatred and curses, as he laid his hand to her unmoving breast.

Elorie, Elorie! Driven by the conscience of a Keeper, she had returned to save the Tower . . . but had she paid with her life? She had gone unprepared, unguarded, into a tremendous matrix operation. He knew how this work drained vitality, exhausting her nearly to the point of death; and even when she was carefully guarded and isolated, this work taxed her to the breaking point! Even guarding her vitality and nervous forces with chastity and sacrosanct isolation, she could hardly endure it! No, she had not lost her powers . . . but was this the price she must pay for daring to use them now?

I have killed her!

Despairing, he knelt beside her, hardly knowing it when Neyrissa moved him aside.

Kennard shook him roughly.

"Jeff! Jeff, she's not dead, not yet, there's a chance! But you've got to let the monitors get to her, let us see how bad it is!"

"Damn you, don't touch her! Haven't you devils done enough—"

"He's hysterical," Kennard said briefly. "Get him loose, Rannirl." Kerwin felt Rannirl's strong arms holding him, restraining him; he fought to reach Elorie, and Rannirl said compassionately, "I'm sorry, *bredu*. You have to let us— damn it, brother, hold still or I'll have to knock you senseless!"

He felt Elorie taken by force from his arms, cried out with his rage and despair . . . then slowly, sensing their warm touch on his mind, he subsided. Elorie wasn't dead.

They were only trying to help. He subsided, standing quiet between Rannirl and Auster, seeing with half an eye that Rannirl's mouth was bleeding and that there was a scratch on Auster's face.

"I know," Auster said in a low voice, "but easy, foster-brother, they'll do everything that can be done. Tani and Neyrissa are with her now." He raised his eyes. "I failed. I failed, *bredu*. I would have broken, if you hadn't been here. I never had any right to be here at all, I'm Terran, outsider, you have more right here than I. . . ."

Unexpectedly, to Kerwin's horror, Auster dropped to his knees. His voice was just audible.

"All that I said of you was true of myself, *vai dom*; I must have known it, hating myself and pretending it was you I hated. All I deserve at the hands of the Comyn is death. There is life between us, Damon Aillard; claim it as you will." He bowed his head and waited there, broken, resigned to death.

And suddenly Jeff was furious.

"Get up, you damned fool," he said roughly hauling Auster to his feet. "All it means is that some of you half-wits—" and he looked around at all of them, "are going to have to change some of your stupid notions about the Comyn, that's all. So Auster was born of a Terran father— so what? He has the Ridenow Gift—*because he was brought up believing he had it!* I went through all kinds of hell in my training . . . *because all of you believed that with my Terran blood I'd find it difficult, and made me believe it!* Yes, *laran* is inherited, but it's not nearly to the extent you believed. It means that Cleindori was right; matrix mechanics is just a science anyone can learn, and there's no need to surround it with all kinds of ritual and taboo! A Keeper doesn't need to be a virgin . . ." He broke off.

Elorie believed it. And her belief could kill her!

And yet . . . she knew, she had been part of his link, with Cleindori; this was why Cleindori had given him the matrix, although his child's mind had almost broken under the burden: so that one day another Keeper could read what Cleindori had discovered, and deliver to Arilinn the message they would not hear from her, read the mind and heart and conscience of the martyred Keeper, who had died to free other young women from the prison the Arilinn Tower would build around their minds and their hearts.

"But we've won," Rannirl said, and Jeff knew they had all followed his thought.

"A period of grace," said Kennard somberly. "Not a final victory!"

And Jeff knew Kennard was right. This experiment might have succeeded, and the Pan-Darkovan Syndicate was now bound in honor to be guided by the will of Hastur in accepting Terran ways. But there had been a failure, too.

Kennard put it into words.

"The Tower circles can never be brought back as they were in the old days. Life can only go forward, not back. It's even better to ask help from the Terrans—in our own way and on our own terms—than to let all this weight rest on the shoulders of a few gifted men and women. Better that the people of Darkover should learn to share the effort with one another, Comyn and Commoner, and even with the people of Terra." He sighed.

"I deserted them," he said. "If I had fought all the way beside them—things might have gone differently. But this was what they were working for; Cleindori and Cassilde, Jeff and Lewis, Arnad, old Damon—all of us. To make an even exchange; Darkover to share the matrix powers with Terra, for those few things where they could be safely used, and Terra to give such things as she had. But as equals; not the Terran masters and the Darkovan suppliants. A fair exchange between equal worlds; each world with its own pride, and its own power. And I let you be sent to Terra," he added, looking straight at Jeff, "because I felt you a threat to my own sons. Can you forgive me, Damon Aillard?"

Jeff said, "I'll never get used to that name. I don't want it, Kennard. I wasn't brought up to it. I don't even believe in your kind of government, or inherited power of that kind. If your sons do, they're welcome to it; you've brought them up to take those kinds of responsibility. Just—" He grinned. "Use what influence you have to see that I'm not deported, day after tomorrow."

Kennard said gently, "There is no such person as Jeff Kerwin, Junior. They cannot possibly deport the grandson of Valdir Alton to Terra. Whatever he chooses to call himself."

There was a feather-light touch on Jeff's arm. He looked down into the pale, childish face of the child-Keeper; and remembered her name, Callina of Neskaya.

She whispered, "Elorie—she is conscious; she wants you."

Jeff said gravely, "Thank you, *vai leronis,*" and watched the child blushing. What Elorie had done had freed this girl, too; but she did not know it yet.

They had taken Elorie into the nearest room and laid her on a couch there; pale, white, strengthless, she stretched her hands to Jeff. He reached for her, not caring that the rest of the circle had crowded into the room behind him. He knew, when he touched her, how deep the shock had been, going unguarded, unprepared into the matrix circle; in days to come, Keepers would learn ways to guard themselves against the energy drains of massive work like this; without the tremendous dedication of lifelong ritual chastity, but with strong safeguards nevertheless. Elorie had indeed been injured; she had come closer to death than any of them would ever want to remember, and many suns would rise and set over Arilinn before her old merry laughter would be heard again in the Tower; but her glowing eyes blazed out in love and triumph.

"We've won," she whispered, "and we're here!"

And Kerwin, holding her in his arms, knew that they had won indeed. The days that were coming, for Darkover and the Comyn, would change them all; both worlds would struggle with the changes that the years would bring. But a world that remains always the same can only die. They had fought to keep Darkover as it was; but what they had won was only the victory of determining what changes would come, and how quickly.

He had found what he loved, indeed; and he had destroyed it, for the world he loved would never be the same, and he had been the instrument of change. But in destroying it, he had saved it from ultimate and final destruction.

His brothers and sisters were all around him. Taniquel, so white and worn that he realized how ruthlessly she had spent herself to bring Elorie back to herself. Auster, with the mold of his life broken, but with a new strength from which it could be forged anew. Kennard, his kinsman, and all the others . . .

"Now, now," said the sensible voice of Mesyr, calm and level. "What's the sense of standing here like this, when your night's work is done, and well done? Downstairs, all of you, for some breakfast . . . yes, you too, Jeff, let Elorie get some rest." With brisk hands she drew up the covers beneath Elorie's chin and made shooing gestures at all of them.

Jeff met Elorie's eyes again, and, weak as she was, she began to laugh; and then they all joined in, so that the corridors and stairways of the Tower rang with shared mirth. Some things, at least, never changed at all.

Life in Arilinn, for now, was back to normal.

They were home again. And this time they would stay.

THE WINDS OF
DARKOVER

CHAPTER ONE

Barron dumped the last of his gear into a duffel bag, pulled the straps tight, and said to nobody in particular, "Well, that's that and the hell with all of them."

He straightened, taking a last look around the neat, tight little world of spaceport living quarters. Built to conserve materials (it had been the first Terran building on Darkover, in the zone later to become Trade City), it had something in common with a spaceship's cabin; it was narrow, bright, clean and cramped; the furniture functional and almost all built-in. It would have suited a professional spaceman perfectly. Ground crews were another matter; they tended to get claustrophobia.

Barron had complained as much as anyone else; saying the place might be a decent fit for two mice, if one of them were on a stiff diet. But now that he was leaving it, he felt a curious pang, almost homesickness. He had lived here five years.

Five years! I never meant to stick to one planet that long!

He hoisted the duffel bag to his shoulder and closed the door of his quarters for the last time.

The corridor was as functional as the living quarters; reference charts and maps papered the walls up to the height of a tall man's eye level. Barron strode along, not seeing the familiar charts, but he did cast a brief bitter glance at the dispatch board, seeing his name there in red on the dreaded rep-sheet. He had five reps—official reprimands—when seven would put one out of the Space Service for good.

And no wonder, he thought. *I didn't get any dirty deal; in fact, they went easy on me. Pure luck, and no credit to me, that cruiser and the mapping skip didn't crash and blow the damned spaceport right off Darkover, and half Trade City with them!*

He set his mouth tight. Here he was, worrying about de-merits like a kid in school—and yet it wasn't merely that. Many people in Terran Space Service went through their whole twenty years without a single rep—and he'd piled up five in one disastrous night.

Even though it wasn't his fault.

Yes it was, damn it. Who else could I blame it on? I should have reported sick.

But I wasn't sick!

The rep-sheet read: gross neglect of duty, grave danger of causing accident to a landing spacecraft. They had found him literally napping on duty. *But damn it, I wasn't asleep either!*

Daydreaming?

Try telling them that. Try telling them that when your every nerve and muscle should have been alert over the all-important dispatch board, you were—somewhere else. You were caught up in a deep dream, bewildered with colors, sights, sounds, smells, blazes of brilliance. You were leaning into an icy wind, under a deep purple sky, a blaze of red sun-light overhead—the Darkovan sun—the sun that the Ter-rans called The Bloody Sun. But you'd never seen it like that, reflected in rainbow prisms through a great wall of crystalline glass. You heard your own boots ringing on ice-hard stone—and your pulse was pounding with hate, and you felt the surge of adrenaline in your blood. You broke into a run, feeling the hatred and blood-lust rise to a crest inside you; before you something reared up—man, woman, beast—you hardly knew or cared—and you heard your own snarl as a whip came crashing down and something screamed——

The dream had dissolved in the thundering nightmare noise of klaxons, the all-quarters alarm of sirens and whoopers and bells, the WRECK *lights blazing everywhere, and your reflexes took over. You'd never moved so fast. But it was too late. You had slammed the wrong button and the dispatch tower was fouled up by that all-important eight-second margin, and only a minor miracle of seat-of-the-pants navigation by the young captain of the mapping ship—he was getting three medals for it—had saved the spaceport authority from the kind of disaster that waked people up—what people were left—in screeching nightmares for twenty years afterward.*

Nobody had wasted words on Barron since. His name on the rep-sheet had made him a pariah. He had been told to vacate his quarters by 2700 that night and report for a new assignment, but nobody bothered telling him where. It was as simple as that—five years in Darkover Spaceport and seventeen in the service had been wiped out. He didn't feel especially mistreated. There wasn't room in the Terran Spaceforce for that kind of mistake.

The corridor ended in an archway; a plaque, which Barron ignored after seeing it every day for years; told him he was now in Central Coordinating. Unlike the building where quarters were located, this one was constructed of native Darkovan stone, translucent and white as alabaster, with enormous glass windows. Through them he could see flaring, blue spaceport lights; the shapes of groundcraft and resting ships, and, far beyond the lights, pale greenish moonlight. It was a half an hour before dawn. He wished he'd stopped for some breakfast; then he was glad he hadn't. Barron wasn't thin-skinned, but the way the men ignored him in the cafeteria would put anyone off his food. He hadn't bothered eating much in the last couple of days.

There was always the Old Town, the Darkovan part of Trade City where he sometimes slipped away for exotic food when he was tired of the standard fare of the quarters; there were not a few restaurants which catered to spacemen and tourists who came for "exotic delicacies." But he hadn't felt like trying to pass the guards; he might have been stopped. They might have thought he was trying to escape an official process. He wasn't officially under arrest, but his name was mud.

He left the duffel bag outside the narrow bank of elevators, stepped in and pressed the topmost button. The elevator soared up, depositing him outside the dispatch room. He lowered his head, passing it without a glance inside and headed for the coordinator's office in the penthouse.

And then, without warning—he was standing on a high parapet, winds flowing icily around his body, ripping at him with enough force to tear his clothes off, ridging his skin with gooseflesh and pain. Below him, men screamed and moaned and died over the sounds of clashing steel; and somewhere he heard stone falling with a great crunching rumble like the end of the world. He could not see: He clung hard to the stone, feeling frost bite with fiery teeth at his stiff fingers, and fought the sickness rising in his throat. *So many men. So many dead, all of them my people and my friends . . .*

He let go of the stone. His fingers were so cramped that he had to pry them off with his other hand. He caught his blowing garments around him, feeling an instant of incongruous physical comfort in the thick fur against his cold hands, and went swiftly, on groping feet, through the blind dark. He moved as in a dream, knowing where he was going without knowing why; his feet knew the familiar path. He felt them move from flagstone to wood parquet to thick carpeting, then down a long flight of stairs and up another flight—farther and farther, until the distant sounds of battle and falling walls were muffled and finally silenced. His throat was thick and he sobbed as he went. He passed through a low archway, automatically ducking his head against the stone arch he had never seen and would never see. A current of chill air blew on him. He fumbled in the darkness for something like a loose hood of feathery textures; he drew it downward swiftly and he thrust his head through the feathers, pulling it down.

He felt himself falling back and in the same instant he seemed to rise, to soar upward and swoop outward on the wings of the feathery substance. The darkness suddenly thinned and was gone, and light broke around him—not through his darkened eyes, but through the very skin of his body—and he felt cold reddish light and frosty clouds. Weightless, borne on the feather dress, he soared outward, guiding himself through the sudden brilliance of dawn.

Quickly he grew accustomed to the bird dress, and balancing on one wing (*It's a long time since I dared to do this*), he turned to look below.

The colors were strange, flat, shapes distorted and concave; he was not seeing them with ordinary mortal eyes. Far below a swarm of men in rough, dark clothing clustered around a rude tower covered in skins, next to an outwork. Arrows flew, men screamed; on the wall a man toppled with a long despairing shriek, and fell out of his sight. He beat harsh pinions, trying to swoop down, and . . .

He was standing on firm flooring, wiping the sweat of terror from his face.

He was here. He was Dan Barron. He was not flying bodiless except for a few feathers over a weird tipping landscrape, fighting a biting current of wind. He stared at his fingers and put one into his mouth. It felt numb, frostbitten. *The stone was cold.*

It had happened again.

It was so real, *so damnably real*. His skin was still gooseflesh and he mopped eyes still streaming from the bitter

wind. *Good God*, he thought, and shuddered. Had someone
been slipping him hallucinogenic drugs? Why would anyone do that? He had no enemies, as far as he knew. He had
no real friends—he wasn't the type to make them at a
strange outpost—but no enemies either. He did his work and
minded his own business, and he knew no one who envied
him either his few possessions or the tough and somewhat
underpaid job he had been doing. The only explanation was
that he was mad, psychotic, freaked-out, off his landing
base. He realized that in that weird dream, obsession or hallucination, he had been speaking and thinking in Darkovan—the strong accented mountain Darkovan which he
understood, but could not speak except for the few words
necessary to order a meal or buy some knickknack in Trade
City. He shivered again and mopped his face. His feet had
carried him within a few feet of the coordinator's office, but
he stopped, trying to get his breath and his bearings.

This made five times.

The first three times had struck him as abnormally vivid
daydreams, born of boredom and hangover and based on his
infrequent but colorful excursions into the Old Town. He
had dismissed them without much thought, even though he
woke shuddering with the reality of the surges of fear or hatred which possessed him in these dreams. The fourth—the
fourth had been the near-catastrophe of the spaceport. Barron wasn't an imaginative man. His possible explanations
went as far as a nervous breakdown, or someone with a
grudge slipping him a hallucinatory drug as a grim joke, and
not a step further. He wasn't paranoid enough to think that
someone had done it for the purpose it achieved, his disgrace and a spaceport catastrophe. He was confused, a little
scared and a little angry, but not sure if the anger was his
own or part of the strange dream.

He couldn't continue to delay. He waited a minute more,
then straightened his shoulders and knocked at the coordi-

nator's door. A light flashed a green COME IN, and he stepped in.

Mallinson, Coordinator of Spaceport Activities for the Terran Zone of Darkover, was a hefty man who looked, at any hour of day or night, as if he'd slept in his uniform. He appeared unimaginative and serious. Any notion Barron might have had about revealing his experiences to his superior died unspoken. Nevertheless, Mallinson looked straight at Barron, and he was the first person who'd done so for five days.

Without preamble he said, "All right, what the hell happened? I pulled your file; you're listed as a damned good man: In my experience, men don't pile up a perfect record and then rack it up like *that*; the man who's heading for a big mistake starts out by making dozens of little mistakes first, and we have time to pull him off the spot before he really piles something up. Were you sick? Not that it's an excuse— if you were you should have reported and requested a relief man. We expected to find you dead of a heart attack—we didn't think anything else would slow you down like that."

Barron thought about the dispatcher's room and its enormous board which patterned all traffic in and out of this spaceport. Mallinson said, not giving him time to answer, "You don't drink or drug. You know, most men last about eight months on the dispatch board; then the responsibility starts giving them nightmares, they start making little fumbles, and we pull them off and transfer them. When you never made even a little fumble, we should have realized that you just didn't have sense enough—the little fumbles are the mind's way of yelling for help, yelling 'This is too much for me, get me out of here.' When you didn't, we should have pulled you off anyway. That's why you weren't cashiered, kicked out with seven reps, and slapped with a millicred fine. We left you on the board five years, and we should have known we were asking for trouble."

Barron realized that Mallinson hadn't expected any answer. People who made mistakes of that caliber never could explain why. If they'd known why they could have guarded against it.

"With your record, Barron, we could transfer you out to the Rim, but we have an opening here; I understand you speak Darkovan?"

"Trade City language. I understand the other, but I fumble in it."

"Even so. Know anything about Mapping and Exploring?" Barron jumped. It had been a ship from M & E which had nearly crashed five days ago, and that sector was in his mind, but a second glance at Mallinson convinced him that the man was simply asking for information, not needling. He said, "I've read a book or two on xenocartography—no more."

"Lens grinding?"

"The principles. Most kids make a small telescope some time or other; I did."

"That's plenty. I didn't want an expert," Mallinson said with a grim smile. "We've got plenty of them, but it would put Darkovan backs up. Now, how much do you know about general Darkovan culture?"

Wondering where all this was leading, Barron said, "Orientation Lectures Two, Three and Four, five years ago. Not that I've needed it much, working in the port."

"Well then, you know the Darkovans never bothered a great deal with small technology—telescopes, microscopes and the like? Their supposed sciences go in other directions, and I don't know much about them either; nobody does except a few anthropologists and sociological experts. The facts remain; we, meaning the Board of Terran Affairs, sometimes get requests for minor technological help from individuals. Not from the government—if there is any government on Darkover, which I personally am inclined to doubt—but that's beside the point. Somebody or other out there, I'm not sure about the details, decided that for forest-fire control and fire watching, telescopes would be handy little gadgets to have around. Somehow the idea crawled up whatever channels it had to come through, and came to the Council of Elders in Trade City. We offered to sell them telescopes. Oh, no, they said politely, they'd rather have someone teach their men how to grind them, and to supervise their construction, installation and use. It's not the sort of thing we can send up a slip to Personnel for and find, just like that. But here you are, out of a job, and lens grinding listed in your comprehensive file as a hobby. Start today."

Barron scowled. This was a job for an anthropologist, a liaison officer, a specialist in Darkovan language, or—*fire watching! Hell, that's a kid's job!* He said stiffly, "Sir, let me remind you that this is out of my sector and out of my specialty. I have no experience in it. I'm a scheduling expert and dispatch man—"

"Not as of five days ago, you aren't," Mallison said brutally, "Look, Barron, you're through in your own line; you know that. We don't want to ship you out in disgrace—not without some idea of what happened to you. And your contract isn't up for two years. We want to fit you in somewhere."

There was nothing Barron could say to that. Resigning before a contract was up meant losing your holdback pay and your fee passage back to your home planet—which could strand you on a strange world and wipe out a year's pay. Technically he had a right to complain about being assigned outside his specialty field. But technically they had a right to fire him with seven reps, blacklist him, fine him, and press charges for gross negligence. He was getting a chance to come out of this—not clean, but not wrecked for good in the service.

"When do I start?" he asked. It was the only question he had left.

But he did not hear the answer. As he scanned Mallinson's face, suddenly it blurred.

He was standing on a stretch of soft grass; it was night, but it was not dark. All around him the night flamed and roared with a great fire, reaching in tendrils of ravening flame far above his head. And in the midst of the flame there was a woman.

Woman?

She was almost inhumanly tall and slender, but girlish; she stood bathed in the flame as if standing carelessly under a waterfall. She was not burning, not agonized. She looked merry and smiling. Her hands were clasped on her naked breasts, the flames licking around her face and her flame-colored hair. And then the girlish, merry face wavered and became supernally beautiful with the beauty of a great goddess burning endlessly in the fire, a kneeling woman bound in golden chains. . . .

. . . "and you can arrange all that downstairs in Personnel and Transportation," Mallinson finished firmly, shoving back his chair. "Are you all right, Barron? You look a bit fagged. I'll bet you haven't been eating or sleeping. Shouldn't you see a medic before you go? Your card is still good in Section 7. It's going to be all right, but the sooner you leave, the better: Good luck." But he didn't offer to shake hands, and Barron knew it wasn't all right at all.

He stumbled over his own feet leaving the office, and the face of the burning woman, in its inhuman ecstasy, went with him in terror and amazement.

He thought, *what in the world—any world—has happened to me?*

And, in the name of all the gods of Earth, space and Darkover—why?

CHAPTER TWO

The breach in the outwork was being repaired.

Brynat Scarface had gone out to watch, and was standing on the inner parapet supervising the work. It was a cold morning and mists flowed up the mountainside; in the chill the men moved sluggishly. Little dark men from the mountains, most of them ragged and still battle-stained, fought the rough ground and the cold stone; they were moved by shouts and the occasional flick of a whip in the hands of one of Brynat's men.

Brynat was a tall man, dressed in ragged and slashed finery, over which he had drawn a fur cloak from the spoils of the castle. A great seamed scar ridged his face from eye to chin, giving to a face which had never been handsome the wolfish look of some feral beast which had somehow put on the dress of a man. At his heels his sword bearer, a little bat-eared man, scurried, bowing under the weight of the outlaw's sword. He cringed when Brynat turned to him, expecting a blow or a curse, but Brynat was in high good humor this morning.

"Fools we are, man—we spend days tearing down this wall," he complained, "and what is the first thing we do? We build it up again!"

The bat-eared man gave a nervous sycophant's laugh, but Brynat had forgotten his existence again. Drawing the fur around himself, he walked to the edge of the parapet and looked down at the ruined wall and the castle.

Storn Castle stood on a height defended by chasms and crags. Brynat knew he could congratulate himself for the feats of tactics and engineering which had broken the walls and poured men through them to storm the inner fortress. Storn had been built in the old days to be impregnable, and impregnable it was and had remained through seven generations of Aldarans, Aillards, Darriels and Storns.

When it had housed proud lords of the Comyn—the old, powerful, psi-gifted lords of the Seven Domains of Darkover—it had been known to the world's end. Then the line had dwindled, outsiders had married into the remains of the families, and finally the Storns of Storn had come there. They had been peaceful lords without any pretense to be more than they were—wilderness nobility, gentle and honorable, living in peace with their tenants and neighbors, content to trade in the fine hunting hawks of the mountains and sell fine wrought metals from the forges of their mountain tribe, which dug ore from the dark cliffs and worked it at their fires. They had been rich and also powerful in their own way, if by power one meant that when word went forth from the Storn of Storn, men obeyed; but they smiled instead of trembling when they obeyed. They had little contact with the other mountain peoples and less with the lords of the farther mountains; they lived at peace and were content.

And now they had fallen.

Brynat laughed smugly. In their prideful isolation, the Storns could no longer even send for help to their distant lordly neighbors. With care, Brynat would be established here as lord of Storn Castle long before the word went out through the Hellers and the Hyades that Storn Castle had a new lord. And would they care that it was ruled no longer by Storn of Storn, but by Brynat of the Heights? He thought not.

A cold wind had come up, and the red sun was covered

in scudding clouds. The men toiling at the lugged stones were moving faster now to keep warm in the biting wind, and a few flakes of snow were beginning to fall. Brynat jerked a careless shoulder at Bat-ears, and without looking to see if the little man followed—but woe to him if he hadn't—strode inside the castle.

Inside, far from watchers, he let his proud grin of triumph slide off. It had not been all victory, though his followers revelling in the rich spoil of the castle thought it had been. He sat in Storn's high seat, but victory eluded him.

He walked swiftly downward, until he came to a door padded with velvet and hung with curtains: Two of his mercenaries lolled here, drowsing on the comfort of cushions; an empty wineskin showed how they whiled away their guard. But they sprang up at the sound of his heavy tread, and one sniggered with the freedom of an old servitor.

"Ha, ha! Two wenches are better than one—hey, Lord?"

Seeing Brynat scowl the other said swiftly, "No more weeping and wailing from the maid this morning, Lord. She is still, and we have not entered."

Brynat scorned answer. He moved his hand imperiously and they flung open the door.

As the door hasp creaked, a small blue-clad form sprang up and whirled, long red braided hair flying about her shoulders. The face had once been piquantly lovely; now it was swollen and dark with bruises; one eye was half shut with a blow, but the other blazed in quenchless fury.

"You whelp of a bitch-wolf," she said low, "take one step further—I dare you!"

Brynat rocked back loosely on his heels, his mouth drawn to a wolfish smile. He set hands on hips and didn't speak, surveying the girl in blue. He saw the white, shaking hands, but noted that the swollen mouth did not tremble nor the eyes drop. He approved with inward laughter. Here he could feel genuine triumph.

"What, still unreconciled to my hospitality, Lady? Have

I offered you word or deed of insult, or do you blame me for
the roughness of my men in offering it?"

Her mouth was firm. "Where is my brother? My sister?"

"Why," he drawled, "your sister attends my feasts
nightly; I came to invite you to attend upon my lady wife
this morning; I believe she pines for a familiar face. But, my
Lady Melitta, you are pale; you have not touched the fine
food I sent to you!" He made a low, burlesque bow and
turned to pick up a tray laden with wine and rich food. He
proffered it to her, smiling. "See, I come in person, at your
service—"

She took one step, snatched the tray, picked up a roast
bird by one leg, and hurled it into his face.

Brynat swore, stepping backward and wiping the grease
from his chin—with a great burst of laughter. "Zandru's
hells! *Damisela*, I should have taken you, not the whimpering, whining creature I chose!"

Breathing hard she surveyed him defiantly. "I'd have
killed you first."

"I make no doubt you'd have tried! Had you been a man,
the castle might never have fallen—but you wear skirts in
place of hose and the castle lies in ruins and my men and I
are here and all the smiths in Zandru's forges can't mend a
broken egg. So I advise you in good sadness, little mistress:
wash your face, put on your fine robes, and attend on your
sister, who is still Lady of Storn. If you have good sense,
you'll advise her to have patience with her lot, and you shall
both have robes and jewels and all things that women prize.

"From you?"

"Who else?" he said with a laughing shrug, and flung the
door open to the guards.

"The Lady Melitta is to come and go as she wills within
the castle. But attend me, Mistress—the outworks, the para-
pets and the dungeons are forbidden, and I give my men
leave—hear me well—to stop you by force if you attempt to
go near them."

She started to hurl a curse at him and then stopped herself, visibly toying with the thought of what even limited freedom could mean. At last she turned away without a word, and he shut the door and moved away.

Perhaps this would be the first step in his second victory. He knew, though his men did not, that Storn Castle conquered was only the first victory—and hollow without the second conquest. He bit off another curse, turned his back on the room prisoning the girl and strode on. Upward and upward he went, high into the old tower. Here there were no windows. There were only narrow slits which admitted, not the red daylight but a strange, eerie, flickering blue light like chained lightning. Brynat felt a strange, cold shiver pass over him.

Of ordinary dangers he was fearless. But this was the ancient Darkovan sorcery, the bare legends of which protected such places as Storn Castle long after their other defenses had fallen. Brynat clutched the amulet round his neck with suddenly nerveless fingers. He had guessed that the old magic was merely a show, had hardened his mercenaries to storm the castle and had won. He had caroused in Storn Castle and had laughed at the old tales. Their magic hadn't saved the castle, had it? He had thought it a show to frighten children, no more harmful than the northern lights.

He strode through the ghostly flickers, through a pale arch of translucent stone. Two of his hardened and brutal men, the most nerveless he could bribe to the task, lounged there on an old carven settee. He noted that they were neither gaming nor drinking, and that their eyes were averted from the arch beyond, where a flickering curtain of blue light played like a fountain between the stones. There was naked relief in their faces at sight of their chieftain.

"Any change?"

"None, Lord. The man's dead—dead as Durraman's donkey."

"If I could believe that," Brynat said between his teeth and strode boldly through the curtain of blue flame.

He had been through it before and it had been his bravest act—bold enough to dwarf the single-handed taking of the last barbican. He knew his men held him in awe for it, but this alone he did not fear. He had seen such things beyond the mountains; they were fearsome, indeed, but harmless. He felt and endured with distaste the electric tingle, the hairs bristling on head and forearms. He stiffened his backbone against the surge of animal fear and strode through.

The blue light died. He stood in a dark chamber, lit with a few pale tapers in fixed cressets; soft hangings of woven fur circled a single low couch, on which a man lay motionless.

The still form seemed to glow softly in the darkness; he was a slender, frail man, with pale hair streaming from a high forehead and deep-sunken eyes. Though he was still young, the face was drawn and stern. He wore a tunic and plain hose of woven silk, no furs and no jewels but a single star-shaped stone like an amulet around his neck. His hands looked white, soft, and useless—the hands of scribe or priest, hands which had never held a sword. The feet were bare and soft; the chest did not stir with breathing. Brynat felt the old frustrated fury as he looked down on the pale, soft-looking man. Storn of Storn lay there, helpless—yet beyond Brynat's reach.

His mind whirled him back to the hour of the castle's fall. The servants and soldiers had been seized and subdued; trusted men had been sent to bind, but not to harm, the ladies. The younger Storn, no more than a boy and bleeding from many wounds, Brynat had spared with grudging admiration—a boy to defend this castle alone? The lad was dungeoned, but Brynat's own surgeon had dressed his wounds. Storn of Storn was Brynat's real prey.

His men did not know; they had seen only the spoil of a rich house, the power of holding an ancient fortress where they could be secure. But Brynat sought choicer game: the talismans and powers of the old Storns. With Storn of Storn in his hands, a Storn of the true blood, he could wield them—and Storn, he had heard, was a fragile, sickly, un-warlike man—born blind. Hence had he lived in retirement, leaving the management of his castle to his young sisters and his brother. Brynat had maidens and boy; *now for the feeble Lord!*

He had found his way through weird lights and magical fire curtains to the private apartments of the Lord of Storn—and found him escaped; lying unrousable in trance.

And so he had lain for days. Now Brynat, sick with rage, bent over his couch, but no stir of muscle or breath revealed that the man lived.

"Storn!" he bellowed. It was a shout that he felt must rouse even the dead.

No hair stirred. He might as well have howled into the winds around the parapet. Brynat, gritting his teeth, drew the skean from his belt. If he could not use the man, he held one power, at least: to send him from enchanted sleep to death. He raised the knife and brought it slashing down.

The knife turned in mid-air; it writhed, glowed blue, and exploded into white-hot flame from hilt to tip. Brynat howled in anguish, dancing about and shaking his burnt hand, to which the glowing skean clung with devilish force. The two mercenaries, trembling and bristling in the blue lights, faltered through the electrical curtain.

"You—you called us, *vai dom?*"

Savagely Brynat hurled the knife at them; it came un-stuck and flew; one of them fumbled to catch it, yelled and shook it off to the floor, where it lay still hissing and siz-zling. Brynat, with a low, savage stream of curses, strode from the chamber. The mercenaries followed, their eyes wide with terror and their faces like animal masks.

In marmoreal peace, far beyond their reach in unknow-able realms, Storn slept on.

Far below, Melitta Storn finished bathing her bruised face. Seated before her toilet table, she concealed the worst of the marks with cosmetics, combed and braided her hair, and brought a clean gown from the press and donned it. Then, conquering a sudden spasm of sickness, she drank deeply of the wine on the tray. She hesitated a moment, then retrieved the roast bird from the floor, wiped it, and, deftly tearing it with her fingers, ate most of it. She did not wish Brynat's hospitality, but sick and faint with hunger she was useless to herself or her people. Now, with wine and food, she felt a measure of physical strength, at least, returning. Her mirror told her that except for swollen lip and darkened eye, she looked much as before.

And yet—nothing could ever be the same.

She remembered, shuddering, the walls crashing with a sound like the world's end; men surging from the gap; her youngest brother, Edric, bleeding from face and leg and white as a ghost after they tore him away from the last defenses; her sister Allira, screaming insanely as she fled from Brynat; the mad screams suddenly silenced in a cry of pain—then nothing. Melitta had run after them, fighting with bare hands and screaming, screaming until three men had seized and borne her, struggling like a trussed hen, to her own chamber. They had thrust her roughly within and barred the door.

She forced away the crowding memories. She had some freedom, now she must make use of it. She found a warm cape and went out of the room. The mercenaries at the door rose and followed her at a respectful, careful ten paces.

Apprehension throbbed in her, she walked through the deserted halls like a ghost through a haunted house, dogged by the steps of the strange brutes. Everywhere were the marks of siege, sack and ruin. Hangings were torn away, furniture hacked and stained. There were marks of fire and smoke in the great hall, and, hearing voices, she tiptoed past; Brynat's men caroused there and even if he had given orders to leave her alone, would drunken men heed?

Now, where is Allira?

Brynat, in hateful jesting—had he been jesting?—had referred to Allira as his lady wife. Melitta had been brought up in the mountains; even in these peaceful days she knew stories of such bandit invasions: castle sacked, men killed, lady forcibly married—if rape could be called marriage because some priest presided—announcement made that the bandit had married into the family and all was peaceful—on the surface. It was a fine subject for sagas and tales, but Melitta's blood ran cold at the thought of her delicate sister in that man's hands.

Where had Brynat taken her? Doubtless, to the old royal suite, furnished by her forefathers for entertaining the Hastur-Lords should they ever honor Storn Castle with their presence. That would be the sort of mixed blasphemy and conquest that would appeal to Brynat. Her heart racing, Melitta ran up the stairs, knowing suddenly what she would find there.

The royal suite was a scant four hundred years old; the carpeting felt new underfoot. The insignia of the Hasturs had been inlaid in sapphires and emeralds over the door, but hammer and pick had ripped the jewels from the wall and only broken stone remained.

Melitta burst into the room like a whirlwind, inner conviction—the old, seldom-used, half-remembered knowing inside her mind, the scrap of telepathic power from some almost-forgotten forefather—forcing her to look here for her sister. She sped through the rooms, hardly seeing the ravages of conquest there.

She found Allira in the farthest room. The girl was huddled in a window seat with her head in her arms, so quenched and trembling that she did not lift her head as Melitta ran into the room, but only cowered into a smaller and smaller bundle of torn silks. She started with a scream of weak terror as Melitta put a hand on her arm.

"Stop that, Allira. It's only me."

Allira Storn's face was so bleared with crying that it was

almost unrecognizable. She flung herself on the other girl, wrapped her arms round her, and burst into a hurricane of sobs and cries.

Melitta's heart quailed with sickening pity, but she grasped Allira firmly in both hands, held her off and shook her hard, until her head flapped loosely up and down. "Lira, in Aldones' name, stop that squalling! That won't help you—or me, or Edric, or Storn, or our people! While I'm here, let's think. Use what brains you have left!"

But Allira could only gasp, "He—he—huh—Buh—Brynat—" She stared at her sister with such dazed, glassy eyes that Melitta wondered in a spasm of terror if harsh usage had left Allira witless or worse. If so, she was frighteningly alone, and might as well give up at once.

She freed herself, searched, and found on a side-board a half-empty bottle of *firi*. She would rather have had water, or even wine, but in these straits anything would do. She dashed half the contents full into Allira's face. Eyes stung by the fiery spirits, Allira gasped and looked up; but now she saw her sister with eyes at least briefly sane. Melitta grasped her chin, tilted the bottle and forced a half-cup of the raw liquor down her sister's throat. Allira gulped, swallowed, coughed, choked, dribbled, then, anger replacing hysteria, struck down Melitta's arm and the cup.

"Have you lost your wits, Meli?"

"I was going to ask you that, but I didn't think you were in any shape to answer," Melitta said vigorously. Then her voice became more tender. "I didn't mean to frighten or hurt you, love; you've had more than enough of that, I know. But I had to make you listen to me."

"I'm all right now—as much as I can ever be," she amended, bitterly.

"You don't have to tell me," Melitta said quickly, flinching from what she could read in her sister's mind; they were both wide open to each other. "But—he came and mocked me, calling you his lady wife—"

"There was even some mummery with one of his red-robed priests, and he sat me in the high seat at his side," Allira confirmed, "with knife near enough my ribs that I didn't dare speak—"

"But he didn't harm you, apart from that?"

"He used neither knife nor whip, if that's what you mean," Allira said, and dropped her eyes. Before the accusing silence of the younger girl, she burst out, "What could I have done? Edric dead, for all I knew—you, Zandru knew where—he would have killed me," she cried out on another gust of sobs. "You would have done the same!"

"Had you no dagger?" Melitta raged.

"He—he took it away from me," Allira wept.

Melitta thought, *I would have used it on myself before he could make me his doxy-puppet in his high hall.* But she did not speak the words aloud. Allira had always been a fragile, gentle girl, frightened by the cry of a hawk, too timid to ride any horse but the gentlest of palfreys, so shy and home-loving that she sought neither lover nor husband. Melitta subdued her anger and her voice to gentleness. "Well, love, no one's blaming you; our people know better and it's no one else's business; and all the smiths of Zandru can't mend a broken egg or a girl's maidenhead, so let's think what's to be done now."

"Did they hurt you, Meli?"

"If you mean did they rape me, no; that scarface, a curse to his manhood, had no time for me, and I suppose he thought me too fine a prize for any of his men offhand—though he'll probably fling me to one of them when the time comes, if we can't stop it." In a renewed spasm of horror, she thought of Brynat's rabble of renegades, bandits, and half-human things from far back in the Hellers. She caught Allira's thought, even the brutal protection of the bandit chief was better than that rabble's hands. Well, she couldn't blame Lira—had she had the same choice what might she have done? Not all porridge cooked is eaten, and not all brave words can be put into acts. Nevertheless, a revulsion she could not quite conceal made her loose her sister from her arms and say dispassionately, "Edric, I think, is in the dungeons; Brynat forbade me to go there. But I think I would feel it if he were dead. You are more psychic than I; when you pull yourself together, try to reach his mind."

"And Storn!" Allira broke out again in frenzy. "What has he done to protect us—lying like a log, safe and guarded by his own magic, and leaving us all to *their* tender mercies!"

"What could he have done otherwise?" Melitta asked reasonably. "He cannot hold a sword or see to use it; at least he has made sure that no one can use him for a puppet—as they are using you." Her eyes, fierce and angry, bored into her sister. "Has he gotten you with child yet?"

"I don't know—it could be."

"Curse you for a witling," Melitta raged. "Don't you, even now, see what it is he wants? If it were only a willing girl, why not one—or a dozen—of the maids? Listen. I have a plan, but you must use what little sense the gods gave you for a few days at least. Wash your face, robe yourself decently, try to look like the Lady of Storn, not some camp follower tom from the kennel! Brynat thinks he has you tamed and well-married, but he is a ruffian and you are a lady; you have the blood of the Seven Domains; you can outwit him if you try. Play for time, Allira! Have the vapors, play at mourning, put him off with promises—at worst, tell him that the day you know you are pregnant you will throw yourself from the battlements—and *make him believe it*! He daren't kill you, Allira; he needs you robed and jewelled in the high seat beside him, at least until he can be sure no follower or enemy will try to topple him from this height: Put him off for a few days, no more, and then—"

"Can you waken Storn to help us?" Allira gasped.

"By all the gods, what an idiot you are! Storn in trance is all that keeps us safe, Lira, and gives us time. Storn roused and in his hands—that devil's whelp would stick a knife in

Edric's guts, toss me to his soldiers for a few hours' sport while I lived, and who knows if he'd even want a child from you? No, Lira, pray Storn keeps safe in trance till I can think of a plan! You do your part, keep up your courage, and I'll do mine."

In her heart a small desperate plan was maturing. She dared not tell Allira. They might be overheard, or, if she formulated it in words, there might be among Brynat's rabble, some half-human telepath who would win favor from his outlaw lord by bearing tales of the plot. But a seed of hope had been born in her.

"Come, Allira, let us dress you as befits the Lady of Storn and bedazzle that ruffian into respect," she said, and prepared, again, to face Brynat without revealing anything.

CHAPTER THREE

Barron had been in the service of the Terran Empire since he was a lad in his late teens and he had served on three planets before coming to Darkover. He discovered that afternoon that he had never left Terra. He found it out by leaving it for the first time.

At the designated gate from the Terran Zone, a bored young clerk looked him over as he examined the slip from Transportation and Personnel, which stated that Barron, Class Two, was being released on liaison assignment beyond the Zone. He remarked, "So you're the fellow who's going back into the mountains? You'd better get rid of those clothes and pick up some sort of suitable outfit for traveling here. Those togs you're wearing might do for the Zone, but back in the hills you'll get frozen—or maybe lynched. Didn't they tell you?"

They hadn't told him anything. Barron felt nonplussed; was he expected to go native? He was a Terran Empire liaison man, not a secret agent. But the clerk was the first person since the accident who had treated him like a human being, and he was grateful. "I thought I was going as an official representative. No safe-conducts, then?"

The clerk shrugged. "Who'd give it? You ought to be planet-wise after five years here. Terrans, or any Empire men, aren't popular outside Trade City. Or didn't you bother reading Official Directive Number Two?"

"Not the fine print." He knew that it made it illegal, on penalty of instant deportation, for Empire men to enter, without permits, any portion of the planet outside the designated trade zones. Barron had never wanted to, and so it never entered his head to wonder why. An alien planet was an alien planet—there were thousands of them—and his work had always been inside the Zone.

But it was no longer.

The clerk was feeling talkative. "Almost all the Terrans in Mapping and Exploring or the other liaison jobs wear Darkovan clothes. Warmer, and you don't collect a crowd that way. Didn't anybody tell you?"

Barron shook his head stubbornly. He didn't remind the clerk that nobody had been telling him anything for some days. In any case, he was feeling stubborn. He was doing his proper work for the Empire—he was officially appointed to it—and the Darkovans were not to tell him how to dress or act. If the Darkovans didn't like the clothes he was wearing; they could start learning the tolerance for alien customs which was the first thing required of every man who accepted work for the Terran Empire. He was satisfied with his light, warm synthetic tunic and breeches, his soft, low-cut sandals, and his short lined overcoat, which kept out the wind. Many Darkovans had adopted them in Trade City; the clothing was comfortable and indestructible. Why change it? He said a little stiffly, "It isn't as if I were wearing Spaceforce uniform. I can see where that might be a breach of good taste. But these?"

The clerk shrugged enigmatically. "It's your funeral," he said. "Here, I imagine this is your transport coming now."

Baryon looked down the roughly cobbled street, but saw no sign of any vehicle approaching. There were the usual crew of loungers, women in heavy shawls going about their business, and three men leading horses. He started to say "where" and then realized that the three men, who were coming straight toward the gate, were leading *four* horses.

He swallowed hard. He had known in a general way that the Darkovans had small technology and used no motor transit. They used various pack and draft animals, indigenous relatives of the buffalo and the larger deer, and horses—probably descended from a strain imported from Nova Terra about a hundred years ago—for riding. It made sense. The Darkovan terrain was unsuited to roadbuilding on a large scale, the population didn't care about it and in any case there were none of the massive mining and manufacturing operations which are necessary for surface transit. Barron, safely inside the Zone, had noticed all this and his reaction had been "So what?" He hadn't really cared how the Darkovans lived; it had nothing to do with him. His world was spaceport dispatch: spaceships, cargo, passenger transit—Darkover was a major pivot on long-distance hypertravel because it was situated conveniently between the High Arm and Low Arm of the Galaxy—mapping ships, and the various tractors and surface machinery for servicing all of those. He was not prepared for the change from spaceship to pack animals.

The three men paused, letting go the reins of the horses, which were well-trained and stood quietly. The foremost of the three men, a sturdy young man in his twenties, said, "You are the Terran representative Daniel Firth Barron?" He had some trouble with the name.

"*Z'par servu.*" The polite Darkovan phrase, *at your service*, brought a faint agreeable smile from the young man as he replied in some formula Barron couldn't understand and then shifted back to Trade City language, saying, "I am Colryn. This is Lerrys, and this, Gwynn. Are you ready? Can you leave at once? Where are your baggages?"

"I'm ready when you are." Barron indicated the duffel bag, which held his few possessions, and the large but light case which held the equipment he must use. "The bag can be knocked around as much as you like; it's only clothes. But be careful not to drop the crate; it's breakable."

"Gwynn, you see to that," Colryn said. "We have pack animals waiting outside the city, but for the moment we can carry them with us. It isn't easy to manage pack animals on the streets here, as narrow as they are."

Barron realized that they were waiting for him to mount. He reminded himself that this assignment was all that stood between him and ruin, but that didn't seem very important at the moment. He wanted, for the first time in his adult life, to run. He set his mouth hard and said very stiffly, "I should warn you, I've never been on a horse in my life."

"I am sorry," Colryn said. His politeness was almost excessive. "There is no other way to go where we are going."

The one introduced as Lerrys swung Barron's duffel bag up to his saddle. He said, "I'll take this, you'll have enough trouble with your reins, then." His Terran was substantially better than Colryn's, being virtually accentless. "You'll soon pick up riding; I did. Colryn, why don't you show him how to mount? And ride beside him until he gets over being nervous."

Nervous! Barron felt like snarling at the youngster that he had been facing strange worlds when this boy was playing with his toys, then he relaxed. *What the hell, I am nervous, the kid would have to be blind not to see it.*

Before he realized how it had happened, he was in the saddle, his feet slipped through the high ornate stirrups, moving slowly down the street and away from the Terran Zone. He was too confused and too busy keeping his balance to give it a single backward look.

He had never been at close quarters with Darkovans before. At the restaurants and shops in Trade City, they had been dark impassive faces serving him and strangers at a safe distance to be ignored. Now he was among them for an indefinite period of time, with only the most casual of warnings, the dimmest of preparations.

This never happened in the Terran Empire! Damn it, you were never supposed to be assigned work outside your specialty; then if they actually sent you into the field on a strange planet, you were supposed to get all sorts of briefing and training! At the moment it was taking all the concentration he could muster to stay on his horse.

It was the better part of an hour before he began to relax, to feel that a fall was less imminent, and to spare a few minutes to look at his three companions.

All three were younger than Barron, as well as he could judge. Colryn was tall, lanky yet delicately built, and his face was narrow and fine, with a shadow of brown curly beard. His voice was soft, but he seemed unusually self-possessed for so young a man, and he talked and laughed with animation as they rode. Lerrys was sturdy, with hair almost red enough for a Terran, and seemed hardly into his twenties. Gwynn, the third, was swart and tall, the oldest of the three; except for a nod and brief greeting, he had paid no attention to Barron and seemed a little aloof from the younger men.

All three wore loose heavy breeches, falling in flaps over high, carefully fitted boots, and laced tunic-like shirts in rich, dark colors. Gwynn and Colryn had thick, fur-lined riding cloaks, and Lerrys a short loose fur jacket with a hood. All three wore short gauntlets, knives in their belts and smaller knives in pockets at the top of their boots; Gwynn had a sword as well, although for riding it was swung across the crupper of his horse. They all had hair cut smoothly below their ears and a variety of amulets and jewelry. They looked fierce, bright and barbaric. Barron, aware of his own thoroughly civilized clothing, hair, grooming and manner, felt queerly frightened. *Damn it, I'm not ready for this sort of thing!*

They rode at first through cobbled streets, between the crowded houses and markets of the Old Town; then along wider stone roads where the going was smoother, between high houses set back behind gardens and unfamiliar high towers. Finally the stone road ended to become trampled grass and the riders turned aside toward a long, low enclosure and through wooden and stone fences and gateways into a sort of compound of reddish, trampled earth, where several dozen unfamiliarly dressed men were doing various things: loading and unloading animals, saddling and grooming them, cooking over open fires or on braziers, washing and splashing in a wooden trough, and carrying buckets of feed and water to the beasts. It was very cold and very confusing, and Barron was glad, at last, to reach the lee of a rough stone wall, where he was permitted to slide from his horse and turn it over, at Colryn's nod, to a roughly dressed man who came to lead it away.

He walked between Gwynn and Lerrys, Colryn remaining behind to see to the animals, under a shelter roofed and walled against the wind. Lerrys said, "You're not used to riding; why don't you rest while we get food ready? And haven't you any riding clothes? I can bring your bag—it would be better to change into them now."

Although Barron knew that the youngster was trying to be kind, he felt irritated at the continued harping on this point. "The clothes I have with me are just like this; I'm sorry."

"In that case you'd better come with me," Lerrys said, and led him out of the shelter again, through the opposite end of the long enclosure. Heads turned to follow them as they passed; someone shouted something and people laughed loudly. He heard repeated murmurs of *Terranan*, which didn't need any interpreting. Lerrys turned and said firmly, "*Chaireth.*" That caused a momentary silence and then a brief flurry of quiet words and mutters. They all moved away with some deference as the young redhead motioned to them. Finally the two came out into a market or shop—mostly clay jars and coarse glassware, a multitude of loose garments lying over baskets and barrels. Lerrys said firmly, "You can't possibly travel into the mountains in the outfit you're wearing. I don't mean to sound offensive, but it's impossible."

"I wasn't given any orders—"

"Listen, my friend"—Lerrys used the Darkovan word *com'ii*—"You have no idea how cold it gets, traveling in the open, especially back in the hills. Your clothes may be warm"—he touched a fold of the light synthetic—"but only for conditions between walls. The Hellers are the very bones of the earth. Your feet will be sore, riding in those things, not to mention—"

Barron, now fiercely embarrassed, had to say flatly, "I can't afford it."

Lerrys drew a deep breath. "My foster father has ordered me to provide everything that is necessary for your well-being, Mr. Barron." Barron was surprised at the manner of address—the Darkovans did not use honorifics or surnames—but then, Lerrys apparently spoke excellent Terran. He wondered if the young man were a professional interpreter. "Who is your foster father?"

"Valdir Alton of the Comyn Council," Lerrys said briefly. Even Barron had heard of the Comyn—the hereditary caste of Darkovan rulers—and it silenced him. If the Comyn had anything to do with this and wanted him to wear Darkovan clothes, there was no use arguing.

After a brief period of spirited bargaining of which Barron—who knew considerable of the Darkovan language, more because he was quick and fluent at languages than because he had been interested—could follow very little, Lerrys said, "I hope these will meet with your approval. I knew you would not care to wear bright colors; I do not myself." He handed Barron a pile of clothing, mostly in dark fabrics that looked like linen, with a heavy fur jacket like the one he himself was wearing. "It's hard to manage a cloak, riding, unless you grew up wearing one." There was also a pair of high boots.

"Better try the boots for fit," he suggested.

Barron bent and slipped off his sandals. The clothing seller chuckled and said something Barron couldn't follow about sandals. and Lerrys said fiercely, "The *chaireth* is Lord Alton's guest!" The merchant gulped, muttered some phrases of apology and fell silent. The boots fitted as if they had been made for him, and though they felt strange along his ankles and calves, Barron had to admit they were comfortable. Lerrys picked up the sandals and stuck them in Barron's pocket. "You could wear them indoors, I suppose."

Barron would have answered, but before the words reached his lips a curious dizziness swept over him.

He was standing in a great, vaulted hall, lighted only by a few flickering torches. Below him he could hear the shouts of drunken men; and he could smell torches, roasting meat, and an odd acrid odor that confused him and made him feel sick. He grasped at a ring in the wall, found that it was not there; the wall was not there. He was back in the blowing wind and cloudy sunlight of the fenced compound, his pile of clothing fallen to the grass at his feet, and young Lerrys staring up at him, shaken and puzzled.

"Are you all right, Barron? You looked—a bit odd."

Barron nodded, glad to conceal his face by stooping to gather up his clothing. He was relieved when Lerrys left him in the shelter and he could sink down on the rough floor and lean against the wall, shuddering.

That again! Was he going mad? If it had been due to the stress of his job, now that he had been removed from the dispatch board it should have stopped. Yet, although brief, this time had been more vivid than the others. Shivering, he shut his eyes and tried not to think until Colryn, coming to the edge of the open wall of the shelter, called to him.

Two or three men in rough, dark clothing were moving around the fire; Colryn did not introduce them. Barron, in response to gestures, joined Gwynn and Lerrys at the trough where men were washing. It was growing dusky and the icy evening wind was coming up, but they all washed long and thoroughly. Barron was shivering uncontrollably and thinking with some longing of the Darkovan fur jacket, but he took his turn and washed face and hands more than he'd normally have done; he didn't want them to think Terrans were dirty—and in any case riding had left him dirtier than pushing buttons and watching circuit relays. The water was bitterly cold, and he shook with the chill, his face bitten by the bitter wind.

They sat around the fire out of the wind, and after murmuring a brief formula, Gwynn began handing food around. Barron accepted the plate he was given; which held some sweet boiled grain covered with a splash of acrid sauce, a large lump of meat and a small bowl of thick bittersweet stuff vaguely like chocolate. It was all good, although it was hard to manage the tough meat which the others sliced into paper-thin slices with the knives in their belts; it had been salted and dried in some manner and was almost like leather. Barron pulled a pack of cigarettes from his pocket and lighted one, drawing the smoke gratefully into his mouth; it tasted ambrosial.

Gwynn scowled at him and said in an undertone to Colryn, "First the sandals and now this—" looking with direct rudeness at Barron, he asked a question of which Barron could make out only the unfamiliar word *embredin*. Lerrys raised his head from his plate, saw Barron's cigarette and shook his head slightly, then said "*Chaireth*" again, rather deprecatingly, to Gwynn and got up to drop down beside Barron.

"I wouldn't smoke here if I were you," he said. "I know it is your custom, but it is offensive among the men of the Domains."

"What was he saying?"

Lerrys flushed. "He was asking, to put it in the simplest possible terms, if you were an—an effeminate. It was partly those damned sandals of yours, and partly—well, as I say, men do not smoke here. It is reserved for women."

With an irritable gesture Barron ground out his cigarette. This was going to be worse than he thought. "What's that word you used—*chaireth*?"

"Stranger," Lerrys said. Barron picked up a lump of meat again, and Lerrys said, almost apologizing, "I should have provided you with a knife."

"No matter," Barron said, "I wouldn't know how to use it anyway."

"Nevertheless—" Lerrys began again, but Barron did not hear him. The fire before them slid away—or rather, flared up, and in the midst of the flames, tall, bluish, and glowing, he saw—

A woman.

A woman again, standing in the midst of flames. He thought he cried out in the moment before the figure changed, grew and was, again, the great chained Being, regal, burning, searing her beauty into his heart and brain. Barron gripped his hands until the nails bit into the palms.

The apparition was gone.

Lerrys was staring at him, white and shaken. "Sharra," he breathed, "Sharra, the golden-chained—" Barron reached out and grabbed him. He said, hoarsely, disregarding the men at the fire, which was once again the tiny, cooking fire, "You saw it? *You* saw it?"

Lerrys nodded without speaking. His face was so white that small freckles stood out. He said at last with a gasp, "Yes, I saw. What I can't understand is—how *you* saw! What in the Devil's name are you?"

Barron, almost too shaken to speak, said, "I don't know. That keeps happening. I have no idea why. I'd like to know why you can see it, too."

Struggling for composure, Lerrys said, "What you saw— it is a Darkovan archetype, a Goddess form. I don't completely understand. I know that many Terrans have some telepathic power. Someone must be broadcasting these images and somehow you have the power to pick them up. *I*—" He hesitated. "I must speak to my foster father before I tell you more." He fell silent, then said with sudden resolution, "Tell me, what would you rather be called?"

"Dan will do," Barron said.

"Dan then. You are going to have trouble in the mountains; I thought you would be an ordinary Terran, and not aware—" He stopped, biting his lip. "I am under a pledge," he said at last, "and I cannot break it even for this. But you are going to have trouble and you will need a friend. Do you know why no one would lend you a knife?"

Barron shook his head. "Never occurred to me to ask: Like I said, I can't use one anyway."

"You are a Terran," Lerrys said. "By custom and law here—a knife or any other weapon must never be lent or given, except between sworn friends or kinfolk. To say 'my knife is yours' is a pledge. It means that you will defend the other—therefore, a knife or any weapon, must be bought, or captured in battle; or made for you. Yet," he said, with a sudden laugh, "I will give you this—and I have my reasons." He stooped down and drew a small sharp knife from the pocket in his boot. "It is yours," he said, suddenly very serious. "I mean what I say, Barron. Take it from me, and say 'yours and mine.'"

Barron, feeling embarrassed and strange, fumbled at the hilt of the small blade. "Mine, then, and yours. Thank you, Lerrys." The intensity of the moment caught him briefly up into it, and he found himself staring into the younger man's eyes almost as if words passed between them.

The other men around the fire were staring at them, Gwynn frowning in surprised disapproval, Colryn looking puzzled, and vaguely—Barron wondered how he knew—jealous.

Barron fell to his food, both puzzled and relieved. It was easier to eat with the knife in his hand; later he found it fitted easily into the little pocket at the top of his boot. Lerrys did not speak to him again, but he grinned briefly at Barron now and then, and Barron knew that, for some reason, the young man had adopted him as a friend. It was a strange feeling. He was not a man to make friends easily—he had no close ones—and now a young man from a strange world, guessing at his confusion, had thrust unexpected friendship on him. He wondered why and what would happen next.

He shrugged, finished his meal, and followed Colryn's gestured directions—to rinse his plate and bowl and pack them with the others and to help with the spreading of blankets inside the shelter. It was very dark now; cold rain began to spray across the compound; and he was glad to be inside. There was, he realized, a subtle difference in the way they treated him now; he wondered why, and though he told himself it made no difference, he was glad of it.

Once in the night, wrapped in fur blankets, surrounded by sleeping men, he woke to stare at nothingness and feel his body gripped with weightlessness and cold winds again. Lerrys, sleeping a few feet away, stirred and murmured, and the sound brought Barron back to the moment.

It was going to be one hell of a trip if this keeps on happening every few hours.

And there wasn't a thing he could do about it.

CHAPTER FOUR

A voice called in Melitta's dreams.

"Melitta! Melitta, sister, *breda*, wake! Listen to me!" She sat up in the dark, desperately grasping at the voice. "Storm" she gasped, half aloud, "is it you?"

"I can speak to you only a little while like this, *breda,* so listen. You are the only one who can help me. Allira cannot hear, and in any case she is too frail and timid, she would die in the hills. Edric is wounded and prisoned. It must be you, little one. Dare you help me?"

"Anything," she whispered, her heart pounding. Her eyes groped at the dark. "Are you here? Can we escape? Shall I make a light?"

"Hush. I am not here; I speak to your mind only. I have tried to waken hearing in you for these last four days and at last you hear me. Listen, sister—you must go alone. You are only lightly guarded; you can shake them off. But you must go now, before snow closes the passes. I have found someone to help you: I will send him to you at Carthon."

"Where . . ."

"At Carthon," the fading voice whispered and was silent. Melitta whispered aloud, "Storn, Storn, don't go," but the voice had failed and faded into exhaustion. She was alone in the darkness, her brother's voice still ringing like an echo in her ears.

Carthon—but where was Carthon? Melitta had never been more than a few miles from her home; she had never been beyond the mountains and her ideas of geography were hazy. Carthon might be over the next ridge, or it might be at the world's end.

She flung agonized queries into the darkness. *How can I, where shall I go?* But there was no answer, only darkness and silence. Had it been a dream born of her frenzy to escape, or had her brother in his magical trance, somehow managed to reach her mind in truth? If it were so, then she could do nothing but obey.

Melitta of Storn was a mountain girl with all that implied. The prime root of her being was the clan loyalty to Storn, not only as her elder brother, but as the head of his house. That he was blind and incapacitated, that he could not have defended her and her sister and younger brother—not to mention their people—in this crisis, made no difference. She did not censure him even in her thoughts and believed, when Allira did so, that the girl's sufferings at Brynat's hands had turned her brain. Now he had laid the task on her to escape and find help, and it never occurred to her not to obey.

She rose from her bed, pulled a fur robe around her shoulders—for the night was bitterly cold and the stone floors had never known fire—and thrust her feet into furry socks, then, moving surely in the dark, found flints and tinder and struck a small lamp—so small that the light was not much bigger than the head of a pin. She sat down before the light, cheered a little by the tiny flame, and began to plan what she could do.

She knew already what she must do—escape from the castle before snow closed the passes, and somehow make her way to Carthon, where her brother would send someone to help her. But how this could be accomplished, she found it hard to imagine.

Guards still followed her at a respectful distance, everywhere she went through the halls. Dark and late though it was, she was sure that even if she left her room they would rouse from where they slept and follow. They feared Brynat more than they longed for sleep. Their fear of him was made clear to her when she realized that not one of them had ventured to lay a hand on her. She wondered if she should be grateful for this, and thrust the thought aside. That was to fall into his trap.

Like all mountain girls, Melitta was enough of a realist to think the next logical step: could she seduce one of the guards into letting her escape? She thought it unlikely. They feared Brynat, and he had ordered them to let her alone. More likely the guard would accept her advances, take what she offered, then go directly to Brynat with the story and win approval of his chief as well. After which, Bryant might well punish her by turning her over to the outlaws for a plaything. That was a blind alley—she could have made herself do it, but it would probably be no use.

She went to the window, pulling her furs closer about her, and leaned out. *You must be gone before the snow closes the passes.* She was a mountain girl, with weather and storms in her blood. It seemed to Melitta that she could almost smell from afar, borne on the chill night wind, the smell of far-off clouds pregnant with snow.

The night was not far advanced. Idriel and Liriel swung in the sky; Mormalor, faint and pearly, hung half-shadowed on the shoulder of the mountain. If she could manage somehow to leave the castle before dawn . . .

She could not go now. Brynat's men were still at their nightly drinking party in the great hall; Allira might send for her still, and she dared not be found absent. But in the hours between deep night and dawn, when even the air was sluggish, she might devise a plan, and be far away before midmorning discovered that she was not in her room. She closed the window, cuddling herself in the furs, and went back to make plans.

Once out of the castle she wondered where she could go. It would be to Carthon, wherever that was, eventually. But she could not make Carthon in a single night; she would need shelter and food, for it might be a journey halfway to the world's end. Once clear of Castle Storn, perhaps some of her brother's vassals would shelter her. Although they were without power to protect against Brynat's attack, she knew that they loved Storn and many of them knew and loved her. They would at least let her hide among them for a day or two until the hue and cry died down; they might help provide her with food for the journey, and it might be that one of them could set her on the road to Carthon.

The nearest of the great lords were the Aldarans, of Castle Aldaran near High Kimbi; they had, as far as she knew, no blood feud with Storns and no commitment to Brynat, but it seemed unlikely that they would, or could, come to the aid of Storn at this time. Her grandmother's kinfolk had been Leyniers, related to the great Comyn Domain of Alton, but even the Comyn Council's writ did not run here in the mountains.

It did not occur to Melitta to censure her brother, but it did occur to her that, knowing himself weak, he might well have attempted to place himself under the protection of one of the powerful mountain lords. But always before, the chasms and crags surrounding Storn had made them impregnable; and—a Storn swear fealty to another house? Never!

He could have married Allira—or me—to some son of a great house. Then we would have blood kin to protect us— bare is the back with no brother to guard it!

Well, he had not, and the time for fretting was long past—*chickens can't be put back into eggs!* The evil bird that had hatched from this oversight was out and flying, and only Melitta had the freedom and the strength to save something from the wreck.

Carrying the tiny lamp, she went to her chests. She could

not go in long skirts and mantles. At the bottom of her chest was an old riding cloak, woven of thick heavy fabric from the valley and lined with fur; it was not rich enough to rouse greed in anyone she passed, but it was warm and durable. There was an old and shabby pair of her brother's riding breeches, patched with leather, which she had worn for riding about the estate; it was a wiser choice than her own long, loose riding mantle. She added a knitted blouse, a long, thick, lined tunic, socks knitted from the spun fur of the forge folk, and her fur boots. She made a small parcel of a change of linen and some small trinkets, which she might sell or barter for help on the way. Finally she braided her hair and tied it into a woolen cap. This done, she put out the lamp and went to the balcony again. Until this moment, the actual preparation for the journey had obscured the really basic fact: exactly *how* was she to get out of the castle?

There were secret passages. She knew some of them. There was one, for instance, leading from the wine cellars near the old dungeon. The only thing necessary was to get into the wine cellar so that she could get into the secret passage. Perfectly simple. And what would her guards be doing while she descended the stairs and went into the wine cellar, conveniently managing to leave them outside? Drinking wine? That might be fine, if she could get them drunk enough, but they would certainly be suspicious at anything she offered them, on guard for a trick.

Another exit from the castle—calling it secret was a mere technicality, a way of saying that it had been unused for years and nobody bothered guarding it any more—was the passageway that led down into the cliffs and the abandoned forges where, in an earlier day of Darkover, the dark, stunted mountain people had worshipped the fires that lit their forges. There they had made the ancient swords and the strangely propertied artifacts which those who had never seen them used, called magical. The fires and forges had been silent for centuries, the little people withdrawn into the deeper hills; the Storns had come long after they were gone. As a child Melitta, with her brothers and sister, had explored the caves and abandoned dwellings of the forge folk. But they, and all their magic, were gone. Their poor and scattered remnants now dwelt in villages near Storn, and they had been captured and driven along with the farm folk; they were more helpless than Melitta herself.

She looked over the balcony again, her mouth curving in what might have been a smile in better days. *I need wings,* she thought. *My guards are too much afraid of Brynat to molest me here; while I stay in this room, they will stay outside in that hallway, and swear to him that I am inside here. I should have managed these things better; I should have spent my childhood in a room with one of the secret passages. I can think of a dozen ways to get out of the castle — but I have to get out of this room first, and I can't think of a way to do that.*

A faint glimmer of light wavering beneath her showed her that, on a lower floor and some rooms away, Allira moved in the Royal Suite. She thought, despairingly, *Storn should have wakened Allira. There is the old hidden way from the Royal Suite, down into the cliff people's village. Allira could simply wait till Brynat was sleeping, and slip away. . . .*

Mad schemes spun in her mind. She had access to her sister; the guards would follow her to the doors of the Royal Suite but not follow her inside; could she manage to get in there and find the old entrance to the passage? At what hour could they be safe from Brynat's intrusion? Could she count on Allira to trick him, drug him, even hold him in talk or in sensual play while she, Melitta, slipped past?

I dare not depend on Allira, she thought with something like despair. *She would not betray me, but she would not have courage to help me; or risk angering Brynat, either.*

If I went down to her rooms, with the guards following me — how long could I count on being alone with her before

*they summoned Brynat, or grew suspicious when I did not
return? And if I vanished from her rooms—they would tear
her to pieces, to find out what way I had gone, and I would
be pursued before the sun was well up. That's no help.*

But the thought persisted. It might very well be her only
chance. It was, of course, to risk everything on one throw; if
Brynat returned while she was with Allira, something might
rouse his suspicions and she would be consigned to securer
custody. For all she knew, her guards had orders to report to
Brynat if she and her sister spoke together for more than a
few minutes.

But if no one knew I was with Allira?

How could she get to Allira's room unseen?

The old Darkovans had mastered the secrets of such
things. The magic electrical net which protected Storn's
trance was only one of the powers with which Melitta was
familiar—but none of them were of use to her now. There
were magical cloaks which threw a veil of illusion around
the wearer and let them walk unseen, by bending the light,
but if Storn had ever owned one, Melitta did not know
where it was, or how to use it. She could slip up to the Sunrise Tower, if she could get there, and pull the magical bird
plumage over her head, and fly out and away from the castle—but only in illusion. What she saw would be real
enough—Storn, she knew, had watched the battle that
way—but her body would lie in trance in the Tower, and
sooner or later, she would be drawn back to it. That was not
the kind of escape which would do any good. I need wings,
she thought again. *If I could fly right off this balcony and
down into that same Royal Suite where Brynat has taken Allira . . .*

She stopped in mid-thought, grimly. She had no wings.
Thinking about them was no good. But she had two sturdy
arms, two sturdy legs, ten strong fingers and she had been
trained since childhood in rock climbing.

She went to the edge of the balcony, fantasies and plans

vanishing in a cold, realistic assessment of the problem. She could not fly down to the Royal Suite. But, with strength, caution, and good luck, it was remotely possible that she could *climb* down to it.

She leaned over, fighting a sudden surge of dizziness. A hundred feet of rough, sheared stone fell away into a chasm below. But the castle wall was not sheer, not smooth. Centuries ago, it had been built of rough stone, the very bones of the mountain, hewn in great lumps and cemented into place with ancient tools which would have blunted too swiftly if the stone had had to be smoothed. A wealth of window ledges, archer's slits, balconies, outside stairways and projections lumped and ridged the gray sides of the old castle.

When I was a child, she thought, Storn and I used to climb everywhere. I was whipped once for frightening our nurse out of her senses by climbing to a third-level balcony and making faces at her from the arbor. I taught Edric to climb on the balconies down lower. I've never climbed this high—I was afraid of falling. But this part of the castle should be as climbable as the lower part.

She knew that if she fell she would be broken on the crags far below. *But why should I fall from two hundred feet in the air, if I could manage not to fall from fifteen feet?*

You never thought about that because it wouldn't have mattered if you did fall from fifteen feet, her common sense told her, but she hushed the voice, packed up the thought into a tiny box, shoved it into the back of her mind and left it there. *And suppose I do get killed,* she told herself defiantly. *Edric didn't mind risking being killed in the siege, or if he did mind, he risked it anyway. I took bow and arrow myself, and I could have been shot or knifed down on the ramparts. If I was willing to die then, in the hope of defending Storn Heights, then why should I hesitate to take the same sort of risk now? If I get killed, I get killed, and at least*

*I won't have to worry about Brynat's rabble lining up to take
turns raping me.*

It wasn't exactly a comforting thought, but she decided
that she could make it do for the moment. She hesitated only
a moment, her hands on the railing. Off went the fur-lined
gloves; she thrust them deep into the pockets of Edric's
breeches. She buttoned the cloak back and tied it into the
smallest possible compass at her waist, hoping it would not
catch on a projection of stone. Finally she slipped off her
boots, standing shivering on the stone balcony, and tied
them together by their laces round her neck. If the thongs
caught on a stone she might strangle, but without boots she
would be helpless in the snow, and her trained weather sense
told her that the snow could not be very long delayed. Then,
without giving herself time to think, she swung herself up
and over the edge of the balcony, sat there for a moment taking the exact bearings of the room and balcony she
wanted—forty feet below her and almost a hundred feet
away to the left—and slipped down, lodging her stockinged
feet in a crevice of the stone, finding a handhold to spread-
eagle herself against the rough wall.

The crevices between the stone seemed smaller than
when she had climbed about on them as a child, and she had
to move by feel on the cold stone. Her feet ached with the
cold before she had moved five yards, and she felt first one,
then another of her nails split back and break as she clutched
the dark, rough stone. The moonlight was pale and fitful,
and twice a white streak that she took for a crevice in the
paleness turned out to be a crumbling, evil-smelling bird-
dropping. But Melitta clung like a limpet to each crevice,
never moving more than one hand or one foot until she was
securely anchored in some new hold.

Evanda be praised, she thought grimly, *that I'm strong
and tough from riding! If I were a girl to sit over my sewing,
I'd drop off in two yards!* Even strong as she was, she felt
every muscle trembling with cold and tension. She felt, also,

that in the pale moonlight, she must be clearly visible against the side of the castle, a target for an arrow from any sentry who happened to look up on his rounds. Once she froze, whimpering as a small light and a fragment of voice, blown on the wind, came round the corner, and she knew one of Brynat's soldiers on some business below passed beneath her. Melitta shut her eyes and prayed he would not look up. He did not; he went on singing drunkenly and, almost exactly beneath her, a hundred feet below, and on the narrow path between the castle and the cliffs, opened the fly of his breeches and urinated into the abyss. She held herself taut, trembling against hysterical laughter. After what seemed an hour he stooped, picked up his lantern, shrugged his clothes into place and stumbled on his way again. Melitta thought she had forgotten how to breathe, but she managed it again, and forced her taut fingers, gripping at a stone, to move again toward the lighted balcony below.

Inch by slow inch—a finger, a toe, a cold yard at a time— the girl crept like an ant down the wall. Once, her heart flipped over and stopped as a pebble encrusted in cement broke away under her fingers, and she heard it slide away and ricochet off a projection beneath her, rebound with what sounded like gunfire off the rocks below, and finally clatter into the darkness. Every muscle tight, she held her breath for minutes, sure that the sound would bring soldiers running, but when she opened her eyes again, the castle still lay bathed in the empty light of the setting moons and she still clung to the wall in her comforting solitude.

The moonlight had dimmed considerably past the shoulder of the mountains, and thick mists were beginning to rise below, when at last her feet touched the stone of the balcony and she let go and slid, dropped down on the stone railing, and crouched there, just breathing in deep gasps of relief. When she could move again, she slipped her hands into her gloves, her feet into the fur-lined boots, and wrapped herself tightly in the cloak, grabbing it tight to lessen her shivering.

The first hurdle was passed. But now she must get inside
and attract Allira's attention without running the risk that
Brynat would see. She had come too far to be stopped now!

She crept like a small shaking ghost across the stone balcony and pressed her face against the veined colored glass,
joined with strips of metal, which closed the double doors of
the balcony. The doors were bolted inside and lined with
heavy thick curtains of tapestry, and Melitta had a sudden
hysterical picture of herself perched out there like a bird for
days, uselessly rapping like a bird at the glass, unheard, until
somebody looked up and saw her there.

She also feared that it might be Brynat who drew aside
those curtains and looked straight out into her eyes.

She tried to force herself to approach the window, but
the picture of Brynat's fierce face was so compelling that
she literally could not make herself raise her hand. She knew
he was behind that tapestry. She sank down, nerveless and
shaking, and waited, her mind spinning.

*Storn, Storn, you came to me before, help me now!
Brother, brother! Gods of the mountains, what shall I do?*
She begged and commanded her weak limbs to move, but
she kept on crouching there, frozen and motionless, for what
seemed like hours. Finally, slowly, her frozen body and
brain began to work again, and she began to think.

*When we were children, Allira and I could reach one an-
other's minds like this. Not always and not often, but if one
of us was in danger the other would know; when the wild
bird pack had her cut off on the island, I knew and I brought
help. She was fourteen then, and I was only eight. I cannot
have lost that power, or Storn could not have reached me
tonight. But if all my mind is giving off is fear, Allira
wouldn't know if she did hear me; she'd think it was just part
of her own panic.*

She had had almost no training. Storn, being blind and
thus debarred from the usual pursuits of men of his caste,
had explored the old telepathic ways. But to his brother and

sisters, these had been dreams, fantasies, games and tricks—
pleasant perhaps for pastime, but not worthy of serious
study. There was too much else that was real and present and
necessary to the moment. Melitta spent a moment berating
herself for not spending more time with Storn learning about
the old speech of mind to mind, but common sense came to
her rescue. She reminded herself of the old proverb, *Fore-
sight could make wise men of Durraman's donkeys!* She
might as well blame herself for Allira's not having been
married to a strong husband with eighty fighting men to defend them.

She put her hand out to rap on the glass sharply, and
again the clear picture of Brynat looking out into the storm
came to her; it was so instant and compelling that she physically shrank back and pressed herself against the railing,
folding herself up into her cloak. It was just in time; a
browned hand drew the tapestry aside, and Brynat's scarred
visage turned from side to side, trying to penetrate the darkness.

Melitta shrank against the railing and tried to make herself invisible. After a minute that seemed endless, Brynat
turned away and the lamp went out. The tapestry dropped
back into place. Melitta dropped, gasping, to the stones, and
lay there trying not to breathe.

Time dragged. The moon set, and the shivering girl grew
colder and colder. After hours, so long that she began to
wonder if the sun would come up and find her there, a thin
fine rain began to fall, and this spurred her; she realized that
whatever she risked, she must be gone by sunrise; she must
be somewhere that she could lie hidden by day. Even if she
must chip the glass of the doors and cut Brynat's throat
while he slept, she must make some move!

As she poised her muscles for action, a faint light glimmered again between the tapestries. Melitta gathered herself
to spring against the bolts; then a fine hand moved through
the gap, the bolt shuddered in the wood and her sister Allira,

wrapped in a long woolen shift, her hair disheveled, thrust the door outward and, her eyes great and staring, looked straight into Melitta's face.

Melitta raised a hand to her mouth, frightened of Allira's nerves and a sudden outcry, but Allira only clasped her hands to her heart with a gasp of relief. She whispered, "I knew you were there, and I couldn't believe—Melitta, how did you come here?"

Melitta replied only with a jerk of her head toward the rocks and a whispered "No time now! Brynat—"

"Asleep," Allira said laconically. "He sleeps with one eye, like a cat, but just now—never mind that. Melitta—are you armed?"

"Not with a weapon I could kill him with, without outcry," Melitta said flatly. "And you'd still have his men to deal with, and they would be worse." Watching Allira flinch, she knew that her sister had already considered and rejected that escape.

"The secret passage through the old cliff-town; have any of Brynat's men discovered it?"

"No—Melitta, you cannot go that way; you'll be lost in the caves, you'd die in the mountains if you ever found your way out—and where would you go?"

"Carthon," Melitta said briefly, "wherever that is. I don't suppose you know?"

"I know only that it's a city beyond the passes, which was great in the days of the Seven Domains. Melitta, are you really going to dare this?"

"It's this or die here," Melitta said bluntly.

"You seem able to stand it here, though—"

"I don't want to die."

Allira was almost sobbing and Melitta hushed her roughly. It was not Allira's fault that she was so timid. Perhaps even such protection as Brynat could give seemed better than a desperate trek through strange crags, passes and mountains. *Maybe I ought to be like that too,* Melitta

thought, *maybe that's a woman's proper attitude, but I sup-*
pose there's something wrong with me—and I'm glad. I'd
rather die taking the chance of doing something to help
Storn.

But the brief moment of censure for her sister passed.
After all, Allira had already faced, or so it seemed to Allira
herself, the worst that could happen to her; what more had
she to fear? By escaping now, she would only lose the life
she had saved at such cost.

"You must go, then, before sunrise," Allira said with
quick resolution. "Quick, while Brynat sleeps and before the
guards come in"—a brief flicker of something like her old
smile—"as they do each night, to make sure I have not
killed him while he sleeps."

The wind blew briefly into the room and was barred out
again as the two girls slipped inside. Brynat lay sprawled
and ugly in the great bed, breathing stertorously. After one
blazing look of hate, Melitta averted her eyes, creeping past
him silently, holding her breath and trying not to think, as if
her very hate might wake their enemy. She breathed more
freely when they were in the ornate reception room of the
suite, but her hands were still clenched with tension and terror.

There were the carven chests, the hangings and the
strange beasts around the elaborate false fireplace. She
pressed the hilt of the marble sword there and the stone slid
away, revealing the old stair. She clutched Allira's hands,
wanting to say something but falling silent in desperation.
She went forward. Whatever happened, she was safe or
dead.

Allira might somehow summon up the courage to
come—but the escaping, Melitta knew with a practical
grimness, was only the beginning. She had a long way to go,
and she could not encumber herself with anyone who did
not share her own desperate resolve; at this point, even if Allira had begged to come with her, she would have refused.

She said briefly, "The guards outside my room think I'm still in there. Try anything you can to keep them from finding out how I've gone. You saw nothing; you heard nothing."

Allira clutched at her, a frightened hug and kiss. "Shall I—shall I get you Brynat's knife? He would search me for it, but when he didn't find it, he'd only think he lost it."

Melitta nodded, a tardy spasm of admiration for her frightened sister touching her. She stood frozen, not daring to move, as Allira crept back into the bedroom, and then returned with a long, unsheathed knife in her hand. Allira thrust it into the top of Melitta's boot. Allira had something else in her hand, wadded together in a torn linen coif. Melitta glanced hastily at the soggy mess; it was a torn half-loaf of bread, some cut slices of roast meat, and a large double handful of sticky sweets. Uncritically, she wrapped it up again and put it into her deepest pocket.

"Thank you, Lira. It will keep me going for a day or two, and if I don't find any help by then, it's no use anyhow. I must go; it will be light in three hours." She dared not frame a goodbye in words; it would have loosened the floodgates of her fear. "Give me your gold chain, unless you think Brynat will miss it; I can hide it in a pocket and the links will pass current, though it's not as good as a copper one would have been."

Allira smiled a wavering smile. "The amulet didn't protect me, did it? Maybe it will do better for you. Lucky charms protect you only if you have your own luck." She pulled off the long chain, looped it twice and put it over Melitta's head. Melitta clutched at the small amulet, suddenly touched—Allira had worn it since she was three years old; it had been their mother's and grandmother's.

She said quietly, "I'll bring it back," gave Allira a quick kiss, and without another word, plunged into the long deep stairwell. She heard Allira sob softly, as above her the passage darkened and the light went out.

She was alone in the depths of the castle.

CHAPTER FIVE

"We should reach Armida by nightfall." Colryn drew his horse to a walk in the neck of the narrow pass, waiting for the others to draw abreast of them, and looked across at Barron with a brief smile. "Tired of traveling?"

Barron shook his head without answering. "Good thing, because, although the Comyn Lord may want us to break our journey there for a day or two, after that we start into the hills."

Barron chuckled to himself. If, according to Colryn, they started into the *hills* tomorrow, he wondered what they had been traveling for these past four days. Every day since they had left the plains where the Terran Trade City lay, they had been winding down the side of one mountain and up along the side of another, till he had lost count of the peaks and slopes.

And yet he was not tired. He was hardened now to riding, and sat his horse easily; and, although he would not have known how to say so, every inch of the road had held him in a sort of spell he did not understand and could not explain.

He had expected to travel this road filled with bitterness, resentment and grim resignation—he had left behind him everything he knew: his work, such friends as he had, the whole familiar world made by the men who had spanned great giant steps across the Galaxy. He had been going into exile and strangeness.

Yet—how could he explain it even to himself?—the long road had held him almost in a dream. It had been like learning a language once known but long forgotten. He had felt the strange world reach out and grip him fast and say, "Stranger, come; you are coming home." It gave him a sensation, of riding through a dream, or under water, with everything that happened insulated by a curtain of unreality.

Now and then, as if surfacing from a very long dive, the old self he had been, during those years when he sat at the dispatcher's board in the Terran Trade City, would come to the surface and sit there blinking. He tried, once, to make it clear to himself.

Are you falling in love with this world, or something? He would breathe the cold, strangely scented air, and listen to the slow fall of his horse's hooves on the hard-frozen road, and think, *What's wrong? You've never been here before, why does it all seem so familiar?* But familiar was the wrong word; it was as if, in another life; he had ridden through hills like these, breathed the cold air and smelled the incense that his companions burned in their campfires in the chilly fog of evening before they slept. For it was new to his eyes, and yet—*it's as if I were a blind man, newly seeing, and everything strange and beautiful and yet just the way I knew it would be. . . .*

During these brief interludes when the old Barron came to life in his mind, he realized that this sense of *déjà vu*, of living in a dream, must be some new form of the same hallucinated madness that had cost him his job and his reputation. But these interludes were brief. The rest of the time he rode in the strange dream and enjoyed the sense of suspension between his two worlds and the two selves which he knew he was becoming.

Now the journey would break, and he wondered briefly if the spell would break with it. "What is Armida?"

Colryn said, "The estate of the lord Valdir Alton, the Comyn lord who sent for you. He will be pleased that you speak our language fluently, and he will explain to you just what he wishes." He looked down into the valley, shading his eyes with his hand against the dimming sunlight, and pointed. "Down there."

The thick trees, heavy gray-blue conifers that cast dark spice-smelling small cones on the ground, thinned as they rode downward, and here and there in the underbrush some small bird called with perpetual plaintiveness. Thin curls of mist were beginning to take shape in the lowlands, and Barron realized that he was glad they would be indoors before the nightly rain began. He was tired of sleeping on the ground under tarpaulins, though he knew that the climate was mild at this season and that they were lucky it was only rain and not snow. He was tired, too, of food cooked over open fires. He would be glad to sleep under a roof again.

He guided his horse with careless expertness down the slope, letting his eyes fall shut, and drifted off into a brief daydream. *I do not know the Alton lords, and I must keep my real purpose secret from them, until I am certain they would help and not hinder. Here, too, I can find some information about roads and the best way to travel—snow will close the passes soon, and before then I must somehow find the best road to Carthon. The way to the world's end . . .*

He jerked himself out of his dream. He wondered what rubbish was he daydreaming. Where was Carthon, for that matter, *what* was Carthon? As far as he knew, it might be the name of one of the moons! *Oh, hell, maybe I've seen it on a survey map somewhere.* He did look at such things now and then when he had nothing better to do. Perhaps his unconscious—they said the unconscious mind never forgets anything—was weaving dreams with these half-forgotten fragments.

If this went on, he'd be ready for Bedlam. *Ready? Hell, I'm going Tom-o-Bedlam one better!* His brain juggled with scraps of a song learned years ago on another world; it was about the world's end.

"I summoned am to journey
Three leagues beyond the wild world's end,
Methinks it is no journey . . . "

No, that's wrong. He frowned, trying to recapture the
words; it fixed his mind on something other than the
strangeness around him.

Lerrys drew his horse even. "Did you say something,
Barron?"

"Not really. It would be hard to translate unless—do you
understand the Terran language?"

"Well enough," Lerrys said with a grin.

Barron whistled a scrap of the melody, then sang in a
somewhat hoarse but melodious voice:

"With a host of furious fancies
    whereof I am commander,
With a burning spur and a horse of air,
Through the wilderness I wander;
By a queen of air and darkness
I summoned am to tourney
Three leagues beyond the wild world's end;
Methinks it is no journey."

Lerrys nodded. "It does seem a little like that sometimes," he said. "I like that; so would Valdir. But Armida
isn't *quite* at the wild world's end—not yet."

As he spoke, they rounded a bend; a faint smell of wood
smoke and damp earth came up to them from the valley, and
through the thin mist they saw the great house lying below
them.

"Armida," said Lerrys, "my foster father's house."

Barron did not know just why he had expected it to be a
castle, set high among impassable mountain crags, with ea-
gles screaming around the heights. On the downslope, the

horses neighed and picked up speed, and Lerrys patted his beast's neck.

"They smell their home and their stable-mates. It was a good trip; I could have come alone. This is one of the safest roads; but my foster father was afraid of dangers by the way."

"What dangers?" Barron asked. *I must know what I may face on the long road to Carthon.*

Lerrys shrugged. "The usual things in these hills: catmen, wandering nonhuman bands, occasional bandits—though they usually prefer wilder country than this, and in any case we aren't enough to tempt the more dangerous ones. And if the Ghost Wind should blow—but I'll be frightening you away."' He laughed. "This part of the world is peaceful."

"Have you traveled much?"

"Not more than most," Lerrys said. "I crossed the Kilghard Hills leading out of the Hellers with my foster brother, when I was fifteen; but it wasn't any pleasure trip, believe me. And once, I went with a caravan into the Dry Towns, crossing the passes at High Kimbi, beyond Carthon—"

Carthon! The word rang like a bell, kicking something awake in Barron and sending a jolt of adrenalin into his system; he physically twitched, missing the next sentence or two. He said, cutting almost rudely through the younger man's reminiscences, "Where and what is Carthon?"

Lerrys looked at him strangely. "A city; or it used to be; it lies well to the east of here. It's almost a ghost town now; no one goes there, but caravans go through the passes; there's an old road, and a ford of the river. Why?"

"I—seem to have heard the name somewhere," said Barron lamely, and lowered his eyes to his saddle, using as his excuse the horse's increasing pace as the road leveled and led toward the low ramparts of Armida.

Why had he expected it to be a castle? Now that he was at the gates, it seemed reasonable that it should be a wide-flung house, sheltered by walls against the fierce winds from the heights. It was built of blue-gray stone with wide spaces of translucence in the stone walls, behind which lights moved in undefined patches of color and brilliance. They rode through a low arch and into a warm, sheltered court-yard; Barron gave up his horse to a small, swart man clad in fur and leather, who took the reins with a murmured formula of welcome. The Terran slid stiffly to the ground.

Shortly afterward he was beside a high blazing fire in a spacious, stone-flagged hall; lights warred with the dark be-hind the translucent stone walls and the wind safely shut outside. Valdir Alton, a tall, spare, sharp-eyed man, wel-comed Barron with a bow and a few brief formal words; then paused a minute, his eyes resting on the Terran with a sudden, sharp frown.

He said, "How long have you been on Darkover?"

"Five years." Barron asked, "Why?"

"No particular reason, except that—perhaps it is that you speak our language well for such a newcomer. But no man is so young he cannot teach, or so old he cannot learn; we shall be glad to know what you can teach us about the mak-ing of lenses. Be welcome to my hearth and my home." He bowed again and withdrew. Several times during that long evening, the warm and plentiful meal, and the long, lazy pe-riod by the fire—which came between the end of supper and the time they were shown to their bed—the Terran felt that the Darkovan lord's eyes were resting on him with a curious intentness.

Some Darkovans are mind-readers, I've heard. If he's read my mind; he must have seen some damn funny things in it. I wonder if there are loose hallucinations running around the planet and I've simply caught a few somehow.

Nevertheless, his sense of confusion did not keep him from eating hugely of the warm, good meal served for the travelers, and enjoying the strange green, resinous wine they drank afterward. The fuzziness from the strong wine seemed to make him less confused about the fuzziness

which blurred his surprise at all things Darkovan, and after
a while it was pleasant to feel simply drunk instead of feeling that he was watching the scene through two sets of eyes.
He sat and sipped the wine from the beautifully carved,
green crystal of the goblet, listening to Valdir's young foster
daughter Cleindori playing a small harp which she held on
her lap, and singing in a soft pentatonic scale some endless
ballad about a lake of cloud where stars fell on the shore and
a woman walked, showered in stars.

It was good to sleep in the high room hung with translucent curtains and filled with shifting lights; Barron, accustomed to sleeping in a dark room, looked for twenty minutes
for a switch to shut them off, then gave up, got into bed and
lay watching them drowsily. The shifting colors shifted his
mind into neutral gear, and produced colored patterns even
behind his closed eyelids, until he slept.

He slept heavily, dreaming strange swooping dreams of
flight, watching landscapes tipping and shifting below, and
hearing a voice calling in his dreams, again and again, "Find
the road to Carthon! Melitta will await you at Carthon! To
Carthon . . . Carthon . . . Carthon. . . ."

He woke once, half-dazed, the words still ringing in his
ears when he thought sleep had gone. Carthon. Why should
he want to go there; and who could make him go? Banish-
ing the thought, he lay down and slept again, only to dream
again of the voice that called—murmuring, beseeching,
commanding—*"Find the road to Carthon . . ."*

After a long time the dream changed. He was toiling
down endless stairs, breaking sharp webs with his out-
stretched hands, blinded except for a greenish, phosphorescent glow from damp walls that pressed all around him. It
was icy cold, and his steps came slow, and his heart beat
hard, and the same question pounded in his head: *"Carthon.
Where is Carthon?"*

With the sunrise and the thousand small amenities and
strangenesses of life in a Darkovan home, he tried to drive

the dream away. He wondered again, dispassionately, if he was going mad. *In God's name, what spell has this damned planet woven around me?*

In an attempt to break the bondage of these compelling dreams or sorceries, half through the day, he sought out Lerrys and said to him, "Your foster father, or whatever he is, was supposed to explain my work to me, and I'm anxious to get started. We Terrans don't like idling around when there is work to be done. Will you ask your father if he can see me now?"

Lerrys nodded. Barron had noticed before that he seemed to be more practical and forthright than the average Darkovan and less concerned with formalities. "There is, of course, no pressure on you to begin your work at once, but if you prefer it, my guardian and I are at your service whenever you wish. Shall I have your equipment brought up?"

"Please." Something he had said touched Barron with incongruity. "I thought Valdir was your father."

"Foster father." Again Lerrys appeared to be on the point of saying something, but he withheld it. "Come, I'll take you to his study."

It was a smallish room, as Darkovans counted space. Barron thought that at home it would have been a good-sized banquet hall. It looked down on the enclosed court; with alternating layers of glass and translucent stone. It was bitterly cold, although neither Valdir nor Lerrys appeared to suffer from it; the two wore only the linen shirts Darkovan men wore beneath their fur tunics. Outside below them, men were coming and going in the courtyard; Valdir stood and watched them for some minutes, while seeming courteously not to notice how Barron hung over the one small brazier to warm his hands; then he turned back, smiling in welcome.

"Last night in the hall I could give you only formal greetings; I am very glad to see you here, Mr. Barron. It was Lerrys and I who arranged that someone from the Terran city should come to teach us something of lens grinding."

Barron grinned a little sourly. "It's not my regular work, but I know enough about it to show beginners. So you arranged for me to come here? I thought you people didn't think much of Terran science."

Valdir gave him a sharp look. He said, "We have nothing against Terran science. It is Terran *technology* we fear—that Darkover will become just another link in a chain of worlds, all as much alike as sands scattered on the shore, or weeds along the path of the Terrans. But these are matters of politics—or, perhaps, of philosophy, and to be discussed over good wine at night, not offhand while we work together. I think you will find us ready to learn."

For the last several moments, while he spoke, Barron had been conscious of some low-keyed irritation, like a sound just at the edge of consciousness, which he couldn't quite hear. It made his head ache, and made it hard to hear Valdir's words. He looked around to identify, if he could, what was making the—noise? He couldn't quite hear it. He tried to concentrate on what Valdir was saying; he had missed a sentence or two.

"—and so, you can see, in the foothills, the sight of a sharp-eyed man may be enough, but in the high Sierras, where it's absolutely imperative that any trace of fire must be discovered before it gets out of hand, a lens—what do you call it, a telescope?—would be an invaluable help. It could save acres and acres of timber. Fire in the dry season is such a constant hazard—" He broke off; Barron was moving his head restlessly from side to side, his hand to his forehead. The sound or vibration or whatever it was seemed to fill every crevice of his skull. Valdir said in surprise, "The telepathic damper disturbs you?"

"Telepathic which? But *something* seems to be making one hell of a racket in here. Sorry, sir—"

"Not at all," Valdir said. He went to what looked like an ornamental carving and twisted a knob on it; the invisible

noise slackened, and Barron's head quieted to normal.
Valdir looked surprised.

"I am sorry; not one Terran in five hundred will know
such a device exists, and I had simply forgotten to discon-
nect it. My deepest apologies, Mr. Barron; are you well?
Can I offer you anything?"

"No, I'm all right," Barron said, realizing that he was
back to normal again, and wondering what the gadget was.
He had the usual Terran notion that Darkover, being a planet
without a great deal of manufacturing or technology, was a
barbarian one, and the idea of some sort of electronic device
functioning out here well beyond the Terran Zone seemed as
incongruous as a tree growing in the middle of a spaceport.

"Is this your first trip into the mountains?" Valdir asked.

"No, but the first time I had crossed the plains." Barron
caught himself. What was the matter with him? That gadget
and its weird noises seemed to have unsettled his brain.
"Yes, I've never been outside the Terran Zone before this."

"Of course you haven't seen any real mountains yet,"
Lerrys said. "These are just foothills, really, compared to the
Hellers or the Hyades or the Lorillard Ranges."

"There's quite enough mountain for me," Barron said. "If
these are foothills, I'm not in any hurry to see anything
higher."

As if to refute what he had said, a picture sprang to swift
life in his brain: *I had expected Armida to be like this, a
great gray peaked castle lying beneath the chasmed tooth of
the mountain, beneath the snow-laden crag with its high
plume of snow.*

Barron let his breath out as the picture faded, but before
he could think of anything to say, the door opened and
Gwynn, now wearing what looked like a green and black
uniform, came in, accompanied by two men carrying between them Barron's crate of lens materials and grinding
tools. They set it down, under his instructions, and removed
the heavy straps, buckles and padding which had protected

it on the trip. Valdir thanked the men in an unfamiliar dialect, Gwynn lingered to ask a couple of routine questions, and when the men went away, Barron was once more composed and in possession of himself. *Okay, maybe I've had something like a nervous breakdown in the Terran Zone, and it's still showing in intermittent brainstorms. It doesn't necessarily mean I'm going insane, and it certainly needn't inhibit the work I'm going to be doing.* He was glad to have the chance to collect himself by talking about familiar things.

He had to admit that for men without a standard scientific education, Valdir and Lerrys showed a good deal of comprehension and asked intelligent questions about what he had told them. He gave them a very brief history of lenses—from microscope to telescope to refracting lens for myopia, to binocular lens.

"You realize this is all very elementary," he added apologetically. "We've had simple lenses from our pre-history; it's a pre-atomic development on most planets. Now we have the various forms of radar, coherent light devices, and the like. But when men on Terra first started experimenting with light, the lens was our first step in that direction."

"Oh, it's quite understandable," said Valdir, "you needn't apologize. On a planet like Terra, where the random incidence of clairvoyance is so low, it's perfectly natural that men would turn to such experiments." Barron stared; he hadn't been apologizing.

Lerrys caught his eye and gave Barron a brief, humorous wink, then frowned slightly at his guardian, and Valdir caught himself and continued. "And of course, it's our good fortune that you have developed this technique. You see, Mr. Barron, here on Darkover, throughout *our* pre-history, we were a world where the so-called ESP powers were used, in place of gadgets and machinery, to augment and supplement man's five senses. But so many of these old powers have been lost, or forgotten, during what we call the Years of

Chaos, just before the Compact, that now we are forced to supplement our unaided senses with various devices. It's necessary, of course, to be very careful which devices we allow into our society; as the history of all too many planets will show, technology is a two-edged weapon, which can be abused more often than it is used. But we have studied the probable impact on our society quite carefully, and decided that with elementary caution the introduction of lenses will do no palpable harm in the forseeable future."

"That's good of you," said Barron ironically. If Valdir was conscious of the sarcasm he let it pass without comment. He said, "Larry, of course, has a fairly good technical education, and can make things clear to me if I can't understand. Now, about power sources for your machinery and equipment, Mr. Barron. I trust you were warned that very little electricity is available, and only in the lowest of voltages?"

"That's all right. I have mostly hand equipment, and a small generator which can be adapted to work by wind power."

"Wind is something we have plenty of back here in the mountains," said Lerrys with a friendly grin. "I was the one who suggested wind power instead of storage batteries."

Barron began putting the various bits of equipment back into their case. Valdir rose and went to the window, pausing beside the carved ornament which hid the strange electronic gadget. He asked abruptly, "Mr. Barron, where did you learn to speak Darkovan?"

Barron shrugged. "I've always been fairly quick at languages." Then he frowned; he had a good working knowledge of the language spoken in the city near the Trade Zone; but he had given what amounted to a long and fairly technical lecture, without once hesitating, or calling on the young man—Larry or Lerrys or whatever Valdir called him—to interpret. He felt strangely confused and troubled. *Had* he been speaking Darkovan all that time? He hadn't stopped to think what language he was speaking. *Damn it, what is wrong with me?*

"Nothing is wrong," said Lerrys quickly. "I told you, Valdir. No, I don't understand, either. But—I gave him my knife."

"It was yours to give, fosterling, but I don't disapprove."

"Look out," Lerrys said quickly, "he can hear us." Valdir's sharp eyes swept in the direction of Barron, who suddenly realized that the two Darkovans had been speaking in yet another language. Barron's confusion made him angry. He said, with dry asperity, "I don't know Darkovan courtesy, but among my people it is considered fairly rude to talk over someone's head, *about* them."

"I'm sorry," Lerrys said. "I had no idea you could hear us, Dan."

"My foster son, of all people, should know about latent telepaths," Valdir said. "I am sorry, Mr. Barron; we intended no rudeness. Telepaths, among you Terrans, are not common, though they are not unknown, either."

"You mean I'm reading your minds?"

"In a sense. It's far too complex a subject to explain in a few minutes. For the moment I suggest you think of it as a very good sort of talent to have for the work you're going to be doing, since it will make it easy for you to talk to people, when you know only a little of their language."

Barron started to say, *But I'm no telepath, I've never shown any talent for that sort of thing, and when the Rhines gave me the standard psi test for the Space Service, I tested out damn near flat negative.* Then he withheld it. He had been learning a lot about himself lately, and it was certain that he wasn't the same man he had been before. If he developed a few talents to go with his hallucinations, that was perhaps the law of compensation in action. It had certainly made it easier to talk to Valdir, so why complain?

He finished carefully putting the equipment in the crate, and listened to Valdir's assurances that it would be securely wrapped and crated for the trip up to the mountain station where he would be working. But when, a few minutes later, he took his leave and went down the hall, he was shocked and yet unsurprised to realize that Valdir's voice and Lerrys' continued, like distant whispers inside his head.

"Do you suppose the Terrans chose a telepath purposely?"

"I don't think so, Foster Father; I don't believe they know enough about choosing or training them. And he seems too surprised by the whole thing. I told you that from somewhere he had picked up an image of Sharra."

"Sharra, of all conceivable!"—Valdir's mental voice blurted out in astonishment and what seemed like dismay. *"So you gave him your knife, Larry! Well, you know what that will mean. I'll release you from your pledge, if you like; tell him who you are when it seems necessary."*

"It's not because he's a Terran. But if he's going to be running around Darkover in that state, someone's got to do something about it—and I can probably understand him better than most people. It isn't all that easy, to change worlds."

"Don't jump to conclusions, Larry. You don't know that he's changing worlds."

Larry's tone in answer sounded positive, and yet somehow sad. *"Oh, yes, he will. Where would he go among the Terrans, after this?"*

CHAPTER SIX

Melitta crept down the long, tunneled stairway, groping through the darkness. After the faint light from the cracks behind her had died, she was in total darkness and had to feel each step with her feet before setting her weight on it. She wished she had thought to bring a light. But on the other hand, she would need both hands to find her way and to brace herself. She went carefully, never putting her full weight on a step without testing it. She had never been down here before, but her childhood had been soaked in stories of her Storn forefathers and the builders of the castle before them, and she knew that secret exits and tunnels could be honeycombed with nasty surprises for people who blundered through them without appropriate precautions.

Her care was not superfluous. Before she had gone more than a few thousand feet down into the darkness, the wall at her left hand fell away and left her feeling a breath of dank air which seemed to rise out of an immense depth. The air was moving, and she had no fear of suffocation, but the echoes stirred at such distance that she quailed at the thought of that drop to her left; and when she dislodged a small pebble with her foot and it slipped over the edge it seemed to fall forever before landing at last, a distant whisper, far below.

Abruptly her hands struck cold stone and she found that

she had run into a blank wall. Taken aback for a moment, she began to feel about and discovered that she was inching, foot by foot, along a narrow shelf at the foot of the stairs. She felt her hands strike and break thick webs, and cringed at the thought of the unseen creatures in the darkness that had spun them; she had no fear of ordinary spiders, but who could tell what horrors might spawn here, out of sunlight since the beginning of the world, and what they would crawl over in the darkness and what ghastly things they would find to eat. She braced herself, setting her small chin, thinking, *They won't get to eat me, anyhow.* She gripped the hilt of her knife and held it before her.

To her left, a small chink of pale greenish light wavered. Could she have come to the end of the tunnel already? It was no normal daylight or moonlight. Wherever the light came from, it was not outside. The ledge suddenly widened and she could step back and walk at ease instead of inching along.

The greenish light grew slowly, and now she saw that it came through an arched doorway at the end of the stone passageway along which she walked. Melitta was far from timid, but there was something about that green light which she disliked before she saw more than a glimmer of it, something which seemed to go beneath the roots of consciousness and stir old half-memories which lay at the very depths of her being. Darkover was an old world and the mountains were the most ancient bones of the world, and no man knew what might have crawled beneath the mountains when the sun first began to cool, ages ago, there to lie and grow in unseen horror.

She had been walking silently in her fur-lined boots; now she ghosted along, hardly disturbing the air she walked through, holding her breath for fear it would disturb some hidden *something*. The green light grew stronger, and, although it was still no brighter than moonlight, somehow it hurt her eyes so that she slitted them to narrowness against it and tried not to let it inside her eyelids. There was something very awful down here.

Well, she thought, *even if it's a dragon, it can't be much worse than Brynat's men. At worst a dragon would only want to eat me. Anyhow, there haven't been any dragons on Darkover for a thousand years. They were all killed off before the Ages of Chaos.*

The doorway from which the green light emanated was very near. She felt the poisonous brightness as a positive assault on her eyes. She stepped to the doorway and peered through, holding her breath against screaming at the ghastly glare which lay ahead.

She could see that the green light came from some thick, poisonous fungus that grew in the slow currents of air. The room ahead was high and arched, and she could see carvings covered with fungus, and at the far end, blurred and overgrown shapes which had once been a dais and something like chairs.

Melitta took a firm hold of her nerves. *Why should it be evil just because it's green and slimy-looking,* she demanded *of herself. So is a frog, and frogs are harmless. So was the moss on a rock. Why should plants growing in their own way give me this overwhelming feeling of something wicked and sinister?* Nevertheless, she could not make her feet move to take the first step into that arched room. The green light made her eyes ache, and there was a faint smell, as if of carrion.

Slowly, as her eyes grew accustomed to the green, she saw the things that crawled among the fungus. They were white and sluggish. Their eyes, great and curiously iridescent, moved slowly in her direction, and the girl felt her stomach heave at that blind regard. She stood there paralyzed, thinking frantically, *This must be new, they can't have been here all along, this passage was in good shape forty years ago; I remember my father speaking of it, though he hadn't been down here since years before I was born.*

She stood back, studying the green stalactites of fungus and the crawling things. They looked dreadful, but were they dangerous as well? Even though they made her skin crawl, they might be as harmless as most spiders. Perhaps, if she could simply summon up the nerve to run through them, that was all that was needed.

A small restless rustle behind her made her look down. Near her skirts, sitting up on his hind legs and surveying her with curiosity, a small red-furred, rodentlike animal hung back from entering the cave. He gave a small, nervous chitter which seemed to Melitta to mirror her own apprehension. He was a dirty-looking little creature, but by contrast with the things in the green cave he looked normal and friendly. Melitta almost smiled at him.

He squeaked again and, with a sudden burst of speed, set off running through the fungus.

The green branches whipped down on the little creature: It screamed thinly and was still, smothered in the green, which seemed to pulse with ghastly light. Through the phosphorescence the small golden-eyed horrors moved, swarmed, and moved away. Not even the bones were left; there was only an infinitesimal scrap of pinkish fur.

Melitta crammed her fist in her mouth to keep from screaming. She took a convulsive step backward, watching the slow subsiding of the fungus. It took some minutes to subside.

After a long time her heartbeat slowed to normal and she found herself frantically searching for solutions. *I wish I could get through here somehow and lure Brynat's men down after me,* she thought grimly, but that line seemed to go nowhere.

Fire. All living things fear fire, except man. If I could carry fire . . .

She had no light; but she did have steel and tinder in her pocket; on Darkover to be outdoors without the means of making fire in the snow season, was to die. Before she was eight years old she had known all the tricks of firemaking anywhere and everywhere.

Trying not to breathe hard, she pulled out her firemaking materials. She had nothing she could use for a torch, but she tore off her scarf, wound it round a small slab of rock, and set it alight. Then, carrying it carefully in front of her, she stepped into the fungus cave.

The green branches whipped back as the firelight and heat struck them. The sluggish crawling at her feet made her gasp with horror, but they made no effort to attack, and she began to breathe again as she began to walk, steadily, across the cave. She must go quickly but not too fast to see where she was going. The scarf would not burn more than a minute at most. Fortunately the patch of green seemed to be less than a hundred yards; beyond the further arch was darkness again.

One of the crawling things struck her foot. It felt squishy, like a frog, and she gasped, staggered a little for balance, and dropped the blazing scarf. She swooped to retrieve it . . . .

A high shrill yeeping came from the crawling thing. The green fungus near her feet moved, and Melitta held her breath and waited for it to strike.

The blazing scarf touched the green branch and it caught fire. A blaze of ghastly green-red light licked up to the ceiling; Melitta felt the blast of heat as the fire blazed up, catching branch after branch. In half a minute the walls of the cave were ablaze; the small crawling things screamed, writhed and died at her feet as the green branches, agitating violently, struggled to get out of range, were caught by the blaze and burned.

It seemed an eternity that she stood there in terror, trying to draw her clothing back from the flames, her ears hurting with the screams and her eyes burning from the greenish tint of the fire. Rationally she knew that it must have been only a few minutes before the flames, finding nothing more to feed on, sank and died, leaving her alone in unrelieved, blessed darkness.

She began to move slowly across the cave, in the remembered direction of the other door, holding her breath and trying not to breathe the scorched, poisonous dust of the burnt fungus. Under her feet it crumpled unpleasantly and she hated setting her feet on the ground, but there was no help for it. She kept moving, numbly, in the direction of that remembered patch of darkness beyond the fungus cave.

She knew when she had passed through it, for almost at once the air was cleaner, and under her feet there was nothing but hard rock. There was also faint light from somewhere—a glimmer of moonlight, perhaps, from a hidden airshaft. The air felt cool and sweet; the builders of these tunnels had gone to some pains to make them pleasant to walk in. Far off she heard a trickle of water, and, her throat still full of the dust of the burnt fungus, it was like a promise.

She went down, moving toward the sound of distant water. Twice she shrank, seeing on the walls a trace, hardly more than a smear, of the greenish stuff, and made a mental note, *If I ever get back I'll come down and burn it out. If not, I hope it grows fast—and Brynat comes down here some day!*

After what seemed like hours of slow descent she found the water—a trickling stream coming out of the rock and dripping slowly down along the stairs beside her path. She cupped her hands and drank. The water was good, and she drank well, cleansed her grimy face, and ate a few bites of food. She could tell, by the feel of the air on her face, that the night was far advanced. She must be safely hidden by morning.

Must I? I could lie hidden in the tunnel for a day or two, till pursuit quiets.

Then she knew she could not. She simply could not trust Allira that much. Her sister would not intentionally betray her; but if Brynat suspected Allira knew, he would try anything to extract the information from her. She had no faith in Allira's ability to resist questioning for any length of time.

As she went downward, she realized that the slope of the tunnel was lessening, until she walked on a grade that was just downhill. She must be coming near the end of the long stair. She was a fair judge of distances, and she knew that she had walked a considerable distance in the night; the tunnel must have led far beneath the castle and down into the caves and cliffs beneath. Then she came upon a great pair of bronze doors, thrust them outward, and stood in the open air, free.

It was still dark, although the smell of the air told her that dawn was less than two hours away. The moons had set, and the rain had stopped, though mist still lay along the ground. She looked back at the closed doors behind her.

She knew where she was now. She had seen these doors from the outside when as a child she played in the forge village. She stood now in an open square of stone, surrounded on every side by the doors cut in the cliffs that rose around her. The sky was only a narrow cut above. She looked at the dark house doors, some of them still agape, and thought with all the longing in her weary body of how good it would be to crawl into one of the abandoned houses to lie down and sleep for hours.

She forced herself upright again and went down the path that led between the cliffs. Like the tunnel, the empty forge village would be the first place searched if Brynat managed to force the secret of the passage from Allira. She passed the open-air hearths where countless years ago, smiths had worked, making their beautiful and curious ironwork, copper jewelry and the iron gates of their own castle now crumpled and thrown down in the siege. She cast a look upward. From here she could see a portion of the outworks. Brynat had spared no time in repairing the fortifications of Storn.

Evidently he thought he might have to hold them against invaders.

*He will. I swear it by Avarra and Zandru, I swear it by
Sharra, Goddess of Forges and Fires! He shall struggle ten-
fold . . .*

There was no time for that. If she wanted to make Brynat
suffer, there was only one way to achieve it, she must get
away herself. Her own safety must be the first thought. She
passed the old circle of fireplaces, cold and rusted. Even the
carven image of Sharra above the central forge was dulled
and the gold of her chains, set against the duller metal of
the statue, covered with spiderwebs and bird-droppings. She
flinched at the sacrilege. She was no worshipper of the
Flamehair, but like every child of the mountains, she had a
deep respect and awe for the secret arts of the smith.

*If I come back—when I come back Sharra's image shall
be purified and served again . . .* There was no time for that
now, either.

The horizon was reddening perceptibly when footsore
Melitta, her steps dragging, clung to the doorway of a small
house in a village far below the castle, and beat weakly on
it. She felt at her last strength. If no one heard her or helped
her, she would fall down here and lie there until Brynat's
men found her, or she died.

But it was not more than a few moments until the door
opened a cautious crack, and then motherly arms grasped
her and drew her inside and to a fire.

"Quick—bar the door, draw the curtain—*damisela*,
where did you come from? We thought you dead in the
siege, or worse! How did you get free? Evanda guard us!
Your poor hands, your face—Reuel, you oaf, bring some
wine, quickly, for our little lady."

A few minutes later, drinking hot soup, her boots drawn
off and her feet to the fire, wrapped in blankets, Melitta was
telling a little of her escape to a wide-eyed audience.

"Lady, you must hide here until the search is quiet—" but

their faces were apprehensive, and Melitta said a swift "No. Brynat would surely kill you all," and saw shamed relief in their eyes. "I can lie hidden in the caves up the mountain until darkness tonight; then I can get away to Nevarsin or beyond. But you can find me food to carry, and perhaps a horse that can face the passes."

It was quickly arranged and by the time the day broke, Melitta rested, wrapped in furs and rugs in the labvrinthine caves which had for centuries been a last hiding place of the Storns. For one day she was safe there, since Brynat would surely search nearer places first; and by tonight she would be gone. It was a long road to Carthon.

Exhausted, the girl slept, but the name tolled in her dreams—*Carthon*.

CHAPTER SEVEN

Barron had believed, on the journey from the Terran Zone to Armida, that he had seen mountains. True, his Darkovan escort had repeatedly called them foothills, but he had put that down to exaggeration, to the desire to see the stranger's surprise. Now, half a day's ride from Armida, he began to see that they had not exaggerated. As they came out of a miles-long, sloping pathway along a forested hill, he saw, lying before him, the real ranges. Cool purple, deep violet, pale grayed blue, they lay there fold on fold and height behind height, each successive fold rising higher and farther away, until they vanished in cloudy distances that might have been thunderheads—or further ranges.

"Good God," he exploded, "we're not going over the top of *those*, are we?"

"Not quite," Colryn, riding at his side, reassured him. "Only to the peak of the second range, there." He pointed. "The fire tower is on the crest of that range." He told Barron its name in Darkovan. "But if you look far enough, you can see all the way back into the mountains, as far as the range they call the Wall Around the World. Nobody lives beyond there, except the Trailmen."

Barron remembered vague stories of various groups of Darkovan nonhumans. The next time they paused to eat cold food from their saddlebags and rest the horses, he looked for

Lerrys, who was still the friendliest of the three, and asked him about them. "Are they only beyond the far ranges? Or are there nonhumans in these mountains too?"

"Oh, yes. You've been on Darkover how long, five of our years, and you still haven't seen any of our nonhumans?"

"One or two *kyrii* in the Terran Trade Zone—from a distance," Barron told him, "and the little furred people at Armida—I don't know what you call them. Are there others? And are they all—well, if they're nonhumans, I can't ask, 'are they human,' but do they meet Empire standards for so-called intelligent beings—time-binding culture, viable language capable of transfer to other I.B.s?"

"Oh, they're all I.B.s by Terran Empire standards," Lerrys assured him. "The reason the Empire doesn't deal with them is fairly simple. Humans here don't have much interest in the Empire *per se,* but they are interested in other humans as individuals. The nonhuman races—I'm no expert on them, but I suspect they have never tried to get in touch with the Empire for the same reason they don't have much contact with humans on Darkover. Their goals and wishes and so forth are so completely different that there's no point of contact; they don't want any and they don't have any."

"You mean even Darkovans have no contact with nonhumans?"

"I wouldn't say *no* contact. There's some small amount of trade with the Trailmen—they're what you might call half-human or subhuman, and they live in the trees in the forests. They trade with the mountain people for drugs, small tools, metal and the like. They're harmless enough unless you frighten them. The catmen—they're a race something like the *cralmucs*, the furred servants at Armida. *Cralmacs* aren't very intelligent; feline rather than simian, but they do have culture of a sort, and some of them are telepathic. Their level is about that of a moron, or a chimpanzee who suddenly acquired a tribal culture. A genius among the *cralmacs* might learn a dozen words of a human language but I never heard of one learning to read; I suspect the Empire people gave them pretty wide benefit of the doubt in classifying them as I.B.s."

"We tend to do that. We don't want later squawks that we treated a potential intelligent race as higher animals."

"I know. *Cralmacs* are listed as real or potential I.B.s and let alone. The catmen, I suspect, are a hell of a lot more intelligent; I know they use metal tools. Fortunately I've never been close to them; they hate men and they'll attack when they feel safe in doing it. I've heard that they have a very elaborate feudal culture with the most incredible tangle of codes governing face-saving behavior. The Dry-towners believe that some of the elements of their own culture came from cultural interchange with the catmen millennia ago, but an I.B. xenthropologist could tell you more about that."

"Just how many races of I.B.s are there on Darkover anyway?" Barron asked.

"God only knows, and I'm not being funny. Certainly no Terran knows. Maybe a few of the Comyn know, but they're not telling. Or the *chieri*; they're another of the nearly human races, but they're as far above humans, most people think, as the *cralmacs* are below 'em. It's for sure no Terran knows, though; and I've had more opportunity than most."

Barron hardly heard the last sentence for a minute, in his interest in the nonhumans, then suddenly it penetrated. "*You're* a Terran?"

"At your service. My name is Larry Montray; they call me Lerrys because it's easier for a Darkovan to pronounce, that's all."

Barron felt suddenly angry and irked. "And you let me make a fool of myself trying to speak Darkovan to you?"

"I offered to interpret," Larry said. "At the time I was under a pledge to Valdir, never to mention that I was a Terran—not to anyone."

"And you're his ward? His foster son? How'd that happen?"

"It's a long story," Larry said. "Some other time, maybe.*
In brief, his son, Kennard, is being schooled on Terra with
my family, and I'm living here with *his* people." He scrambled to his feet. "Look, Gwynn's looking for us; I think we
ought to get on. We want to reach the fire tower before
nightfall tomorrow, if we can—the rangers there are due to
be relieved—and it's still a long way into those hills."

It gave Barron plenty to think about, as they rode on, but
his thoughts kept coming back, with an insistence he could
not understand—it was as if some secret watcher, far back
in his mind, kept dwelling on that point almost with frenzy.

*A Terran could pass as a Darkovan. A Terran could pass
as a Darkovan. A Darkovan could pass himself off as a Terran. A Terran could pass as a Darkovan. In these mountains,
where Terran are never seen, a Terran willing to pass as a
Darkovan would be safe from anything human, and attract
no unusual attention from nonhumans . . .*

Barron shook his head. *That's enough of that.* He wasn't
interested in the Darkovan mountains except from the view-
point of doing his job well enough to redeem himself with
the Empire, and get his own job, or something like it, back,
and start over again on another planet, in a spaceport job. *If
Larry, or Lerrys, or whatever he calls himself, wants to
amuse himself living with a family of weird, Darkovan
telepaths and learning more than anyone else cared to know
about nonhuman and such, that's his business; everybody
gets their kicks in his own way and I've known some dillies.*
But he wasn't having any.

He clung to that with an uneasy concentration all that
day, doggedly ignoring the beauty of the flowers that lined
the mountain road, snubbing Larry's friendly attempts to
pick up the conversation. Toward evening, as the ride steep-
ened, Colryn whiled away the time by singing Darkovan
legends in a tuneful bass voice, but Barron shut his ears and

*cf. *Star of Danger*

would not listen, closing his eyes and letting his horse take the road along the mountain trail; the horse knew more about it than he did.

The sound of hoofs, the slow jogging in the saddle, the darkness behind his closed eyes, was first hypnotic, then strangely familiar; it seemed normal to sit unseeing in his saddle, trusting himself to the horse beneath him and his other senses alert—the smell of flowers, or conifers, of the dust of the road, the sharp scent of some civet-smelling animal in the brush. When Lerrys drew abreast of him, Barron kept his eyes closed and after a time Lerrys spurred his horse and overtook Colryn. Colryn went on singing in an undertone. Without knowing how he knew, Barron recognized that the singer had shifted to the opening bars of the long *Ballad of Cassilda*.

How strange it sounded without the water-harp accompaniment. Allira played and sang it well, though it was really a song for a man's voice:

> The stars were mirrored on the shore,
> Dark was the dark enchanted moor,
> Silent as cloud or wave or stone,
> Robardin's daughter walked alone.
> A web of gold between her hands
> On shining spindle burning bright,
> Deserted lay the mortal lands
> When Hastur left the realms of light.
> Then, singing like a hidden bird . . .

He lost track of the words, hearing a far-off hawk cry and the small wounded scream of some animal in the bush. *He was here, he was free, and behind him, ruin and death.*

The song went on, soft and incessant;

> . . . A hand to each, he faltering came
> Within the hidden mountain hall

Where Alar tends the darkened flame
That brightened at Cassilda's call. . . .
And as his brilliance paled away
Into the dimmer mortal day,
Cassilda left the shining loom,
A starflower in his hand she laid;
Then on him fell a mortal doom:
He rose and kissed Robardin's maid.
The golden webs unwoven lay . . .

His mind spun in a strange dream as he listened to the
song of the love of Cassilda, the sorrows of Camilla, the
love of Hastur and the treachery of Alar. *It must be strange
to be Comyn and Hastur, and know oneself sib to the
God. . . .*

I could use a god or two for kinsmen now!

*What are these old gods really? The forge people used to
say that Sharra came to their fires—and they didn't mean
the spirit of fire, either. The old telepaths could raise powers
as far beyond my bird forms, or the fire shields, as these are
beyond a Trailman's knife!*

"Barron! Don't fall asleep here, man; the trail gets dangerous!" The voice of Gwynn, the big Darkovan, broke into
his dream, and Barron shook himself awake. Was it another
hallucination?—No, only a dream. "I must have been
asleep," he said, rubbing his eyes. Gwynn chuckled. "And to
think that five days ago you'd never been in the saddle. You
learn fast, stranger. Congratulations! But you'd better keep
your eyes open from here; the path gets rough and narrow,
and you probably have better judgment than your horse—
even though there is an old proverb that says, 'on an uphill
road give your horse his head.' But if you fell here—" He
gestured at the thousand-foot drop on either side of the pass.
"We ought to try and get through and down into the valleys,
before nightfall. There are Ya-men around these heights, and

perhaps banshees; and although there's no sign of the Ghost Wind, I'm not any too eager to meet them just the same."

Barron started to ask what they were and stopped himself. *Damn it, I don't care; I'm already too entangled in this business, and Gwynn and the others are here to guard me.* There was no reason he should think about these supposed dangers or even know what they were.

Nevertheless, the unease of the others penetrated to him, and he found himself pulling close to them in the narrow neck of the pass. It was almost an anticlimax when they topped the pass without incident and began to ride downward.

They camped that night in the valley under a shelter of the gray-blue boughs, which smelled of spice and rain; there was less talk and singing than usual. Barron, lying awake in his blankets and listening to the nightly rain sliding off the thick boughs, felt an apprehension he could not check. *What a hell of a world, and why did I have to get stuck in it?*

Already he had half forgotten the delight and fascination he had felt during the first journey through the foothills. It was part of that strangeness within which he wanted to forget.

They arrived at the ranger station late the next day; Barron, unpacking his crates by lamplight in the large; airy room allotted to him, realized grudgingly that at least Valdir had spared no pains to make a guest comfortable. There were ample shelves and cupboards for his working tools, benches and space with good light—the pressure lamps produced unusual amounts of light from the relatively crude fuels extracted from resins and oils of the local trees. A broad window of clear glass—not common on Darkover, not much desired, and evidently provided for the comfort of the Terran guest—provided an unbelievable panoramic view of mountains, and ridge after ridge of forested and rocky slopes and heights. As Barron stood at the window, watching the huge red sun of Darkover setting behind the peak—

the mountains here were so high that the sun was hidden
even before the night's mist formed—he was touched again
with that uncanny sense which made his heart race; but by
sheer force of will he kept himself from succumbing to it,
and went out to explore the station.

From where it sat at the top of one of the tallest peaks, it
commanded a view—even without climbing to the tower
behind—of what seemed like hundreds of square miles of
forested country; Barron counted fifteen small villages, each
lying sheltered in a fold of the hills, each only a cluster of
dim roofs. At this distance he could see why telescopes
would be needed; the view stretched so far that it vanished
in haze through which no unaided eye could penetrate and
which could easily hide a thin coil of smoke. He could even
see the faraway roofs of Armida, and, high in the hills, a dim
pale spire which looked like a castle.

"With your lenses," Larry told him, joining him at the
doorway of the station, "we will see forest fires while they
are still only small blazes, and save our timber. Look." He
pointed to the side of a faraway ridge which was a black scar
in the green. "That burned five years ago; it was out of control only for a day or two, but even though every man from
seven villages turned out, we lost I forget how many square
miles of good timber and resin trees. Also, from here, we
could see and give the warning, if bandits or something attacked."

"How do you give warning? There seem to be no sirens
or any such things here."

"Bells, fire beacons—" He pointed to a high pile of dry
weed carefully isolated behind a ditch filled with water,
"And also, signaling devices—I don't think I ever knew the
Terran name for them." He showed Barron the shiny metal
plates. "Of course they can only be used on sunny days."

"Heliograph," Barron said.

"That's it."

Barron had expected to feel like a fish out of water, but

the first few days went smoothly enough. There were six men at the ranger station, serving tours of duty of fifteen days each and then being replaced by others, in a staggered rotation system which sent three new men every seven days. Currently Gwynn was in command of the station. Larry seemed a sort of supernumerary, and Barron wondered if he was there only to interpret, or to keep an eye on the stranger. From something Gwynn said, he eventually decided that Larry was there to learn the management of the station, so that he could take his place in a series of responsible duties held in sequence by all younger men of Darkovan families. Colryn was there as Barron's assistant, specifically to learn the work of lens-grinding and to teach the making and use of the telescopes and lenses to any of the rangers who were willing to learn.

Barron knew, from his orientation lectures years ago, that Darkover was a world without complex technology or industry, and he had expected that the Darkovans would not be very adept at learning what he had come to teach. He was surprised to see the swiftness with which Colryn and the others picked up the rudiments of optics, his instructions on the properties of reflected and refracted light, and, later, the technical work of grinding. Colryn in particular was apt at picking up the technical language, the meticulous scientific techniques; so was Larry, who hung around when he was not out on patrol, but then Barron had expected it of Larry, who was a Terran and seemed to have at least the rudiments of a Terran education. But Colryn was a surprise.

He said as much one afternoon, when they were working in the upstairs workroom; he had been showing the younger man how to set and adjust one of the complex grinding tools and how to check it with the measuring instruments for proper set. "You know, you really don't need me," he said. "You could have picked this up on your own with a couple of textbooks. It was hardly worth Valdir's trouble to bring me all the way out here; he could simply have gotten books and equipment from the Terran Zone and turned them over to you."

Colryn shrugged. "He'd have to have me taught to read 'em first."

"You can speak some Terran Standard; you wouldn't have that much trouble learning. As nearly as I can tell, the Darkovan script isn't so complicated that you'd have any difficulty with Empire letters."

Colryn laughed this time. "I couldn't say. Maybe if I could read at all, I could read Terran Standard. It's nothing I've ever stopped to think about."

Barron stared in frank shock; Colryn *seemed* intelligent enough! He looked at Larry, expecting to exchange a look of consternation at this barbarous planet; but Larry frowned slightly and said, almost in reproof, "We don't make a fetish of literacy on Darkover, Barron."

Suddenly he felt condemnatory and like a stranger again. He almost snarled, "How in the hell does anyone learn anything, then?"

He could see Colryn visibly summoning up patience and courtesy toward the boorish stranger, and felt ashamed. Colryn said, "Well, I'm learning, am I not? Even though I'm no sandal-wearer, to sit and wear my eyes out over printed pages!"

"You're certainly learning. But you mean you have no system of education?"

"Probably not the way you mean it," said Colryn. "We don't bother with writing unless we're in the class that has to spend their time reading and writing. We've found that too much reading spoils the eyes—weren't you telling me, a few days ago, that about eighty per cent of your Terrans have imperfect vision and have to wear false lenses to their eyes? It would seem to make more sense to set those people to doing work which doesn't need so much reading—anyway, too much writing things down spoils the memory; you don't remember a thing properly if you can go and look it up. And when I want to learn something, why should I not learn it the sensible way, from someone who can show me if I am doing it properly, without the intermediary of printed symbols between us? With only a book to learn from, I might misunderstand and get into the way of doing things wrong, whereas here, if I make a mistake you can set me right at once, and the skill gets into my hands, so that my hands will remember how the work is done."

Not really convinced, Barron let the discussion drop. He had to admit that the arguments were singularly coherent for someone he now had to reclassify as an illiterate. His systems of thinking were shaken up; communications devices had always been his field. Colryn said, evidently trying to bend over backward and see his point of view, "Oh, I didn't say there was anything wrong with reading, in itself. If I were deaf or crippled, I'm sure I would find it useful—" But understandably, this did not calm Barron's ruffled feelings.

Not for worlds would he have admitted what was really bothering him most at the moment. His hands went on, with almost automatic skill, adjusting the delicate micrometric measurements on the grinding tool, and connecting it to the small wind-powered generator. While Colryn was talking, the argument somehow seemed familiar. It was as if he had heard it all before, in some other life! He thought, with black humor, that if this went on, he would come to believe in reincarnation!

His eyes blurred before him, colors running into one another and blearing into unfamiliar patches, shapes and groups without reference. He looked at the equipment in his hands as if he had never seen it before. He turned the pronged plug curiously in his hands; what was he supposed to do with this thing? As it focused and came clear, he found that he was staring wildly at Colryn, and Colryn looked strange to him.

All the strange colors flooded together again and sight went out; he found himself standing on a great height, look-

ing down at a scene of ruin and carnage, hearing men shrieking, and swords clashing. As it blotted out sight, he found
himself once again looking up at rushing flames, and in the
midst of the fire was a smiling woman, flame-haired; lapped
in fire as another woman might stand beneath a waterfall.
Then the woman faded and was only a great female shape,
fire-crowned and golden-chained. . . .

"Barron!" The cry cut through his consciousness and he
came briefly back, rubbing his eyes, to see Colryn and Larry
staring at him in consternation. Larry caught the lens machine from his hands as he swayed and crashed to the floor.

When he came to himself again, water trickling down his
throat, they were both staring down at him with troubled
concern in their faces. Colryn was apologetic: "I think
you've been working too hard. I shouldn't have gotten into
that argument with you; you have your ways and we have
ours. Have you had seizures like this often?"

Barron simply shook his head. The argument hadn't
bothered him that much, and if Colryn wanted to explain it
away as an epileptic fit or something of that sort, that was all
right with him and probably a saner explanation than whatever it really was. Perhaps he was suffering some sort of
brain damage! *Oh, well, at least when it happens out here in
the Darkovan mountains, I'm not likely to be responsible for
crashing a couple of spaceships!*

Colryn might have accepted this explanation but it was
quickly obvious that Larry hadn't. He sent Colryn away,
saying that he was sure Barron wouldn't feel like working
for the rest of the day; then he began slowly to put the lens-
grinding equipment away. Barron started to get up and help
him, and Larry gestured to him to stay put.

"I can manage; I know where this stuff goes. Barron,
what do you know of Sharra?"

"Nothing—less than nothing." *It's damned unhandy having a telepath around.* "You tell me."

"I don't know that much. She was an ancient goddess of

the forge people. But gods and goddesses, here on Darkover, are more than just something you say your prayers to, or burn incense to, or ask for favors. They seem to be real—tangible, I mean."

"That sounds like rubbish, gobbledygook."

"I mean, what they call gods, we'd call forces—real, solid forces you can touch. For instance—I don't know much about Sharra. The Darkovans, especially in the Comyn, don't like to talk about Sharra worship. It was outlawed years ago; it was thought to be too dangerous. Also, it seemed to involve human sacrifice, or something like it. What I mean is, the forge people called on Sharra, using the proper talisman or whatever—these things concentrate forces, I don't know how—and Sharra would bring the metallic ore up out of the mountains for them."

"And you a Terran? And you believe all that stuff? Larry, there are legends like that on every planet in the Empire."

"Legend be damned," said Larry. "I told you I don't think they're gods as we use the term. They may be some form of—well, entity or being—maybe from some other dimension. For all I know, they could be an invisible race of nonhumans. Valdir told me a little about the outlawing of Sharra worship—it happened here in the mountains. His people, the Altons and the Hasturs, had a lot to do with it; they had to go into the hills and confiscate all the talismans of Sharra so that the forge people couldn't call up these forces any more. Among other things, I gather, the fires sometimes got out of control and started forest fires."

"Talismans?"

"Stones—they call them matrix stones—blue crystals. I've learned to use them a little; believe me, they're weird. If you have even rudimentary telepathic force, you concentrate your thoughts on them and they—well, they do things. They can lift objects—psychokinesis—create magnetic fields, create force-field locks that no one can open except with the same matrix, and so forth. My foster sister could tell you more about them." Larry looked distressed. "Valdir should know, if Sharra images can even get to you, a Terran. I should send to him, Barron."

Barron shook his head urgently. "No! Don't trouble Valdir; this is my problem."

"No trouble. Valdir will want to know. Valdir is of the Comyn. He must know if these things are coming into the mountains again. They could be dangerous for us all, and especially for you." He smiled a troubled smile. "I shared a knife with you, and it is a pledge," he said. "I have to stand your friend whether you want me to or not. I'll send for Valdir tonight."

He finished closing the box with the lens blanks, and turned to go. "You'd better rest; nothing is urgent, and I have to go out on patrol," he said. "And don't worry; it is probably nothing to do with you. You have evidently picked up something that is loose in these mountains, and Valdir will know how to deal with it." He paused at the door, said urgently, "Please believe that we are your friends, Barron." He left.

Alone, Barron lay on the wide bed, that smelled of the resin-needles used to stuff the mattress. He wondered why it seemed so urgent to him that Valdir should not be sent for. He heard Larry ride away with the patrol; he heard Colryn singing downstairs; and he heard the wind rise and begin blowing from the heights. He got up and went to the wide window. Down in these valleys and hills lay villages of unsuspecting men, little knots and nests of nonhumans in the thickest and most impenetrable forests, and birds and wildlife; they would be safer for protection against forest fire and raiding bandits—catmen and nonhumans and the terrible Ya-men. He would help with that, he was doing good work; why then was he gripped by this sense of fearful urgency and despair, as if he sat idling while around him a world fell into ruins? Disoriented, he covered his eyes.

It was quiet at the station. He knew that in the tower a

ranger in the usual green and black uniform scanned the surrounding countryside for any signs of smoke; the resin trees, in spite of the nightly rain, were so volatile, that an unexpected thunderstorm could strike one and send it ablaze. The only sound was the wind that never changed and never died; Barron hardly heard it now. And yet there was something—something in the wind. . . .

He tensed, throwing the window open and leaning out, closing his eyes the better to focus attention.

It was almost imperceptible except to senses sharpened like his—almost lost in the overpowering smell of the resins—a faint, sweet, yellow-dusty smell, almost lost, borne on the wind. . . .

The Ghost Wind! Pollen of a plant which flowered erratically only once in several seasons—was released in enormous quantities, scattering its scent and queer hallucinogenic qualities from the valleys to the heights; blessedly rare, it produced euphoria and a queer drunkenness and, occasionally, if one breathed too much of it, brain damage in men. It released the animal instincts of rage and fear and anger, sending men cowering in corners or raving on the hills. But into the nonhumans it went deeper, penetrating into their strange brains and releasing very old things, very terrible things. . . . The catmen would howl and strike and kill wantonly, and the Ya-men—when it reached the Ya-men—

He moved fast. He was not Barron now; he was not conscious of himself or who or what he was, he knew only that he must act to warn the others at the station, to warn the men in the valleys to take shelter. It would not be strong enough for any ordinary nose to smell for two or three more hours, and by that time the rangers would be too far from the station to take shelter, and the nonhumans would already be out and ravening. By the time the Ghost Wind was strong enough to affect humans it might even be too late to take shelter.

His vision was blurring. He closed his eyes, the better to let his feet find their way around, and ran down the stairs. He heard someone call to him in an unfamiliar language, pushed past and ran on.

The beacon. He might light the beacon! He did not know the alarm systems here but the beacon would certainly alert everyone to danger. There was a fire burning in the lower hall, he could feel its heat on his face. He bent over, carefully reaching, picked out a long stick blazing at one end and cool and charred at the other. He ran with it in his hand out the door and across the graveled horse path and the lawn; almost falling into the ditch around the beacon, he thrust the blazing torch into the tinder-dry wood and leaped back as it flamed up and a tall column of fire reared to the sky. Then someone yelled at him, hands were gripping him, and Colryn was demanding, as he held him in a steel-strong grip, "Barron, damn you, have you gone mad? That's going to rouse the countryside! If you were a Darkovan, you'd be hanged on the spot for raising a false fear!"

"False fear be——" he swore atrociously. "The Ghost Wind! I smelled it! By night it will be everywhere!"

His face slowly blanching, Colryn stared at him. "The Ghost Wind? How do you know?"

"I smelled it, I tell you! What do you do here to rouse the countryside for taking shelter?"

Colryn looked at him, only half believing but gripped by his obvious sincerity. "The beacon will alert them," he said, "and I can signal with the mirror, after which they will ring bells in the villages. We have a good alarm system here. I still think you're insane, I don't smell it at all, but then for all I know you could have a better nose than mine. And I won't take a chance on letting the Ghost Wind—or the Ya-men—get anyone." He shoved Barron out of his way. "Look where you're going! Damn it, what's the matter, are you *blind*? You'll be in the ditch in a minute!" He forgot Barron again, and ran toward the station for the signaling device.

Eyes closed, Barron stood listening to the beacon crackle. He was aware of the pungency of the burning beacon and through it, the growing, sick scent of the pollen-laden Ghost Wind blowing from the heights.

After a while, still disoriented, he turned and made his way, on faltering feet, inside the station. Colryn was on the tower, signaling. Paradoxically, the thing which surprised Barron most was that he was not surprised at himself; he had a vague sense of split selfhood, in the same sort of divided, underwater consciousness that he had felt once or twice before.

The next hour was insane confusion: shouts and voices, bells beginning to ring in the villages below, and the rangers at the station running about on errands they didn't bother explaining. He kept his eyes closed against further disorientation and kept out of the way. It seemed natural to sit by while others acted; he had done his part. Presently men came riding up the slope in crazy haste and he became aware that Larry had come in and was standing with Colryn in front of him.

"What happened?"

"He smelled the Ghost Wind," Colryn said tersely.

"And in good time," Larry said. "Thank the gods we have warning. I had just barely begun to wonder if I smelled it myself when I heard the bells and ordered everyone back— but it's still so faint I can hardly make it out! How did you know?" he demanded. Barron did not answer, but only shook his head. After a little while Larry went away.

He thought, *I have done a foolish thing; before, he only suspected something strange, but now he will know, and if he does not, Valdir will. Valdir is Comyn and he will know exactly what has happened.*

I don't care what they do to the Earthman, but I must get away. I should have kept quiet and escaped in the confusion of the Ghost Wind.

But I couldn't let them all go through that danger; and

Lerrys would have been caught on the hills. I owe him some-thing. There is a blade between us.

Nothing human will dare to move in these mountains tonight. I must lie low and keep from attracting any more at-tention to Barron until then.

And then—then I must be gone, long gone, before Valdir comes!

CHAPTER EIGHT

It seemed eternities that he watchfully waited, that curious doubled consciousness keeping him nerve-strained, but holding himself back from being noticed. He kept out of the way while the men at the station hurried around, making all secure as the wind rose higher, screaming around the corners of the station and the fire tower. The sickish smell grew stronger by the moment and he fancied he could feel it penetrating to the rest of his nose, into the brain, subtly eating away at his humanity and his resolution.

Nor were the others unaffected; at one point Colryn stopped in his work of nailing heavy shutters tight and bent over, crouching, his arms wrapped round his head as if in terrible pain. He began a low, crazy moaning. Gwynn, hurrying through the room on some errand or other, saw him there, went to him, knelt beside him, put an arm around his shoulders and talked to him in a low, reassuring voice, until Colryn shook his head violently as if to clear it of something. Then he stood up and swung his arms, swore, thanked Gwynn and went on with his work.

The man who was not sure at the moment whether he was Dan Barron or someone else, stayed where he was, fighting for self-control; but he was not unaffected. As the wind rose and the smell of the Ghost Wind grew stronger, strange images spun in his mind—primordial memories laden with

fear and terror—frightening hungers. Once he jerked upright from a waking nightmare of kneeling over a prone
man, tearing at his throat with his teeth. He shuddered, rose
and began to walk feverishly around the room.

When all was secure they sat down to food, but no one
ate much. They were all silent, all tormented by the rising
scream of the wind, which tore at their ears and their nerves,
and by the spinning of vague hallucinatory images in their
eyes and their minds. Barron kept his eyes closed. It seemed
easier to eat that way, without the unfamiliar distraction of
sight.

Halfway through the meal, the faraway shrieking began;
a high, keening, space-filling howl and yelp that rose higher
and higher, through the audible frequencies, and seemed to
go on even after it could be heard no more.

"Ya-men," said Gwynn tersely, and let his knife drop to
the table with a clatter.

"They can't get into the station," Colryn said, but he
didn't sound sure. No one after that made much more than a
pretense at eating, and before long they left the food and
dishes uncleared on the table and went into the shuttered and
barricaded main room of the station. The yelping and howling went on—at first distant and intermittent, then constant
and close. Eyes closed, Barron saw in his mind's eye a ring
of towering plumed forms, raging and shrieking and hurling
themselves, in a maddened dance, around the peak of the
hill.

Once Colryn tried to drown out the sound by beginning a
song; but his voice died away, halfway through the first
verse.

The night wore on. Toward the deepest part of the darkness, the pounding and banging began; it sounded as if a
heavy form hurled itself, again and again, against the barred
doors, and fell back, howling with bruised, insensate rage.
Once begun, it went on and on, until their nerves were
screaming.

Once Larry said low in the darkness, "I wonder what they're really like? It seems hell that the only time they come out of the deep woods, they're maddened—and we can't communicate with them."

Gwynn said, with bleak humor, "I'll unbar the door, if you want to try a little nonhuman diplomacy."

Larry shuddered and was still. Colryn said, "Upstairs in the lens-grinding room there's a glass window. We could get a look at them from there."

Gwynn refused, with a shudder, and so did the other rangers; but Colryn, Larry and Barron went up the stairs together. It was something to do. At this height, the window had not been covered or barricaded. They did not light the lamp, knowing the light would attract the howling nonhumans outside. They went to the glass and, cupping their hands around their eyes, peered through.

Outside, though he had expected it to be dark and stormy, it was clear moonlight—one of the rare nights on Darkover when rain and fog had not blotted out the moons. The air seemed filled with swirling dust, through which he saw the Ya-men.

They were hugely tall, nine feet at least, and looked like tall emaciated men, wearing plumed head-dresses, until he saw their faces. They had huge heads and terrible beaked faces like strange birds of prey, and they moved with a clumsy swiftness that was like the wind-tossed branches of the trees which dipped and surged at the edge of the clearing. There were at least three dozen of them, it seemed, and perhaps more. After a little, as if by common consent, the men turned away from the window and went down the stairs again.

Barron, about to follow them, remained behind. The strangeness was growing in him again. Something turning like a thermostat in his brain told him that the tide of the Ghost Wind had turned. There was no change in the slamming noise of the wind, nor in the howling of the nonhumans, but he *knew*.

They will be gone long before dawn. The wind will die and there will be rain. Only the mad and the desperate travel on Darkover by night, but I—perhaps I am both desperate and mad.

An enormous crash, and cries from downstairs, told him that the slamming attack of the nonhumans had crashed an outbuilding. He did not go down to investigate; it was not his affair. Silently, moving like an automaton, he went in the darkness to the chest of drawers where he kept his clothing: He discarded the thin indoor garments he was wearing, put on leather riding breeches, a thick woven shirt and a heavy tunic. He slipped into Colryn's room and appropriated the man's heavy, fur-lined cloak. He had a long way to ride and a cloak was better than a jacket. He regretted that he must steal a horse, but if he lived, it would be returned or paid for, and if not, he reminded himself of the mountain proverb, "when Eternity comes all will be understood and forgiven."

He cocked a practiced ear; the wind was definitely quieting. In another hour the Ya-men would be gone, the restless impulse that had led them there entirely gone; they would waken to terror and strangeness and creep timidly back to their caves and nests in the deepest woods. *The poor devils must feel damn near as strange as I do.*

The slamming of the wind was subsiding and even in the incessant howling there were gaps now, intervals grew wider and finally lessened to nothing. Peering through the glass, he saw that the clearing was empty. Not more than half an hour after that, he heard the other men coming up to the large room where they slept. Someone called, "Barron, are you all right?" He froze, then made himself answer in a sleepy, resentful mutter.

In a few more minutes a silence lay over the fire station, broken only by the snores of exhausted men in the far room, and the rattle of occasional branches in the dying wind.

Peering through the glass, he saw that fog was rising. There would be rain and it would lay the last traces of the poison from the Ghost Wind.

All was quiet, but nevertheless he waited another hour, to dispel the chance that one of the men, sleeping lightly after fear and tension, would waken and hear him. Then, moving with infinite caution so that the stairs would not creak beneath him, he stole downstairs. He made up a parcel of food from the leavings on the table. They had left the doors barricaded, but it was no great trouble to unfasten the bars and take them down.

He was outside, in the bitter cold and fading moonlight of the mountain night.

He had to find a clawed tool to unfasten the bars they had nailed over the door of the stable, and in order to use it, confused by its unfamiliar weight in his hand, he had to close his eyes and let the inner reflexes take over. He thanked his fate that the stable was at some distance from the house, otherwise the racket he made as he wrestled with the heavy boards would certainly have wakened even such weary sleepers, and they would have come down raising an outcry against thieves. He got them loose and stole inside.

The stable was warm, dark and friendly-familiar with the smell of horses. He shut his eyes to saddle up the horse; it was easier to handle the harness that way. The beast recognized him and neighed softly and he began to talk to it soothingly in an undertone. "Yes, fellow, we have a long ride tonight, but quiet, do you hear? We must get away quietly. Not used to going in the dark, are you? Well, I am, so don't you worry about that."

He dared not mount and ride till at some distance. Taking the bridle, he led the horse carefully down the slope and down the mountain road, then paused to take stock. He was ready; he closed his eyes to orient himself. He must go over the ranges and past the castle he could see from the fire tower, skirt the bends of the River Kadarin and beware of trailmen in the forested slopes on the near side. Then the road toward Carthon lay clear before him.

He was warmly clad. He had a good horse; it was Gwynn's, which was the best, one of the finely bred blacks which the Altons bred for the rangers. He had heard Gwynn boast that Valdir had broken this one with his own hands. It was a crime to deprive the ranger of such a beauty; yet—"Necessity would make a thief even of a Hastur," he reminded himself grimly. Yet another proverb came to mind: "If you're going to steal horses, steal thoroughbreds."

He was well provided with money. Nudged by his subtle prodding, Barron had had Valdir change his Terran credits for Darkovan coins.

He spared a thought for Barron. It was almost a pity to do this to the Earthman, but he had had no choice. One of the greatest of crimes on Darkover, ever since the days of the Compact, was to take over another human mind. It could only be done with a latent telepath, and telepaths on Darkover were aware, and they guarded against such invasion. He had hoped to find an idiot mind, so that he would be robbing no man of his own soul. But instead, as his mind ranged in the desperation of trance, unbound by the limitations of space, he had touched Barron. . . .

Were the Terrans even human? In any case, what did it matter what happened to these invaders on our world. Barron is an intruder, an outsider—fair game.

And what could I do, blind and helpless, but this?

At the foot of the path leading to the fire station, he came to a halt and swung into the saddle. He was on his way.

And for a bare instant Dan Barron, confused, disoriented, surfaced as if coming up from a long, deep dive. Was this another hallucination—that he was riding along a dark road, faint dying moonlight overhead, icy wind whistling around his shoulders? No, this was real—where was he going? And why? He shuddered in terror, jerking on the horse's reins. . . .

He disappeared again into fathomless darkness.

The man in the saddle urged his horse to top speed; by dawn he wished to be hidden from the station by hills, so that when he emerged again, if they sought him from there he would simply be another man on horseback, moving on his lawful occasions through the countryside. He was very weary, but as if he had taken some euphoric drug, not at all sleepy. For the first time in his sheltered, invalid's life he was not resting inert, waiting for someone else to take action. He was going to do this himself.

He had stopped briefly three times to let his horse rest and breathe before the great red rim of the sun peered over the hills. He found a sheltered clearing and hobbled the horse. He rolled himself in his blanket and slept for an hour, then rose, ate a little cold food from his saddlebag and was on his way again.

All that day he rode through the hills, keeping to little-known roads—if Larry had sent for Valdir the one thing he did not dare was to meet Valdir on the road. Valdir had the old Comyn powers, which made his own look feeble by contrast. Valdir would know at once what he had done. The Storns had no traffic with the Comyn; certainly they would not come to his aid, even in this emergency. He must keep clear of the Comyn.

Toward noon it became cloudy, and Storn, looking up, saw gray caps hanging over the far hills. He thought of Melitta making her way toward Carthon from the far side of the Kadarin, and wondered, despairingly, if she could make her way across the passes in time. Snow must be falling on the heights; and in the hills there were bandits, trailmen, and the terrible banshee birds, which hunted anything living and could disembowel man or horse with one stroke of their terrible claws. He could do nothing to help Melitta now; he could help them both best by bringing himself safe to Carthon:

All that day he met no one on the road except an occasional farmer working in his fields, or, in scattered villages, miles apart, women chatting in the streets with rosy children clustered around them. None of them paid attention to him, except in one village where he stopped to ask a woman selling fruit by the road for a drink of water from her well; he bought some fruit, and two small boys sidled up to admire the horse and ask, shyly, if it was of the Alton breed, which gave him a moment's shock.

A *Storn of Storn, fugitive and thief!*

He slept again in the woods, rolled in his cloak. Toward afternoon of the second day he heard hoofbeats on the road, far off, ahead of him. Riding after, hanging at a distance lest he be seen and the horse, perhaps, recognized by the wrong people, he found that the small road he was travelling spread out into a wide, graveled surface, almost a highway. He must be nearing the Kadarin. Now he could see the riders ahead of him. They were a long line of men wearing cloaks of unfamiliar cut and color—tall men, sandy-haired, fair, and fierce-looking. Only a few of them had horses; the others rode the antlered, heavy-set pack beasts. He recognized them—Dry-towners from Shainsa or Daillon returning home after trading in the mountains. They would not recognize him and they would have no interest in him, but, as was customary in these lands, they would let him travel in their company for a small fee, since everyone added to their band was an extra protection against bandits or nonhuman attackers.

He spurred his horse and rode after them, already rehearsing what he would say. He was Storn of Storn Heights, a man who need fear nothing in foothills or mountains.

He could ride with them almost as far as Carthon.

He was safe now. He prayed, with gut-wrenching intensity, that Melitta had had equal luck—that she, too, was safe. He dared not let his mind range backward to Storn Heights, to the castle where his body lay entranced behind the blue fire, guarded by magnetic fields; that might draw him back.

He dared not think of Allira, brought to a bandit's bed, or to Edric, wounded and alone in the dungeons of his own castle.

He sent his hail ringing out after the caravan and saw the riders stop.

CHAPTER NINE

They rode down into Carthon at midmorning, as the morning mist was beginning to burn away under the quick, hot sun.

For five days they had ridden through diminishing mountains and foothills and now they came between the hills into the wide plain which lay in the bend of the River Kadarin— where Carthon lay bleaching on the plains. It had the look of incredible age; the squat buildings were like mountains leveled by the erosion of millennia. It was the first part of Darkover that he had seen where there were no trees. The Dry-towners had been silent and apprehensive moving through the mountainous forests; but now, with the ancient city lying in their gaze, they cheered visibly. Even their pack animals quickened their steps, and one of the men began to sing a heptatonic melody in a rough and guttural dialect that Storn could not understand.

For Storn—despite his fear of being overtaken, the constant and growing sense that he was pursued, and his endless apprehension for Melitta, struggling somewhere in the snows and passes around High Kimbi—the journey had been magical. For the first time in his life he tasted freedom and even adventure; he was treated as a man among men, not as a handicapped invalid. Deliberately he had suspended his fears for his sister, the thought of Edric and Allira in danger and captivity, and his own sense of guilt for breaking one of the most rigid of Darkovan taboos—the meddling with another human soul. He dared not think about these things; if he let his mind roam back or forward, he risked losing control of the man he had mastered; once, in fact, in the night while Storn dreamed; Barron had wakened in astonishment and terror, looking around at the unfamiliar surroundings and ready to panic and run wild. Only with difficulty had Storn resumed the upper hand. He could feel somewhere, at a level beyond his control—in that ultimate fastness of the human spirit where not even a telepath or Keeper could penetrate—Barron watched and defied him. But Storn kept control. He told himself now that even for Barron's sake he must maintain surface control—among Dry-towners, a Terran would not be permitted to live. Small was the contact between Terran and Darkovan in valley and mountain country; with the Dry towns it was absolutely minimal. Many of them had never seen or heard of the Terran Empire cities, and in the Dry towns any stranger walked with his life in his hands. An off-wonder could not have maintained safety for a single day.

As they reached Carthon, Storn realized that his single-minded enjoyment of the journey was of necessity coming to an end. Carthon had been deserted years ago by the valley lords, who had withdrawn into the mountains when the fertility of the land failed and the river changed its course. It had become a no-man's-land, inhabited by the flotsam and jetsam of a dozen civilizations. At one time, Storn remembered—he had traveled here twice in his boyhood, with his late father, long before assuming the heirship of his house—it had been the haunt of half a dozen bands of mercenaries, recruited from mountain bandits, renegade Dry-towners and the gods alone knew what else. It had been Storn's thought that here he might hire one of these bands to aid in freeing High Windward. It would not be easy—Brynat had had no easy task and a captain of that quality would not be simply dislodged—but Storn knew a trick or two, besides knowing every niche of the castle. With an able band of mercenary soldiers he had no doubt of his ability to recapture his home.

He had urged Melitta to meet him there because he was, or had been at that time, uncertain of the ultimate degree of control he could establish over Barron. He could have sent her alone, keeping only telepathic contact with her; but he was not sure of her continuing ability to maintain rapport over long periods of time and distance. What Storn knew of the old Darkovan *laran* powers was of necessity incomplete and based on trial and error. Only the long, idle childhood and adolescence of a man born blind had given him leisure and impetus to explore them, and he had had no teacher. They had been a way to alleviate his terrible boredom and the feeling of worthlessness felt by a physically handi-capped man in a society which put great reliance on strength, physical skill and action. He knew that he had ac-complished a great deal for a man with his handicap, even in the fields proper to a man of his family and caste: he could ride; he could climb skillfully in his own mountain cliffs and crags with little help; and he administered his own estates, with his sisters and young brother at his side. In fact, not the least of his pride was in that he had won, and kept, the loy-alty of his younger brother in a society where brothers were often bitter rivals and he could easily have been relegated to the background, with Edric taking his place as Lord of Storn. To them—until Brynat had appeared and made war— he had seemed strong and competent. Only when the castle was under siege had he tasted the bitterness of helplessness.

But now the other things he had explored were coming into their own. His own body was guarded against Brynat, and he was free to seek help and revenge—if he could get it.

The red sun was high and warm, and he had thrown back his riding cloak when they rode through the gates of Carthon. At first glance he could see that it was unlike any of the mountain villages they had ridden through; it felt,

sounded and smelled like no Darkovan city he had ever
known. The very air was different; it smelled of spice, incense and dust. It was obvious to Storn that in the interven-
ing years more and more Dry-towners had moved into
Carthon, possibly in search of the more abundant water from
the Kadarin River, or perhaps—the thought crossed his
mind—feeling that the lowlands' and valleys' peaceful peoples would lie there at their mercy: He dismissed the thought
for later worry.

Nevertheless he felt apprehensive. He was less confident
in his ability to win help in a predominantly Drytown area.
Traditionally they had their own concerns and their own culture; he could offend them fatally by a chance word. From
what he had heard and what he had seen traveling with these
merchants in the last days, their prime motivation was the
scoring of points in an elaborate, never-ending game of
prestige. No outsider could hope to win anything in this
game, and Storn, traveling in their company, had been ignored, as men intent on a gambling game will ignore the cat
by the fireplace.

It was humiliating, but he knew it was safer that way. He
had no knowledge and no skill in knife fights, and they lived
by an elaborate dueling code under which the man who
could not defend himself to the death against enemy or
friend was dead.

It was a forlorn hope that he could find Dry-towner mercenaries here. Still, there might be mountain or valley bands
here, even though the predominant culture now seemed Dry-
town. And even Dry-towners might be tempted by the
thought of sacking Brynat's riches. He was prepared to offer
them all the loot of Brynat and his men. All he wanted was
the freedom of Storn Castle and peace to enjoy it.

They had passed the city gates, giving their names at the
outworks to fierce-looking, bearded men; Storn saw with relief that some of them wore familiar mountain garments and
heard them speaking a dialect of his own language. Perhaps

they were not all Dry-towners here. The city was wide-flung, not like the huddled mountain villages cramped be-hind protective walls or the *forsts*, the forest forts behind high stockades. The outworks seemed little manned. Every-where were the tall, fair-haired Dry-town men, and women walked in the open dusty streets—slender Dry-town women, sunburnt and swift, carrying their heads proudly and moving in the tiny chiming sound of chains, the jew-elled fetters that bound their hands, restricted movement and that proclaimed them chattel to some man of power and wealth.

At the main square of the city the caravan turned purposely toward the Eastern quarter, and Storn was reminded that their agreement terminated here. Now he was on his own—alone, in a culture and country strange to him, where any moment might bring some fatal blunder. But before he began to rack his brains as to how he could best explore the possibilities, the leader of the caravan turned back and said bluntly, "Stranger, be reminded that in our towns all strangers must first pay re-spects at the Great House. The Lord Rannath will be better disposed toward you if you come of your free will in courtesy, than if his men must hail you there to give an account of your-self."

"For this my thanks." Storn gave the formal return and thought that these Dry-town newcomers had indeed moved into Carthon in quantity; nothing like this had obtained when he came there as a boy. The bitter thought crossed his mind that this Lord Rannath, whoever he might be, had no doubt moved into Carthon much as Brynat had moved into Storn Castle, and with as much authority.

It was nothing to him who ruled in Carthon. And in the Great House he might learn what he wanted to know.

In Carthon all roads led to the central plaza of the city. There was no mistaking the Great House, a vast structure of curiously opalescent stone lying at the center of the main plaza. Low, dusty beds of flowers grew in great profusion in the outer courts, and the Dry-town men and women came and went through the halls as if moving in a formal dance. The women, safe and insolent behind the protection of their chains, cast him sidelong smiles and bright-eyed glances, and murmured phrases he could not well understand. Only the repeated murmur of *charreta* was familiar; it was another form of *chaireth*, stranger. *Stranger indeed*, he thought with a flash of unaccustomed self-pity. *Doubly and trebly stranger, and just now without even the time and freedom to answer these bold looks . . .*

He had expected to be stopped somewhere and asked his business, but evidently formal manners either did not exist here or were so alien that he did not recognize them as such. Following the shifting crowds he finally came into the main hall, and realized that it was evidently the hour for audience.

Elegance and a bleak luxury there was, but it was barren and alien here; this room was meant for rich hangings and the luxurious furniture of valley nobility. Stripped to the bare Dry-town manner it seemed as if it had been looted; the windows were bare, letting in harsh light, and there were no furnishings apart from low pallets and a great central throne-like chair on which lay a crown and sword, with hieratic formality in their arrangement on the gold cushion. The throne was empty. A young man, his chin just fuzzed with blond beard too sparse for shaving sat on a pallet beside the throne. He wore a fur shirt, cloak and high, exquisitely dyed and embroidered leather boots. As Storn approached him, he looked up and said, "I am the voice of the Lord Rannath; I am called Kerstal. My house is the house of Greystone. Have you feud or sworn blood with me or against me?"

Storn desperately mustered what little he knew of Dry-town customs. He started to answer in the formal and stilted Cahuenga tongue, *lingua franca* of Darkover between mountain and valley, Dry-town and river folk, then suddenly dropped the pretense. He said, drawing a deep breath and stiffening his backbone, "Not to the best of my knowledge, no; to the best of my knowledge I have never heard of your house and, therefore, I have never offended against it, contracted debts to it, nor do they owe me anything. I come here as a stranger, strange to your customs; if I offend against them, it is done unwittingly and seeking peace. On my last visit to Carthon the Great House was vacant; I offer such respects as a stranger should—no more and no less. If other courtesy is required, I request that you tell me."

There was a little chiming of chains as the women in the hall turned toward him, and a small breath of surprise ran all around the room. Kerstal seemed very briefly taken aback by the unaccustomed answer. Then he said, with a brief nodding of his head, "Bravely spoken and no offense given or taken. Yet none walk in Carthon without leave of the Lord Rannath and his House. Who is your liege lord and what business brings you here?"

"As for my liege, I am a free man of the mountains, with fealty sworn to none," Storn returned proudly. "I am my own man, and in my own place men give me loyalty at their own will, not from constraint." It flashed over him that pride would serve him better here than any other commodity. Drytowners seemed to respect arrogance; if he came as a suppliant, they might kick him out without listening. "My house is the house of High Windward, in the Domain of the Aldarans, ancient lords of the Comyn. As for my business here, it is not with you; does your custom require that I must make it known? In my place, a questioner must show that his question is neither idle curiosity nor prying malice; if it is otherwise here, show me reason to respect your customs, and I will do so."

Again the little ripple of surprise ran round the room and Kerstal moved to lay his hand on the hilt of the sword which lay on the vacant throne, then paused. He rose to his feet, and now his voice had courtesy rather than negligence. He said, "In the absence of sworn blood feud between us, then, *charrat* of the house of Storn, be welcome in Carthon. No law requires that you make your affairs known, if they are your own—yet a question locked behind your lips will be forever unanswered. Tell me what you seek in Carthon, and if I can honorably answer, it will be my pleasure to do so." A faint smile touched his face, and Storn relaxed, knowing he had won. Dry-towners valued control above all else; if a Dry-towner relaxed enough to smile, you were probably safe with him.

Storn said, "My ancestral house has been attacked and laid under siege by a bandit known as Brynat Scarface; I seek men and aid to redeem my house's strength, honor and integrity." He used the word *kihar*, that untranslatable idiom for face, personal integrity and honor. "My kinsmen and the women of our people are at their mercy."

Kerstal frowned faintly. "And you are here, alive, and un-wounded?"

"Dead men have no *kihar*," Storn answered swiftly. "Nor can the dead come to the aid of kinsmen."

Kerstal paused to consider this. Behind them, in the outer hallways, there was a stir and an outcry, and some vague familiar sound in that cry touched every nerve in Storn to immediate response. He could not identify it, but something was happening out there. . . .

But Kerstal paid the noises no heed. He said slowly, "There is some justice in that, stranger of Storn, and—your ways are not ours—no ineradicable loss of honor. Nevertheless, our people will not, I warn you, become entangled in mountain feuds. The House of Rannath does not sell their swords in the mountains; there is enough *kihar* to be found on our own plains."

"Nor have I asked it of you," Storn replied quickly. "When last I visited Carthon there were many who were willing to sell their swords for the chance of reward. I ask only freedom to seek them."

"Freedom of that sort cannot be denied you," Kerstal replied, "and if your tale is true, the House of Rannath will not forbid any free and unsworn man to give you his service. Speak then your name, *charrat* of Storn."

Storn drew himself up to his full height.

"I bear my father's name, with pride," he said, and his voice, although it sounded strange to himself, rang loud and clear—a strong bass voice—through that hall. "I am Loran Rakhal Storn, Lord of Storn, of High Windward."

Kerstal looked at him flatly and unreadably and said, "You lie."

And all around the hall, another sound ran; Storn had never heard it before, but nevertheless, he could not be mistaken. All around the hall, men were drawing their swords. He cast one quick look around.

He stood in a ring of naked blades.

CHAPTER TEN

Melitta had stopped struggling now. She walked between her captors, her head down, thinking bitterly, *I've failed. It wasn't enough to fight my way across the passes, hiding from banshee birds at night, getting lost in the snow, the horse freezing to death in the heights. . . . No, I manage to get all the way to Carthon and the first thing that happens is, I'm grabbed up as soon as I walk into the city!*

Think, Melitta, think—there must be a way. What do they want with you, what law have you broken? Storn would never have sent you here if it was impossible for you to find help. But did Storn know?

She drew herself up to her full height, wrenching herself to a stop between the tall, fair-haired men. "I will not go another step before I am told what is my offense," she said. "I am a free woman of the mountains, and I know nothing of your laws."

One of the men said briefly "Masterless wenches"—the word he used was untranslatable into Melitta's own language, but she had heard it used as a particularly filthy insult—"do not walk free here in Carthon among decent people, no matter what your custom may be beyond the Kadarin."

"Have you no courtesy for the customs of strangers?" she demanded.

"For customs in common decency," said one—the dialect so thick and barbarous that she had trouble understanding— "but every woman who comes here must be properly owned and controlled, and her master known. It is for the Lord of Rannath to say what shall be done with you, wench."

Melitta relaxed her taut muscles and let herself be drawn along, among staring men and the soft laughter of the women. She saw their chained hands with something like horror, and was shamed for them and astonished that they could hold up their heads and walk with something that looked like pride. Seeing their robes and their fair hair bound with ribbons and jewels she was more than ever conscious of her travel-worn riding cloak, the patched and faded breeches she wore—even the relatively free manners of mountain girls on Darkover did not accept breeches for riding, and only desperation had driven Melitta to wear them— and her hair, damp with sweat and dirty and straggling with the dust of the road. She, flushed dull red. It was no miracle indeed if they thought her the lowest of the low. She wanted to cry.

Lady of Storn, she thought. *Yes, damn it, don't I just look like it!*

They were going through a bare archway now and she saw men and women gathered in a ring around a throne where a standing man, one of the fair-haired Dry-towners but taller and better dressed than most, was questioning a man in mountain clothing. Her captors said, "The Voice of Rannath is not at leisure; wait here, wench." They relaxed their grip.

Melitta's command of Cahuenga was not very fluent, and she stood without listening, trying to recover her own self-possession and glad of the respite. What could she say to convince the lords of this city that she was a free and responsible human being and not a chattel to come under their stupid laws about women? Perhaps she should have sought help in the foothills. The Comyn lords at Armida and at Castle Ardais were no kin to her family but they might have shown her hospitality and then she could have proceeded to Carthon dressed as befitted her rank, and properly escorted. She had heard that the lord Valdir Alton was a wise and enlightened man who had done much to safeguard his own people against the raids of mountain bandits and had led an expedition to root out the *forst* of the notorious Cyrillon des Trailles. Everyone in the Kilghard hills, Storns included, had slept safer in their beds after that. *Certainly he would have been willing to come to our aid against Brynat,* she thought.

She was not trying to follow the conversation between the man her captors had styled the Voice of Rannath and his prisoner, but the prisoner caught her attention. He was unusually tall, with reddish-dark hair and a heavy and somber face, with something strange about his expression and eyes. She wished she could see him more clearly and understand his words. She could see that he was making some impression on the Voice of Rannath, for the Dry-towner was smiling. Then, before Melitta's electrified ears, the very voice and accent of her brother rang through the hall, drawing her upright in a frenzy of bewilderment.

"I am Loran Rakhal Storn, Lord of Storn, of High Windward!"

Melitta stifled a cry. It had evidently been the wrong thing for him to say; the smile was gone from Kerstal's face. He rapped out something and suddenly every man in the room had drawn his knife and they were closing in on the unlucky stranger at the center of the circle.

Kerstal said, "You lie. You lie, stranger. The son of Storn is not personally known to me; but his father is known to mine, and the men of Storn are known to our house. Shall I tell you how you lie? Storn men are fair-haired; the eyes of Storn men are gray. And it is known to me, as it is known to every man from the Hellers to Thendara, that the Lord of Storn has been blind from birth—blind beyond cure! Now state your true name, liar and braggart, or run the gauntlet to save your wretched skin!"

And suddenly, with a gasp of horror, Melitta understood. She understood what Storn had done—and quailed, for a thing that was a crime beyond words—and why he had done it, and what she must do to save them both.

"Let me through," she said, her voice clear and high. "He lies not. No Storn of Storn lies, and when my words are heard let any who belies us call challenge on either or both. I am Melitta of Storn, and if the House of Storn is known to you, father and son, then look in my face and read *my* lineage there."

Shaking off the hands of the startled men who held her, she made her way forward. The closed ring of knife-wielding Dry-towners parted before her and closed after her. She heard a rippling whisper of wonder run round the circle. Someone said, "Is this some Free Amazon of the lowlands, that she walks shameless and unchained? Women of the Comyn Domains are shamefast and modest; how came this maid here?"

"I am no Free Amazon but a woman of the mountains," said Melitta, facing the speaker. "Storn is my name and Storn is my household."

Kerstal turned toward her. He stared at her for some minutes; then his hand fell from his knife hilt, and he bent in the formal bow of the Dry-towners, his hands spread briefly.

"Lady of Storn; your heritage speaks in your face. Your father's daughter is welcome here. But who is this braggart who calls kin with you? Do you claim *him* as kin?"

Melitta walked toward the stranger. Her mind was racing. She said quickly, in the mountain tongue, "Storn, is it you? Loran, why did you do it?"

"I had no choice," he replied. "It was the only way to save you all."

"Tell me quickly the name of the horse I first learned to ride, and I accept you for who you are."

A faint flicker of a smile passed over the stranger's face. "You did not learn to ride on a horse, but on a stag pony," he said softly, "and you called him *Horny-pig.*"

Deliberately Melitta went to the stranger's side, laid her hand in his and stood on tiptoe to kiss his cheek. "Kinsman," she said slowly, and turned back to Kerstal.

"Kinsman of mine he is indeed," she said. "Nor did he lie when he named himself Storn of Storn. Our mountain ways are unknown to you. My brother of Storn is, as you say, blind beyond cure and thus unable to hold *laran* right in our house; and thus this cousin of ours, adopted into our household, wears the name and title of Storn, his true name forgotten even by brother and sister, *nedestro* heir to Storn."

For a moment after she spoke the words she held her breath; then, at a signal from Kerstal, the knives dropped. Melitta dared not let her face, show relief.

Storn spoke softly: "What redress does the Great House of Rannath give for deadly insult?"

"I am the Voice of Rannath only," Kerstal countered. "Learn our customs another time, stranger."

"It seems to me," Storn said, his voice still gentle, "that Storns have suffered grave ills at your hands. Deadly insult given to me, and my sister—" His eyes turned on the two men who had haled Melitta into the Hall. "Is this your courtesy to strangers in your city?"

"Amends shall be made," Kerstal said. Beads of sweat stood out on his forehead. "My House has no quarrel with you, Lord of Storn; be then our guests and receive gifts consonant with your quality. Let the exchange of courtesy wipe out memory of offense given or taken."

Storn hesitated, his hand on the hilt of his knife, and Melitta, reading the gesture with astonishment, thought, *He's enjoying this; he half hopes that Kerstal will call challenge!*

But if this was Storn's intention, he remembered his primary intention in time. He said, "Be it so, then. My sister and I gratefully accept your hospitality, kinsman of Rannath," and all round the circle, there were small sighs and stirs of relief or, perhaps, of disappointment.

Kerstal summoned servants and gave orders, then detained Storn a moment with a raised hand. "You claim this woman, then? See you to it that she does not walk abroad free in defiance of our customs!"

Melitta bit her tongue on an angry retort, feeling Storn's hand dig hard into her shoulder. This was no time to start any further arguments.

A few minutes later, they were in a large guest room, bare as all Dry-town rooms, with little more than mats on the floor and a shelf or two. When the servants had withdrawn, Melitta faced the stranger who bore her brother's voice and manner. Left alone with him, she hardly knew what to say.

The stranger said softly, in their own language, "It's really me, you know, Melitta." He smiled. "I must say—you came at exactly the right moment. We couldn't have planned it better!"

"No planning of mine, but good luck," she conceded. She sank down wearily. "Why did you send me here?"

"Because at one time there were mountain-born mercenaries all through this part of the country, gathering at Carthon. Now, with the Dry-towners moving in here, I'm not sure," Storn said. "But we are free; we can act. We could do nothing, now, at High Windward." He threw himself down on one of the pallets. Melitta too, was tired beyond words and she was also ill at ease with a man who still seemed a stranger to her. At last she said, "Who is—the man—"

"His name is Barron; he is a Terran, an off-worlder. His mind lay open to me; I scanned his future and saw that he would be coming into the mountains. And so—" Storn shrugged. Another of those silences fell between brother and sister, a silence which could not be talked about. They both knew that Storn had broken an ancient taboo, forbidden

from the earliest years of the Darkovan Compact. Even
though the victim was a Terran, the horror remained with
Melitta.

They were both relieved when servants of Rannath entered, bearing trays of food, and a pair of chests which, the
servants explained, were gifts from the House of Rannath to
the Lord and Lady of Storn. When they had gone away
again, Melitta rose and approached the pile of gifts, and
Storn laughed softly. "Never too tired to be curious—just
like a woman! As a matter of fact, Melitta, enjoy these gifts
with clear conscience—Rannath's Voice, or whatever that
official calls himself, knows that he is purchasing immunity
from a blood feud that would run for years and cost him a
hell of a lot more than this! If we were Dry towners, that is.
He'll despise us a little because we can be bought off, but I
for one don't care a scrap for what a patch of unwashed Dry-
towners think about us, do you? I accepted the gifts because,
among other things"—he surveyed her—"you looked as if
you could use a few gifts! I've never seen you look so hoy-
denish, little sister!"

Melitta felt ready to cry. "You don't know half of where
I've been, or how I've had to travel, and you're making fun
of what I'm wearing—" Her voice broke.

"Melitta! Don't cry, don't—" He reached out and took
her into his arms, holding her tight, her face on his shoulder.
"Little sister, *breda, chiya . . .*" He cuddled her, crooning pet
names from their childhood. Gradually she quieted, then
drew away, vaguely embarrassed. The voice, the manner,
were her brother's, but the strange man's body and touch
were disconcerting. She lowered her eyes, and Storn
laughed, embarrassed.

"Let's see what Kerstal has sent us, and we'll see how
high he rates the *kihar* of the House of Storn."

"Not cheaply, at any rate," Melitta said, opening the
chests.

There was a sword of fine temper for Storn. He buckled

it on, saying, "Remember, these are Dry-towners—it does not mean what it would mean in our mountains. Worse luck, or it would be a pledge to come to our aid." With the sword was an embroidered vest and baldric. For Melitta, as she had hoped, were gowns of linen trimmed with fur, hoods and coifs—and a gilt chain with a tiny padlock. She stared at that, unbelieving.

Storn laughed as he picked it up: "Evidently he thinks I'm going to put you on a leash!" Then, as her eyes flashed again, he added quickly, "Never mind, you don't have to wear it. Come, *breda*, let us eat, and then rest for a little while. We're safe here, at least. Time enough tomorrow to think about what we're going to do, if Rannath decides that no one here can help us."

CHAPTER ELEVEN

Storn had proved an accurate prophet. However eager the House of Rannath might be to avoid a lengthy blood feud with the Storns, the word had evidently gone out all over Carthon; no one was "at leisure," as he told them regretfully, to pursue a war in the mountains.

Storn, privately, didn't blame them. The Dry-towners were never at ease in the foothills, let alone in the high passes; and the House of Rannath had enough to do to hold Carthon, without scattering such armies as he could command on missions in the far Sierras. For that matter, Dry-town mercenaries, unskilled at mountaineering and ill-guarded against snow and cold, would be more trouble than they were worth. They needed mountain men, and there were none in Carthon.

When the brother and sister insisted on taking their leave, Kerstal besought them to stay and managed not to sound nearly as insincere as they both knew he was. When they pleaded urgent necessity, he found Melitta an excellent riding horse from his private stables and pressed it upon her as a gift.

"And thus," Storn said cynically as they rode away from the Great House, "the Voice of Rannath serves his lord by cutting another tie with the mountains and making it less likely that more mountain folk will come here. That makes it more convenient for the few who remain in Carthon to go elsewhere—I wonder what happened to all the Lanarts? They used to hold land near Carthon," he explained, "and they were a sub-clan of the Altons, along with the Leyniers and the people of Syrtis. I hope the damned Dry-towners haven't killed them off by entangling them in blood feud and picking them off one at a time; they were good people. Domenic Lanart offered his eldest son in marriage to you, once, Melitta."

"And you never told me."

He chuckled. "At the time you were eight years old." Then he sobered again. "I should have married you off, both of you, years gone; then we would have kinfolk at our call. But I was reluctant to part with you. Allira had no great wish to marry. . . ."

They both fell silent. When they spoke again, it was of the past of Carthon and how it had fallen to this deserted state. Not until they were free of the city did Storn again broach the subject of their next move.

"Since Carthon has proved a false hope—"

Melitta broke in: "We are within a few days ride of Armida, and Valdir Alton has banded together all the men of the foothills against bandits—look what he did against Cyrillon des Trailles! Storn, appeal to him! Surely he will help us!"

"I cannot," Storn said somberly. "I dare not even meet with Valdir's men, Melitta. Valdir is a Comyn telepath, and has Alton powers; he would know at once what I have done. I think he already suspects. And besides"—he flushed darkly, ashamed—"I stole a horse from one of Alton's men."

Melitta said dryly, "I wondered where you got such a beauty."

Storn's own thoughts ran bitter counterpoint. *Valdir's foster son pledged himself with a knife—but it was to the Earthling, Barron. He knows nothing of me and has no friendship for me. And now that road is closed, too. What*

now? He said at last, "We are far kin to the House of Aldaran. I have heard that they, too, are a rallying point for the
people of the mountains. Perhaps they can help us. If they
cannot help us for old kinship's sake, perhaps they will
know where we can find mercenaries. We will go to Aldaran."

Melitta, reflecting that meant recrossing the Kadarin and
turning back into the mountains, wished they had gone there
first; but then she remembered that Storn—Barron—had
come all the way from the valley lands far to the other side
of the foothills. Carthon had been the best intermediary
place they could locate, and furthermore Storn had had
every reason to believe they could find help at Carthon. It
was the strangest thing; when she did not look at him, it was
easy to believe she rode with her brother Storn; the voice,
unfamiliar in timbre and tone, had still her brother's familiar mannerisms and speech rhythms, as if it came filtered
through distance. But when her eyes alighted on the strange
figure which rode so easily on the great black horse—tall,
dark, sullenly alien—the unease overtook her again. What
would happen if Storn withdrew and she was left alone with
this stranger, this off-worlder, this unbelievably alien man?
Melitta had thought, after her terrible trek through the
mountains, that she had little left to fear. She discovered that
there were fears she had never thought of before this, the unknown hazards of an alien man, an alien mind.

She told herself, grimly, *Even if he gets out—he couldn't
be worse than Brynat's gang of toughs. I doubt if he'd want
to murder me, or rape me.* Surreptitiously she studied the
strange face, masked in her brother's familiar presence, and
thought, *I wonder what he's really like? He seems a decent
sort of man—no lines of cruelty, or dissipation—sad, if
anything, and a little lonely. I wonder if I'll ever know?*

The third evening out of Carthon, they discovered that
they were being followed.

Melitta sensed it first, with senses abnormally sharpened

by the tension and fear of the journey; as if, she was to say later, "I'd gotten in the habit of riding looking over my shoulder." She also suspected that she was developing, perhaps from contact with Storn or from some other stimulus, from a latent telepath into an actual one. She could not at first tell whether it was by the impact on her mind, or through some subliminal stimulation of her five sharpened senses—sounds too faint to be normally heard, shapes too distant to see—in any case it made little or no difference. When they found shelter in an abandoned herdsman's hut on a hill pasture, she finally told Storn of her suspicions, half afraid he would laugh.

Nothing was further from his mind than laughter. His mouth pinched tight—Melitta knew the gesture if not the mouth—and he said, "I thought so, last night; but I thought I listened only to my own fear."

"But who could be following us? Certainly none of Brynat's men, at such a distance! Men from Carthon?"

"That's not impossible," Storn said. "The House of Rannath might not mind seeing another of the old mountain families disappear—but then, sooner or later he might have to deal with Brynat's raiders himself. Raiding parties have been known to come as far as Carthon, and I dare say he would find us more towardly neighbors than the Scarface— he might not help us, but I doubt if he would hinder. No, what I fear is worse than that."

"Bandits? A raiding nonhuman band?"

Somberly, Storn shook his head. Then, seeing Melitta's fear, he tried to smile. "I'm no doubt imagining things, *breda*, and in any case we are armed."

He did not say what he most feared: that Larry, through sworn friendship and fear for Barron, might have set Valdir on his track. He had not meant any harm—quite the opposite. But Barron had twice—or was it three times—asked questions about Carthon. It would have been simple enough to trail him there. And if no Terran had come there—well,

Valdir at least would know what he had done and why Barron the Earthling had vanished. From what little Storn knew of the Comyn, once on the track of such an offense against the ancient laws of Darkover, they would make little of chasing him over half a world.

And when they caught him—what then?

With the uncanny habit she was developing, of reading his thoughts (Had he done well, to waken *laran* in the girl?), Melitta asked, "Storn, just what *are* the Comyn?"

"That's like asking what the mountains are. Originally there were seven Great Houses on Darkover, or Domains, each with a particular telepathic gift. If I ever knew which House had which Gift, I have forgotten, and in any case, generations of inbreeding and intermarriage have blurred them so that nobody knows any more. When men spoke of the Comyn, they usually meant Comyn Council—a hierarchy of gifted telepaths from every House, who were responsible, first, for surveillance over the use of the old powers and gifts of the mind—and later, they gained temporal power, too. You've heard the ballads—originally the seven houses were descended from the sons of Hastur and Cassilda, so they say. It might even be true, for all I know, but that's beside the point. Just now, they're the givers of law—such law as there has been since the Compact—all over this part of Darkover. Their writ doesn't run in the Dry towns, or in Trailman country, and the mountain people are pretty much out of their orbit—you know as well as I do that we mountain people live under our own customs and ways."

"They rule? Doesn't the King rule in the lowlands?"

"Oh, yes, there is a King in Thendara, ruling under the Comyn Council. The kingship used to rest with the Hasturs, but they gave it up, a few generations ago, in favor of another Comyn family, the Elhalyns, who are so intermarried with the Hasturs that it doesn't make much difference. You know all this, damn it, I remember telling you when you were a child, as well as about the Aldarans."

"I'm sorry, it all seemed very far away." They sat on blankets and furs inside the dark hut, crouched close to the fire, although to anyone accustomed to the fierce cold of the mountains it was not really cold. Outside, sleety rain whispered thickly along the slats of the hut. "What about the Aldarans? Surely they're Comyn too?"

"They used to be; they may have some Comyn powers. But they were kicked out of Comyn Council generations ago; the story goes that they did something so horrible nobody knows or remembers what it was. Personally I suspect it was the usual sort of political dog-fight, but I can't say. No one alive knows, except maybe the Lords of Comyn Council." He fell silent again. It was not Comyn he feared, but Valdir, specifically, and that too-knowing, all-reading gaze.

Storn did not have to be told how Melitta felt about what he had done. He felt the same way himself. He, too, had been brought up in the reverence of this Darkovan law against interfering with another human mind. Yet he justified himself fiercely, with the desperation of the law-abiding and peaceful man turned renegade. *I don't care what laws I have broken, it was my sisters and my young brother in the hands of those men, and the village folk who have served my family for generations. Let me see them free and I don't care if they hang me! What good is an invalid's life, anyhow? I've never been more than half alive, before this!*

He was intensely aware of Melitta, half-kneeling before the low fire, close to him on the blankets. Isolated by the conditions of his life, as he had been till now, there had been few women, and none of his own caste, about whom he could care personally. To a developing telepath that had meant much. Habit and low vitality had made him indifferent to this deprivation; but the strange and newly vigorous body, in which he now felt quite at home, was more than marginally aware of the closeness of the girl.

It crossed his mind that Melitta was extraordinarily beautiful, even in the worn and stained riding clothes she had re-

sumed when they left Carthon. She had loosened her hair
and removed the outer cloak and tunic; under it was a loose
rough linen shift. Some small ornament gleamed at her
throat and her feet were bare. Storn, weary from days of riding, was still conscious of the reflex physical stir of awareness and desire. He let himself play at random with the
thought, perhaps because all his other thoughts were too disturbing. Sexual liaisons between even full siblings in the
mountains were not prohibited, although children born to
such couples were thought unfortunate—the isolated mountain people were too aware of the dangers of inbreeding.
With the grimmest humor he had yet felt, Storn thought, *In
a stranger's body even that would not be anything to fear!*

Then he felt a sudden revulsion. The stranger's body was
that of an alien, an Earthling, a stranger on their world—and
he had been thinking of letting such a one share the body of
his sister, a Lady of Storn? He set his jaw roughly, reached
out and covered the fire.

"It's late," he said. "We have far to travel tomorrow.
You'd better go to sleep."

Melitta obeyed without a word, rolling herself in her fur
cloak and turning away from him. She was aware of what he
was thinking, and intensely sorry for him, but she dared not
offer him overt sympathy. Her brother would have rejected
it as he had done all her life, and she was still a little afraid
of the stranger. It was not the low-keyed throb of his desire,
which Melitta could feel almost as a physical presence,
which disturbed her, of course. She did not care about that.
As with any mountain girl of her caste, she knew that, traveling alone with any man, such a problem would in all prob-
ability arise. With Storn's own person she might not have
thought of it, but she was much more aware of the stranger
than Storn realized. She had been forced to think about this
eventuality and to make up her mind about it. She felt no
particular attraction to the stranger, although if his presence
had been uncomplicated by the eerie uncanniness of know-

ing that he was also her brother, she might have found him intriguing; certainly he was handsome, and seemed gentle and from the tones of his voice, likable. But if she had even inadvertently roused desire in him, common decency, by the code of women of her caste, demanded that she give it some release; to refuse this would have been wrong and cruelly whorish. If she had been unalterably opposed to this possibility, she would not have agreed to travel entirely alone with him; no mountain girl would have done so. It would not have been impossible to find a traveling companion in Carthon.

In any case, it seemed that at the moment the matter was not imminent, and Melitta was relieved. It might have been entirely too uncanny; *like lying with a ghost,* she thought, and slept.

It was still dark when Storn's hand on her shoulder roused her, and when they saddled their horses and began to ride down the dark mountain path, they rode through still-heavy sleet which only after an hour or more of riding turned into the light rain which presaged dawn at this latitude and season. Melitta, cold and shivering, and even a little resentful, did not protest; she simply wrapped her cloak over her face as they rode. Storn turned into an inordinately steep and forsaken path, dismounted and led her horse along the slippery path through the trees until it was safe to ride again. She was thinking, *If it is Comyn on our trail, we may not be able to lose them. but if not, perhaps we can shake off our followers.*

"And we may gain two or three days ride on them this way, if they are not accustomed to the mountain roads—they or their horses," Storn said, out of nothing, and Melitta understood.

All that day and the next they rode through steeper and steeper mountain paths, with storms gathering over the heights, and at night they were too exhausted to do more than swallow a few mouthfuls of food and roll, half asleep already, into their blankets. On the morning of the third day after they had first sensed that they were followed, Melitta woke without any uneasy sense of a presence overshadowing their moves, and sensed that they had lost their followers, at least for the moment.

"We should reach Aldaran today," said Storn, as they saddled, "and if what I've heard is true, perhaps even the Comyn don't care to come this far into the hills. They may be sacrosanct in the lowlands, but not here."

As soon as the mist cleared they sighted the castle from a peak, a gray and craggy height enfolded and half invisible in the hills; but it took them the rest of the day to approach the foot of the mountain on which it stood, and as they turned into the road—well-traveled and strongly surfaced—which led upward to the castle, they were intercepted by two cloaked men. They were asked their business with the utmost courtesy but nevertheless entreated to remain until the Lord of Aldaran knew of their coming, with so much insistence that neither Storn nor Melitta wanted to protest.

"Inform the Lord of Aldaran," said Storn, his voice sounding gray with weariness, "that his far kinsmen of Storn, at High Windward, seek shelter, counsel and hospitality. We have ridden far and are weary and call on him in the name of kin to give us rest here."

"Rest in safety is yours at the asking," said the man with exquisite courtesy, and Melitta sighed in relief; they were among people of familiar ways. "Will you wait in the gate house, my lord and *damisela*? I will have your horses looked to. I cannot disturb the Lord of Aldaran without his consent, but if you are his kinfolk, I am sure you need not wait long. I am at your service, and there is food for all travelers if you are in need of it."

Waiting in the bare, small gate house, Storn smiled briefly at Melitta; "Aldaran keeps the old ways of courtesy to strangers, whatever else may have befallen his household."

In an almost unbelievably brief time (Storn wondered if some signaling device had been used, for there hardly seemed time for a messenger to come and go to the castle on the heights) the guard returned: "The Lady Desideria bids me conduct you to the main house and make you welcome, Lord and Lady; and when you are rested and refreshed she will receive you."

Storn murmured to Melitta, as they climbed the path and the steps leading upward, "I have no idea who the Lady Desideria is. Old Kermiac would hardly have married; I suspect it is one of his son's wives."

But the young woman who greeted them was no man's wife. She could hardly have been more than fifteen years old. She was a striking red-haired beauty whose poise and self-confidence made Melitta feel shy, countrified, and ill at ease.

"I am Desideria Leynier," she said. "My foster mother and my guardian are not at home; they will return tomorrow and give you a proper welcome." She came and took Melitta's hands in her own, searching her face with gentle eyes. "Poor child, you look tired almost to death; a night's sleep before you face your hosts will do you good; and you too, Master, you must rest and not stand on ceremony. The Storns are unknown to me but not to my household. I give you welcome."

Storn returned thanks, but Melitta was not listening to the formal words. In the presence of this queerly self-possessed child, she sensed something more than poise; an awareness, an inner strength, and the touch of an uncannily developed sensitivity, so far beyond her own as to make her feel like a child. She made a deep reverence. *"Vai leronis,"* she whispered, using the ancient word for a sorceress wise in the old skills.

Desideria smiled merrily. "Why, no," she said. "Only one, perhaps, who has a little knowledge of the old crafts— and if I read rightly, child, you are no stranger to them! But

we can talk of that another time, I wished only to give you
welcome in my foster parents' name." She summoned a servant to conduct them, and herself went before them along
the long halls. It was evidently a busy hour before the
evening meal; people went back and forth in the halls, including some tall thin men whose presence and careless regard made Storn draw breath and clamp his fingers hard on
Melitta's arm.

"There are Terrans here—this deep in the mountains," he
whispered, "what in the name of Zandru's hells is going on
here at Aldaran? Have we walked from the trap to the cook
pot? I would not believe that any Terran alive had ever come
into these mountains. And the girl is a telepath—Melitta,
keep your wits about you!"

Desideria turned Storn over to a servant and conducted
Melitta into a small room at the top of a tower, one of four
tiny pie-shaped rooms on that level. "I am sorry the accommodations are not more luxurious," she apologized, "but
there are a great many of us here. I will send you wash
water, and a maid to dress you and although you would be
more than welcome in the hall, child, I think you would be
better to have dinner here in your room, and go to bed at
once; without rest you will be ill."

Melitta agreed gratefully, glad that she need not face so
many strangers tonight. Desideria said, "He is a strange
man—your brother," but the words held no hint of a prying
question. She pressed Melitta's hands and kissed her cheek.
"Now rest well," she said in that oddly adult way, "and don't
be afraid of anything. My sister and I are near you in the
rooms across the hallway." She went away. Left alone,
Melitta took off her dirty and cold riding clothes and gratefully accepted the services of the quiet, incurious maid who
came to wait on her. After bathing and eating the light, delicious food brought to her, she lay down in the soft bed and
for the first time since the alarm bell had pealed Brynat's

presence at the walls of Storn, she felt she could sleep in peace. They were safe.

Where is Storn? Is he, too, enjoying the luxury of safety and rest? Surely he must be mistaken about Terrans here. And it's surely strange—to find a vai leronis *deep in the mountains.*

CHAPTER TWELVE

Storm woke in the early light, and for a few minutes had no notion of where he might be. Around him were unfamiliar airs and voices, and he lay with his eyes closed, trying to orient himself, hearing footsteps ringing on stone, the sound of animals calling out for food, and strange voices rising and falling. They were peaceful morning sounds, not the sounds of a home in the hands of conquerors, and then memory flooded back and he knew he was in Castle Aldaran. He opened his eyes.

A curious apprehension lay on him, he did not know why. He began to wonder how long he could keep the upper hand over Barron—if it would be long enough to carry through his aims before he lost hold and found himself back in his own body, lying helpless in trance, guarded against personal attack, but still unable to do anything for his family and his people. If that happened, he had no illusions about what would happen, sooner or later. Barron would go his own way, confused by a period of amnesia or perhaps false memories—Storm really did not know what happened to a man in Barron's position—and Melitta would be left alone without anyone. He would never know what happened to her in that case, he supposed.

And he did not want to return to his own body, blinded and helplessly imprisoned. If he did, what would happen to

Barron, an Earthman alone in these strange mountains? For the very sake of his victim, he must maintain hold at all costs.

If there *were* Terrans at Castle Aldaran, what could it mean? Sick with unanswered and unanswerable questions, he flung back the covers and went to the window. Whatever happened in the end, he would enjoy these few days of sight out of a lifetime in darkness. Even if these days were his last.

From the window he looked down at the commotion in the courtyard. Men were going to and fro with an indefinable sense of purposiveness, there were Terrans among them, a few even in the leather dress of the spaceports—*how do I know that when I see it, never having been there?*—and after he had watched a while there was a stir among the men. One man and two uniformed attendants rode through the gate.

The man was tall, dark-bearded, well past middle age, and had an air of authority which reminded Storn vaguely of Valdir, although this man was clearly one of the mountain people. Storn realized from the hubbub surrounding him that he must be looking down at the arrival of the Lord of Aldaran. In a few hours he must face this man and ask for his help. Deep depression lay on Storn, for no discernible reason. Could even a whole army, if Aldaran were willing to put it at his disposal (and why should he?) dislodge Brynat? Storn Castle had been besieged before and it had never even been necessary to defend it. *Now that Brynat holds it, could anyone retake it? Army? We would need a god.*

The scene below melted away and Storn seemed to see within himself the great chained shape of Sharra, flame-crowned, golden-chained, beautiful and awesome. It was the vision he had seen when he lay helpless and blind behind the magnetic force-field at Storn Castle, his body tranced, his mind free ranging time and space in search of help from *somewhere.*

Sharra again! What does the vision mean? Melitta came for him late in the forenoon with Desideria, who told them that her guardian was ready to receive them. As he followed the girls down the long corridors, stairs and hallways, Storn was quietly evaluating the poise, the strength and the obvious telepathic awareness of this very young girl, and coming up with a disquieting answer. She must be a Keeper—one of the young girls trained from infancy to work with the old matrix crystals and screens which would have made the few things at Storn Castle look like children's toys. But, overhearing snatches of conversation between them—Desideria seemed to have taken a fancy to Melitta, and talked to her freely—he gathered that there were four of them. In the old days a matrix circle, isolated from the world and giving all their time to it, had barely managed to train one Keeper in about ten years. If Aldaran had managed to train four in the few years since Storn had been here last, what was going on in this place?

But when he asked her a random question, using the polite form of address, *leronis*, Desideria gave him a merry smile and shook her head: "No, my friend, I am not a *leronis*; my guardian does not like the word and its connotations of sorcery. I have been trained in a skill which anyone can learn who is a good telepath, just as anyone who is strong and fit enough can learn hawking or riding. Our world has accepted foolish ideas like sorcery for all too many years. Call me, if you like, a matrix technician. My sisters and I have learned this skill, far better than most; but there is no need to look at me with reverence because I have learned well!"

She went on looking at him with a girlish, ingenuous smile, then suddenly shivered, flushed and dropped her eyes. When she spoke again it was to Melitta, almost pointedly ignoring Storn.

He thought with a certain grimness, *Training or not, she is still conventional in the old ways—and I owe my life to*

that. If she were old enough to look at it that way—a trained
telepath of her caliber need only look at me to know what I
have done. Only the convention that girls of her age may not
initiate any contact with men other than their blood kin, has
saved me so far.

The thought was strangely poignant—that this young girl
of his mountain people, of his own kind and caste, and
trained in all those things which had been the major solace
of his life, was so guarded against him—and that he dared
not reach out to her, mind or body. He felt as if he could
have wept. He set his lips hard and followed the girls. He did
not speak again.

Aldaran received them, not in a formal audience chamber
but in a small, friendly room low in the castle. He embraced
Storn, calling him cousin, kissed Melitta on the forehead
with a kinsman's privilege, offered them wine and sweets,
and made them sit beside him; then he asked what had
brought them there.

"It is far too long since any of your kinsmen have visited
us at Aldaran; you live as isolated at High Windward as ea-
gles in their aerie. It has come to mind in the last year or so
that I have neglected kinship's dues and that I should ride to
Storn, there is much astir in the mountains these days, and
no one of our people should hold himself aloof too far; our
world's future depends on it. But more of that later, if you
are interested. Tell me what brings you to Aldaran, kinsman?
How can I help you?"

He listened to their story gravely; with a gradually darkening and distressful face. When they had finished, he spoke
with deep regret.

"I am ashamed," he said, "that I offered you no help before this, to prevent such a thing. For now it has happened,
I am powerless to help you. I have kept no fighting men here
for more than thirty years, Storn; I have kept peace here and
tried to prevent feuds and raids rather than repelling them.
We mountain people have been torn by feuds and little wars

far too long; we have let ourselves go back to barbarian days."

"I, too, had no fighting men and wanted peace," Storn said bitterly, "and all I gained from it was Brynat's men at my outworks."

"I have Terran guards here and they are armed with off-world weapons," Aldaran said. "Would-be invaders knew enough, after a time or two, to let us alone."

"With—weapons? Force weapons? But what of the Compact?" Melitta gasped in genuine horror. The law which banned, on this world, any weapon beyond the arm's reach of the wielder, was even more reverenced than the taboo against meddling with the mind. Aldaran said quietly, "That law has delivered us to petty wars, feuds, murders and assassins. We need new laws, not stupid reverence for old ones. I have broken the Darkovan code and as a result, the Hasturs and the Comyn hold my family in horror; but we are at peace here and we have no hooligans at our doors, waiting for an old man to weaken so that he can be challenged and set down as if the stronger swordsman were the better man. The law of brute force means only the rule of the brute."

"And other worlds, I believe," Melitta said, "have found that unrestricted changes in weapons leads to an endless race for better and better weapons in a chase to disaster which can destroy not only men, but worlds."

"That may even be true," Aldaran said, "and yet look what has happened to Darkover, in the hands of the Terrans? What have we done? We refused their technology, their weapons, we insisted on refusing real contact with them. Since the Years of Chaos, when we lost all of our own technologies except for the few in the hands of the Comyn, we've slipped back further and further into barbarism. In the lowlands, the Seven Domains keep their old rule as if no ships had ever put forth into space. And here in the mountains we allow ourselves to be harassed by bandits because we are afraid to fight them. Someone must step beyond this deadlock, and I have tried to do so. I have made a compact with the Terrans; they will teach us their ways and defenses and I will teach them ours. And as a result of a generation of peace and freedom from casual bandits and learning to think as the Terrans think—that everything which happens can and must be explained and measured—I have even redis-covered many of our old Darkovan ways; you need not think we are totally committed to becoming part of Terra. For in-stance, I have learned how to train telepaths for matrix work without the old superstitious rituals; none of the Comyn will even try that. And as a result—but enough of that. I can see that you are not in any state to think about abstract ideas of progress, science and culture as yet."

"But what all this fine-sounding talks means," said Storn bitterly, "is that my sister and brother, and all my people, must lie at the mercy of bandits because you prefer not to be entangled in feuds."

"My dear boy!" Aldaran looked aghast. "The gods help me; if I had the means to do so, I would forget my ethics and come to your aid—blood kin is not mountain-berry wine! But I have no fighting men at all, and few weapons, and such as I have could not be moved over the mountains." Storn was enough of a telepath to know that his distress was very real. Aldaran said, "We live in bad times, Storn; no cul-ture ever changed without people getting hurt, and it is your ill-fortune that you are one of those who are getting hurt in the change. But take heart; you are alive and unhurt, and your sister is here, and believe me, you shall be made wel-come here as kin; this is your home, from this very day forth. The gods seize me, if I am not as a father to you both from this moment."

"And my sister? My brother? My people?"

"Perhaps some day we will find a way to help them; some day all these mountain bandits must be wiped out; but we have neither the means nor any way."

He dismissed them, tenderly. "Think it over. Let me do what I can for you; you certainly must not return to throw your lives after theirs. Do you think that your people really want you to share their fate now that you have escaped?"

Storn's thoughts ran bitter counterpoint as they left Aldaran. Perhaps what Aldaran said made sense in the long run, in the history of Darkover, in the annals of a world. But he was interested in the short run, in his own people and the annals of his own time. Taking the long view inevitably meant being callous to how many people were hurt. If he had had no hope of outside help, he would gladly have sent Melitta to safety, if nothing more could be salvaged, and been glad there was a home for her here. But now that hope had been raised for more, this seemed like utter failure.

He heard, as from a distance, Desideria saying to Melitta, "Something draws me to your brother—I don't know; he is not a man whose looks I admire, it is something beyond that—I wish I could help you. I can do much, and in the old days, the powers of the trained telepaths of Darkover could be used against intruders and invaders. But not alone."

Melitta said, "Don't think we are ungrateful for your guardian's good will, Desideria. But we must return to Storn even if all we can do is to share the fate of those there. But we will not do that unless all hope is gone, even if we must rouse the peasants with their pitchforks and the forge folk of the hills!"

Desideria stopped dead in the hallway. She said, "The forge folk of the caverns in the Hellers? Do you mean the old folk who worshipped the goddess, Sharra?"

"Indeed they did. But those altars are long cold and profaned."

"Then I can help you!" Desideria's eyes glowed. "Do you think an altar matters? Listen, Melitta, you know, a little, what my training has been? Well, one of the—the powers we have learned to raise here is that associated with Sharra. In the old days, Sharra was a power in this world; the Comyn sealed the gates against raising that power, because of various dangers, but we have found the way, a little—but Melitta, if you can find me even fifty men who once believed in Sharra, I could level the gates of Storn Castle, I could burn Brynat's men alive about him."

"I don't understand," said Storn, caught in spite of himself. "Why do you need worshipers?"

"And you a telepath yourself, I dare say, Storn! Look—the linked minds of the worshipers, in a shared belief, create a tangible force, a strength, to give power to that—that force, the power which comes through the gates of the other dimension into this world. It is the Form of Fire. I can call it up alone, but it has no power without someone to give it strength. I have the matrixes to open that gate. But with those who had once worshiped—"

Storn thought he knew what she meant. He had discovered forces which could be raised, which he could not handle alone, and with Brynat at his gates. He had thought, *If I had help, someone trained in these ways—*

He said, "Will Aldaran allow this?"

Desideria looked adult and self-sufficient. She said, "When anyone has my training and my strength, she does not ask for leave to do what she feels right. I have said I will help you; my guardian would not gainsay me—and I would not give him the right to do so."

"And I thought you a child," Storn said.

"No one can endure the training I have had and remain a child," Desideria said. She looked into his eyes and colored, but she did not flinch from his gaze. "Some day I will read the strangeness in you, Loran of Storn. That will be for another time; now your mind is elsewhere." Briefly she touched his hand, then colored again and turned away. "Don't think me bold."

Touched, Storn had no answer. Fear and uncertainty caught him again: If these people felt no horror of breaking the Darkovan League's most solemn law, the Compact against weapons, would they have any compunctions about what he had done? He did not know whether he felt relieved or vaguely shocked at the thought that they might accept it as part of a necessity; without worrying about the dubious ethics involved.

He forced such thoughts from his mind. For the moment it was enough that Desideria thought there was a way to help. It was a desperate chance, but he was desperate enough for any gamble, whatever that might be—even Sharra.

"Come with me to the room where my sisters and I work," she said. "We must find the proper instruments and—you may as well call them talismans, if you like. And if you, Storn, have experimented with these things, then the sight of a matrix laboratory may interest you. Come. And then we can leave within the hour, if you wish."

She led the way along a flight of stairs and past glowing blue beacons in the hallways which Storn, although he had never seen them before, recognized. They were the force beacons, the warning signs. He had some of them in his own castle and had experimented until he had learned many of their secrets. They had given him the impregnable field which protected his body and had turned Brynat's weapon, and the magnetic currents which guided the mechanical birds that allowed him to experience the sensation of flight. There were other things with less practical application, and he wanted to ask Desideria question after question. But he was haunted by apprehension, a sense of time running out; Melitta must have sensed it too, for she dropped back a step with unease.

He tried to smile. "Nothing. It's a little overwhelming to learn that these—these toys with which I spent my child-hood can be a science of this magnitude."

Time is running out. . . .

Desideria swung back a curtain, and stepped through a

blue magnetic shimmer. Melitta followed. Storn, seized by indefinable reluctance, hesitated, then stepped forward.

A stinging shock ran through him, and—for an instant Dan Barron, bewildered, half-maddened, and fighting for sanity, stared around him at the weird trappings of the matrix laboratory, as if waking from a long, long nightmare.

"Storn—?" Desideria's hand touched his. He forced himself to awareness and smiled. "Sorry. I'm not used to fields quite as strong."

"I should have warned you. But if you could not come through the field you would not have enough knowledge to help us, in any case. Here, let me find what I need."

She flicked a small button and motioned them to seats.

"Wait for me."

Slowly, Storn became aware of the strange disorganizing humming. Melitta was staring at him in astonishment and dismay but it took all his strength not to dissolve beneath the strange invisible sound, not to vanish. . . .

A telepathic damper. Barron had been aware of one, at Armida, with his developing powers, he had just been disturbed at it, but now . . . now . . .

Now there was not even time to cry out, it was vibrating through his brain—through temporal lobes and nerves, creating disruption of the nets that held him in domination, freeing—Barron! He felt himself spinning through indefinable, blue-tinged, timeless space—falling, disappearing, dying—blind, deafened, entranced. . . . He spun down into unconsciousness, his last thought was not of Melitta left alone, nor of his victim Barron. It was Desideria's gray eyes and the indefinable touch of her compassion and knowledge, that went down with him into the night of an unconsciousness so complete that it was like death. . . .

Barron came to consciousness as if surfacing from a long, deep dive.

"What the bloody hell is going on here?" For a moment

he had no idea whether or not he had spoken the words aloud. His head hurt and he recognized the invisible humming vibration that Valdir Alton had called a telepathic damper—that was all his world for a moment.

Slowly he found his feet and his balance. It was as if for days he had walked through a nightmare, conscious, but unable to do anything but what he did—as if some other person walked in his body and directed his actions while he watched in astonishment from somewhere; powerless to intervene. He suddenly woke with the controlling power gone, yet the nightmare went on. The girl he had seen in the dream was there, staring up at him in mild concern—his sister? *Damn it, no, that was the other guy.* He could remember everything he had done and said, almost everything he had *thought*, while Storn commanded him. He had not shifted position but somehow the focus had changed. He was himself again, Dan Barron, not Storn.

He opened his mouth to raise hell, to demand explanations and give a few, to make everything very clear, when he saw Melitta looking up at him in concern and faint fright. Melitta! He hadn't asked to get involved with her, but here she was and from what he could realize, he was her only protector. *She's been so brave; she's come so far for help, and here it is within her reach; and what will happen if I make myself known?*

He was no expert on Darkovan law and custom, but the one thing he did know from walking with Storn for seven or eight days was that, by Darkovan standards, what Storn had done was a crime. *Fine—I could murder him for it, and God willing, some day I will. That's one hell of a thing to do to a man's mind and body! But none of it was Melitta's fault. No. I'll have to play the game for a while.*

The silence had lasted too long. Melitta said; with growing fear in her voice, "Storn?"

He made himself smile at her and then found it didn't take an effort. He said, trying to remember how Storn had spoken, "It's all right, that—telepathic damper upset me a little." *And boy, was that a masterpiece of understatement!*

Desideria came back to them before Melitta could answer, carrying various things wrapped in a length of silk. She said, "I must go and make arrangements for transportation and escort to take you into the hills near High Windward, to the caves where the forge folk have gone. You cannot help in this, why not go and rest? You have a long journey behind and ahead, and difficult things—" She glanced up at Barron and quickly away, and he vaguely wondered why. *What's the matter with the red-headed kid?* He suddenly felt faint and swayed, and Desideria said quickly, "Go with your brother, Melitta; I have many plans to make. I will come for you at sunset."

Too disoriented and confused to do anything else, Barron let Melitta lead him through the suddenly strange corridors to a room where he knew he had slept the night before but which he had never consciously seen before. She stood looking down at him, distressed.

"Storn, what's happened? Are you ill? You look at me so strangely—*Storn! Loran!*" Her voice rose in sudden panic, and Barron put out a hand to quiet her.

"Take it easy, kid—" He realized he was speaking his own language and shifted back, with some effort into the tongue Storn and his sister spoke together. "Melitta, I'm sorry," he said with an effort, but her eyes were fixed on him in gnawing horror and understanding.

"The telepathic damper," she whispered. "Now I understand. *Who are you?*"

His admiration and respect for the girl suddenly grew. This must have been just about the most terrifying and disconcerting thing that had ever happened to her. After she'd been so far, and been through so much, and with help so near, to find that her brother was gone and she was alone with a stranger—a stranger who might be raving mad, or a homicidal maniac, and in any case was probably mad—and she didn't run or scream or yell for help. She stood there white as a sheet, but she stood up to him and asked, "Who are you?"

God, what a girl!

He said, trying to match her calm, "I think your brother told you my name, but in case he didn't, it's Dan Barron. Dan will do, but you'd better go on calling me Storn or some of these people may get wise. You don't want that to happen when you've been through so much, do you?"

She said, almost incredulous, "You mean—after what my brother's done to you, you'll still help me? You'll go back with us to Storn?"

"Lady," said Barron, grim and meaning it more than he had ever meant anything in his life, "Storn is the one place on this damn planet that I want to go more than anything else in the world. I've got to help you get those bandits out of your castle so that I can get to your brother—and when I get my hands on him, he's going to wish he only had Brynat Scarface to deal with! But that's nothing against you. So relax. I'll help you play your game—and Storn and I can settle our private difficulties later on. Good enough?"

She smiled at him, setting her chin courageously.

"Good enough."

CHAPTER THIRTEEN

There was an airplane.

Barron looked at it in amazement and dismay. He would have sworn that there were few surface craft on Darkover; certainly no fuel was exported from the Zone for them, and he had never known of one being sold on Darkover, except one or two in Trade City. But here it was, and obviously of Empire manufacture. When he climbed into it he realized that all the controls had been ripped out; in place of an instrument panel was one of those blue crystals. Desideria took her place before it, looking like a child, and Barron felt like saying, "Hey, are *you* going to fly this thing?" But he held himself back. The girl seemed to know what she was doing, and after what he had seen on Darkover, he wouldn't put anything past them. A technology which could displace possession by another mind was worth looking into. He began to wonder if any Terran Empire man knew anything about Darkover.

Melitta was afraid to climb into the strange contrivance until Desideria comforted and reassured her; then, looking as if she were taking her life in her hands and didn't care, she climbed in, resolved not to show her fear.

The queer craft took off in an eerie silence. Desideria put on another of the telepathic dampers inside, saying almost in apology, "I am sorry—I must control the crystal with my own strength and I dare not have random thoughts intruding." Barron had all he could do to endure the vibrations. He was beginning to guess what they were. If telepathic power were a vibration, the damper was a scrambler to protect the user of the force from any intruding vibrations.

He found himself wondering what Storn would have thought of covering in a few hours, the terrain which he and Melitta had covered so laboriously, on foot and horseback, in several days. The thought was unwelcome in the extreme. He did not want to think about Storn's feelings. Nevertheless, his beliefs about the backwardness of Darkover had been gravely shaken in the last few hours. Their refusal of weapons other than knife and sword now seemed an ethical point—and yet Aldaran, too, seemed to have a valid ethical point, that this kept them struggling in small wars and feuds which depended for their success on who had the stronger physical strength.

But don't all wars depend ultimately on that? Surely you don't believe that rightness of a cause would mean that the right side would be able to get the biggest weapons? Would the feud between Brynat and Storn be easier settled if both of them had guns?

And if this was an ethical point rather than a lack of knowledge, was it just possible that their lack of transit, manufacturing and the like might come from preference rather than lack of ability?

Damn it, why am I worrying about Darkovan ways when my own problems are so pressing?

He had deserted his work with Valdir Alton's men at the fire station. He—or Storn in his body—had stolen a valuable riding horse. He had probably irredeemably ruined himself with the Terran authorities, who had exerted themselves to give him this job, and his career was probably at a permanent standstill. He'd be lucky not to find himself on the first ship off Darkover.

Then it struck him that probably he need not go. The Empire might not believe his story but the Altons, who were telepaths, certainly would. And Larry had given him friendship, while Valdir was interested in the field of his professional competence. Perhaps there would be work for him here. He suddenly faced the awareness that he didn't want to leave Darkover and that he had at last become caught up in the struggles and problems of these people whose lives he had entered against his will.

I could kill Storn for what he did—but damn it, I'm glad it happened.

But this was the briefest flash of insight, and it disappeared again, leaving him lost and bewildered. During the days as Storn he had grown used to Melitta's companionship. Now she seemed strange and aloof and when he tried to reach out and touch her with his mind, it was an almost automatic movement and the low-keyed vibration of the telepathic damper interfered, making him feel dull, sick and miserable. He had expected to feel more at home flying than riding horseback but after a short time all he wished was that the flight would be over. Melitta would not look at him.

That was the worst of it. He longed for the flight to be over so that he could speak to her, touch her. She was the only familiar thing in this world and he ached to be near her.

Inconsistently, he was distressed when the flight ended and Desideria brought the craft expertly down in a small valley as quietly as a hovercraft. She apologized to Melitta for not coming nearer to Storn, but explained that the air currents around the peaks were violent enough to crash any small craft. Barron wondered how a girl her age knew about air currents. *Oh hell, she's evidently something special in the way of telepaths, she probably feels 'em through her skin or her balance centers or something.*

Barron had no idea where they were. Since Storn had never seen the place—being blind—Storn's memories were no good to Barron. But Melitta knew. She took charge, directing them toward a mountain village where Darkovans swarmed out, welcoming Melitta with delight, and showing Desideria a reverential awe which seemed to confuse the young girl—the first time Barron had seen Desideria taken aback—and even make her angry.

"I *hate* this," she told him, and Barron knew she still thought she spoke to Storn. "In the old days there might have been some reason for treating the Keepers like goddesses. But now we know how to train them, there is no *reason* for it—no more than for worshipping an expert blacksmith because of his skill!"

"Speaking of blacksmiths," said Barron, "how are we going to round up these forge people?"

She looked at him sharply and it was like the first time she had seen him: She started to say, "You and Melitta will have to manage that; I have never been among them," and stopped, frowning. She said, almost in a whisper and less to Barron than herself, "You have changed, Storn. Something has happened—" and very abruptly turned away.

He had almost forgotten that to her he was still Storn. Elsewhere the masquerade was over; the village people ignored him. He realized that if these were people who lived near High Windward, they would know all the Storns.

He did not try to follow what Melitta was saying to the villagers. He was definitely excess baggage on this trip and he couldn't even imagine why Melitta had wanted him to come back to Storn with her. After a time she came back to Storn and Desideria, saying, "They will provide horses and guides to the caverns of the forge folk in the hills. But we should start at once; Brynat's men patrol the villages every day or two—especially since I escaped—just to make sure that nothing is happening down here; and if it were known that they had helped me—well, I don't want to bring reprisals on them."

They started within the hour. Barron rode silently close to Melitta, but he didn't try to talk to her. There was some comfort in her mere presence, but he knew that she felt ill at ease with him and he did not force himself on her. It was enough to be near her. He spared a thought for Storn, and this time he pitied him. *Poor devil, to have come so far and been through so much and then be forced offstage for the last act.*

He supposed Storn was lying entranced, high in his old wing of the castle, and if he was conscious at all—which Barron doubted—not knowing what had happened. *Hell, that's a worse punishment than anything I could do to him!*

He had been riding without paying much attention to where he was going, letting the horse choose his own road. Now the air began to be filled with the faintly acrid smell of smoke. Barron, alert from his days at the fire station, raised his head to sniff the wind. but the others rode on without paling attention.

Only Melitta sensed his attention and dropped back to ride at his side. "It's not fire. We are nearing the caverns of the forge people; you smell the fires of their forges."

They rode up along a narrow trail that led into the heart of the mountains. After a while Barron began to see dark caves lining the trail. At their entrances, small, swart faces peeped out fearfully. There were little men dressed in furs and leather, women in fur cloaks who turned shyly away from the strangers, and wrapped in fur, miniature children who looked like little teddy-bears. At last they came to a cavern gaping like a great maw, and here Melitta and Desideria alighted, their guides standing close to them in a mixture of fear and dogged protectiveness.

Three men in leather aprons, bearing long metal staves and with metal hammers thrust into their belts—hammers of such weight that Barron did not think he could have lifted them—strode out of the cavern toward Melitta. Behind them the fearful people came up and gathered, surrounding them. The three men were dark, gnarled, short of stature but with long and powerful arms. They made deep bows to the women. Barron they ignored, as he had expected. The central one, with white patches in his dark hair, began to speak;

the language was Cahuenga, but the pronunciation so guttural and strange that Barron could follow only one word in
three. He gathered, however, that they were making Melitta
welcome and paying Desideria almost more reverence than
the village people had done.

There followed a long colloquy. Melitta spoke. It was a
long speech that sounded eloquent, but Baryon did not understand. He was very weary, and very apprehensive without knowing why, and this kept him from the attempt to
reach out and understand as he had done with Larry and
Valdir. *How the devil have I picked up telepathic gifts anyhow? Contact with Storn?* Then the white-haired forge man
spoke. His was a long chanting speech that sounded wild
and musical, with many bows; again and again Barron
caught the word *Sharra.* Then Desideria spoke, and again
Barron heard *Sharra,* repeated again and again, to cries and
nods from the little people gathered around them. Finally
there was a great outcry and all the little people drew knives,
hammers, and swords and flourished them in the air. Barron,
remembering the Dry-towners, quailed, but Melitta stood
firm and fearless and he realized it was an acclamation, not
a threat.

Rain was drizzling down thinly, and the little people
gathered around and led them into the cavern.

It was airy and spacious, lighted partly by torches burning in niches in the walls, and partly by beautifully luminescent crystals set to magnify the firelight. Exquisitely worked
metal objects were everywhere, but Barron had no leisure to
examine them. He drew up beside Melitta as they walked
through the lighted cavern corridors, and asked in a low
voice, "What's all the shouting about?"

"The Old One of the forge folk has agreed to help us,"
Melitta said. "I promised him, in turn, that the altars of
Sharra should be restored throughout the mountains, and
that they should be permitted to return, unmolested, to their
old places and villages. Are you weary from riding? I am,

but somehow—" she spread her hands, helplessly. "It's been so long, and now we are near the end—we will start for Storn, two hours before the dawn, so that when Brynat wakes we will surround the castle—if only we are in time!" She was trembling, and moved as if to lean on him, then straightened her back proudly and stood away. She said, almost to herself, "I cannot expect you to care. What can we do for you, when this is over, to make up for meddling in your life this way?"

Barron started to say, "I do care, I care about you, Melitta," but she had already drawn away from him and hurried after Desideria.

With jewel lights and with music provided by small, caged tree frogs and singing crickets, there was a banquet that evening in the great lower hall. Barron, though he could eat little, sat in wonder at the silver dishes—silver was commoner than glass in the mountains—and the jeweled, prismed lamps which played unendingly on the pale, smoke-stained walls of the cave. The forge people sang deep-throated, wild songs in a four-note scale with a strangely incessant rhythm, like the pounding of hammers. But Barron could not eat the food, or understand a word of the endless epics, and he was relieved when the company dissolved early—he could understand enough of their dialect to know that they were being dismissed against the ride before dawn—and one of their guides took them to cubicles carved in the rock.

Barron was alone; he had seen Melitta and Desideria being conducted to a cubicle nearby. In the little rock room, hardly more than a closet, he found a comfortable bed of furs laid on a bed frame of silver, woven with leather straps. He lay down and expected to sleep from sheer exhaustion. But sleep would not come.

He felt disoriented and lonely. Perhaps he had grown used to Storn's presence and his thoughts. Melitta, too, had withdrawn from him and he was inexpressibly alone without her presence to reach out to, in that indefinable way. He re-

flected that he had changed. He had always been alone and
had never wanted it any other way. The rare women he had
had, had never made an impression on him; they came, were
used for the brief emotional release they could provide and
were forgotten. He had no close friends, only business associates. He had lived on this world and had never known or
cared how it differed from Terra or from any other Empire
planet.

Soon it would be over, and he did not know where he
would go. He wished suddenly that he had been more re-
sponsive to Larry's proffered friendship; but then, Storn had
spoiled that contact for him, probably for all time. He had
never known what it was to have a friend, but then he
had never known or realized the depths of his aloneness,
either.

The room seemed to be swelling up and receding, the
lights wavering. He could sense thoughts floating in the air
around him, beating on him, he felt physically sick with
their impact. He lay on the bed and clutched it, feeling the
room tipping and swaying and wondering if he would slide
off. Fear seized him; was Storn reaching out for his mind
again? He could *see* Storn, without knowing how it was
Storn—fair, soft-handed and soft-faced, lying asleep on a
bier of silks—face remote and his human presence simply
not there at all. Then he saw a great white bird, swooping
from the heights of the castle, circling it with a strange musical, mechanical cry and then sweeping away with a great
beating of wings.

The room kept shifting and tipping, and he clung to the
bed frame, fighting the sickness and disorientation that
threatened to tear him apart. He heard himself cry out, unable to keep back the cry; he squeezed his eyes tight, curled
himself into a fetal position and tried hard not to think or
feel at all.

He never knew how long he lay curled there in rejection,
but after what seemed a long and very dreadful time he came

slowly to the awareness that someone was calling his name, very softly.

"Dan! Dan, it's Melitta—it's all right; try to take my hand, touch me—it's all right. I would have come before if I had known—"

He made an effort to close his fingers on hers. Her hand seemed a single stable point in the unbelievably shifting, flowing, swimming perspective of the room, and he clung to it as a man cast adrift in space clings to a magnetic line.

He whispered, "Sorry—room's going round. . . ."

"I know. I've had it; all telepaths get this at some time during the development of their powers, but it usually comes in adolescence; you're a late developer and it's more serious. We call it threshold sickness. It isn't serious, it won't hurt you, but it's very frightening. I know. Hold on to me; you'll be all right."

Gradually, clinging to her small hard fingers, Barron got the world right-side up again. The dizzy disorientation remained, but Melitta was solid, a firm presence and not wholly a physical one, in the midst of the shifting and flowing space.

"Try, whenever this happens, to fix your mind on something solid and real."

"*You* are real," he whispered. "You're the only real thing I've ever known."

"I know." Her voice was very soft. She bent close to him and touched her lips gently to his. She remained there, and the warmth of her was like a growing point of light and stability in the shifting dark. Barron was coming quickly back. At last he drew a deep breath and forced himself to release her.

"You shouldn't be here: If Desideria discovers you are gone—"

"What would it be to her? She could have done more for you; she is a Keeper, a trained telepath, and I—but I forgot, you don't know the sort of training they have. The Keepers—their whole minds and bodies become caught up into the work they do—must keep aloof and safeguard themselves from emotions—" She la ughed, a soft, stifled laugh and said, almost weeping, "Besides, Desideria doesn't know it, but she and Storn—"

She broke off. Barron did not care; he was not interested in Desideria at the moment. She came close to him, the only warm and real thing in his world, the only thing he cared about or ever could . . .

He whispered, shaken to the depths, half sobbing, "And to think I might never have known you—"

She murmured, "We would have found one another. From the ends of the world; from the ends of the universe of stars. We belong together."

And then she took him against her, and he was lost in awareness of her, and his last thought, before all thought was lost, was that he had been a stranger on his own world and that now an alien girl from an alien world had made him feel at home.

CHAPTER FOURTEEN

They started two hours before dawn in a heavy snowfall; after a short time of riding on their thickset ponies the forge folk looked like polar bears, their furred garments and the shaggy coats of the ponies being covered with the white flakes. Barron rode close to Melitta, but they did not speak, nor need to. Their new awareness of one another went too deep for words. But he could feel her fear—the growing preoccupation and sense of desperation in what they were about to dare.

Valdir had said that the worship of Sharra was forbidden a long time ago, and Larry had been at some pains to explain that the gods on Darkover were tangible forces. *What was going to happen? The defiance of an old law must be a serious thing—Melitta's no coward, and she's scared almost out of her wits.*

Desideria rode alone at the head of the file. She was an oddly small, straight and somehow pitiable little figure, and Barron could sense without analyzing the isolation of the one who must handle these unbelievable forces.

When they came through the pass and sighted Storn Castle on the height, a great, grim mass which he had never seen before, he realized that he had seen it once through Storn's eyes—the magical vision of Storn, flying in the strange magnetic net which bound his mind to the mechanical bird.

Had I dreamed that?

Melitta reached out and clasped his hand. She said, her voice shaky, "There it is. If we're only in time—Storn, Edric, Allira—I wonder if they're even still alive?"

Barron clasped her hand, without speaking. *Even if you have no one else, you will always have me, beloved.*

She smiled faintly, but did not speak.

The forge folk were dismounting now, moving stealthily, under cover of the darkness and crags, up the path toward the great, closed gates of Storn. Barron, between Desideria and Melitta, moved quietly with them, wondering what was going to happen which could make both Melitta and Desideria turn white with terror. Melitta whispered, "It's a chance, at least," and was silent again, clinging to his hand.

Time was moving strangely again for Barron; he had no idea whether it was ten minutes or two hours that he climbed at Melitta's side, but they stood shrouded by shadows in the lee of the gates. The sky was beginning to turn crimson around the eastern peaks. At last the great, pale-red disc of the sun came over the mountain. Desideria, looking around her at the small, swart men clustered about her, drew a deep breath and said, "We had better begin."

Melitta glanced up uneasily at the heights and said, her voice shaking, "I suppose Brynat has sentries up there. As soon as he finds out we're down here, there will be—arrows and things."

"We had better not give him the chance," Desideria agreed. She motioned the forge folk close around her, and gave low-voiced instructions which Barron found that he could understand, even though she spoke that harsh and barbarian language. "Gather close around me; don't move or speak; keep your eyes on the fire."

She turned her eyes on Barron, looking troubled and a little afraid. She said, "I am sorry, it will have to be you, although you are not a worshiper of Sharra. If I had realized what had happened, I would have brought another trained telepath with me; Melitta is not strong enough. You"—suddenly he noticed that she had neither looked directly at him, nor spoken his name, that day—"must serve at the pole of power."

Barron began to protest that he didn't know anything about this sort of thing, and she cut him off curtly. "Stand here, between me and the men; see yourself as gathering all the force of their feelings and emotion and pouring it out in my direction. Don't tell me you can't do it. I've been trained for eight years to judge these things, and I know you can if you don't lose your nerve. If you do, we're probably all dead, so don't be surprised, whatever you see or whatever happens. Just keep your mind concentrated on me." As if moved on strings, Barron found himself moving to the place she indicated, yet he knew she was not controlling him. Rather, his will was in accord with hers, and he moved as she thought.

With a final, tense look upward at the blank wall of the castle, she motioned to Melitta.

"Melitta, make fire."

From the silk-wrapped bundle she carried, Desideria took a large blue crystal. It was as large as a child's fist, and many-faceted, with strange fires and metallic ribbons of light. It looked molten, despite the crystalline facets, as she held it between her hands, and it seemed to change form, the color and light within it shifting and playing.

Melitta struck fire from her tinderbox; it flared up between her hands. Desideria motioned to her to drop the blazing fragment of tinder at her feet. Barron watched, expecting it to go out. Desideria's serious, white face was bent on the blue crystal with a taut intensity; her mouth was drawn, her nostrils pinched and white. The blue light from the crystal seemed to grow, to play around her, to reflect on her—and now, instead of falling, the fire was rising, blazing up until its lights reflected crimson with the blue on Desideria's features—a strange darting, leaping flame.

Her eyes, gray and immense and somehow inhuman, met Barron's across the fire as if there were a visible line between them. He almost heard her voice within his mind. "*Remember!*"

Then he felt behind him an intense pressure beating up— it was the linked minds of the forge folk, beating on his. Desperately he struggled to control this new assault on his mind. He fought, out of control, his breath coming fast and his face contorted, for what seemed ages—though it was only seconds. The fire sagged and Desideria's face showed rage, fear and despair: Then Barron had it—it was like gathering up a handful of shining threads, swiftly splicing them into a rope and thrusting it toward Desideria. He almost felt her catch it, like a great meshing: The fire blazed up again, exuberantly. It dipped, wavered toward Desideria.

It enveloped her.

Barron gasped almost aloud and for a bare instant the rapport sagged, then he held it fast. He knew, suddenly, that he dared not falter, or this strange magical fire of the mind would flare out of control and become ordinary fire that would consume Desideria. Desperately intense, he felt the indrawn sigh of the men behind him, the quality of their worship, as the fires played around the delicate girl who stood calmly in the bathing flames. Her body, her light dress, her loosely braided hair, seemed to flicker in the fires.

With a scrap of awareness on the edge of his consciousness, Barron heard shouts and cries from the wall above, but he dared not cast an eye upward. He held desperately to the rapport between the girl in the flames and the forge folk.

An arrow flew from nowhere; behind them someone cried out and an almost invisible thread broke and was gone, but Barron was barely conscious of it. He knew without full consciousness that something had roused the castle, that Brynat's men knew they were under strange attack. But his mind was fixed on Desideria.

There was a great surge of the flame, and a great shout

from behind them. Desideria cried aloud in surprise and terror and wonder, and then—before Barron's eyes, her frail fire-clad figure seemed to grow immensely upward, to take on height, majesty and power. And then it was no delicate girl who stood there, but a great veiled Shape, towering to the very height of the outworks and castle, a woman in form, hair of dancing flame, tossing wildly on the wind, wrapped in garments of flame and with upraised arms from which dangled golden chains of fire.

A great sighing cry went up from forge folk and village people crowded behind them.

"Sharra! Sharra, flame-haired, flame-crowned, golden-chained—Sharra! Child of Fire!"

The great Shape towered there, laughing, tossing arms and long fiery locks in a wild exultation. Barron could feel the growing flood of power, the linked minds and emotions of the worshipers, pouring through him and into Desideria—into the flame-form, the Form of Fire.

Random thoughts spun dizzily at the edge of his mind. *Chains. Is this why they chain their women in the Dry towns? The legends run, if Sharra ever broke her chains the world would explode in flame. . . . There is an old saying on Terra that Fire is a good servant but a poor master. On Darkover too; every planet that knows fire has that byword. Larry! You! Where are you? Nowhere here; I speak to your mind, I will be with you later.*

He dropped back into rapport with Desideria, vaguely knowing he had never left it and that he was moving now outside normal time and space perception. Somehow Storn was there, too, but Barron shut out that perception, shut out everything but the lines of force almost visibly streaming from the worshipers—through his body and mind, and into the Form of Fire. With multiplied perception he could see into and through the Form of Fire—see Desideria there looking tense and quiet and frail and somehow exultant—but it was not with his eyes.

Arrows were flying into the crowd now, dropping off men who fell strangely rapt and without crying out. One arrow flew into the Form of Fire, burst into flame and vanished in soundless, white heat. The Form loomed higher and higher. There came a loud outcry from behind the castle walls as the great Form of Sharra stretched out arms with fingers extended—fingers from which ball fires and chain lightning dripped. The men on the walls shrieked insanely as their clothes burst into flame, as their bodies went up in the encompassing fire.

Barron never knew how long that strange and terrible battle raged, for he spent it in a timeless world, beyond fatigue and beyond awareness, feeling it when Brynat, raving, tried to rally his fleeing, burning, dying men; sensing it when the great Form of Fire, with a single blow, broke the outworks as if they had been carved in cheese. Brynat, desperate, brave against even the magic he did not believe in to the very end, charged along the walls, beyond the reach of the flames.

From somewhere a great white bird came flying. It flapped insanely around Brynat's head; he flung up his arms to batter it away, while it flew closer, stabbing with its glittering metallic beak at his eyes. He lost his balance, with a great cry; tottered, shrieked and fell, with a long; wailing scream, into the ravine below the castle.

The fires sank and died. Barron felt the net of force thin and drop away. He realized that he was on his knees, as if physically battered down by the tremendous streams of force that had washed over him. Melitta stood fixed, dumbfounded, staring at the heights.

And Desideria, only a girl again—a small, fragile, redhaired and white-faced girl—was standing in the ring of the dying fire, trembling, her dress and hair unscorched. She gestured with her last strength and the fire flickered and went out. Spasmodically, she thrust the blue stone into the bosom of her dress; then she crumpled unconscious to the ground, and lay there as if dead.

Above them the great wall of the castle breached, with none left to resist them except the dying.

CHAPTER FIFTEEN

The forge folk picked up Desideria with reverent awe and carried her, through the break in the walls, inside the castle yard. They would have done the same to Barron, except that he made them put him down, and went to Melitta, who stood weak-kneed and white. The forge folk disposed of the dead simply, by tossing them into a deep chasm; after some time the wheeling of the *kyorebni*, the corbies and lammergeiers of Darkover, over the crags marked their resting place. In their enthusiasm they would have thrown the wounded and dying after them, but Barron prevented them and was astonished at the way in which his word was taken for law. When he had stopped them he wondered why he had done it; what was going to happen to these bandits now? There weren't any prisons on Darkover that he knew about, except for the equivalent of a brig, in Trade City, where unprovoked fighters and obstreperous drunks were put to cool off for second thoughts; anyone who committed a worse crime of violence either died in the attempt or killed anyone who might try to prevent him. Perhaps Darkover would have to think about penalties less than death, and he frankly wished Aldaran the joy of the task.

At Melitta's orders they went down into the dungeon and freed young Edric of Storn, whom Barron found, to his surprise and consternation, to be a boy of fifteen. The terrible wounds he had sustained in the siege were healing, but Barron realized with dismay that the child would bear the scars, and go lame all his life. He welcomed his rescuers with the courtly phrases of a young king, then broke down and sobbed helplessly in Melitta's arms.

Allira, numbed and incoherent with terror—she had not known whether they were being rescued or attacked by someone eager to replace Brynat—they found hiding in the Royal Suite. Barron, who had formed a strange picture of her from Melitta's thoughts, found her to be a tall, fair-haired, quiet girl—to most eyes more beautiful than Melitta—who came quickly back from terror. With dignity and strength, she came to thank their helpers and place herself at their service, and then to devote herself to reviving and comforting Desideria.

Barron was almost numb with fatigue, but he was too tense to relax even for an instant. He thought, *I'm tired and hungry, I wish they'd bring on the victory feast or something,* but he knew firmly in his mind, *This isn't the end. There's more to come, damn it.*

He realized with disbelief that the sun had risen less than thirty degrees above the horizon; the whole dreadful battle had been over in little more than an hour.

The great white bird, glittering as if formed of jewels that shone through the feathers, swooped low over him; it seemed to be urging him upward. Melitta behind him, clutching at his hand, he climbed the long stairs: He passed through the archway, through the blue tingle of the magnetic field and into the room where the silken bier lay. On it lay the form of a man—sleeping, tranced or dead—like a pale statue, motionless. The bird fluttered above it; suddenly flapped and dropped askew to the floor, lying there in a limp dead tangle of feathers gleaming with jewels, like some broken mechanical toy.

Storn opened blind eyes and sat up, stretching out his hand to them in welcome.

Melitta flew to him, clasping her arms around his neck, laughing and crying at once. She started to tell him, but he smiled bleakly. "I saw it all—through the bird's eyes—the last thing I shall ever see." He said, "Where is Barron?"

Barron said, "I am here, Storn." He had felt that at this moment he would be ready to kill the man; now he felt all his rage and fury drain out of him. He had been a part of this man for days. He could not hate him or even resent him. What could he do to a blind man, a frail invalid? Storn was saying in a low voice, ridden with something like shame, "I owe it all to you. I owe everything to you. But I have suffered for it and I will take whatever comes."

Barron did not know what to say. He said roughly, "Time enough to settle that later, and it won't be me you have to settle it with."

Storn rose, leaning heavily on Melitta, and took a few fumbling steps. Barron wondered if he were lame, along with everything else, but Storn sensed the thought and said, "No, only stiff from prolonged trance. Where is Desideria?"

"I am here," she said from behind them, and came forward to take his hand.

He said, almost in a whisper, "I would have liked to see your face once, only once, with my own eyes." He fell silent with a sigh. Barron had no longer any anger against Storn, only pity; and he knew, with that new and expanded awareness that was never to leave him, that his pity was the worst revenge he could have taken on the man who had stolen his work, his body, and his soul.

A horn sounded far below them in the courtyard, and the women rushed to the window. Barron did not have to follow them. He knew what had happened. Valdir Alton, with Larry and his men, had arrived. He had followed them through half the mountains, and when he lost them, had come directly here, knowing that sooner or later, it must end here. Barron no longer wondered how his masquerade had been known for Storn. Larry had been in rapport with him too long for any surprise.

Storn drew himself upright, with a quiet assumption of courage that did much to dilute the pity and redeem him in Barron's eyes. "My punishment is in Comyn hands," he said, almost to himself. "Come, I must go and welcome my guests—and my judges."

"Judge you? Punish you?" Valdir said, hours later, when formalities were over. "How could I punish you worse than the fate you have brought on yourself, Loran of Storn? From freedom you are bound, from sight, you are blind again. Did you really think it was only to protect their victims that we made what you have done our greatest taboo?"

Barron had found it hard to face Valdir; now, before the man's hard justice, he looked directly at him and said, "Among other things, I owe you for a horse."

Valdir said quietly, "Keep it. His identical twin and stable mate was being trained for my guest gift to you when you had finished your work among us; I shall bestow him upon Gwynn instead. I know you were not responsible for leaving us so abruptly, and we have you—or Storn," he smiled faintly, "to thank for saving the entire station, and all the horses, the night of the Ghost Wind."

He turned to Desideria and his eyes were more severe. He said: "Did you know that we had laid Sharra, centuries ago?"

"Yes," she flared at him, "your people in the Comyn would rob us both of Terra's new powers—and Darkover's old ones."

He shook his head. "I am not happy with what the Aldarans are doing. But then, I am not entirely happy with what my own people are doing, either. I do not like the idea that Terra and Darkover shall always be the irresistible force and immovable object. We are brother worlds; we should be joined—and instead—the battle between us is joined. All I can say is—God help you, Desideria—any god you can find! And you know the law. You have involved yourself in a private feud and stirred up telepathic power in two who did not have it; now you, and you alone, are responsible for teaching your—victims—to guard themselves. You will have little leisure for your work as a Keeper, Desideria. Storn, Melitta and Barron are your responsibility now. They must be trained to use the powers you broke open in them."

"It was not I all alone," she said. "Storn discovered these things on his own—and it will be my joy, not my burden, to help him!" She glared at Valdir defiantly, and took Storn's pale hands between her own.

Larry turned to Barron, with a glance at Valdir as if asking permission. He said, "You still have work with us. You need not return to the Terran Zone unless you like—and, forgive me, I think you have no place there now."

Barron said, "I don't think I ever did." Melitta did not move, but nevertheless he felt as if Melitta had come to stand beside him, as he said, "I've never belonged anywhere but here."

In a queer flash he saw a strange divided future; a Terran working both for and against Terra on this curiously divided world, torn relentlessly and yet knowing where he belonged. Storn had robbed him of his body and in return had given him a heart and a home.

He knew that this would always be his place; that if Storn had taken his place, he would take Storn's, increasingly with the years. He would master the new world, seeing it through doubled eyes. The Darkover they knew would be a different world. But with Melitta beside him, he had no fears about it; it was a good world—it was his own.

DARKOVER

Marion Zimmer Bradley's
Classic Series

Now Collected in New Omnibus Editions!

Heritage and Exile
0-7564-0065-1
The Heritage of Hastur & Sharra's Exile

The Ages of Chaos
0-7564-0072-4
Stormqueen! & Hawkmistress!

The Saga of the Renunciates
0-7564-0092-9
The Shattered Chain, Thendara House
& City of Sorcery

The Forbidden Circle
0-7564-0094-5
The Spell Sword & The Forbidden Tower

*"Darkover is the essence, the quintessence, my most
personal and best-loved work."*
—Marion Zimmer Bradley

To Order Call: 1-800-788-6262

DAW 6

Julie E. Czerneda
THE TRADE PACT UNIVERSE

"Space adventure mixes with romance...a heck of a lot of fun."—*Locus*

Sira holds the answer to the survival of her species, the Clan, within the multi-species Trade Pact. But it will take a Human's courage to show her the way.

A THOUSAND WORDS FOR STRANGER
0- 88677-769-0

TIES OF POWER
0-88677-850-6

TO TRADE THE STARS
0-7564-0075-9

To Order Call: 1-800-788-6262